WORDS OF FURY

- Words of Power volume 2 -

Ritchie Valentine Smith

Whatever has happened before, from now on everything can be different…

Words of Fury:

By the same author:

Fantasy novels
'Words of Power'
'Words of Fury'
To come
'Words of Darkness'
'Words of Light'

Other novels
'Fortune'
'Winning'
'Risk'

Plays
'Rocket Man' **(Edinburgh & London 2003)**
'Kiss' **(London 2011)**

RVSMedia 2017.

Words of Fury:

Author's dedication:
This is for Tony and Louise Richards

'**I say unto you, Love your enemies, bless them that persecute you, do good to them that hate you.**' (Matthew 5)

'**Don't mistake my kindness for weakness.**' – Al Capone

PART ONE

There is a war between darkness and light in every world, including our own. In samurai Japan, where the Empire of Albion and new faiths have arrived, the city of Jade has been lost. Those who led the fight to save the city are using a balloon to get to sanctuary, but their great enemy – a half-human face of incredible forces in this universe – is in pursuit...

Prologue to Part One: *Half of Heaven*

Man woke up shivering, turning his shoulders restlessly in the cold. He had been dreaming about Jade, that wonderful cosmopolitan port city in Japan, and the fight there against Albion and the Lord of the North. In the aftermath, he and his friends had escaped. Now, their balloon sailed fourteen thousand feet above sea-level, and the thin chill air was making him breathless.

Why did I wake? Something bad ahead...?

But what? Man considered what it might be, hanging by his hands from the rigging-ropes. The ropes held the bench he sat on with the others. He was Emmanuel, though usually Man to his friends and to others.

Up above, he saw how the bright shining constellations stretched to the horizon. In this dark and cloudless night the

Words of Fury: 3

Milky Way was a glowing river which a hero could sail.

The rigging creaked again, though not enough to wake the others. Then the Lady Joah turned her head.

Emmanuel?

His mind spoke back to hers. *I feel something wrong!* – What?

'We always knew *he* would pursue.'

They had their enemy the Lord of the North, who was much, much more than a person. Man had half hoped *he* had been left behind, and was about to argue an optimistic case. Instead, he gasped – because up ahead half of heaven was being shaken. Magical forces ran like a waterfall of power from miles above all the way down to sea-level.

'Look at that! Joah, it's like the stars are going to be ripped out of the sky. That has to be the enemy – *him*.'

When their balloon touched that force it would be over – after a long dreadful fall to the sea.

'Yes, Emmanuel. The Lord of the North is doing something colossal.'

'Do you know what?'

She considered, touching her red sash. 'I think he's building a trap.'

'For *us?*'

'Who else?'

There was a partial Moon to give them light, so, when Man turned to look, the samurai lady was no longer an exquisite ghost. Moonlight showed what their struggle back in Jade had done. She had fought bravely, like Man, but she too was stained with blood and was exhausted – and their fight was far from over.

'We both see what comes is deadly,' he told her. 'Still you are brave.'

She touched the tiny crucifix at her throat, and when she half turned he felt her warm breath on his cheek.

'No! Man, I am only good at overcoming fear; that merely seems like bravery.'

'You are too modest.'

'I am fooling you, then – but not myself. *He* is a face of some of the most profound forces in the universe. His power has long made me afraid. If we cannot get ourselves to The Waning of the Moon, we are finished.' The look she gave Man pierced his heart. 'Ahead may be our murder-place!'

Words of Fury:

Man looked again at the shivering chaos they were being driven towards. Lady Joah was right about the scale of that power. For the very first time, he considered surrendering.

Then he turned to her. 'Lady, you're too young and pretty to die.'

'Perhaps *I* am! But what about you?'

He touched the strong curve of his jaw and laughed.

'Too young. Now, look ahead. Think of escape. There must be something we can figure out.'

The enemy was there, with a trap miles across already laid, a magic trap certain to bring them down. If a woman acted to counter the trap, *he* would know at once and respond. In the same way, any other man using magic would be recognized as an enemy by the Lord of the North. So how could it be done?

There must be some escape possible, by clever trick or act of bravery.

Man tried very hard to see it.

Words of Fury:

CONTENTS:-

Prologue to Part One: *Half of Heaven*

Chapter One: *No Way Through*
Chapter Two: *When His Trap is Ready*
Chapter Three: *Fill Your Hearts with Fear*
Chapter Four: *Immediate Surrender*
Chapter Five: *Vulnerable Emotion*
Chapter Six: *Flesh Like Glass*
Chapter Seven: *We Must All Face Monsters*
Chapter Eight: *Other-World Monsters*

Chapter Nine: *Unless There Is A Miracle*
Chapter Ten: *Impossible Things*
Chapter Eleven: *This Is War*
Chapter Twelve: *In War the Unlikely Happens*
Chapter Thirteen: *We Must Walk this Path*
Chapter Fourteen: *Now I Believe!*
Chapter Fifteen: *I Will Dare Anything and Everything!*
Chapter Sixteen: *After So Much Pain*
Chapter Seventeen: *Up Towards the Mountain*

Prologue to Part Two: *Heaven, or Hell?*

Chapter Eighteen: *A Light That Never Goes Out*
Chapter Nineteen: *Some Other Peril*
Chapter Twenty: *A Dead End*
Chapter Twenty-One: *A Crossing Perilous*
Chapter Twenty-Two: *Ominous Truth*
Chapter Twenty-Three: *Honor Is My Gift to Give*
Chapter Twenty-Four: *Enough Enemies*
Chapter Twenty-Five: *We're Running for Our Lives*

Chapter Twenty-Six: *The Steel Angel*
Chapter Twenty-Seven: *Will Your Caution Get Us The Eye?*
Chapter Twenty-Eight: *The Disciple I Loved Most*
Chapter Twenty-Nine: *Expect Nothing*
Chapter Thirty: *Perhaps More Than a Man*
Chapter Thirty-One: *The Boldness*
Chapter Thirty-Two: *We Thought We Were Heroes*

Chapter Thirty-Three: *We Have Made Our Stand*

Chapter Thirty-Four: *A Place Already Full of Magic*
Chapter Thirty-Five: *A Miracle*
Chapter Thirty-Six: *My Daughter*
Chapter Thirty-Seven: *I Have Loved, Too*
Chapter Thirty-Eight: *The Price*
Chapter Thirty-Nine: *That Isn't Logic, But It Is Magic!*
Chapter Forty: *We Have Darkness In Our Light*

Prologue to Part Three: *A Mile of Freezing Storm*

Chapter Forty-One: *Every Diabolical Legion*
Chapter Forty-Two: *We Must Move On!*
Chapter Forty-Three: *Stars and Galaxies*
Chapter Forty-Four: *The Connection is Live*
Chapter Forty-Five: *You Have No Dominion*
Chapter Forty-Six: *Now We're Prisoners*
Chapter Forty-Seven: *Unconditional Love*
Chapter Forty-Eight: *Sanctuary*

THE WORLD OF 'WORDS OF POWER'

COPYRIGHT INFORMATION AND AUTHOR'S WEBSITE

Words of Fury:

Chapter One: *No Way Through*

The sky ahead of them shook again and again. There was no way through *his* magical clawing that Man could see – and he had looked long and hard. He leaned down from the swaying bench to rub the bronze casket lashed below.

'You're hoping for luck?'

The sleek metal case held the Eye of Jade, one of the mightiest power gems known and a certain target for the Lord of the North.

Better to destroy it, and ourselves too, than let it fall into *his* hands...

Man straightened up, wishing that he still had access to its power.

'At least a touch of good fortune.' He pulled a rueful face. He was young and normally confident, but worried now. 'If only the Eye would like me again...'

Now, as they were blown forward, he and Lady Joah watched their doom together.

'I can see little detail of *his* weaves, but I see their power.'

She smiled wanly, and played again with her sash. 'A man's magic is hardly visible to other men; only the effects. There's no way through what I see coming.'

'It's the same, reversed, isn't it? A woman's power is easily noticed by men. So if you do something – '

'Then *he* will at once see *me*, and strike back, and it will be over.'

'I already feel *his* character.' Man considered, all his senses alert. 'He's brutally self-confident; he knows *exactly* how to win – or he thinks he does.'

'You sound overawed.'

'That's how the Lord of the North wants me to think. So if I know how he wants me to think, maybe I can do something different.' Man gave a grim smile, feeling slightly dizzy from the lack of oxygen. Power still fountained up and then down. 'But I see things in *him* I see in me – things I don't like. And he *is* over-confident.'

She took his wrist, held it desperately. 'Can you act against him?'

'We can't fight *his* magic head-on.'

'Then we're done?'

Suddenly Man was decisive; an idea had come, though only

half formed. 'I think there's a way even *he* might be fooled.'

She let go of his hand. 'How? And who might do that? Mother Zandar is too remote and my father is imprisoned back in Jade, and they are both far stronger than us.'

The idea was firming up in Man's mind. 'There is us, you and I together.'

'But who are *we*, unschooled as we are, to even try?'

That annoyed Man, who had a temper.

'Lady Joah, my father was Lord of Arms of all Albion, and you are the daughter of Lord Okada of the Jade, one of the most powerful men in this whole country. *I* used the Eye of Jade to rock an entire city. Joah, we're strong. We *are*. Especially together!'

He twisted about, put both his hands onto her head. She leaned back in annoyance, but he persisted. There was flickering light in his mind, silver swirling with gold, his diminished power and hers, and then their two magics became one.

He gasped. Through the eyes of Joah, a woman of power, Man could see the enemy's weaves rising from where *he* was at his work. Man saw a first veil of fiery red, backed by another veil that was a poisonous glowing violet.

Man saw what was coming. 'If we pass through his magic, the balloon carrying us will be ripped apart – and it's a long way down!'

He felt Joah shudder. 'Does he want us to stop? I don't see how we can!'

So she thought they would likely die?

He wanted to seize her, reassure her, kiss her.

He did none of these things, only tried to prepare magic of his own. The red and purple veils falling out of the sky miles above them and then all the way down to the sea came closer and closer.

'We're going to fall,' she said calmly, 'and that will be the end.'

He saw there was a possible weakness in the great fountain of power. Where two different weaves met he saw a gap. In spite of the high-altitude cold he was sweating and nervous, but he took a necessary risk and used magic to push the balloon hard left towards the seam. He heard the rigging-ropes creak as the balloon slewed over to one side, and Faslane, his fellow from Albion, snored. Neither the Voice from Afar nor Man's samurai friend Yoshi stirred.

Not enough power, thought Man. I must move us further...
'*Wish me luck with the weaves!*'

'Man, surely that's too much power; he *will* see us!'

True, he *should*. Only, my power is now a mimic of *his*, and I'm pushing us in the same direction as the wind *he* made...

Fire licked towards them, hot and red although icy cold. Man shivered.

'We won't get through, my Man!'

'We might.'

The balloon shuddered, and Man spread his fingers to make a larger parting in the enemy's force.

'Then he'll see us!'

'Maybe not. *I'm pretending to be him...*'

He gave the balloon a few more pushes, guiding them out of the final clawing reds. They had safely passed through, to the space beyond.

'I don't see how you survived even one challenge!'

She sounded amazed. Though there had been no alert, and he felt satisfied over that, there was a bigger risk to come. Those dangerous, clawing shades of red were behind them, but still the stars shook and the deadly violet barrier was glowing ahead. His skin tingled; he knew the purple veil contained an even more deadly negative energy.

'It's getting worse,' she told him quietly. 'The Lord of the North is still building up his magic, though the centre of the enemy's power is far away and I cannot see what is waiting for us there.'

'It won't be a handshake and a free ticket to one of the Voice's concerts, that's sure!' He laughed, a little wildly. 'Or maybe *he* will be right there, and it will be!'

He was still carefully watching the last and most dangerous veil. It was like a living violet net, painfully bright. He had to use even more power to push away those violet claws. The whole balloon shuddered. Electric-purple flashes surrounded them, and they both flinched though the blasts of light were silent.

He looked down, and from the sheer mad height he felt sick. Yet somehow the swaying balloon stayed whole.

Man exhaled, wondering at their good luck, wondering if *he* had really not noticed them.

He closed his eyes, let his soul go looking for their great enemy...

'Emmanuel!'

Nothing; they were *still* undiscovered.

'Emmanuel!' Joah sounded shocked, and entirely without gratitude. 'I never ever imagined escape was possible!'

He waited for a better reaction. When it did not come his smile faded and he pulled his hands off her head.

The connection was broken; they were separate again. Without the use of her eyes all he could see ahead was the same colourless clawing, and he watched to see if there was any change.

'I wonder if *he* knows we've escaped?'

She gestured with empty hands. 'I don't think he even knows we're here, at least he doesn't yet. But look at those lines of force still coming up! He is working on something gigantic.'

Man took a burning breath. 'Whatever it is, it's still hours away.'

Joah sighed. 'The Lord of the North, when he springs this trap... Oh, if only we could reason with him, or plead...'

Man turned his head, to dispute the soft things she had just said.

'Lady Joah, *don't* imagine you can reason with him, still less plead. That was *his* best chance, right here – and we got past. In the morning, everything will look very different.'

'Yes, I suppose, for the dark of night is *his* time.'

It was strange how resigned she seemed.

'What about the others?'

'Let them sleep on, Emmanuel, and you, too. If you and I together cannot fight *him* directly, what could even the Voice from Afar do?'

The Voice was was a sweet wild child of Albion descent. She was now a famous singer in the port of Jade who did magical things with music and sound. Man loved her, too, and was awed by her touch of what might be musical genius.

One day they might both go back to Albion, and be famous for very different reasons, but that day was not yet.

Ahead, heaven continued to shake with *his* power. Man knew the Lord of the North was close and had set that giant trap, but he trusted Lady Joah.

Soon he fell into an exhausted sleep.

Hours passed; he dreamed of falling, right to the centre of the Earth. Transparent walls showed red-hot rock pressing down. It was terrifying. But in his dream he was with someone very

Words of Fury:

important, who *had* to be protected.

Then a hand was shaking his shoulder.

'Emmanuel-John, we need you!' Lady Joah said. *'Please wake up!'*

The dawn was a pink promise beyond his closed eyes, but he kept his eyes shut. Then the bench was kicked so hard he almost tumbled from it.

He blinked madly. The sunrise was an immense display that dazzled. In its centre bloody red was turning to white-hot gold.

Their bamboo bench swung perilously on the ropes that stretched down from the frail balloon. Man saw all his friends were awake now. The women were on either side of him, while the other men perched on the two bench ends. From the expressions Man saw they were all as afraid as he was.

'Ah, I feel the Lord of the North is very close.'

The Voice from Afar had spoken.

The bench was buffeted again. Man snapped: 'You're right. That's no caress!'

Now Yoshi eyed him, blearily. He was a very cool young man, stylish in his green and gold kimono and red leggings, though he too was blood-splashed. His swords had proved crucial to their fight back in Jade.

'Tell me something I don't know, my Man!'

'It won't be long till we are brought down.'

Lady Joah was interrupted by Faslane. He was the mariner newly come from Albion, earthy, powerful-looking and smart. 'My lords, ladies, surely we have to do something?'

'Put heat into the balloon, and we'd soar away!'

Joah responded, 'If we use magic, dear Voice from Afar, he'll know *exactly* where we are.'

'Surely he knows already?' said Yoshi.

'No – because so far *his* strikes have missed.'

'So far!' Yoshi was angry. 'Faslane is right; it's necessary to act.'

'I know it is,' said the Voice. She pulled at her long, disarranged blonde hair. 'For last night I dreamed of the future – of what will happen should we fail.'

Man had to know. 'How will it be?'

'If *he* kills us and takes the Eye, *his* world will come to pass. Cold earth only, with humanity bred to be slaves in *his* prison tunnels. And elsewhere only a cold, cold imitation of life upon this earth – till beyond the end of time, forever.'

Words of Fury:

The Voice sometimes had the gift of Foreseeing. That, especially said in such a powerful, mournful tone, silenced everyone.

Man stared at the shimmering weaves over the still-dark sea, turning his head from side to side. 'You women, what do you see?'

The Voice answered. 'I don't know what he's making, but his weaves stretch for miles.'

'How long till we hit the trap?'

'*He* has had time enough to make it inescapable, my Man,' said Joah softly. 'All the time there is.'

Man was furious with that negativity; but how could he argue?

Yoshi ran fingers down the bandolier of throwing knives strapped to his chest. 'I hate being helpless. I like to fight! You people with the power, tell me how!'

Joah spoke quickly. 'We mustn't be rash! – If we keep walking small and work no magic, perhaps we can escape.'

Yoshi sounded even angrier. 'He bangs on the balloon so that we're like monkeys being shaken out of a tree! *He wants to kill us!* Your "perhaps we can escape" isn't good enough!'

'Don't forget that Man has the Eye, the greatest of all power gems!'

Though it was after a long and dark night, Man could tell Joah had found her shining enthusiasm again. But he said nothing now. *I don't want to tell them.*

Joah continued, 'Now look ahead, everyone! Please! Across the sea – look below the dawn – there is Mount Unzen! Look!'

Emmanuel did look. Many, many miles away there was land visible below the blinding sunrise – the Unzen peninsula. It was dark and indistinct land, but real.

Joah explained more. '*There* is hope! *There* is sanctuary! On the other side of the mountain is The Waning of the Moon! In that place are scholars and fighters from all over the known world, and they can teach us how to prevail.' She turned to Man, visibly excited. 'Oh, *there* is our promised land!'

On this side of the mountains the land was still dark. But on the other side, where the Waning was, Man knew there would be light.

'I do see that,' he told them all, 'but only because of you, Lady Joah. Because of you I do believe – and I hope.'

She raised two fists, ecstasy on her face.

Words of Fury:

'Yes, have hope in Mother Zanadar, and in that place! For the Waning is where the Lady Naosuke spoke of *you* so many centuries ago, my Emmanuel. Her Prophecies say we *can* win. And when we get there, there will be welcome and protection for all! You and I, Man, and our Voice from Afar, can become everything in magic we might possibly be! And *then* we fight *him*!'

It was a long journey they had to make and Man knew that a mere touch from *him* on their balloon would make it burst. But whatever the danger they were on their way.

Words of Fury:

Chapter Two: *When His Trap is Ready*

In that dark hour just before dawn the Lady Berenda was on the galley deck, tall and in black. She raised her head and peered through the fine-mesh black veil she wore. She had once styled herself 'the Tears', and back in Jade had given Emmanuel a bloody mark on his face. Now, she knew, Man had her in his soul.

She had brought the three boats here before the enemy's balloon could arrive. She knew something of her master's plan – she was the Lord of the North's beloved familiar, after all – and was content to serve it. The galley's blood-red sails had been taken down at her order, and now the crew waited for sunrise. It had been a night of sweaty effort, and fear from all the world-shaking *he* did.

This low, sleek galley with twenty-two long oars per side was packed. The specially selected purity police were wearing the broad black sashes that gave them their nickname. Though Lord Oatha was officially their commander, and chief of all the purity police in Jade province, all those men were secretly sworn to *his* service; and each man knew that the Lady Berenda was *his* chief interpreter on Earth.

Dawn came now, sudden and blinding white.

Berenda turned to the weather-beaten pirate captain – a shaggy-bearded and truculent man – and withdrew her veil to show off her winning smile. 'We are in the right place, and the other galleys too. Take in the oars.'

He glared back at her from under bushy brows. 'You have us hurry a long, sleepless night, and at dawn – way out at sea – we just stop!'

'Yes.'

He came aggressively close, bristling chin out and breath sour.

'What exactly are we waiting for?'

His dislike of women at sea had long been plain. Berenda hated him back, but to keep the peace for now she merely re-fastened her veil and made her response polite.

'For a miracle.'

His moustached lip curled. 'What does that mean?'

'Even if I was allowed to say, I would not spoil the wonder of it by telling you.'

He scowled back at Berenda, clearly furious. Then he spat

over the side.

Behind her veil, she glared at this mocker and felt fury flood her. She would teach this scum a lesson, and she raised a hand to do it, but beside her now her aide Hagiwara pointed up into the sky.

'Our cold Lord is at work! The sky is shaking! Look!'

Hagiwara was a burly man, though round-shouldered. The fool actually sounded triumphant, as if he had achieved something himself.

Often Berenda disliked Hagiwara, who took his privileges as a man for granted – but he had his uses. Berenda decided to postpone her revenge.

'Now I feel our enemies. See, Hagiwara, the balloon-riders are coming, just as our master foretold. Alert the crew!'

Hagiwara had the common touch, that was true. He was a black sash for Lord Oatha, and as a male he was notionally in command here. Of course he knew her supreme rank in the Lord of the North's service, so he was usually deferential – on the outside.

He bellowed, 'Our enemies are high above, and coming from the west! There are five of them, hung from a clear balloon! Keep watch!'

She watched as Hagiwara looked round with a pleased face. He had a certain small ability in using the power and he certainly enjoyed giving orders.

The crew were still resting at the oars, and there was yet another angry exchange between her and the captain before the oars were taken in. The crew, all pirates and mostly Korean, were waiting for her to give the commands now. Berenda could tell that by the fearful glances they gave her.

Hagiwara spoke quietly to her. 'Up on the balloon, how high d'you think they are?'

'Not high enough to be safe!'

Now Man had a very pleasant surprise, which he could not quite believe – till the Voice from Afar confirmed it.

'I don't feel *him* any longer. He's gone!'

Yoshi lolled back and began to laugh. 'As easy as that? We chat a little, we wean ourselves from fear, and *he* vanishes and we're safe?'

'Don't believe he's gone for good,' Man told his oldest friend.

'Yes!' said the Voice. 'I'm still aware of his masculine power,

Words of Fury:

which is vast, and he's a trickster, too. This is most likely another trick – so he might still be waiting to pounce!'

'I've just had a very bad thought.' Man shifted uncomfortably, and the woven-bamboo bench shifted too. 'What if he's gone to The Waning, to attack it before we get there?'

The Voice from Afar stared worriedly at Man. 'I hadn't thought of that.'

Faslane pulled a face sour enough to scare cats away from milk. 'So we turn up to your sanctuary, and make ourselves prisoners?'

'Our Waning of the Moon will not fall easily, even to *him*. It is a psychic fortress protected by magic.' Joah sighed. 'Perhaps he has other duties – there's his fight in Ezo, don't forget.'

'Or he will strike at us when his trap is ready!' Man was gloomily thinking of the snare ahead. 'He has already damaged the balloon – and us!'

For some reason that made brave Yoshi laugh again.

'My Man, cheer up! Take off that sombre face! For now, *he* has gone, so relax. But – I must insist – whatever you do, don't start snoring. Last night you were an all-night earthquake, just when I needed sleep!'

That made Man grin back. Yoshi was a high-born samurai and a low-life-loving poet. He was also Man's oldest friend in this place of his exile.

'If you don't like the company here, leave.'

'Why, I might! I might step off into empty air and surprise you all by walking! – True, vertical walking is unusual, but I have seen it done.' Yoshi had once watched Man and the Voice come stumbling together out of a blue sky, supported only by their magic. 'But, at least till *he* comes back, can't we forget our worries?'

'How?' asked Joah.

'Each of us will have a special way, I imagine. Man here will think of eating and drinking and – well. The Voice from Afar will hear music. For me, as it is a splendid morning now, if somewhat garish-bright for my superbly refined taste, I may compose. "Dawn at high altitude – Below, splashes of shade..."'

Joah grumbled, 'Your modesty isn't superbly refined! – Yoshi, why is it you men always want poetry when prose is needed, and the other way round also?'

Man let loose: 'To annoy you women!'

'Leave me to my dreams! I am an artist!' Yoshi closed his

eyes and he sighed theatrically. 'Perhaps *he* really is gone for good. For now, let's enjoy how we float on, in a peaceful, silent world, buoyed up by sunlight. Meanwhile, I will create a pure *haiku*...'

'I love your bard-words, Yoshi, but we must discuss our situation practically.'

Yoshi opened his dark eyes and now he touched his sword-hilts. 'Joah, here's practicality! If we are cut down from this height...'

'That would be death for all of us,' Man said, 'but at least we would be free of *him*!'

'You really are cheerful, aren't you?' After a moment Yoshi spoke again. 'Surely being so high must make us hard to see.'

Man made himself sound careless and jaunty: 'It depends who's looking.'

'You all tell me *he* is,' Faslane responded. 'And as we're at the mercy of the wind, it must be obvious where we are going.'

Joah said, 'That's inevitable.'

'Why?'

'Because *he* already knows.'

Faslane was disquieted. 'Then shouldn't we change direction?'

'How, sea-pilot?' Joah's voice was sharp. 'How?'

'By use of magic?'

'We cannot and must not! You're right that this wind could be changed by magic, but *any* serious use of that will draw *him*.'

'You're sure, Lady Joah?' Faslane asked her.

'Quite sure.'

Man frowned, wondering if all this talk was a distraction from decisions, with lingering conversation replacing hard-headed action. Yet Dirk Faslane, with his accent from the Empire and his cool, calm air, always inspired a certain confidence.

'So there is nothing to be done?' Faslane asked. 'Surely there is...'

'We might try to look ahead, perhaps,' said the Voice. 'There is a skill called "Far-Seeing" which Lady Joah and I know a little of...'

The talk continued; Man let it go on uninterrupted. They made silent headway, blown at a speed they could not feel towards the sunrise glare. Man knew that every yard gained was precious.

Man began looking down at the sea so far below, which was still in pre-sunrise gloom. He had noticed movement there.

'I think some boats are ahead,' he announced.

'You must have good eyes,' Faslane said grudgingly. 'It's dark down there, dark as *his* Hell.'

'Look east, a couple of miles – three boats sailing in line abreast. Can you see?'

Three blurred shapes sailed on in the gloomy twilight.

'I think they are galleys.' Faslane turned his head. 'Friends? Or foes? Whichever, they're in an unholy rush.'

'It could be Fukuzawa down there, come to help us?' the Lady Joah ventured.

Fukuzawa was a famous fighting captain from Jade, Joah's city. After Joah's father Lord Okada was overthrown, Fukuzawa had thrown in with Lady Joah and the other rebels.

Sudden pain stung Man's face, aggravating him.

'I respect Fukuzawa's fighting spirit, but even if that is him, what difference does one galley and a handful of fighters make? Anyway, that's three boat-loads below, not one, and I'm guessing they're not Fukuzawa, they're enemies.'

'Man, I wish you'd change your name to "Mr Optimism" and make your nature follow!' Yoshi said fiercely.

The Voice said quietly, 'Emmanuel is right to beware: I feel the ice-taste of *him* down there – and I've met him and his before!'

'So they *are* enemy agents!'

The Lord of the North's followers had killed the Voice's parents when she was little more than a toddler. She could recognize the enemy.

Then Yoshi raised his head. 'They've downed their sails!'

Man stirred. 'Were the sails pirate red, or Nippon white?'

'It was too dark to tell.'

They flew on, at the same speed as the prevailing wind. That meant they were catching up with the three motionless galleys.

Joah shuffled her bottom on the bamboo of the bench, trying not to look down now that the fall was so visible. 'I'd still like to think that is our friend Captain Fukuzawa below, but they might be enemies.' She drummed the fingers of one hand on her knee. 'They can't have seen us before, when it was dark, and I doubt they can now. We're hung from a transparent bubble, the five of us. We must be hard to see.'

Man continued to look east.

Words of Fury:

Except for the boats, he saw nothing untoward – although he touched his sword-hilts again. A samurai always liked to know his swords were close. Then he realized they were gently sinking, and that was poor news. When would they have to land? If they dare not use magic, a half hour or so. Would that get them to solid earth? No; they would likely drown – or fall into *his* trap.

The sun struck the sea below. Now the water there was a silver-and-blue dazzle.

Yoshi clenched his fists. 'Three bloody boats. Three hundred people, maybe... If they're the opposition, that's a lot.'

Then Man's face stung again, and he flinched. It was the wound he had received back in Jade – the Tears' bloody, toothy kiss.

It's like *she* just bit me again!

He winced as he felt the pain go even deeper. Slowly now he felt the hope and faith in him all draining away. It was as if everything good and bold in him was escaping through that wound.

What's doing this to me? Surely it can't be *her?*

Man touched the sore spot again; and suddenly he knew there was only defeat ahead. Japan would be lost, and he and his friends with it. There was still his original home, the mighty steam-powered Empire of Albion, but how could it stand alone against the Lord of the North?

There was only a mean-spirited anger left in him. 'Lady Joah!' Man felt the kind of secret despair that so easily turns into blustering fury. He had to speak out ill truths in an ill way. 'The magic we're swinging from won't lift us over that mountain, and the balloon's coming to the end of its life.'

Joah's voice matched his in sharpness. 'Man, our enemy *can* be defeated; he is *not* God!'

Man touched his wound yet again as he stared back at Joah.

'What do *you* know about the Lord of the North?' He grabbed her forearm, shook it. 'Have you met him?'

She tried to pull away, but he was too strong. 'Why do you say that? Of course I haven't.'

'I have!' he told her.

'What?'

'He came to me in my cell in your father's fortress. And do you know how the cold lord looked? Do you?'

She shook her head.

'He was Satan – with a smile!'

Immediately power whip-cracked the air ahead – *his* power. A touch from it would gut their frail bubble.

'Man, you've led him to us!' said Joah.

Yes; Man had called on the cold darkness.

Now it arrived.

The ropes jerked. The world held its breath, and so did they. Then *his* magic yanked at the rigging and their bench twisted all the way around and then spun dizzyingly back. Their seat bucked backwards. Man held tight to the safety rope across his lap and tried not to look down or throw up. He felt air-sick; sea-sick with added dimensions.

He wished with all his heart he had not named the enemy.

When next *he* struck, the bench they sat on was tossed around like a cork on a rough current.

It was almost impossible to stay seated. Man realized he was holding Joah's arm strongly enough to hurt. He let go and saw he had left marks in her flesh. He had wronged her badly before, hurt her now, and done even more wrong to them all when he had named that name.

Now the Voice from Afar pointed up. 'Look!'

Man saw their giant soap bubble was badly distorted and leaning over to one side. He grimaced.

Joah raised a hand, then lowered it without making magic. 'Man, the balloon... How much more can it stand?'

'How much more can *we* stand?' the Voice complained.

Man eyed the clear-skinned shape. It was twisted, and it shook.

'It's only a soap-bubble the Voice and I enlarged with magic, and our spell is beginning to fail. The heated air is leaking. Another blow from *him* and we'll be finished.'

It was a cry of pain from the Voice, as if from a wound. 'Ah!'

Joah leaned closer to Man, almost cheek to cheek. Her honey-and-brown eyes flashed. 'Man? Will you protect us?'

He had to be honest. 'I can't.'

'Back in Jade – '

'This is different!' He wondered how desperate and cowardly he was sounding, and he was ashamed of himself. 'That's *power* up ahead, miles across and miles high.' He shivered. 'In this weather there are lines of force that have seized us and they're too strong to break.'

The Voice cried out. 'But you fought *him* before! You used

the Eye!'

Man saw his hands were shaking. His mouth turned dry.

He knew what the symptoms of fear were.

'I know what I did. I suppose I could try again.'

'Of course you could!' said Joah.

Yoshi was savage. 'Freeze you for a fool, Man, don't listen to Joah! Last time the Eye made your heart stop.'

'I only know what you all told me.' Man had no memory of his death at all. 'And, Joah, I'll always owe you. Because of you, I didn't stay dead.'

'"And yet, it *wasn't* the end..."' She was quoting the Naosuke Prophecies word for word, frowning at Yoshi. '"For he lived again." Man, it was a miracle, your resurrection!'

Man doubted it had been a miracle; more likely it had been Joah's courage and some blind luck. The Lord of the North had the deep death magic – entropy, Joah's father Lord Okada called it – and it was very, very hard to fight that. Jade itself had been a magical place – cosmopolitan, welcoming, and as wild and free as any city in the realm could be. It had to be taken back, but that was for the future.

Now, in this desperate moment, Man tried to work magic as he had done during the fight in Jade. He worked his fingers as hard as he could, muttering spells to make use of the Eye's might. He was sweating and fearful – he really didn't want to die again – but he tried *everything* to make use of the power, so that he could help his friends.

Nothing.

Man closed his eyes now, scrunching them till all he could see was red chaos. He tried to speak directly to the green power of the Eye, but he couldn't form words. Sickness welled up in his stomach; nothing was coming back from the great power gem in its bronze casket below.

All was futile. The Lord of the North's trap was close and so their situation was desperate; but the Eye of Jade and its power might as well have been upon the Moon.

Man's lack left him furious with himself. He touched his cheek, where the pain from the Tears' kiss was biting very hard. The Voice saw that, so she pressed a hand to Man's brow.

'You're at fever-heat! You're ill!'

Man pushed away her helping hand, though even that small effort made him dizzy. 'Leave me alone!'

Her brows compressed. When she reached out – she was

something of a Healer – she touched the exact inflamed spot.

'Ow!' he said, furious. Then duty made him apologize. 'I'm sorry. I know you're trying to help.'

'Oh, Man! *What* did *that* to you?'

He was sweating an unreasonable amount now and breathing heavily. He suddenly developed double vision, and seemed to see the Tears eyeing him back in the music room in Jade. He remembered her magic, remembered the webs of ice descending on his flesh. It was as if *she* was right here, gloating, ready to give him yet another ill touch.

'It was the one you played your koto for.'

'*The Tears!*'

'Yes; her.' He pushed the Voice's hand away from his face again, seeing the calluses from her musicianship. His own strength felt queerly diminished. 'The wound on my face is a love-bite from her.'

'Why didn't you tell us?'

'Why bother?' Man looked down the immense plunging distance to the sea. It was as if he looked upon his own open grave, but somehow now he hardly cared. He just sneered, 'I'm bored with bad news.'

'I will try proper healing of your wound as soon as I can. If I fail, then the Lady Joah will try.'

'Thanks for your optimism! And if she fails?'

There was no answer to that from the Voice. Instead she rubbed at her bare sunburned neck and shoulders. 'Do you others feel that chill?'

Man already knew it was *his* unearthly power that had drawn heat out of their atmosphere. He turned away from his so-called 'friends' with another sneer.

The Voice asked, softly, 'Man? What should we do?'

Before Man could speak, Faslane gave his own opinion. 'We're really on show up here. I think we should come down.'

Man frowned, trying to think tactically. 'I take your point, Master Faslane, but height might be our advantage. Even *he* may not want to bring us down – at least, not yet.'

Yoshi had turned. 'What do you mean?'

'We're over deep water. If the Lord of the North crashes us, won't he lose the Eye? A quarter-mile of ocean would be quite a barrier, even for *him*...'

'There!' said Joah, as if mere words made them safe.

Yoshi was more suspicious, of course.

Words of Fury:

'Don't you think *he* may prefer us out of the game, right along with the Eye? Often it's better to wipe out an enemy even if you don't gain a captive.'

'Then more fool *him!*' said Man, unaccountably angry. He rubbed his hurt face again. 'The Eye is a power in its own right. If he can, the Lord of the North should just *take* it!'

He saw Joah had fearful eyes now, and she stared to one side and then the other, and then behind. Man knew what she was looking for: another dread sign of *him.*

But the Voice misread what was happening. 'Lady, I see you keep looking back towards Jade city! With your father in so much peril...'

This touched something raw in Joah. She kicked her feet out, helplessly angry.

'You think that I want to return to my father? Well, of course I do! I want to help him fight foul Oatha, who won the city by trickery! Voice, my heart aches for my noble father, for my sister, and for my home! I would do *anything* to free my city, anything!'

'I know you would,' said Man, suddenly wondering if she would betray them all, now or in the future, to help her father.

Then the steel in Joah showed. 'But helping my family is *not* my duty now. I must get you all to Mother Zandar and to The Waning of the Moon, and I *will!*'

'Amen,' said the Voice, very quickly.

Man turned to Lady Joah. 'Might I borrow your eyes again? I'd like to take a look at what he's doing.'

She scowled. 'Leave it for now.'

He blinked, surprised at her unhelpfulness.

Yoshi complained, then. 'It's turning hot!'

It was, so they sipped some of their remaining water, but not much. Unless something changed, Man knew it would be noon or later before they reached land and even a chance of fresh water.

Faslane was still peering forward. 'What's that ahead?'

Man had felt the power, along with the two women. He looked, and saw chaos in the blue sky ahead – mad, rippling motion. Power throbbed above that whole area beyond the hove-to galleys. They felt the vibrations even here.

'Water magic, and cold,' the Voice said said.

'That's *him,*' Man said, feeling an icy thrill run along his spine. 'That's his trap!'

Lines of force previously laid down by *him* suddenly

coalesced. They all could see dread energy rising, like water running upwards.

Then the shimmering stabilized. Inside that giant magic, Man saw smeary white clouds had swirled up in a triangular pattern.

A few minutes passed, with the temperature all the time plunging. There was thickening fog ahead, and perhaps something else that Man strained to see.

Faslane gestured again.

'In God's name, what's inside the mist? Do you see shapes moving there?'

'No,' the Voice answered. 'I think it's just the one huge thing.'

Ahead, Man glimpsed something in the fog. He peered harder. Then the mists ahead of the flying balloon partly cleared, and the sun sparkled on a mass large as a mountain. Only, that mountain had a shape.

Man's heart seemed to freeze. He swallowed, and leaned back. He was very afraid now.

'*I think it's alive!*'

It looked like a giant was clambering up from the sea, and the giant looked like *him*.

Words of Fury: 25

Chapter Three: *Fill Your Hearts with Fear*

'Will our lord attack them in the air?' Hagiwara asked Lady Berenda, making a big smiling show of deference that only made her more contemptuous of him.

She deigned to explain. 'If Man and the Eye and Book are drowned here... It's deep water. A recovery would be difficult, you see, though of course our master can do miracles.'

'Ah! So our lord may have to let them fly on?'

'Be patient! You are not *his* general yet. Accept *his* plan!'

Would the lord of night follow her suggestions? Or would he simply strike directly at his enemies riding below the balloon?

She opened her mouth to give another sharp order, but then her skin tingled, first outwardly and then within. It was *his* special kiss, telling her he had arrived.

'I feel him right here, right now!'

In her black robes, Berenda arched her back and sighed. *He* was here in the overwhelming sky above her, in the sunlight that glittered raw and bright on the sea beside her. His strength was always increasing, and when he had the Eye...

Her heart beat faster.

Now Berenda felt *him* stretch down. She saw how the air glimmered where he touched the waves. Instantly the air turned freezing cold.

He *had* accepted her advice!

Man acknowledged the scale. 'Look at the size of him!'

A giant head and shoulders had emerged from the sea. The huge face was higher than they were flying. Man saw the Lord of the North had a vicious smile that showed spiked teeth.

'God,' the Voice said, 'but he's *ugly!*'

Man couldn't disagree.

Silvery ice-blades had formed in the Lord of the North's hollow eye-sockets and they were whirling round like scimitars. In the gap representing the nostrils, two larger blades were opening and closing like scissors. Where the mouth was, a sucking force began roaring, as if a giant rudely inhaled.

Man felt dark pain pulse again in the wound on his face. He felt even more certain that their enemy's path to victory was clear and that *he* could not be defeated. Man saw written plainly in Joah's expression what a disaster their future would be.

'We'll be swallowed whole.' Lady Joah sounded desperate.

Now she stared at the shining ice structure. 'When we hit, it will be the end!'

'Then stop us hitting it!' said Yoshi. 'Man! You women! Surely there's a way of getting out of this trap?'

As *he* inhaled more, sucking them on, the wind also speeded up, driving them towards death. From all round, *his* terrible voice began to thunder.

'COME DOWN, YOU PEOPLE IN THE AIR! EMMANUEL! LADY JOAH! LAND! ONLY IMMEDIATE SURRENDER TO MY SERVANTS BELOW WILL SAVE YOU!'

'He knows who we are and where we are!'

Man leaned forward, his fists clenched. 'If we put heat into the balloon...'

'If we could, we would then rise, though he would see us,' the Voice ventured. She rubbed at her bare arms. 'Only I can't help do that – for my power has been quenched by *his!*'

'Voice, even if you or I could act, *he* would indeed see – and strike.' Then Joah slowly turned her head. 'Man? You already know as a male he would notice you less. You might even do as you did before and disguise yourself... What can you do?'

Man gave Joah a sickly smile. He had hoped he would not be called upon.

'Last night I acted only through you, Joah. Now this duty must pass to another.'

Faslane was pointing at him. 'Lord Emmanuel, you have to act!'

The truth came tumbling out of Man.

'This isn't just a temporary quenching caused by *him*. My strength is gone. Whatever great magic all of you, or the Prophecies, expect of me now, *I can't do it.*'

Joah was frantic. 'But there are things you have to do; *have to*. And back in Jade you fought *him* and *his* and we escaped!'

'Yes, but in the process I had the power burned out of me!' His insides churning, his face aflame, Man tried to explain. 'Except for a trickle, there's no magic left. When it comes to fighting the Lord of the North – well, I am a dead man!'

They all stared at him; his bleak words were devastating.

Yoshi spoke: 'I've seen a dead man fight!'

'Not this time.'

Joah spoke calmly now. 'Then I do not think we have any good choices left. Nothing about this is in Lady Naosuke's revelation – nothing. We're off the map! We can crash from a

Words of Fury:

height and all die, or come down to surrender. I suppose that's why those boats are placed below.'

'Rotten choices, both,' Yoshi said.

Lady Joah tried to be dignified. 'My friends, we only have minutes.'

'I know that, brave Lady,' said the Voice from Afar. She pointed at the towering, half-mile-tall self-image of ice. 'If I could sing that barrier down, I would, but its scale is way beyond me.'

'IF YOU CONTINUE TO FLY FROM ME, I WILL TAKE WHAT YOU HAVE STOLEN ANYWAY, AND AS PUNISHMENT I WILL EAT YOUR FLESH ALONG WITH YOUR SOULS!'

Man heard the terrifying certainty in that voice. *Eat our flesh,* and *our souls...*

Yes, the Lord of the North has won. We are being sucked on towards that gaping mouth. I wonder what it will be like to be eaten...

Yoshi shook a fist at *his* approaching image. 'If I end up being swallowed, you self-pleasing bastard, I hope I give you indigestion!'

Faslane gave a weak chuckle.

Everyone had admired the young samurai's defiance, but this time Yoshi spoke quietly. 'If the only alternative to our landing is destruction, what else can we do but come down?'

Faslane agreed. 'We'd still be alive.'

'No, we would not!' said the Voice. 'Believe me, brave man of Albion, I know what would happen! There would be no mercy from *him* in the end.'

It had to be talked about, didn't it? Man turned away from the half-mile tall Lord of the North.

'Not even if I gave myself up, somehow, and brought the Eye with me to give *him?* Might that save all of you, if not me?'

'We *cannot* surrender, Emmanuel, and certainly not with the Eye!' The Voice's eyes flashed at him. 'What would your father do? Be unmanned and tame, or fight?'

Man clenched both fists again, this time around his sword-hilts.

'He would fight. And I would, too. It's just I don't see *how...* I mean, look!' Man pointed. Ahead, he saw the glittery whirling shapes come ever closer – *his* deadly weapons, made of hard ice. He saw the thing's gaping mouth sucking in air, saw the sharp ice teeth within. Their enemy was flinging ice blades from the half-mile-tall obstacle. Most were going down but many were flying up, and the fragments made terrifying screaming noises as they flew. 'That's death ahead – for all of us!'

Then something terrible happened: that great ice mouth smiled.

Faslane said, 'Is *he* actually inside that pig-ugly giant? *Is he?*'

Man felt Joah touch his arm.

'His deepest magic must be there. If we were very strong we could hurt him...'

She left the rest unsaid: But we are not very strong...

Suddenly Man knew the one thing he could do.

In a heartbeat Man's short sword was in his hand – the blade used for ritual suicide. Man looked down, and saw his own pale distorted face reflected in the steel. He tried to see the soul behind the green eyes and measure the depths of that soul's courage, but he was inscrutable even to himself. He had been brought here from a different continent, for a purpose still obscure. For a while he had gained new friends, and a home; but in his despair he saw his life differently. He had lost both parents, lost his country, lost himself.

I mustn't be taken alive, that I know. And this way I'll take the Eye with me!

Joah turned to stare at him, her eyes widening.

'Man, stop! You don't know what you're doing!'

'Yes, I do,' he told her, shifting the blade into both hands and pointing it at his stomach. 'There is deep sea below to be my grave. And you *know* that death is better than surrender.'

'Please, no!' Tears had come to her eyes, but her voice was still strong. 'Do *not* make an end of yourself prematurely!'

Man saw then that she truly loved him.

'Lady, I have the Eye and its Talking Book in the casket below. If *he* gets them, and me, isn't that utter disaster for the world?'

She was crying openly now. 'I cannot lie to you.'

'But when I cut them loose, Eye and Book will go into the sea and they will be lost – and I with them. After that *he* will never read the Book, nor touch the Eye, nor me.'

'You will be dead, and then Prophecy cannot be fulfilled!'

Man weighed all that up. What should he do? Act as a samurai, and die? But what if suicide took his soul and the Eye to some dark place where *he* ruled?

Words of Fury:

'Lady Joah, surely my capture by the Lord of the North will end the world... I can't let that happen, and I *won't!*' Man put the point of his short blade to the left of his navel. For one last time he looked at Joah, who had said she loved him, and whose father had replaced his own. Her brown eyes had that soft gold in them, but now they were judging as well as loving. 'I can take the Eye down with me and lose myself in the embrace of the sea! I have the courage; I can do that.'

Can I, really?

Her expression had changed; it was as if a harder, more calculating Joah – a sly stranger – peered out from her face.

'You know best what to do.'

He suddenly knew he had been using Joah's words to delay and to excuse himself. He had been too much of a coward to take action before, but now he would *have* to let himself die, with no hope of renewed life, rather than let the ancient enemy win.

Man looked down at his short sword. The point had already drawn blood. He had to prove his courage to her, and also to himself. If that meant death, so be it.

'*I must not lose to him.* And if I die while keeping the Eye away from him, then I *haven't* lost!'

Man held his short sword ready to slash the ropes binding up the Eye in its metal casket, though he'd use one hand to hold on to it. With the other hand he would cut himself open, and, dying, fling himself with the casket off the bench.

He felt that irrevocable choice as a relief.

But before Man could cut, Faslane spoke.

'My lord Emmanuel, don't! There's no escaping him that way!'

Man had focused on the absolute beyond this life. He was irritated by the interruption.

'What?'

Faslane insisted, 'You won't be lost deep in the sea now, nor will your Eye. Lord Kinross, look down!'

Man did, and saw the sea all round that giant *him* had turned white. On the frozen sea the three ice-bound galleys were already disgorging the beetle-shapes of men.

Faslane said, 'You'd end on the hard ice, and then they'd take the Eye off your corpse!'

Man saw it all now. 'We've been gamed; we've lost.' Suddenly he was in a rage. 'That bitch the Tears is below! She's been working on my mind! Ah, it would have been better to

Words of Fury:

throw ourselves down earlier, all of us, and die with unmarred souls!'

Man made himself look ahead, to where they were being sucked. Inside that gaping mouth their balloon would be ripped into rags; and the Lord of the North would win.

He began counting away the last sixty seconds of his life.

We're dead, dead, *dead*, he thought then, and *he* has won!

Even to Berenda there had only been a shimmering at first, spread out north and south. Then the sea had suddenly flattened, as if giant hands pressed down on the swell, and soon the seawater there froze white.

From further to left and right salt water had blasted upwards in mile-high arcs, with rainbow effects in the sky. Then those arcs began to freeze.

It was not subtle – her lord was rarely that, and never when in a fury – but his work was always effective. The frozen base already stretched for over a mile. She saw how quickly he built up huge ice bones and then laid ice flesh upon them. A roughly triangular shape was forming, half a mile high.

He was risking exhaustion by working at this intensity. Berenda's concern rose. Perhaps she should advise him to ease off?

No; *he* knew best, now and for always.

Here in the cold a white mist formed. Soon Berenda could see no more than fifty paces ahead, then twenty, then five. This thick fog dulled all sounds and made the chilled world blank and wet and mysterious.

In his rough voice the sea-captain cursed the strangeness. What few faces she could still see stared at her in horror. Their feelings didn't count, of course. She began to laugh at them, remembering their numerous slights. Then it occurred to her that a mutiny might be dangerous. She prepared to do violence with her power.

Hagiwara was shivering violently, his eyes frightened though he tried to keep anguish out of his voice.

'What is happening? Even if the balloon *does* fly over, how can we see it? And if we can't see it, how can we act?'

She silenced him with a gesture. 'Faith gives me eyes to see, and I have a mouth to speak.'

The freezing grew worse. There was ice everywhere – on the furled sails, on the rigging, on the decks, and on human flesh.

Words of Fury:

The sea-ice all around held the galley tightly. She heard strained boat-timbers begin creaking. In the fog, dangerous ice-pieces fell. One sharp piece wounded a rower.

She only laughed. '*His* victory *will* come!'

The sea-captain looked at her as if she were mad. Then he turned, to shout out orders. 'Oars, back in the water! Steersman, head us west!'

Black-veiled Berenda seized the thick arm.

'Stay your words, you coward! Your oars are no good on *his* ice!'

On his own galley, the captain always got his own way.

'You crazy bitch! The sea is frozen and it's likely trapped us! If it gets worse the ship's sides will be stove in!'

It was so cold now many of the men were screaming in pain. She saw those close enough to have readable expressions agreed with the captain.

'You've brought us nothing but bad luck, Satan's whore,' he told her. 'Soon we'll sink under the weight of your madness! Well, that won't happen; we go back!'

To deal with this she had to come out of her ecstasy completely, though she hated to lose communion with *him*. She stepped up to the doubter.

'You, sea-captain, talk much too much and see too little.'

He sneered. 'Who are you to tell me anything? You keep giving these hints that you are close to *him*, but what proof is there?' He dared to raise his fists against her. 'What proof?'

The thick, eerie fog meant they could barely see one another now.

'There is this,' she said.

Finger-rings sparkling with power, Lady Berenda put both her hands to her veil and drew it up until her face was fully revealed.

Berenda saw blood flood into the seaman's face. But it was not desire; it was fury and contempt.

'This proves only that you're ugly!'

Incredibly, she felt hurt. 'Oh, you are low!'

He guffawed. 'You give only hard words and soft looks! Am I supposed to be impressed?'

'No, you're supposed to be my victim!'

With a gesture, she paralyzed the man. Held still, a sudden sweat sprang out on his face. Berenda tapped his mouth with one finger. Her touch made his tongue thicken, till that swollen thing could not form words at all. It grew and grew, till it hung down from his mouth – a pink, foot-long penis.

Every man who saw that sickly miracle groaned; some touched their own private parts to ward off the evil.

Fog began to clear from the air, and more and more of the crew could see the horror. Now she tapped a forefinger on his eyeballs, first one unblinking brown sphere and then the other. Instantly both eyes swelled. She released him, to let him feel the pain more.

He put his hands to his face, crouching over and moaning. He tried to push his swelling eyeballs back into their sockets, but it was no use. Both his eyes turned first pink and then red, swelled to fist-size, and then burst.

The sea-captain was in agony, but what was in his mouth meant he could not even cry out – though other men screamed. He fell to his knees on the deck, choking, and began tearing at his own throat.

'All of you, see what happens if you oppose our lord!' said Berenda. She pointed at a trio of wailing, frost-covered seamen. 'You three! String him up by his hands!'

As the fog cleared, the captain was hung from his own foremast. Twenty feet above the deck he kicked out and tried to scream through what was choking him.

It much amused her to see how the pink penis still waved.

Except for the muffled howling, that was that. Berenda looked around at the crew, ready to hurl dangerous but taming magic. There was no need, though. Making an example had worked. The chief mate succeeded to the captaincy, and that was the end of any disputes.

'Look at *him!*' said Hagiwara. 'Look!'

Ahead, ice rose up: a sheer cliff half a mile high – the head and shoulders of her lord, and his partly concealed face. She wanted to fall down and worship his image, but duty called. Instead she pointed upwards, spoke for all to hear.

'Look above and see our master! Fill your hearts with fear, and worship him!'

She gestured at the shining face above them all. It might be foreshortened and grotesque, but it was colossal.

'This is *him*, here to catch the balloon and its crew. There are five of them, being driven by *his* wind. So, when our enemies fall, I want you men to go onto the ice! Claim what you find as *his*, five bodies and a bronze casket, and you will be rewarded.

Words of Fury:

Fail our master, and you will die!'

'They're going through the mouth?'

'Yes, Hagiwara; he will *swallow* them – *and then he will eat!*'

She was laughing. She felt wonderful.

Hagiwara still seemed worried. 'Have they no allies?'

She was more than confident. 'Nothing human could help them now.'

Words of Fury:

Chapter Four: *Immediate Surrender*

A silent, pink dawn had been breaking at The Waning of the Moon when two women in white crossed the meditation garden and headed down towards the deep levels. Though nobody expected physical threats here, they were followed by three bodyguards: elite Sword Maidens.

One woman was dawdling and reluctant. This was the senior Sister, Daisen.

'Holy Mother, Emmanuel and the others fought an air-battle over Jade?'

'Yes.' The other woman in white was the famous Mother Zandar, and she strode on with determination enough for a dozen, even though a narrow white bandage was over her eyes. 'Sandella did a remote viewing and saw Man bring down an Albion airship – '

'The "flying snake" killed! I wish I'd seen *that!*'

'And then he drove off a black battleship, also from the Empire of Blood.'

Daisen slowed. 'He wasn't just lucky?'

'You mustn't disrespect the power of Prophecy!'

'I don't, Mother. I mean, you tell me they are riding a soap-bubble – "riding the winds" as the Prophetic Books say! I only hope their grip on Prophecy, or their good luck, holds.' Daisen lowered her voice. 'You are certain we must steer them to danger?'

'We must do what is necessary.'

'To dispatch a war party to help them was good of you – but such a small party!'

'Far-Speaker Keli is with Sweet Snake and her Maidens, there to open a line of communication that will allow me to advise our friends.'

'Is advice enough?'

Zandar laughed. 'If the advice is good, and it's *my* advice!'

The dark, steep stairs gave onto a large underground waiting room. Zandar took comfort from the sight of the familiar walls with their faintly luminous painted icons. They were powerful saints indeed: St Peter with his keys, St George in samurai armor slaying a dragon, and the Virgin herself in glowing gold.

Two dark corridors led off, left and right. The iconic saints gazed on as Zandar headed down the right-hand one. Daisen pulled closed the metal-barred gate and locked it behind her.

Words of Fury:

They left their escort, Winter Morning the she-captain and the others, here.

'If our young friends die because of what I do, Daisen, the responsibility will be mine. But remember Emmanuel has been lucky before, fighting *him*.'

'I hope we have the same luck if *he* comes here!'

Mother Zandar turned to her friend.

'Daisen, cheer up! There are wards around the whole of The Waning. That keeps this place safe even from the Lord of the North.'

'There are no guarantees.'

'No, but even if there were guarantees coming, which there aren't, I would not wait! Our friends need help *now*. When dawn comes and *he* can see...' Zandar let the sentence trail off.

They walked the underground corridor. Once they were in their own secluded, plain cell, Zandar locked its metal gate, too, then closed the wooden door which was carved with lucky charms.

Daisen put a hand on her arm. 'Is our mere Far-Seeing so dangerous to *this* place?'

In wall-niches, two candles within glass lit the room. Zandar checked all was secure.

Now she could speak freely. 'We cannot only look. We must send forth our souls. If we then touch *him*, as we might, of course that is a risk.'

'But we have the benefit of – '

'In the fight Man got badly hurt, and he may not be willing to work the Eye.'

'A serious injury?'

'It was a deadly bite given by *his* agent, "the Tears".'

'You mean he is *dying*?'

'From a kiss, if you look at it that way.'

Daisen was shaken; it took her seconds to make even an appearance of calm. 'Can young Emmanuel be healed?'

'If we can get him here, I will try. If I obtain the Eye and use it, I might feel optimistic.'

'But, Mother, what if our Emmanuel dies during the journey?'

'He might die on the "midnight beach", or before, or after. But I am prepared to risk that – as he must, though all unknowing.' Mother Zandar gave a grim smile, rather impressed by her own ruthlessness. 'I now mean to steer them away from *his* path and towards that beach.'

'But you can't even be sure Monster Beach *is* the "midnight beach" of Prophecy!'

'There is no certainty for any of us now.'

'They may all die.'

'If that is their fate, then so be it. To serve Prophecy I will do everything, risk everything – and you must help.'

Zandar gave that warrior smile again and laid down on a futon. She realized how very quiet it was here; quiet as the grave.

Daisen sat and laid her back on the stone wall.

'Sister, are you ready to dream-walk?'

She sensed how Daisen closed her eyes, then opened them again. Her eyes, Zandar remembered, were a warm, piercing brown.

'No, Mother.'

Zandar's teeth ground together. 'You are unwilling!'

'I'm terrified! If we go searching, I fear *he* will find *us*.'

'Daisen, beloved – it must be done, and you know it.' She took Daisen's wrist. 'Will you come with me?'

There was a deep sigh. 'If you go, I will follow.'

'Thank you. Now, look at the map for me.'

Daisen spread out the great chart on the floor beside her. It showed the Shimabara peninsula and the sea around it. She put a fingertip on a spot out to sea, west of the land.

'Last night we worked out that by dawn the balloon should be over open sea, thirty miles off the west coast.'

'And where are they?' Zandar asked.

Daisen closed her eyes for several heart-beats, then opened them again.

'About where we predicted, and their course is the same, which is suspicious in itself.' Daisen's finger traced the calculated course. 'It seems they will still make landfall over this place, Four Rocks.'

'No.'

'I've been there. It's unimportant – and safe.'

'Their being safe is wrong – and impossible.'

'Mother! I hate it when you sound so brutal!'

'We are running out of time. Now we *know* the balloon *must* land on "the black shore" and they *must* confront monsters, though they die doing it. *That* is Prophecy!'

Daisen audibly swallowed, and eyed her, but to Zandar's relief she did not argue. Zandar had felt enough pricks of

Words of Fury:

conscience already.

It would not be easy for her and Sister Daisen to project themselves so far, and harder still to do it with such a subtle use of power that *he* might not see them. But Zandar believed they might go unseen when they dream-walked, at least for a while.

So Mother Zandar began the necessary spell. She used Latin. When those words of power were spoken, the air in the cell trembled, though nothing physical happened.

'He's trying to suppress opposing magic, Daisen.'

'With some success!'

'And I feel his thinking. Come sunrise, something immense is planned...'

'But you don't know what?'

Zandar sighed. 'No, Sister. But it is gigantic, so let's hope we don't have to face it.'

Then their joint magic worked. Their two souls rose up, hand in hand. When the walls and mad, elegant towers of The Waning were left behind, they flew west over the Shimabara mountains, to the sea.

It was still dark below, though dawn had come back home. Zandar scanned for thoughts at high altitude. Joah especially was both very familiar and very strong-souled.

A few minutes passed, as the stars faded.

Zandar heard herself worrying. 'I don't feel them, Daisen. Do you?'

'No, Mother. But I do feel *him*, continually – so he is in the hunt. And if our friends have passed away, or are in his hands, I would not hear them, would I?'

The realization of *his* presence was making Zandar feel ill. Nevertheless, she scanned the heavens. For a quarter hour they went from north to south, then a few miles west, and finally back east.

'There is no balloon,' said Daisen, with finality. 'He has intercepted them and eaten them up. We are wasting our time.'

Then Zandar sensed aggressive male power approaching them. She turned her head, trying to see what was happening. 'It's *him*! And if *he* catches us, it is death!' Zandar swallowed. Though the Lord of the North had already blinded her, she hadn't expected to be this scared. She said aloud, 'Stand down, Daisen, and return home.'

'No! – Unless you come with me.'

'I don't need you now that I can see.'

'If you can "see", Mother, so can *he*! If you stay, you will reveal yourself.'

Her own unfortunate turn of phrase had made her wince, but Zandar kept trying to see with her power, while avoiding his intense magic.

'He has created some kind of power centre at sea-level, though his weaves go well above. He's doing something, and I want to see it.'

'What's the point? That's *him* right here – too big to fight! Please come home!'

Zandar raised her head and broke concentration. Her vision of the distant sea vanished. Surely withdrawal wasn't what Daisen wanted? Surely Daisen was wholly committed to the fight?

She said it very delicately. 'Would you have me run?'

'If they have encountered *him,* they are dead or his prisoners.'

'I will not give up, as long as there is life in me! My title is "Mother", and that means love!'

'You cannot hope to rescue our friends *or* the Eye!'

'You are right; I cannot hope. But that is no limitation. As long as I have the courage to act, I *may* act, even without hope.' Zandar scanned more sky. Then she saw some tiny flicker of movement. 'I see something!'

'Is it them?'

Zandar concentrated. Lady Joah? Emmanuel? Sitting together on that bench below the balloon?

'It is hard to see with magic, now *he* is so powerful that he interferes with everything! Oh, I wish we had some strength to search physically at sea. We have so few human forces now!'

'When Shogun Anamizu called on us to help fight *him* up North, we had to respond. But you're right. Now we can barely staff The Waning.'

'We have allies coming.'

'You truly believe that Lady Rishiri and the Princess are your allies?'

'Allies to me, Daisen? Perhaps not. To *him*? Never. They *will* know their duty.'

'*If* they come! – And, God knows, a part of me hopes they don't!'

Zandar waved a hand. 'Enough! I have seen something that just might be them!' She squinted her dead eyes, but then

Words of Fury:

disappointment crashed down. 'Nothing! It was only a few seabirds flocking together in a line.'

'They are dead, Mother!'

'We don't *know* that.'

But surely, thought Zandar, if they are still sailing the sky they will soon be revealed? Or is Daisen right, and something terrible has happened? What if there is nothing to see, now, nothing to find?

She did not want to encounter *him* again, and a part of her wanted to head home.

Nevertheless, she focused her mind again. Now the clear light of dawn revealed something new – it was hardly more than a row of dots, but it was something.

Her quick magical gesture brought her closer.

'Daisen, look! Two girls, with three young men. Emmanuel, with beloved Joah alongside! And they really are riding below a *soap bubble!*'

For one moment Zandar felt contact with Man, who actually seemed to be staring at her, but then his thoughts faded. She frowned at what she had seen in him. There had been poisons in his soul: guilt and fury, and a frightening lack of self-confidence.

This Tears has poisoned him, he cannot now use the Eye – and so we have *already* been defeated...

'Mother, look what lies ahead of them! Look!'

She saw it. '*He* has made an idol of himself *half a mile high!* That's a colossus, to be worshipped!'

'From the sheer scale of *him*, I might worship him myself.'

Zandar laughed. 'I used to tell men that size isn't everything! Of course, they never believed me...' She turned her gaze to the sea below the idol, and saw boat-masts. 'He has turned much of the sea to ice, and I see there are three galleys trapped in it.'

'Are they *his?*'

'I can't tell. So far below the balloon, what good could they do him?'

Then Zandar found out.

The deep, sure voice shook the universe. 'COME DOWN, YOU PEOPLE IN THE AIR! EMMANUEL! LADY JOAH! LAND! ONLY IMMEDIATE SURRENDER TO MY SERVANTS BELOW WILL SAVE YOU.'

Zandar saw their faces, Joah, Emmanuel, the three others. Except for the one male stranger she saw how very young they were, and how very afraid.

'Oh, what power he has!'

Zandar did not turn to see her friend's fear. 'He can be fought!'

'An ant might fight a tiger, but to what effect? Mother, be sensible! Withdraw!'

Their friends flew on towards that gigantic and icy Lord of the North.

'I did not come here to be sensible. Now be quiet!'

'IF YOU CONTINUE TO FLY FROM ME, I WILL TAKE WHAT YOU HAVE STOLEN ANYWAY, AND AS PUNISHMENT I WILL EAT YOUR FLESH ALONG WITH YOUR SOULS!'

'He has the ice-teeth to do it!'

'Yes, he has. Daisen, when they hit him *they* will be dead, and the Eye lost...'

Daisen was almost screaming. 'Is that your responsibility?'

'Yes!' Zandar felt anger flood her, an anger powered by fear as well as by love. 'Yes, it is! For everyone who turns their back to the evils of this world is helping evil!'

Afraid, Daisen wiped away a tear. 'If even one of them sacrificed himself or herself, and lessened the load...'

'It must be *all* we save, or none. Christ died for *everyone*. – Ah!'

'He has seen you!'

At his thought-touch, Zandar's flesh crawled. 'Yes.'

'Mother, *run!*'

Words of Fury:

Chapter Five: *Vulnerable Emotion*

The Lord of the North knew exactly where Zandar was. His huge and ugly spirit-form flicked towards her, fast as a striking snake. There was a sensation of rough masculine hands upon her naked soul. Terror crawled on icy spider-legs over all Zandar's body.

Her breath caught; desperate to get away, she back-flipped.

Somehow *he* lost his grip on her, but Zandar knew Daisen was right. There was no way to keep safe except by running.

She didn't run. Instead, she rose as unobtrusively as she could. Then she was deathly quiet, floating and not thinking or feeling, only watching *him* below.

His giant head-and-shoulders would be visible for fifty miles. From mere sight of this, how many people would come to worship him? She feared the number would be large. As for herself, she felt only fear so great she could not fear him more.

I've been blinded, but *this* may be worse...

She stayed still as death as his spirit-soul searched for her.

While he did that, she used her power to scan his giant self-image.

It was bad news she whispered to Daisen. 'Daisen, there is no way the balloon can get through. This graven image is beyond my power to break.'

'Then come home!'

Mother Zandar saw the balloon had been driven close to the ice-idol. She heard the young people on the bench begin screaming. For one poignant moment she let herself look upon them with something *he* would never have: compassion.

The one moment of vulnerable emotion was enough. He sensed it, sensed her, transported himself above, and began to focus his power.

The image was undignified but deadly: an evil boy, focusing a burning-glass upon insects...

Zandar felt pain begin. 'He has me now, but I cannot desert my friends!'

'Do you think even your *death* will distract him enough to help them?' Daisen shrieked.

Zandar knew the cold, cruel answer to that. His energy on her skin was like being scalded by cold, and she knew she could not endure it long. Lying there on the futon, Zandar was already panting from pain.

Nevertheless, she somehow bore the pain, and then she

shoved hard, so that her living arms generated magical motion. Many miles away the bench swung up like a pendulum – and it stayed up. Now the bench was leading the way, with the huge globe of the balloon following. You could have drawn a horizontal line straight through both.

That had taken *him* by surprise. Was her timing right? It had better be.

She *saw* them on the bench, waving their arms, about to be swallowed by his spike-toothed mouth. Yes, he would eat them, all five.

She drew back both her arms, concentrating all her power – and then she drove her two clenched fists forward as her friends plunged into the gaping mouth.

As they neared the giant image, Joah heard Man shouting as if all this was her fault.

'I wish I'd thrown myself down! I could have taken the Eye with me and kept it from *him* forever!'

'You would have died!'

'We're going to die anyway, stupid!'

They were jerked up, screaming. Now they all went flying feet-first towards *him* and his savage mouth. Joah held onto the safety rope with both hands, terrified by the constant shaking and the sheer drop below and even more by the hideous face ahead.

Their enemy was going to swallow them whole. In a last useless gesture of self-protection Joah held her forearm up high and spoke a shielding charm.

There was nothing more she could do. As she neared *him*, the deadly cold he radiated bit at her flesh. For her and all her friends this was death.

Then the ice face exploded.

Her power went smashing through his sneering mouth and deep into him. He felt that; he roared with pain as pieces of ice teeth whirled away. Now, with two hand-jerks that used her thumbs, Zandar ripped his mouth wide open.

That pleased her. Perhaps her friends could get through.

Then she saw that monstrous throat still had fangs of ice inside. Now she mouthed something not a prayer – she still had some Sword Maiden habits which a high marriage and then holy orders hadn't cured – and hit out with her hands again and again.

As she tried to enlarge the wicked mouth, ice-shards flew away. Her hands hurt terribly now and were visibly bloody. As always, magic exerted a price. But now the mouth was torn open. – Though perhaps not wide enough for the full, round balloon to pass?

With incredible delicacy, she massaged the frail balloon into a different shape, narrower and longer.

Their enemy reacted: he laughed at her.

'YOU ARE BLINDED AND YOU ARE WEAK! LEAVE THEM, ZANDAR, OR YOUR SOUL IS FORFEIT!'

'Daisen, they're inside him, and I can't protect them anymore!'

'Then leave them,' Daisen said, weeping, 'and come home!'

What else could Zandar do? It wasn't a conscious decision, but she awoke back in the thinking cell.

'I have saved myself, but at what cost! I have left my young friends... Hate me, Daisen!' Instead of receiving hatred, she felt Sister Daisen take her right hand in both of hers. In this touch Zandar felt pure undying love. 'Daisen, that comforts me! Even if the flesh dies, love can continue.'

'Forever.'

Berenda stood on the ice-shrouded galley, looking up proudly. Her lord's creation would swallow his enemies; there could be no escape. Gladness beat in her heart. Around her men howled as frost bit into their flesh, but that was nothing to her.

Then an impossible thing happened. There was a thunderous explosion high in the ice. His face on the idol was suddenly terribly disfigured – from another's magic!

Berenda wanted to dance out her fury. Then she saw giant pieces of ice flying down towards her.

There was no time for protective magic. In terror, she covered her face with her hands. Most of the ice came crashing down on the frozen water in between Berenda's galley and *him*, but some hit the boat. Newly wounded men screamed. Next, a giant piece crashed to starboard, so big it smashed right through the sea-ice and created a wave that washed over the gunwale and took with it a man. Now more deadly pieces, some weighing tons, crashed down around the galleys.

Where was the help from her master? Where was his love, when she had done so much for *him*?

Suddenly he left.

Why, she didn't know. She had been promised things by him, and now he had run.

A man's voice wailed: 'His image is cracking! Look! *He* has been broken!'

She was going to silence Hagiwara, but when she looked up at the towering figure she realized it was true. A crack had ripped all the way down from the hole blasted through his face. She saw it slowly widen. From top to bottom the graven image began splitting.

But her master *could not* fail. This was all so *wrong*.

Now sunlight came through the gap, lighting up the galley. A quarter-mile stretch of the broken image, topped by *his* ruined face, began to lean towards her.

At first it went slowly, but as it tilted further it gathered speed. This was hundreds of thousands of tons of ice tipping over, maybe millions of tons – a mass far beyond her power to affect. Berenda knew it would smash the galley and drown them all.

Somebody screamed, 'This cannot be! I have been given *promises*!'

She realized the voice was her own.

In that moment, she lost her faith forever.

From the impact, waves rose up everywhere. She wondered what it would be like when she drowned.

When Zandar returned to the fight, she guided the bench and those who clung to it through the opened-up mouth, with the sausage-shape balloon behind. Then Zandar once again struck out.

While clearing away his ice teeth she saw right into him, saw his immense power and his obsession with the Eye. She could see it now as he saw it, glowing at white heat and deadly dangerous, with a strong link to both Joah and Man – and if that link was broken by their deaths...

She saw the horror he anticipated. At once her imagination put into his mind the eruption as the Eye cracked the sea-bottom and turned square miles of ocean into a hurricane of hot rain...

She saw his fear flare. Then he was *gone*.

He had chosen self-preservation.

'Where did he go, Mother?'

'Daisen, there are *incredible* energies within the Eye. If the

Words of Fury: 45

two who are partially attuned should die ... well, when the link goes those energies will probably be released.'

'What does that mean?'

Zandar's mouth twisted as she kept her trembling arms raised. By magic, she was both carrying the bench and pushing it on, though she was at the limit of her endurance.

'I would want to be further off than The Waning if that happens, and even then there would be no guarantee that I would survive – and it is the same for *him*.'

They were beyond his smashed mouth, in the chill tunnel of ice. Joah looked behind, to see the translucent balloon-shape following them. It had somehow been distorted into a long cylinder only just narrow enough to get through.

'What if we hit the walls?'

The balloon seemed to bounce from wall to rough wall and its gleaming skin showed dents that took a moment to heal, but it somehow stayed whole.

'Yes!' said Faslane, roaring as only that roaring man could. 'We might escape *him* yet!'

Then they were right through, just as the bench slewed down. Direct sunlight shone on them, and that light was like a promise fulfilled.

Joah had had dark moments, but now she was exultant. All her prayers had been answered, though she knew *he* could still strike them dead.

'We're alive!' said Man, and he sounded amazed.

'Yes, I prayed, and all of us are alive!' said Joah, suddenly seeing that life itself is an answered prayer.

She and the others were still swinging wildly below the balloon and all the shaking was making her sick, but her soul was triumphant.

'Look behind!' said the Voice.

Joah did, to see the ice idol crack apart. Huge sections began to separate. Soon they fell, and slumped into the sea. This raised a tidal wave, which spread out in all directions. She blinked at its speed. It left only wrecked ice-islands behind it.

'That's the end of *him*, and that'll be the end of *her*.'

Man had sounded vindictive, but he could hardly be blamed.

Joah herself still felt joy. They were drifting powerlessly before the wind, with the greatest enemy in the world still wanting to locate them and destroy them, but Joah knew their

Words of Fury:

luck had changed.

Mother Zandar saw the idol break and fall in the water, and that was very satisfying. But she knew *he* would return, to find the balloonists and kill them.

So Zandar had no choice. Though it might mean her death, she had to lure the Lord of the North away, and there was only one guaranteed way to do that.

Of course Daisen saw what she wanted to do. 'Mother, you've done enough. For now, he is gone; come home!'

'I cannot, till I have diverted *him* from our friends and restored them to the road they must follow.'

'Mother, to send them to that cursed place would make you as cruel as *him!*'

'It is a necessity.'

'And if they die there, on the dark-as-midnight beach?'

'Then that is God's will, but we will know we tried!'

She let the balloon fly on, and flung spells of misdirection and disguise all around it. Every yard gained now was a yard that put her friends further away from him and closer to sanctuary.

The balloon sailed east; she prayed.

Then *he* returned. Making that giant self-image had drained him, but he was still incredibly powerful. He focused on her with everything. Again she felt his attention like an agonizing freeze that burned. Then he started hitting out. She tried to dodge his blows, but he struck savagely and sometimes connected.

Zandar knew, and had often said, that *he* was a face of profound forces, and he had already blinded her. But he had weaknesses, for example little self-control. When she twisted away from him he bulled straight past her, furious.

She had eluded him yet again, and that gave her satisfaction.

'Daisen, I have given our friends time!'

'But how can it be *enough* time?'

So she stopped dead, a mile and a half up in the air, and then showed him her soul.

At once he flew towards her. Zandar flung herself away, dancing her mind among the clouds that haunted the blue arch of the morning sky. Suddenly she was high on all the magical power she was employing. She even began wondering if she might lead him right to The Waning.

If he can be lured close, and my sisters use all their power, perhaps even he *can be smashed...*

Words of Fury:

Would he be lured?

She knew it was possible.

Anger made him too chaotic in his mind to act against her, and that gave her precious moments to mind-speak directly to those with magic.

'Sweet Joah, my Emmanuel, and you the Voice from Afar, can you hear me?'

She felt their assent.

'He is mad with fury now, so perhaps I can divert him from you, but afterwards *you* must outsmart *him!* Think of how to do that. Remember, he knows where you are going!'

'We're headed over Mount Unzen to The Waning.' She saw how Man's hands closed on his sword-hilts. 'So he *will* find us!'

'Emmanuel, you must evade him and then find your way back to Prophecy. For *your* end will mean the world ends!'

'Oh, Mother, Mother!' said Joah.

'That end may yet come.' Zandar choked on this bitter truth, watching *his* fury as it shook a cubic mile of air. 'But worry about yourselves. Your balloon is too fragile to fly on. Without my protection it would not have survived. You must land soon – you won't make it over the mountains.'

Now Man spoke, sounding aggrieved.

'So at best we can only hurry to a doubtful landing, and then walk over a bloody *mountain* – at risk *all* the time! Can't you give us more?'

Zandar realized how sorely Emmanuel had been wounded both in flesh and spirit.

Then she saw *him* coming again.

'I have given you more than you know, young Man! Quickly, all of you, see what is in my mind!' She tried to project a spell of invisibility into the minds of Joah and the Voice, though it was probably beyond them. Still, she had tried. Then she gave them some prophetic lines about the midnight-black beach.

Suddenly agony struck.

'Ah!' Zandar moaned. 'Now *he* has me.'

She was distantly aware of how her body writhed about on the futon. She wondered if she should have talked more openly about the beach and its horrors, but it was too late now.

'I will lead him away if I can, but...'

When that sentence stayed unfinished Joah addressed the empty air. 'How long have we got?'

'At worst *no time at all!*'

Words of Fury:

'If I check my map,' Yoshi began.

'I cannot stay to hear! There is strange land ahead, different to ours. If you have the courage to land there and face down monsters, *his* power in such a place will be weak! Keep Emmanuel safe, and the Eye of Jade, and the Talking Book. That will make any sacrifice of mine worthwhile. Know that I love you all!' It was a hoarse whisper that hardly sounded like Mother Zandar at all. 'Ah! *He* has hurt me!'

He hurt her more. There was pulse after pulse of pain, even though the Lord of the North never quite caught her directly. Meanwhile, Zandar was leading him further and further east, to The Waning of the Moon. This was the only place whose power might possibly damage him. *He* tried to follow her swift, twisting course over the water, but he was projecting himself from much further away, and lacked her agility.

Eventually, he slowed. He was just there, high above the blue sea a few miles off the coast. She had a sense of *his* tired mind focusing elsewhere. Was he going to stop following her, turn back and strike at the balloon? Or was this all a trick?

Zandar had to presume he would attack her friends again, so she stopped and once more showed her soul to *him*.

It had been a trick.

He struck instantly.

She felt his power overwhelm hers; she was exhausted. She swooned before his assault, and it was all she could do to fall helplessly away from this monster.

He followed after, and she felt his power closing on her legs like the jaws of a shark. When she was held, he squeezed her hard.

Words of Fury:

Chapter Six: *Flesh Like Glass*

Lady Joah saw Man was staring beyond the horizon, into infinity. 'When he made that ice-god... I never imagined even *he* could have so much power!'

'Please don't give up,' she said quickly. She was stunned that even brave Emmanuel could be brought to such a low.

'He iced miles of sea! He could do it to a whole city!'

She knew suddenly that *he* or one of his agents had touched Emmanuel deep in the soul.

'Perhaps – though back in our beloved Jade he didn't. It's true the Lord of the North is strong, but *he* made a titanic effort, and it's weakened him.'

Joah sensed that much about the Lord of the North. But then she saw Man's face turn sour again. He looked over his shoulder, and shuddered as the ice-wreckage dwindled behind them.

'You know they will talk of what *he* did here for a thousand years... *He* will be back, and when he finds us...'

'Let's celebrate what *we* have done,' the Voice said. 'We have flown many miles, and so far he hasn't laid a weave directly upon us. Lady Joah, now *he* has been lured away, let us make a wind to drive ourselves over the mountains!'

Joah leaned forward across Man and spoke to the other young woman.

'Anything done with more than a flick of power will show him where we are!'

'So we should do nothing?'

This voice snapped with command. 'I agree with you, Voice; we should risk *some* decisive action.'

'Lord Yoshi!' said Joah in distress, feeling this disagreement was almost treachery. Yoshi was a noble; surely he would do what was right?

But the Fujiwara heir continued, 'What are our alternatives to flying on? Come down in the sea and likely drown? Or get to land, but *only* if we are lucky, and touch down on an unknown shore with a long dangerous trek ahead?'

The Voice said simply, 'Neither plan sounds good. I'd rather fly straight to The Waning! So why don't we try to do that? *He* is no longer suppressing our powers. *He* is no longer even here!'

'No,' Joah said stubbornly, 'he'll locate us.'

'If you can do something, Lady Voice, you must do it soon!

Words of Fury:

We're falling, see?' Faslane told them all. He was looking hard at sky, sea, and the approaching shore – and now at the Voice. 'Lady, if you hope to reach the shore, let alone fly over yonder mountain, do something now.'

'I will,' said the Voice.

'No!' said Joah, loudly. 'You play into *his* hands!'

The Voice slowly turned her head. Within the wayward mass of golden hair, her expression set hard. 'I think not. I think the one acting as if on *his* side is you!'

There was a shocked silence. Joah swallowed, hiding her face from the bright sunlight.

Is *he* somehow here with us right now, stirring up all this depressing treachery?

Joah wasn't sure if she was responding to the Voice, or to her own thoughts. 'That's ridiculous.'

'We must evade *him* now,' said the Voice. Joah knew the girl from the port was theatrical and flighty, but far from weak. The Voice from Afar had a stubborn quality of her own. 'We could go higher by putting a little heat into the balloon.'

'You'd wreck it,' said Man.

'I could be gentle – gentler than you can imagine, you rough man!'

The Voice's lovely smile took most of the sting from that rebuke, but Man did not retreat. 'Joah was right. If you show your power, *he* is sure to notice.'

'Hear him, girl!' said Joah. 'We must be patient.'

Now the Voice, that foreign girl who had been orphaned and once been poor as dirt, turned to face the daughter of the city's overlord.

'I know that you are the great lady, and I suppose that I am nothing in your sight. You call me "girl", though we are much of an age. Yet I too am Christian, and I too have soul power. We don't know how long *he* will keep away, but for the moment we are *free*! Please, let's not be cowards, let's act!'

Joah had stiffened as the other spoke. She suspected she had plain fury on her own face, though she knew this was not the time to express it. That would only make things worse. As they stared at one another for long, long seconds Joah's anger slowly died away. She read a supreme sincerity and goodness in the wayward foreign girl.

That goodness, and the Voice's mention of her faith, were commanding. For now at least all Joah's indecision and fear melted away.

So, with no more words, the two of them joined hands over Man's lap, linked their powers and made a strong though subtle weave. When Joah nodded, the Voice made a single right-handed gesture. Over their heads, power flared sun-bright within the balloon.

They all felt heat on their faces. With the air newly re-heated within it, the balloon might have been kicked upward; Joah felt it rush dizzyingly higher. She saw the sea below retreat, the details there shrinking and shrinking into a blue blandness marred only by an expanding misshapen circle. She knew that was the tsunami created when *his* idol collapsed into the sea.

Man said, 'We're going up. Voice, you played that beautifully!'

He had sounded admiring, Joah noted with some jealousy. Not that she *was* really jealous, of course, it was just that...

After a minute, Joah saw they were perhaps five thousand feet up and still ascending. What they could see of the horizon was many miles off. From all the way up here they looked down onto what seemed like mountain-ranges of pure white.

Yoshi was clearly awed. 'Look how the clouds have built up! They are like immaculate, shining snow, heaped up by the gods!' Then he turned to Man. 'We could even hide in these clouds, do you think?'

Man said only, 'Joah? Voice? Is there no more you ladies can do?'

Joah took that as a criticism and snapped, 'I have done everything that was possible, and more!'

Now Man glared at her. When she saw that, Joah glared right back at him. But then she saw the Voice from Afar lean back and give Man a very, very languid look.

'I enjoyed exercising my power before, dear Emmanuel. There is more that *I* will try – Mother Zandar had it in mind for us, though it may not work.'

Joah saw her hands and lips move, in the strange interrelated manner that indicated a spell. There was a faint deep music in the air that had no obvious source. Then the Voice made a casual-looking gesture with her left hand.

For Joah the quality of the light suddenly changed. Then she looked down at her own left hand and gasped.

Her flesh was now like glass – quite translucent. Her hand had almost vanished.

'Look at us!' Joah said in wonder. Even the strong bones of Joah's forearms, legs and pelvis were barely shadows. The others, she saw, were just the same – ghostly and very hard to see. 'I have disappeared!'

'Aye, we're bloody invisible!' Scots Faslane made much of this small miracle, laughing with gusto. 'That'll make it easier to slip by *him*.'

'Yes,' Joah said, wondering if the Voice's spell might save them, wondering why she, herself, hadn't suggested the same thing. 'We are hidden in the best way possible, in plain view.'

Words of Fury:

Chapter Seven: *We Must All Face Monsters*

Mother Zandar came to herself panting on the sweat-soaked futon.

'Mother! You escaped *him!*'

'Not exactly.' Zandar's voice rasped, much like *his*. If this was a victory, however small, why did she have the taste of terror in her mouth? 'I think he has followed me...'

For a moment, Daisen cupped her hands to hold Zandar's face. 'You are safe in this sanctuary.'

'I know.'

'Are our friends also safe?'

As she remembered *his* touch, Zandar could not even speak. She still quivered from the horror of his rough embrace.

'I got them through the ice!' she said eventually, though there was more amazement in her voice than firm triumph. She wondered if the Voice from Afar and Lady Joah had understood her last messages. 'And when *he* retreated, I was able to advise them...'

'You gave instructions about the "midnight beach"?'

Zandar raised a hand.

'My predecessor Lady Naosuke did not give instructions – so I do not. I do no more than guide. I told them only that they need to cross strange land, where *his* power will be less.' Zandar grimaced at the risks she was making her friends take. 'What is on Monster Beach is made clear by the very name – but I believe they must go there.'

'It is too cruel to to steer them towards such peril.'

'Daisen, when our time comes we must all face monsters.'

Daisen wrung her hands together. 'Mother!'

'We are protected here, but our friends are not, even if they tried my invisibility spell. When I sense he has returned to the hunt...' Zandar took a breath, her heart thumping. She didn't want to face the Lord of the North again, but she knew she had to. 'I will be bait again. It is necessary.'

'You're so tired you're shaking! Take one more risk and he'll catch you!'

Zandar waved a hand, and then changed the gesture so that Daisen brought her water in a cup.

The water had been chilled by magic, and to Zandar it tasted like liquid music. In gratitude, she sighed and then closed her dead, hidden eyes.

'How strange, that a cup of water can bring us so near Heaven...'

'Only when it is so wanted and so needed, Mother. Otherwise it is ordinary.'

Zandar luxuriated over the taste and the chill.

'Mother, where is *he* now?'

There was a sudden, vast knocking. The entire ring-walled Waning shook.

'Guess!' Zandar managed a brief laugh as the impact came again. It was like a blow upon a stout door, though Zandar knew this door would not be forced open easily. 'For now, here is the best place to have him. He's trying to force his way in, and that takes up his time and energy. No-one here will open the way for *him*, and our fortress has deep-magic wards. Every minute *he* wastes threatening us is a minute he is away from our friends.'

But at every strike the stone floor and walls trembled, and the pounding grew steadily worse.

'He is giving me a headache.' Daisen touched both temples, then sighed.

'He has great power, true. And there is more to think of! In no variant of the Prophecies I have read is there mention of *him* as a giant idol.'

'What does that mean?'

'I fear it means we are in unknown territory and have no maps.'

'Then we must have faith!'

Zandar knew she lacked the faith Daisen mentioned. In her mind, Zandar saw a catastrophic bursting of the balloon and a deadly fall. She saw many evil things ahead, and few good.

'If they face monsters, I want to believe they will be supported by Prophecy. But what if I am wrong, and they die?'

'There is no comfort I can give, Mother, if your faith gives none.'

'The instant *he* leaves this place is the instant I follow him.'

'Will the Lord of the North trail the balloon again, or go back North?'

'I think it will be the balloon for now, but of course he wants to conquer Rumoi and the entire North – as a start!'

As she said 'Rumoi', Mother Zandar had put her right hand above the clay relief model she had been working on.

The brown-grey clay had been sent here from the great Northern island Ezo, by Lady Egawa. Rumoi was the port city

Words of Fury:

there that was the Imperial armies' headquarters. Using the gifted clay, Zandar and Irizo had modeled all of Ezo, showing mountains and inlets and cities like Rumoi itself.

No doubt Zandar's intention was plain.

'No, Mother! Rumoi is too far from here! If *he* sees you there he'll kill you!'

Did she dare go so far from all the protections of home? Zandar's hand hovered above the clay model, which embodied a powerful spell. When she *did* touch that clay, her soul would go North, and *he* would know, and leave the balloon alone and pursue her.

Her fingertips almost touched the model city: Rumoi.

If *he* was threatened there, surely *he* would go there?

'I have to distract our enemy, for I sensed another plan in his mind that may yet bring down our friends and seize the great Eye.'

Daisen was emphatic. 'It will be *deadly* to go where *he* is strongest!'

His great fists were still beating on the ancient wards. It was almost like the tolling of a solemn bell.

Zandar pulled her hand away from the clay model, wondering how long the Lord of the North would pound away here.

She was thinking aloud, now. 'There was that servant he has, or *had*, the Tears... That his-her magic of hers had great power, but also some subtlety. I suppose she is dead. But hers would have been a wonderful soul to save...'

'The Tears is *his* willing slave! Her soul is dark as night.'

'Night is always followed by day.'

'That's empty word-play! Perhaps nobody is born condemned, but those who turn to *him* later in life have condemned themselves, and *stay* condemned.'

'Daisen, that is wicked! Those who repent *can* be saved!'

'What, even *him* above us now?' It was almost a sneer from Daisen. 'You might have done something with *her*, but you can't imagine that you could bring *him* to repentance!'

'I have always had a powerful imagination, Daisen.'

His hammering ceased. The sudden silence made Zandar raise her head.

'He's stopped.' With her power, Zandar scanned the horizon, and saw him moving. 'He's heading back to the sea west of Shimabara, to hunt them again!'

'You cannot stop him.'

'Can't I?'

Zandar moved to touch the clay of Rumoi, but then hesitated.

He must not catch me... That would be worse than death. Yes. And yet I must risk it...

With no more hesitation Zandar put a forefinger onto her magic model and touched the port city Rumoi.

Immediately, she was *there* – in the cold blue sky above that place, being bait.

But *he* did not follow her; he stayed west of Shimabara. He was hunting Man and the Eye again. So now Zandar radiated power till she burned like a star; she called out to him in loud mind-speech, insulting and defiant.

Still he did not come. What if he ignored her attempts to lead him away? What if the Lord of the North stayed in the hunt down there in the South, and caught them?

That would be disaster.

She shouted out in mind-speech. 'World, look! There is that worm called "the Lord of the North"! There is that pitiful coward, hiding away from a woman!'

He came after her so fast he took Zandar by surprise.

From a few yards off she saw his face.

In soul-form his appearance was rawly male and terrifying. The eyeballs were solid white. In his body huge muscles bulged everywhere, like a caricature of moronic manliness.

In the moment before he reached her his ravings shook the sky.

While his own speed carried him forward, Zandar fell back.

She let him catch up with her again, then risked everything to whirl around his presence. If she could keep him here, on the balloon they could escape!

She was mocking him, there in the sky above the port he wanted to own.

I am here! she said to him. *If you are so almighty, you stinking imitation of a man, come take me!*

He lashed out again and again, but he could not quite hit Zandar directly.

Over Rumoi the sky rippled as the two incredible magics contended. Male magic and female magic went tearing at their opposites till the sky shook and lightning played to the delayed sound of thunder.

Words of Fury:

Her use of the power was intoxicating, as it always was. She began to laugh, in spite of what he had done to her before and the worse things he might do now. They had an audience below, Zandar presumed. She felt both sides looking up at the fight from around the embattled city, and she wanted to put on a show. She could hardly defeat *him*, but to make him out a fool would be good for her own side.

Rumoi was too far for her to work with light, but she wrote with clouds high above the port.

FIGHT THE LORD OF THE NORTH! FIGHT HIM AND THE ENTIRE WORLD WILL HELP YOU!

'Fight him!' Zandar murmured to herself. He was powerful; but there was a whole world to set against him, a whole world to keep free. 'He *can* be beaten!'

But now he came after her even more quickly than before.

To avoid him, she worked her way high above Rumoi, seeing the coast dwindle till the walled port city was far below. The coast road and a mountain road led to its gates. Imperial forces held it, though most regiments were well inland. Several miles off the shore she saw three great sphere-ships, partly submerged. That was surely *his* invasion force. She wondered if she might shake *him* off before striking at the ships, but *he* was still following her.

Now Zandar wondered if she should have been more explicit to Joah and the others. Perhaps she had been wrong to doubt their courage, been guilty of that too-familiar crime: lack of faith.

They believe in me; I *should* believe in them!

Had she earned her friends enough time? She hoped she had, because some instinct told her she was soon going to pay the supreme price.

Zandar went on soaring up. Finally she was so high that the blue sky had turned black and the stars came out. There was no oxygen here and the cold was sub-zero, though neither lack of air nor heat mattered much to a naked soul thirty miles up. Zandar zig-zagged madly, trying to see where *he* was.

'He's right on top of you! You *must* come home!'

It had been Daisen's voice, from an immense distance.

As so often, Daisen was right. Zandar sensed *him* above.

It was time to go, so now Zandar moved away from the great northern island Ezo, intending to get *him* to follow her.

It worked. Now *he* came after her. Only, he was faster as well as stronger. She thought she heard him snarling. Though he struck again and again, she dodged him, turning more quickly than he could, and he missed her narrowly every time though he still pursued.

'Daisen, he's after me, but I'm going to lead him right to The Waning.'

'He'll be a rotten visitor.'

'Get the other women of power together, and we can really make him feel unwelcome!'

She flew over the Sea of Japan and had the great isle Honshu to her left. Off to her right, beyond the sea, was great T'zina, and beyond that was mountainous Tibet and the Roof of the World.

He came after her again and then again.

I'm not far from home, she thought. She was excited. I have my chance. And if the others assemble and use all the Waning power gems... Well, there's a small chance he will end crippled, or even dead!

Soon there was Kyushu close ahead. She *would* get to The Waning and all the comforts of home. She felt a glow of optimism now, and tried to speak to her girls and to Man. There were new warnings to give them. While mind-speaking, she crossed rugged Kyushu as quickly as she could, heading all the time for home.

That was to do the obvious.

When she neared the gigantic Waning Moon, *he* was already waiting.

She ran right into him, and they grappled, spectral limbs entangled. She struck out at the Lord of the North, clawing and vicious, hoping that her Sisters in the fortress might see and help.

That didn't happen immediately. She continued to fight, very close to him indeed. She was reading horrific things in his mind, which her young friends had to know about. With her last strength she reached out to Joah and to the Voice from Afar. There was contact, and she rejoiced; then her power failed.

In a place distant from them Zandar's head sagged forward. She was exhausted.

He took advantage. He followed her, and she knew he would soon catch up. Now she could taste the full acid power of his fury and hate. He had hatred that could freeze the Earth.

She tried to accelerate down to the sea, but *he* was faster now. The soul of Zandar hit the water and blue warmth drowned

Words of Fury:

her. Still he followed... She was twisting desperately among the warm currents as the Lord of the North's projected soul threshed after her.

She rose to the surface just ahead of him, but then felt his power closing on her legs like the jaws of a shark. When he pulled her back she knew she was facing death and worse.

With sanctuary almost in sight, he finally pinned her in place. The soul of Zandar wriggled, but she could not escape the blow she saw coming nor escape what would happen after.

'Daisen, he's going to eat my soul!'

Now Mother Zandar was caught, the man-thing smiled delight.

'Sister Daisen and Mother Zandar!' That voice was barely human, with an incredible deep throb. 'We have *properly* met now, haven't we? I look forward to ... enjoying you both.'

There was only one thing to do.

Instead of trying to fly away, she performed a tight turn – and drove right into him. The two spirits smashed together. She hurt him, but also felt the ghost of herself being violated; he was with her and within her.

After the one flash of agony she fell through an empty universe, paralyzed and helpless, and saying only one last thing: '*Satis est, Domine, satis est.*'

It's enough, Lord, it's enough...

She tumbled over endlessly, falling further and further from home. She felt the taste of blood in her mouth, there was a blank whiteness in her mind which echoed the blank white of this reality. She realized with sorrow that this would be the end.

In another place, in another world, there was screaming desperation from Daisen, but Zandar could no longer hear.

In the thinking-cell Daisen had seen how *his* force held Zandar in the air three feet above the futon, as if she were a doll struggling in a giant's hands.

'Daisen, he's going to eat my soul!'

Sister Daisen saw the ugly picture that was in Zandar's mind; she recoiled in horror. Then in the outer world she saw *him* first squeeze and then strike full-force; and Zandar's soul and her consciousness were smashed.

'*Oh, God!*' Daisen cried. 'She's gone!'

At first Man had not felt Zandar fight so many hundreds of miles to the north, but there on the rocking bench the three of them with magic had felt her approach, and now they felt her sudden removal from life.

'Oh, sweet Lord, that is such pain! Mother Zandar...!'

There was no response from the holy Mother, and Man knew no response would ever come, now. Joah began to weep.

The Voice could not believe it. 'Ah, surely our brave holy Mother will be back! Surely she – she cannot be *dead!*'

Man swallowed. Was this truly the end?

'I don't understand!' said the Voice. Man turned his head to see she, too, was crying. 'She was speaking to me about the evil things in *him*... How can she just be – '

Faslane asked, 'Do you mean that your holy Mother is dead? You *know*?'

Lady Joah said it: 'We know.'

The Voice from Afar gave a gasping sob. It was a moment before she could speak.

'She can't be dead. I won't believe that goodness can be destroyed so easily!'

Man felt sickened. He knew there was nothing realer than loss. He had lost his own mother long ago, then his father, and finally his country. Now the loving Mother Zandar had also been taken, and the world was that much closer to its cold, loveless end. Something wonderful *had* existed, but now it had vanished, imploding and leaving only cold absence behind.

'She is gone up,' said Joah. 'And, Voice, though goodness cannot be destroyed, it cannot always live on in *this* world!' Joah sounded firm, though tears ran down her face. 'That's why there's a Heaven.'

'Without *her*,' said the Voice, 'how can we prevail?'

Nobody answered that. Nobody could.

Man, too, was desolate. From this moment, he felt, nothing good could happen.

There was a blast of *his* power, channelled through Zandar into the thinking cell. The soundless explosion was all blinding light. Daisen staggered back from it with both hands raised. She banged into the wall behind, moaning. After-images filled her vision with purple and red, so thick and chaotic as to make her sightless.

Perhaps it had been like this when Mother Zandar was blinded...

But even that thought was not the worst. Daisen choked back sobs. Two realities had connected: *he* was coming here.

She continued to squint at the glare through held-up hands. The light had some dark shape moving in it. She looked down at once, sick to her stomach, and rammed fingers into her mouth to stifle renewed screaming.

Two realities had connected: *he* was coming here.

Now a big black steel gauntlet, on a man's big arm, came out of the wall. She saw the steel hand strike sparks from the stone wall as it lashed out.

Yes; it was *him*.

She fell to her knees, too terrified to pray, barely ducking below his steel hand as it clutched at her.

Now the battle here was lost, Daisen decided to take Zandar and carry her away. She moved quickly, dodging his grasping hands. The body was light and slack. Even when Daisen dragged Zandar up from the futon there was no reaction from her. Daisen sheltered in a corner, wanting to time her run to the cell door. She held Zandar close, but there was no heartbeat. Mother Zandar the holy – she was *dead*.

More plated-steel arms came out of the walls and ceiling. It was impossible for Daisen to dodge all of them, though she tried. Twice lengths of hair were torn out; once her clothing was seized though she was just able to tear herself away.

She was sobbing in terror, still holding her deceased friend. The soul was gone, but she wanted to save the body from violation.

The white glare intensified, though the light was somehow freezing cold too. Flakes of snow fell from the shivering air now and piled up ankle-deep on the stone floor. In the glare was *his* terrible shape. Daisen was screaming out loud as she tried to do something to soften that searing light and reverse the icy cold. She made a feeble motion with one hand, to try to hold off his magic with her own.

She failed, utterly. Now *he* was chuckling, and right here.

'*I will have you all, I will!*'

He had entered this sacred place; entered her.

Her own endless screaming was the last thing Daisen remembered.

Words of Fury:

Chapter Seven: ***We Must All Face Monsters***

It was strange to be invisible, but the Voice from Afar thought it would be effective. They were all sitting like ghosts on the half-seen bench. Still, she knew she had to speak about the things she had read in Mother Zandar's mind. It would be upsetting for everyone if she had to do what was right against the others.

Before she could talk of that she saw something ahead flicker for a moment. She sat bolt upright.

'I just felt *his* magic! It's as the holy Mother said! A dangerous male spell, spreading out on the coast!'

'He's back?' Man tried to push himself away from this bad news.

'I don't know where he is, though I felt *him* beating hard on something ahead of us.' Suddenly the Voice from Afar knew they would not make it over the mountains by balloon; it was made by magic and it would fail them. She shivered. 'Man? Joah? There was something in our holy Mother's mind... In Prophecy, are there lines about a "midnight beach"?'

Man snapped, 'It's noon, as far from midnight as you can get!'

'But Mother Zandar believed we must go to a dark shore, and somehow cross it. If we do not, our mission fails.'

'What dark shore?' Man leaned forward, both fists clenched, a glassy ghost. Then he looked at Joah. 'Why didn't *you* say something?'

'There's nothing to say, because the Voice has misinterpreted.'

'No! The knowledge was in *her* mind, and I must respect that, Lady Joah.' The Voice swallowed. She tried again to recover Zandar's thoughts from her own mind. 'We must move from our present course. It will call for a weather-weave; but perhaps if done with subtlety *he* will not notice.'

'What if you are doing *his* bidding?' Joah asked, voice savage.

'I – I really don't think I am.'

'That is no assurance,' Joah told her, cuttingly.

The Voice was shocked by the anger and aggression among her friends. Might it be *his* work? Was one among them, or even more, on *his* side?

That was a very ugly thing to consider.

She pleaded with them, 'Have a little faith in Mother Zandar and me. Is that too much to ask?'

'It's not too much to *ask*, dear Voice, but maybe it's too much to grant.'

The Voice felt outnumbered. 'Yoshi, can you show us your map? Master Faslane, I'd like to know where we will cross the coast.'

Yoshi eyed her.

'You really want us to change course, don't you?'

'I want to reach the place mentioned by holy Zandar, yes: the "midnight beach".'

The Voice had been trying to speak pleasantly, but now Yoshi too was glaring at her from a face like stone. Resentment grew in her. Then another thought came, this one very hard to take. Was brave Yoshi become an enemy?

She really didn't want to think that.

The Voice saw Yoshi pull something from his pouch. He unfolded the bright painted silk, then passed it to her.

She spread the map out on her lap and saw with sudden delight that it was bewitched. Magic of the as above, so below, kind made it show the Shimabara peninsula ahead in full, living color and three dimensions. She saw actual movement as rivers ran and a few high clouds were eased along by the same wind that moved their balloon.

The green coast ahead was mapped clearly. Near the far coast was a ring-walled fortress, shown on the chart in perfect miniature: the Waning of the Moon itself.

On this coast was a charred, semi-circular bay, nothing like any other geographical feature.

'This black bay here must be "the midnight beach"!'

Lady Joah took the map. She turned to Faslane, her expression cold.

'You are a pilot, are you not?'

'Aye, I am; time-served and commissioned,' said the Albion seaman.

'If this wind holds, where will we land?'

The Voice watched Faslane closely as he took the map and turned it so that it was a match for the coast ahead. He looked ahead at that shore, checked the small compass he had. Finally he murmured a calculation.

'Well?' she heard Man ask, sharply.

'In an hour we will make our landfall well north of yon black beach.'

Words of Fury:

Now the Voice put herself back into the conversation. 'But holy Zandar herself advised us to go there to the beach! Her voice was in my mind, clear as the daylight!'

Yoshi said scornfully, 'Did she know everything in advance? If so, why didn't she tell us all, earlier?'

The Voice glared at him.

In a peace-making gesture, Faslane shook the map in his two broad callused hands.

'If we land, this map will be priceless...'

Joah's voice remained cold. 'Where exactly *will* we land?'

Faslane thumbed a coastal spot.

'Unless we change course as the Lady Voice wishes, we will come to "Four Rocks".'

'I've been there,' said Yoshi. 'I went with my esteemed father, hunting for *his* Sons and Daughters.'

Man took an interest. 'So there's *his* evil in Four Rocks?'

Yoshi was quietly scornful. 'We found exactly nothing, and the place is obscure and insignificant – exactly the landing-place we want.'

'No!' The Voice was insistent. 'We must follow the holy Mother's advice.'

At once Yoshi took back his map. The Voice knew suddenly there *was* going to be an argument, and probably a bitter one. Yoshi was no longer the charming poet who had worked with her on songs. Now he gave her another ice-cold look, and then spoke with deliberation to the Voice and Joah both.

'You two look up to Mother Zandar. You have placed her on a very high pedestal indeed.'

The Voice touched her crucifix.

'As she deserves, friend Yoshi.' Then her voice turned tragic. 'Or did, when she lived.'

'You'd know her quality better than I. But in this, trust me, her advice was bad.' Yoshi showed them the blackened bay – first on the map, then the black coastal smudge in reality. 'Not only is this beach not safe, it's crazily *un*-safe!' The Voice flinched back, for Yoshi was giving her the kind of slit-eyed stare that would be appropriate in a duel to the death. 'Do you know what they call it? Let me tell you! That's *Monster Beach!*'

Faslane and Man both shifted uneasily; they took what Yoshi was saying very seriously.

Yoshi crumpled the map up and put it back into his pouch. His face was stone.

Words of Fury:

The Voice from Afar wanted to take back the map, and so take command. She could not, only speak from the heart.

'My dear friends, aren't there lines in the Prophecies that imply we *will* meet monsters? And ahead on the coast is *his* trap. We are vulnerable. We must follow the Prophetic signs and the holy Mother!'

'A trap ahead?' said Joah, with scorn. 'So what do you want us to do? Head for a place where *he* is strong?'

'No, I want to go where his power is weakest. Mother Zandar said this beach is strange and there *his* power is less.' The Voice pressed on, hoping she might persuade Joah. 'So, in the name of Lady Naosuke, dead these three hundred years, in the name of God, we must change course!'

The Lady Joah folded her hands together.

'Voice, you're quite wrong; we can't risk changing course.'

Those words hurt the Voice from Afar much as blades might have done. Wouldn't they ever accept her? But now she saw Man didn't believe her either, and that was worse.

'Voice, this "trap" of his – I just don't see it,' he told her bluntly.

She blazed up. 'Why would you? It's subtle work for a man, you *man*! Oh, why do you doubt me, my Emmanuel? I know what I know.'

'Then why don't I know it? Or the Lady Joah? Are you saying we are both blind, or just stupid?'

Men so lacked patience! Like the Lord of the North, Man was all masculine impulse, and that might one day be his ruin.

'Please, I must follow the truth of my vision, and turn us south to the beach Mother Zandar mentioned.'

'No!' The ghost of Yoshi seemed to be scowling at her. 'This is madness. Only *he* would want us to land among monsters!'

'I don't care what *he* wants! He isn't even here! What about what Prophecy demands? What about me?' Now the Voice raised a translucent hand, began to twirl it around. Some subtle threads of weather power combined to push the balloon south of its original course and then still further south. 'There. That will serve!'

An appalled silence fell.

Then Yoshi said, 'You have just killed us all.'

When Sister Daisen came round again she was on the floor with her eyes tightly closed. The cold thinking cell smelled rank;

male-animal sweat.

So *he* was here! He really was! Her flesh crawled.

What to do? Daisen was still partly blinded and partly deafened. Play dead, longer? She tried not to move, not so much as flicker her eyelids, so very much wanting not to draw attention.

I am so weakened now, what can I do? Should I cry out for help? But there are no adepts here...

She wondered how much she had been hurt. From the pains all over her body, badly.

Playing dead might keep her safe for a time, but what about the others? Even the brave Sword Maidens, let alone the clerks and the menials and the unworldly scholars, could not defend themselves from *him*...

As it was, she was powerlessly wondering what had happened. Beyond this cell The Waning was deathly silent. Perhaps he had already massacred everyone...

Daisen dared to open her eyes. There were flickering obscure shadows on the walls, thrown by the one wall-niche candle that was still burning – but she was alive. Did that mean he had only overlooked her as he went off to deal out more death, or was he waiting? She was conscious now, but she only wanted to scramble away on hands and knees, while weeping and begging for mercy. It was impossible to fight him physically, and his magic had already penetrated their defenses.

Even if *he* is no longer here, most likely *he* has gone into the Waning for a mass killing. So I must try something...

Daisen rolled up onto her knees and straightened her back, but pain exploded in her head and she fell down flat again.

It took a while to recover. Then, instead of hiding, she armed herself with what little magic she could summon and got to her hands and knees. Her vision was blurred, but she saw Zandar sprawled in the shadows. There was no blood visible on the open-mouthed body, but her chest did not move and that made Daisen acknowledge her superior's death. Tears came first, and then despair. Nevertheless, she had to touch; only the cold, cold flesh would tell her for certain.

She started to crawl towards her friend, but then somehow found the strength to stand up. After a moment, when she shivered from the cold left here, she staggered to the futon.

Was there any hope? She took up the familiar hand.

It was already cooling, indeed almost cold, and there was no pulse. Zandar's wide-eyed, shocked face did not change.

Daisen wept unrestrainedly. There was no help she could give Mother Zandar; that story was done. With her free hand, she closed her old friend's eyes.

Then she limped to the cell doorway. The wooden door had been splintered, and the metal gate burst. A gap had been driven through that would have let pass a giant. She touched one bent iron bar. The metal was still icy cold, no doubt from *him*. *He* would have frozen the metal till it became fragile as glass, and then forced his way through.

Where did the Lord of the North go then?

She gathered her weakened powers, hoping she might somehow surprise him, but knowing how small her chance was. She sidled out of the doorway. Her hands were ready to throw death, but her hands were weak and trembling...

Nevertheless, Daisen knew she would have to fight.

'Sword Maidens! Send to our adepts! Our holy Mother has need of them!' She had not shouted, only spoken in a dry scared whisper. There was no reply. 'If anyone is alive to hear me, to arms! *He* is here, murdering all those he touches!'

Her voice had been an uncertain hoarse bray, barely enough to carry. Still that small effort was too much. Daisen sank to her knees again.

Then she heard a footstep. Down the darkened passageway she saw a human outline, too large to be any normal man; it had to be *him*.

The brutal thing striding towards her was the last thing she remembered.

Man saw the effect of Yoshi's words. The Voice from Afar looked devastated. Miserably she shook her head. 'You are all supposed to be my friends! I have killed no-one. I truly want to protect us and get us to safety. Why won't you believe that?'

Man saw the ghostly outline of burly Faslane take her hand and squeeze it.

Well, Man thought, the man of mystery from Albion was giving comfort before any surrender...

Yoshi wasn't giving up. 'Lady Joah, Man? You do see this is madness, don't you? Can't we turn back to our original course? Four Rocks could not be safer!'

The balloon lurched and they almost fell from the bench. Man looked up at the misshapen sphere. One way or another, their flight wasn't going to last much longer.

'There is nothing we can do to restore the balloon,' said Joah. She sounded very weary. 'Nothing we can do to the wind. It's out of our hands.'

Now they were committed, Man looked ahead. He could see the wide black beach in detail. He saw a few bizarre-looking smoothed-off black crags there – as if some parts of this shore had been melted into dark glass and somehow sucked up. Then he realized there was an overall shape.

'That bay is half of an up-tilted disc. The rest of it must be underwater. Put the two halves together and you have a perfect circle! And look at that!'

On the black sand, glistening snail-trails of what looked like melted black glass criss-crossed.

Man leaned over and gripped his friend's forearm.

'Yoshi? What do you think made those trails?'

Yoshi said, with an undisguised shudder, 'Monsters?'

Man tried to keep any panic out of his voice. 'Can we fight these "monsters" without magic?'

'I shouldn't think so. This place is deadly.'

Man turned to glare at the Voice. She had brought them here, and he wondered if she had joined *him*. But her face was so innocent he could not believe that.

About half a mile offshore they passed through a barrier that made Man's skin thrill painfully. He flinched, hearing gasps all around. Then he saw he could see his own hands, and see the others. Even the soap-bubble balloon was faintly visible again.

'When we crossed the line into this "place of otherness", our invisibility failed,' said Joah, obviously quoting. 'Here the rules are different.'

Man saw a tiny hope in that. 'So it's harder to do our magic, or keep up spells, because we're in a kind of alien world... But then *his* magic should be lessened, too.'

'That makes sense,' said Yoshi.

'Reality simply *is*,' Joah told them. 'It is not obliged to follow our rules of rationality.'

'I think you mean "realities *are*",' Man responded. 'Many worlds are round the corner, including wherever this black land came from...'

'What if it came from Hell?' the Voice whispered.

That silenced everyone.

'If not from there, I think – I *feel* – this land truly is from another world!' She turned to glare at Yoshi. 'A world free from *him*, perhaps!'

'But we are in this world,' Man said gently. 'Where is this trap of *his*, which you mentioned?'

Perhaps the Voice read his mind again – she was always good at that – but when she spoke she sounded nervous. 'Man, we made a balloon from a soap-bubble and our magic, but now we've come to the end-game.'

'Don't land on the beach!' Yoshi roared. He turned to scowl at the Voice. 'I curse your Prophecy!'

The Voice was shocked, and so was Man. When he looked down again they were only a hundred and fifty feet above the water, and the wind was blowing them on.

'We're falling.' Faslane ground big fists together. 'What do we do?'

The Voice answered. 'We must do as Mother Zandar said: land, and cross the beach.'

'This place kills!' Yoshi turned his head, anger and desperation showing in his eyes. He really saw no future at all here. 'Man? Can you help?'

When Man reached into himself for one last time he was still empty. 'It's no good. I'm done.'

Yoshi turned his head. 'What of you, Lady Joah?'

'Lord Yoshi, magic is a thing involving mood and self-confidence; all I feel now is dark. I can't do much, even if we are being herded towards death.'

When Man heard that, he raged.

'I can still let the Eye go, casket and all, into the sea!' As the wind drove them, Man had the strong impression that someone, or something, wanted them to crash here. 'What we want no longers matters; we're coming down.'

Joah was looking desperate. 'But we carry the Eye of Jade!'

'We do.'

'Can you look after it, Man?'

'I can't swim with that weight!' Man saw her eyes widen. 'Lady Joah, are you worried about swimming? Should I help you? You mustn't drown!'

'I don't need any man's help, Emmanuel. Forget me, and look after the Eye!'

The hot salt smell of the sea was suddenly overwhelming. Man began panting through his mouth like a dog, wondering if they would drop into the water here or crash on the shore.

What's the difference in the end?

Now Faslane leaned forward. 'Princess Joah? Your ancient lady with foreseeing powers – Lady Naosuke, I mean, the authoress of the Prophecies – did she predict what will happen now?'

Joah had a princess's self-confidence, which Man had always admired. It seemed lessened, now. 'There are ambiguities in her prophetic books.'

'Yes, Lady – but will we survive?'

'I have faith; all will be well.'

'For all of us?' Faslane was insistent now. 'Is it certain we will *all* live on? Or will some of us die?'

Joah turned away.

'Look! We're almost at *his* trap!' The Voice's eyes had gone very wide. 'Can't you see it?'

Yoshi was still angry. 'You see *his* work easily, Lady Voice!'

'You didn't find me so despicable when we read Rumi together and worked on songs!'

Man still saw nothing; he wondered if the Voice had been turned.

The Voice was standing up. 'We're crossing the coast, where his snare is!'

'Oh, God!'

Man saw the Lady Joah cover her face with her hands.

There was a flash of silver that left the balloon ripped; they fell like stones.

Man saw the Voice had been ready for the trap, ready for the balloon to shred. She made the shapes of magic even as they plummeted, hands threshing about as if she was conducting some exciting music, and said words of power. Then her healing magic pulled the ragged balloon back together, more or less, and refilled it with hot air.

They had dropped a long way, but they were still floating – just.

'Man, we're actually lucky! This land is alien to *him*, too! Here he's less! Anywhere *except for the black beach* his trap would have been full-strength and ripped us and the balloon wide open!'

That was a scrap of good news.

'Will he know his snare has been triggered, and come?'

'He might!'

Words of Fury:

That would be bad, if *he* came searching.

Even with the Voice's magic supporting it, the balloon was sagging. They swept forward, pushed on by the wind, but they were getting lower and lower.

Man braced himself, hands stretched out on the safety-rope – the Voice on one side, Lady Joah on the other. Man's dangling legs were splashed up to the knee by a wave, and then they all bounced up again. There was a crooked black sea-stack to their left and now the black shore was close, no more than fifty yards away.

He saw they wouldn't make it.

He wondered if the weight of the Eye in its casket would drown him.

The balloon dragged them on, though it was finally deflating. Sea washed over their legs up to their waists.

He shouted out, 'When we hit, dive forward and *swim* – or you'll tangle with the balloon magic and drown!'

Instead, they all rolled backwards. Someone's elbow hit him hard in the face. Man's head went underwater. He struggled upright, spluttering, and when they were lifted out of the water one last time he called out, 'Yoshi, help me! We must save the Eye!'

Then he went rolling forward into the waves.

He struck the water at a steep angle. The others splashed about on the surface while the bench was pulled deeper – along with the casketed Eye. He held on to the bench with one hand, and with the other he found the Eye's rope-lashed casket and then worked his fingers to unfasten it.

A bubble belched out of his mouth. The salt water seemed to make everything slippy, and he was going deeper. He worked on the casket knots till the bronze shape came free, but the casket was so heavy it slipped through his hands.

So the Eye was drowned, its Talking Book with it.

He began to drown. That was terror enough, but the thought of losing the Eye was worse. The water here was deep and those precious things might be lost forever.

He splashed up to the surface, panting. Yoshi was with him.

'We have to stay here!'

Yoshi spat out seawater. 'The Eye's below, right?'

'Yes!' Man sucked in air. 'I'm going to try and find it, walk it out if I can. Follow me!'

Man went head-down, then kicked his legs up. Salt water

forced itself unpleasantly into his nostrils. With his hands, he pulled himself down towards sea bottom.

It was slick black rock he found, and black sand sloping away. A few brightly colored fish slipped by as he went after the casket.

He touched bottom again.

No bronze-casketed Eye here, nor here, nor here...

Then where was it?

There was no magic to help him. Though he was already short of breath, Man refused to give up and he stayed underwater. Then he saw a glint of metal in the blue twilight. He swam closer. It was the Eye's bronze casket. Relief filled him. He caught a trailing rope. Using this, he tried to lift the casket off the sea-bottom. His legs and free arm threshed uselessly. He could not swim this weight back to the surface. So he settled his feet into the soft sand and lifted up the casket using both hands.

Was he strong enough to walk with the Eye?

I'd better be...

Man held that weight to his chest. He was just able to make progress, although his feet scrabbled over the soft sand and he was at permanent risk of falling. If he did fall, he knew he would lose the casket for good.

It was a slow walk and soon his held-in breath was burning his lungs. What if he died here? What good would that do anyone? Surely he should lay down this burden and save himself?

Then there was no air left. Pain stabbed his chest.

He knew he would have to leave the Eye – or die.

Words of Fury:

Chapter Eight: *Other-World Monsters*

If I drop the casket, though *I* might then live, *the whole world dies...*

Man had always been stubborn; he stayed stubborn now. He kept the casket clutched to his chest, though dark cobwebs gathered in his mind and he knew he was about to drown.

Then something strange happened.

There was green light leaking from inside the casket. Was the Eye actually waking? Man realized the green flashes now had the rhythm of his heartbeat. He felt powerful now. Perhaps the Eye was on his side and he wouldn't die...

He saw underwater for hundreds of yards – schools of fish, the black rocky outcrops – though everything had that green Eye-magic tinge. He sensed something move in the water, and turned his head. Yoshi was alongside, pointing at his own mouth and then Man's.

It's better than dying, Man thought. His mouth streamed bubbles as he let Yoshi do what they'd heard pearl divers sometimes did.

Yoshi blew the breath of life into his lungs. Then Man's friend gave a double thumbs-up sign and went back-stroking away.

Man hoped he was going for more air.

The new oxygen was a big help, though it could not last long. Man walked on through the water, legs sinking into the black, feeling gritty sand get in between his toes. He felt waves swirl over his head.

Then Joah was beside him. She pushed her lips onto his in an underwater kiss, and breathed new air and new life into Man. When his lungs were inflated she pulled away, smiling. She waved with underwater slowness then swam away, a mermaid in a silk kimono.

Bouncing weirdly, Man went trudging towards the light. Another step underwater, then another... He might live. If he did, he would fight on, get to The Waning, learn, then go back to Jade and try to rescue it from Oatha, if he could.

He saw the rippled surface of the sea overhead, and then his head broke through. He gasped fresh air, still holding on to the casket.

Yoshi was lazily backstroking here where the water was chest deep.

Words of Fury:

'On the whole, I'd rather not get used to kissing you – and you could have shaved.'

Man coughed out one laugh. 'So could you!'

The undertow pulled at Man's legs. It was difficult to stay upright, but he managed. The Eye and its Book were safe, now, and held to his chest.

'I got to kiss Lady Joah.' Man showed his teeth – more of a supreme effort than a smile, since the casket was so heavy. 'That was a pleasure.'

'I suppose she and I saved the Eye – and your life.'

'If I wasn't out of breath from being a hero, I'd thank you,' Man said.

'Sweet Joah is divine!'

Yoshi was looking at something. Man turned, to see the princess from Jade standing in knee-deep seawater. She stared not at him, but at the rope-trailing casket of bronze which he had clasped to his chest. She was dripping and bedraggled, with her wet black hair loose and wild now, but somehow all her dignity was intact.

'Yes,' Man said softly, looking at those lovely brown-and-honey eyes, the lovely feminine shape. 'She is divine.'

Man got out of the surf and walked several paces before he grounded the casket. He looked down. The wet bronze box was beautifully worked with pictures and words written in dead languages, but when his magic reached out, or tried to, there was no sign of life now.

Suddenly his heart spoke, a cry that was pure loss.

'I made a city shake with the Eye! I fought the Lord of the North with the Eye! And now there's nothing from the Eye *I* am nothing!'

Joah came forward quickly. She embraced him, pulled his head down to kiss his mouth.

'Keep the faith, my Man! To all of us you are wonderful!'

Her affection was grounding.

'I will keep faith, Joah,' he said, holding her. Then Man let her go. 'It'll be a long walk, if we go by foot. Or do we stay here, and hope Fukuzawa finds us before any pirates do?'

'We must get to The Waning of the Moon. How, I don't quite know – but I don't care, just as long as we get there!'

Man bowed to her.

Suddenly Joah gave him her wonderful bright smile again. She pressed water from her clothing and hair with magical hands, then fastened her padded over-kimono tightly. Then she turned to eye Man, critically.

'You're dripping wet. Come here.'

Her warm hands pressed onto his hair, his clothes, sometimes onto his bare flesh. Water oozed from Man's clothes and evaporation left them dry.

'Your touch is a pleasant tingle,' he said.

'Not always!'

Joah had a big scabbarded knife hanging from her red sash. She did not look anything like a shy sweet girl any longer. Though as care-worn as the rest of them in her crinkled clothes, she looked alert and dangerous.

She had changed, and Man approved.

'Yes, you're dangerous in your own way.'

'If you only knew, my Emmanuel...'

He kept his voice low. 'Other than our blades, we're relying a lot on words, aren't we? Especially the words Lady Naosuke left behind.'

'But there *are* words of power. Aren't there?'

'There are,' he admitted, even though he had lost faith in them.

'So we are not weaponless. Now, what of this place?'

Man looked around even more carefully. Were there really monsters here? The occasional twisted glass column rose up strangely, while black sand sloped gently up from the beach. The sweltering air had a strange dead quality to it, he thought. Then his gaze was drawn to the vertical cliffs nearly three quarters of a mile away – walls two or three hundred feet high, neatly and unnaturally cut.

Neatly and unnaturally *cut*? Was that possible? As if by a knife wielded by some giant?

Man thought first of *him*, coldly cutting up the land. Then he thought of some kind of overwhelming magic, which could take slices of land from world to world. Or was it a purely physical power tha had cut here, something scientific, which Futurists like Lady Joah knew about? Man turned to ask her.

Perhaps Joah read his mind. 'This is a *very* odd world, Man.'

'So is ours.'

'Especially your part!'

Man laughed along with the others. 'Doesn't it feel strange, here!'

At once Faslane asked, 'Strange?'

'As if the laws of nature themselves are different in this place. – Yoshi, where are your monsters?'

Yoshi's voice was low. 'I see nothing of them. I wonder if they died. I hope they did.'

'That would be a piece of luck,' Man said. 'Should we go?'

They walked on together, heading east. Beyond the cliffs mountains lifted. The black sand had a strange crusty texture underfoot – at least, a crusty surface, but there were large hollows below the surface. Man tried to puzzle out how the hollow places could exist.

Then Yoshi fell forward. Man saw the sand had swallowed his right leg up to the knee. Electricity snapped at him, big sparks bright enough to see in daylight. He had shouted out in pain.

Man had his sword ready, but there was nothing to kill yet. He felt the sweat run down his face.

Yoshi grimaced, pulling out his leg and rubbing it.

'It's like the sand here is sometimes solid, but sometimes it runs like water... Is it magic?'

'Might be,' Man admitted, grudgingly. 'Might just be static electricity.'

Lady Joah turned to him. 'Should we go forward again, Emmanuel?'

It would be dangerous; he could tell that. But, with all eyes now on him, Man took the responsibility.

'Yes, and I will lead.'

'No,' said Lady Joah and Yoshi, together.

He knew he was young, a foreigner, and in the eyes of Albion a traitor's son. But now he claimed his title.

'I am The One Who Will Change; so follow me!' He led off up the beach, ankle-deep in the hot soft black sand. Will I fail, he wondered, and lead everyone to destruction? To cheer himself he quoted his father, though not so loud that the others could hear. 'A brave leader always says "follow".'

After a moment he dared to look over his shoulder.

They had followed him.

The pace he set was easy, though the Eye on his back was a burden. Then he saw something ominous. Humped areas in the sand were slowly circling them.

'Stop!' Man looked around quickly, sword drawn. A black shape raised out of the sand and then withdrew, and there were others. 'It's as if we're on a black sea and surrounded by sharks.'

When they advanced again, the disturbed areas circled them more and more closely. Man was beginning to understand how other-world monsters might function here.

'Watch out on all sides! I think they're swimming through the sand.'

'Stop moving in step!' Joah shouted, dread in her voice. 'They sense vibrations!'

Yoshi's eyebrows rose. '*You* know something about this place?'

'Do you?' Man demanded.

'I just know Lady Naosuke's Prophecies! "Monsters of an alien blood / Roaming a shore of otherness dark"!'

'Whatever *that* means,' Man said. 'I wish these Prophets and poets would use plain speech!'

'I'll try not to take that personally!' Yoshi called out to him.

Lady Joah was looking over the shimmering black expanse of sand that separated them from the sheer cliffs.

'It must be do-able, this journey – do you think?'

The Voice from Afar responded. 'It is what was prophesied; that much we know. A march across this darkness, climb the cliffs and then the mountains, and then there will be The Waning of the Moon, and safety.'

Yoshi pulled a face. 'Are you sure about the safety?'

'No, but I am sure about the Lady Naosuke and what she was guided to foresee.'

'Let's go on,' said Man to everyone, 'but take it easy, and let's not look like bait.'

A few yards were gained, and Man felt his pulse slow. It *was* possible to make safe progress.

Then Faslane whirled around. Man saw there was some kind of commotion in the sand beside him. Faslane had his fighting-iron raised, but the pair of giant black claws that emerged between his feet clashed shut anyway.

That could be a terrible wound...

The claws withdrew into the sand. Man called out, 'Are you all right?'

Faslane put one hand on the family jewels. He was sweating. 'These things are fast.'

'Not too fast to fight, I hope,' Man murmured. He turned his head around, checking a full circle. 'Yoshi? What monsters live here?'

Words of Fury:

Yoshi's fingers played on his bandolier of throwing-knives. 'My uncle never said.'

'But he told you they were dangerous?'

'He used stronger words!'

'Though he lived?'

'Unlike the rest who were shipwrecked with him.'

'What happened to them?'

'They were eaten alive.'

Man took that in. Eaten alive was how the Voice from Afar's parents had died.

'Yoshi, you just made me lose my appetite!'

A monster crab erupted out of the sand between Man's legs and knocked him down.

Words of Fury:

Chapter Nine: *Unless There Is A Miracle*

Man had to bounce back onto his feet to front up this black-and-red giant. The crab was as large as a pony and it moved with unexpected waspish speed. One huge claw struck at Man's chest. He parried it with his sword, but the blow forced him back a step. Yoshi came in on the monster's other side and used his own katana to duel the claw there.

Man reckoned they could hold off two monsters, with luck, but any more would make the odds impossible. Even with just this one opponent for both men it was dangerous work. From behind, Man felt the two young women raise small fast spells to fling blinding sand at the other circling creatures.

This crab whirled around, and its right-hand claw struck at Man's shoulder and knocked him down.

Am I done for?

'I'll help you!'

Faslane was here. He struck out with his fighting-iron, though it was so short it kept him dangerously close to those clashing claws.

Man stood up, feeling for damage in his shoulder-joint and his collar-bone. If anything was broken he would be terribly handicapped.

Yoshi was cutting, while Faslane smashed his spiked weapon through the crab's shell. They broke pieces off, and then Yoshi managed to lop an eye-stalk.

'Yes!'

Man felt relief. The three of them closed in to finish the crab off. The two samurai swords stabbed the thing as Faslane smashed its legs.

But before Man and the others could quite kill it, a thing surged out of the sand ten yards off and galloped towards them. It was a black lobster the size of a small horse and it flourished saw-edged claws.

Man moved to intercept it, hearing the others smash the crab. But just before the lobster-thing reached him it dug itself in, spraying sand.

It left a giant mole-hill behind. Man felt a momentary impulse to jump into the hole and follow it.

'There's a half-dozen of them, at least!' said Faslane. 'Look! They're circling us!'

He waved at the humped disturbances.

Words of Fury:

Man was cursing now – too many enemies! Was that lobster thing under him? He sensed something moving through the sand below his feet. It might be ready to shrug through to the surface and eat! He rubbed at his sore shoulder.

To Man's right, now, Yoshi shook his sword in his two hands. He wanted to get attention while staying silent. Then he pointed with his blade.

At first Man saw nothing; then he realized there was a hump in the sand moving towards his friend. This monster emerged right in front of Yoshi, a many-legged, scuttling black crab three yards across. Its eyes turned on waving stalks as it sidled from side to side.

Man made a motion to Yoshi with one hand. 'Don't make any sudden movements! That is a *king* crab!'

As he said that, the crab came forward – and then vanished into the sand in front of Yoshi.

This was the time of maximum danger. Yoshi stood poised, his sword out, slowly turning round. Where had the thing gone?

Then sand crumbled under Yoshi, making him slip forward and put both hands to the ground. A crab-claw came out and snipped at his forearm. When Yoshi pulled back, his sword was dangling weakly and Man saw there was blood spurting from a very bad wound; lots of red blood, from a grievous injury to the sword-arm.

Man realized Yoshi was half useless now. His heart went out to his friend. For as much as thirty seconds it had felt very good to be brave. Not any more, not after Yoshi had been disabled.

For Man, courage was now a concept in the past tense.

'We can't cross this sand,' wounded Yoshi said. 'I don't care what it says in Lady Naosuke's books! For us to get over the sand would take a miracle – or a bloody army!'

And we have neither, thought Man. If we had spear-men, if we had men with long shields, perhaps we might win through – but even if this journey is in Prophecy it is *impossible* to make it!

He heard Yoshi muttering as Faslane wrapped a bandage around his forearm. The cloth quickly turned blood-red.

'Lord Yoshi, you're right!' Faslane was rattled, and that made him rage. 'I see a half-dozen humps in the sand, every one showing us a killer!'

Man saw the seaman's heavily muscled chest heave. He was a brave man, but his eyes already had the thousand-yard stare, and he waved his fighting-iron up and down as if he had a whole

Words of Fury:

world to fight.

'The Lady Naosuke made prophecies: she says we *must* cross.'

'The attempt would be death!' Faslane insisted to the Voice.

'Surely we can get over somehow, Dirk Faslane?'

'No.' Faslane shook his shaggy head. 'Voice, dear wonderful Voice from Afar, you have no weapons, only your magic, and the Lords Yoshi and Emmanuel are only two. That isn't enough!' Faslane turned to Yoshi. 'Sir, you are a warrior. What do you say?'

Yoshi lowered his splendid sword, which was in his left hand. He was still looking at his ruined sword-arm, which Faslane had wrapped up to staunch the blood.

'You already know what I think – and now I think it even more.'

The Voice kneeled, and took Yoshi's bloodied forearm between her hands. Man saw his wounded friend twitch, and then suddenly smile. After the Voice from Afar released his arm, Yoshi unwound the bandage to show off a limb which was unscarred and perfect. Man waved a hand at the Voice, to show his admiration. Then Man turned to look at Lady Joah, careful not to move his feet in case that alerted monsters.

'Joah? What do you say?'

'We cannot retreat,' she said dreamily, though her face ran with perspiration. 'That would mean we have failed. But we cannot advance.'

'Well, we bloody well can't stay here!' said Yoshi. 'So what does that leave?'

After overseeing the executions of the Christians, Lord Oatha came out onto the castle roof-terrace. Here the signalers were hard at work.

'What news from out at sea? Is Fukuzawa captured?'

The senior signaller bowed low and checked his records on the slate log.

'No news of that renegade ship-captain, sir, but your loyal forces have arrested eighty-seven foreigners and other dubious people.'

'They are in our holding cells?'

'They are, sir, or on their way.'

'Excellent. I have the techniques to get truth out of any man – or woman.'

Words of Fury:

Lord Oatha was a very bulky man, with furious, piercing eyes. He raised a hand to wipe perspiration from his face. It was sweltering. He had defeated Lord Okada and taken his high office and his castle home, but there was still much more to do.

'Is even a legend like Fukuzawa so important?' Old grey-haired Yamagata sneered at Fukuzawa's misplaced loyalty. 'That fool is only one man.'

'A single leader can be worth a whole army,' Oatha explained to his followers. 'We do not have full command of the sea or the sea-coast yet, but I intend to get it – and Fukuzawa will oppose me.'

Aoki, the tall young man who was his deputy, was very polite to Oatha.

'Only a third of Lord Okada's sea-force left with Captain Fukuzawa, sir, and it's clear that he wants to find the Lady Joah –'

'And commit treason with her!' Oatha interrupted. 'Yes, I know. But she went flying away on the Foreigner's balloon, and now they are gone, maybe even dead.'

'Fukuzawa should have accepted the judgement of heaven, and not gone looking for Okada's daughter – for you have legally outlawed that "Lady" Joah, and those others!' said Yamagata.

'The law is powerful, but less so than swords, eh?'

'Most people accept you, lord.' Yamagata was very pompous. He had a patriot societies' black dragon tattooed on his wrist. 'Those few who do stand against you must be made not to.'

'Those nails will be hammered flat,' Oatha promised, knowing he needed full control of the shipping-lanes of the sea as well as control of the land. He was willing to use pirates, outlaws and even *his* servants to achieve that. Though his bargain to win Jade meant that much of his force had been sent to conquer The Waning of the Moon, he was very confident – and he had almost always been lucky.

The handful of black sashes with him were here only to receive his orders, and Oatha was pleased with how they all jostled each other to give extravagant praise. Only young Aoki said little. Oatha knew his notional deputy clung onto an exalted idea of his own independence. Aoki was of high lineage and even higher education. Once, Oatha had approved of him, as a usefully respectable face of black sash power.

Now I have less need; now the world must deal with *my* face, ugly though it may be.

Words of Fury:

'I spoke well in Jade Hall, eh?' Oatha laughed coarsely. 'I rammed some truths up some quivering behinds, eh? And did you see the faces when I had that Christian arrested!' He chuckled again. 'Anyway, you all understand? The wall around Foreign Town will be a proper barrier again: a ghetto. And from now the churches and chapels there will stay closed, till the fines are paid.'

'Excellent!' said Yamagata, slapping his knees. 'That vile faith of Christ's is a pollution meant to weaken us!'

'If they pay the mass fines, what then?' asked Aoki.

'Then we increase them.'

'You mean to bleed them dry; I see it. But what if they protest?'

'There is my answer to protest.'

Lord Oatha gestured down at the blackened iron cages. There he had burned alive the Christian man he had arrested, along with his family. It had been most amusing. The charred corpses would remain on show on the public burning-ground – and they would not be the last human sacrifices.

'Religious liberty has long been guaranteed in this free city,' Aoki pointed out.

'This is a *polluted* city,' Yamagata told him, braying, 'where vermin foreigners threaten our pure blood and our ways!'

Oatha said easily, 'That "liberty" was under the leadership of Lord Okada, a proved traitor. Now he is yesterday's man, these so-called "freedoms" must be ended. But for now, hint that further money will let the Christians stay free. Same way, when mass arrests start, we will let some of them be ransomed.' He rubbed his inflated thighs, and thought hungrily of naked Lady Oki. 'A little hope can be a good narcotic, eh? Of course, ultimately, they will be made to vanish...'

'We will run an extermination program?'

'You have seen it begin, young Aoki.'

That fool's death had been an instructive example to the populace. Pastor Ruhr had spoke in favor of Okada and against the black sash rule of Oatha; he and his wife and his three daughters had paid the price.

Oatha smiled to himself. Terror was the best teaching-aid.

Then he thought of foreign enemies, and looked over the rest of his domain.

The city of Jade still smelled of smoke from the fires started by Albion's airship. Man and the others had destroyed the

Words of Fury:

fighting balloon before the entire city could be torched. Many buildings had been wrecked, though, and a few still smoldered.

On the north side the shipyards had mostly been burned.

Aoki pointed there. 'Steel Angels are picking over the wreckage. I presume they're looking for illicit technology.'

'For which *Okada* will get the blame,' said Oatha. 'Those Angel things are dangerous. I would not willingly quarrel with them.'

As he spoke, some cold presence insinuated itself into Oatha's mind. When prompted by it, he re-examined what had happened.

There had been panic. Even after the Albion balloon was brought down in flames and Albion's paddlewheel steam-ship was driven away there had been riots and then looting. Oatha remembered that scene by scene; it was as if someone was closely examining his mind. He stared into nothing.

'Jade was being gravely hurt by Okada's changes, and so I acted, but still these vile foreigners scream for what they call freedom and change!'

That statement was approved. Then there was a mental question about who had overall control now.

'Okada's partisans have no leader, and I have him and his family as hostages. Of course, foreigners especially do not love me, of course Okada still has support – but now my forces are everywhere. Soon the one called Emmanuel will be taken or killed, and the gem called "the Eye" recovered – and then all will be well!'

From the unknown came agreement. Lord Oatha was the right man for this duty; was strong, and would prevail.

Who is *that?* he wondered, as the cold presence withdrew. I hope it was not the Lord of the North!

It had nothing like the power of *him*, but perhaps it had been a high Son of the Cold. Oatha scowled: *he* was an annoying power to placate.

Oatha stepped back into the cool, shady family rooms. Before he could speak, there was a disturbance outside, a flapping shadow that briefly killed the sunlight, and then shouting.

Aoki rose immediately, and looked to his master.

Oatha nodded permission. But when Aoki stepped outside he returned immediately, with eyes wide. 'Lord! Asking for you – it's a Steel Angel!'

Oatha sprang up, agile for one so heavy. His open-handed blow almost took off Aoki's cheek.

'Liar!'

'You – ' The young man's left hand cupped his left cheek, which turned white for a moment while the rest of his face flushed. 'I don't lie. Look outside, Lord!'

Oatha, grumbling, stepped out.

There he met the alien.

The thing was in mirror-shine armor, with the wide angel's wings now folded behind its back. Its face was hidden by a steel mask, from where its breath rasped strangely.

Oatha held down the fear that had come. He stared at the thing, heart hammering. A long sword was strapped to the Angel's back. Some said the Angels had their faces concealed because they only had one face: they were not true humans, only copies.

He had had secret dealings with the Angels before – had told them about that shipment of forbidden medicines from T'zina, for example, which had effectively killed Okada's only son.

Here, all four of Oatha's samurai guards had their swords drawn. They were all sweating with the heat and with fear. Cube Castle Angels were fearsome opponents.

He knew a display of courage would impress his men.

'I am Oatha, Lord of the Jade city now. Do you want to ask a favour, Angel?'

The Angel pointed through the doorway and Oatha backed up there. The Angel followed, and then placed a small cube on the table by the door. It was made of some glimmering black material.

The cube spoke. 'Oatha? Are you there?'

A machine which *speaks*? It was a distorted barbarous speech, admittedly, and barely understandable – like someone speaking through a tube from centuries past.

Oatha swallowed. Was this his chance to join the great ones, or would he be destroyed?

Oatha had never been any kind of coward. He made a violent gesture, then spoke.

'I am right here, Angel friend. Your enemy The One Who Will Change – *if* he was truly the one prophesied – has fled.' He tried to smile at the Angel, wondering what those half-concealed eyes could read in his expression. 'And the Lady Joah, that

Words of Fury:

Okada witch-girl, is with him.'

'Yes,' said the brassy voice from the black cube, 'they are together, and they live. That we/I know. But where are they? They have broken with the past and they must be stopped.'

'I agree,' said Oatha, staring at the buzzing cube. 'Of course, if you need information from me, there has to be a trade, or...'

'This city of yours stands on the edge of destruction! Did you not see the images shown before? If this city cannot be corrected, it will be burned!'

A city-burner! That dreadful weapon... But if this city died, Oatha did not want to die with it. He much preferred to rule it.

'Angel friend, I will happily tell you what I know. They left here using a balloon. The wind has taken them south and east, across the sea towards Shimabara.'

'More! Especially about this "Emmanuel"! More!'

Oatha found he too was sweating. It was clear that the Man Beyond Age, who ruled Cube Castle and had the Steel Angels to do his bidding, had identified young Emmanuel as an agent of change.

'As well as this "Emmanuel" there's a whole group of them, two green girls strong in the power and two other men. I understand they are aiming for The Waning of the Moon. That's the bastard monastery full of your enemies, with Christians, Buddhists and Muslims all plotting to make changes to this world.'

There was silence as that information was digested. The Steel Angel stood like a statue, utterly still. The Waning was one of the very, very few places – mostly shrines devoted to the deepest magic – where the Steel Angels could not go.

'The Waning on the eastern side of Shimabara?'

'Yes.'

'We/I know of it.'

Oatha blurted, 'I have sent men there already – and if you want I will send more. The One Who Will Change is my enemy, too.'

'We/I intend to see him eliminated. The power of magic has been returning to this world. That infection must be sterilized. Therefore its strong practitioners must be removed and its tools taken.' There was another pause, and Oatha feared some impossible demand was coming, and then it did come. 'We/I must have what you call "the Eye of Jade".'

'No! That gem is for *me*!'

Words of Fury: 87

'Negative! We/I must have it. Or this city of yours will burn!'

Was this a bluff? Oatha tried to smile and look callously confident, wondering if his expression would be understood. Then he admitted the truth to himself. The faceless, eternally re-born ruler of black Cube Castle really meant it.

If he disobeyed the Angels, the city of Jade would be burned.

At once Oatha became pleasant, wanting to win these strange persons over.

'Look, I'll help you. Go looking for the fugitives yourself, I mean yourselves. I've given you clues. A balloon is crossing the sea towards the Shimabara peninsula, and it's making for The Waning of the Moon!'

'We/I will look, but know this: we/I *will* be back. Listen out for us/I when we speak!'

Oatha could only watch as the mighty Angel exited the room, stepped out onto the roof-terrace and then flew away.

'Yoshi, I don't know what to do now! I don't even understand how we are still alive!' said the Voice, distressed. 'Two crabs done for and that giant lobster hurt, but there are many more here and we have taken wounds!'

Man agreed with her about everything. Two of the wounds were his, one slash on each leg below the knee. He had been bleeding heavily. Fortunately healing had stopped that. Nevertheless he was sweating and his sword was actually shaking in his hands. The hot one-eyed glare of the sun was painful, and there were mirages glimmering ahead as well as more monster claws. They had only made a few dozen yards from the sea. He didn't see how they could pass over all this midnight-black beach.

'And yet it must be done, to fulfil Prophecy!' said the Voice from Afar, clenching her small fists. 'It must be done!'

Lady Joah remained distant. 'Lady Naosuke saw that it might end for us here, and said so.'

That wasn't exactly cheering, and what the Voice said next wasn't either.

'I wanted us to land here, I thought we *had* to, but I don't want to die...' She shuddered. 'This place will kill us all!'

Yoshi spoke. 'Maybe we can find another way to The Waning of the Moon. Is that possible?'

'It may be possible,' said Lady Joah, 'but it is not Prophecy. If we can't cross this beach we have failed ourselves, and the world.'

Berenda knew that Emmanuel was alive, and not far. From the galley deck, under the ruse of billowing white sails, she stared up. The sky was shimmering blue. It was a beautiful, gusty day, full of sunshine, although hot and humid. Though she no longer had access to *his* help, Berenda still had confidence in herself, and felt sure that she could take on Emmanuel and his party and seize the Eye.

'Is there something new up there?'

'Perhaps there is, Hagiwara.'

Berenda sensed her enemies were close. Her hands were ready to fling magic, just as soon as she saw the balloon. She *could* take the great power gem; for wasn't she a power in her own right? She could change in any way she wanted. She had even imagined herself coming to believe in good – as if someone was on her side and praying for her.

'Love your enemies, bless them that persecute you, do good to them that hate you.'

Somehow those words compelled, though to her the sentiment made no sense. To do good, to *be* good, for no reward... That seemed both stupid and too hard.

But it came to her that now she *could* change, she would have to.

I used to believe I was loved by *him*, but I see now I was only a fool fooling myself; and *that* is the hard truth I cannot forgive.

The self-image of ice *he* had made half a mile high had been a miracle, but the miracle had failed.

She should have been killed, and her lord had not intervened to help. Only her last-instant magic had saved the galley and most of its crew, when she had made her protective bubble. Afterwards they had risen to the surface, bobbing among giant ice-floes grinding away and a tsunami – a wall of water moving away more quickly than a hurricane wind.

There had been no word from *him* then and silence since. She was alone in an empty world that was without meaning.

Berenda paced the deck, growing ever angrier about how he had deserted her.

In time I might have other loves and might even turn to other gods, but *him* I cannot continue with. Now what if I follow the balloon crew for my own purposes, and take the Eye for my own?

Words of Fury:

I can do it, and I will!

She felt very determined. The giant shape of ice, and indeed all *his* powers and bold talk, seemed no more than expired fantasies now. The Lord of the North was in the past. She squinted ahead into the future, wanting her enemies in her power, and most of all wanting the Eye.

That might be enough to challenge even *him*.

The day's loveliness somehow made everything worse for her. Nature was beautiful and eternal; she was neither. The white sails flapped as the galley came about.

She was following the balloon's set path, though she had yet to see it. The men, who had once crowded to thank her for saving their lives, now sat muttering. The galley proceeded by sail, going high and then low over the swell of the sea.

Now she turned, to study how the boat was rigged – checking the sails, the taut ropes, and the careful man at the tiller who never spoke except to ask practical questions. The sails, of course, were all white.

Hagiwara had asked about that. 'Why take down the red sails, and fly white!'

'There are certain folk I want to take by surprise.'

'Our enemies?'

She made a chopping gesture. 'We will bring them low and take the Eye.'

'I fear they are already low; landed,' Hagiwara murmured. He kept looking at the shore, which was as rugged as most of Japan. 'We should gather reinforcements and attack.'

'They still fly to Four Rocks.'

The new captain grimaced, but stayed very polite. 'Lady, are you sure? Before, you said that they *would* be brought down – that it was *certain* – when *he* made the graven image of ice.'

She put her hands to her veil, as if about to lift it.

'I mean no disrespect! I beg you, listen. Even if they're really above us, how can you expect me to sail fast enough to outpace the wind?'

She let her veil drop, amused by the man's relief when she concealed her face again. There was power even in a hard look.

'I don't care what you do, just beat them!'

'But how?'

She stared at the man's desperate, sweating face. Then she raised both arms, and something happened. The white sails rattled. A great calmness, as of exhaustion, settled over the sea.

Words of Fury:

As the wind died, the sails sagged, useless now.

The captain gave her a fearful sidelong look. He had learned the power of magic.

'Yes, this lack of wind will stop the balloon.' Berenda smiled. Of course, she could not negate the weather for long. It wasn't only fighting Nature; other magic had been worked in this area, some of it very powerful indeed. When the wind returned, she would order the sails raised again, but for now they rowed on, heading for the destination she had been given and others doubted. 'Most convenient – for us! Now we can overhaul them by using the oars.'

The oars came out; men sweated and muttered though no one dared complain out loud.

'You are now willing to check the coast?' Hagiwara asked her.

They were nearing the shore, but she was preoccupied.

She spread her hands. 'They are not here, but you may look for them as we pass.'

'Thank you.'

Then there was a shout from the foredeck. 'People on shore! People on shore, signaling!'

It was weird how the hot wind had died away. Man felt something odd in the sweltering atmosphere now, a touch of magic.

The Voice put a hand on her crucifix. Her face looked desperate.

'I was wrong to think we could cross this black beach, and I apologize for bringing you all here.'

Faslane had been looking out to sea, but now he turned to her. 'So we need a boat?'

'Unless there is a miracle, there will be no boats,' said the Voice, her eyes self-condemning.

Man was more than worried. If they couldn't go forward and they had no friends to help them get back to sea, what would happen? But he already knew: come night, the monsters would emerge, and eat.

'We know Fukuzawa was following us. He might still arrive!'

Joah turned, her expression dark. 'And if he doesn't, Man?'

He looked out to sea, desperate for help to come. Then he saw something, right on the horizon. 'Hey, what's that?'

The others all turned very carefully, so as not to disturb the sand. They had learned to fear what lived here.

Out to sea a bare mast-top had appeared. Man was suddenly excited. 'Perhaps that is Fukuzawa.'

Twin masts seem to slowly lift out of the sea-haze.

'It is a galley,' Faslane said as it approached. 'A Jade-type design, I'd say.' He eyed the approaching craft. 'Now the sails are furled. The wind has died there.'

They stood under the blazing sun. Were those furled sails white, or enemy red?

'What if it's not a friend? *He* must know we are here. What if it isn't Fukuzawa at all, but agents from *him?*'

'If it's no a friend, you might want to get some more praying in,' Faslane said to the Voice, wry as ever.

Was it Fukuzawa coming? Then Man asked himself another question: Or is this some enemy, in disguise?

Man realized how dry he was. He unpacked a water bottle, though he only took a sip. This water might have to last. He remembered the Lord of the North when he was made of ice, and how *he* had fallen into the sea. A few melted slivers of that flesh would be welcome now.

Man watched the galley approach. He touched the stinging wound on his face, where a female enemy had drawn blood while kissing him. The Tears, he thought, is... But he had no words to describe her dark and dangerous splendor, still less to pass judgement.

The galley rowed steadily closer. Though it was still too far out for Man or anyone to recognize it, he felt some connection.

'They're coming here! They must be looking for us!' He punched the air.

'That must be Captain Fukuzawa! Oh, sweet Jesus,' the Voice said, 'if it is, we're saved!'

'Lady, *he* has more agents than we know. What if it isn't your friend?' Faslane asked.

Man's cheek stung sharply but he was determined to ignore it. He took off his own sash and waved it frantically. 'Joah, everyone – wave what you can and pray!'

Man watched the galley, wondering if their signals had been seen. He was suddenly uncertain about everything.

What if the galley is enemy? Or what if it's a friend, but doesn't see us and turns away?

Our luck together is bad, but without my friends my own luck is even worse. And what about my chance to go home? I bet that's lost forever!

When the black steamship from Albion had come and attacked their city Jade, all he had had to do was turn traitor, and it would have taken him home.

But Man was proud to be Okada's adopted son and he hadn't turned. He had fought that ship and its airship. And then he had spoken to Albion's battleship, and to history, with his magically amplified voice.

'I COULD CHEERFULLY DESTROY YOU – AND YOU WOULD DESERVE IT.'

He had let that linger. On the black ship they would have waited for his magic to destroy them.

'BUT I WILL NOT. I WILL SHOW YOU A MERCY YOU DID NOT SHOW TO MY PEOPLE OF JADE.

'SO GO NOW! GO IN PEACE! AND TELL THEM ALL IN ALBION WHAT HAPPENED HERE!'

The black ship had gone; and if it made it back they might even speak well of Albion's exiled son.

Yes, they very well might! And that could still turn into my ticket home, and acceptance when I get there!

Man shifted his feet, the casket below him. The sun was burning the left side of his face. He watched the galley.

One day he might return to the Empire, but that day was not yet. The Lord of the North had to be fought here. And Man did not mistake his position; most likely he would die the final death in this foreign land.

'They are coming here, aren't they?' the Voice asked, with hope and no certainty.

The sea-haze thickened.

'I can't tell!'

'Surely they must be coming for us!' the Voice murmured, wringing her hands.

Man knew that was her wishful thinking: for suddenly now the galley turned north.

He stared. 'It's going to pass us by!'

'Who is that?' demanded Faslane. Then he became angry. 'Why did they turn away?'

'Does it matter?' Man asked. 'Now there will be no help.'

'Then we are only the walking dead.'

Even Yoshi had lost courage? Man turned his back to the water and stared at the black sand. The distance to the steep cliffs seemed immense. He squinted at the flickering mirage-effects of heat on the black sand.

'It doesn't look like anything is moving now,' he said, mostly to himself.

'No,' said Faslane. His voice sounded unnaturally flat. 'Actually, if you look closely you can see there's nothing growing here; nothing. Very few birds fly over and – have you noticed? – none of them land.'

Man stared. 'You're right.'

'We can't worry about that now!' Yoshi said promptly. He actually sounded gay; but perhaps his lightheartedness was just an act. 'You tell me Prophecy dictates we move inland. If so, let's do it, and make those monsters scared of us!'

Man kneeled, and carefully re-tied the ropes to the Eye's casket so that he could sling it like a knapsack. He rose again, putting the weight between his shoulders. The Eye was a burden, but he was man enough for it.

Better to die on your feet than...

He raised his voice. 'Let's go!'

'There were people on shore, really there were!' Hagiwara seemed determined to complain, but Berenda eyed him with indifference. 'Lady, we should turn back and investigate. It could be *them*.'

'I think not. I was told they were going to Four Rocks.'

'Surely I can persuade you?'

She considered, touching her chin.

Should I turn back? Or should I trust what I learned from my former master, and go on to where they will land?

Probably Hagiwara saw something, and it won't take long to check.

'Our friends won't forget us!' said the Voice from Afar.

Nobody replied to that. The mood among them was grim hopeless determination. Man wanted to say something to raise morale; but it would have been like telling tasteless jokes at a funeral.

They had packed carefully. There were some basic supplies and a little drinking water, though Man wondered how long they would last. They stepped off over the sand, and he saw the humps that indicated monsters.

Yoshi had his map again. 'There are a few passes across the mountains, and then The Waning of the Moon is not far.'

Words of Fury:

The Voice held her head in her hands. 'How can we survive the journey? How?'

Then Joah spoke.

'Stop!' she said. 'Stop, and look out to sea!'

Faslane turned, pointed. 'That galley has returned – or another!'

Man only saw bare masts. The sails, whether red or white, were down.

'They're heading in our direction!' Joah said. 'Do you think they're friends?'

'They're not coming back from the north, the way that other galley surely would. – Are you *sure* they're on our side?'

'Maybe we shouldn't have signalled.' Man stared, desperate to know if it was a friend coming, or a foe. 'Maybe that boat is full of bounty-hunters!'

Yoshi stared hard at the galley. 'Fukuzawa, or an enemy? Who can tell me which?'

Nobody answered.

Faslane turned his head to Man. 'Lord Emmanuel, if it is your Fukuzawa, will he see us and land? And even if he does meet with us and is willing to transport us, dare we risk those pirates?'

'We risked being flown about under a soap-bubble, and we risked monsters here.'

Faslane glanced over his shoulder. The black sands were empty, and they shimmered in the great heat. 'I see no monsters now.'

The Voice shivered. 'Except perhaps for ourselves.'

'That is quite profound,' Yoshi murmured without taking his gaze from the masted vessel. 'I will quote it, if my epic about us is ever written!'

Man laughed. 'Are we that short of toilet rags?'

'Ha! There goes your chance of literary immortality! Now, your position in the story will be comic relief: you will be a flatulent, cowardly clown!'

'You have me on all three counts,' Man admitted. 'Especially the first.'

'Even our beans are patriotic!'

'If that galley is really Fukuzawa's,' Joah said firmly, 'perhaps we might use it to evade Prophecy rather than fail it.'

Man frowned at Joah's own evasion. Wouldn't leaving this beach still mean they had failed the world, even if they saved

Words of Fury:

themselves? She seemed oddly complacent about it. To Man, now they had failed to cross Monster Beach – presumably the black midnight beach Naosuke had seen in her visions – it seemed they had failed Prophecy, failed all mankind, and the future itself.

While the others debated, Man reached behind and touched the bronze casket – for luck, or from hope, or to placate a possible enemy, he could not have said which.

The galley came closer.

Man still couldn't decide whose side it was on.

Words of Fury:

Chapter Ten: *Impossible Things*

After she entered the Waning's Map Room, she-captain Hanake closed the door carefully behind her. The door was both armored and hexed, and closing it made the long, long chamber soundproof.

The Sword Maiden wore long braids with gold and silver beads threaded there. Hanake was young for her rank, very leggy and fit, and confident in almost all circumstances. Ignoring the incredible paintings and the maps of lost lands upon the walls, she turned towards where Sulina and High Healer Irizo knelt on opposite sides of a low table.

Without speaking, Hanake bowed very low.

'Well, she-captain?'

'Elder sister, I went down the stairs as instructed, but the gate to that floor is still locked.'

'You didn't try to get in?'

'I followed your orders, so no.'

'And when you called out?'

'There was no response from the Sword Maidens on duty, nothing from Elder Sister Daisen, and nothing from holy Mother Zandar.'

'Then our Mother may be...' Irizo did not complete the sentence, but her expression told its own sad story.

Sulina was a very senior adept, and a luscious-fleshed woman. Her tart tongue and intelligence had always impressed Hanake.

Hanake watched as Sulina unrolled a living map of The Waning, its ring-walls and moat – and defensive magic. Hanake saw how her hands trembled. Lady Sulina nervous? Another bad sign. Sulina stared down where the paddy fields were a natural green and the sacred river flowed like quicksilver around Miracle Island, then around the Waning fortress. Everything, including the great waning Moon itself, was shown in three dimensions.

Sulina's fingers continued to play, but when she looked up her face seemed calm.

'You saw bodies?'

'I could not see down the corridor where the thinking-cells are, and so saw nothing of our holy Mother and Sister Daisen.' Hanake took a breath. 'But I felt death, and at the gate to that corridor I saw three Sword Maidens sprawled on the floor. They did not move.'

Irizo almost growled. 'Did you see signs of *him*?'

'High Healer?' Hanake was shocked. 'Would I know him, if he had disguised himself or come as an avatar? I don't know. But though I shouted I saw no sign of life.'

'You called loudly?'

Hanake touched her sword's hilt.

'I have drilled troops in the open. I can shout very loudly.'

'I can imagine,' Sulina said dryly.

'There was no response from Mother Zandar or Sister Daisen. I now volunteer to go looking for them. I can get keys, or force the gates.'

Prime Healer Irizo made a sudden gesture. 'Join us, please.'

The she-captain kneeled with them. 'This has the feeling of a council of war.'

'There is no war here,' Healer Irizo told them, pointedly.

'There *was* no war, but it has arrived.'

Hanake understood Sulina's point, but hesitated to clarify it. 'The great knocking was *him*?'

'Yes, and it could be worse. We fear *he* may still be within.'

'Here?'

That is a *truly* terrifying thought, Hanake acknowledged.

'It may be that the Lord of the North lies in wait; it may even be that the wards have trapped him.' Sulina gave a very thin smile. 'I think I will use my power to feel things out.'

As the other woman focused her mind prior to the dangerous expedition, Hanake glanced at the Map Room walls. Some maps went back to the elder days. One huge canvas was the Popple Map, dated 1733 and said to show the Hidden Continent. There were other city and country names out of legend, and place-names and even written scripts she'd never heard of or seen before.

The paintings were more striking, as they were mostly the products of occult dreaming. They were often grotesque, but sometimes beautiful. She saw city towers that could not exist, so tall were they. She saw a jungle of unearthly blue, and next to it a sea that was being sailed by mastless ships. She saw an immense striped world with rings around it, and other impossible things.

Hanake prided herself on being down to earth; but she had always found these pictures unsettling.

Sulina twitched out of her trance, touched her chin with a single finger. 'I feel no living spirit in the cells. None that I know, at least.'

Words of Fury:

Hanake couldn't stop herself blurting it out. 'Our Mother has been kidnapped away, or is dead?' Then Hanake felt a disturbance more profound than fear. No-one that Sulina knew... 'Or holy Mother Zandar might have been *turned?*'

'Perhaps.'

'Holy Mother of –'

Sulina raised a hand, to override the she-captain.

'You need to know that our Mother and Daisen were spirit-walking outside the protection of the wards, to escort a very important party here. The party included Lady Okada-noh-Joah, a gaijin adept known as "the Voice from Afar", and a young man who *may* be The One Who Will Change.'

'Elder Sisters, this is hard to take in. You have no contact with that party?'

'Not unless our Mother and Daisen managed it,' said Sulina, after a moment. 'They would have tried, for that party was bringing the Eye of Jade.'

Hanake was aghast. 'You say "was"? So now the Eye might be with *him?*'

'If I knew more, she-captain, I would tell you,' Sulina said.

Hanake nodded, feeling grim. 'Now we truly, truly need our holy Mother.' She looked at the others, in turn. 'Even if it is bad news we find, surely we must to try to get in.'

Irizo stirred. 'If Mother Zandar is enmeshed in magic and lives on, it might endanger her if we break in – break in against her instructions, I must add!'

'I know, Healer,' Sulina said. 'But there was that pulse of magic down there that was *male*. We must admit we have been penetrated; war *has* begun.'

A flicker of horizontal motion caught Hanake's eye.

'Look!' she said. They all turned, to the picture that showed giant towers on a waterfront. 'Why, that tower is on fire!'

That was one of two impossibly tall buildings, each with a corrugated grey hide. Gigantic quantities of grey smoke poured from the wound in its side, almost hiding the red flames within.

The fire was very high up. For long seconds that turned into minutes they all watched the tower burn.

Hanake was wondering why the sight was so distressing. After all, it could only be some fantasy, another world, not real...

Then their healer spoke. 'What is falling from the tower?'

Hanake hoped it was only her imagination – but she shuddered. Were those tiny falling shapes people?

Words of Fury:

Yes.

Many people must have been in that gigantic funeral pyre. More jumpers stepped into space. Some stepped off hand in hand with others.

Irizo said, 'I cannot believe this!'

Hanake had fought in wars. 'I can. It is *his* cruelty.'

'My God!' said Sulina, flinching back.

Something flying had struck the other tower and the blast spewed debris for hundreds of feet. There was a ball of fire in the tower from that explosion. Now this tower, too, began to burn.

'We have towers in this place,' Sulina said softly. 'Are we being warned...?'

Healer Irizo was quietly praying. Then one tower collapsed. Now Irizo looked upon all the burning and smoke, and quietly crossed herself. Her expression turned hard, then, and she turned to address Sulina and Hanake.

'We must find out what has happened here.'

'Find out *whatever the consequences?*'

'Yes.'

'High Healer, I ... am afraid,' said Sulina.

Hanake felt a rising sense of dread. 'What if we find *him*? It can only be *him* who broke our barriers! And *he might still be here!*'

They were all gravely silent. In the painting the second tower went down, in a soundless maelstrom of smoke and dust. That seen, Sulina rose, and then Hanake.

The Healer looked at them. 'I wish you both well, and I will pray for you now – and always. Please think of some way to tell me what you find – even if it is *him.*'

'We will try, sister.'

When Sulina left, she-captain Hanake followed.

Man asked himself the same question over and over. Who is on that galley? Oars cut into the water. From here, the rising and falling oars looked much like beating wings. Soon Man saw the samurai crowding at the boat bows. The figurehead there was painted lurid red: Hachiman, the warriors' god.

The oars chopped the water twice in the reverse direction and now the galley grounded gently in the black sand just to the right of the looming sea-stack.

In spite of himself, Man began to grin. They would be given safe passage now, and he was also unexpectedly glad to see the fierce old man himself.

They were hailed by Fukuzawa. 'Little lord Kinross, idling on a beach!'

'Not so little and never idle, but it's me!'

Man recognized other faces. Ozawa waved down, and so did Sanada. Friends!

As he felt their affection, Man's heart leapt.

A flexible boarding-ladder was let down. Two lithe brown seamen stripped off and dived in to help them board Fukuzawa's galley.

Lady Joah went up first. Her wet clothes were clinging and the colorful kimono silks almost transparent. When she stepped over the gunwale, Man saw that everyone within sight bowed very low. The Voice went next, though she was received with polite nods rather than bows. Faslane followed, received still less warmly.

Man wondered what his own reception would be; for he was as foreign as Faslane.

Then Yoshi was climbing on board. Once there Man saw him proudly raise his arms to display the Emperor's Man tattoos on his forearms. Samurai, many in chainmail or plate armor, bowed low to him and suddenly there was lusty cheering. Of course, Yoshi was charming, handsome, and famous for his poetry and his combat skills, and he knew how to cultivate popularity.

His face fits, Man thought dismally.

Still worrying about his reception, Man put the Eye's casket back on his back and then hurried up the boarding-ladder.

On deck, friends crowded round.

'You rode that balloon, and we followed you!' Sanada said. He was as he always was, plump, sincere and likeable – though maybe a little nervous among the hard veterans that Man saw here.

'Our Man fought the Empire of Blood as well as the Lord of the North!' Joah said loudly, no doubt to make sure all the men on board heard. 'He killed Albion's night-flying snake!'

'I saw it happen,' Fukuzawa acknowledged. 'By this Emmanuel our city was saved.'

There was more cheering. Man wondered now why he had felt so uncertain.

'So is Prophesy fulfilled!' said Joah. 'Rejoice, and follow my

Emmanuel!'

Man tried to be quietly polite as he spoke to his oldest friends.

'Please don't tell the world again – or me – that I'm "The One Who Will Change"!'

'But you are!' cried Sanada.

Man tried to insist: 'I don't mind doing the right thing, but not as a puppet.'

As if he hadn't spoken, Sanada gestured to the crowd, turning Man all the way around.

'Here is the hope of the world!'

Man didn't argue, for he saw now he was something for Sanada and others to believe in. He put down the casket and began toweling his hair dry.

Fukuzawa eyed Man, then Lady Joah. 'Did you see *him*, as a great statue of ice?'

'We did, and then we saw him brought down.'

Fukuzawa laughed. 'Quite a splash, but we rode it out.'

Joah said softly, 'From the great seaman Fukuzawa I would have expected no less.'

The scarred face beamed pleasure at the compliment. 'You escaped *him*, too. You are lucky, my Lady Joah – or your destiny is very strong.'

'I hope you're right about both. We have many enemies.'

Fukuzawa nodded. 'We don't have enough men here to re-take Jade, Lady Joah, but this force is a start. There are pirates around, in the pay of our enemies, but I can take you anywhere.'

'I appreciate that – and you.' She pulled a face. 'We were supposed to cross the black beach as Prophecy said. Alas, that was not possible.'

'Where do we go, then?'

'Shimabara port,' she said, looking over at Man and Yoshi. Man didn't disagree; nor did his friend. 'Then we will go inland, to The Waning of the Moon.'

Fukuzawa began shouting orders. Oars pushed them off from the beach and then turned them south. The white sails rustled as the rigging worked them up, and Man saw in delight how the sails caught the wind and bellied out. Suddenly they were leaving Monster Beach behind.

Still, Man felt a pang. In departing from the route laid down in Prophecy, surely they had let down the world? That thought bothered him greatly, but there was nothing he could do now;

nothing. He saw the Voice looking over at him in a way that showed she shared his feelings, though Lady Joah just seemed glad to be away from immediate danger.

Fukuzawa pointed. 'There's someone new you should meet, lordling. This is Two Heads.'

Man turned, then stared in disbelief.

'You could've called him Three Heads – if you wanted to lie.'

This was a hulking but misshapen pale-skinned man, typical of the Siberian tribes the Lord of the North drew on. His right shoulder was immense, though the other was weaker – but the first thing Man's eye was drawn to was the two heads. One was suitably large and craggy, the left more delicate. He had a big axe resting on his right shoulder and was wearing chainmail torso-armor that was too small to fasten over his giant chest. Two sets of eyes blinked, one set blue, one brown.

'Lord Kinross.' The big head nodded as the smaller head kept watch. 'I am glad to fight alongside you.'

Fukuzawa lowered his voice. 'He is a creature made by *him*, in the breeding-tunnels, to fight in *his* armies, but being shaped so, the mockery became too much.'

Man's mind was working quickly. He glanced over at Yoshi.

'Made for the Lord of the North... So he will know about *his* plans! Something, at least. Two Heads may be incredibly valuable.'

Then Ozawa came. He was smiling broadly.

'I have brought you tea, Emmanuel, in the Albion style.'

Man wrapped his hands around the hot bowl, sipped the spirit-laced chai and honey. He smiled back at his friend.

'Ah, that's good!' Now Man turned to speak to Lady Joah. 'I'm worried. Didn't Mother Zandar *want* us to cross that beach?'

Joah hesitated. 'The Voice from Afar thinks so.'

'And you?'

'I think we must surrender ourselves to destiny.'

Man nodded, reluctantly. He preferred to follow his own path. He had never liked being a tool.

'Well, the port of Shimabara is only half a day away by water.'

Joah bowed low, giving Man great face. Man sipped the brew, which invigorated. Wind thrummed in the rigging as the galley cleared all the black coastal sea-stacks. Clean salty air swept over them as they turned south.

Suddenly Man felt fantastic. With his own luck flowing, with friends like these, he could do anything. There *was* such a thing as destiny.

Ozawa gestured at the veterans he had with him.

'We have a small army for you, Emmanuel.'

'An army is great!'

Yoshi came ambling over, somehow looking both stylish and dangerous in his green and gold kimono and his frayed red leggings. 'Maybe not the "small" part.'

'Ozawa-san,' Man said, 'your men all look fierce.'

'They are hand-picked: some of Yoshi's and some my own.'

Yoshi agreed. 'These men are superb – but ready to learn from you, Emmanuel.'

'You must have worked hard to persuade them to throw in with a foreigner like me.'

Yoshi laughed.

'Some volunteered?' Man asked.

'Every last man here, my Emmanuel, and more were asking!'

Man felt his mouth sag open.

'A moment, please!' Fukuzawa dropped his voice to speak to Man privately. 'Foreigner-Sir, is it true that State Secretary Sukomo gave my lord the Five Touches?'

'It is true,' Man responded. 'Sukomo poisoned Lord Okada, and did the same to Lady Oki, and to Lady Joah here.'

Nostrils flared. 'Ah! So she is *dying*!'

'There will be help for her at The Waning, which is one reason why we must get there quickly. And, for what it's worth, Sukomo acted on Oatha's behalf.'

Fukuzawa spat over the side. 'Those black sashes! Ah, the cowardly way they work!'

'I hope Oatha will learn what happens to those who love evil.'

Fukuzawa's savaged face crumpled. 'Worldly preferment.'

'Captain!' Man was shocked. 'Was that a joke?'

The scarred face glared again. 'You fool! I never *ever* joke.'

Then Fukuzawa leaned towards Man, very close, threateningly close. He looked unblinkingly ferocious – till he winked and laughed a guttural laugh.

Man still felt warm surprise when a lean young samurai came over. He was pale, and younger than the twenty- and thirty-something veterans.

'We all wanted to work with you, lord. It was a revelation, your war knowledge from Albion.'

'War is different in E'ropa. There is less thought of individual honor there, and more thought of effectiveness. – Ashida, isn't it?'

'Yes, Lord Emmanuel.'

'In battle here, great warriors on either side step forward, proclaim their lineage, and issue challenges. It makes surprise almost impossible, and a general is always aware that his supposed allies may turn against him.'

'That does not happen in your E'ropa?'

Was there treachery back in Europe? Of course, though Man thought it best to downplay it.

'Warring there tends to be between nation-states; so to change sides does not show loyalty to a liege-lord, it is treachery to the realm.'

'I see.'

'My father believed in the constant re-invention of tactics. "Endless surprises and striking-power produce success".'

'Very wise.'

'And very effective. I remember him saying that often... Against the Lord of the North we must be equally determined – and flexible.'

'Yes,' the young man said. 'And I am.'

When Ashida went Yoshi explained. 'When you had us fight the Kuninaka clan in the fog – a clever idea I would never have thought of – his father was not at the gathering-point afterwards.'

'So? Most likely he had already died.'

'Ever since then there have been whispers of cowardice against the father, so of course Ashida has been tainted.'

Man found his fists were clenching. Young Ashida was about his own age, and fatherless.

'I hate people who put the sins of the fathers onto the sons! And I *hate* behind-the-back whisperers!'

Then the boy seaman up the mainmast shouted down. 'Masts in sight! West of north-west, maybe five miles!'

At once Man climbed part way up the rigging till he saw red topsails.

'Red sails ho!' He called down, 'That boat's a pirate junk.'

Faslane scrambled up beside Man. 'It is – and it's coming after us!'

Words of Fury:

'And not to talk about poetry!' said Yoshi, lounging on deck.

Fukuzawa began steering away, to get his passengers to Shimabara without a fight. Man watched the junk. Flying fish leapt out of the sea round them, little flashes of silver.

Faslane was soon beginning to smile. 'As you'd expect, we're faster.'

Man scrambled back down. The Voice was leaning on the gunwale. She basked in the sun and seemed not to care about the spray or the pursuit.

'Even here there is strange earth below – see? – which is enough to reduce the powers of our enemy. We may not even be seen by him.'

Man looked over the side. The water was crystal clear, but below was black sand. Then he heard another wail from the look-out.

'Sails ho! Red sails ahead!'

Ahead were two more boats, one not far from the shore and the other three or four miles out to sea. Every bellying sail was red.

'They're trying to cut us off,' said Faslane. 'This is a trap.'

Fukuzawa was prowling the deck from bows to tiller, his body language speaking of grave concern.

Yoshi was looking ahead. 'But we may have enough speed to get between... Ah!'

Man saw what Faslane had seen. There was a new enemy, a swift galley. It was far to the west but it also began heading for them.

'Four, against the one of us!' Man looked behind; the first junk was still in pursuit. He turned from Faslane to Fukuzawa, asked them both the same question. 'Must we fight? If so, can we fight them all?'

Fukuzawa frowned at the world. 'Four to one against us, maybe six to one in manpower...'

Yoshi was staring at the enemy and absently fingering his sword-hilts.

'Even to battle a single junk would be hard, though one we could by-pass. But so many...'

Ozawa straightened. 'So now we fight?'

Chapter Eleven: *This Is War*

Fight? Or run? As Man stood there, one simple truth blazed in his mind. We must make *sure* the Eye is not lost!

He realized suddenly that he did not really believe in the samurai honor code nor in Albion's knightly equivalent. He was his father's son; like the Lord of Arms of all Albion, he believed in winning – and winning now was getting to The Waning of the Moon, with everyone safe and the Eye with them.

Man said to Fukuzawa, 'I don't care how it might look! Can we run?'

The sea-captain snarled, 'Three enemies ahead, another behind – they have us trapped.'

Only then did Yoshi speak. 'Man, if they close in on us, is it best to drown the Eye?'

'It's a weapon neither you nor I can use,' said Joah. She looked angry with herself for speaking. 'We should discard it.'

Man snarled. Pain had suddenly stabbed from his cheek-wound to his brain.

'No, never! – You want it *yourself!*'

She said nothing to that, only flapped at her face with a fan she had obtained somewhere. Man realized he had again said something close to unforgivable.

'We can't parley with those boats, I suppose?' the Voice asked.

'Evening Land pirates?' Man was scornful, upset by the pain he had caused and by the pain in him. 'At best, they'd agree to take us alive – but then we'd be sold to Lord Oatha or to *him*. I'd rather drown.' Then he spoke only to Joah and Yoshi, 'But I'm not throwing the Eye and the Talking Book away! We *fight!*'

Two Heads was silently fingering his great axe.

Shortly the first Evening Land junk was closing in. Through the sea-haze Man saw men crowd the gunwales, and many waved swords or axes or spiked fighting irons. It was a crew two or three times the size of their own. He wondered why they weren't waiting for the other boats. Perhaps the rewards for seizing the Eye were just too great.

Fukuzawa beckoned Man over. As always, a helmet hid most of his disfigured face. He leaned forward, spoke with terrible intensity.

'*Are you what they say?*'

Man was tempted to make some great claim, but instead he

was honest.

'I can't magic us out of this battle, if that's what you're asking.'

'Your story is that we are weak and old-fashioned here, and we cannot prevail.'

Man felt the weight of destiny. There were choices to be made, producing success or failure – a terrible responsibility.

'What do you want from me?'

Those eyes were very fierce. 'An answer!'

What would my father say now? It'd be easy to lie, to gain this man's support, but...

To Fukuzawa, Man's silence was aggravating.

'You claim nothing, gaijin? Then I can't believe you are "The One Who Will Change"!'

The wind picked up and the red-sailed junk altered course. Now it was sailing straight for them, as if the intention was to ram.

Man settled his feet. 'I can make no promises.'

'Your honesty repels me.'

'It should not, for I *do* offer this realm loyalty, and I do ask for your help, though in return I offer things beyond value.'

'What?'

'The Eye of Jade, and someday the help of Albion!'

Suddenly Fukuzawa was smiling. 'Ah, they used to say The One Who Will Change would ride through the air to battle a monster. And you *did*.' The older man's eyes seemed to blaze. 'I thank you for it, Lord Emmanuel, for I love the city of Jade, and that sky-snake would have burned it to the ground.'

On impulse, Man hugged him. He was embracing a bloody legend, but the legend was looking up at him with respect. Man realized he was the younger and stronger man.

'So what do you want me to do, Emmanuel? I can put you and your friends ashore, while I lure the enemy away.'

'But that's the end for you! I can't let you do that!'

Suddenly, Fukuzawa kneeled before Man. 'Let me give you the gifts I can!' He took both of Man's hands in his own. 'I know from the Lady Joah you need men to cross that beach – and that you *must* cross, to save us. Take the men here! Let me help you!'

Man was deeply moved. For the first time in an age he felt like his father must have. His two strong arms raised Fukuzawa to his feet again.

'Even if you give me all these men I cannot give you

certainty, Captain!'

'This is the end of times. There can be no certainty for anyone.' Now Fukuzawa looked at Lady Joah, who looked back sternly. 'Will you two please instruct me?'

Fukuzawa resumed his place by the tiller-man. The junk was still closing.

Now Man saw Yoshi whisper to one of the crew. Other samurai were leaving messages with Fukuzawa's sailors, to be passed on if Fukuzawa ever made port.

'It's for my father, Man. I wanted to tell him what Joah said about the high Son of the Cold in Jade.'

'Will he listen?'

'I don't know! But anything that helps our side is worth trying. Don't fool yourself: when Oatha and his "patriots" run Jade, all you foreigners will be walled in, and then your religions and you will be wiped out!'

Man imagined the burning of holy books, the screaming anger of crowds, the mass arrests, and the mass-murders. 'You know this for certain?'

'That's my honest prediction based on the intelligence I have; so listen. And because *he* and all of *his* will be on Oatha's side, we need any help my father can give us – even though he now hates me almost as much as he hates you.'

Faslane kept going from side to side of the galley, looking at the shore, looking up at the sails, looking at all four enemies.

'Four against one is terrible odds!'

'There are more,' Joah said, in a flat voice. She waved a hand at the sea. 'More enemies out there.'

'You see *his* servants?'

'Yes, and *his* power, all around. I have done wrong, I fear, but I can see much.'

Joah folded her hands together and then her eyes closed; but she did not look calm. She looked frightened. Then, very strangely, Man felt his skin prickle. He saw Joah's head jerk back.

'What is it?'

'I feel – cold. I feel the power of the Lord of the North!'

Incredibly, snowflakes began to fall.

Joah caught one flake on a fingertip. She looked at it as it melted away. Perhaps she saw that as an omen, for when she looked up Man flinched from the pain in her eyes.

'We have gone beyond the bounds of that strange black land

Words of Fury:

where *he* was less. Now he is great again.'

'Then surely it's better to be back on shore!' Man turned away from her, shading his eyes to look back at the bay. Twisted black glass columns rose out of the turbulent water, often wider at the top, as if melting rock had been sucked up from under the sea. Waves battered their bases. 'Dare we risk it?'

Joah was dry-washing her hands. 'Could Fukuzawa land us before the enemy strike?'

'Man,' the Voice said, 'I have my faith back. There *is* a story already written for us, and we must get back to it. The black beach, the monsters – well, if that is our Prophesied destiny...'

'I don't believe!' Man said suddenly. More snowflakes fell. 'I never have believed!'

The Voice from Afar kissed his unwounded cheek. 'Perhaps it's enough if we believe in you.'

Faslane came close. 'If you bring all these samurai, we have a genuine chance to cross the beach!'

'Even if I do, many of us will die. Perhaps you, Master Faslane.'

'Then so be it!'

Man acknowledged this man's loyalty, too. Suddenly he felt a growing and very personal anger, directed against the Lord of the North. His heart began to beat faster, flooding his system with hot determination.

He was ready to fight, and the others saw it.

'The Lady Joah is right about the power of story, too,' Yoshi said. 'Stories live and stories change us. Your Bible stories, Voice. Or that Albion drama you took me to see.'

'"*Romeo and Juliet*"? You were so shocked!'

Man saw the enemy was closing in; soon the fight would start.

'I was, dear Voice, even more when I borrowed the book and read it. Two mad young hearts, defying their families in every way – of course they deserved death!'

'Yoshi!' Now it was the Voice who was shocked.

'I took it as an exercise in justice at first, but it was justice so savage it broke my heart! But then I changed.' Now Yoshi turned to Man, who was still watching the approaching enemy. 'That's because of you, my brother.'

'Me? How so? I know what I like, most of the time, but I know nothing about art.'

'I saw their story in a different way because of your story.

They were young and in love, their love had a marvelous intensity, and they risked everything for it. They dared to break the rules, which is how change happens. It doesn't matter what tradition and family say! They *loved!* What they deserved was life!'

'Yes,' said the Voice, 'just as we deserve life. And, if you think about it, they *have* life. Romeo and Juliet will live forever – and that's the power of a well-told story.'

'It is. The man's poetry is somewhat erratic for my taste, but he can tell a timeless tale. Tell me, Man, is your "Shakespeare" still alive?'

Though Yoshi was a poet, Man was not, and he had only a small familiarity with Albion's drama.

'I have no idea. If he is, maybe you can get to meet him.' He looked over at the enemy junk again, crammed with Evening Land pirates and black-sashed purity police. 'If we survive.'

'Our story will survive,' said the Voice, 'whatever happens to us now. We should land upon that beach, because *that* is our story. Or, to put it another way, we must fulfill Prophecy.'

It sounded too poetic for Man, but he accepted what his friends said.

'Very well, we follow the authored story. – Monster Beach it is! Captain Fukuzawa, are you willing?'

'Look!'

Man turned again. Faslane was pointing dramatically to the north-west. A black squall rushed visibly over the dark-green sea towards them, flattening the big waves as it came on.

Faslane barked, 'That's a storm and a half!'

Joah was staring. 'It's not natural! Somebody wants to end our story at the wrong place.'

'Then we'll have to stop whoever it is,' Man said firmly, though he had no idea how.

Sleet struck at them. In an instant, they were all soaked.

She shrieked, 'Captain Fukuzawa, turn towards the wind!'

'What? Into the storm? Where that junk is coming?'

'Yes! I have seen the future... Turn!' Joah was transfigured. In her, faith and certainty had come together: it was as if a bright light was shining out of her. 'We must turn!'

Man suddenly believed in her. 'Captain, do it!'

Fukuzawa cursed under his breath, but he turned his boat into the storm-wind and into the path of the pirate junk and set the oars beating. As their galley crested one huge wave its bows

Words of Fury:

reared up, and when it crashed deep into the maddened sea heavy spray broke right over Man and the others. A wailing samurai was swept overboard.

Man saw how lightning flickered ahead, among black, corkscrewing thunderheads. The pirate junk had stayed with its sails set and it was running them down.

Fukuzawa screamed at Man, 'If that boat and mine survive the storm there'll be a head-on collision! They'll sink us!'

Man saw that was true, but his faith didn't fail.

'Hold to this course!' he bawled. 'Hold on!'

The black wind hit. A man went flying, his shocked upside-down face going past Man. Man was blown off his feet and sent rolling over the galley deck. When he managed to get up, he blinked away blinding rain and threw a fearful glance back towards the tiller, which was swinging. No doubt the tiller-man had gone overboard too.

Faslane went to the tiller and tried to work it. Man stumbled across the crazily pitching deck to help him. They heaved together.

'I've never felt anything like this before!' Faslane was just inches away from Man, which was the only reason Man could hear. 'This must be magic!'

Their oarsmen moaned. Oars had crashed together; only a few of the men were fast and strong enough to take the oars back aboard.

'For the love o' God!' Faslane said. 'Say your prayers, for we're dead!'

Man saw it was too late for prayer, or even a miracle.

The Evening Land junk, a few rags of red sail still set, was bearing down on them on a collision course.

'Don't pull away! Straight ahead!' said Joah.

Though there was now an aggression in her that made her look like her sister Oki, Man and Faslane heaved on the tiller-bar, setting it straight again. They obeyed Joah, even though it would be a head-on collision. The junk had no ram that Man could see but it was so much heavier than their own galley that it was certain to sink them.

What's Joah doing? We will be wrecked, and the Eye lost to humanity. Surely what's happening now is *his* plan!

Perhaps Joah read his mind, for she shouted out: 'Have faith!'

The wind strengthened to beyond hurricane force. Man saw

two more samurai hurled over the side. Ahead, the Evening Land junk lost the last red sailcloth and rigging, and then the entire foremast snapped off at the base loud enough for Man to hear. But the big boat plunged on.

Faslane bawled at Joah. 'It's going to hit us! Brace!'

Joah did not move. She stood at the gunwale, both fists clenched, head lowered. Man saw the power of her weaves shimmer around her.

Would it be enough? It couldn't be. Northern wind blasted both boats, actually driving their galley backwards. Next, only yards away, the junk seemed to rear up at the bows. Man knew they were all dead.

Joah pointed her two forefingers and said something.

At once their enemy was swamped by a great wave that came out of nowhere – a wave forty feet high – which swept the junk's decks. Men were knocked away along with anything not fixed. The junk somehow had its bows forced down and Man saw water overwhelm it.

It sank in seconds, taking most of its crew with it. Its truncated masts scraped on the galley's hull as it went below them.

'Lord Jesus Christ ha' mercy!' Faslane said, crossing himself. He explained to Man, 'It's horror to any sailor to see other seamen drown – even if they were enemy.'

Joah was panting hard. 'Blame the Lord of the North! Oh, blame *him*, and not me!'

She was weeping. Man went over and held her, as the winds began their rapid dying. He turned his face to the heavens. The black sky was clearing. For now, they were saved. Then he looked at Joah again, there in his arms. She was looking where the junk had drowned. She had killed many, and she was heartbroken.

'I must not think of the casualties, must I?'

'Think of a whole world that must be saved!'

'At such a cost?'

'This is war; and you are a heroine! Thanks to you we're still alive, and have hope!'

Now Joah began to smile: at first a very sad smile, which suddenly turned wonderful.

Man reached out for her right hand, and kissed it. She flushed, her lovely eyes sparkling. He held her fingers against his cheek where he had been wounded. Then she touched a finger to

Words of Fury:

his lips, looking so beautiful now he might have cried.

'Look beyond!' Fukuzawa grimaced. 'We still have those other enemies! Three boats!'

To the west and to the south, still cutting them off from the sea-passage to Shimabara, were the other two Evening Land junks, and the enemy galley.

Joah said at once, 'My power is exhausted!'

Fukuzawa turned to Man. 'What do you want me to do?'

'Put us on the beach.'

Proud Joah turned to Fukuzawa. 'Yes, land us!'

Fukuzawa spoke quietly. 'I will round that sea-stack there and put into the cove beyond.'

'But won't they follow us?' Man asked. The sea-stack was a mile away, and though they would beat their enemies there their enemies could also land.

'They won't have time. I will go back out to sea fast and be your decoy, Lord of Albion. By the time they catch us and we fight, by the time I am destroyed, you should be well inland.'

'Whatever chance *we* have, you'll have none! You and your men will die instead of me, *for* me!'

'Lord Kinross,' Fukuzawa said hotly, 'I am samurai. What I have lived for is to die in the right way. If I help save my country, how better?' Without further speech he turned to the replacement tiller-man. 'Take us to the shore!'

Men scrambled again to man the oars. The sea was curiously flat and windlessly calm now, so the junks could do nothing and the enemy galley was still far away. The samurai began rowing. Man tried to focus whatever power he had left to give help, and perhaps the galley slid more easily over the sea than before.

Dead ahead, he saw black sea-stacks that were jagged boat-rippers. But Fukuzawa worked his boat well, and his men oared the galley into a gap between two spits of glassy rock. There was a cove there, with shining black sand. They grounded in it.

Fukuzawa was screaming. 'Quickly! Off my boat and onto land!'

Man led the others in jumping off, their packs and weapons held above their heads. He went splashing through knee-deep surf up the beach. Fifty people followed. When Man was just beyond the waterline he turned to watch.

Fukuzawa backed the oars, making a quick turn as soon as he had sea-room. As the oar-master's drum began to beat again, the captain looked back once from the stern. Then he turned away.

'Fukuzawa will fight,' Yoshi said quietly, 'even if the Evening Land pirates outnumber him three to one.'

'I know he will. The question is this: can he possibly win?'

Man turned his back to the black beach, climbed up slick rock and then squirmed forward.

He had to see.

Words of Fury:

Chapter Twelve: *In War the Unlikely Happens*

Hanake followed Sister Sulina down the stairs, her sword drawn.
 Is *he* waiting for us?
 Hanake said nothing out loud, though even in deadly battles she had never felt closer to death. A line of Sword Maidens was on the stairway behind her, ready to pass on good news or bad.
 These stairs gave onto a large, barely-lit cellar room. In a sign of *him*, it was freezing cold.
 'Look, Sister!' said Hanake in amazement. 'Now the walls are bare!'
 The painted icons were gone – the fighting Saints and the Madonna.
 Sulina responded. 'I would like to think St George and our other patrons came off the walls and fought for us, and so did the Mother of God.'
 Now Sulina unlocked the first gate, to the large cellar. She advanced slowly into the gloom, the fingers of her right hand tapping on the jewel between her breasts – the Diamond Heart.
 'The bodies!' Hanake said, pointing in the gloom with her sword.
 Each one was a Sword Maiden in blood red, armed and once fierce.
 Now they were dead.
 Hanake stared. Two Sword Maidens lay just outside the gate to the thinking cells – obviously dead, as there was ice on their blue flesh from *his* touch. But by a small table sprawled Winter Morning herself, still breathing.
 'What can the senior she-captain tell us?' Sulina murmured, clearly reluctant to go to the actual cell Zandar had used. She fluttered her right-hand fingers over the veteran Sword Maiden. 'Alive, yes – but *changed*.'
 For a moment Hanake kneeled to study her superior. Winter Morning was indeed breathing, though the wide-open eyes that stared at the ceiling seemed dull and lifeless.
 Blinded, perhaps...
 Hanake rose.
 Our chief duty is to find out if *he* is still here. If he is, then ... shortly I will be dead.
 She stepped over the bodies and with one hand quietly shook the iron gate to the corridor of cells. 'It is still locked.'
 'That doesn't mean much when we deal with *him*.' Sulina

raised the diamond in her hand and looked into it. 'Power has been used, but I don't see man's magic now.'

'No? Is that some trick to put us at our ease?'

'She-captain, we are neither of us at our ease.'

'True.'

It was always cool here, but today it was freezing. That was *his* work, Hanake knew. There was also a rank, male-animal-in-a-cage odor, which she wondered about.

'Now I must unlock this gate, and then...'

Sulina would go down this corridor, towards where *he* had been. In spite of Hanake's protests, she would go alone.

Sulina suddenly turned, eyed her. 'Let me quote you: this gate being still locked could easily be a trick, to "put us at our ease".'

'I quote you back: "we are neither of us at our ease".'

Sulina lowered her gem and sighed. 'I still feel no life in the thinking-cells – but that might be some spell of disguise.'

'Let me come with you!'

'Wait five minutes, then call. If I do not respond – and it must be my voice in response, not *his* – please tell your Sword Maiden shadowers what has happened.'

'What will have happened?'

'I will be dead.'

'What do I do then?'

'If you can – and this is a request, not an order – please come looking for me. If that is too dangerous, as I suppose it will be, then I *order* you to leave and report back to the High Healer.'

Hanake looked into the dark corridor ahead. A flicker of light came from one cell. There was no other illumination.

Sulina unlocked the thick-barred metal gate, hesitated, but then locked it again behind her. She gave Hanake the key. 'You know what to do.'

Then Sulina went down the corridor, alone.

That was about the bravest thing that Hanake had ever seen.

She called out over her shoulder. 'Sword Maidens! Elder Sister Sulina has locked the gate and left me the key, and now she goes forward with the Diamond Heart. In five minutes, if she has not returned, I will go looking for her!'

Early on in her waiting she felt a faint skin-prickling, indicating female magic was being used. An adept might have been able to say it was Sulina herself, or Daisen, or the holy Mother. Hanake did not have that sensitivity.

If I get through this I'll suggest triple-manning the wall and closing the gates, Hanake decided. *Of course, if he is already here, and about to unleash himself...*

Five minutes after Sulina had gone, Hanake went to the gate.

'Sister Sulina?'

Hanake's voice was distorted. She realized how scared she was. But there was no possibility of disobeying war orders, so she would obey. Behind her another senior Sword Maiden watched, to bear witness in case Hanake encountered *him*.

'Elder Sister! Do you hear me?'

That call produced the same lack of response as before. It was as if Sulina had died – or been *taken*. Hanake had to fight off a superstitious feeling that the Lord of the North had already killed Sulina and was waiting for more prey.

She shouted behind her, 'Sword Maidens! I am going in. Be ready for anything!'

She unlocked the corridor gate and advanced, sword out.

It was very cold here. When she came to the cell, there was still the same soft light flickering from within. Wary, she called out. 'Elder Sister?' When there was no response, Hanake swallowed another lump of pain. 'Mother Zandar?'

Hanake held her sword in her two hands. If *he* was within, if *she* moved quickly enough...

'Does anyone hear me?'

It was another moment before Sulina answered – if it was Sulina.

'I am here, Hanake. Forgive me for not answering you.'

'What happened?'

'I could not speak...'

'Elder Sister? Has – the worst happened?'

'Yes.'

Still Hanake did not enter. Some things you just did not want to see.

Then, shuddering, she stepped through the burst wood and metal gates and went on into the cold, cold cell.

Daisen was here, standing up. She looked exhausted – as if roughly woken from a long nightmare. She and Sulina were both gazing down. Hanake had to brace herself now. Some deaths were minor; other deaths were major; this tragic death would make history.

Noting the deep scours on the stone walls and floor, Hanake

came to join the others. 'I see you gave her back her dignity.'

Daisen wiped away tears. 'She deserved no less.'

'I know,' Hanake said, in a broken voice.

The three women around the death-bed looked at the sacred corpse.

Daisen spoke without turning. 'Sulina, how are the wards of protection?'

'The many layers still shield our fortress.'

'Somehow *he* got in. I hope, *only* by way of our holy Mother, entering her as she lost her fight...'

'We still have some protection, though I wonder how much,' said Daisen.

'I think it must be "enough", otherwise the Lord of the North would be sitting here in state.'

'You are wise as always, Sister Sulina.'

Hanake saw Daisen's face was etched with stress, though you would not have known that from her voice.

Then Daisen threw Sulina a sharp glance. 'You kept quiet the news of her death?'

'Yes,' said Sulina. 'We three are the only ones who know for certain. Oh, and the Lord of the North, I suppose.'

'*Him*,' said Hanake, feeling distaste soil her mouth. 'But others must soon find out. And then there'll be the obvious effect on morale.'

'She-captain, you prepare for war.'

'I do.'

Another silence, for Daisen was deep in mourning. 'Ah, she looks at peace. She is immaculate.'

'Might Healer Irizo be consulted?' Hanake said, most politely.

'Why?' asked Daisen. 'Death cannot be healed.'

'True,' said Hanake, 'but the senior she-captain is still breathing.'

Daisen turned to Hanake. 'Help our Mother; then you may aid Winter Morning.'

Hanake pulled a white sheet over the unmoving body and wrapped it up as in a shroud. Even then the two women did not turn away from the surprisingly small corpse. This lack of decision unnerved the senior Sword Maiden. She turned to Daisen.

'We do not know where the Lady Joah is, do we?'

'Last seen hanging beneath a leaking balloon,' said Daisen.

Hanake took a breath. 'So she might also be dead?'

Daisen straightened. 'The party from the balloon, we really should have met them as they landed, but it is too late now.' She shivered. 'I think *he* left because he thought he would get the Eye. And he *will*, if they have landed anywhere except the black shore!'

Sulina insisted, 'They are not weaklings! Surely they will try to come here?'

'They will try, yes! Pray that they succeed.' Daisen's voice was rough now. 'What else has happened? I know Sandella has been dreaming of some disaster in the North? Is *he* at Rumoi, taking the city? Ah!' It was a cry of pain. 'Already Jade has fallen! Though the war has hardly begun, we are losing.'

'Our adepts might have guessed that.'

'Who?'

'Young Sandella,' Sulina admitted.

'You told her everything?'

'No; I said that our Mother was ... not currently available. But she was determined, because of another fearsome dream about Rumoi.'

'What dream was this?' asked Hanake.

'The Lord of the North struck Rumoi from the sea.'

'Rumoi is where Sandella's sister Kinshi is, on active service under Lady Egawa. This could be very important indeed. Did you permit her to pass on details to her sister, and so to Lady Egawa?'

'It was only a dream. And Rumoi is a strongpoint. A direct attack there seemed unlikely.'

Hanake raised an eyebrow. So there had been no warning given!

'In war the unlikely happens.'

'Yes, so in the end I sent Sandella away to mind-call her sister.'

'At least Lady Egawa will be forewarned.'

'If Sandella actually spoke to her sister.'

'She may not have done?'

Daisen lifted empty hands. 'Can't you feel it? The Lord of the North is blanketing everything.'

Sulina gave a worried look. 'Is there *any* chance of that alliance with great Albion, as our Mother wished?'

'Only if young Emmanuel lives.'

'If Emmanuel dies...' Sulina's voice cracked.

'Then *he* will win everything.'

That silenced them all. Hanake saw that hope had died here; and it might not be resurrected.

'Man, I also must be a witness,' Yoshi said from behind. 'Fukuzawa will fight, and this will deserve a poem.'

'What about our men?'

'Ozawa will not move till you tell him.'

Without another word, still looking out to sea, Man made a space. Yoshi wriggled up beside Man, head low in case their enemies were looking. Man really wanted to be out there on the galley, which was oaring away quickly now. But the sea-captain was dying a hero's death so that his friends could escape. How much help did a man need to do that?

Lady Joah squirmed in between the two men without speaking. They both felt her soft, elastic curves against their own hard bodies, but said nothing.

She was muttering under her breath as the three boats closed in.

'This is strange land. Here my tired magic is made small.'

'It's the same for me,' Man admitted. 'I can't help either.'

Fukuzawa's galley was a quarter-mile out, with the enemy galley and a junk closing in.

'It'll happen a half-mile off shore,' Man predicted. 'A three-on-one fight.'

The high-sided junk from the Evening Land had a foredeck catapult. As it let fly, Man winced. The heavy bolt went through Fukuzawa's mainsail. Suddenly Fukuzawa turned, in one swift move that put distance between his vessel and that junk and brought his own galley next to the enemy galley: from pursued to pursuer.

Now Fukuzawa's men stood up with bows. Arrows flew – fire-arrows.

'What a brilliant surprise!'

Man saw several small fires take hold on the enemy. Frantic men tried to fire-fight, but soon part of the rigging as well as the reefed head sail was burning. The rowers lost their rhythm.

'That's done damage to the most maneuverable enemy,' said Yoshi, in approval.

The junk let rip with two more catapult bolts, and Man whistled in disbelief as one killed Fukuzawa's replacement tillerman. In the moments Fukuzawa's boat was out of control the

Words of Fury:

enemy galley swept closer and grappled. Hands heaved on those two lines and brought the two vessels side by side, though flames were flickering over the pirates' boat. Then Man saw armed shrieking enemies board Fukuzawa's vessel.

Man saw Fukuzawa dart left, right, killing an enemy on each occasion. Red-flighted arrows stuck out from his armor, though as yet he did not seem much hurt.

Fukuzawa cleared his foredeck of enemies, though he had lost his helmet and his carved-up face was visible. Nevertheless, more pirates and black sashes pressed up the companionways to the raised decks fore and aft.

Joah shook Man's shoulder. 'If there is anything you can do with the Eye, do it now, or Fukuzawa will die and they will come for us!'

Man rested his hands on the casket, and he tried to touch the power it contained. There might have been a single flash of green from within, but no more.

He shook his head, ashamed. She turned away, scowling, and Man felt disliked.

Yoshi drew back. 'We should go.'

'Oh, look now!' Joah said.

She reached out to take Man's hand. He felt her small fingers hold his. Whatever this was, it was hardly hatred.

Yoshi reached over Joah and pulled at Man's shoulder. 'Come on.'

'No! I have to see!' Now Man pointed. 'The fire-arrows have worked!' Flames showed red-orange on the enemy galley. 'It isn't over!'

They saw that Fukuzawa's boat had slid away from the enemy. Clever use of his few manned oars kept Fukuzawa on the far side of the pirate galley to the junk, and the surviving enemies on Fukuzawa's boat were quickly killed.

'That was well done!' said Man.

Meanwhile, Fukuzawa had freed his vessel from the grapple-lines and now his fire-arrows struck the junk too. But enemy bowmen had replied, and Fukuzawa's own galley had fires on it, too. Yellow flames rose from all vessels, grey smoke billowing above.

Through the smoke, Man looked at the ghostly shape of Fukuzawa's craft. Rain, he thought. Lots of rain on Fukuzawa's boat and only there! His fingers flexed...

Nothing happened.

Words of Fury:

Fukuzawa's men extinguished the fires on board, while Man saw the pirate galley continue to burn, losing sails, rigging and finally masts to the furnace. Men threw themselves from the burning wreck into the sea.

'Two down!' said Man.

But now the junk closed in, fifty yards from Fukuzawa, thirty yards, less.

Junks were slow, so why didn't Fukuzawa get away?

Man watched the fight in despair; but when the junk was close enough Fukuzawa and three of his seaman began throwing things into the bigger enemy boat – things that trailed smoke through the air.

'Fire-grenades!'

'Which *you* introduced, my Man,' Yoshi said.

Four explosions of fire, then five, then six...

The young samurai continued, 'Now Fukuzawa will make them burn!'

For the junk, right from the start it looked bad; a yellow flickering of flames from six locations and palls of smoke. The other sea-going junk came in to help instead of attacking Fukuzawa. It was also hit – sails, masts, everywhere – with fire-arrows.

'Fukuzawa is fighting brilliantly. Look at him!'

Probably it was Man's imagination – but he seemed to hear Fukuzawa shouting in triumph. Somehow, Fukuzawa's handful had taken the battle to their enemies.

Fukuzawa's men went back to their oars; the oarblades cut deep into the water, driving the galley on.

'He's getting away!' said Joah, overjoyed.

She was wrong.

'I don't believe it!' Man responded. 'Fukuzawa's going back to the fight!'

Smoke and the sea-haze were grey palls preventing clear vision, but Man had a last glimpse of the captain patrolling his burning deck with a raised sword. Then the grey smoke swirled, concealing all. Nevertheless, the great death-cry came faintly from inside the smoke. 'Fukuzawa! Okada! The Lord Emmanuel!'

Man, shocked but touched, turned to Yoshi. 'The man knows how to fight.'

'For a samurai that's a proud epitaph.' Yoshi rose. 'Fukuzawa will die for a purpose. Now we must take the chance

Words of Fury: 123

he earned us.'

They scrambled back, then trotted up to the others.

At Ozawa's direction, the samurai had formed up so as to watch all sides. Man saw they all wore swords, which many had drawn. Others had bows. Some held small shields, others long shields. Several had naginata spears, and Man was especially glad to see the spear-heads glinting in the sun now the wooden sheaths were off. Trained naginata men could stand off horsemen.

These men looked fit, alert, competent. They were ideal.

'Fukuzawa took the fight to them!' Man explained. His voice was suddenly breaking. Fukuzawa had given up his life for Man himself and for all these others. 'Fukuzawa has given us the time we needed...'

Man took a deep breath. 'You men should all know that we now follow Prophecy. The Lady Lalla Naosuke has said that we must cross this "midnight beach" on our way to safety at The Waning of the Moon. We go there so that I can change things, to fight *him!*' Man took another breath. 'Thank you all for your faith. I will not let you down. Beware of what is under the sand – giant crabs and giant lobsters.

'Now, give your officers and me a moment and we will decide on the command.'

Faslane nodded grimly, arm around the Voice. In his free hand he bounced his fighting-iron. 'Can we really cross this Beach of Monsters?'

'We must.' Joah pointed at the distant mountain crest that rose above the green cliff-tops beyond the beach. 'For Shimabara is behind Mount Unzen there.'

In other words, Man thought sourly, safety is miles off.

Man felt his best friend's hand on his shoulder. Then Yoshi turned to Ozawa. 'What should be the chain of command?'

'I know the men, so I suggest I field-command, of course under you.'

'Agreed, Ozawa-san, although the Lord Emmanuel should be in ultimate charge.'

'*Me?*'

Now Yoshi showed the expression of an officer prevented from doing his duty.

'Who else?'

Man swallowed. Fifty persons, some his dear friends, were now his responsibility. So was the destiny of this world – unless

Words of Fury:

he said no.
    He thought about it, but he didn't say no.

Words of Fury:

Chapter Thirteen: *We Must Walk this Path*

Berenda's galley had avoided the sea-fight. The sea was dead calm again, so sails were useless. In the hot sunshine, sweating and complaining men used what oars had survived the tsunami.

Hagiwara found himself speaking.

'Lady, surely we might have stayed?'

She tapped her fingers along her thighs and her veiled face did not even turn. The horizon ahead is much more interesting to her, Hagiwara thought, because beyond it is her heart's desire: Emmanuel and the great Eye, and her own glory...

Her wonderful voice was rough. 'Why should we?'

'We could have seen Fukuzawa's defeat, even helped it. Fukuzawa's legend may be immortal, but he is not!'

'So?'

'So the five we seek might have been with him.'

'Our enemies were not with Fukuzawa.' Of course the veiled face was unreadable, but he sensed held-back anger. 'But if you *really* wanted to play the hero there, why didn't you?'

'What?'

She spread her hands now, flourishing her long fingers. He remembered how she had plucked out music from stringed instruments – and plucked out eyes from defiant human faces.

She placed one finger on his forehead.

The sea abruptly sagged below Hagiwara, or perhaps it was just his stomach reacting to her magic. He was made to remember the dreadful burning smells – sailcloth, wood, human flesh – from Fukuzawa's fire-arrows and fire-bombs. At the mere thought of burning to death, Hagiwara flinched. He was brave, but not brave enough for that.

'What do you want us to do now?'

'Follow me.'

'When we do find him, will this Emmanuel be – dangerous?'

Berenda touched her cheek.

'With the wound I gave him, will he even be alive?'

Man touched the stinging wound on his face. He winced, then turned to Ozawa. 'Who will be below you?'

Ozawa pointed out one thick-set samurai wearing a horned helmet; he had plate armor on his chest and arms and wore grey cotton leggings. 'If I go down, put Ugaki in charge. He's tough and steady.'

Words of Fury:

Ugaki raised thickly-muscled arms in acknowledgement. Man waved back.

Ozawa continued, 'Below Ugaki, the other two seniors will be Yonai there –'

Man nodded at the slim man with the smoldering eyes. 'I remember him from the fight at Yomiba.'

Yonai bowed low.

'Then you'll recall that Yonai's an excellent rider and archer, and a fast runner. Also, he's a believer.'

'In what?'

'In you.'

'I wish he'd chosen someone better to put his faith in.' Man looked round at the carefully-arranged ranks of samurai. 'Who else?'

Ozawa pointed. 'The scar-faced man over there. Kido!'

Kido was on the far right flank. He turned his head back, grinned. 'I hear you, sirs! Ozawa-san, then Ugaki-san, then Yonai, then me!'

Ozawa lowered his voice. 'Not as clever as the other two, maybe, and he'll need you to lead with ideas as well as your presence, but he's got an iron soul and never gives up.'

Man spoke in a similar low voice to Ozawa and Yoshi. 'What about Ashida there?'

Ozawa said gravely, 'Too young. Besides, the men doubt his luck – and his character.'

Man nodded in understanding. The taint...

All the chosen men acknowledged Man by bowing to him, then left the ranks at Man's gesture and stood with him.

Man squared his shoulders, trying to keep his face haughty. It suddenly came to him that the troops might not obey him. He looked at their hard, closed faces. Who was he, to give such men commands?

They might even laugh!

Man whirled out his long sword – a perfect draw. 'When I tell you, move up the beach, but go slowly and *don't* walk in step! There are giant lobsters and crabs hiding in the sand, listening for us!'

Was he doing this right?

Joah took a step forward.

'I want all of you to know the Lord Emmanuel is the predicted one. Prophecy says we must travel with him across this alien sand to help our own realm – by getting him to The

Words of Fury: 127

Waning of the Moon!'

Suddenly all the others lifted their own blades, shouting and giving air-punching salutes. They showed they were true believers.

'Banzai! Banzai! Banzai!'

Then the approval became more personal. 'The One Who Will Change! The One Who Will Change!' The majority already convinced by his legend chanted, 'You are the one we will follow to Hell!'

Man knew now that he would indeed be followed. With his sword, he pointed up the beach.

'When we meet the monsters, kill them.'

To his surprise, his voice hadn't sounded uncertain at all.

The first fifty yards went well. Then one alert scout at the head of the formation warned of something moving in the sand.

'Hold it!' Man called out generally, and then he addressed the point man: 'That could be one of the creatures!'

Nothing happened except that hot-air mirages shimmered. Lady Joah fastened a sweat-band over her forehead and then threw a questioning look at Man.

'You two stay together, please,' Man requested, 'and we will look after you.'

'Whether we want to be looked after or not!' the Voice accused.

Man reassured her. 'We'll all look after each other.'

Then the lead scout stepped out again. A pair of black claws speared up from the sand and closed on human flesh.

Man saw the shrieking samurai pull away from the crab, but the great claws had ripped open all his right side. He stumbled to his knees with bloody entrails hanging out, and then a single clash of claws cut off his head. Fast archers put three arrows deep into the giant crab's body-shell, but without any effect Man could see. In seconds the thing had chopped the body into bloodily convenient pieces. Then its lesser claws flung the fragments into a hidden mouth.

One of us lost already!

When all the human body parts were gobbled up the crab vanished into the sand, leaving only a kind of bloodstained mole-hill behind.

Man swallowed, sickened. Would being eaten be the fate for them all? He wondered again why they were all risking their lives. Because of a woman dead these three hundred years, or because the Voice and Lady Joah believed those uncertain and ambiguous words...?

But we all have to be believers, now: don't we?

Yoshi made slow exercises with his sword.

'I like to have crab for lunch,' he said, 'not be its lunch!'

The sand erupted one giant crab. Man saw a big samurai run to meet it. Ugaki was skilled with his katana when he duelled. Chunks of the tough claws flew as the crab sidled forward. Man watched, trying to learn the best tactics.

Ashida and another spearman came and speared the thing from both sides. It lashed out, but the men stabbed till the shell was pierced in many places. Only then did the monster slow.

'Stand back!' Man ordered. 'If it's dying, let's see how long it takes!'

Ashida moved to cover Man. Man waved fingers back, still watching the thing.

It was shaking madly, with its many legs and claws quivering. It died slowly, but finally it died.

'One down!' Man called, smiling at Ashida.

Ashida gave his sunniest smile back, knowing that the green young foreigner had accepted his friendship. He saw Man was rubbing his inflamed right cheek as he stood joking with the others. Then more monsters appeared in the distance and their force moved to full alertness.

Ashida was thinking of other things.

This Emmanuel-John Kinross is dubious in every way; he is a nonentity who has somehow been accepted here. Should I kill him, or get the monsters to do it?

Ashida watched small, brief fights ripple up and down their skirmish line. He saw some blood drawn and he put on a concerned face; but he felt nothing.

He had no love for these men. They had been there when his father died, but *they* had come back in honor, to more honor. Ashida had had to fight for a place among this élite and his place was aggravatingly low. Nobody had *quite* accused him of being a traitor's son, since there was no proof and making such an accusation would lead to a death-fight, but the feeling was always there.

To try to make up for those doubts Ashida had tried and tried, training even harder than the others, and putting on a

Words of Fury:

friendly face always. In his fighting skills he considered he was now the equal of most of these men, though it hadn't gained him acceptance.

Then there was religion...

To Ashida, Man Kinross was a posturing outsider in this land of the gods. But many of the other men were followers of the Lady Naosuke and her Prophecies. Several, Ashida knew, had even visited her shrine at The Waning of the Moon. And when there had been that fire-fight in the sky over Jade, with Man apparently saving the city – Ashida doubted it – most of them had thrown in with Man completely. To them, Man was the one promised in the Prophecies, and now many *worshipped* the Albion lord.

That acceptance was so unfair that it made Ashida's soul writhe.

Didn't the others know they were supporting a foreigner who could *not* be The One Who Will Change, whatever he pretended or got others like Lady Joah to claim on his behalf? He just couldn't be!

As well, this Man had caused Ashida's father's death.

Therefore he deserved to die.

Ashida gave the foreigner his best smile and came closer, naginata held level.

A single spear-strike, and the outsider will be dead!

Man sidled forward again and at once Ashida came with him. That was a brave and skilled young man. Then Man heard a shout. He whirled round with his sword high and saw the largest crab yet come out of the sand. It ripped off a samurai's right arm and swallowed it. Then the crab galloped straight for the Voice and Lady Joah.

Man threw himself in front of the monster and impaled one big claw. They fought.

This monster was powerful enough to lose many episodes of a fight, while Man knew if he made a single mistake he would end up dead. Nevertheless he didn't retreat and struck again and again with his sword. Fragments of the claws flew about as Man fought the thing to a standstill. A spear man took his chance and closed in from the flanks, driving in his sharp point. Man took advantage of the diversion to come close and lop off the eye-stalks.

Even though he had blinded it, the creature still threshed

Words of Fury: *130*

about and flourished saw-edge claws.

Then Ashida drove his spear in, and twisted it.

Man gasped his thanks, 'I'm grateful, Ashida-san! That thing took a dislike to me, I believe.'

Ashida, too, was panting. His spear shook in his hands.

'Ashida!' Man called loudly. 'Thanks for the killing!'

The young man turned his body and head. Still holding his spear, he gave Man a narrow-eyed stare.

Man blinked. That look had been disconcerting. He felt an impulse to ask Ashida about it. Instead, he turned to address the company.

'I want alert men around Lady Joah and the Voice from Afar! Remember, these things can come out anywhere!'

Five men went there, a protective circle. Three other men helped the wounded, though the one-armed man holding in his glistening, bloody entrails had to be dispatched and left on the black sand.

They went on another dozen yards. Then a new enemy emerged; a black lobster. Its claw snapped closed on a samurai's calf. Man saw him fall, screaming. A younger samurai jumped over the wounded man to save him from the monster.

It was Ashida again.

The black lobster hissed; but Ashida struck with his spear towards its eyes and he almost got them, though they were not on stalks as the crabs' eyes were. He had perhaps taken the monster by surprise, for the thing reared back and up, its vulnerable light-colored underside now revealed.

Now Ashida plunged his razor-sharp spear into lobster flesh and then turned it in the wound.

'Well done!' Man called. 'Now finish the thing!'

Four or five more stabs did it. Then Ashida looked over his shoulder at Man.

Man waved a hand back. 'I'm glad you're here!' Then he spoke to Lady Joah in a low voice. 'We're losing so many men I don't know if this journey is possible. Maybe we should have tried another way.' He had hoped she might cheer him up, but now he saw something not quite right in her expression. 'What is it?'

She came close, wiping at her sweat-sodden face. 'I have not the confidence I pretend.'

Man felt something cold close in around his heart. 'What do you mean?'

'I brought you here in ways that you do not know, foul ways sometimes...'

Man's frown deepened. 'That's cheerful,' he said, turning to irony in the Albion style. 'But it's also too late.'

She looked guilty and miserable, but she was far from weak.

'Yes. Now there is no alternative. We must walk this path, my Emmanuel.'

Realizing that, Man risked another soft step ahead, and then another. More sweat trickled off his face. Flies buzzed around him, as if he was already dead meat.

Ashida had three times delayed taking action, but he would not delay a fourth time.

Only, this Emmanuel had been brave, and then kind; and the others clearly loved him.

All that made Ashida consider. Even Lord Okada's daughter Lady Joah was deeply involved with Man, and Ashida had long looked up to her and her sister Oki. He turned now to stare at the lady from Jade. Joah looked noble, if sad, and it was clear she was devoted to Man.

Surely it is my duty to execute him; but what if killing him is wrong?

When they'd covered three hundred yards, with twice that distance to go, a giant lobster emerged right where Ashida was, talking. Maybe Ashida had been distracted, for when he whirled around, Man saw him slip, his spear-point uselessly high. The lobster arched up, giant claws poised to come down and rip Ashida apart.

Sanada rushed to get ahead of Ashida and protect him, and he did.

Man expected him to strike the underbelly at once. But, though his surprise appearance made the lobster wriggle back, Sanada froze.

'Archers!' Man yelled, and then he was running, long sword raised.

Sanada would likely die, but Man would risk everything to protect him and the equally young Ashida. A barbed arrow struck deep into the thing, and then a second arrow – with no effect that Man could see. He got to Ashida just as the lobster struck.

Man pushed Ashida out of danger.

The big claw closed around Man's neck.

That is, it would have done, but Man had already ducked, his unbreakable sword raised in his two hands.

Then the claw caught Words of Power, twisted, and Man's sword went flying.

Man was empty-handed and off balance.

I'm *dead*...

He felt rather than saw Ashida move up towards him. In front of Man the thing drew its claws back, ready to strike. There was one unbearable moment when nothing happened, and when he turned his head he saw something strange in Ashida's smooth young face.

Then the youth turned from Man, and drove his long spear deep into the lobster-thing. He shook his blade in its innards and sang out with murderous joy, 'Enjoy this, enjoy, enjoy!'

As Ashida twisted the naginata, Man snatched up his fallen sword and struck. First he severed the right claw, then struck into the body. Yellow liquid splashed out of the wound. The lobster gave a weird wail and then huddled up, all its remaining claws drawing in. Most likely it was dying.

Then it sprang forward, knocking down Ashida, left claw raised to snap him in two.

Man and Sanada struck together. Sanada went for the giant lobster's nearer eye. Man side-stepped to give a two-handed blow, and cut off its remaining claw. Now Man struck through the lobster's hard shell deep into its body. He felt exhilarated from the danger and the killing.

When Ashida rolled to his feet again the three men hacked at their enemy together. Ugly with gaping wounds, the monster now stretched itself out. Its smaller claws and tail were still flexing but it was beginning to die.

'Another one down!' Man said then.

'Yes, Lord Emmanuel!' Ashida responded, breathing heavily. He turned. His expression had more puzzlement than gratitude. 'You saved my life.'

'You saved mine, and for that I honor you. Whatever has happened before, from now on everything can be different...'

'And you saved me too, One Who Will Change!' Sanada shuddered, looking back at the yellow-bleeding wreckage. 'It was like a bad dream. I remember wanting to... But Ashida got there first, and...'

Man nudged him, not taking his attention from what was

happening elsewhere.

'If you hesitated, what of it? You helped kill a monster!'

'Yes, Emmanuel.' Sanada's face suddenly brightened. 'And now I am a man among men!'

Man smiled at that, feeling good because his friend Sanada did. But then Yoshi threw him a worried look. It didn't take a profound intellect to interpret Yoshi's expression. Should they retreat?

Man sighed. 'It's tempting, but it isn't the Prophecies – or possible.'

Perhaps Joah understood, for she pointed ahead.

'See the shimmering in the air over the cliffs? I think that's the boundary between our own world and – whatever this world is, or was.' She turned to look at the others with hesitant hope. 'Remember, this land is so different that *his* power is here made small.'

That was a small but real comfort to Man, and – he turned to look – the same small comfort for Yoshi.

It was good to have any hope.

'You are a friend of Mr Foreigner and the Lady Joah?'

Sanada glanced over at the lean young man beside him. Sanada was trying to stay close enough to the Voice to guard her, though he saw the occasional mutual anger between her and the Lady Joah and he wondered about it.

'I have that honor, Ashida-san.' Sanada wiped a sodden sweat-cloth over his face, disliking this heat and the glare of the sun. 'I sense you are full of questions?'

'The Prophecies,' Ashida began, though he did not finish.

'What of them?'

'They are really about *him*, the Foreigner?'

Sanada was emphatic. 'They *are*.'

'You are a disciple, Sanada-san?'

'I saw him bring down a flying snake. I know of other miracles he has done. The hateful one we do not name knows him to be an enemy – therefore I am Emmanuel's friend, and his follower too.'

'I heard you call him "the hope of the realm".'

'He is. And he is the hope of Albion, too – and most likely the world. I would go on with him forever, if not for my own role in the Prophecies.'

'You have a role?'

'I believe I am that "young man" who must die defending the Voice and Lady Joah.'

'That is very loyal.'

'Without those women, Emmanuel cannot prevail.'

And those two young goddesses now seem to dislike one another, and I do not know how that can be changed...

Sanada and Ashida trudged on together on the uncertain sand.

'Sanada, can you teach me faith?'

'Stay with me. Perhaps then faith will come. I have seen miracles and will tell you about them. Perhaps you and I can become "we"; perhaps we can fight together, and if necessary die together.'

'So that others might live?'

Sanada found he was giving the other young man a big beaming smile.

'So that others might live.'

The sun was moving behind them now. It was a golden afternoon, though still burning hot. Man felt optimistic. By a miracle, he had been given these brave companions; he might yet go a very long way before he died, perhaps even the great distance he had to.

Yoshi came to walk with him, checking that everyone paced irregularly so as not to attract the monsters.

'They're all being careful,' said Man. 'Nobody wants to be eaten, not when we see an end to this part of the journey.'

'We're half-way over the beach, maybe?'

'I'd say so. We've taken casualties, but this is do-able.'

'All for you.'

'All for the world,' Man corrected. 'And for *our* world, not this one. I think we're in a bigger story than we know.'

'Always, Man. And when we get to The Waning, what then?'

'We heal up, we train up, then we make use of the Eye to take back Jade and fight *him*. And then there's Albion...'

Another quick bout of fighting left one samurai wounded and two giant lobsters speared to death. Man paused the advance while the Voice from Afar and the Lady Joah took the man and used Healing to restore him.

'That might've been you,' said Yoshi, watching.

'True; or you, come to that.' Man thought of Mother Zandar, then. 'All of us will have to make sacrifices to get to The Waning.'

Words of Fury:

A few buzzards circled overhead; they never landed. Then three monsters briefly emerged from the sand, though they did not stay on the surface long.

Man found time to have a word. 'Yoshi? Do you think these things are under conscious control?'

His samurai friend shook his head. 'If there was intelligence, they'd all attack at once and we'd be *dead.*'

They continued the slow careful advance. Man was thinking they might make it. The everyday world was only half a mile away, after all.

It was as if that complacent thought was overheard. Two more pugilist crabs came up on their left, and a lobster thing to the right rear. Then another lobster emerged ahead along with a long-clawed crab, and that made five attackers.

The humans made a fighting circle, which the monsters scuttled to surround. Man saw long spears could hold the things off, but as long as this fight continued his own side could not advance. The vicious claws struck so that shields were battered noisily and swords were struck aside. Not many humans had been wounded yet, but they were not winning.

Man suddenly realized that *this* might be the end.

Ozawa stayed in the same place, the rock of this defensive circle. Man was mobile and went everywhere, giving a vital defensive sword-slash in one place, a word of encouragement in another. Often he stopped to see how the fighting played out. They needed to develop smart tactics against their foes. Ugaki and Man himself were sometimes strong enough to front up the creatures directly, but other men needed silkier and more defensive skills.

Man saw the warriors looking at him, often with confidence, but sometimes dubiously. Ashida's stare was particularly puzzling, as it changed so much.

When things quieted, with three more creatures destroyed, they started to advance again. Man was far from sure that they would make the jungle line before sunset. They found their way onto one of the glistening, glassy trails, but the glass crust was sometimes only an inch thick or less. When it was so thin it broke under human weight.

'This is all taking up time!' said Joah, distressed. 'We're well into the afternoon!'

Their shadows had indeed lengthened.

'I know what'll happen if these things attack us in the dark, but there's no alternative to caution,' Man said, though he wondered if he was doing the right thing in moving so cautiously.

'Eyes left!' sang out a bowman. 'More claws in the sand!'

'More coming on the right!' said a spearman. 'More and more!'

'I'm getting a bad feeling,' Man said, as much to himself as to Yoshi.

Then the foremost scout reported, from thirty yards ahead.

'There's an area of fused glass here, solid as a rock! Fifteen yards long and ten across!'

'How solid?' Man called.

'It takes *my* weight, Foreigner-Sir! And it'll be too solid for those monsters to stick their heads through it!'

Without orders, three samurai ran towards the place of safety. He saw Ozawa raise a hand to stop them, but it was too late. Perhaps it was the multiple footfalls together, but now Man saw the sand erupt. There were crab giants and lobster giants, maybe a dozen, and all closing in. The humans were surrounded, and in a mad fight. Man saw at once that the odds were insurmountable.

'Everybody get onto the rock!' he shouted.

Yoshi and Man were probably the fastest with weapons, so they were the rearguard with two spearmen to back them. But more and more things boiled out of the black sand and attacked the desperate column.

'Form a circle on the rock!' Ozawa shouted now. 'Yonai! Put the women in the middle!'

Man cut away at whatever threatened. Yellow liquids splashed; fragments of claws and shell flew. He hoped he could fight long enough for the others to get to safety. But there were so many enemies! He saw claws rising everywhere, saw those hideous mouths chomping away. He slashed again, cutting off crab legs.

Some of their party got onto the hard place and Man heard them raise a cheer. He finally backed his way there, stepping up onto the glass, glad he had made it. But as he saw the brutal reality of their position – in the baking sun, outnumbered and surrounded – he felt raw fear.

Already they had barely enough men to man their battle-line. They were going to lose.

Words of Fury:

He saw a crab come scuttling fast onto the low rock and head for Ozawa. Man kneeled and drove his Words of Power all the way into the crab's gaping mouth, and then he ripped his sword all through the body shell. The crab flipped over. On its back, it bled a yellowish liquid with the smell of the sea, quivered its huge claws, then died.

Ozawa turned. 'Thank you, Lord Emmanuel!'

'You are as polite as always.'

'There's some reason I shouldn't be?'

Man laughed, impressed by Ozawa's grace under this terrible pressure.

They all fought on, defending their tiny glass island.

Man found himself alongside Faslane, who was a fighter if not a trained samurai. He had picked up a small shield, and his spiked fighting-iron was covered in creatures' flesh. He was staring at the oncoming enemies, beating his shield and in the same rhythm chanting in what Man presumed was Scots poetry. He finished: 'Welcome to your gory bed – or to victory!'

The monsters came again.

The humans chopped and speared and struck out with their swords. It continued for what seemed like a long time.

Finally, there was a lull in the fighting.

Now Ashida edged round till he stood side by side with Man, spear ready. 'Was it like this, in your father's victories against *him*?'

'Worse.'

'Worse?'

'Yes, because *he* had human allies, and when we killed them, we sometimes felt guilty, and the world called us the Empire of Blood.'

Another many-legged crab came galloping over the sand, and Man and Ashida dispatched the thing together.

A wounded samurai was assisted away by Sanada to their circle's centre. There, Man saw both women used rags and medical creams to bind up the wounds they could not fully heal. Somehow in all this blood and chaos they remained tender.

'The women have healing hands,' Ashida said. 'What they do might make one believe in miracles.'

'Amen, brother!' said Man, and Ashida blinked as if the claim to brotherhood was surprising. 'I wonder how many there are?' Man asked.

Faslane wrinkled his nose. 'It can't be that many in the

Words of Fury: 138

immediate area, but if they're being summoned...'

Man stared at him. 'Do you think they are? Being called here from another world?'

'I bloody hope not!' Yoshi answered. 'We can't fight a whole planet!' Now he looked round, eyes concerned. 'This hero business – ! In future I'll stick to poetry.'

It had all gone quiet now, except for the distant washing sound of the surf.

Then more monsters came out of the black dunes, too many to count – ahead, around, behind, claws snapping together.

They attacked at once.

Words of Fury:

Chapter Fourteen: *Now I Believe!*

When Hanake followed Daisen and Sulina into the Map Room, she had to stare. In the picture, the giant towers were now only smoldering ruins.

Was this the future of the Waning of the Moon, too? Was this how it would end?

Tears came to Healer Irizo's eyes. 'Daisen! Oh, I'm so glad you lived ... but you're alone.'

'Yes. Though she fought bravely, Mother Zandar is gone.'

'What happened, sister?'

'Our great enemy linked himself to the holy Mother; in the moment of her dying, *he* stepped through.'

'Holy Mother of God!' Irizo crossed herself. 'So our wards had no effect!'

Sulina now took her place alongside tired, subdued Daisen, kneeling opposite the High Healer. In Zandar's absence, nobody was at the table's head. At its foot, Hanake sat down unobtrusively, cross-legged.

Daisen took a sip of water. 'The Lord of the North killed our loving heart, and that is more than enough.'

'It is,' said Irizo, 'but why did he go?'

Daisen frowned, trying to recover the memories.

'I think *he* left us only because some trap he had set was sprung. Otherwise I suppose he would have stayed here to finish the job.'

'Have we almost been lucky?' Hanake asked.

'Not if the Lord of the North went to his trap and seized our young friends and the Eye!'

Irizo was appalled. 'Oh, what if *he* has caught them!'

Sulina reacted quickly to that. 'I am not certain he has.'

Irizo shifted about. 'We should send more help to where our friends have landed: Four Rocks, wasn't it? I know we sent two full Sisters, but we can dispatch more.'

Daisen spoke slowly. 'That may not be any use. At the last, you see, our holy Mother was thinking of a different variant of Prophecy, thinking they could, would, and *should* land elsewhere... A "midnight-black beach".'

'She sent them *there?*'

'You sound outraged, Healer. If it is true Prophecy, it *must* be fulfilled to find that happy ending. If what Emmanuel and Joah do is not what is prophesied, then we are without a route-map for the terrible journey we all face!' Now Sulina turned to Hanake. 'She-captain, can we send out more search parties and cover both Monster Beach and Four Rocks?'

'I think we might dispatch a dozen strong parties – or one force six hundred strong, with as many Sisters as you deem appropriate.'

'I think not,' said Daisen, more hesitant now than the others had ever heard her. 'We have this sacred place to defend, and any rescue party we sent would be outnumbered.'

Healer Irizo blinked. 'How so?'

'Oatha is invading; and as well as his own purity police he now has the resources of the city of Jade.'

Hanake had to be direct. 'Surely he can't plan to take this place?'

'He, and his overlord, do want us to fall. So we need our defenses here ... and yet we also need the Lady Joah and the Lord Emmanuel...' Daisen's words trailed off. 'I cannot square that circle.'

Hanake said, 'Oatha is an evil man. Is he confirmed as *his?*'

Sulina responded to that. 'There are hearts already so dark that *he* cannot always turn them to himself. For a long time we have thought Lord Oatha may be one such. But any force Oatha sends here will operate knowingly or unknowingly on behalf of the Lord of the North.'

Hanake cracked her knuckles. 'What about the Sisters already sent to Four Rocks?'

'For two days now there has been silence from them,' said the High Healer.

'If they are dead,' Daisen said, with some of her previous brusqueness, 'then *he* has force enough at Four Rocks to murder two full Sisters.'

Hanake grimaced. 'Then let's hope our friends did divert to Monster Beach.'

Sulina sat up straight. 'My fellows, we need to get Emmanuel and Lady Joah *and* their power gem here. What else can we do to make that happen?'

Man was fighting alongside the others in this last and greatest crisis. He saw thickets of claws, some dripping human blood. He whirled around and struck off the claws. He saw crab-eyes on stalks and lopped them off too. Enemy creatures came and then he hacked them apart, and though it was dangerous it felt very

Words of Fury:

good. To Man, successful violence almost always felt good.

Man was turning his head to see what Joah and the Voice were doing when he heard Ashida call out a warning.

He whipped back round, sword out. He should already have been dead, because the crab reared over him. It was held away only because Ashida had got in between the two pairs of claws and was clattering his naginata from side to side to keep the pairs apart. The slim teenager was very fast and Man knew Ashida had saved his life. Ashida drove his blade deep into the thing's innards. The terrible mouth opened in pain.

Now Ashida jumped back to re-join Man, but a side-swipe from the left-hand claw knocked him down. Man took a pace forward and sliced off that claw, then the other. So handicapped, the crab was smashed by Two Heads.

As he got to his feet Ashida just stared at Man.

'You have saved me – again!'

Man yelled, 'Watch out!'

This crab was huge, and it came galloping through a gap in the defense towards Lady Joah and the Voice.

Ashida stepped forward to fight, but he had been taken by surprise. He was immediately overwhelmed. One claw knocked away Ashida's spear, and the other claw crunched around Ashida's legs and then jerked him off his feet. He was held upside-down in the air and shaken.

Man was horrified to see Ashida's torn legs were at wrong angles and bleeding badly. He was going to strike the crab with his Words of Power, but dangling Ashida protected the creature, and now it hopped towards Joah.

She stood up, shocked. Man grabbed Ashida's spear and started to run to her, but Sanada was already coming over from the left. Suddenly Man wondered if this was the time for Sanada to die.

Before Sanada could arrive Man was there in front of Lady Joah, and he had the spear. Now he thrust it deep, and twisted it savagely till the crab dropped its victim. Ashida fell to his knees, screaming in pain, and when he feebly raised his sword the remaining claw closed around the wrist of his sword-hand.

'No!' Man said.

The claw snapped shut. Hand and sword fell away together and more of Ashida's blood spurted, just as Sanada drove his spear into the mouth.

Man cut off both claws, but it was all too late for the horribly wounded Ashida. With Two Heads guarding his back, Man and Sanada dragged the youth away.

'Joah!' Man was screaming for help for his bleeding savior. 'Voice from Afar! Get over here!'

Sanada helped Man pull Ashida to the makeshift medical centre. The women were both on their feet, staring down in horror. Man went on his knees, a young man before an equally young man, and scrabbled for strips of cloth that would serve as tourniquets.

'Ashida-san, you took that for *us!* For the women, and me!'

'Yes.' Ashida was hunched up and mumbling, and his smashed-bloody legs were hanging uselessly. 'I was wrong before. Now I *believe!*'

'You have taken my place,' said Sanada, shocked.

Ashida's remaining hand suddenly closed on Man's left wrist. 'You must fight on for us all! Yes, you must fight!'

Man lost control, then. He went back into battle in an almighty fury. When he stepped off the rocky islet his sword chopped faster than it had ever done before. Giant creatures challenged him, but he cut up them up. Stalked eyes, claws, and pieces of armored hide all flew.

'Come back, Man! They'll eat you!' Yoshi screamed.

Man was far out on the sand now, and surrounded by the creatures; but as they came for him he killed them. Perhaps this madness was what the Lord of the North wanted, but it didn't seem important to Man that if he took too many risks he would die.

The only thing important now was revenge.

Finally Yoshi pulled Man back from yet another brutal encounter, this one with a giant-sized crab that had main claws as long as a man's body.

'You thrice-damned fool!' Yoshi swore, while trying to rush Man back to the hard glass. 'You can't kill every monster! Try, and you will die here, and all the sacrifice will have been for nothing!'

Man realized he had been screaming as he demolished the things. His head was spinning from effort and from the Tears' poisoned kiss, and he was no longer in the berserker mood. He felt obliged to do what Yoshi said. Once he was back on the island he lowered his sword, utterly weary.

He wondered how many creatures he had killed himself. It must be a half-dozen or more, but it was not nearly enough. He

Words of Fury:

had fought, so had the others; but they were losing.

Now it may be time for us all to die...

Man saw the human casualties still being treated in the middle of the glass platform. He went there now, though he had avoided that butcher's shop before.

Joah and the Voice stood above two prone wounded men in the middle of the rocky islet. Joah looked desperate, her kimono disarranged and blood-spattered. The Voice was weeping. She was not made for this kind of ugly desperate fight.

Then Man saw the two women turn east, and make identical chopping gestures. An attacking lobster was hacked almost in two, but Joah sagged. Man saw the women were now too weary to defend themselves with magic.

The Voice from Afar bent over again, working with a writhing man who had lost both legs below the knee.

It was Ashida, and of course his sword-hand was also missing. She had put tourniquets upon all three lopped limbs, but his face was ashy from blood-loss and his mouth twitched.

Her weeping was uncontrollable now. 'We'll get you home, and then you'll be all right. Ah, don't worry!'

Elsewhere, steel struck crab shells and lobster shells. Occasionally a samurai grunted in effort; otherwise they were too tired to speak now.

Here, Man looked down at the ruined teenager.

'I know the Prophecies said that some young friend would die for me and the women, but I thought it would be Sanada, and he thought that too. *Why are you dying for me?*'

There was no coherent reply. Man squatted beside Ashida, but looked at the Voice.

'He must have admired me.'

'He did – does!'

'But before this, he looked at me so strangely that I thought, and I know it's crazy, that he hated me...'

The Voice from Afar still wept. 'Whatever he *was*, he's like the rest of us, now: he *loves* you! He has *died* for you!'

Ashida croaked, 'You talk about me as if I had already passed on.'

She was suddenly very cool, very firm. 'It won't come to that. Just rest, now. Soon it'll be sunset, and cool.'

'If I could ... have water.'

Man gave him the few sips they could spare, and then held Ashida's remaining hand. There was really nothing to say.

Ashida was simply going ahead of them, wasn't he?

Yoshi stalked over, and screamed at Lady Joah, 'We're at the end, now! Can't you do war magic?'

'We have killed those creatures just as you have!'

'That's not enough.' He glared and pointed a finger at the samurai lady. 'You must get us help!'

'What help?'

'These friends of yours, the Sword Maidens and Zandar's adepts – where are they?'

Lady Joah bowed very low, shamed. 'If they knew where we are, I am certain they would come, Lord Yoshi!'

'Your "if" is hopeless!' Yoshi grabbed her shoulders, pulled her up. It was the sort of rule-breaking Man himself might have done. 'They have to come soon, or not at all!'

This was desperation shocking to see, and Man was shocked, for Yoshi was famous for his wry self-control. Then Yoshi put his hands on his head and seemed to shake it, and himself. When he straightened up he managed his usual impish grin.

'My mouth spoke without permission.'

'I know how that can be,' Man admitted.

'You know that we're doing all this for you, so that you can do this for the world?'

'I know.'

Yoshi turned to Joah. His sweaty, strained face was cool again. 'If you helped us with your magic, dear Lady, maybe we could all grow wings and flap our way to The Waning!'

'I would do that if I could,' she said, her eyes shining.

Man's breath was rasping in his throat. He rose, rubbed Joah's head, touched Yoshi's shoulder, then held the Voice close for a moment. These were his best friends. Though Man was ashamed he could not do more to help, there could not be better people to die alongside.

Ashida suddenly raised his head, looking from Yoshi to Man.

'Look at me... Look... You know what you must do!'

'No!' The Voice was screaming again. 'I tell you, it'll be all right! I can heal you, I can!'

For one last time Ashida sat up, erect and proud and forcing a smile. He met Man's eyes.

'I see what you are and I'm glad I helped you, Lord Emmanuel. But ... I am nothing, now. No samurai, not like this...

Words of Fury:

I cannot live with the shame!'

That was plain, and all the men understood. Man and Yoshi exchanged glances. This would be the first of many, no doubt.

As an act of mercy, in one whirling sword-stroke Yoshi cut off his head.

So died Ashida, the sacrament of his blood going over Man, the Voice from Afar, and Yoshi.

Man stood away from the rolling head, the slumped corpse. It had been a death in the samurai tradition; nevertheless he was sickened.

Yoshi touched his shoulder. 'We must go back to the fight.'

'I know.'

They did, together.

There were always more enemies now, and the samurai war-whoops had long since died away. Man saw that such a fight as this, on such a hot day without even time to take water, was beginning to exhaust even these hand-picked warriors. He was himself panting all the time, and conscious of how dry and painful his throat was.

The horrible rattling of the claws was still rising in volume. All around them claws still rose out of the black sand, waved, snapped shut – sometimes on the defenders' weapons, sometimes on a defender's flesh.

Man saw the others could not fight much longer and only magic enabled Man himself to continue. He tried to clear his head and look round. From here he could see their whole, small position. It was obvious now; it would not be much longer till they were overrun.

He saw Sanada come back to the fight though he was visibly desperate. Sanada had doomed himself by coming on the journey.

Is that something else I must blame myself for? And the women, what of them? Won't they die, too! Oh, we're all going to die! We are outnumbered by all these monsters, and more are coming all the time, and soon they will feast on our corpses!

He met Yoshi's eyes, and saw the desperation lurking just behind the sparky self-confidence. Man clenched his fists. They would all perish here, for an impostor, for a fool: for Man. He felt despair. He fell to his knees, wanting to pray but somehow not knowing how.

He had a sudden strong sense that there was a presence here, and perhaps it was Mother Zandar, though he feared it might be *him*. Man tried again and again to call her, but there were too many voices in his head and too much noise from the fighting here.

If her soul had somehow lingered, could he reach her?

'Mother Zandar!' His voice was raised, as if in some religious rite. 'If your soul hears me, I ask for your help!'

Anything?

'Help us! Somebody please help us!'

Nothing at all.

Zandar was *good*, but that wasn't enough. Mother Zandar might be the epitome of goodness, but he had been forsaken, and lost his faith.

Then he remembered where the power was, and in desperation Man turned there. His plea wasn't in words, but it was understood.

The voice that came in reply was very deep, like great boulders rumbling together, though it also came from within Man.

'EMMANUEL! ACKNOWLEDGE ME!'

Immediately Man changed his mind. What he was doing was treachery! He tried to ignore that demand, though he was desperate for help and still in praying posture. His head felt as if somebody was pounding it with a rock. He touched his swollen cheek, and winced. Yes, that had been a poisoned kiss, and now... Now he was *weak* and letting his friends *die*.

Suddenly all the fury in him was turned against himself.

I'm to blame for what's happened! I had faith in my destiny, just when I shouldn't! I should've died earlier or turned in a different direction! Now I'm letting my friends die – though I'd do *anything* to save them!

A long dark shadow fell across Man.

Man didn't look up. He knew there was true, terrifying strength in this universe, and without faith in goodness that was what he reached out to now – to *him*. He had the sudden sly feeling that he would get back all the power he needed and wanted – *all* of the power – if he would only serve.

'ACKNOWLEDGE ME AND BE SAVED!'

Everything else went silent.

When he dared look up, Man saw the giant black knight from a previous nightmare: *him*.

The Lord of the North stood eight feet tall. His face-guard was open to show the savage mouth, though his eyes remained shadowed.

'LITTLE MAN!' The voice now was ear-splittingly loud, so that Man had to bend over and put his hands over his ears. 'YOU HAVE DISAPPOINTED EVERYBODY!'

'I didn't want to!' That had sounded petulant; what came next sounded merely weak. 'I'm sorry!'

'THIS IS YOUR ONE CHANCE TO SAVE YOUR FRIENDS. YOU MUST ACCEPT ME INTO YOUR HEART, OR YOU AND THEY DIE!'

He was surprised by his own courage when he answered. 'You are the Father of Lies. I won't sell myself!'

'EVEN YOUR FRIENDS HAVE FOOLED YOU. ONE IS FALSE!'

'Name him! Or her! *I'm not scared of the truth!*'

'YOU ARE! FOR THE CIRCLE OF DEATH TIGHTENS, BUT YOU REFUSE TO ADMIT IT.'

It was as if Man was inside a soundproof glass jar. Outside, in pale colors and slow motion, he saw his human friends were losing the fight against those ghastly creatures.

'YOUR FRIENDS WILL DIE HERE!'

That stabbed him to the heart.

'Let me help them, you murderer!'

'MURDERER?' The head leaned down. 'HOW DO YOU THINK YOUR FATHER WON HIS BATTLES?'

'That was war!'

'WHAT I DO, TOO, IS WAR – FOR SOMETHING MUCH MORE IMPORTANT THAN INSIGNIFICANT ALBION, LET ALONE YOUR SOUL!'

Somehow this dark knight seemed hollow, compared to when Man had confronted him with Mother Zandar's help. Nevertheless Man sensed great power within touching distance. If he could even touch it, he would shake this world...

'HOW MANY DIED IN YOUR FATHER'S BATTLES?'

Man stared at the face he could not see. 'Thousands, I suppose. But it was for Queen and country!'

'HE CAUSED HUNDREDS OF THOUSANDS TO DIE, BUT HE DID WHAT WAS NECESSARY. YOU, TOO, MUST DO WHAT IS NEEDFUL.' The voice was one vast jeer. 'AND DON'T IMAGINE THERE IS HELP COMING. YOU MUST HELP YOURSELF. CAN YOU?'

Something odd was happening. Man was no longer frightened.

'I'd die to save my friends! Let me help them and then maybe I'll help you!'

Man turned his head, to see the two women were both looking at the closing-in battle – but he knew this conversation was as important, or even more important. If he said the wrong thing now, the world would die.

'Why am I so significant?'

'YOU HAVE INHERITED POWER, IN A WORLD WHERE SUCH POWER CAN DO EVERYTHING! THINGS COME FROM THE OTHER WORLDS – DREAMS, EVEN PEOPLE.' The metal-protected head leaned down again. 'DO YOU SEE WHAT THAT MEANS?'

'Others can come here and change things, and we can go to other places and do the same!'

'YOU SEE IT.'

'But I'm important to my friends, and I must help *them!*'

Man walked away to join the battle again. He felt ready for self-sacrifice. If he was so important, let the Lord of the North allow him to save his friends, or they would go down together!

But he walked into an invisible wall and came bouncing off. The Lord of the North really had sealed Man off.

Now Joah banged hard on the barrier, mouthing something.

She thinks I'm a *coward*, hiding here!

The voice roughened. 'YOUR FRIENDS CANNOT SEE ME, BUT THEY CAN SEE YOU – SAFE, AS *THEY* DIE!'

'I can't give up my soul. Please! There must be something else!'

He saw the Voice break off from a magic-making gesture. She tumbled forward, and now a crab-claw closed in on her hair and with terrible slowness yanked her off her feet.

'I HAVE SPEEDED UP TIME FOR US, BUT STILL YOU ONLY HAVE SECONDS. YOU WILL THEN SEE THAT GIRL EATEN ALIVE, AND ALL THE OTHERS. AFTERWARDS I WILL RAISE THE SHIELD AND LEAVE YOU TO THE MONSTERS.'

Man saw, in slow motion, the Voice dragged forward. The crab's other claw opened wide.

'EMMANUEL-JOHN ARTUR KINROSS, LOOK INTO YOUR SOUL AND FREE WHAT IS THERE – OR YOUR FRIENDS DIE!'

He realized he was sobbing.

There was only one thing he could do; he did it. He gave that

Words of Fury: 149

word of obedience to *him*.

The cold lord faded away and the barrier vanished.

He saw the creatures had surrounded the glass islet on all sides. They were so many they were certain to win.

Man looked into himself for self-confidence and power. This time he saw great things within. He became aware he held a monstrous amount of energy; he felt like a volcano ready to erupt. He pointed two flat hands at the crab about to cut the Voice in two.

Man the volcano erupted.

He exploded the crab. Its top shell flew away in pieces. He saw the Voice pull away from the remains.

'Man, I thought... Thank you!'

He didn't answer her, just killed another monster, and then another. He turned in a full circle, throwing fire from extended hands, destroying many creatures and whipping the others back with lightning.

Man rotated both hands – and white-hot fire flared up all around their island, a terrible Man-made heat that made the samurai duck.

All the monsters on the surface burned, but still he kept on to finish the job. He killed deep into the earth. A few burned sand-creatures came twisting up and died in the open air.

In the backwash of the heat Man could smell broiled lobster and crab. His power had heated the black sand so much it melted. Now pools of molten lava bubbled around their islet. Fumes and smoke swirled around, blinding them, choking them. Sanada went down, retching.

Now Man could hardly see. In the smoke, a figure approached. Man raised his sword, two-handed. Was this *him*, come to claim a soul?

Yoshi came close, his face dripping sweat, and leaned one hand on Man's shoulder.

'Well done, my Man! But how did you do that? I thought you'd lost your power!'

Man looked up, but there was no Lord of the North here now. He was with his friends, wondering exactly what he had promised the enemy.

'How did I do that? I have no idea.'

He had decided to say nothing about the Lord of the North.

Sanada's laughter turned a touch hysterical. 'You overcooked lunch!'

Words of Fury:

Man said only, 'You've heard the phrase "well-done"? Now you've seen it.' He started to laugh, too, but then he was coughing.

Joah was here. 'You've killed every living thing for fifty paces, but we can't walk on molten sand! We're still trapped!'

'You think so?' Man asked her, bold again. 'I think not.'

He corkscrewed both arms, and then pointed up at the sky.

Words of Fury:

Chapter Fifteen: *I Will Dare Anything and Everything!*

Man's every gesture now generated energy, and the air itself trembled with his magic. In a few minutes he saw a column of dark raincloud form overhead.

The war party looked up in astonishment as Man's pillar of cloud quickly expanded and blocked out the sun. Soon after that the rain came flooding down.

Man saw the rainwater sizzle and steam on the molten sands, cooling everything off. Rain also fell on the desperate faces, chill and at first welcome. Soon sheets of falling water cascaded down on Man and the others, blindingly thick. It continued till they were all sodden. He flinched; this was too close to drowning. He knew he was overdoing his magic, but he wasn't sure he could stop. Even the flood of rain wasn't the end, though. Hailstones fell, large enough to strike painfully.

'Man?' Yoshi was shouting over the noise. 'Man, is this your work? If so, it isn't safe!'

'No, it isn't safe,' said Man. 'It's magic.'

The hailstorm suddenly stopped, to Man's relief. He felt a woman's touch strong in the mix: but who? He saw the Voice from Afar looking at him, a few curls of her wetted-dark hair turned around one finger. Had *she* saved them?

The sky cleared completely, scrubbed clean by the wind. The sun was shining down on the steaming land, there was a rainbow, and they were still alive. In spite of their hurts the men suddenly began to cheer.

'Thank you, Lord Emmanuel. You have saved us,' Ozawa said.

Lady Joah had recovered her samurai poise, thumbs in her red sash where the long knife hung in its sheath.

'You've been our salvation, Emmanuel.'

'Thank you.' He bowed to them all. 'But now we must go on.'

Berenda had collected some new followers in two more boats, so in this golden afternoon over a hundred and fifty black sashes landed with her. They took over the dozen or so stilt-legged houses of this fishing village, where four very tall rock spires loomed. She saw there was little visible damage from the tsunami; could *he* or some agent have helped this locale survive?

But *I* was not helped! Berenda thought, in a fury all over again.

Words of Fury:

At her order the Four Rocks locals were rounded up, brought to the beach, and made to lie down with their mouths open to the sand. Small children cried. Their mothers were too terrified to comfort them.

As the senior black sash, Hagiwara was notionally in charge. Therefore Lady Berenda spoke through him, with the obvious questions coming first.

Where had the balloon landed? Where were Emmanuel and party now? Who had the Eye?

The folk pretended ignorance.

She picked out four of them. She was hot and perspiring with hurt and rage.

'Hagiwara, get my questions answered!'

Soon, Berenda saw four limbless bleeding bodies on the sands in front of her. They were dying badly, crying out and writhing like worms. The others were still prostrate in front of her. Several had wet themselves; almost all wept and begged; but that did not move her.

It was late afternoon now and it bothered Berenda tremendously that the Eye could not be felt by her. It was as if it had been taken out of this world completely!

Ah, she thought, when I find *them*, I will find *it* – and take all for my own! Then the gospel I will preach to the world will be self – self – *all* myself! And either the world will be my humble servants, or it will be dead!

Berenda shook her clenched fist over the prostrated locals.

'I know the balloon has landed – a great bubble of air, with five persons swinging below! So where are the Foreigner and his friends?'

The response was moans and wails. She grimaced, made a magical gesture.

All four men screamed, each one struck blind.

'Silence!' she said. 'I can give you back the light of this world, but only when I have the truth out of you!

'You must obey! See, times have changed. There is one who will be above our Shogun, even above our Emperor – *and I speak with his voice!* Fear me, love me, and *obey me!*'

'Fine sentiments, Lady – though not when applied to you.'

Berenda whirled around, taken by surprise. 'What?'

The woman walking towards her was tall and willowy, with a rounded, perfect shape revealed by the tight silk kimono. She was perhaps the most beautiful woman Berenda had ever seen.

'There is nothing they can tell you while I live. Nothing useful to you, that is.' The beauty's hand waved over the tortured fisher-folk, and her slanted eyes were commanding. 'My spell has silenced them.'

This woman was *his* agent here. Berenda could tell. Her heart sank, though her rage mounted. Surely this was Berenda's enemy, though she did not dare kill.

Surely she dared not kill...

I will dare anything and everything! I am no servant now. Others will serve me!

She powered up her magic to confront this stranger.

The woman only raised manicured hands, somewhere between a gesture of dismissal and a welcome.

Berenda tried to make it a sneer, but it was only a tremulous question.

'Who are you?'

The perfect beauty parted her perfect cherry-red lips in perfect scorn. 'I am just what you think. I am *his*.'

'Then prove it!'

The other woman laughed. 'Why should I, handmaiden? *I* am *his* agent here – and you are not.' She stepped back daintily, eyeing tall Berenda up and down. 'Look at you! Quite the giant, eh?'

Immediately Berenda felt huge and unsexed. Her cheeks flamed. The woman made it even worse by smiling.

Berenda bared her teeth.

'Giantess perhaps – but *his*,' she lied quickly. Often *his* servants fought among themselves. Queller had murdered to gain his high place in Jade, she remembered. It was all about competition. 'You should not doubt *his* esteem for *me*.'

'I know who you humbly serve.' The woman eyed her large hands, till Berenda flushed and hid them away. 'From your rings of power.'

'All gifted from my master.'

The beauty parted her kimono. Between the perfect breasts a ruby pendant hung.

'This is what *I* had from him. A greater gift than he gave you, see?'

Berenda did see, and also feel the red throb of power from the gem. She was horrified she was less than this other woman. Her lost faith in the Lord of the North turned to fury again.

Then those other emotions vanished, dissolved by her bitter, bitter loneliness.

I am alone, Berenda thought. I am no longer beloved; but I have no master now. I am free, but there is no delight in being so alone.

The other woman tossed her head so that the magnificent mane wafted. 'Even my own ruby gift is not a match for the Eye, but ... I think we need privacy. Come!'

Berenda had to follow the swaying hips. It was even worse to see the leering smiles of her followers also following those rounded shapes.

They both went up a steep footpath, to a house built into rock. Within it was a kind of luxury – bright painted hangings, a woven rug upon the plain mats, and excellent utensils. There was also a magnificent high-backed chair carved from wood of different colors. Berenda had never seen anything like it.

The woman sat down upon her multi-hued throne, waving a hand at the low stools before it.

'Take your ease, giant. There is no need to exchange names.'

'No,' said Berenda. True names had true power, and also produced vulnerability. She lowered herself awkwardly and stuck out her long legs. She had never felt more oversized and clumsy, or more ignorant. What were *his* plans now? She felt a sick sensation that she was so wholly excluded from them. It wasn't just fear, though most of it was. 'You have been waiting long?'

The woman ignored that.

'Two nights ago I went in dream to "welcome" two sisters of the enemy.'

Berenda was shocked; but that boast might even be true. 'Sisters from The Waning of the Moon? Two *full* sisters?'

'Indeed. They had been sent to Four Rocks to find and help The One Who Will Change.'

Berenda shifted. 'Are they still here?'

The goddess laughed. 'I killed them. I did our master that service. The Lord our master had a trap here – the *real* trap, not that half-mile-tall nonsense you were concerned with...'

'I see the plan now! The balloon and unsuspecting crew would fly over Four Rocks when it triggered *his* magic, and be brought down here.'

'Yes. The fall would likely kill all the passengers but leave the Eye of Jade free to be collected – by me, for *him*. So you were

Words of Fury:

nothing to him, all along.'

Berenda's soul rejected that hard truth.

'I was important to him! I was, I was!'

'Perhaps; perhaps you *were* important.'

Berenda's mind was spinning. 'When was the trap sprung?'

The woman caressed the ruby, which now glowed with a blood-red light.

'Several hours ago.'

'I see! So now you have the Eye!'

'I?' The gem-caressing continued, but the eyes had narrowed. 'Have *you* not brought it?'

'What? Do you imagine I would give the mighty Eye to *you*? Lady, *I* am his lovely chosen!'

'You are "lovely"? You are his "chosen", you say?' The woman looked at Berenda with scorn. 'You think too much of yourself. Know that I have been *his* for all my life – which is one hundred and seventy three years.'

Berenda showed her shock. It was true! His chosen could live forever!

'In every way you are not what you seem.'

'No more are you. But, since you are *one* of our lord's, and hardened to some small extent, I will reveal myself truly.'

The woman made a simple out-spreading gesture with her two hands.

Berenda flinched away, choking back a scream.

In raw reality, the enthroned crone was like an animated corpse several days dead. She had one eye that was a milky white and no more than three blackened teeth left in her mouth. She wriggled about, relaxing, and even from there her bad breath revolted Berenda.

Berenda might have changed her allegiance, but still she had to proclaim her achievements.

'You belittle me, you ugly thing, but I was at the ice-wall for *him*! I nearly died there, for *him*!'

The laughter was like a bullfrog croaking. 'Your life has no significance for him above, still less your dying.'

Berenda saw it all, now. The crone spoke truly. The great ice-wall that almost killed her was only another scheme among *his* many, and she herself was nothing to him.

'I have been betrayed!'

'How can a mere tool be "betrayed"?'

Berenda had a sickening certainty that she was indeed only

one tool among many. It was right that she had repaid *his* betrayal with her own, but now her pain spoke. 'How I have *suffered!* Oh, I was promised more, and I deserve more!'

The one good eye cocked. 'Now, the Eye... If you give it to me now – then *perhaps* I will let you live, if you humble yourself enough.'

Berenda felt sick inside from all the betrayal; in her anger, she scrabbled for some pride.

'I am not good at being humble.'

'You will learn.'

'No, I will not! Now where is the Eye? I *demand* to know!'

The old crone pushed herself up. 'Bitch, you speak out of turn!'

The jewel glowed bright red, giving the room a furnace appearance and a furnace heat. Suddenly Berenda began to sweat. She had not expected so much power to be exercised so soon.

She was afraid.

The old woman smirked. 'Feel my power! ...Oh, you *do*... So come here in humbleness, you dog-dirt, and lick my boots!'

The woman's expression was a goad, but Berenda had to recognize the power of her ruby. She scrambled over on hands and knees, trying to make her expression submissive.

'You are learning, wench.'

'Yes, yes,' said Berenda. 'I have learned so much!'

Berenda's vision was all red rage. Instead of lowering her face towards the old woman's stinky footgear, she stabbed a finger into her chest.

The woman choked, her eyes rolling up in surprise. Berenda had stopped the old woman's heart. She fell over and rolled away.

She was quite dead.

Berenda was squatting now, panting madly. What had she done? Murdered one of *his* high servants!

I will be tortured *endlessly* for this...

She stared down at the corpse. It was nothing in itself, but the power gem...

That living jewel is the only witness. What if I take her ruby, to help me find the Eye? – Well, when I have the Eye, I may be too powerful for even *him* to conquer!

So Berenda emerged from the cliff house dangling the ruby pendant. She ambled back down to the beach as queen of everything.

The living dead were sobbing and moaning still. She pointed a finger, though she knew the men could not see.

'Tell me where the balloon went, you blind scum! It must have flown very close to this place! – Tell me what you saw!'

There were incoherent moans, but no direct answers.

Berenda felt a long moment of terror. Was it possible the boy Emmanuel and the others had been *allowed* to land? What if the boy had already been turned by the Lord of the North? Was he, right this moment, being welcomed by her master with true love?

She began shaking at the unfairness of it all.

Man led the way. He had to pick carefully over the solidified sand. His rain had cooled the surface, but sometimes the crust of glass broke and sandaled feet went into what was still boiling-hot sand. Then there were bad burns and yells of pain.

Nevertheless, they went on; Prophecy was fulfilled.

Man felt good, and that worried him greatly, for he had made that gesture of obedience to the Lord of the North.

Have I given up something important? He considered carefully as he walked. I don't *think* I have changed... If there's a touch of darkness in my soul, I do not feel it.

In spite of what he had said to the Lord of the North, Man didn't feel inclined to throw himself at the feet of that cold, implacable entity. He was still a free man. He felt truly powerful now, and afraid of nothing!

'Man,' said Yoshi, 'you're smiling!'

'Yes,' Man answered.

He felt marvelous. Though it was still a quarter-mile to the cliffs' curving wall, and those cliffs were high and steep, everybody expected success.

Yoshi suddenly laughed.

'I bet you wish we'd captured some of those beasts. You like lobster, I know, and crab!'

'Only in their place – hot on a dish in front of me.'

Another two hundred steps or so and Man knew they would be safely off the black beach. Even the Eye's casket, slung over his shoulder again, was a bearable burden.

Lady Joah glanced over at him. 'I think there is magic in these cliffs.' Her face was alert, but knotted with tension. 'Something was put there to guard our own land from *this* dark place.'

That made sense.

Then the Voice shrieked. Man felt a shadow cross him. He whirled round, the Words of Power ready.

Something new had risen out of the sand to stop them – a gigantic coal-black human hand. A line of other huge hands had appeared along the foot of the cliffs.

All statues. They *had* to be statues.

Then Man saw the nearest giant hand reach out for the Voice. Man saw the entire line of hands grasping, to keep his party away from the cliffs. All his people were backing up now. First their retreat was a stumbling backwards walk, then a trot, then a panicked run.

Man went with them.

Then he stopped.

What is this? We're being driven back to the beach! It mustn't all end here! The Waning is ahead, a better world is ahead, but only if I can get the others out of this.

He *had* to act...

'Turn back, everybody! But watch out! I'm going to use fire again!'

And he did.

From the flicks made by his hands light and fire flashed forward. He blasted fire so that three of the hands burned, producing thick black smoke. Then he hit part of the cliff-face till it collapsed. He struck again to clear an upward path through the jumbled rocks, though the effort was tasking. Shortly the choking stink of burning was all around. Man blinked through the swirls of dark smoke.

'Run to the cliffs and climb!' he yelled, somehow knowing it might be too late. He felt weird magic shimmer all round. 'Run!'

It was not a sprint over the shifting black sands, for they were assisting the wounded and still carrying their loads. Man lifted up one hurt samurai himself, but thick-bodied Ugaki came over. He was bandaged up, but he took the weight of the wounded man off Man and elbowed Man away.

'Your magic is needed, lord!'

It was; so Man would have to be the last to go.

As the others stumbled towards the cliffs through the line of hands, he stood alone, turning to face the afternoon sun. When all appeared to be safe, Man began walking backwards. He felt the magic split around him, like Moses when the Red Sea parted.

Words of Fury:

He looked over his shoulder, to see the others go scrambling up the fallen rocks as quickly as they could, though some stopped to beckon him.

He turned and ran forward, and began to drag himself up the cliff, using the bushes that hung there. The Eye was a serious weight on his back, but he carried it with determination. Sweat dripped from his face; but he never stopped trying to make progress. On hands and feet he forced his way up. A waterfall had cut a path of sorts, which he could sometimes follow.

There was dangerous magic swirling behind him. He hoped it would stay behind.

Then a shout came. 'Man! We're here!'

Elbow raised to knock branches aside, he crashed through more greenery. There was a stitch in his side and he was panting, but now he saw the others. Safe with them in that green twilight he could finally stop, and he did.

He had made it. He had fought monsters on the midnight-black beach, as Prophecy required, and he had lived.

They had assembled on a ledge, still breathing heavily, squatting with their backs to tree-trunks. A few tiny, colorful birds darted about in the gloom. This was everyday Nature, good and wholesome, whereas Man knew Monster Beach down below was alien.

Yoshi said, 'Man, you look exhausted.'

'I am beyond exhaustion. It'll be days before I can power up with magic again.'

Yoshi clapped Man on the shoulder.

'Six dead and three walking wounded,' he said, but then Man saw his tense expression relax. Now there was wonder on his face. 'But the rest of us made it. Emmanuel, you led us through the Beach of Monsters. Nothing will stop us now! I see destiny.'

'I,' said Joah, 'see the hand of God.'

Berenda had felt it, when Man and the others crossed back into this world. That was strong magic at play. Berenda *felt* her enemies. Somewhere close, Emmanuel and the others had escaped some mighty peril, and now they shared joy and shared love.

She hated them for that.

Still, Emmanuel was sick, though he did not know how bad

it was – and in some subtle and recent way *he* had touched Man in the soul. Lady Joah – that prattling, arrogant girl – had delayed death in her too, from the Five Touches.

If they're dying, I win! *As long as I get the Eye!*

This was a good place, Man decided: a flat ledge the samurai could secure, with fresh water. And there was a view, all the way to the sea.'

They made camp under a rocky outcrop where water tumbled into a pool. No-one could attack from above, and it would be impossible to come in force from below. Ozawa put guards out to protect both ends of the camp, and a detail filled water-bottles while others began cooking.

It was golden dusk, now. The sun had dropped to the horizon. Man just sat, glad to rest with the others. His exhausted legs dangled over the sheer drop. The black beach glistened in the declining sun, black-glass whirls frozen there forever in weird postures – as if they had once been alive.

'That beach is alien,' said the Voice from Afar.

'True, but look beyond it,' said Man, softly. 'There is the sea we came from...' He waved a hand. 'The silver-shining sea.'

'In that direction is our city,' said Joah. 'Jade; home.'

Man heard the yearning in her voice, and wondered again if the love of her birthplace might make her vulnerable. Nevertheless, he was content to sit. The blue water had hazed over with cloudy sunset pink. Behind them, to the east, Man felt Mount Unzen as a brooding presence.

'Ozawa has sent out scouts, two north, two south, and two inland towards the mountains. We need to know if black sashes are already here, or friends of *him*. Then we want to find a trail for tomorrow, ideally one that goes directly east.'

'A trail that takes us north might be better – you know, past that place Four Rocks. It'd be longer, but also unexpected.'

'Four Rocks wouldn't have been lucky for us,' said the Voice.

Lady Joah sighed. 'We'll never know, now.'

'North or south are our best choices, unless we want to go mountaineering. If we can't find a suitable quiet trail,' Yoshi said, almost to himself, 'we may have to use a better road.'

Man asked, 'Is there a problem with that?'

'All good roadways are always heavily used, so we'd be noticed. Also, on a good road our enemies will be able to move their forces up and down at will. By now they might even have cavalry here.'

'Do you *really* think Oatha can have horsemen chasing us?' Ozawa responded to that.

'Emmanuel, he will have been preparing his treason for months or even years.' He turned to Yoshi. 'Though your father never knew it?'

'Oatha has made his feelings plain for years. So you could be right, Ozawa-san; there might be hundreds of his men here.'

'Or only a recently-arrived handful,' Man speculated.

Yoshi snorted. 'The pessimist changes!'

'This is all guesswork,' Man admitted. 'But I do take your point. We must be ready for anything. We *are* being pursued.'

'Yes, those boats –' Faslane began.

'What's that?'

Joah had pointed due west, towards the bloated orange half-sun.

Man squinted at the movement. 'Looks like beating wings.'

Faslane stared too, then pulled back from the brink. 'Is that what I think, heading here?'

'I believe so,' Yoshi answered bleakly. 'It's a Steel Angel from Cube Castle. And I have the feeling it's looking for us.'

Sunset dipped the thing in blood. Man guessed the hovering Angel was about four hundred feet up and twice that distance away, beating its great wings so that it could hover in the same place. Its helmeted head was always turning, scanning the black beach and the green heights where they were. It looked so utterly unnatural that everyone felt frightened.

Man said, 'Yet another set of enemies!'

'Don't speak!' Yoshi told them all. He lowered his voice. 'It might have super hearing – or super vision.'

Man didn't want to take on anything with super powers, not even with magic. He had rarely seen Angels before, but they were armored and their human strength was amplified.

'We've heard nothing from them in Albion for a hundred and forty years.'

Man snapped, 'Faslane, this isn't *your* Empire!'

The steel Angel came closer.

Man continued to glare, feeling the threat. He clenched his fists. 'Has it seen us?'

Joah had turned her head to follow it.

'I can't tell.'

'I'm glad we're in cover,' Faslane murmured.

'Perhaps it has seen us, it just doesn't want to alert us,' Man said, angrily.

After several seconds it flew north.

'Gone!' said the Voice from Afar, relieved.

'Maybe it'll come back, with reinforcements!'

For a minute no one spoke, digesting that thought.

Eventually Yoshi made a comment. 'Evil bastards, the Angels are. They're few – but too strong to fight.'

Joah sounded more tranquil. 'They want to destroy certain possible futures, Emmanuel; that is why we Futurists oppose them. They are enemies of change.'

Man shifted about. 'I hope they never find us.'

Joah hesitated. 'They might, you know. I think Lady Naosuke saw that possibility... Do you remember the lines?'

'Try me.'

'"Like a steely angel made of history, / Fighting magic and hearts true."'

The Prophecies again! And more enemies!

Man scowled at those abstruse words. Would he never get away from other people's ideas of his destiny?

Full sunset came. Slowly all the land below went dark.

Words of Fury:

Chapter Sixteen: *After So Much Pain*

When Man was alone, he beckoned Yoshi. When he came, Man asked only one low-voiced question. 'What are the names of those who died?'

Yoshi studied his friend. 'You really need to know?'

'Those men died for a chance of a better future. They died for *me*...'

Man listened to Yoshi recite, committing the martyrs' names to memory, resolving to honor their sacrifice in the best way, with victory.

When he said nothing more, Yoshi backed politely away.

Man stayed sitting there. A sea breeze came. He found it refreshing as it cooled the evening. From somewhere came the floating, mournful notes of a shakuhachi – the bamboo flute beloved in Japan.

A few yards off he saw Yoshi beckon Ozawa over and then sit down with Two Heads. They began questioning the escapee.

The Lord of the North was based in the Arctic north. Though he had not been attacked there for centuries, there was always the chance of discovering some weakness. Where exactly where his bases and ports? What was his strategy?

From what Man could hear they weren't getting very far. He sighed. Intelligence was priceless; anyone who had studied Sun Tzu – or Man's own father – knew that. Two Heads sounded like he had a good soul, but Man doubted he had much intelligence in any sense.

Next, Man considered what the Lord of the North had said earlier. A secret enemy, here on their journey? His gaze flicked over to Faslane, who squatted by the campfire in spite of the humid evening warmth. Now that was a man of mystery... And yet, just as easily, the enemy could be one of the samurai. Ugaki, perhaps? Or what about Yonai or Kido?

He didn't want to think it was Yoshi, or the Voice, or the Lady Joah – but he worried a lot about himself.

Berenda hated the idea that she had been misled, that all this time Emanuel and the others might have been elsewhere. She *could* have been fooled. They *could* have been where there were monsters, not here at Four Rocks at all...

Berenda came back to watch Hagiwara at work. He was very experienced and he liked to be thorough.

Eventually he stood up from yet another corpse, wiping the blood and flesh from his hands.

'Lady Berenda, they know nothing.' He had one fist cupped. 'But we have tried. Here, look...'

Berenda looked down into her own palm, as he tipped eyeballs into her hand. Then her own eyes widened, and she flung the souvenirs away.

Then she went mad.

It felt that she was looking down on someone else, with all her wails and her inconsolable moans, her apologies and pledges. It was as if she hated what she had herself ordered, but surely that could not be?

So, divided in herself, she gestured her drama for everyone to see. It was a drama so powerful that many kneeled and a few men even fainted; but Hagiwara left her and turned back to the torturing.

Hagiwara squatted down by one sniveling youth, who shivered dreadfully and held one hand over an empty eye-socket.

Hagiwara considered the obvious: taking the other eye. These men had to talk; it was as simple as that. Oaths of loyalty like Hagiwara's, sworn to the Lord of the North, could not be withdrawn, and Hagiwara *had* to deliver.

My son Hagiwara, the Lord of All had said in that last dream, *do not fail me. For if you do, your end will be unspeakable...*

Hagiwara knew he might be made to answer for this delay; he had to speak.

He found her by the dark sea.

'Please, Lady Berenda, let's just march inland tomorrow morning, and look for Man and Joah there.'

'I was told the landing would be here, at Four Rocks.'

Hagiwara dragged the captive youth forward. 'You, talk!'

The youth howled at his merciless touch.

Hagiwara leaned over menacingly. 'You admit you saw the balloon, so tell me where it came down!'

'It was blown over the coast south of this place! Where it landed, sir – we did not see! I think it was Monster Beach but *I don't know!* I beg you, believe me!'

Hagiwara flung the boy down.

'So many stories spoken after so much pain cannot be completely false.'

So that, thought Berenda, was the truth about this agony; all had been done in error, and for nothing. She remembered the eyeballs in her palm, as squishy as ripe grapes. That had been her doing, really. She had lost her soul, and for what?

When *he* said they would be here, was I lied to, by my former lord?

Deep in thought, Berenda circled the weeping youth.

No; even though the mundane call him the Father of Lies, he would not so disrespect his own schemes. So either my lord changed his mind, and for some reason chose not to tell me, or the error that was made was *his*.

She thought her way through her dilemma, knowing she *had* to sound confident.

'You say they're at Monster Beach, Hagiwara? Well, they could hardly have crossed *that* quickly, so if we move now there is a good chance we can intercept them – and the Eye – by morning.'

If I *can* take the Eye, I will be very powerful indeed. I could stand to anyone and perhaps rule the world...

'How will we do that?'

She made a gesture, to the leader of the black sash cavalry.

Nagaoka came up to her quickly. He was a loud-mouth, annoyed he had missed most of the torturing. Now he waved a hand over the hostages, radiating impatience.

'Lady, are there more questions to ask, or have we done with them?'

Berenda realized that if she was merciful now and let these fisher-folk go, news of the black sash landing and her own error would get out. Then *everyone* would know she was here, misled and a fool.

On the other hand, no one kept secrets better than the dead.

'Nagaoka, Hagiwara, and all you others!' There was never any mercy, not really. With full attention paid to her, Berenda pointed at the unarmed villagers. 'Kill them all!'

Man helped Yoshi look over the sentries. After Yoshi pronounced himself satisfied, they returned to the campfire, whose cheery orange blaze was carefully hidden.

'We seem secure enough here,' said Man.

Yoshi rubbed at his weary face. 'With *him* after us, and the Steel Angels too?'

Words of Fury:

'I was trying to be optimistic.'

'For once! Still, it's quite an adventure we're having, eh?' Now Yoshi grinned. 'My epic will be unbelievable – in a good way.'

'If you live to write it, I will live to talk about it.'

'"If" – the biggest small word in existence.'

Man sniffed something appetizing.

'There's a good meal to come?'

'These veteran samurai are very efficient – they cook as easily as they kill. Also, they drink!' Now Yoshi called everyone round, and broke out some dark-glass bottles from his baggage. He addressed them all, grinning. 'From Fukuzawa, this special drink! It's for Kiku No Sekku Festival. So we far we have escaped monsters in human shape and monsters not in human shape; let this continue!'

'I'll drink to that!' the Voice said, reaching for a cup. 'And to Captain Fukuzawa, who was so very, very brave!'

'And I will drink to you,' said Yoshi, 'and apologize for how I doubted you!'

'We all have doubts,' said Joah.

The bottles went round. Each person poured out a little, just a symbolic taste of a fine past and an equally fine future.

Yoshi was bouncing with energy, though his joy was largely relief. It was only then that Man realized how heavily his friend's responsibilities had weighed on him.

Yoshi raised a cup. 'Now, everyone!'

'A moment!' Man had lifted his hand. 'To all the fallen!' He named Ashida first, and then every other one. 'That their sacrifice be not in vain!'

They all drank. It was a powerful dark saké with a surface thick as a broth and an odd flowery aftertaste.

'More!' the Voice said, brightly. 'Oh, please, more!'

'Yes, I could get used to this,' Man announced, remembering many mad nights in the Floating World area of Jade. He passed the bottle on, wiping his lips with the back of one hand. 'What is it?'

'The most exquisite saké I know, flavored with chrysanthemum petals.'

There was the smell of gohan coming from the hidden campfire, that thick, hunger-satisfying steamed rice.

Yoshi raised his empty cup, frowned into it. 'Who drank all that?' He whirled round with incredible speed and pointed at the

Words of Fury: 167

Voice. 'It was you!'

She drank her own share and smiled. 'I plead guilty, my lord. And I'd like to be guilty all over again, if it pleases you.' She made her smile broaden and made a smooth dancer's twirl. 'It'll certainly please me.'

Yoshi back grinned at her. 'Plenty of time for a refill. See!' He drank again. 'Or two or three more refills...'

'You'll be falling over,' Man said.

'Oh, I never get drunk,' Yoshi said, raising his cup again.

'Never?' Man raised an eyebrow in ironic response. He had seen his friend get in several drunken scrapes, and the reverse was true, too. The two of them, often with the Voice accompanying them, were well known on the more dubious streets of Jade city.

'Not my definition of drunk, anyway.'

'What definition is that, friend Yoshi?'

Man had spoken without turning, wondering if he had just seen some dark shape fly across the stars. A Steel Angel? If he wasn't so exhausted he might have tried for some magical perception, but as it was... Anyway, whatever it might have been, it was surely gone, and there was no point worrying the others, was there?

'Oh, being drunk is falling about.' Yoshi drank again, then burped. Yoshi was with his friends after a vital victory, and he was cheerful. 'Hey, Voice from Afar! Drunk... I mean, really drunk... What is your definition?'

The Voice also drank deeply. 'Talking nonsense.'

Man was laughing. 'I do that sober and so do both of you!'

'In my case – speaking as a poet – that's the divine intoxication of art, my Man!'

The Voice from Afar turned to Yoshi to discuss drunkenness in more depth. 'Talking incredible lurid nonsense – or you talking poetry! Then throwing up.'

They all laughed again. Yoshi poured out more drink. He was relaxed and happy. He turned to the Voice again and raised his cup of the tongue-rollingly-good saké in a salute to her.

She responded with a coarse port chant, pulling up her kimono to let the men see her long legs, which she moved very sensually.

'A man loves a woman, every night...'

Yoshi's eyes gleamed. 'His hands, tongue and his – ' Yoshi made a vulgar but vital gesture '– giving sweet delight!'

'And the woman says then...'

All around the campfire they were applauding and laughing, knowing the punchline, shouting it out together.

'"Make love! Don't fight!"'

Yoshi shook a clenched fist, a wild grin on his face. 'And he does make love, he does!'

A voice said their meal was ready.

Man sighed, joining the others to take a rice portion which was served in steel helmets.

He sat down. His appetite was huge as an empire, but it was about to be satisfied.

What had the Lord of the North said? Alternate worlds... Man remembered those words of *his*, a little dizzied from the strong drink on an empty stomach.

What might those other worlds be like? he wondered. Earths where women rule? Or where two-headed folk are the majority? Worlds where the Moon is inhabited? Worlds where the stars really are in reach?

Alternate worlds that might reach out here, and be reached in turn by visitors like me or my friends from our world...

He realized he hadn't known his own universe until today. Now he knew it was infinite in possibility – where the river of time can change course, or even go backwards to take us to the very beginning of everything!

He knew he had the Lord of the North to thank for that knowledge.

Man, trained to be careful, was still looking all round – over dark Monster Beach to where the sea glimmered. Soon it would be time for sleep. He felt ready for that. Then he looked over his shoulder. There, somewhere over the high mountain, was Shimabara town and their mysterious destination, the psychic fortress known as The Waning of the Moon. But there *he* claimed he also had friends.

Man sighed, regretting his promise to the Lord of the North, but still thinking it had been necessary. He touched his inflamed cheek. His headache was back, but there was help waiting at the Waning, wonderful help. Mother Zandar had trained others, and when he was healed those disciples would train him to use the Eye – and he *would*. Though his death in this struggle was almost certain, he had accepted his destiny, and he wanted to go on right to the very end.

'I will serve a high purpose – and save many lives...'

Words of Fury:

Now he looked out to sea again. It was a deep ultramarine. Sparkling lights, faint as stars, were heading inshore.

Joah came, and asked him softly, 'Might they be something ordinary? Perhaps night-fishing boats?'

'I doubt it. Most go south – to round the rocky tip of this place. I have a feeling they'll land men.'

'So you think they are enemies, Emmanuel?'

He looked up; he couldn't make out Joah's expression.

'I do.'

'Many enemies you have, and I too.' She had spoken so sadly that he thought of the Five Touches, and her own likely but untimely and tragic death. Her expression was still lost in the shadows. 'But you are also loved.'

He rose, and touched Joah lightly on one silky cheek. Oh, she was very lovely. He heard her intake of breath and then her long sigh. He suddenly felt the power and goodness of this woman, as well as her erotic power.

Should they kiss, now? He kept his hand on her. Yes. They should. She wanted that; so did he. A finger-kiss? Or with the lips?

He hesitated to do that intimate thing, but he was happy to pay compliments. 'You have won me over, Lady Joah.'

'Won you?'

'I have been tempted towards ... another track. But now ... '

'Ah,' she said, in a strange throaty voice. 'Temptation.'

Suddenly Man saw again that black knight; saw *him*. 'But I will turn my back on that path. I will faithfully serve the vision in the Prophecies, and their interpreter, you.'

'You think that's what I want? Your service? Or, rather, all that I want, or desire, from you?'

The word 'desire' had had a strange yearning sound when she spoke it. Perhaps there had even been a catch in her voice. He felt a throb of corresponding emotion in him so powerful it was overwhelming. He saw Joah, no lady in his fantasies, rolling naked with him, kissing, biting, scratching...

Man lowered his hand, not because he did not want to touch her, but because he wanted far more. Even in the dark he felt an equivalent yearning come from her. She had much love to give, and she deserved to get it all returned.

Yes, but no lasting love can come from a dead man – and that's me.

'Go to sleep, lovely Joah. At first light we rise and head for this "Waning" of yours, and it'll be a hard race. If the black sashes catch us, or if that unlovely the Tears comes close…'

'I know it will be hard: but we have passed one trial, and now that we have the Prophecies say our journey doesn't end yet. We will go on, my Emmanuel.'

He nodded back. Night was *his* realm, as was nightmare, and cold, and death, but now Man would sleep. He was far from unhappy. Tomorrow would be another perilous journey, and they had taken casualties, but he was beginning to think they might make it.

Words of Fury:

Chapter Seventeen: *Up Towards the Mountain*

The mass murder was quite a procedure, since some villagers managed to run and had to be caught again. Hagiwara was annoyed by the noise as he worked to letter tiny characters onto a message-scroll, which he then slipped into a tube he tied to a carrier pigeon's leg, repeating the process with another bird. Then he released both.

They circled twice, and then headed out to sea. One would be with Lord Oatha in hours, telling him that this first detachment had safely landed but the Eye was not seized yet. The other message would say much the same and go to the High Son of the Cold in Jade.

Hagiwara rose, now, keeping a wary eye on Berenda's turned back.

'Are you sending good news, sir?' Nagaoka asked, keen as a young officer should be.

'We haven't captured our enemies, so how can the news be good?' The corners of Hagiwara's mouth turned down. 'Tomorrow we *must* find them.'

'South of here, we were told.'

'That black beach is impassable.'

'Then surely they died there, lord?'

Hagiwara rubbed his face, mused out loud. 'The Lady thinks not.'

'I do!' She had come upon them silently, her black robes extending out like raven wings. Then Berenda suddenly stood upright. 'I have felt *him* – the Lord Emmanuel, with his friends!'

'Alas,' Hagiwara said soothingly, 'it's too late for us to close on him tonight.'

'You fool! Don't you see that this is our chance?' Berenda whirled around on their horsemen. 'What are you waiting for! Mount up, and get inland of the black beach! Intercept them!'

'You want us to find this Emmanuel? Now?' It was obvious Nagaoka was reluctant. 'Lady ... you say he's strong ... and it's *dark* ...'

'There will be light for you!'

'Even so, won't they have magic?'

'So do we. You two at the front, raise up your lances!'

The first men did, and then at Berenda's gesture a painfully bright light blazed at the two spear-tips. It seemed to Hagiwara that the metal itself was burning. He flinched, and the horses neighed in agitation in spite of their training for war.

Berenda called, 'When you find them, Nagaoka, immediately send me messengers to let me know where they are!'

'But – what do we *do?*'

'Kill them all, and get the Eye! Now go!'

Hagiwara watched the last of them mount up, saying nothing at all. This conflict was becoming far-reaching, and he would prefer that it stayed far.

Berenda stroked her face through the veil.

'I felt betrayed; therefore I felt hurt. Ah, my arrogance, my fool's fury! But now...'

Hagiwara saw that she had the ruby power gem. So Berenda must have killed *his* other high servant. He shivered, in the great dark. When the high ones fight, the low folk suffer.

'Now, Lady?'

He had heard the uncertainty in her, which she immediately concealed with pious words.

'Hagiwara, I am only a single finger on his hand. Right now *he* is working to take Jade, take The Waning here – and also the city Rumoi, far in the North. I fear he may be distracted; there may be errors made.' Berenda's smile was full, and perhaps a little crazed. 'Yes, there may be errors made – but *his* victory will be *my* victory!'

'Yes, Lady.' Her piety had seemed hollow, but what came next was clearly her true feeling.

'Emmanuel and his friends will never reach The Waning of the Moon. I will seize them long before!'

She was ecstatic, but Hagiwara's mind was going over the incredible truth. A barrier of ice a half-mile high, and somehow the enemy had broken through, to face monsters which they then escaped! Four pirate ships onto the enemy's one, and the enemy had won!

He tried to tell himself there was nothing to fear.

We have the Lady Berenda here; and above her we have *him*. So we cannot lose, in Jade, or here, or in Rumoi. Surely we cannot lose?

He watched Nagaoka's sixty horsemen leave the camp, led by the flaring lances. They rode up towards the mountain till they vanished in the dark.

Words of Fury:

PART TWO

In the world of this book, those on the side of light must get to The Waning of the Moon – though their great enemy the Lord of the North will do anything to stop them. If they fail, their world, and our world too, will end...

Prologue to Part Two: Heaven, or Hell?

As soon as he opened his eyes, Man looked around. He was standing in some dark place.

If this isn't a dream and this place is real ... is it Heaven, or Hell?

From the frozen absence of life it wasn't hard to guess. This world was flat and very cold. Dead ice glimmered everywhere, slippery under his feet when he moved. The sky was sunless, a starless dead black.

I hope this is a dream. If this world is real, it already belongs to the enemy.

Now memories came. Man remembered escaping the city of Jade by flying away with his friends. Then there had been a sun-drenched black beach, and a long fight with monsters. Man's side had taken casualties, but afterwards they had found a safe place to sleep; probably he was still there, dreaming.

Only, all nightmares were the enemy's, and now Man felt a *serious* enemy was coming. Man carried two samurai swords and he knew how to use them. His soul-power – his magic – had once been very strong.

But this enemy is way too powerful...

Now a voice rumbled: 'Yes, *I* am too powerful for *you*! Cold night is *my* realm, and so are nightmares, and death itself.'

He tried to laugh. 'This is only a dream. What rotten taste I have – I'm actually dreaming *you*.'

'No, Emmanuel, you are here in the world to come – *my* world! Look upon it – and then look upon *me!*'

The voice was so loud it made Man flinch. When he did look North, there was his enemy in all-black armor – a hundred miles tall.

'You are mankind's deadly enemy,' said Man.' You are the Lord of the North.'

Words of Fury:

'I am the culmination of *everything* – for you, too.'

'No. Whatever I said before, now I reject you! I am not yours, nor ever will be!'

'Too late, Man! You have already lost. You cannot save your new homeland, try though you may; and I am already at the dark heart of the Empire you left behind. Look down again!'

When he did, Man recognized this dark land.

It was home. Or, at least, the home he came from.

I have one foot in the West Country at Tintagel where I was raised, and the other on the Thames near London. If this isn't my Albion, it is an echo in a parallel world – or it is the future.

This country-spanning view was possible only because he was a giant himself. That cheered him. He watched his enemy and stretched his long limbs, then touched the hilts of his two swords. Perhaps the fight wasn't quite impossible.

His opponent thought differently.

'I have already killed your mother, and your father also! You didn't know that, but now you do. You have no chance.'

That string of lies didn't produce fear; it just made Man hate *him* even more.

So did the truth Man gave back. 'And you killed Mother Zandar at The Waning of the Moon, who was going to accept the Eye of Jade from me. Well, you won't ever get it from me – you murderer!'

'She was barely an obstacle.'

As Man heard *his* contempt he felt anger build. This would be a death-fight, and he wanted to be ready. He and his friends had been tasked with getting the power gem 'the Eye' to safety. The Lord of the North wanted it.

Over my dead body...

'Don't imagine you have a destiny, Man. You are only a blood sacrifice. And your friends here will also die when I defeat you.'

It didn't seem important to Man that he was still so very afraid. He felt fury, but he also knew he had to do the right thing. This was cold implacable evil right in front of him, and it had to be fought.

'You do not speak, boy. You should. Take a chance on my mercy, and surrender!'

Man let his fingers creep towards his sword-hilt.

'Boy, you still say nothing. You are too proud! You think because you are middle-named "Artur" you can be a king and

Words of Fury:

save a kingdom. No! Any more than you can save Japan here, no matter what is prophesized.' The vast armored figure leaned down. 'Run, Man, or fight me and die.'

Man drew his sword as he came leaping forward, and struck out with it. His aggression took the other by surprise. He hit the armored chest hard. Metal parted, and perhaps flesh.

'*That* was for Mother Zandar!' Even the one hit was encouraging, but Man did more. '*That* was for my father!'

The shadow-black giant had been cut and also forced back. Man felt hope, till the enemy hit back at him.

As Man took each sword-blow he grunted, for the enemy was *strong*. Man had to step back from Albion onto the frozen Straits; he felt sea-ice crunch. Another step back and he was in France.

The Lord of the North has driven me from Albion...

'Yes, Emmanuel, and my victory over you will seal the fate of this world!'

Man sensed that was true; nevertheless he did not weaken in any way. 'The rubbish you speak, I wish it would seal up your lips!'

'My voice is history; hear me and tremble!'

Man said in contempt, 'You think you speak words of power, but it's wind!'

That clearly annoyed the giant. Now there were no words, only more sword-strokes. Man was forced further back, right through France and south-east onto the icy Middle Sea.

Entropy had taken all warmth from this world. It was truly the Lord of the North's. Man saw life here had died – the price of losing to *him*.

Suddenly Man was inspired: he *was* life, defending itself against death. He defended this world that was a defiled echo of his own. He slowly backed away to Egypt where he straddled the frozen Nile, biding his time and waiting for his arrogant opponent to make a mistake.

Still that Albion long-sword clashed against Man's lighter samurai blade. Over Arabia the two opposing powers fought on for many minutes. Still Man was driven east, and then south of the ankle-high Himalayas into India.

I can't see *his* face, thought Man, though I should know it...

Then his enemy's blade nicked a shoulder. It was an inconsequential pain, but Man began to bleed. He was gasping too and suddenly he knew he could not carry on for much longer.

Words of Fury:

The light was dying and it was getting colder. Man was so cold that his teeth were chattering.

He was on the high plateau of Tibet now, parrying, and somehow still resisting that overwhelming power. Shortly he was driven onto the great plains of China.

I must fight on, or *he* will win the world. Only, I need more than my own words to win!

He was losing this fight and there was no help coming. He knew that now. Mother Zandar was dead. Lady Joah, the Voice, and his best friend Yoshi were not even in this dream.

The giant leaned in and gave more blows. Man was backed up into Korea, the Evening Land. Being there didn't last long, and behind him another sea had to be stepped over. When he did, stepping onto Japan, he took another smash-down blow which put him on one knee. It could have been finished then, but the Lord of the North always did like to gloat. By sprawling away Man escaped *his* follow-up – a death-blow that hacked a new valley into Japan.

I won't last long, unless I can think up some trick or get help...

Man still tried to fight the giant who had driven him here, but the enemy's blows were too strong and *he* was too tall. Man was diminished, a toddler trying to defeat a full-grown man. Each blow seemed more powerful than the one before. He wondered how bad dying in a dream would be.

There was only one place that might give assistance: the great fortress-monastery The Waning of the Moon. That was where his long retreat was ending. Besides, there was no other place to go. From here on there was only the vast uncrossable Pacific.

He promised himself, 'I must get to friends before I – '

A bass roar: 'Do you think friendship will save you? Do you think love will save you?'

'Yes.'

'No! You think of The Waning of the Moon, but you will never get there! Even if you did it would not save you – for now you die!'

The great enemy and Man both raised their swords. Man saw cold eyes, squinting at him through a face-guard. Though he knew he must lose, Man would not surrender.

Then someone spoke: 'Believe in the light!'

Somehow those words helped, and he gave his next

Words of Fury:

chopping strike everything.
    When the two blades struck that elemental clash showered sparks across the whole world and beyond. For one eternal moment the universe was full of light.

Chapter Eighteen: *A Light That Never Goes Out*

Sister Daisen had been the late Mother Zandar's chief aide. She had been dream-walking in search of Man. But just as she found him, just as she glimpsed his dream, his fight began.

Man against the Lord of the North was impossible – and you *could* die in a dream, of course. That would end everything, for Emmanuel's lost soul would stay wandering endlessly and aimlessly till the end of time.

She felt both angry and sick with concern.

My dear Emmanuel, you *must not* die! Oh, if only I could do more to help you!

Here he still had the Prophecies to fulfill, whether he wanted to or not. She watched helplessly as the swords struck, and Man was slowly forced back across half the world. This could only end in tragedy.

Then a blast of light came and she could see no more.

For a moment after waking Daisen couldn't even distinguish between the end of Man's dream and the depressing white reality around her. The whitewashed cell was lit by the same candle-in-glass as before, and her friend Zandar was in a white shroud. Their most significant person had been martyred here by the Lord of the North. And the coming of the light in Emmanuel's fight had been meaningless, for he was too young to be fighting *him* with any hope.

I know young Man fought monsters, but he *will* be destroyed before reaching sanctuary here at The Waning. There is only obliteration ahead, and then the dark and the cold.

Somehow the light stayed shining in her memory, though.

She was here with the defeated dead, but she found a little courage.

I don't *know* how it will end, so I must *not* surrender hope!

However, there seemed to be no mystery here, only death. She rubbed her face and thought more about hope. Then she sidled past the vividly-painted, carefully-placed screens to look upon the corpse.

Daisen had kept vigil here all night, but no miracle had happened. Zandar was still dead.

As she had always known he would, the Lord of the North had won.

And yet...

Daisen went outside. A single Sword Maiden sat cross-legged, opposite.

'You are the one called Ice?'

The woman was surly. 'That's me, Elder Sister.'

Daisen eyed her. 'Did you see a bright light here?'

'I saw no light to speak of.'

It was clear. Mother Zandar was dead; Emmanuel of Albion would follow.

Then there really was light. Daisen turned quickly.

It was only Sulina, holding up a lightstone. She was the senior adept here, fleshy, clever, and warm-natured. Daisen saw that, for her, she was ungroomed, with darkness under her sad eyes.

'I felt something happen here.'

Daisen shrugged. 'Everything is the same bad. The city of Jade has been lost to our enemies. Young Sandella has been having terrible dreams about Rumoi and our forces defending it. And now...'

Sulina raised the light. 'What?'

'I dreamed of Emmanuel, the boy Man, but he was in a fight with the Lord of the North.'

'Emmanuel is lost!'

'Probably.'

'Daisen, he *must* succeed, or this world entire will fall!'

Ice shifted her weight, watching both women.

'I know that. Man was on his way – but he may not arrive.' Daisen pushed open the cell door. 'Please come in.'

Sulina had been going to look at Mother Zandar's corpse, but now Daisen saw her avert her gaze.

'Thank you for staying with her, Daisen.'

'It was one of the last things that I may do for her, Sister Sulina. But how are you? By your look, you have not slept.'

'No,' said Sulina. 'I have been trying to keep things moving.'

Daisen humbly took second place. 'What do you think we should do?'

'Our original plans are irrelevant now. Our Mother gone... Lady Joah and Emmanuel dying, and their dangerous journey incomplete...' Sulina grimaced. 'What if they are killed?'

Daisen stood tall. 'It would *not* be the end. We might still recover the Eye of Jade – a supremely powerful weapon. And Princess Anamizu and Lady Rishiri are coming. We have a chance.'

'To fight *him*, and prevail?'

Words of Fury: 180

'To survive.'

The 5 a.m. bells sounded then. It was pre-dawn; the Hour of the Hare, which would be followed by another two-hour slot named after the Dragon.

When the death bells began to ring, Sulina gave a sigh.

'After Mother Zandar's funeral we will meet and make plans.'

'Sulina, you are a truly strong character,' said Daisen, approving it.

'Am I? I suppose I am, or at least strong enough to face the truth. I do not have the Foretelling, Sister Daisen, and I know we will likely lose – but I do know how to hope. In that alone am I like our late holy Mother. I have this hope above all: that one day there will be *someone* in the world powerful enough to strike out against *him!*'

'Hope is a wonderful thing, Sulina.' The faint noise of the funeral bells became louder, and then the opening door let them both hear footsteps in the corridor outside. 'Here come the others.'

'No,' said Sulina. 'No.'

There was a strange quality in her voice. Daisen whirled round, to see Sulina was pointing down at the white-wrapped corpse.

'She is breathing! Zandar is back from the dead!'

Daisen went down on her knees to celebrate.

Man rolled over in his sleep. His mind was a jumble of flashbacks. In this life he was travelling with his friends and the Eye of Jade. Though more enemies were landing, there was sanctuary ahead. But he knew it might be the real Lord of the North he faced in his dream and that had made him afraid.

Then he heard his long-lost mother, rocking him in her arms after a childhood nightmare. 'There *is* a light that never goes out...'

I *do* believe in the light, he thought; and I always will.

He rolled over again, so comforted that he was instantly in a deep sleep. He did not even realize he had been wounded.

When Mother Zandar heard the sound of bells and the words 'back from the dead', she began to pull white bindings away from her face.

There were four women around her futon: Daisen, Sulina,

Words of Fury:

High Healer Irizo, and the young she-captain Hanake.

'Mother?' asked Daisen. 'Have our prayers been answered?'

Sulina spoke sharply. 'Or are you some *kami*, only pretending to be her that we loved?'

Zandar felt very remote from this room. What was this world? What was *she*?

'Will you answer us?'

Zandar sat up and rubbed at her blindfolded eyes. Her mouth was desert-dry. She was wondering whether this was some subtle episode in the afterlife. Heaven, or Hell, or some in-between limbo?

'When *he*...' Zandar felt herself choking. Then she found her courage. 'The Lord of the North came here, didn't he?'

Daisen answered. 'Yes.'

'Is he still here?'

'What?'

Zandar was explicit. 'Did we surrender?'

'No,' said Daisen and Sulina, together.

'Thank God!' Zandar shuddered. Daisen touched her hand, then helped her escape the shroud. 'Otherwise *he* would have won the world!'

It was too late for magic, but not for faith. She had helped Man against *him*; and she felt good about that.

After a minute, Daisen spoke. 'Mother, is Man saved?'

'I don't know!' Zandar was fully alive again. 'We helped him in the dream, but he is still in danger. Only, I don't know *how* he is in danger – or *where*...'

'Mother, do not distress yourself. Here.'

Now Zandar received water and green tea from Daisen's hands. Two sips from each cup, and then she returned them.

Zandar knew she was not far from being broken. She had fought *him* several times, and every time the same thing: I fight, and I lose!

'Now,' said Daisen, still speaking gently, 'can you use your power to Far-See what has become of Man, and identify this danger?'

'We are still in *his* embrace here! The Lord of the North's magic is everywhere outside.'

'I know.'

'You might be asking me to do the impossible.'

'I ask it anyway.'

Sighing deeply, Zandar summoned up her magic.

In her mind's eye now she began to see things. She saw the Lord of the North in his half-mile-tall self-image made of ice. With her help, that huge idol had disintegrated. She saw the black sand beach that had erupted monsters when her young friends had landed, but she saw them winning through.

'The powers Man and the others faced were unstoppable. They had been sure to die.' She took a breath. 'But in both crises they got through. That was a double miracle.' Now her voice was pleasingly strong. 'Man is sleeping – but I feel danger around him!'

'What danger?' asked Sulina.

'I can't quite see, but when I do I will send adepts with power gems, all that we can spare. Novice Keli and her party are not enough. Man needs many more swords on his side, and Sisters!'

There was silence around her futon.

'Am I no longer obeyed?' She remembered how she herself had overthrown her drunken, wild predecessor, Lady Rishiri. Had the same thing happened to her, with another now chosen? 'Tell me!'

'Holy Mother, it is not so easy.'

This voice belonged to Hanake, the long-braided Sword Maiden.

'You wear the torc of she-captain-in-chief!'

'Yes, Mother. Winter Morning ... when she was in the fight with *him*, something in her broke.'

Zandar was appalled. 'She cannot fight?'

'No, Mother. But I can.'

On impulse, Zandar reached out and touched Hanake's wrist. 'I see you are worthy. Now, speak.'

'We were already short of fighting power, for we obeyed the Exalted and the Shogun, and sent our regiments to Ezo to fight *him*...'

'Surely we can still send a few battle-companies west!'

'Mother, as you ... slept ... news came.' Hanake spoke gently. 'Black sashes and others – many *his* sworn servants – have been landing.'

This was bad news indeed. 'We can't spare any force to send to young Emmanuel?'

'Mother, we have our walls to defend.'

Zandar saw it plainly, now. 'Man and the others are a million miles from safety. In every way *he* is winning! *His* tactics

Words of Fury:

fooled us! It is all hopeless!'

She sensed how the others were staring, shocked at this change in her.

'Forgive my moment of weakness. There will be ways to outsmart even *him*! Let me look now.'

Zandar checked the west coast with her power, but her glimpses were few and out of focus. *He* was still drawing veils of interference over what was real. She saw Four Rocks, the fishing-village which was now full of enemies. She saw the black beach, but it was empty.

'Emmanuel and Joah have moved on.'

'Are they heading into one of *his* traps?'

'They are in danger, rely on that.' Then Zandar turned her face to Daisen. 'I can now see Emmanuel and Lady Joah!' Zandar was having difficulty in expressing herself. She hoped those problems were just temporary, though now her small frame shook. 'As our friend Man sleeps he is being watched by enemies, a spy of some sort or a traitor!'

Daisen touched her shoulder.

'Can you warn him?'

Zandar tried, but then *his* interference thickened, and she lost sight of Emmanuel and the others. It was still dark there; and that was *his* time.

'I cannot get through – *he* is too strong. But Man *must* be told!' Zandar shivered. She knew the spy watching Man was linked to very powerful enemies. 'Fetch me Sandella and the Diamond Heart!' The message was sent, but Zandar was unhappy. 'That will take too much time... – If *I* can't wake Man, perhaps I can get Lady Joah to...' She murmured under her breath, then shook her head wildly. 'Joah cannot hear me either!'

'Then what do we do?'

'I will try Joah's sister.'

'Will Lady Oki help? *Can* she help?'

'Sulina, Oki had better be able to! They must wake up, locate and destroy the spy, or that will be the end!'

Her desperation silenced the room. But even though she had been hurt and defeated, Zandar was still in charge. She drew back her shoulders, touched her temples, and mind-spoke with all the power she had.

'OKI! LADY OKI, HEAR ME!'

Words of Fury:

Lady Oki rolled over, moaning. She was dozing off a saké hangover, as dawn's rosy fingers began to pull the night away from Jade. She had not slept well, though she knew her sister and the others had crossed Monster Beach. They'd taken losses, but Joah, Yoshi and Man were still alive.

Yes, but holy Mother Zandar was dead.

Oki seemed to hear an oddly familiar voice, but it was from far away. Her nightmares were important, not some fantasy voice.

In her first nightmare Oki had seen her beloved Jade become Lord Oatha's completely. She saw the people of Foreign Town forming up in long lines – thousands of men, women, weeping children – before being led off to the execution ground for beheading.

The second dream had seemed a great improvement, at first. In this dream she was the all-powerful princess of the city, giving orders to the cringing world. Oatha was no longer there. But above the city stood a gigantic statue made entirely of black: the Lord of the North.

She felt sickened. What if that was a Foretelling? What if she really would come to serve *him?*

'Never!'

And yet last night Lord Oatha had celebrated and so she had been obliged to celebrate too. The city's conqueror had been boasting like *him* about how the city would be purified of foreigners, especially Christians; he had dropped smiling hints about mass-murder...

Everything horrible his young deputy Aoki had told Oki was coming true.

Oki removed her mind's eye from the horror of that triumphalist statue. Was that a Foretelling? It certainly had the feel of one.

Meanwhile, the voice came.

'OKI! LADY OKI! DON'T YOU KNOW ME?'

Then overwhelming male power quenched the female voice.

Who had been speaking? Oki touched her pounding head. Her mouth was sticky and foul. Last night there had been much saké. She remembered black sashes making toast after violent toast. She had drunk each one. She remembered dancing girls from the port, shaking bare breasts to applause. She had clapped loudly, screaming with laughter too, her fan and all decency left somewhere.

Words of Fury:

Shame hit her now. To think she had been in a drunken celebration, while her father was in the death-cells below!

Her cheeks flamed; suddenly she sobbed.

'Oh, how could I do that?'

For the third clear time that voice came again. 'OKI! HEAR ME WHEN I CALL!'

'I don't know who you are!' she mind-spoke crossly. 'Be clear!'

She rubbed sticky eyes to see her sleeping room was scattered with finery. There were kimonos of the finest silk, high-heel shoes in E'ropan style. On the futon-side table were little piles of gems. She picked up a few of the stones – green emeralds, rubies, a large sparkling diamond.

Oatha's gifts... In reality, Oatha's robberies.

Of course, Oatha could now do as he liked – and he was. That man was *full* of fury. She remembered a thing Mother Zandar had once said to her and her sister Joah: 'In the dark time to come, money will become a lie that loses all its value, and religion won't be love, it will be ten thousand competing voices shouting out hatred a million times over.'

She heard that urgent, desperate voice again... That voice, was it her conscience? Three times ignored, should she now answer? She ought to.

The inner shoji was opened. A naked man stood there.

The young samurai Aoki smiled down at her.

Oki gaped back, blushing. He was lithe and very attractive, but, especially after what they had done last night, his presence here was dangerous.

'Do you think we dare bathe together, wonderful Oki? You said we could trust your maid.' Aoki was still smiling, and surely he was much more important to her than some spirit voice in her head? 'I remember last night, even if you don't...'

'I only remember the saké! And the bare-breasted dancing! Oh, Aoki-san, if Lord Oatha finds us together, you *know* what he will do!'

Aoki only laughed; a fit and lethally trained young man, in his prime and utterly confident.

'Let us talk of us. Do you still "love" me?'

'I cannot commit myself! For my family's sake, I may have to be bound to Oatha!'

'I am Oatha's legal deputy, am I not? And he is still promised to your sister.'

'He could break that promise in a moment and he probably will now she has gone with Emmanuel! Oatha is all the law.'

'MY OKI!'

Suddenly Oki recognized who was contacting her. She burst into tears of joy.

'Mother Zandar! Oh, praise, *you live!*'

'MY SOUL WILL LIVE, WHATEVER HAPPENS. – NOW, PLEASE LISTEN.'

Oki tried to wipe away her tears. If Zandar lived, there was hope for the world!

'OKI, YOUR SISTER AND EMMANUEL WHILE SLEEPING ARE BEING WATCHED BY AN ENEMY. I CAN'T WARN THEM – *HE* IS INTERFERING. WAKE THEM!'

Oki tried.

'Sister Joah! Emmanuel! Can you hear me?'

Nothing. Only a sense of something overbearing; a crushing force trying to blanket all magic.

'Mother, I can't reach them either! But I do have news of my own. Last night I learned that Oatha has hired thousands of masterless samurai to assault The Waning. He's commandeered a fleet to transport them. Some have already sailed!'

'YOU SHOULD HAVE TOLD THE WANING IMMEDIATELY!'

Fending off Aoki with one hand, Oki bent her head in shame. She should have spoken, of course she should. Now, she was ready to weep again, but not in joy.

'I know, Mother. I am – so very ashamed.'

'WE WILL BE OUTNUMBERED BUT WE ARE READY TO FIGHT. HOWEVER, WE NEED YOUR SISTER AND EMMANUEL!'

'I hear you!' Oki put fingers to her temples and tried to make her thoughts more powerful. 'Joah! Sister!' She tried harder until she thought her skull would explode. 'Emmanuel! Oh, *hear me!*'

There was no reply, and little sense of her sleeping sister except the knowledge that she was alive.

'What are you doing?' Aoki held her with sweet intimacy, touching her breasts. 'Who are you talking to?'

Though she loved being in this strong man's arms, she had to pull herself away.

Then Oki began to see. There was a camp, on the ledge of a high cliff. In the grey light of dawn Oki saw a girl, wiping hair

Words of Fury:

from her bleary eyes.

'Mother Zandar, I see Joah! But I can't get her to talk! – Should I try Man again?'

There was no reply. Suddenly Oki realized she was on her own. Her violet eyes went very wide; she raised a hand to ward off Aoki and his endearments.

If she didn't succeed in helping Man everything would go bad. She had sometimes felt a little envy over the famous Mother Zandar's power in magic, but now wished she had the holy Mother right here with her.

'Emmanuel! Man! It's me, Oki!'

There was only greyness, and silence, and no reply at all.

'Man, we have fought with swords and kissed with fingertips and with lips! Oh, don't you know me? *Emmanuel!*'

There was no reply, but now Oki made a connection with their living souls. From the little encampment she felt a faint throbbing of human thought. The power of her magic was very great, but making it stretch so many miles was hard. She feared that if she had to release it abruptly, the backlash might wipe her mind.

In spite of the danger, Oki focused.

Joah was asleep again, dreaming of some romantic man. Yoshi had poems running through his brilliant, eloquent mind, though there was also something dark there. Emmanuel-John had in his mind a loving warm presence from long ago, and Oki suddenly realized it must be his lost mother.

All were in danger, now, because something she could not make out was watching.

'DAUGHTER... HARD TO...'

In the unreal confused dark pool of dream-talk, Oki suddenly felt the presence of Zandar again. The link strengthened; it was very powerful, because it was made out of love.

'Mother, what must I do?'

'SPY FROM... TELL...'

'Tell Man *what?*'

The link with Zandar suddenly expanded, to include a power gem and some other strong female at The Waning of the Moon. All this amplified Oki's power. Now she understood what the spy was, and she shouted with her mind.

'WAKE UP, EMMANUEL!'

Chapter Nineteen: *Some Other Peril*

Woken, Man gasped. At once his swords came into his hands. He jerked up from his bedroll, scanning the ghost-grey morning. His mother was gone, and that one-on-one fight with *him* was over for now, and just as well. This was some other peril, but what?

'YOU ARE BEING WATCHED!'

He looked around but he could see no danger. It was barely dawn, with pink coming beyond the mountains. Only, that young female voice had been full of fear, and it was familiar.

Then he looked up.

By some illusion of magic, Lady Oki was there and looking down. Her face was perhaps ten feet across and thirty feet above the earth.

Words came into his head, though her image's lips did not move.

'THERE'S A SPY CLOSE! FIND IT!'

He rose immediately, mostly undressed but entirely alert. A black sash, or perhaps a hovering Steel Angel? 'A spy... Where?'

Suddenly he felt all four minds in the link: Lady Oki was back in Jade and her sister was right here, but over the mountain was Mother Zandar and some other powerful female.

Zandar was *alive!* Man's spirit rejoiced.

When Joah realized Mother Zandar was vital again, she began weeping in joy. 'Back from the dead!'

The linked minds spoke inside Man.

'SOMEONE IN CUBE CASTLE IS WATCHING YOU. THAT LINK HAS TO BE BROKEN OR THE SPY WILL LEAD YOUR ENEMIES HERE!'

He remembered seeing that Steel Angel yesterday. He had both his swords out, though he wondered dismally if he could really fight a man in powered armor. Everybody knew that magic and refined metal did not mix; perhaps a Steel Angel would be immune to his power as well as his swords.

He used his left hand to signal to the three patrolling sentries – be on guard, but the danger is not immediate. Two Heads and the Voice came over. Somehow the Albion girl sensed what was happening should not be interrupted. She held away the two-headed giant.

Man saw no sign of any steel-encased man-thing. 'Where is it?'

'LET US GUIDE YOU!'

He stood tall. 'Do it!'

The four women were working together with great skill as well as power. When they touched Man, he felt something release in him. While his body slumped back, some fiery masculine force escaped. He let the two sisters and Zandar and this other guide his soul.

Earthbound reality fell away. He was clawing with his arms at the air and he saw the campsite dwindle.

Soon he was level with the mountains. To the east, dawn split the grey cloudscape with veins of gold. He could see for miles in every direction, from the dark sea west to the sunlit sea east.

'YOUR ENEMY IS BELOW! THE CASTLE WORD IS "DRONE". SEE IT?'

Language had begun to fade; but Man's every sense was intense – sight especially. He was, he realized now, a living bird of prey: a great eagle. He followed the females' instructions, dropped down a few hundred feet and saw the thing which was circling their camp far below.

The drone looked like a wide-winged hawk, but it was beating its wings too regularly to be natural.

His own thoughts turned simple and savage. He stayed focused on the mechanical bird; then his wings pulled in and he began to dive.

'BE CAREFUL!' said four voices chanting as one. 'IT MIGHT HAVE POWERS!'

Man was nothing but an eagle now. He dropped down a thousand feet to the mech-bird – and his talons ripped through it. As he gutted the thing, electricity shocked him and left him paralyzed.

The drone had been dangerous. As it tumbled away there were wires revealed and flying sparks. By magic Man knew it had been sending pictures back to Cube Castle, though that had stopped now.

It's been brought down – *but so have I...*

What had been a man fell with the eagle, still watching the mechanical thing below.

The eagle tumbled, knowing this fall would kill.

Fifty feet above the camp, the man within the eagle finally died. That meant the eagle could fly free again. He beat his powerful wings, cawing in triumph. A few people pointed up and shouted sounds which were called 'words'. But that was back in the human world. Now Man was an eagle.

He began to fly away from the desperately waving people.

He would never inhabit human flesh again.

Oki still sat chest-deep in steaming bathwater. With her Far-Sight she had followed Man as he ripped open the drone.

Joah mind-spoke to her. 'Man killed the thing! Now call his soul back!'

'I?' Oki turned and pushed excited, loving Aoki away. 'Please! Go dress! I need time alone to do vital magic!' Then she spoke to Joah again. 'The last thing you want is a troop of Angels on your trail...'

'Help me!'

Oki reached out with her power towards that imperious flying creature: was that a vital spark within, was it Man, what Christians like her sister called a soul?

'I think I've found him but I don't know if I'm doing this right!'

'Speak to him! You were *always* the one he looked up to...'

'But you know him better now, Joah, and you are closer!' Oki gasped. 'Do something! I've lost him!'

Oki felt her sister also extend her magic; but Man was not even touched, still less released.

'Oki – *I can't free him!*'

Even when Oki found the bird of prey again she felt only the eagle's triumphant savagery, and not Man's complex spirit. Was he lost forever?

She felt frightened.

'Man put his soul into the eagle, sister Joah. If he doesn't come back, he is dead as a man!'

Joah said with surprising heat, 'Are you are afraid for him? Why? You never even liked him!'

Oki closed her eyes. Even if the room had not been steamy already, her face would have gleamed with sweat.

'If Man is lost, you know what happens. It will be the end of humanity!'

'Yes, but now he's pure eagle, I have no remedy,' her sister said. 'Have you?'

Joah's thoughts were a tart taste in Oki's mind. What had happened to her plum-sweet sibling? Oki realized Joah had grown up and they had grown apart.

Words of Fury:

Emmanuel, as a man, *had* to be reawakened!
But now there was shouting outside.
Oki's eyes opened. The spell was broken; Man was lost.
The shoji slid aside. Through the steam, a man's grinning face peered in. Instantly Oki was conscious of her pink nakedness; almost as quickly, conscious of fear.
'Lord Oatha!'
She dropped lower in the bath till the scented foam covered her to the chin.
What if Oatha has already gone to where I was sleeping? Then he will know about Aoki and me!
Man was lost, she was lost, and she had never been more afraid.

Joah felt her sister depart, but her own voice and others babbled frantically away – mere empty sounds to the eagle, who felt that this was the morning of the world. To be a wild and predatory hunter was the finest thing in creation.
Joah's voice was suddenly loudest. 'Mother Zandar! He is flying away! He will be lost!'
'BRING HIM BACK!'
'I don't know how!' said Joah, miserably. 'I can't!'
'YOU MUST!'
What could she do? Was it over?
The eagle that contained Man's soul flew on, leaving Prophecies behind, leaving the future behind, leaving humanity behind.

Somebody right in front of Man was screaming at him, and this person slapped his human face.
'You piece of dirt!' she said.
Man was back in his body.
It was Joah, her hand raised to strike again. She was almost spitting, she was so furious. 'Don't you dare leave us, you coward!'
He felt a rush of red anger and of course he had two bare blades ready. 'You dare call me – '
'I would say anything, the more hurtful the better,' Joah said. 'I had to hit you!' She put her hands on his shoulders and as he looked down he saw her emotions had utterly changed. What had happened before was only an act. Now she was watching with honey-eyed concern. 'I *had* to bring you back!'

'With shock tactics and foul words!'

'With whatever it took! Or would you rather stay as an eagle?'

His sight had cleared and he was human again. He saw everyone in the camp was watching him. He gave a brief laugh, and put away his swords. As so often, Joah was right.

'You've won me over. I know I have a mission. Things must be changed.'

'Well, then,' she said, in a voice an impatient schoolmistress might have used, though she was smiling, 'stay with us, and be human.' She stared at him. 'You're bleeding! How did that happen?'

He touched his bloodied shoulder and shivered.

'If I told you I was hurt by *him* in a dream, would you believe me?'

'Of course!' She traced a fingertip along the rounded muscle of his upper arm, healing the cut and the rent in his plain kimono. 'And your face is all red on one side.'

'You slapped me hard!' Now Man blinked. 'But this isn't from *you!* It's from the Tears!'

Tenderly, Joah touched his cheek. 'This thing I cannot heal.'

He didn't want to hear that, and he pulled her hand away.

But there were other new things for Joah, and because of one she looked joyful. 'Oh, Mother Zandar lives! And she can help us – help *you*.'

'That,' Man said, 'is the most cheerful thing I've heard since – since Yoshi wrote me out of his epic!' He was still looking at Joah. Mother Zandar could help her, too, with the Five Touches of poison – he hoped. 'And dear Oki... Wasn't she here, too?'

Joah gave him a very direct look. Was she angry about something?

'She is still in Jade. With... With the Five Touches enslaving her, how could it be otherwise?'

'Ah, poor Oki! And poor *you*!'

'Yes. I must die soon, I suppose. But not unfulfilled – and not without fighting back!'

Then Oki's face reappeared up above. It was vaguer than before; she was under strain.

'I am sorry but I have to go. I have a guest I...'

'Who?' Man shouted, suddenly jealous. Someone was alone with Oki at this early hour? 'Who?'

As Oki's magic faded, so did her face.

Words of Fury:

Man turned on Joah, unexpectedly enraged. 'What's happening with your sister? Who is she with?'

Joah's nostrils flared. 'Nothing you or I can help with – is the answer to *both* your questions!'

Now Joah moved away, sat down and huddled up in her quilted over-kimono by the grey ashes of the fire. Man was wondering what she knew about what was happening to Oki.

'I hate Oatha, too!' she said to no-one.

Man felt disturbed. What was going on back in Jade?

That gross man, Lord Oatha, stood in her doorway. His face was one selfish, lippy leer, and she felt dread.

'I must request that you leave me now,' Oki said, knowing that she had no power to make Oatha go. Her heart was beating madly. If Oatha knew what she had been doing with lovely Aoki... Almost fainting, she slid back into the bloodheat water.

Oatha continued his leering; he was a dangerous man looking at a possession.

'Your voice is high, my lady. You must be excited.'

Her lip curled. 'Not in any good way!'

His smile broadened. Then he backed out of the room and slid the shoji closed.

She dared to breathe again.

Oatha had gone, for the moment. Her heart beat at her chest like a hammer.

Now Aoki stepped into view, naked except for sandals, as lithe as a leopard. His mouth was quivering.

'That dirt, assembled into a man! I want to kill him.'

'I know you do!' She closed her eyes, shook her head. Would this nightmare ever end? Right this minute Man was sailing away into oblivion... Oki opened her eyes, hoping that it would all come right. 'Oatha had his swords and you're naked! Who would win?'

Aoki said nothing for a moment.

'Oh, don't look surly! That makes you small. When you're yourself, dear Aoki, you're a beautiful wild warrior.'

He laughed, very handsome and fully aware of it, but his eyes were still serious.

'You know he will be back, Lady Oki.'

'I know it. Well, we must certainly conspire to produce his downfall now; or we are dead.'

'True.' He touched her bare shoulder, rubbed the bare flesh.

'For you saved me now and perhaps yourself only by fanning the flames.'

'That's so,' Oki admitted. Her heart was pounding, and she wondered if her addiction to excitement was dangerous. 'But I'm expert at flame-fanning. I never get burned.'

Aoki looked at her.

'Lady Oki, there is always a first time.'

Joah was obviously in no mood for conversation, so Man let her alone.

After his use of overwhelming magic on the beach yesterday he was self-conscious about how the others would see him. Most seemed comfortable, though wary. A few looked at him with explicit pride, as if his power was something good which they all shared.

Ugaki was openly grinning at Man; but he was an admirer of violence. When Man turned away, the rough voice addressed him.

'Monstrous hard fighting, Mr Foreigner.'

Ugaki ambled over, with bloody bandages still round his neck and more around one arm. No healing, then? Man was wary of this man who was as tall as he was and more powerfully built. Someone like Ugaki would be an excellent tool for the Lord of the North…

'Yes,' Man agreed, politely. 'We were fighting hard monsters.'

'And more to come, eh?'

Without answering, Man edged away to make a space on the log where he was sitting. He was wondering if he could get this possible enemy to make a slip.

Ugaki did not sit down. 'I have been thinking.'

'Yes?'

'I will probably die on this journey, and then my life will have been…' Ugaki shrugged. 'For what, exactly?'

Man was surprised this cold veteran was making conversation. It came to him again that Ugaki, stone-faced and famously violent, would be an excellent agent for the Lord of the North. Man wondered if there might be a murder bid now; the Lord of the North and his agents would want Man dead. He moved one hand very slightly, so he could more easily get to his short blade.

Ugaki still stared down: an ugly, angry man. And yet…

Words of Fury:

And yet he too had a soul, which might be saved. Man probed, gently.

'You're here and you may die – to defend us against the Lord of the North. Or do you have another, darker reason to be here?'

The smile on Ugaki's face stayed mirthless, though Man did not feel an immediate threat in him.

Man continued, 'Or do you question samurai life in general, Ugaki-san?'

'You read me like an opened book, Lord Foreigner... Ah, I had four sons, once.'

'And now?'

Ugaki sat down, bulldog jowls hanging. 'Two are already dead, doing their samurai duty.'

Did Ugaki want sympathy? In flash of understanding Man saw that he did. He probed more.

'And the two sons who live?'

'One is brave enough. And a fool. A strong-willed brave fool, much like his father.'

Man regarded the older warrior. 'And the other?'

'Oh, we never got on, and he thinks I look down on him. I know I never meant much to him. At eighteen he shaved his head and became a Buddhist bonze and scholar. I've not seen him for many years now. I don't suppose I will see him again, not in this life.'

Now Man saw all the sadness, all the regret.

'Ah, Ugaki-san! And he was the one you loved the most?'

The man looked away, and then spoke with slow dignity. 'Yes. He was the one I loved the most. – Now, please excuse me. I have said too much.'

Man watched him stride slowly away.

Ugaki may really believe he will die, Man thought, and is thinking now of all he has left undone, all the things unsaid... Man sighed; and his own thoughts turned in a similar direction. There was his father, disappeared and almost certainly dead back in Albion. There was Man's own life here, ruined forever because Oatha had seized the city of Jade.

Yoshi had been smiling around with his usual charm, but when he looked over at Man his face turned serious again and he came over.

'Friend Emmanuel, it seems the Steel Angels and Oatha are joining our main enemy.'

Joah answered from behind Yoshi.

'Better presume we have three sets of enemies: science, and magic, and plain evil.' She shivered, and said bleakly, 'And I feel them all, not far. We must be very careful here!'

'We will be. I have my scouts out.' Yoshi lowered his voice. 'All our enemies want *you*, Emmanuel.'

'Why?' Man asked, harshly. His cheek burned and his head was pounding again, though instinct told him to be a man and not reveal a weakness. 'To see if my death will be amusing?'

Yoshi paused a moment.

'You, Man, are from a different continent and in every way you represent change. And whether or not Oatha is a Son of the Cold, he is powerful – and he hates you and everything you stand for.'

Joah was bitter. 'Oatha is winning, Lord Yoshi. I carry the poisonous evidence in my body.'

Man thought about it; then his stomach turned over. 'Oatha will do as he likes; because he may have won Jade permanently.'

Joah was shocked. 'How so?'

'Who's going to take the city back from him? The Emperor? No. The Shogun and his forces? Well, they're up in Ezo, aren't they?' There was so little going for Man and the others, and time was against them. Suddenly Man felt dread, for himself and for his friends. 'Unless we get to sanctuary soon – '

'From the Five Touches I will be dead, and it is little better for you,' Joah said. 'I know, Emmanuel.'

He felt the pain in her, and in himself. He didn't expect to live a long life, but it would be wrong beyond anything for brave and loyal Joah to die.

Yoshi turned back to Man. 'To the Angels, you're better dead. The Lord of the North wants you dead or turned to him. And if we lose but you somehow live on, Oatha and his purity police will make sure you'll be on the run here forever.'

'Then I would have to go to Albion.'

'Perhaps that's the idea?'

Man felt great hurt, and that as it so often does turned into anger. 'I thought I had a home here!'

'Why resent *us*,' Yoshi said quietly, waving a hand towards Faslane the sea-pilot, 'when your own people came thirteen thousand miles to kill you?'

That thought had been ominous; but Man had learned to not entirely distrust Dirk Faslane.

He walked away and sat down by himself, by the remains of one of last night's fires. Elsewhere, others wolfed down cold pickled vegetables and rice, but he had no appetite.

He wondered if he had really changed allegiance, and if he should confess.

I had to do something back on the beach, or we would have all died! – And I did not *quite* pledge allegiance!

He decided to never think of the Lord of the North again. That way, surely, he would keep his freedom – and his soul.

Without that link, though, what power was left to him? Especially given the way all magic locally was being suppressed by the Lord of the North.

Man saw there were big stones round the circle of grey ash, most large enough to be adequate trials of strength. He looked around carefully, to be sure he was unobserved. Then he stared at one head-sized boulder opposite him. He imagined lines of force going out there, cradling the stone, lifting it up. He concentrated; he remembered how mighty he had been back on the black beach, and now he reached out...

Nothing happened.

He tried to remember linking with Oki and Joah, before, how that had worked and how the power had flowed.

Still nothing happened.

Have I let my power slip away again? I can't let myself be powerless! If I am unmanned, in the next crisis we will be destroyed! What must I do to regain my strength?

Then in his secret soul he opened up one memory, and he saw again that huge man in black armor and he heard his hyper-confident bass voice, and...

The boulder suddenly rolled over. Man stared, his hands tingling from use of magic. He half-saw lines of glowing power reaching out from him to the stone, which rolled over again more quickly than before.

Then he levitated the stone a good foot above the earth. He could feel the tension in his shoulders and arms; his head pounded, and he was sweating with effort as the stone floated towards him. He swallowed, lost belief; and the boulder tumbled into the pool of ash, from where a grey smoke rose.

In the ashy smoke, just for a moment, he seemed to see the black-armored Lord of the North.

Man felt his stomach turn; but perhaps that was the wrong reaction. He had his power back, even if the Lord of the North

had helped.
 Yes, he helped me! So doesn't that make me *his*?
 He felt sick again, sick to his stomach.
 It better not…

Words of Fury:

Chapter Twenty: *A Dead End*

The Lady Berenda had once been the Lord of the North's most faithful servant 'the Tears', and – as she thought – his most beloved follower.

But now she knew the truth. She had only been a tool, and nothing to him.

She had spent a very bad and very lonely night here at Four Rocks, after killing *his* high agent and taking her ruby power gem. All night, in that house overlooking the beach, Berenda kept the ruby in her fist, and that fist she kept close to her heart. She sometimes shivered, sometimes sweated; she was lost between two utterly different and contradictory worlds.

I have betrayed *him*, my master. Oh, I deserve to be beaten and degraded!

She had writhed about, tearlessly weeping.

I thought I knew better than him! Mad to think that way, but I did. But from *him* all I will get now is death!

She let the taste of that develope.

No; I refuse to die at *his* hand. Instead I must follow the path I have chosen – of disobedience, of freedom.

She had used the power of the ruby – and it was a considerable power – to weave forces that suppressed magic locally. It would have no effect on The Waning, but it would interfere with lesser powers close by and also help hide her from *him*.

She had enjoyed experimenting with the gem, which was amenable. She had played some cruel tricks on people, but they were nothing to the cruelties she would inflict on Man and those two girls. The anticipation of that made her smile.

And when Nagaoka and his horsemen find our enemies I will *destroy* them – and enjoy the process!

Yet, when she thought over some of the shocking things that she had done, or been made to do, they mostly disgusted her now. She remembered being given a handful of human eyeballs; and the memory of their ripe-grape feel made her shudder.

That shudder was a surprise. Perhaps she had been changed even more than she had imagined.

Berenda had been born different, and raised lonely. She had long ago come to *him* on that basis, full of her hurts and unsatisfied longings. She had been encouraged to nurse her grievances by him, to think the worst of everything and everyone, and then encouraged to take endless revenge on the world.

All she had really done, of course, was to mindlessly serve *him*.

Yes, who is *he*, really? Out at the ice, he *lied* to me, and then left me to die...

She suddenly imagined being good, and being loved for herself. That pleased her so much it brought tears to her eyes. She thought of a new self, a self that was looked up to by everyone.

As Berenda drank local saké and ate sushi fish, she thought of the power of love.

Why have I *never* felt really loved? *He* had his chance and he failed me. Now I want a clean break, I do. I might now escape from slavery to *him*, and then turn my heart and soul in a different direction.

'I *can* change – and I *will!*'

That decision, as well as the cups of saké, warmed her. Words came to her again. *Love your enemies, and...*

'No!' She swallowed. 'I have enemies I *hate!*' She was suddenly shivering. 'Turn to good? Is that even possible?'

Berenda thought again of that power held in her fist. As the gem powered up, cold ember-red light appeared from between her fingers.

With this power I can change things to suit myself, and stop being a follower!

She looked hard into that blood color, which began to pulse in time to her heart-beat.

'Where *are* my enemies? Show me!'

Now she suddenly saw a vision, people assembled around a pool of water.

It was them. They had lived, and they were not far.

She came out of the trance, and stumbled half-naked outside. She began shouting.

'Clear the camp right away!' Sleepy sentries stared; other men looked out from bedrolls as still others slept. In the night more reinforcements had arrived. 'Those with horses mount up! It isn't too late to catch our enemies!'

The camp became a chaos of packing. The pink sky turned blue. She saw carrion birds picking at the dead.

'All of you, up!' She made this very loud. '*Find me Emmanuel! Find me the Eye!*'

A sentry called, 'Third scout back!'

Man looked, but then something thrashed up from the wall of green jungle and zig-zagged just overhead. Ducking men shouted in alarm. Man saw the thing circle the pool. It wasn't flying comfortably and wires leaked out of it, but the mech-bird was moving.

'We need to kill it for good.' Yoshi was furious.

Lady Joah agreed. 'If it brings Steel Angels here, we are done...'

Yoshi touched his bow and made an unobtrusive request to Man.

Man understood. He threw up his right arm, hand flat, fingers together: stop. Everyone became still.

Man alone made some wild, attention-getting gestures, while his friend put an arrow to his bow. The mechanical bird whirled closer to Man, hovering awkwardly about fifty feet up to see what he was doing.

Man saw Yoshi take aim – hold the aim – then loose an arrow.

It was a wonderful shot. Man could tell that by the big grin Yoshi showed even before his arrow brought down the thing.

'Look!' Yoshi went ambling over, and picked up the wide-winged drone. 'It was in flight, and a single arrow brought it down!' He exalted himself. 'Oh, I'm good, aren't I?'

Man took the thing from him. Now he held it, it was obvious the mechanical bird had never lived. He looked into the odd wide-awake eyes; but then the glassy eyes moved in separate directions and the tail suddenly curled as it tried to twist out of his hand.

'It's still alive!'

Immediately Man began to smash the thing on a rock. There was another flash and then a burnt smell.

Man flung the remains off the cliff.

'It's dead now!'

'But it might already have passed on our location.' Yoshi was serious again. 'There may be armored Angels on our trail soon – as well as *him*.'

Man stared bleakly down at where he'd thrown the wreckage. The practical war-maker in him spoke.

'Then we have to get out of here.'

'Yes, for now they know their creature is dead, surely Steel

Angels will investigate.'

Joah was nodding to herself. 'You know it isn't magic in that drone; it's technology, much as Futurists understand it – or your Albion, Man.'

Albion had its engineering marvels, and made some use of electricity. But Man knew his country had nothing so advanced as that mechanical bird.

Joah looked directly at Man, her expression hard. She really has changed, he thought. What happened to that sweet girl who said she loved me?

'When my young brother the heir was very ill, drugs to help were coming – against all precedent and law – from T'zina, sometimes called China. The Angels somehow learned of it and destroyed the ship. My beloved baby brother died in agony – to help stop "progress"!' Joah's eyes softened now. 'That broke my mother's heart and so she died. Do you understand now why I want freedom, and why I was *proud* to swear the oaths of Futurism?'

Man said only, 'If you and Yoshi are trying to convert me, I will listen. But, for now, perhaps we should be concentrating on our own situation.'

'You Water Tiger,' Joah said; an astrological reference that made Man self-assured, noble-natured – and a little pompous. 'I appreciate your noble concern.'

Yoshi looked up at the sky, looked at the wall of jungle. 'As soon as the last scout checks in, we move on!'

At that, the Voice scowled prettily, first at him, next at the kettle.

'Oh, Lord Yoshi, I swear I'd kill for a cup of hot tea first.'

'Then rather than murdering someone, make tea!'

The Voice tapped the kettle hung above the dead fire and sighed. Of course, it was stone cold.

Man saw the Lady Joah eye the tousled foreign girl. Then Joah reached out and put her hands on either side of the tin kettle. She glanced over at Man for a moment, a look that might have been angry. Then Yoshi stepped away, his eyes going wide.

Man too had felt a flicker of heat pass him. Joah pulled her hands away, shaking them, grimacing. The bubbling kettle had boiled over.

Joah rose. 'I grow stronger every day. How sad that it does nothing to make me happier.'

Eyes watched her walk off.

Words of Fury: 203

As the men formed into line to take hot tea, Man saw the last scout arrive. He went over with Ozawa and Faslane, and Lady Joah came back.

By the time the scout finished reporting, tea had been drunk and Yoshi was already consulting his map.

'Two main choices to get us south. The easiest and fastest road is the coast road here, which is an Imperial way, but of course it is well-used and we could not be secret.'

'What's the alternative?' Man asked.

Yoshi put finger and thumb on the magic silk, spread them apart to increase the scale. He showed them a tiny irregular pathway into the mountains. 'We might go between the peaks, here – see the path?'

Man squinted down. 'That looks like a bridge.'

'The path must be being upgraded. If so, it'll be quite a short cut. So, what do you think?'

'Without tree cover we'd be easy to spot up there – should a Steel Angel or a drone come along.'

'True, though isn't the coast road also exposed?'

'There really are no good choices, are there? Of course, the coast road is better...'

'And quicker. What do you all think?'

Ozawa answered first. 'Lord Yoshi, surely our general location is known, and our destination? We must hurry – on the best road we can take.'

Yoshi looked over at Lady Joah, then Man; neither disagreed with Ozawa.

'Then let's use the best road – if the scouts advise it.'

Man and the others nodded acceptance. The last scout, though, made some negative points.

Yoshi scowled. 'It seems the coast road is already busy, maybe too busy to risk. Man?'

'Then we should cross the mountains.'

Without speaking to any of the others Yoshi loudly clapped his hands.

'Everyone, we move!'

The Voice sidled over.

'Man, what will happen now?'

'Now?' Man touched his sword-hilt, suddenly seeing a bleak future. 'We will be hunted. I'm only glad we have two or three hours before Angels can come here from Jade.'

'Are you sure?'

That was Faslane, now putting his beefy arm round the Voice from Afar.

'What do you mean?' Man asked.

'You're presuming those Angels have to come here all the way from Jade. What if some Angels overnighted locally? Lord Emmanuel, our enemies might only be minutes away!'

Yoshi led them away from the ledge, up a narrow steep trail partly hidden by over-arching tree-branches.

'Do you think they're after us, Man?'

'They're bound to be. Steel Angels, Oatha's people, and *him*.'

Yoshi glanced up at the greenery. 'At least for now it's easy to stay hidden.'

'Easy to stay hidden, but progress is slow.'

They kept in shelter as best they could, giving orders through hand-signals. Even though they had scouts out, Man still had a strange strong sensation that he and the others were being followed. He glanced up at the sky when he could, but he saw little except flashes of sun. There might be mech-birds circling, or even Steel Angels; he could not see. Grim-faced, he touched his sword-hilts, wondering what the Prophecies said about this part of their journey to sanctuary.

Morale was good, though the temperature and humidity were both high. Men sweated, the young women glowed. But they all pressed on with determination, their optimism began to increase, and Yoshi was soon smiling.

'Nobody's following us, Man. Even if there are Oatha's purity police here, so what? We're elite. We're going to make it!'

They walked on quickly through criss-cross light. It felt good to make this progress. Man insisted on leading some of the time, though of course they had their specialist scouts ahead.

Then Yonai came close to Man.

'You are looking strange, Lord Kinross. You may not be well and, please, you should slow down.'

'What?'

The fellow pointed. 'Your face is pale on one side and red on the other.'

'So?'

Yonai squinted. 'In the redness, is that a wound-mark?'

'No!' Man said roughly, turning away. Though he continued to trot, he suddenly felt the bite throb. He didn't like to be reminded of the Tears and her toothy kiss, but she too was on their trail now and Man knew it. The pain got worse, affecting his mood.

He went over to Yoshi for a change of subject. 'How close is the coast road? How near is Mother Zandar?'

'The Imperial way is a half mile. The Waning of the Moon is still miles away over the mountains.'

A little further on they climbed out of the jungle. Here, they found what the map had shown. A roadway stretched north and south, left and right, clinging to the flanks of the mountain.

Man suddenly realized he was panting. A good flat road seemed very appealing.

He had started to speak to his friend to advocate this easy way when he saw his friend's expression. 'Yoshi, you seem edgy!'

'I feel we're being watched.'

'I felt the same,' Man admitted. There was the high rocky crown of one of the mountains above, though no human observers were there, and no mech-birds were flying that he could see. 'Are we being observed magically?'

Lady Joah sighed. 'There is female magic coming from The Waning of the Moon, and *his* magic criss-crossing it, so everything is hard to make out.'

'What about the road we take?'

'Either way there's not much cover. Perhaps the better road is the better option.'

It was true the mountain slope ahead was green-speckled only in places. Otherwise it was bare rock.

Man stepped back into the jungle to consult the others. 'Should we take this road?'

Ozawa made the first comment. 'The scouts saw traffic on it, though it looks empty now.' He grimaced. 'It only takes one person to see us.'

Ugaki threw in, 'Would even a few armed enemies be such a danger? We are an elite force; why should we be afraid of mere humans?'

That was a good point, Man thought.

Then the Voice from Afar came running, her kimono skirts raised around her knees.

'I don't know if it's through magic or through the air, but I hear horses!'

Man waved frantically. 'Everybody get off the road and take cover! Hide!'

They did. Now a warm shadow-cave hid them all in humid

green twilight.

'Voice, who is coming?'

'I don't know!'

Yoshi grunted: 'Enemies, I bet.'

Man listened intently, first to the air, then with one ear pressed to the hard earth. Horsemen, for certain. Without rising, he turned his face to Joah. 'Is that help?'

'I *hope* so, but I don't know!'

So her knowledge of the Prophetic books was not useful now, and her own far-seeing magic was weak...

The drum sound of galloping grew louder. Man heard raised voices in the air. Then riders appeared on the left – from the north. It was a column of black-armored cavalry riding two abreast. They carried lances and had two cipher banners raised high. Every last one wore black sashes – the torturers' uniform.

The lead rider was a brittle, arrogant man he and Yoshi had twice crossed: Nagaoka.

Man flinched deeper into the shadows. Nagaoka was vicious. Man saw the riders were looking from side to side, but they were moving so fast it would be difficult to see faces in the greenery. He could not count accurately, but there were over fifty.

He heard Yoshi whisper, 'I think we could take them, even though they're mounted.'

'We can't afford more casualties.'

Yoshi shrugged. 'Anyway, I don't believe they saw us.'

'Can they be so stupidly impatient?'

'They are Oatha's, if that answers your question. I'm sure you recognized the banners and some faces too – including Nagaoka.'

'That charmer!' Man spat on the ground.

'No Hagiwara, nor Aoki, nor anyone very senior, you notice?'

'So if anything goes wrong, all will be deniable!' Man saw it. 'Ah, if Lord Oatha loses interest in theft and murder, he could go to court and take up politics...'

They waited, considering whether to cross the road. Man wanted to; but some instinct made him cautious.

Another party came galloping past. The rearguard was a half-dozen strong.

When they had gone, Man asked the Voice and Joah, 'Did you feel magic, either male or female, in either party?'

Lady Joah answered. 'There are men and women of power

all around, but most are miles away.'

Man considered. 'It's ominous they were so many, isn't it?'

'Of course,' said Ozawa. 'But, Lord Emmanuel, you and the Eye are very much wanted. I think we have to assume many enemies have landed.'

And so far no Sword Maidens to help out!

Man stood up. 'Joah, do the Prophecies say how we should reach The Waning?'

'Prophecies are *not* road-maps, Emmanuel.'

Man eyed her. Where was her fighting spirit now? He pulled a face. 'I think we've lost this road.'

'Yes,' she said. 'It's time for the mountains.'

After going another mile down the road Nagaoka pulled savagely at his horse's bridle. He had learned his cruelty in an excellent school, and he applied it equally to animals and to humans.

'They cannot have come further than us! Lady Berenda promised us they have no horses!'

'They are likely hiding, the cowards!'

'Let's find some more peasants and torture the truth out of them!'

Nagaoka considered, then sent two separate trios of horsemen on ahead to check the road for Man and the Lady Joah and the others. The Lady Berenda had sent him out last night, with burning steel lances to illuminate the way. That had been spectacular, and it was frightening to see metal burning. As soon as the lances burned away he had been forced to make camp by the side of the highway, though he had started again at first light.

Now one of the rankers pointed up.

Nagaoka squinted into the sky. There was something circling, three or four hundred feet up. It had beating wings, but it didn't seem to be flying naturally.

'Is that thing looking us over? What is it?'

'It could be a mechanical bird,' said a young samurai from Jade. 'Cube Castle sends them, and sometimes Steel Angels follow.'

The thing swooped lower – though still out of bow-shot. It crossed over a hundred feet above and then resumed its circling. Nagaoka began to curse under his breath.

Everybody knew Cube Castle's ruler was mad, but no doubt his Steel Angels wanted Emmanuel and the Eye of Jade. What if they got Man first?

Words of Fury:

Nagaoka felt a flush of fear and anger.

If Man and the rest are not on this road, is there some other pathway they might take?

'Bring me the map again!' This map was crude, but it served its purpose. In a moment he looked up from it. 'I think they have taken a short cut through the mountains. I am going to follow them.'

It took a while for Lady Oki to get her father to the family roof terrace. Oatha's guards were everywhere in the castle now, and it had been made clear to both Okadas that any escape attempt, any rescue attempt, would mean death.

When they were finally alone, in one corner overlooking the morning bustle in the port, she explained how her sister and the others had killed the mech-bird.

'Then Joah headed off, and you already know their destination,' she said, meaning The Waning of the Moon.

'I do, Daughter-Dear; so must others.'

'But I have hope.'

Her father raised an eyebrow. 'Even for Emmanuel, whom you so much despised?'

She hesitated, but then spoke her mind.

'If he is against Oatha, and he is, then I am on his side. Not as a true believer – but I *am* on his side.'

Her weary-eyed father did not reply, only watched more Steel Angels fly about Cube Castle. Most were flying away though some were returning to the gigantic coal-black fortress. Three others constantly circled, presumably airborn sentries.

'If that mechanical bird saw enough, then right now Angels will be pursuing your sister and Emmanuel.' Okada's big fists clenched on nothing. Now he had no swords to touch. He was physically very powerful still, but in every other way she knew the greatest man of Jade had been reduced. 'If they know exactly where to go...'

'I hope they don't, and why should they? Man killed their spy!' Oki knew how worried her father was. She tried to make the conversation lighter. She gestured at the armored flyers. 'They flutter like – doves to the cote, don't they?'

She saw a great anger in her father, then, although it was hidden the instant after it showed.

'I see these "Angels" as vicious hornets. They are vile things out of the past, all born from one blood and sworn enemies of progress.'

'What does that mean, "born from one blood"?'

Okada shrugged, irritably. 'I believe "cloning" is the precise word.'

Oki had listened to her sister talk of the Futurists and their secrets; she had a pleasant smug sense that she knew more than her father.

'Why are they so against change?'

'Oh, that depends on which chronicler of times past you believe, if any.' He touched his chin. 'Some say there were once thirty thousand million humans on this Earth, or perhaps on another just round the corner. Thirty billion, poisoning and polluting, dying... The Cube Castles were put in cities to keep humanity as something ... manageable.'

'Do you mean mass murder?'

He glared at her, though she knew she was not the cause of his fury.

'Daughter-Dear, even now Angels strike out against the sciences, and engineering, and knowledge, and the making and transporting of medicines.'

She flourished her fan. 'Like the medicines that might have cured my little brother?'

'Yes, Oki. They sank that ship. And so my only son died.' He turned his gaze away from glossy black Cube Castle to his violet-eyed daughter. 'That, truly, broke your mother's heart.' His mouth showed pain, now. 'Just as the application of the Five Touches' poisons to you and your sister broke mine.'

'Oh, Father-Sir! We cannot give up! Oatha is not immortal; he can die like other men.' She lowered her voice, thinking of what she had been discussing with Aoki. 'And he *will*, perhaps quite soon.'

He took her hand, squeezed it. No doubt he guessed she had been plotting. 'You must be careful!'

She disengaged. 'I always am. And, even now, we have many helpful friends!'

'True, daughter. We do have many friends. But now Oatha has many, many swords.'

She rose, the wonderful child that he loved so much. She was graceful and deadly. 'Then I must seek swords, too.'

He held her hand again and this time refused to let her go. 'Do not imagine it's only you and I at risk! We saw what the Angels showed us, on their castle wallscreen. That was a whole

city burning – maybe *this* city!'
'In wartime.'
'What time do you think *this* is?'

After Oki had gone, Lord Okada stayed up on the roof terrace. From here he looked down upon his city. 'Or what had been his city.

Incredible to remember that great fighting airship from Albion, and how it bombed *my* port. Thank the Infinite that Emmanuel saved us! If I had weapons like that, I would take on the Lord of the North, take on the whole world!

If I had weapons like Albion's, if I wasn't a prisoner here, if I wasn't dying like my daughters from the Five Poison Touches...

Now Okada made himself look upon the purity police headquarters and the execution ground below its walls. Pastor Ruhr, a Christian, and all his family had been burned alive.

Okada knew that his own end would most likely come there, under unbearable torture before the eyes of the world.

He clenched his fists as he looked upon the blackened corpses. He had little hope for his daughter Oki, and less for himself. But he wondered if his daughter Joah and her Emmanuel might somehow escape their enemies and begin the fight-back.

Man and the others were following a trail little better than a footpath now. As they climbed higher it was almost pure rugged rock around them. The soil was in handfuls, though clumps of green grass and bright flowers flourished in a few places.

But they saw nobody, and nobody was chasing them now.

That was just as well, because Man became breathless if he forced the pace too much. Twice he saw Yonai looking at him, and the slim man's face showed concern. Then Ozawa sent him on ahead as a scout.

Yoshi was in the lead alongside Man, but now he stopped and looked back down on the good road they had decided not to take. Man saw his friend's face change, so he too turned to look.

Riders were milling on the road.

Yoshi stared. 'The same black sashes?'

'I think so. – Yes,' said Joah. Then she turned to Man and his friend. 'But they may not know we're here.'

'No, but they'll come looking. We haven't escaped.'

Man said quietly, 'Then let's beat them over the mountain.

Words of Fury:

Even with their horses I think we can!'

Man led off now, forcing the pace. The hot sun was pounding down and heat shimmered over bare rock.

They went further up this split, steep land. There were huge boulders around, and a tangy whiff of volcanic sulfur. A 'hell', they called that here. Near the Jade city Christians had once been sacrificed in one such boiling-place. He remembered visiting the place with the Voice, who had cried.

'Yoshi, you like poetic images. Is this Hell we're heading towards, while being pursued by *his* demons?'

'Why, *this* is Hell – nor am I out of it!'

Man laughed; Yoshi was certainly eloquent. As Man trotted on, he saw there were many birds circling above, but he did not recognize anything mechanical.

Then why do I feel so unsafe?

He saw that the Voice, too, was looking uneasily into the sky.

'The way that one flies... And now it's circling.'

The wings beat very regularly, Man saw.

'Lots of birds circle,' said Yoshi.

Man frowned. He feared the 'bird' up there was a mechanical drone.

A scout came sprinting back, panting so he had to communicate by hand-gestures.

Yoshi let him catch his breath and speak, and then he turned to Man. 'Yonai is staying ahead. No side-trails are suitable, my friend. We have to continue straight on, but the way is clear.'

'We'll be easy to spot and there may be a drone above us!'

Yoshi said heatedly, 'There's no alternative, unless you want to go back. Do you?'

'Of course not.'

'So it has to be this path. The terrain will slow down any mounted force, and we could find places to fight rearguard actions.'

Faslane frowned. 'My lord Yoshi, what if they're already ahead?'

'I don't feel enemies ahead, and I still thank God we have this chance!' said the Voice from Afar.

So they went on.

To their right the mountainside fell away steeply into a rocky gorge. Nobody would come at them that way.

Of course, Steel Angels could fly...

Words of Fury:

Man looked up into the air. Though he could see no enemies, he felt another pulse of magic. This land really was being dueled over.

'Look behind!' the Voice said.

Man did. On the rocky ridge they had crossed over – a mile away and well down – a party of horsemen in black armor was now following their trail.

Yoshi began to curse. 'They're closing!'

'Yes.' Now Man turned to Yoshi. 'They already outnumber us! D'you think they've larger forces close by?'

Yoshi's face was grave.

'You can put your manhood on a chopping-block and bet it on that being the case.'

'And if there's another lot ahead... This path would be very easy to block.'

They had stopped, and for some reason they all felt a strange reluctance to push on.

'Maybe we should have stuck to the good road, Yoshi,' Man said.

'I thought you disliked second-guessers! Me, I *hate* having my decisions second-guessed!' Yoshi looked even grimmer now as he raised his voice. 'Faster, everyone!'

They went scrambling over the rough spots, looking round all the time.

Man knew they could not beat well-handled horses, though. And any kind of a fight involving strong magic would reveal their position.

Man kept looking around, though he tried to smile. These men were veterans, but they were running from pursuers, who were gaining. It was very important to avoid panic – but he could see other heads as well as his turning to see how close their enemies were.

They climbed up through more sulfurous rocks.

Yoshi jumped up onto a higher ledge and looked back. 'They're only minutes away!'

Man said quickly, 'Then we should set up an ambush, Yoshi.'

'That will only delay them!'

The lack of fight surprised Man. 'Yoshi, these passes are narrow. A few heroes could stand off hundreds of men for hours. It would be like Thermopylae!'

'Even a few heroes are more than we can spare.'

That didn't make much sense. Though he continued to run

uphill Man came closer to his friend, so he could speak in private.

'I don't want to take any more losses either, but what else can we do?'

Yoshi's lips tightened, and he gave no answer.

'We have horses, Nagaoka-san, so we are faster!'

Fast enough, though? Nagaoka was not certain. And how long would this path be suitable for horses?

It was already even steeper than before, and stinking like a hot and sulfur-choked Hell. Nagaoka was sweating inside his helmet and armor.

The track became less and less suitable for horse-riding. Finally, Nagaoka had to dismount and lead his horse up the trail. It was frightened by the sheer drop to the right and sometimes its hoofs scrabbled madly. Once it almost slipped off the path, which would have dragged Nagaoka off too.

This was no place for horses, Nagaoka knew that. But now the enemy were so close he could almost smell them. Nagaoka outnumbered them, and he and his men were armored.

Nagaoka pushed on.

The trail entered a great steep-sided gorge, so narrow and deep it was black dark down there.

Man and Yoshi looked over the dizzying plunge to their right, then exchanged glances.

'That would be an excellent barrier!'

'It would indeed, if we were on the other side of it.' Man heard the frothy river far below. 'And the enemy were on this side.'

Yoshi managed a wan smile as he trotted on. They were on the left wall, climbing up in single file, with sheer rugged cliffs on both sides. 'I like this notion better: if only we were all at The Waning, and they were dead!'

'Mother Zandar's is just beyond the mountain – we're not so far.'

'But so are they – not far from us, I mean!'

In this crisis, Man tried to appeal to the Eye and Book yet again, saying words of power under his breath.

As before, there was no reply. He felt as much as saw a strange ripple cross the sky, and felt a moment's chill that made him think of *him*; but there was no time to investigate.

Then he stopped. 'Look! That's a dead end!'

Ahead, their trail was buried under a tumble of rocks. A landslide had swept across the path. To the right was the same impassable deep gulf.

'Why didn't Yonai tell us?' said Man, savage in his frustration.

'They'll catch us within minutes,' Ozawa said. 'Lord Yoshi, may I have the honor of commanding our rearguard?'

In admiration of his bravery, Lady Joah touched Ozawa's shoulder.

Words of Fury:

Chapter Twenty-One: *A Crossing Perilous*

Mother Zandar had her head bowed over the map, her fingers spread there. A few chalk-marks in red showed where they had sent their aid parties, though the positions were no more than best guesses.

Then there was a pulse of the power. It had a dark male taste to it. Zandar raised her head. 'Did you feel that, Daisen?'

'That was surely *him*, focusing somewhere up in the mountains... Has he found Man?'

'The Lord of the North touched *someone* but I don't *think* it was our Emmanuel. I think it was a traitor that he was helping.' Zandar brushed her fingers over the contour lines of the peaks, and the few ragged lines which showed mountain paths. She grimaced. 'For a moment I could see the scene.'

'Where are they?'

'I don't know, exactly. I saw them going through a high pass somewhere in the mountains, just where we *don't* have reinforcements!'

'We could not expect Man and the others to be mountain-climbing, Mother, and we cannot be everywhere.' Daisen sighed. 'If only we could communicate with them!'

'If they get to the east side, Novice Keli might find them.'

'We can't instruct her, or at least give guidance?'

'No, it's almost impossible to mind-speak, with *his* power contending against our own.'

Daisen tried for optimism. 'It might be well for us that *his* own might hides our friends from *him*.'

'I hope you're right. But they are outnumbered and miles away.' Zandar clenched her fists. 'Yes, *he* has found one of his own traveling with Man and Lady Joah! I wish I knew who! Oh, surely I must go out to match myself against *him!*'

'Doing so would be infinitely stupid.'

'You chide me, Sister Daisen!'

'That is my duty, and I do it out of duty – and love.'

'Yes. You do.'

But Zandar felt aggrieved to be so very far from the action. There were Sisters already sent there, and young Keli to open a channel of communication. But because of *him* that might not work, and all the furious pride in Zandar made her want to go out and fight on the front line herself.

Then a breathless novice came scampering in.

'Holy Mother, holy Mother! I have come from the adept room!' Abruptly the girl straightened up and tried to look suitably meek. 'Lady Sulina asks you to come as soon as you may. The enemy is landing.'

Daisen was curt. 'That is already known.'

The novice gave a half curtsey. 'This is new, elder Sister; these landings are on the *east* coast.'

A dead end ahead? Then they were trapped, weren't they? Beside Man, heads turned back unhappily. Looking backwards they couldn't see their pursuers at the moment, but the enemy were certainly close.

Man was determined not to panic. Maybe there would be a way through the boulders, or some other way to escape?

'Surely a well-established path can't end this way! And Yonai the scout hasn't returned to say we are trapped!'

Joah leaned on Man, and said breathlessly, 'We're almost at the crest. If we can only cross here, afterwards it's all downhill, and then The Waning will be in sight!'

She had sounded desperate – and Man looked at her, suddenly wondering what signs of the deadly Five Touches he might discern in her. For Joah was dying. She knew it, and he knew it too.

We are all desperate to be saved, he thought. If only we *can* be...

Yoshi finished conferring with Ozawa. 'Man, please go on with Joah.'

'While you fight to cover our retreat?'

'If we need to, we will,' Ozawa replied.

'We have to cross here, somehow, and you and Lady Joah should go first.'

Man could not disagree. He stepped forward to the unstable mass of boulders. The mess loomed higher to his left and there was the same sheer drop to his right. He began to pick his way through the stones, many of which moved, Joah just behind.

She said only, 'If even a few more stones fall the path will be swept away.'

A hope came to him. 'Can *you* do that by magic, after we have all passed?'

She looked up at the heavens. He stopped now, expectant. But then she shook her head.

He was angered by her lack of zest. 'Now it's always bad

Words of Fury:

news!'

'Man, it will be impossible for the enemy to ride horses over these stones, and very hard and slow to lead them.'

That was true, and when he picked through the last stones he saw something that cheered him. The path became a broad, rough ledge. Two hundred yards ahead was a rope bridge which crossed the deep gulch. Yonai was waiting there for them, on this side of it.

'Look, my Man! This path is hope in itself. We can use it, and the bridge, to go on!'

He helped her down, and then they both ran to the bridge, and Yonai.

The slim man looked nervous, but determined.

'Take it easy as you cross! I know these country bridges. Single file, spread well out, and don't march in step!' He was talking to Joah, wanting her to go first. 'For now we're safe. The enemy isn't in sight yet.'

Yonai beckoned her forward, but Man spoke crossly as he turned to look over his shoulder.

'They may not be in sight, but they're only minutes away!'

It happened in an instant.

When he turned back Man saw a blur, and then Yonai was behind Joah and pulling her onto the bridge. His long knife was held to her throat. Joah was his human shield.

'Now get away, foreigner! *You* will not cross, not if you want Lady Joah to live!'

Man realized that slim, deadly Yonai must be a Son of the Cold. Yonai's eyes were glazed over with fear and something that Man thought could only be some bizarre sort of hope. Perhaps Yonai was fool enough, or desperate enough, to imagine there would be gratitude from his master the Lord of the North.

In spite of the threat Man took a small step closer, wondering if a throwing-knife might possibly do it, or if he should try his magic.

'I'm watching you!' said Yonai the traitor. '*You*, gaijin!'

Man stopped and glared. He was furious but helpless, wondering if he should wait to see what Joah or the Voice might do.

Now Yonai turned his head and raised his voice. 'All of you, back off twenty paces! Especially you, foreign Voice! Back away and don't try anything! Not a gesture of magic, not a syllable of song!'

Words of Fury:

'I see now why you hid your power!' said the Voice from Afar.

'Of course, for you do not like the master I serve!'

Man flexed his fingers, imagining them closing by magic around Yonai's throat; but nothing happened.

'Why are you doing this, Yonai?' asked the Voice. 'I thought you were a good-hearted man! Do you truly want to give us all to *him*?'

Man saw Yonai's face was now glistening with sweat and muscles twitched there. Yonai was not certain this would work.

Yoshi was in a fury. 'Yonai, you are a traitor to mankind! Let the Lady Joah go! We cannot, we must not, be captured!'

Though he looked again for Nagaoka and the other enemies, Yonai's long knife had stayed at Joah's throat.

'I was brought over to *him* long ago. Today, all your souls will follow. And it's best! Don't you know *he* is the Lord of Entropy? If we resist, he can make this whole land freeze over, and us with it!'

'Yonai – ' began Joah.

'Be silent, witch!' said Yonai, and he cut her at the side of the neck.

That painful show of bright blood made Man decide he had to act, but Yonai shouted as if he had read Man's mind.

'Foreigner, don't try anything! I have some power myself, so if I am harmed in any way, even if you make me die, I have spelled my right arm to drive this blade up into her brain!'

The Voice said to Man, 'Please! What he says is true! I can see the weave. It'll be Lady Joah's death!'

Joah said nothing, though her usually proud and warm eyes now looked fearful. Man wondered again what effect Sukomo's poisons were having on her and her fighting spirit. Even a delay getting her to The Waning could be fatal.

'There might still be a good end for you!' Ozawa said. 'Release her, and then you can go and commit an honorable seppuku!'

Yonai made some brutal suggestions to Ozawa; none involved honor.

'The black sashes will be on us within minutes,' said Ozawa now, to Man and Yoshi.

To Man, it was looking like *he* had won.

What did the Prophecies have to say? Was there anything he could use? Man muttered some recalled words to himself, 'gulf'

Words of Fury:

and 'a crossing perilous'. That sounded relevant, but those words were usually read as metaphors. This gulf was real.

He knew he had to help Joah. He wondered if he grabbed a throwing-knife, flung it hard – ah, Yonai was beyond easy range, and knew it!

Perhaps Yonai read Man's mind again, or at least his face, for now he shouted out.

'Foreigner, look what you're making me do!' He cut Joah again, this time under the chin. Blood trickled down onto a garment already bloodstained. 'You see? I have life and death at my command!'

No, Yonai, Man thought, you don't. You only have influence over death...

The traitor was screaming out. 'Back away, all of you, or she dies! Raise a bow to me, and she *will* die!'

Man raised his empty hands and took a first step backwards, then another. There was no way to take this enemy by surprise. Even an arrow-strike that killed Yonai would leave lovely Joah dead!

Sickened, Man realized her life might well end here, on this obscure bridge over an obscure mountain river.

He tried to reach into himself for power, but there was no contact. He flushed, feeling like a stupid boy. He and the others had lost without even fighting.

'Please let her go,' said the Voice to Yonai. 'Even if you have hurt her, I have healing powers!'

'Your power doesn't matter,' Yonai responded, 'for I have the help of *him*. You cannot raise the dead; only *he* can!'

'You are completely wrong!' the Voice said bravely. 'There are miracles, and there is love and mercy for all!'

Yonai spat towards her, and then his lips pulled back from his teeth and he showed the world a terrible, animal snarl.

'Back away, or I start serious cutting!'

Man gestured; all the others did back away, except for Yoshi and the Voice and Man himself.

From behind, Ozawa called out softly, 'I see riders back along the trail.'

Man turned his head. At the top of the landslip he saw a flash of bared steel and a man leading a horse. Another few minutes and the enemy cavalry would be here, and then they'd mount up, and charge, and then...

Then it will all be over, thought Man.

'I think we've lost,' Yoshi said. Then tension suddenly went out of his body and he turned a hopeless face to Man. 'Ah, freeze the world! It's over!'

Man had heard something he recognized only too well: despair.

Then he saw Ugaki come marching towards them.

Another traitor! Ugaki? Yes, Man thought, it could easily be him...

But Ugaki bared his teeth at Yonai, and if looks really could kill Yonai would die in agony.

'Stand away, you ugly bear! Or I will strike her down, and then you!'

But Ugaki came on anyway and somehow Man couldn't move to stop him.

Lady Berenda rode on quickly, the mounted force just behind her and the troops on foot following them as best they could. They were closing in on Nagaoka, and she knew he was closing in on the Eye.

'That must make us three hundred strong now, and we also have you and your ruby!' Hagiwara told her. 'Nagaoka will probably be enough, but, if not, soon as we get to the foreign bastard ourselves we'll teach your Man a final lesson, eh!'

She hoped and intended to teach Man several lessons, and all the time she held the ruby gem in her right hand.

She had already seen an easy way to help goodness. What if she held Nagaoka back now and let Man escape? Afterwards she could shadow Man's party and secretly help him till he was safe in The Waning of the Moon.

In that way she could *prove* that she had changed. Man's party was not far ahead. If there was combat, she could be a secret heroine.

Saving Man and the Lady Joah meant there would be sanctuary for Berenda herself among the women of The Waning. Berenda knew her power would put her among the highest there, and all manner of good things might then happen.

In her mind she saw a future when she joined with Man. They shared the Eye, rescued Jade, then saved Rumoi – and that meant they saved all the Land of the Gods from *him*.

Berenda rode on, very satisfied.

Nagaoka heaved his horse up by the bridle. It raised a hoof,

Words of Fury: 221

angry and reluctant. He was panting, and these big stones were very hard to walk upon, especially for the horses. A couple had already been lost to broken legs. But now he made it past the landslip. Up ahead, Nagaoka saw the enemy. They had bunched up, mostly looking back at him. Beyond, the Foreigner and others were standing off from a plank bridge. This was held – most strangely – by one man holding a girl in bloodied garments.

Nagaoka realized an ally was holding the narrow footbridge, and given the numbers he had with him it was already too late for all the enemy to cross over.

'We have them!' he exulted. He was pleased now that he hadn't sent any more messengers, because this was his chance. How the Lady Berenda and Hagiwara would reward him! 'They'll have to surrender!'

Man heard an enemy arrow hiss by his head, and then a shouted countermand about taking 'them' alive. He saw a few of his own side grab their bows, but all the different threats had affected them and they moved uncertainly. The enemy were arriving one at a time, but soon they would form up and attack.

Ugaki had stopped. Now Man looked hard at Yonai. He kept his voice calm. 'What do you think you can achieve?'

'Your capture, foreigner!' Yonai laughed, though his voice sounded half-mad. 'I have to hand you over to *him*, though I do not hate you.'

'Then show mercy!' the Voice called out. 'For we must love one another or die!'

'Yap away, port girl,' Yonai sneered. His expression was as ugly as his soul. 'Mouth your Christian nonsense! A little delay will be enough to seize you all, and when *he* is grateful *I* will be rewarded!'

'Yes, you will be rewarded, Yonai.' Yoshi spat. 'Your name will spell out vileness till the end of time!'

'Time ends when my master decides; and not before!'

Man looked over his shoulder. Twenty or thirty enemy were already here on the ledge, with their horses. It wouldn't be long till they all mounted up and charged.

If he only had his power, he could push the landslide a little further, and sweep away those enemies and the narrow path itself.

Lady Joah's eyes met his; he saw she had understood and

Words of Fury:

approved of his plan. Man took deep breaths, and tried to reach out for the all-powerful Eye...

Nothing.

'We only have a few minutes!' said the Voice, who had also understood.

'I'm trying!'

And he was; then Man suddenly felt a connection with *him*, and something terrible happened. He didn't understand it but he knew something within him had changed for the worst. Suddenly he *felt* Yoshi in him – and he felt a raw fury strong enough to scour life from the world.

Yoshi began to move, eyes flat with rage.

Man didn't recall seeing anything like that on his friend's face before. Now Yoshi looked terrifying, with a rage to equal the Lord of the North's own. He took a step forward.

Yonai stared back at the young Emperor's Man, with something not quite human looking out of his eyes. Then, with Yoshi still glaring at him, Yonai looked deep into Man's own eyes. Man felt his own mind somehow link to his best friend's, though he still stared at Yonai, who was in the link too.

The three-way connection was made.

Now Yoshi was within Man and acting through him, as Man realized when he found himself puppet-mastered into making magical gestures.

Man made a spell and it worked at once. In response to it, Yonai's weapons flew away from him and there was a ripping sound as his clothes were torn off. He was naked now, mouth a big 'o' of surprise. Man saw he was still clutching a shocked Lady Joah, and his knife.

To save her, Man began to run.

Suddenly Joah and Yonai were parted. There was a popping noise that was almost drowned out by Yonai's screaming.

Man stopped, shocked. Yonai had been turned into two men.

There was naked Yonai, skinned alive and dripping blood. The other Yonai was his ripped-off human skin.

'You are two-faced, Yoshi!' screamed Yonai.

'Well so are you, you bag of skin!' said Yoshi.

'There's another of us, Emperor's Man, so you still lose!'

The two Yonais raised their arms, mirror images of one another. As the bleeding remains of Yonai continued to scream, his lidless eyes bulging with agony, the man made of baggy skin and the bloody-bodied human danced arm-in-arm, madly whirling.

Man saw the horror, and wondered if he was going to be sick.

Then Yoshi came stamping forward. He took Yonai by the neck and took the animated skin into his other hand. He shook both, savagely – and then flung them into the gorge.

The bloody skin flapped down, but skinless Yonai quickly tumbled those hundreds of feet, bouncing from rock-face to rock-face into the final darkness. He screamed and screamed and screamed.

Man watched Yoshi watch the dying man fall.

What had just happened? And was there really another traitor? Man had thought it might be Ugaki but now...

Yoshi turned, his expression harsh. Before Man could say or do anything, he gave a command.

'Archers! You give us covering fire! The rest of you, over the bridge, fast!'

He waved again and was obeyed.

Man looked back up the trail. Two hundred paces away, above the rockslide, he saw the held-high banners of the oncoming force. Those already on the flat ledge had formed up for a charge.

Maybe skilled archers fighting from cover could hold them off till everyone had crossed over, but Man doubted it. Anyway, the enemy would cross, too, and they had the numbers...

'Archers!' boomed Ugaki. 'Shoot!'

Man had his own longbow out. He could fire arrows further than most, so he had decided that he would cover those going over the bridge. He shot at the horsemen two hundred paces away, as did Ugaki.

'Five down!' said Ozawa, as the black sashes tried to duck out of sight close to the cliff-face.

Man nocked another arrow.

'I wish it was fifty of the bastards down! Now, please, Ozawa-san, get everyone across!'

As the Voice comforted Lady Joah, the others hurried over the rope-hung planks that crossed the big drop. But they could only go one at a time. Then Faslane more or less dragged the Voice away, too. They all knew she was not made for the bloody work.

When everyone else had crossed Man too backed away over

Words of Fury:

the bridge to the other side. The plank bridge swayed and a few times he almost fell. He glimpsed the floor of the gulley hundreds of feet down, where the stream tumbled madly in deep shadow. There was no sign of Yonai. Man wondered how many more traitors there might be among his friends. Then he thought of how the Lord of the North had touched him; and for one bitter moment he wondered if he himself might be the new betrayer Yonai had mentioned.

Archers gave covering fire to help Man cross, and from behind he heard horses and enemy men scream from hits.

Once Man was on the other side he, Joah and Yoshi stood in the scant shelter of a tree-grown boulder. He gestured into the gulf.

'If it wasn't for the bridge, we'd be safe. That gap would keep off an army – unless they can fly!'

Lady Joah calmly fanned herself, as the Voice from Afar worked to remove all trace of the bloody cuts on her. 'My Man, the bridge *is* here.'

She was truly law-abiding, wasn't she? Man smiled; for *he* was *his* father's son!

'Then we must bring it down.'

'Emmanuel! This must be part of a lost Imperial way!'

So what? – Though he didn't say that aloud.

'Bring it down, and we'll delay the pursuit for hours, especially if they stay with their horses.'

Yoshi tugged at the rope supports of the bridge and then produced his short sword and started to saw through. He stopped, looking up in disgust. 'Entwined steel is the core – and magic!'

'Enemy advancing to the bridge!' someone called. 'They're going to cross!'

Man clenched his big fists. 'If I could have moved that landslide even a little...!'

'You couldn't, or you didn't, so let's fight it out here!' said Yoshi.

The first half-dozen enemies jumped off their horses and made for the bridge, shields raised.

'I have a notion,' Man said, remembering how Joah had put a great deal of heat into a kettle to boil water. 'Lady Joah!'

Joah stepped away from the Voice, still bloodstained though healed. She eyed Man. Though she was disheveled and grimy, she looked so noble and brave that Man felt a renewed surge of feeling for her. Then he took her right to the end of the bridge, seeing the enemy beginning to charge across it.

Two Heads passed them. Under him, the bridge supports creaked. He was head and shoulders taller than most men, and his weight matched. He stood up with his long axe raised high. Unsurprisingly, that stopped the other side advancing – for now.

Man knelt to check with his fingertips the two thick ropes that supported the swaying plank floor. Two thinner ropes, at waist height, were only guide-ropes.

'Joah, the bridge floor is wood, but the ropes are wound around metal chains. If you can do your fire-making trick...'

'My "trick",' Joah said, sourly. 'You want magic hot enough to melt metal, and you call it a "trick"!'

'He means no disrespect for the female Art,' Yoshi said smoothly. He kicked Man on a shin. 'Do you?'

'Of course not!' Man rubbed his shin and hoped his grimace could pass for a smile. One enemy arrow brushed past his shoulder. 'Joah, they'll take the bridge by sheer force of numbers.'

At that, Joah kneeled. She put her hands around one thick rope. She didn't look very confident as she murmured something Man did not catch. Another arrow went past his face, but it seemed unimportant now and his own side was firing back.

Enemies had got half way over the footbridge.

Man saw the rope between Lady Joah's hands was smoldering. Would that be enough? There was steel twined within.

He looked up, to see the first enemy arrive, his shield raised. Two Heads struck out and smashed the shield. This first man reeled backwards off the rope-and-plank bridge.

It didn't matter. Man knew they were so many they were certain to get across.

When Man looked down again he saw molten metal dripped from between Lady Joah's hands. The first chain parted, the surrounding rope on fire, and when she made a spread-fingered gesture this fire spread to the wooden flooring. She did the same to the other floor rope, and when that chain melted too she touched the two side ropes and made them flare with fire for a dozen feet or more.

A full column of the enemy came charging. Man went behind Two Heads and braced himself, long sword and short sword both out. Joah stood back alongside the Voice.

Words of Fury:

The ropes were burning, now. Then suddenly all this end of the bridge was on fire.

'Come back!' Man said to Two Heads, and the big man began backing off the bridge.

Man pulled Two Heads from the burning planks. Fire made pleasing orange trails along the footway – a flaring acid eating away rope and wood. Smoke, all grey, swirled up. Man felt a sudden wash of heat.

The black sashes stopped, seven or eight of them on the bridge. They saw what was coming, but on the narrow footbridge it was impossible to turn quickly.

Then this end of the bridge came away. Man saw all the long length of it tumble into the deep gulley. The enemies went with it.

In relief, he started to laugh.

'If they keep using horses that will delay them by hours,' Yoshi said sternly. 'And if they leave their horses behind, they still lose time – and their big advantage.'

Man looked up at the rugged peaks. Mount Unzen was beside Mount Kunamini. The mountains were a considerable barrier.

'Now we'll have a breathing space.'

'We will indeed.' Yoshi made rallying gestures to the column. 'Archers, stay for five minutes and keep firing! The rest of you, come! For the moment we've outpaced our enemies, and once we get over the mountains there'll be friends waiting!'

Men cheered.

Chapter Twenty-Two: *Ominous Truth*

Nagaoka saw the Foreigner's men vanish into the pass on the other side. They would soon be over the mountains, and then it would be an easy path for them to The Waning of the Moon.

The bridge continued to burn.

What will Hagiwara-san say when I tell him of this escape? Or Oatha? And what of the Lady Berenda? Ah, if it wasn't for the burned bridge, Nagaoka thought in a fury, we *would* have had our enemies...

He turned.

'You! Messenger! Back to Master Hagiwara and the Lady Berenda! Tell them – tell them how I tried, but – but – the other side ran!' Now he cupped his hands round his mouth and bellowed to the others. 'The rest of you listen! There must be another trail over the mountains and we will find it and then catch our enemies again! So follow me – for your lives!'

'A bridge brought down, not a man of ours lost, and a few obscene gestures given as we leave!'

Man heard the familiar accent. He turned his head to see Faslane rubbing his palms on his kilt and enjoying a gloat. They were all going in single file along the rough trail now, with the bridge out of sight.

'Aye, milord Emmanuel, this magic of yours has its uses.'

Man saw the Voice hold Faslane's big hand for a moment. Man was surprised to feel a certain jealousy. After all, the Voice's prime relationship was to her musical art; and though she was very, very attractive she had always made it clear she was a free spirit.

Nevertheless, he had always loved her loving nature, and he did not take kindly to losing her attention to another man.

Jealousy is a sin, he told himself in annoyance, and also a barren, useless feeling ... which is, sadly, very strong.

They were all enjoying some optimism now, though. Although it was a hot day, this narrow steep gulf was shady, and soon their trail would take them out of the mountains. Then, Man knew, they would be safely on the eastern side, and much closer to The Waning.

Yoshi led them. His face showed cheery confidence, though he set a very brisk pace.

Without moving his lips, because he did not want to be

overheard nor have his lips read, Man murmured to Joah.

'Remember, Yonai said there was another traitor with us.'

'He could have been lying.'

Man replayed the memories. 'I think not.'

'With that much pain and shock, I suppose you're right.' She sighed as she jogged on. 'Treachery. And when it must be one of us, when it already has been one of us…!'

'Joah, we must find that traitor. He, or she, could betray us any time.'

She grimaced. 'Yonai almost named him!'

'Almost, he did,' Man said. Then he added, with significance, 'But Yoshi – who he called "two-faced" – silenced him.'

'You suspect your own best friend?'

'Well, there is one alternative; but that's too terrible to think about.'

Man saw the touch of pink that came to her face as he thought of the obvious culprit.

Who called on the Lord of the North, earlier? Who let the Cold Lord touch his heart?

With a sensation part sinking and part freezing, Man answered his own questions.

I did…

This path twisted round another shoulder of bare mountain. Suddenly there was a narrow but clear view east, where the trail ahead was finally heading down. There, a flat luminous blue gleamed.

'Look!' Man said. 'The sea! The sea!'

Yoshi produced his map again, and huddled with Ozawa, Man and Lady Joah. They traced their tiny footpath into larger roadways and discussed possible routes to The Waning of the Moon.

Man said finally, 'It looks like a choice between going straight down to the sea and taking the easy coast road, or sticking to some obscure high trail for a while. What do you think, Ozawa-san?'

Ozawa stroked his chin and for one terrible instant Man saw him as a traitor, figuring out how to lead them all into some trap.

'We think there are no enemies on the other side of the mountains, but it's best to stay cautious.'

'If the enemy can't find us, he can't attack,' Man agreed.

So they turned right, staying high. It was a slower smaller

Words of Fury:

path, though clearly more secret. This rough rarely-used track took them up the high flank of a mountain. Below, to their left, there were forests, their jungle-green already turning to yellow. Summer was almost over. When Man looked further away down the sloping earth he saw thickets of bamboo, tea plantations and, where there was plentiful water, rice paddy fields.

Then they reached the high point of the ridge. Looking south from there Man saw a sight to awe and silence, and it did – except for Yoshi, who was never without words.

'That is a miracle, written by magic in stone!'

It was The Waning of the Moon they all saw. Above it, Man saw a scimitar of stone, which stabbed the sky.

'You see why this place has its name?' Joah asked.

Now Man saw what the giant curve represented.

'I do, Lady. That sweep of stone is a waned Moon!'

This giant arc was like twin horns, which towered several hundred feet above the fortress's odd, irregular tower-tops. Below the towers, Man glimpsed the top of high ring-walls. The walls were said to be tall enough to defy a vast army – which was just as well.

As they went on without even a glimpse of opposition, Man almost relaxed.

'I suppose we will soon encounter friends, do you think? These Sword Maidens of Mother Zandar must be close.'

'They're probably west, down towards the coast, defending it,' Yoshi said. 'In the meantime, I could eat a horse.' He looked directly at Man. 'Actually, I could eat you. Without seasoning.'

Man hoped it was a joke. He smiled politely, though he was still angry with his friend and full of doubts.

'Man? To be serious, now ... Yonai.'

'Your hatred turned my magic against that man – without my consent!'

Man realized that this sounded accusing. Did he really so mistrust his friend? And if he did mistrust, did he want Yoshi to know?

Yoshi flushed.

'What else could I do? I know he might have given us another traitor's name, but – oh, look, I know I lost control!'

Man had never seen his friend's self-control crack before. Nevertheless, he made himself do as his father would have done, and put a possible enemy at ease.

'It was well done, Yoshi. You freed Joah and put down a

mad dog.'

Yoshi gave a grimace that might have passed for a smile. 'There's an enemy close to us, though.'

Man tried to divert the conversation; he didn't want Yoshi to know that he was suspect. 'How can that be? We are all friends –'

'I do not trust your man Faslane and never have,' Yoshi said at once. He glared at the sea-pilot, who did not notice because his back was turned.

Man didn't exactly rush to Faslane's defense. 'You have no particular reason to think he might betray us, do you?'

'If I did, he would be dead.'

They followed the path towards The Waning.

'I don't know if I believe Yonai,' Man said slowly, weighing it up. 'What if it was just a fiction from the Father of Lies, meant to stir us up against each other?'

'What if it was the truth?'

'I've still got faith in all of us. Don't you?'

'I am an Emperor's Man, Emmanuel, suspicious of everyone.'

'Long ago you were suspicious of me.'

'But not now!'

'Men like Ozawa – it's unthinkable it could be one of them! For they fought with us, bravely!'

'For a while, so did Yonai.'

There was no answer to that.

The desperate scout came galloping up to Berenda and flung himself out of the saddle.

'Lady, Master Hagiwara, we were so close!'

He looked up in appeal, but Hagiwara was furious.

'You mean that you *lost*?'

'No, no, master! I mean they went over the mountains and we could not follow!'

Hagiwara whirled out his sword. They had three hundred men now, to see this lesson. 'You let the Foreigner escape! You know the penalty!'

'Lord, they cut down the bridge! Master Nagaoka tried his best, and now he's going round the mountains to cross over further south!'

Nagaoka was obviously running away from meeting her, and that was sensible, for him. Nevertheless Berenda raised a hand

Words of Fury:

to stop this beheading, sparing a moment to glare at Hagiwara.

'Nagaoka's men are all mounted. What about the other side?'

'All on foot. We can intercept them before the Waning!'

Hagiwara rubbed his stubbly chin. 'You'd better hope so.'

Berenda leaned forward. 'Where is this bridge?'

The scout pointed east, up into the mountains. 'Along the footpath up there!'

Berenda was secretly pleased by all this delay. 'How much damage did they do?'

'The bridge is rope and plank – you know the kind. It was burnt by witchery from the far end, before it collapsed into the gulch.'

'Does some of it survive?'

He blinked. 'Yes, almost all, but surely it can't be restored?'

She said simply, 'Let's ride on and see.'

I will find my way to the remains of that bridge, and try my magic, and fail with it, and then I will wail in public helplessness that Emmanuel and the others have escaped us and our master. Oh, I will wail, and do nothing to help *him*!

And then, soon, I will receive Emmanuel's gratitude; yes, and the gratitude of all those at The Waning, too!

Now I *hate* the Lord of the North, for all the evil he has done, and for what *he* has done to *me*!

That hatred generated a comforting energy in her.

They cantered along the rough, irregular footpath that Emmanuel and the others had followed previously.

Now Man saw the road ahead passed over a wooden walkway that crossed a broad shallow river, and then led to a village. Smoke rose from smith-work and cooking. The village had perhaps two dozen houses. Two inns were perched on stilts in the fast-flowing shallow water. Ramped footbridges connected both to the shore. Fishing-nets stretched between the stilt houses, where women were thigh deep in the water.

Yoshi sent his men to stop traffic on the road and go into the village, giving orders to set up a security cordon and search all the houses.

Ozawa said only, 'I suggest we do not linger.'

'We will not,' Yoshi promised.

Man looked over his friends, seeing the strain in everyone. The Voice also looked distressed. 'The air is thick with *his* power, and he always was stronger than all of us put together.'

That truth was ominous, even though Man still had the Eye of Jade slung upon his back.

Man said what he'd been thinking for some while. 'It really bothers me that we're on Mother Zandar's territory, and there's not been a single Sword Maiden patrol.'

Faslane got it immediately. 'You mean there may be no help!'

Man clenched his fists, and watched as Yoshi's well-trained samurai spread out through the village. For the villagers that was frightening enough, but there was more to make the locals wide-eyed and set girls to screaming: four pale-skinned gaijin, rarely seen outside of Jade and surely never in a backwater like this, and one of them was an axe-wielding giant with two heads.

Man looked around. 'A commotion in the neighborhood, friend Yoshi.'

'It'll do them good,' Yoshi replied brusquely. 'Broaden their minds.'

In the wait, the Voice nodded at two children, who had been pushing palms against each other and chanting in musical lisps till the strangers interrupted their game.

'Emmanuel, what was that?'

'A folk-chant, of sorts,' Man said idly, hands on his sword hilts and his eyes watching everything. 'I suppose you could call it country music. "Sa - Shi - Su - Se - So!" is a children's speaking game, about food and its seasoning.'

'I liked the rhythm of it,' said the Voice, tapping a forefinger on one palm to aid her memory. 'What does it mean?'

'In the old language from before trade speech, sato is sugar; sa. Shio is salt, su is vinegar. Se, shoyu, is soy sauce. You'll likely know that so, miso, is soya bean paste.'

'Yes! Food again!'

He smiled at her. 'You're hungry too?'

'As if you didn't know!'

Faslane had squatted down to talk to the frightened children, pulling faces to amuse them till one laughed and then the others did too.

Yoshi frowned at this fraternization but said nothing.

In five minutes the first reports came back. This was indeed Waning territory, though no Sword Maidens had been here for a week. There was unsettling news about black sashes landing, though it was all very vague.

Words of Fury:

'So what's the plan?'

'We're exhausted, and we should stay and eat,' Joah told them.

'Very well.' Yoshi pointed. 'We will send two scouts down that road to the coast, and two up the other. Whatever road is free of enemies will suit us.'

'Lord Yoshi, what if neither road is free?'

Yoshi answered Faslane with a scowl. Then he sent the first two scouts running down towards the coast road, and two more by this high inland track. He had told them all to be back within the hour. Yoshi said no more, but his intent, his hope, were both clear. If they found an open road they would soon be at The Waning. If not, they would be in a world of trouble.

Ozawa said to the women, 'We have told the scouts to run separately. If the man ahead is killed or captured, the one behind will return to tell us.'

'And if none of the four return?' Joah asked.

Yoshi gave a crooked grin. 'Then we will make peace with our gods and our ancestors, for we will know we are surrounded.'

Joah looked stern. 'To die bravely is not enough! Man! Ozawa-san! And you, Yoshi! We *must* get to The Waning of the Moon!'

The men stayed silent. In this society women did not normally insist – about anything.

But Joah said even more, now. 'When I say "we" I mean the Lord Emmanuel, the Eye, and perhaps myself. Nothing else can matter.'

Yoshi's reply was surprisingly gentle.

'We understand.'

They went quickly into the village to pick up food and horses. At the inn Yoshi chose, a shoji screen was slid aside; maids bowed them into the premises, the inn-keeper and his wife beaming nervously.

'You know our other guests, sir?'

'Other guests?' Yoshi demanded, half-drawing his sword. Window-screens of oiled silk painted with exquisite flowers let in light. 'Who are they?'

At the far end of the room three rough-looking samurai were kneeling at a low banquet table.

They stood up instantly, hands going to their swords.

Waning of the Moon men? Or Oatha's mercenaries?

Yoshi took a pace forward, sword swinging into his hands the instant after the men drew their weapons.

Man had Words of Power out, ready for the killing to start.

A black sash came out to Lord Okada and spoke without any deference: 'You asked for Irian Dall the gaijin merchant. He is here.'

Now Lord Okada of the Jade was a prisoner on the family level of the castle, with hardly a servant to serve him and no loyal samurai. Therefore he had to make a great effort to save face and look confident – for Oki's benefit as well as his own.

So Okada smiled, like a man at his ease.

'Dall-san is here,' Okada said formally, 'with the Lord Oatha's permission?'

'Of course, sir,' the guard said, actually looking shocked. 'That was the agreement with your protocol office.'

The protocol people were all new and they were not Okada's subordinates; they were his jailers. They followed Oatha's orders.

As for Dall, Okada had long had tentative reports linking the merchant to the underground Futurist network. He hoped to reach out to them through Dall.

It's a hundred-to-one long shot, but I have to try, don't I?

'Allow Dall-san to join me!' Dall might even be the key to escape. As for this black sash, he'd seen the man before, and sometimes the fellow looked regretful. Okada was in desperate search of allies, so he added: 'From here it's a fine view; he'll enjoy it. Please, look yourself!'

'Thank you, Lord.' Oatha's man bowed, though he looked taken aback by the pleasantry. He was small and round-shouldered, hardly warrior material. That might make him more amenable, of course. Okada saw him glance quickly west and east, then he bowed humbly again, with less of the arrogance the all-conquering black sashes usually showed.

'There! Now, what's your name?'

'It's Saikaku, Lord.'

'Perhaps you and I can talk later.' Okada wondered about bribing this man, directly or indirectly. 'Do you have a family?'

'My wife died young, lord.'

'Then I am sorry for your loss. Now bring the merchant here, Saikaku-san, and if you listen, as you must, think well of me.'

The black sash had looked suitably pleased by Okada's interest in him.

Inwardly, Okada seethed at all this indignity, but there was nothing he could do right now. So he undertook what he so often counseled – patience. Dall was immensely rich, and a very prominent man among the foreigners; he was liberal-minded; he might even become an ally...

You're a stupid optimist, now! Okada told himself contemptuously. You clutch at mere straws and hope to build something strong out of them!

The four black sashes at the far end of the balcony regarded him coldly. He knew they, or at least Saikaku, would remain in earshot for all of the conversation. He wondered again if he could do anything with Saikaku.

But this was the most important thing: if Okada said anything treasonous towards Oatha and his black sashes he knew he would be held with no visitors at all, if not put back into a cell or quietly executed.

Nevertheless, I have to try. This city is tilting further and further away from honor. With the black sashes in charge we are half way to disaster.

If the Lord of the North struck now, he'd win...

Okada sighed. What if his own city, Jade, was surrendered to the Lord of the North? What if Ezo was lost to *his* forces, and The Waning of the Moon also went down?

He already knew the answer to all those questions.

It would be the beginning of the end for everything...

Saikaku stood to one side, very politely, as the swarthy, tall merchant bowed low.

Okada raised his right hand in a kind of loose blessing. Dall had trade links to the Banda Islands and monopolized the imports of mace and nutmeg to Jade. He was incredibly wealthy, and that wealth could be put to political use.

Irian Dall said politely, 'Forgive me for saying it, sir, but you do not look well.'

Okada eyed Dall. It was the Five Touches, no doubt. They were delayed-action poisons Oatha had used on Lord Okada. There was also drawn-out stress of his current position.

But leadership is mainly a confidence game, so Okada had to make light of it. 'Oh, there is always strain.'

The big man nodded. Okada saw that, like himself, Dall was

very conscious of the possibility of eavesdropping.

They sat at a low table and there was tea, brought by castle servants, then an exchange of presents. Dall's was a packet of dark powder for an expensive hot drink called caffe, which Okada sent to his daughter along with the instructions for preparing it.

As he and Dall talked about spices and hot drinks the listening black sashes seemed to slowly lose interest, even the man Saikaku. Okada hoped his enemies really weren't focusing on this conversation, for he planned to talk rebellion – if he could do so with any safety.

Now, thought Okada, how do I communicate with this man without using spoken words? If he is what I think he is, we might be able to do that. If he is no more than he seems, there will be no real communication.

Patience, he thought again. I must have patience, and faith...

From under the table Okada produced a cardboard tube, and extracted rolled-up plans. With his strong but artist-sensitive hands Okada laid out the neat inked diagrams on the table, and then explained them to the merchant.

Here was a new, even larger Jade, clean and modern. Here, a public water-garden. Here, a new free hospital. Here, an international college, where different forms of knowledge from the whole wide world would freely compete.

'You have a vision, sir,' Dall said politely. 'It is impressive.'

Okada leaned forward and turned on the power of his personality.

'I do have a vision, a vision of change, and it is impressive!'

Then they got down to business.

'I called you here to make quite sure you know about the greatness, generosity, and open-minded kindness of Lord Oatha,' said Okada, loudly.

Dall eyed him. Okada wondered if he had gone too far in the crudity of his praise. But when Dall spoke Okada was sure he detected irony.

'I am aware of the truth of all that you mention. So is the rest of the foreign community.'

'Excellent,' said Okada heartily, putting his hands together. 'If we are all to have a civilized future, we must work together.'

At the use of the word 'future' Okada made what his own staff had identified as a Futurist recognition sign, touching his two thumbs together and then when he said 'together' his two first fingers.

The Futurists believed in freedom and change. Did Dall recognize their hand-signs? If he did and he admitted it, he would be admitting he was a Futurist, and that was very dangerous.

Dall eyed Okada without expression.

Okada said artlessly, making the sign again at intervals to emphasize certain words, 'Of course, I am not a prisoner here, no matter what some say. I am a guest of Lord Oatha's, resting from the cares of the world.'

Dall said only, 'You are happy?'

'Of course I am. I would never say "no" to wise Lord Oatha, and never seek to escape his noble presence.'

The conversation, with hand-signs, had been this:

'I am a prisoner here. I would say "no" to Oatha, and escape.'

Dall studied the man who had once been all-powerful here. Then he acknowledged Okada with a Futurist hand-sign.

Okada held back an overwhelming excitement, keeping his expression careless and pleasant. He had been right about Dall. Now he had this rich and powerful man here, and he *would* make an ally out of the Futurist. Then many things would be possible – perhaps escape, perhaps an uprising!

It went quickly now.

Dall used the hand-sign to talk in code. 'If I could help you and your daughter escape, I would.'

'Then see what you can do,' Oatha said briskly. 'There are many possible allies! My loyal officers. Foreigners, the foreign religions especially. In fact, all those who hate Oatha – and they are many.'

Dall nodded, though he did not look too hopeful.

'When Pastor Ruhr spoke against him, he was burned along with his family.'

'That horror will sow hate as well as fear; Oatha will make himself even more hated than before, and perhaps the harvest will surprise him.' Okada spoke more, using signs. 'Still, I want you to get our outland community prepared.'

'Prepared for what, sir?'

'Oatha is...' Okada tried to find appropriate words; strong words, but not so strong they caused panic. 'Oatha is no friend of the stranger-outsider, as you know.'

'Unlike you, sir.'

Words of Fury: 238

'Entirely unlike me; I have befriended the world!'

'Your adopted son...'

'Emmanuel is from the Empire of Blood, but he is fine young man.'

'There are many empires, aren't there?'

'There are, in this world and the next worlds.'

'I know, sir.'

Okada wondered if this man had really visited the legendary Hidden Continent. Irian Dall always denied it; but the story did not die... Okada looked at the merchant leader, still reluctant to talk of blood – but then he remembered he was dying, and his daughter was also dying.

There were few threats you could make to the dying.

'Master Dall, as Oatha's position grows stronger, he will strike out against you strangers.'

Dall got it immediately, though he kept smiling.

Okada went to the parapet, gesturing for Dall to accompany him. He looked down then on the execution ground. There were charred bodies chained there. Ruhr the pastor, his wife, their daughters.

'I know Oatha's plans. That family was only the first.'

'But what can we do? We cannot evacuate twenty thousand people! And surely we cannot fight!'

'You may have to.'

'Are you talking – ?'

'Mass arrests and then mass murder.'

That shocked even the imperturbable Irian Dall. Dall's eyes asked, Are you sure?

Okada gave a barely perceptible nod. 'Remember, Emperor and Shogun are not friendly towards Oatha; he has many enemies.'

'That's so, but now he has many swords here.'

'True, and they are cruel swords – though many are mere mercenaries. So if it comes to it, fight, and if you lose, save whoever you can.'

Dall indicated that was a great deal to consider, and at present he could make no commitments.

It was a victory for Okada that Dall was even considering action, though. So a smiling Okada turned their talk to the end-of-season vagaries of the weather, although it was war he was really talking about.

'I will make sure you outlanders are not alone, but I am a

captive. If I was free...'

Again, Dall understood at once. 'If you were free, you could lead a rebellion...'

'I could, and I *would*.'

Okada wondered if Dall would pass that on to the black sashes. If so, Okada knew he had just signed his own death-warrant. Surely not, though! For Dall was a foreigner and a rebellious Futurist.

Lord Okada rose, hands automatically reaching for the sword-hilts that were no longer there. 'I will not detain you.'

Now the far-travelled merchant went onto his knees, took Okada's hand, kissed his jade ring, and murmured quietly in case of eavesdroppers.

'In your city we remember freedom and change, lord. If it comes to it, we will not die quietly, and if we can, we *will* help you – and your daughter.'

Okada smiled grimly.

'I ask no more.'

For another moment Dall stayed on his knees. Then he rose, gave the thumbs and first fingers Futurist sign, and backed away respectfully.

Okada watched him go. It was odd to receive men like this not in state and not with councilors, but as one plain man to another. Odd how good it felt, to be a plain man, talking truth to others.

Next, Okada called for his daughter Oki. It was time to cheer her with good news, but also to warn her.

They stood together, resting their elbows on the balcony with their backs to the guards. Okada saw Oki's face was tired under the make-up. He had to master his own anger at that, so he looked over the city. There was a Buddhist festival on the street, though the chanters stayed well away from Oatha's re-occupied purity prison and the charred corpses outside.

He kept his voice low and tried his hardest to sound positive. 'I met Dall, the merchant. I'm hoping he can help us.'

'He's rich enough – and I've even heard that he's a Futurist.'

'I heard the same. But then I have also heard Joah is a Futurist too.'

'Talk! – Can Dall really do much, Father-Dear?'

'He can; so can others in the foreign community.'

'They would all follow you!'

'Yes, perhaps, but now I'm a prisoner. And so if they do

rebel, it's better I have no advance details.'

Oki's lips were pursed and she was not happy, but Okada thought she took the point.

Then Oki looked over her shoulder, and beckoned.

Jimmoko, her shy young maid, came over with a tray on which was a steaming silver vessel and porcelain cups. Oki waved her away, and poured herself.

'Father? This is the gift from Irian Dall.'

Jimmoko looked anxiously at Lady Oki and Lord Okada, though the Lord of Jade was smiling at his daughter and her domesticity.

'The drink called "caffe"? – Let's try it.'

'It's made from beans harvested around a volcano in Java. Do you know that some of the young people in the port and the Floating World have started going to what they call "caffe houses"?' Oki sniffed the steaming cup dubiously. 'I had it brewed following the recipe Dall-san left. But it's nothing like our cha.'

'It wouldn't be, Daughter-Dear; it's exotic caffe.'

Oki sipped, then pulled a face. Immediately her maid looked devastated.

'Oh, Father, it's so dark and bitter!'

'Like life?' Now Okada sipped dark brew from his own cup. He rolled it around his tongue, and then nodded. 'An acquired taste, but it has a powerful bite: and the bitterness is earthy and refreshing.'

'I understand in some caffe houses they take honey or even milk with it. I don't have my sister's love of things outlandish, but I will try that. – Jimmoko!' Oki summoned her maid, who had least face to lose if the brew was still unsatisfactory. 'Stir honey into this; and a dollop of cream, I think.' As the young maid went off to do this, she turned back to her father. 'Father-Sir, you look poorly! Have you smiled at all, since the Five Touches?'

'I can smile when the company is good,' Okada told her, giving her a true, warm smile. 'And now it is.'

'Thank you.'

'We still have days to cherish.'

'Yes, and for now we can ignore Oatha's poisons – though we won't forget.'

'No,' said Okada, letting his daughter see some of his rage.

When the maid returned, Oki rolled the sweetened,

Words of Fury: 241

creamier brew about in her mouth. 'Oh, now I think I like it! But how odd! Such a dark taste, and yet stimulating...'

'Add it to your potion-books,' her father said, jovially. 'It's another good thing from abroad!'

He was happy to sit with her now, and begin playing her at the game of Go. It was a good contest, which they took slowly as they sipped the caffe.

'In enjoying this drink, Daughter-Dear, are you making a political point? I didn't know you were so in favor of trade.'

Trade was not much liked by the ruling samurai in Japan. It involved crude money and cruder foreigners – and disturbing new knowledge. Jade had been the only city truly open to international trade, and therefore Jade was the richest place in the realm.

'Always I make political points,' she said, smiling. 'Haven't you realized that yet? After all, I am your daughter.'

He rose, embraced her. 'You're too clever for your own good.'

'I'm sure I inherit that from you.'

She was in his arms, his lovely daughter, but he was staring over her shoulder – not at the present-day city but into the lost past. So much was different now; so much had been changed.

'But your looks, they are from your mother.'

Oki looked up at him. 'You never talk of her!'

He quivered, and turned his face away. The large game-board showed that Oki was winning, as often happened now. Equally as usual, his family pride overlaid any feelings of wounded vanity. My girl is smart and lovely, he thought. And dying!

If only Man and Joah could do something! But though they had escaped, they were young and inexperienced. Okada could only hope they might reach The Waning of the Moon. *There* they would have access to true power.

Do you really imagine they'll make it? he asked himself. You know that's next to impossible!

But he remembered how Oki had said she had mind-spoke to her sister, and Joah had survived a balloon-crash and then some monsters on a beach, and was now well on the way to The Waning. So there was hope – surely?

Okada grimaced, touched his right forearm where the skin was still inflamed from traitor Sukomo's Five Touches.

Hope, yes, but not much.

'Father-Dear, I would like to know – is there a picture?'

'Of your mother? Why do you ask?' His voice was throaty. 'And why do you ask now?'

'These are dark days, and I just want to see her, Father-Dear, in the only way I can. Just once, before I die.'

'I kept no likeness of her.' He had been glaring at his beloved daughter; but now he turned his face away. 'It would have been too painful.'

'I understand.' Oki gently disengaged herself from him. 'To come here, to a new place, a new city...and then she dies...'

'Do you remember her at all?'

Even to Okada himself, his voice had sounded oddly hollow. Was it as simple as wanting to shield his daughter from pain, or was there still love in him for the woman who had been his wife, true love and an immense loss, in spite of everything?

'I recall a little, Father-Dear. Hands, touching. A voice late at night when I was ill... I wish I'd known her!'

Ah, my Oki is so young and so bold, Okada thought. She doesn't yet realize that loving makes all the fears worse.

'You,' he said in pain, 'would have respected her as well as loved her. She is, was, very much like you.'

'Really? Then I hope to meet her,' Oki said, accepting death, 'in the life to come.'

Words of Fury:

Chapter Twenty-Three: *Honor Is My Gift to Give*

Man had enjoyed the quickly-eaten feast. He saw their men appear from the other restaurant, looking pleased to be well-fed, and with their energy and confidence restored. Then he saw the three masterless samurai again, and their expressions also made him smile.

'There are the ronin with our men, Yoshi. Don't they look happy?'

'And so they should; for I could have had them killed.'

'Yet you did not.'

'No, Man. I have learned mercy from you.'

Man remembered them standing up in the inn, all three bedraggled and worn. The older one had stopped the others –the thick-set dog-faced man and the thin beardless boy – using their swords, and so saved their lives.

'Why mercy in this case?'

Yoshi looked at the three, considering.

'Three men are useful reinforcements, are they not? As for them as individuals, the older man, Fudai, has been dishonored – '

'And yet you trust him?'

'Ah, I can provide what he wants. I am of the house of Fujiwara, and an Emperor's Man. Honor is my gift to give and Fudai wants his back! The boy is hardly old enough to count and is anyway impressionable. The third... In other circumstances, I would have made him dead. He looks two-faced and violent, but perhaps we can use those qualities.' He glanced over at Man. 'So now you know.'

'Oh, I wasn't questioning your judgment; and of course three new swords can help. I was just asking.'

'If they help us win, then Fudai's good name will be restored.'

In Japanese terms, Man thought, Fudai can be redeemed. There can be salvation for him.

Now Man thought of the secret commitment he had made to the Lord of the North.

I wish it could be the same for me.

Their column formed up on the hard-packed earth road. Looking pleased, Yoshi glanced over at Man.

'We've taken losses, Man, but four good horses and some

ponies, and three new swords – that's a gain.'

Man wore a padded jacket now and had his bow attached to his saddle as well as his two scabbarded swords. He patted the horse, a black stallion, which pulled at the bridle and neighed.

'It is. – Shall we go?'

'Of course. The question is, in which direction?'

'I have a voice, too!' said Lady Joah. Her eyes flashed dangerously at Man, and that reminded him of her sister. 'Please do not insist that we take your *orders*, just because we are females! When the Voice said "vote", she meant all should have a voice!'

'I do not mean disrespect,' Man answered, 'and you should know that. I know we're all in this together.'

'That's the truth!'

Man made an elaborate bow, only slightly mocking. Like the others, his legs were still hurting, but a quick massage had helped. 'Yes; it is the truth.'

Man wondered what it would have been like to spend a lifetime in some obscure little place like this. He had a sudden sense of history flowing past this dot on the map, while the inhabitants came and died and perhaps came again. That was life, the common life of mankind; but the path chosen for him was very different.

Far below, down towards the sea, he saw rice-paddies in watery terraces with peasants working them in the hot sun. It seemed peaceful and untroubled; an immemorial scene. When they headed out on the high path Man looked back over his shoulder, but it was too late for regrets. The village was out of sight.

He looked forward again. Optimism rose in him, and spoke.

The enemy doesn't know exactly where we are. We left the only pursuers on our trail on the other side of a mountain. There should be Sword Maidens out looking for us, and The Waning is not so far. We *are* going to make it!

He looked up at The Waning's crescent Moon again and took comfort from the sight. Their destination was strong; it was a sanctuary. Then a warning shout came from Ozawa, who pointed a finger at the flatter country below.

'Look there! A war party coming up! – And they've seen us!'

Chapter Twenty-Four: *Enough Enemies*

'This might be the road to get us to our enemies, but it is also the road to Hell!' said Hagiwara. He had been forced to ride very carefully along the narrow, steep footpath. 'I even smell sulfur – which stinks like a devil's fart!'

Berenda only laughed. 'Hell is a cold place; you should know that.' She had stayed on her horse too, and now she looked up at the bare, cracked mountain slopes. In some places the cracks were steaming. 'Scout, how far now to the broken bridge?'

'Only a little way, lady!'

She felt great satisfaction. She would perform trying magic, then perform dramatic failure, and then berate herself for that failure.

Meanwhile, the bridge would stay broken. Therefore, unless other Friends of the Cold could come inland in time, Emmanuel and the others would get to sanctuary – because of her good nature. She smiled to herself, this hot summer's day.

There came a sickening surprise.

Berenda suddenly felt *him*, right beside her.

He stood alongside, to her left. Though she was immediately riding hard to get away from him, and *he* did not seem to move at all, she did not increase the distance between them. No matter how she tried he was just there, all too close, tall, implacable and immovable.

The column behind had speeded up to keep up with her. She wondered about the foot soldiers, but that hardly seemed important now.

The all-white eyes of the Lord of the North stared at her. For once, she felt sorrow there, as well as the endless cruel, cold fury.

She read what was in his expression easily, just as she could before – and it was true what he thought.

Yes, she was his betrayer. She *was*.

She wanted to hide, but there was nowhere to hide from *him* and really there never had been.

Now Berenda felt herself read in depth. In response to what he had seen in her, she felt his feelings intensify. His glare held her rigid in the saddle, and her horse missed a step.

The power of his voice shook existence.

'YOU THOUGHT YOU COULD BETRAY ME!'

She wondered then if all the world could hear him, or only her. The volume alone was pain. She moaned between gritted teeth. It would be very bad indeed when he really hurt her.

As the broad ledge narrowed, she reined in, stopped. She began to shiver. She could hardly move as the pain built up; she could only hold up her hand to halt the others.

'I thought that *I* had been betrayed!'

'YOUR ONLY PURPOSE IS TO DO WHAT I WANT. YOU ARE MY SLAVE.'

In her palm was the red-eyed power gem – that tricky weapon. As she slowly powered up the jewel it began to flicker and glow. She surreptitiously took some of that power into herself, wondering if she might fight.

If I had the Eye, I would fight forever!

She gasped out, 'I am close on their trail, lord! Let me follow them! Then I could apologize and serve you again!'

There was no concession from him; he still hated her.

A glow surrounded her, silver in some places, sun-yellow in others. She trembled, daring to fight him for control over her own body. He wasn't quite attuned to the ruby; but *he* had the skill of centuries to fall back on.

The power colors swirled, and sometimes she had the advantage, and sometimes it was *him*.

She fought this avatar of the Lord of the North very hard, but he slowly began to move the hand that gripped the ruby closer to her chest. She was sweating as the half-visible forces wrestled. The glow from the gem was too fierce to look upon, and then even more hot blood-red power glared out of it. Though much of it went to *him*, more went to her. Her hand was shaking, but everything was held in balance. Between them, there was stasis; and forces in the entire universe were now equal. Though he pushed at her, she found she could still resist. She was *his* equal!

She began to laugh, wildly.

It was brave to be good; it was very good to be brave.

She was both, now. She *could* fight him, and with that infusion of faith in herself she did. She moved the power gem inches further away from her body while still drawing energy from it, and all this against *his* will.

She was winning. She dreamed now of having the Eye of Jade; for even *he* could not resist that.

The victorious moment stretched out.

'I'm not going to lose! I won't be your slave again! *I will beat you!*'

Words of Fury:

For minutes, for hours, for long, long days Berenda fought *him* hard. Her hand trembled and she felt it burning with cold – *him*. He was soaking up her attack and now he began responding.

In spite of everything she could do, the gem inched closer to her chest. Her power rose to match *his*, though her head was about to explode with pain. Her hand trembled just above her heart, and then she moved it away from her.

That small triumph made her relax and want to crow.

Then suddenly *he* had all the power. Though her flesh still fought him, her lonely soul was not used to being so strong and faith leaked out of her. When her soul saw the situation it surrendered.

'Mercy! I will do anything that you want! Master, please!'

'WHY SHOULD I BELIEVE YOU?'

There was no good answer she could give. Her own enslaved hand now pressed the gem to her chest. Pain bit into her flesh and ate away at her heart. He was going to eat, and she deserved it. A cold white light filled her.

Then she slid helplessly from her horse, to lie on her back on the roadway dirt.

She heard her horse gallop away.

Her vision should have been full of summer-blue sky, but she could only see a cold blank white. Was she now like Zandar, blinded? Was she like those victims whose eyes she had taken?

She began to sob.

The agony intensified. Now it was as if every nerve fiber in her body was one continuous screech of pain.

'Yes!' She writhed about in surrender. 'I will obey!'

'THAT IS NOT ENOUGH. YOU MUST BE MADE INTO AN EXAMPLE.'

Pain ripped her apart, limb from limb. She heard herself screaming, and then it was impossible even to breathe. She knew that even if she lived through this she would be crippled... She came to again, still shrieking. Pain filled her. She writhed about in a terrifying fit, and frothed at the mouth.

There was a gap in her consciousness, then more pain woke her.

Now she realized she was standing up, naked. People had gathered round to stare. Not one moved to help her. She wept, shamed by her public weakness, knowing that there was more agony to come. She held the burning-hot gem in one hand and

Words of Fury: 248

screamed out his name in pain again and again, as he wrote his name on her flesh.

Now she was branded, the Lord of the North pushed the glowing ruby, still held in Berenda's hand, towards her mouth.

Eat a power gem? 'No!'

'YES!'

Her own hand was made to feed her. In her mouth the jewel was first so cold that it burned. She cried out to him, all her words jumbled; but there was no mercy. When she got the full taste it was hideous: corpse-ashes and decay. Of course she didn't want to swallow this thing, but he made her.

When she tried to gulp it down, she began to choke.

'G – uk – uk!'

Another swallow put it deep inside her. Now its frigid heat began burning through her body. She was sobbing pitifully, banging her fists on her stomach. Soon the gem's deadly light glowed out of her flesh. Even some hard-bitten black sashes shouted at the sight. She was shaking from head to foot now. Would she be destroyed, right in front of them all? Would she be a legendary example of *his* ability to punish?

She shook more and more and then her mind went blank and suddenly she was face down in the dust. She was on her belly, writhing on the ground where the horses had been, and at *his* command licking there.

She remembered picking herself up out of the evil-tasting dirt again and again, but every she time fell back in a faint and was then punished more.

The torture seemed to go on for hours. However, it did not take long to break her.

She sniveled, confessed her weakness, cried out to serve her master again; and in a great pulse of power *he* and she merged. As a mere limb of the Lord of the North she rounded on the men, turned into *him* in his black armor, and spoke to all in *his* giant voice.

'THIS IS NO LONGER MY SERVANT, *THIS IS ME!* BOW DOWN!'

They were sensible; they bowed very low – Hagiwara in the front rank.

She collapsed. Now, she could no longer see.

His voice thundered out of the air. 'I HAVE DISCARDED THIS BODY! LEAVE IT, AND FOLLOW YOUR ORDERS!'

She seemed to hear voices then, ordinary fearful human

Words of Fury: 249

voices. Then horses went galloping away.
   That was the last thing Berenda remembered.

Yoshi turned round and shouted to the column. 'Stay out sight, but form up for a fight! There are horsemen in the trees!'
   Ozawa had worked his katana loose. 'I could not identify the banners, though I suppose they must be black sashes.'
   Man stared at the clump of trees, wondering when the enemy would emerge and the violence would begin. He had somehow expected it would be easy from now on; clearly it wouldn't be.
   Lady Joah said only, 'I had not thought to find enemies east of the mountains.'
   Yoshi said sharply, 'We have found no friends here; none. That alone should have told us something!'
   Joah mumbled hopelessly, 'This land is *his*.'
   But when riders emerged from the greenery below it was Joah who made the crucial observation.
   'Look closely. Now I have hope, for they're not horse-*men* at all!'
   Soon Ozawa's scouts were escorting the party up. All the six women except for one wore blood-red kimonos, and all rode ponies. There was also a tall shaven-headed Buddhist monk on foot, clutching a metal-tipped staff.
   'Sword Maidens!' Man said happily. 'Mother Zandar's help must be on the way!'
   'Perhaps.' Lady Joah frowned down, her honeyed eyes distracted. 'I see a robed Far-Speaker among the women. She should know more.'
   The lead Sword Maiden cantered forward, the white-robed girl coming with her.
   'I am Sweet Snake, leader of this patrol. Sweet in nature I am, but when I fight I am a deadly cobra.'
   Man could believe it. The Sword Maiden was short and looked young, but she exuded healthy confidence. A silver snake charm hung from a necklace.
   'We escorted a Far-Speaker here.' The Maiden pointed at the young girl who wore white, with a crescent moon embroidered on the back of her robes. 'This is Novice Keli.'
   'I am tasked by Mother Zandar to help you.'
   Man relaxed. This was a channel of communication straight to The Waning of the Moon. This was very good news indeed.

Yoshi responded formally. 'I am Fujiwara-noh-Yoshi, and this is my party – the Lady Joah, the Voice from Afar, and captain Ozawa. And here beside me is the Lord Emmanuel from Albion.'

When Sweet Snake turned to Man there might even have been awe in her.

'We were sent looking for The One Who Will Change. Now he is recognized.'

Hands slack on the reins, Man frowned. 'You know me? How?'

'You have the signs outwardly, and in your soul,' said Keli.

Sweet Snake introduced the monk, and then beckoned forward one of the Maidens, who looked exactly like her.

'This is my sister and second in command, Precious Stone.'

An identical twin, thought Man.

A carved semi-precious gem hung on a silver chain from the new twin's elegant neck. Man's attention was held, for when he raised his eyes and met Precious Stone's, he felt a weird shock.

She kept on staring back; their gazes had locked, and somehow he could see into her soul.

Oh, Precious Stone *feels...* But I suppose she hates foreigners. A pity, for this Precious Stone is very pretty indeed.

I do not hate you at all, Emmanuel, said a voice in his head – the Sword Maiden in front of him. She touched her gem.

'You know me, Maiden?'

Yes; from the Prophetic Books I know you!

Man felt the outpouring from Precious Stone's heart. No, she did not hate him; even before this first sight she had loved him.

As Man started to respond, Yoshi overrode him.

'We are glad to have you, friends from The Waning, but you are few. Aren't more coming?'

'Others are out searching, but I can make no promises,' Sweet Snake admitted. 'Much of our force went to Ezo. Others of us garrison the eastern sea-towns to stand off invasion.'

Yoshi was insistent as he spoke to the Far-Speaker. 'Then please tell your sisters at The Waning that we need armed help!'

'I will do what I can, but *he* may not let me speak.'

'A typical man,' Joah murmured.

'Try!' Yoshi ordered.

Novice Keli closed her eyes and folded her hands together. Man saw flashes of her power and felt her reach out. He waited along with the others for success or failure.

Meanwhile, Precious Stone leaned closer to Man.

'You really are monstrous strange.'

He smiled, for he knew it was well-meant. 'I don't think you are disappointed, though.'

'No, my Emmanuel. For you are monstrously attractive, too.'

He bowed mockingly low. 'Thank you; and my heart is no monster's heart, but pure.'

'A pity!' She bowed back, with the same affectionate mockery. 'Otherwise I might ask you for a kiss.'

Man smiled at her, loving her mouth and her hair. It was as if tiny black bushes grew from her otherwise shaved scalp.

'Why not forget the "might" and just ask, Sword Maiden?'

'Now call me by name!' said the girl, who then leaned forward from the saddle and kissed him hard. 'Say my *name*, Man!'

Man touched his lips.

'You didn't ask, you just kissed – Precious Stone.'

'I act boldly – always. And I wanted to know you.'

And now you do.

She smiled, her dark eyes truly bold, and Man returned her look. He felt in a strange way that he had come home.

But what Sweet Snake said then was disturbing, and spoilt Man's good mood.

'Lords, ladies, we must tell you that enemies have landed in force on the east coast.'

Yoshi said angrily, 'We're already being pursued from the west! Does this mean we might soon be surrounded?'

Sweet Snake frowned and fondled her sword-hilts.

'My sword-sisters are fighting hard!' She took a breath. 'But you're right. The enemy are coming inland, perhaps to intercept you.'

That was depressing. So Man had to know. 'How strong are your forces on the coast? Is there a force enough left over to help us?'

Sweet Snake's brown eyes looked from one man to the other. 'What I do not know, I cannot be made to betray.'

'Are enough of you out to hold the road from here to The Waning?' Man felt anguish: so near, and yet still so far! 'Surely there must be!'

'I don't think so, Lord Emmanuel, not given the numbers coming against us.'

'So the road ahead might've already been cut!'

'I can't tell, but it might have been.'

That was very bad news, and Man and the others received it as such.

In response, Sweet Snake made a reassuring gesture.

'Don't think your journey is impossible. We do have a Maiden garrison at Miracle Island, the main crossing-place over the river, and that is not far.'

'That's worth knowing, and we're grateful.' Now Man turned to little Keli. 'Any luck?'

'I'm sorry. There's so much interference from *him*... I just can't get anyone at The Waning to hear me!'

Man digested the new bad news.

The novice added, 'We are here to help you, but the black sashes and all *his* friends want *you*, Lord Emmanuel – and the power gem in your charge.'

'You glimpsed that in their minds?' asked Joah.

'Yes. They do not know exactly where you are, but they do know you are the expected one.'

Man threw his hands up. 'I have enough enemies already!'

'You have many, yes. I see that in your mind... Who is following you most closely?'

Man scowled. 'We've already encountered a mounted force of black sashes. They're about sixty strong, and going south on the far side of the mountain-range. As soon as they can they'll cross over, aiming to intercept us.'

'That is not good. If they can get to Miracle Island before you... Who else?'

Joah answered. 'The main force is led by a woman strong in the darkest shades of the power, though she can use male as well as female force. In Jade, she called herself the Tears. She has repaired a bridge and is following us directly – with *hundreds* of fighters.'

'I think this person might be in the Prophecies! This is bad; very bad. – How would we recognize her?'

This time Man spoke. 'She is tall – not far short of my height – and she has very distinctive black waist-length hair.'

'I will remember about the hair,' Sweet Snake said, 'and so will Keli.'

'How long might we have?'

Sweet Snake answered. 'That depends. But it will take our enemies time to find and seize every path to The Waning.

Words of Fury: 253

Remember, you only need *one* path.'

'But we don't know which path that might be!' Yoshi grimaced. 'So, how much time?'

'Hours, I hope – though it could be less.'

Now Man turned to Yoshi and Ozawa. 'If Keli cannot speak to her superiors, we must go ahead fast! Without communication, there will be no reinforcements. Without reinforcements, we can only run.'

'Run right into trouble?' Ozawa asked.

The senior Maiden looked from Man to Ozawa, then to Lord Yoshi. Her gaze lingered over Lady Joah before she turned back to Man.

'A fast run might be your salvation. Does anyone else know where you are, One Who Will Change?'

Joah answered for him.

'We hope nobody knows exactly. But we were seen earlier by at least one mech-bird, and probably another.'

'So that's the Angels,' said Sweet Snake. 'And also Oatha's purity police, working for *him*.'

Yoshi showed determination. 'I know that sounds bad, but we fought our way out of Jade and we fought right across Monster Beach. We're determined to outsmart our enemies here, outrun them – *and* outfight them.'

'And so are we!' said Precious Stone.

Man stared at this pretty warrior, feeling that connection again.

I hope you fight as boldly as you speak, Man told her.

Even more boldly! Precious Stone responded.

It was very rarely that Man could manage mind-speech, but it seemed he could with her.

Man came closer, spoke privately to her. 'I thought at first you must dislike me.'

'No! I dreamed of you many times, my lord Emmanuel. I am ... impressed to meet you, in the world of the real.'

'Then you have a touch of the power. What did you see of our future, my Precious Stone?'

She did not reply.

'I offer you my plan,' said Sweet Snake. With Keli beside her, she spoke only to Man and Yoshi, though her twin stayed to listen and Lady Joah and Ozawa were also close. 'With your permission, I want to risk going ahead to alert The Waning. I'll send two other horsewomen also.'

'Just three of you? That's not enough to stand off dozens of enemies!'

'No, Lord Emmanuel,' Sweet Snake acknowledged, 'but we know these trails and we are fast and we have been trained for this.'

'True,' said her sister. 'And someone *has* to say we've found you, and get assistance. You are mostly on foot and you do not know this land; you cannot go quickly.'

Sweet Snake looked fondly at her sister, and then at Lilac the other Maiden.

'I will take the high path, Lilac will try to get to Miracle Island, and my sister Precious Stone will risk the coast road. We gallop on ahead by separate routes. If we find reinforcements we will send them to you, while we go on to The Waning of the Moon to get you more help – *strong* help!'

Man foresaw many dangers, and said so.

Sweet Snake shrugged. 'If any of the roads we take to The Waning are blocked, we will return whether that is one of us or all of us.'

Return without help, thought Man. 'What then?'

'Then we will stay with you till the end – whatever that might be.'

'Very well,' Yoshi said. 'Brave Sword Maidens, go, and may your God watch over you!'

Sweet Snake, Precious Stone, and Lilac went galloping away.

Man watched them charge down a road now almost empty. For a moment the two sisters exchanged hand-clasps, or perhaps handed something over one to another; for some reason he thought it might be to do with luck. Then the wind-tossed green swallowed them up.

I wonder if they'll make it, and find us at least one open road. It will be dangerous, but they're locals, and they look confident.

They *might* get away; but what about us?

Words of Fury:

Chapter Twenty-Five: *We're Running for Our Lives*

The Voice was riding alongside Lady Joah, on a white pony similar to hers. The Maidens had been gone for half an hour.

Joah addressed her, quite formally. 'I hope all three Maidens return, with news of three safe routes.'

'Is that likely, Lady Joah?'

'No.' Now Joah showed the Voice a frown that indicated she had been doing a great deal of thinking. 'There is something about our experiences which makes me wonder...'

The Voice picked up the subtlety – the important, hidden inside the casual. Wondering if their quarrel over landing the balloon might have ended, she made her face signal interest.

Lady Joah continued. 'The monsters were real; they drew blood.'

'Yes. And the black beach was in Prophecy, which is now fulfilled.' The Voice became equally cool, equally polite, equally Japanese – and wished she had a fan to flap at her face. 'That's so.'

'You are learning.' Joah smiled. 'You did not even make it a question.'

The Voice had made a conscious decision to avoid the rougher, more flexible language of the port and try to speak to this highborn lady as another would. Japanese culture, and its dialect, was full of complex codes it was shaming to misunderstand.

'No, Lady Joah, for a question demands an answer, and I know that to demand is impolite. Anyway, you will give me the answer anyway – when it suits you, in so very polite a way – so I need not demand it.'

'I don't even have the answer myself!'

'You are thinking, lady; you will find the truth.'

'But I may not like it.' Joah frowned again. 'We have survived, we are here ... only, something about this journey feels *wrong*.'

'Wrong?'

'Unlikely. Unreasonable.' Joah smiled now. 'The exact opposite of unlucky!'

The Voice touched her washed and combed hair. Metal pins bought from the stilt-house village kept it almost as neat as Joah's. She was wearing a crown of woven-together golden flowers while Joah wore blue. In her head the Voice from Afar was working on a war ballad with a chorus about dying pretty, but then she saw the Lady Joah touching the marks where Yonai had cut her, and that was terribly real.

'It was lucky, us finding that village,' the Voice said.

'Real luck will be a safe fast road to The Waning! Still, we ate and bathed back there, and the horses and pack-ponies are useful. That counts as good luck. Though I have doubts about those three ronin Lord Yoshi took on.'

'I suppose the men know what they are doing.'

'*They* will think so!'

The Voice smiled. 'True.'

'We are guarded so heavily I am annoyed. Look!' Joah gestured at their bodyguards. 'Can these men really think we are helpless?'

'The men must think we are under a grave threat, my lady.'

'You are in favor of men, aren't you? Especially Albion men?'

That had been said with humor and warmth. Nevertheless the Voice blushed.

'I like Master Faslane, true, and Emmanuel also.'

'That's two men, both from Albion.'

'Man is one of us, really; Jade is his home. Dirk Faslane is the traveler. The coasts of E'ropa, Africa – many islands... He has been talking to me about what I might do in Albion with my music...'

'And you are tempted.'

'I'd love to travel.'

'With one particular man, or with both?'

The Voice laughed. 'Men always have ideas about what's best... But they mean well, don't they?'

'Men usually do, dear Voice; it's just they're so often wrong.'

'I know you don't want so many guards, but we *are* under threat.'

Joah raised her head. 'You feel it, too?'

'The danger? The violence in our past and to come? I do.' Now the Voice's tone turned tragic. 'How did I come to be here? I am not a brave fighter like you! I'm a musician!'

'Ah, Voice from Afar, I feel the same. I never expected this.'

'No?'

'No! I was always the shyer one, who hung back. And look at me now, fool that I am! I have stumbled into incredible danger!'

'No, you are the Lady Okada-noh-Joah, who is a heroine, in

Words of Fury: 257

the middle of an adventure!' On impulse, the Voice reached over and touched Joah's shoulder. 'I will write a song about you someday, so everyone will know!'

'Thank you.' Joah flashed a smile; all sweetness and shy eyes. 'But I am little more than a runaway, and I think my sister has the heroine role marked for her own.'

'I have seen her sometimes, at ceremonies. Lady Oki is – a commanding presence.'

They exchanged wry glances and then Joah laughed. '"Commanding" is well said. You do not have sisters, yourself?'

'No. I'm an only child, an orphan. I was born at sea, and my parents brought me here when I was very young.'

'And when the Lord of the North struck last time, he took both your father and your mother?'

'He did.'

'I have lost my own mother. I know how it is.'

At the front of the column Man had raised his voice; he was saying that something was impossible. The Voice really wanted to go over and break into that conversation, but knew the men would not allow it.

'Your father was a Christian missionary, wasn't he? From Albion?'

The Voice looked over, and this time her words had an edge. 'You know that much of me?'

'I have heard you sing more times than you know. I was impressed, dear Voice! Also, I know Emmanuel well.'

'He talks about me?'

'Most favorably. – I do know Jade. It must be very hard, to be on your own in a low part of town.'

'It was. But then Pastor Ruhr took me in. He's a good man, and his daughters became like sisters to me. He doesn't exactly approve of my life now, but I sing and play music. That is, in every way, my living.'

'You are a free spirit! Oh, value your freedom!' Joah sighed. 'For I am not free, never have been, and never will be.'

'I am sorry.'

'It is my karma. Ah, my family meant so much, good and bad! I miss my father terribly.'

'I sympathize. I still miss mine.'

The Voice saw Joah glance around with a bleak look.

'The samurai go marching on, but there is not the safety in swords that men seem to think. We will see a higher power at work, when we get to The Waning of the Moon.'

'Where Mother Zandar is again, by a miracle?'

'We are both people of faith; we *know* the age of miracles has not passed.'

'Amen.'

'There at The Waning many adepts practise – and also teach – the white art: magic of the Earth, and Water, Fire and the Air. The holy Mother can help us. It is a cultural centre, too, for music, painting, and poetry. And as well as priestesses who follow Kannon or the Madonna and know the Art, Mother Zandar has Sword Maidens – hundreds of them.'

'Is that what you intend for yourself?'

'I intend to fight, Voice.' Joah sounded utterly determined. 'The Waning of the Moon is a fortress for females. Men are mere guests there.'

The Voice looked at these hard-bitten samurai again, and saw Man, broad-shouldered and walking with determination, laughing with Yoshi over something while Faslane was scowling.

'It will do the men here no harm to be "mere guests" for a while.'

Joah smiled. 'I agree.'

'Of course, I like Emmanuel – I'm sure you do, too – but he can be so prideful and touchy!' The Voice wrinkled her nose, as her pony picked through a potholed section of path. 'These Sword Maidens, do they count as full samurai?'

'In a way. Once they were girls who wished to break free, and learn martial skills as men do.'

'To break free...' the Voice murmured.

'I know! Men make the rules to suit themselves, don't they?' Joah sighed, then looked admiringly at the sea-born girl. 'You are the freest spirit I have ever met.'

The Voice suddenly realized that her curiosity about this highborn samurai lady, and the warm respect she had felt since Joah fought so bravely and unselfishly, were both returned in full measure.

'Tell me, dear Voice from Afar, why do they call you "the Voice", rather than using your name?'

'Ah, what if my given name was clashing syllables that I could not bear to hear, still less speak?'

'That wouldn't give you your present name.'

'No.' The Voice had made that reply echo magically, more than man-deep, and now she spoke in a child's soprano. 'I suppose it's for my love of mimicry – I can imitate any voice – but mainly because I sing.' Her voice was normal now, pleasing as always. 'And using magic, I can sing along with my own voice, and distort it as I please.' Her voice became a breathy, high music that she tripled. 'For I love music. And dancing.'

'Good for you!'

'Do you dance and sing, Princess Joah?'

'I? *Dance* and *sing*?' Joah asked, shocked. 'I am a highborn in a palace, where ceremony binds almost every hour! Why, I only feel free now, because I am away!' She blinked, suddenly realizing it. 'Yes, sweet Voice, free. Now, though I may die, I am truly free at last!'

The Voice somehow plucked details from Joah's mind. She saw petty rules and more rules, and ancient ceremony dictating every aspect of life to a vital young girl.

In spite of those rules she bent forward and kissed the other woman of power.

Joah was shocked. To be touched so, by one of low blood!

Then she smiled. She was free now, and she could make her own rules.

'We quarreled while flying on the balloon and we quarreled upon the black beach, but now we will be friends, won't we?'

'Very good friends,' the Voice said.

They rode on together, warmed by affection. The remaining Sword Maidens stayed with them, the Buddhist priest with the long staff following.

Their column went along roads thickly lined with apple-trees, then climbed up a shoulder of still another mountain. From the highest point they saw again the horned Moon above tall fairytale towers.

'Not so far,' Joah said, although their longed-for destination was still miles away. 'I almost feel I could touch that holy place!'

There, the Voice knew, Joah could perhaps be healed – and Man could be healed of the Tears' toxic love-bite, too.

'We're going to make it, aren't we?'

'Yes, Voice from Afar,' said Joah, smiling. 'I think we are.'

When Berenda came to again, she was face down in the dust she had been made to lick. Hagiwara stood above her, hands on hips.

'You live, lady, which surprises me.'

'And me.' Her voice was a croak. When she looked around, she saw there was nobody else here; not a living soul. 'For there is no mercy, ever. Isn't that so?'

'Of course.'

'And yet I do live, so *he* may yet have use for me...'

'You think? We are in profound disfavor now; both of us, because of you.'

The pain had ceased. Berenda got to her hands and knees, then forced herself to stand. She felt weak and dizzy, but collected her clothes and dressed. Had *he* really left?

'What exactly happened?'

'You were displayed in your agony, you collapsed – and *he* came and showed himself.'

'And showed *me* to all.' She grimaced. 'The others went?'

'They have retreated, and plan to find another path across the mountains. Ideally they will find young Nagaoka and follow him. There is still a chance they can intercept your Man and the others.'

Her right palm bore a burn-mark from the ruby, and she stared at the brand, fascinated. The power gem was still lodged within her, like a vile pregnancy. As for the jewel, there would be another tiny part of her punishment later, when she had to grope for it in her own bodily wastes.

'What do we do now, lady?'

'Do we have orders?'

'No. I suppose that we should follow the others, since that bridge was destroyed. Nagaoka will be guided by our lord to the fight – and the three hundred who used to follow you will follow him.'

'You make it all sound easy.'

'Of course it isn't! When we arrive late to the battlefield, we will have missed *his* victory. Our master will win over Emmanuel and get the Eye – without assistance from ourselves...'

'How then can we win back our high places?'

'How indeed?'

'Perhaps we should run...' Then she pressed hands to her stomach. It was a mere speck of warmth now, but at any time *he* could power up the gem and kill her, burned from within. 'No, no running away. I think we should follow, and make ourselves useful. It was not mercy that led him to avoid killing us; surely he has some plan that might allow us to redeem ourselves. I will go to that broken bridge and see what I can do.'

She made herself walk on, eastwards and upwards. It was a very hot day and she was thirsty, but she had nothing to drink and there were no servants to fetch anything. She had been made to roll in the dirt and was filthy from it, and she knew she was stinking with sour sweat and worse, but that was only part of her penance.

In her mind she saw her master bring The One Who Will Change into his service along with the Eye. Then he smashed down The Waning walls and killed this Mother Zandar, and so won everything.

There really was no place for her.

She was surplus to requirements. There was nothing ahead. There never had been mercy and never would.

She began to weep as she walked.

'Lord, oh my dark Lord, that enemy called Emmanuel *should* worship you, but he does not. Oh, but I gave him the special kiss to make him suffer! Let me make him suffer more!'

After a few minutes Hagiwara spoke. 'Do you really imagine that *he* can have need of *you?*'

'I had his love once!' She cried out, in her pain. 'I did! And I will do *anything* to regain it!'

That might have been sincere, but her previous betrayal was the reason why Hagiwara had been placed with her now. If *his* order came, he would give her death.

Nevertheless he had to respect Berenda's power, so when the veiled lady suddenly stopped Hagiwara stopped beside her. She had turned her head south-east.

'Our enemies – that Mother Zandar – have their headquarters over the mountain. I feel the power of women there.'

That made him consider. 'They are very strong?'

'A few are, but when our lord and master can focus all of himself they won't resist *him* for long.'

'That's excellent.'

'Yes, yes, of course – but we must not be mere bystanders.' She went further into the steep-sided gulley, where the path vanished below a huge landslip. Now she was deep in the shade. 'Somewhere here should be the bridge.'

They came upon it. She went right up to the broken crossing. Hagiwara stayed close to her, trying to seem servile. He looked over with her. The rope and planks hung down in the gulf, the other end burned black.

'This bridge is destroyed, Lady!'

'You still have eyes.'

'Surely we're wasting our time. We can't fly over!'

Her voice hissed. 'Then just what is your solution to our problem?'

Hagiwara stared in consternation at the veiled face.

'Well, we can perhaps climb down the rock face here, cross the river below, and climb up on the other side. Our best men using the right equipment could do it, I think. Us, I'm not sure about.'

'That would take hours!'

'I suppose so, Lady Berenda. But what else can we do? Either we do that, or we must do what Nagaoka did and go looking for another pass... I understand you want to be in at the death of Emmanuel, but what if that is not possible?'

'I have a thing in me to make the impossible possible, and you know it!'

'I mean no disrespect! As for the bridge here, it could maybe be pulled back up and repaired, but we can't connect it to the far side because we can't *get* to the far side!'

'Everything you talk about means delay, and there can *be* no delay.'

She raised her veil, and again Hagiwara saw those striking dark eyes. She was clearly mad, but...

He saw her turn away now and lean far over the gulf. Hagiwara heard her begin to chant. She made gestures, again and again. He moved forward, to be with her. Her face was covered in sweat and showed terrible strain.

As the air over the gorge began to shimmer, Hagiwara's skin prickled.

Then the miracle happened. Way down below, the far end of the rope bridge began to stir. Then it slowly lifted up, though it slipped back again twice. He was actually relieved to see that. He was afraid of the power that she was using and he wanted her to stop.

Instead she gestured even more fiercely, making pulling motions with both hands. Hagiwara saw her power ripple the air again. The charred planks rattled together as the other bridge-end rose, and then the broken bridge extended out horizontally though there was nothing at all to support it. Eventually, he saw the charred end touch the other side of the gulf.

He saw how she stared at it, her head bowed and chest heaving.

Then Hagiwara looked again at the swaying bridge. It was held up now by nothing more powerful than this Lady's will – and her magic.

'I shall cross over, man Hagiwara. But you will go first.'

'Lady, please – '

She turned that striking dark-eyed face to him and glared murderously. 'Do you doubt me and my power – which came from *him?*'

In front of her, Hagiwara went down on his knees, then kow-towed with his head banging the earth. He was overwhelmed by fear.

When he raised his head again she was already walking over without him.

'I don't believe it!' he heard himself say. 'That bridge rests on nothing. She must fall!'

She didn't fall.

At the far side the person who had once called herself the Tears bent to tie together the charred ropes, which she slung over the bridge supports.

That done, the Lady Berenda rose up to her full height.

'Come over, Hagiwara – come quickly, and perhaps *I* will have mercy!'

Hagiwara made sure he came quickly, though the bridge swayed and he was terrified.

Joah spoke with urgency.

'Dear Man, dear Yoshi, there's something happening behind us – back among the mountains. Some powerful magic, with the feel of a man, but also the feel of a woman.'

Man felt a hot flush of pain in his face. Immediately he knew who it was.

Man and the Voice spoke at the same time: 'The Tears!'

He rubbed at the love-bite on his face, which was throbbing from the approach of its maker.

'For a moment her magic was so strong it linked us. I actually *saw* her, at the bridge...' He swallowed. 'She's repaired the crossing and she's come over! She's on our trail again!'

Yoshi said angrily, 'With magic, and lots of swords to back her?'

Man looked around, weighing up the contending forces he sensed. 'The Tears has her strong magic; but does she have a large force with her? Right now, no, she doesn't. And, Yoshi, we're still ahead of them all.'

'Yes, but do we stay ahead?'

'What do you mean?'

'I mean that if we're on foot we're slow and might get caught. So maybe the few of us with horses should just go on?'

Man scowled. 'If others did that, you and I would call it cowardice.'

'Don't fool yourself, my Man. It might become necessary. You and Lady Joah *have* to get to The Waning – the rest of us don't.' Yoshi looked round. There were shadows under his eyes and his expression was grim. 'We're running for our lives.'

Words of Fury:

Chapter Twenty-Six: *The Steel Angel*

Aoki was with Oatha and two other high officers in the black sash headquarters. Oatha was grinning.

'I have a message from Hagiwara, sent from Shimabara this morning.' Bulky Oatha shook the tiny, coded ribbon brought by carrier pigeon. 'He has landed and is closely following the Foreigner and the Eye!'

Old Yamagata made a finger-sign to ward off evil. 'Let us conquer and purify!'

'Let us indeed,' said Oatha, clearly pleased with himself. 'As long as I get the Eye of Jade!'

They went back to the map-table, to finalize the new dispositions of their forces, and the sites of the first camps to concentrate the foreigners. Oatha had already issued orders to raise the Foreign Town walls and work to fortify the gates.

Aoki saw it was all becoming realer and realer. He watched Oatha carefully, nodding bland subordinate approval although he wanted to curse. For when Oatha had moved away Lord Okada's most loyal troops there would be no significant force in the city except for Oatha's own, and what then?

The question answered itself...

Aoki kept a bland approving look on his face; but inside he was horrified. He tried to ask questions, hoping this might slow the process.

'Sir, with Hagiwara and his forces going, should we really rush Okada's regiments away from this city?'

'I must have no armed enemies here when I put down the foreigners,' said Oatha.

Aoki had already passed that news on to Lady Oki, though both could hardly believe it. Mass murder! 'You are still determined?'

'This city must be cleansed.'

Everyone except Aoki liked that. Though he could speak now, and he did, he could not directly oppose them.

'Lord, there's no real support for us from the Shogun nor from the Emperor – not so far – so can we hold the city? What if *he* comes here again?'

'We need not fear the legendary foe, or our internal enemies. Trust me, our position here is safe enough, young Aoki. I'm shipping Okada's regiments away for "coastal defense".' Oatha looked round, the pouchy face pleased with itself. 'Within a week, only forces loyal to me will be in the city.'

Aoki felt furious, but what could he do? Could he defeat Oatha? He had made plans, but it would not be easy. Oatha was cunning as a snake and could strike fast as a cobra.

Nevertheless, it had to be attempted... Oki was right.

When Oatha is dead – best if that can be done in secret – I will get myself announced as his successor. Lady Oki can come out in my support, and Okada's forces should declare for us. Then everything changes.

It was a wonderful daydream, while this was a terrible reality.

Oatha mused on. 'But there is still the Foreigner and his friends to consider – and they have the Eye of Jade.' Oatha tapped a finger on the map, on a place in Shimabara. 'The Waning of the Moon. That's where our enemies are heading.'

'Where *women* rule!' Yamagata took this personally. 'That is beyond unnatural.'

'Of course, and we will make sure everyone knows how unnatural. But now I am moving thousands of men there, to make war on them.'

'Lord,' Aoki said, 'they have power gems of their own.'

'They surely do, and I want them – as much as I want the Eye, and Emmanuel dead.'

A round-shouldered man wearing the black sash came in, bowed low.

Oatha skinned a banana which was blackened to the point of being disgusting, and then slurped it up before giving the man a broad smile.

'Ah, Saikaku! Tell me, who did Okada see?'

'It was as you permitted, Lord.' The black sash spy unrolled a scroll. 'Irian Dall, merchant. And then the architect, Cheng. I have made notes as best I could.'

'Irian Dall, merchant – and vile black-skinned gaijin,' said Oatha, straightening. 'What did you learn?'

'Dall I think is in some conspiracy, though I have no details. He may be a Futurist.'

'You think?' Aoki asked, edging his words with scorn.

'Only my opinion, master,' said the spy. 'But this I know: Lord Okada is encouraging Dall to lead the foreigners in resistance.'

Oatha was very pleased.

'Proved treason from Okada!'

Words of Fury: 267

'There is nothing in writing, lord.'

'Your honest testimony will be enough – and I speak now as the judge in this case.' Oatha gave his self-confident grin. 'And the other "guest"?'

Saikaku said only, 'Cheng is a genuine architect; I have checked. He talked with Lord Okada about plans for colleges and a free hospital.'

'Better if the plan was for human slaughterhouses!' said Yamagata, fiercely.

The spy hesitated. 'But...'

'But what?' Oatha asked.

'I believe Architect Cheng is also a secret contact for China.'

'Therefore dangerous, eh?' Oatha stroked his upper lip. 'T'zina does have some interest here... I wonder if they might try to make use of our late Lord Okada?'

'I will find out for you, lord. Okada does not know I can lip-read. I will keep that secret, and befriend the man.'

Oatha laughed, slapped his knee. 'Play the game with Okada carefully, and you will see that desperate man do desperate things ... and he will suffer because of it. When, that is, I have proof.'

Aoki thought, I'll make sure Oki's father does nothing, so that you *never* get the proof you want!

'I will lure him,' Saikaku the spy said.

'Excellent. But I need honest testimony from you! – Well, fairly honest. I can't demand perfection in liars' lies, eh?'

The men around gave sycophantic laughs and Aoki quickly added his own.

Suddenly Oatha turned savage, and turned to Aoki. 'And the spy in my own black sash ranks?'

Aoki kept his face straight, though he thought his own innards might drop through him. As Oatha turned away again, Aoki wondered if this was a crude trap, or a cruder warning. Was Oatha watching his reaction? He didn't seem to be, but Oatha's cunning misdirections were legendary.

Saikaku looked uneasy. 'I have no hard information, Lord, and could not even guess at a name.'

'Treachery is treachery,' said Oatha.

Aoki met Oatha's eye, and then he looked around at the others. There didn't seem to be a particularly high level of suspicion here, though it wasn't easy to tell. Yamagata, for instance, had a face like an old leather bag – a heavily-used bag that muttered to itself constantly – and was always hard to read.

Oatha had a brush-pen, black ink, and three pieces of writing silk. He wrote, breathed on the scraps, then showed them to Aoki.

'These are the arrest warrants. Immediately I give the order, take the persons named to the death-cells.'

Aoki looked at the warrants as Oatha chopped all three. Was this a goad, to push him into action?

Oatha gave Aoki the first two warrants. 'Lord Okada of the Jade, and his daughter Okada-noh-Oki!'

What about Oatha's notion to marry the Lady Oki, and make use of the power of the Okada name? Was that a discarded scheme? Were all the Okadas only the walking dead now?

Aoki put that disturbing question into a compartment in his mind as his master handed over the third piece of silk.

'Lord, on this warrant – there is no name!'

'That,' said Oatha, 'is for the traitor within our ranks, soon to be named.'

Oatha turned his gaze from man to man. Aoki tried to look hard and indifferent. Inwardly, he was trying to decide if he was about to be named.

Oatha suspects everyone, he suspects the universe! If he thought I was opposing him, surely he would just strike?

I have to bring him down before he does, or I, the Lady Oki, her father and even this mighty city are all finished...

It was then they all heard a rushing-waters sound from outside.

Oatha recognized those sounds as giant wings thrashing.

There was quiet for a moment, except for some cries of alarm. Then the door to the balcony was smashed down. There the thing was. The Steel Angel was metal-masked and terrible, with a spiked mace on its belt and a two-handed sword slung across its back. It came in, wings furled behind it, and placed a small black cube on the table.

'Out!' Oatha screamed. 'Everybody out, and then guard the doors!'

He would deal, because he had to. But he didn't want to be overheard doing it.

The giant Steel Angel stooped close. Oatha stared at the mask, wondering what was beneath it. A clever mechanism? Or was this 'Angel' some strange human?

Words of Fury:

The Angel pointed at the cube and the cube rasped: 'Oatha, your men went after the Eye, but they lost.'

'If it happened, it's only a mishap, and temporary! I did what I agreed!'

There was no reply. Suddenly one side of the cube showed a miniature 3D picture. It was some mountain gulch, where he saw his own black sashes milling around uselessly in front of a broken bridge.

On the other side of the gap he saw others, standing and jeering. Then the mech-bird view shifted to show the other party advancing deeper into the mountain pass. He recognized Lady Joah as she looked back.

Oatha wanted to say the images were lies, but he knew he was seeing the truth.

The same blurred, antique-accented voice came from the device.

'You said you would take back the Eye! But you failed!'

Oatha took off the power jewel he was wearing, and then let it swing from his hand without looking at it. It was needful to threaten, though very dangerous to provoke.

'My men found them, didn't they? This is just a setback.'

'The One Who Will Change must be stopped.'

Oatha shrugged. 'Why are you angry with me? You and I want the same thing: this perfect world never to change. When my power here is absolute that is just what will happen.'

'But things have already changed in this city! Look around you! Foundries; glassworks; colleges of education; new medicines. If this Emmanuel escapes justice, this world *will* change – permanently!'

Oatha realized he was dripping sweat; for he was in the presence of a power so great it terrified. The blank steel face stayed turned to him.

'You want the Eye, and I will help you get it. What more do you want?'

The voice rasped: 'The man "Emmanuel". The one called "the Voice from Afar". This "Joah", the renegade daughter of Lord Okada.'

'I'll get them! I just need a little more time!'

'You know what you risk! For I and I have shown you what may come!'

'You showed me a city burning!'

The voice overrode Oatha's. 'That could happen here! Steel

Words of Fury:

Angels cannot be defeated by anything in this world now... So give me the jewel you have been using!'

The metal giant extended a hand.

But Oatha averted his face from the Angel, and now a glow of power surrounded him.

'I cannot hand over this gem! – No, don't approach me now, or I'll blast you down, metal angel!'

The Angel in the powered armor did not advance; but it did not retreat either. Oatha held on to the glowing gem, as if on to life itself.

'Back off! I mean it!' Oatha's teeth ground together. 'We are allies! Or if you don't want that, we can fight right now!'

'You would be destroyed!'

'Perhaps I would; but then you would lose this city to progress!'

There was no reply.

Oatha pressed home his point. 'I have plenty of force over in Shimabara, and I already know one thing you probably don't – that the Eye can't now be used by this "Emmanuel". So just what are you are afraid of?'

'Of change; of change,' the cube said. The winged Angel backed out of the doorway where the smashed door lay. 'Find out more! Then speak to I/we through the com box. I/we give you till sunset.'

Oatha followed the thing as it backed away outside. Once there was a clear space the Angel spread its wings and took off.

He watched as it flew back towards Cube Castle. Till sunset... He shivered, suddenly.

'Aoki, fetch Okada, and his daughter.'

'Should I bring them here?'

'No, to the death-cells!'

Aoki bowed before leaving.

When he had gone Oatha began shouting.

'Maps! Monster Beach! Mount Unzen!' These places found, he gave orders. 'Send carrier-pigeons to Hagiwara and the others there! Tell them we *must* have the Eye, and by nightfall!'

Oatha shivered again. His right fist clenched on something imaginary – the Jade Eye. He hated even the thought of surrendering its power, especially before he had enjoyed it, but he did not underestimate the Angels. Cube Castle could destroy this city, and himself with it.

I need magical insight on how to locate the Eye.

Words of Fury:

He shouted again. 'Get me the torturers, and then we will visit Okada and his daughter!'

Chapter Twenty-Seven: *Will Your Caution Get Us The Eye?*

Man stayed on his horse, but he remained with the others. Perhaps it was a mistake, but he couldn't and wouldn't leave his friends. That was unthinkable. And, besides, he knew they still had a good chance. Admittedly, though the Tears was well behind, she could now take the same direct route they were taking, and catch up.

Man hoped she wouldn't. He estimated they were no more than an hour or two from safety: that was a fighting chance.

Then he heard that sweet, slightly hoarse voice in his head: Precious Stone.

I think he has withdrawn a little, so perhaps you can hear me, Man – ?

'I can,' he said with his mind, all excited now. 'What news, Precious Stone?'

I headed for the coast road, but there has been a major landing; many ships belonging to the enemy ...

Man found himself cursing under his breath, but then he apologized for being so indelicate.

She laughed. *There is not a word you have used that I did not already know, so what does that say about me?*

It was his turn to chuckle, even though she had passed on some very bad news. The black sashes, many of them in *his* service, would come up as quickly as they could to intercept Man and his party.

'How long can you Sword Maidens resist?'

They will buy you time, my Man; never fear. But how much time I do not know...

He gathered in the reins. 'I wish you'd brought better news.'

I have something good to show you... Watch!

The picture she showed him then proved this bold Sword Maiden was truly bold.

'You are naked!'

Something to look forward to, my hero... Now I will head back towards the high passes as fast as I can. We must join forces there!

'Yes, find us and then take us along a safe path, but be careful looking! The enemy is here!'

I know! They are ahead, with –

'What's happened?' There was no answer. Man straightened

Words of Fury:

in the saddle, worried. 'I'm fearful for you, Precious Stone!'
Then *his* power returned, and silenced the world.
Had she been captured or killed, or just interrupted?
He didn't know.
He spurred his horse, to tell Yoshi, Ozawa and the Lady Joah about the landings, and make a choice with them what to do now.

Man gathered the other leaders together. Now he looked at them, worried to his soul. 'I just heard from Precious Stone; she met the enemy close to the coast, and they are coming inland.'
'What else did she say?' asked Yoshi.
'Nothing that got through. I'm worried!'
Joah looked over, in compassion. 'You are worried for her.'
'Yes. She said she was galloping back towards the high places to meet us, and she saw something, but then *his* magic killed our talking.'
Yoshi looked annoyed. 'She made no suggestion?'
'There was no time.'
Joah grimaced. 'We should stick to obscure trails, then, even if they are not the fastest for us.'
'That makes sense,' Man agreed. 'Is there any point getting to this Miracle Island? Or do we go high and try to stay hidden?'
Yoshi was furious; the strain was telling on him.
'We need decent intelligence about how to proceed, but where is it? Where is your Precious Stone now? Will she really find us? And what about Sweet Snake, and Sword Maiden Lilac? Why aren't they back with help, or at least news?'
Joah said only, 'I feel our enemies approaching us, and Precious Stone has confirmed that. But there is no more we can do now except continue.'
'Not towards the coast, after her warning!' Man said. He ground his teeth together. 'I think we need to go back – *another* delay, when speed is vital!'
So they had to double back towards the mountains, going west away from the invaders on the east coast. Yes, time would be lost, but Man was determined to play this smartly.
They all went on even more hurriedly than before. This was another rough trail, not made for speed. Man saw in the others' eyes they were aware of time counting down too. The land up here was typically rough, with gulleys and streams and small rivers to cross, often by fording. You just couldn't go very fast.

Man saw there were people on the trail, though not many.

'We should have tried for this Miracle Island, maybe,' he said now.

Lady Joah sniffed. 'It won't do us much good if we turn up there and it's deserted, or, worse still, under siege.'

'We might have enough force to break the siege, if there is one!'

He had tried to sound cocky, but in reality Man knew they were in danger. All the time now he glimpsed the crescent sign of The Waning of the Moon. It was huge even at this distance.

'I know that it's miles away,' the Voice from Afar said to Man, 'but I feel I can touch our destination.'

He said only, 'Your faith does you credit.'

She stared back. 'I hope you're not being sarcastic.'

'If you want to label my feelings, try "worry"! I keep feeling pulses of masculine magic, and surely that has to be bad.'

Then the Voice was staring wide-eyed at The Waning.

'It *is* bad. It is *very* bad. Look!'

'Do you really think we can catch up with Nagaoka, and then meet this "Man"?' Hagiwara asked. Berenda and he had just come down out of the mountains, though it was still rough country here.

'Probably not in time to make any difference, for look what is happening!'

Berenda pointed. Stormclouds had gathered over The Waning, black and thick, and now they were beginning to corkscrew.

He was stirring his giant pot of magic.

'See, *his* power has already broken through some of the Waning defenses!'

'That is good news, I suppose.'

She prophesied herself, now: 'When that storm breaks it will be so terrible that The Waning will be cut off.' She turned to Hagiwara, angry with herself and with her fate. 'If our master's cavalry and foot command all the roads to The Waning, and the fortress itself is isolated and besieged by *his* magic, Emmanuel and the others *must* be captured – by Nagaoka or by newly-landed others!'

'So now the Lord of the North is a bare inch from winning everything!'

Her voice broke. 'Yes, so now he has no need of me.'

Words of Fury:

She wept again, head lowered.
What would become of her? Where could she go now?
Her feet dragged in the dust and she saw the lonely life of an exile in front of her.

Oki felt sickening fear in her stomach. This was it, then.
She stood with her father, and stared down at the torture implements on the table in front of Lord Oatha. This was the end, and it would be very, very bad. A dozen black sashes were crowding behind their monstrous leader, filling up the windowless cell.

'I need information about your other daughter, Okada – your sister, Oki. Speak!'

'Never!' Oki told Oatha, though her voice shook.

Her father put his arm around her shoulders and comforted her.

Oatha unpeeled a blackened banana, slurped it up and flung away the skin.

'You must not refuse me,' he said. He lifted up thumbscrews, and then a set of skinning blades. 'Otherwise, neither of you will leave this room alive.'

'We can't be traitors to family, principles, everything!' Oki blurted.

Oatha actually laughed. 'Of course you can. Now, tell me where your sister and this Emmanuel are, and don't lie. I know you've been in contact with the Lady Joah.'

'What do you need to know their location for?' Oki said. 'Do you imagine you have the power to stop them? They have the Eye!'

'Your chit-chat doesn't answer my question, which I must have answered.' Oatha lifted up a blood-rusted saw, showed it to the Okadas and then made sawing motions. 'And I *will* have it answered.'

There was pushing in the throng, and Oki saw the Emperor's Man arriving. As always, Yoshi's father was unsmiling and austere. He was known for his integrity, though. Would the famous Lord Fujiwara intervene to help them? Oki was an Okada, so surely he would!

In the front rank now, Fujiwara made a brief gesture to Oatha.

Even if he is here as a witness only, Oki told herself, that might work to our advantage.

Words of Fury:

Then she thought of that saw, cutting away at her delicate fingers one at a time...

Oatha was snarling his fury. 'Lady Oki! Tell me what you know!'

'No!' she said to that evil man, and to history. 'I won't betray my sister! I don't care what you do to me!'

She remembered Lord Fujiwara from her childhood. He hated children. He had raised Yoshi very coldly. Was he any better disposed towards adults?

Fujiwara eyed her, raised a scented cloth to his nostrils. His eyes were indifferent.

She saw then he was only here as a witness, not as help.

Oatha looked at her for a long time, and then turned to her father. There was a long pause; the two men were staring at one another.

Finally Okada spoke. 'It's no use, Daughter-Dear; really it isn't. Tell him what you know.'

Tears came to her eyes. This was so ignominious and cowardly. To betray her sister, and in public; to describe as best she could where Joah was, tell about her plans...

Okada gave scant comfort. 'Speak. You were in touch with Joah, so tell the man about it. For, one way or another, he'll get it out of us.'

Though she knew her father was right, Oki could only give back the shame of hot tears.

'I wish I was dead!'

Oatha showed her the skinning knife. 'That will be a long, long while yet.'

Nagaoka had led his mounted force straight down from the mountains. Somewhere between here and the coast would be Man and his party, though he didn't know where. At a guess, Man would be mid-way, and his fifty-strong party was too large to hide easily. Nagaoka would slow him, even stop him; then reinforcements would arrive and Nagaoka's side would win.

Almost at once they encountered a Sword Maiden racing on a tired pony, and captured her.

Soon Nagaoka was satisfying himself with her in every way. It was especially good to torture a female.

When he had finished, he beckoned over a courier before wiping blood off his hands.

'Send another carrier pigeon to Lord Oatha, and then go in

person to Lady Berenda and Master Hagiwara. Say that we have encountered many enemies. We battled them heroically, and from prisoners we have learned where the Foreigner and his friends are.'

'Down towards the coast, sir?'

'No.' The rigorous questioning had eventually worked. The Sword Maiden had first been made to howl, and then, eyeless, to talk secrets. Nagaoka pointed back towards Mount Unzen. 'They are still up on the higher ground. Tell our lord and the lady that we're going back to get them...'

The man saluted, then rode away.

When he had gone Nagaoka's confident look turned to fury. He snarled at his men, 'You are all useless! Not one of you guessed they were still hiding up in the mountains, the filthy cowards!' He glared; they lowered their eyes. 'What do you think? You never offer your own opinions!'

A black sash recruited locally responded.

'May I speak, sir? The Waning of the Moon has traditional rights in these parts and the Sword Maidens used to patrol all around here. It's true lots of them went up North with the Shogun, but in their territory shouldn't we proceed with caution?'

'Will your caution get us the Eye?' Nagaoka grimaced. 'We must stop this Emmanuel from getting the Eye to The Waning of the Moon. That place is a true fortress – even if mainly defended by women!'

'I would not like to winkle out enemies from there,' the black sash said honestly. 'Especially not when it is women of power behind those painted walls.'

'I agree! So we must intercept the enemy *before* they gain sanctuary! You heard what I tortured out of the prisoner! The Foreigner and the others are hiding from us back in the mountains!'

Unconvinced eyes watched Nagaoka. He swallowed. If he succeeded, black sash rule might last for a thousand years. But if he failed... Nagaoka was afraid: that was the black sash way. Lord Oatha was a mad brute, always had been. Hagiwara was his true apprentice, and this Lady Berenda even worse.

He was afraid, but he made his decision.

'You heard that Maiden! Lord Yoshi and his party are still up in the mountains – so we'll go get them! Mount up and follow me!'

Oatha left the Okadas down in the cells. In private again, in shadows away from the bright light of day, he licked his dry lips and approached the table with the black cube upon it.

'Do you hear me, Man Beyond Age?'

Nothing.

He pressed the point. 'I am here with the information you wanted; please respond.'

There was a clicking sound. Then the same blurred, accented voice spoke.

'I/we copy you.'

'The one you wanted – that Emmanuel, "The One Who Will Change" – '

'The power gem is first priority.'

Oatha said smoothly, 'That is with him, and I can tell you where he is.'

'I/we listen.'

Now I can pass on what the Okadas said, and I'm saved!

'He and the others are on the east coast of the Shimabara peninsula, not the west coast. They are near The Waning of the Moon, maybe three or four miles north of the place by now, or perhaps a little more. Look around the river there and you will find them.' He hated to say this next thing: but what alternative was there? 'Send your Steel Angels. This is your chance to take the Eye.'

As Man rode, he thought about Precious Stone. Was she actually missing, even captured? Or was she just out of contact? He didn't really know her; and yet he somehow knew she was brave beyond good sense. He writhed about on his horse. What if she missed them now, went on into one of the high passes as she'd said she would, and was then caught? Nagaoka was in the mountains and searching.

Man was miserable, with all this worry about Precious Stone.

They all had to turn south soon, and then take a path to The Waning of the Moon. What else could they do? What more could he, Man, do?

If only Mother Zandar can send us more help...

'Lord Emmanuel!'

Man looked back at Faslane, who was loping along like any of the samurai. His clothes were sweat-stained, and he looked

Words of Fury:

very serious.

Man leaned down from the saddle.

Faslane kept his voice low. 'I want to tell you the whole truth.'

Man stared down. Faslane stared back at Man, unshaven and grim.

Man slid off his stallion and gave it to young Sanada to ride. Sanada had been sweating and panting. Now the plump boy scrambled awkwardly into the saddle. He was a competent rider when the actual reins were in his hands.

Man kept trotting alongside his countryman from the Empire of Albion. There was the feel of unspoken secrets, and the silence between the two was not easy.

At last Man spoke. 'You are not just a sea pilot, are you?'

Faslane kept his voice quiet, though his eyes were busy looking round. He didn't want to be overhead.

'I did not lie to you. But you are right: I am more. And while you're alive to hear and I'm alive to tell you, you need to know more about things in Albion.'

'What makes you say you or I might die?'

Faslane glanced over. 'The ladies are supposed to have magical insight, aren't they?'

'What's the relevance of that?'

'Lord Emmanuel, look at their faces!'

Man did; and both the Voice and Lady Joah looked very unhappy indeed. Of course, they had seen *his* power closing in on The Waning; probably that was why.

But Man himself also felt an increasing sense of doom. He focused his mental energies on this stranger from home. 'Now tell me who you are.'

But Faslane only looked ahead.

Man felt a sudden terrible fury. In his heart, he didn't really want to hear upsetting truths. Even worse, this man could be another traitor. Man put one hand on his Words of Power and with the other tapped Faslane's shoulder.

'You Son of the Cold!' Faslane whirled round with his fighting iron there in his hand; but it was too late, for the sword Man had unsheathed was an inch from Faslane's throat. 'Now only your confession will save you!' Man said savagely. 'Yonai the traitor said another black heart is with us! *You!*'

Now Faslane's eyes looked so far down at the shining blade they distorted. He knew what that steel could do.

'I'm no' what you said! Truly I'm not!'

Man stood there, prepared to kill. The others had stopped walking and they were all staring, but that was distant.

A few drops of perspiration fell from Faslane's chin.

'You are a dangerous man, Dirk Faslane. That I do know. Now you have one minute to either confess or convince me you're not with *him*.'

Faslane licked dry lips. 'I'm no friend o' the Lord of the North!'

'Then who are you with! With those on the black ship?'

'I swear I know nothing of them, or their mission! I am a Queen's man!'

'Exactly what does that mean?'

'I'm Imperial Intelligence.'

Man felt a strong impulse to cut, and almost did. It was surely the double-I which had killed his father! He felt as if someone else had taken control of his limbs, and this person wanted to deal out death. It was very hard to hold back that fury.

'So Imperial Intelligence sent you here to kill me?'

'*How did you know?*'

'For God's sake, remember who my father was and how he was ended! I have insight into dark strategy, Faslane! Now, given what you've just admitted, give me one good reason not to kill you!'

'Because I was given the choice over what to do, depending on what I found. Kill you, yes – if you were a danger to Albion! They say your father was one of *his*, so you might have been, too!'

Yoshi ambled over, an eyebrow cocked at the display of weaponry.

'A warm discussion, Albion style?'

'That's exactly what it is,' Man said, not taking his eyes from Faslane. Then he addressed the man from Albion again. 'What do you think about me now?'

'Now that I know you, I make my choice. My lord, you are deserving, *and I can bring you home!*'

Man felt breathless. Was this safe passage? Then realism kicked in.

'Alive? Or dead?'

'Alive! I will get you home alive, to serve the realm! And you would need my help – you'd *have* to have my help – to cross into Her Majesty's territory!'

Words of Fury:

'I'd get that help from you? You swear it?'

'Aye.'

After another moment Man sheathed his long sword, to Faslane's obvious relief. 'It seems I'm both more popular at home than I thought and *less* popular.' He looked over at Faslane again. 'I still haven't put the thought of assassination out of my mind.'

'I kill only the Queen's enemies!'

'And then you mentioned that the Queen is dead! Where does that leave you – and me?'

'In a place where you can have hope of redemption.'

Man said nothing to that, so Faslane looked at Yoshi.

'Sir, they tell me you are of the noblest lineage possible. I am certain you will understand loyalty and duty. I have been trying to do my duty. I am a senior lieutenant, secretly dispatched here on a mission to meet your friend the Lord Emmanuel and gauge him.'

Yoshi was dangerously quiet.

'And when you have gauged what manner of metal is in him, true metal or false, what then, Faslane of Albion?'

'If I was positive about him, and I am, I should ask him to return with me.'

Yoshi gave Faslane a hard look. 'And if you were negative?'

Faslane flushed. 'You both know!'

Yoshi acknowledged that truth with a gesture, and then signaled everyone to move on. This was a death race they were running, and none of them wanted to lose.

Yoshi gave his most gay smile. 'So now you are positive about my friend – ?'

'Lord Emmanuel, I want you home – on behalf of others far greater than I!' Faslane spoke with force. 'However your father ended, think of the name you bear. The Empire has need of you!'

'And so does this land!' said Yoshi, suddenly furious. 'Don't you understand what we're doing now? We're trying to fulfill a Prophecy, for this Empire's salvation. If we get it wrong, if we fail, *he* wins – everywhere, *forever*.'

Faslane looked from Yoshi to Man.

'I'm a patriot as much as either of you,' Faslane said. 'Of course I put my own native country above this land, but I hate *him* as much as you do, and I'm happy to fight the Lord of the North alongside you.'

When Faslane realized there would be no response, he

simply stayed standing as the column went on and passed him by.

As Man took back his horse and rode along with Yoshi, Yoshi looked over his shoulder.

'I think your Faslane at least has manners – for a foreigner. He's willing to let us two old friends speak in private.'

'Yes.'

'So what do you think?'

Man pursed his lips. 'I think he is no Son; and I think he has finally been honest. But I can't shake off the feeling he has more to tell.'

'He's said a few major things already, hasn't he?' Yoshi sounded somewhere between awed and amused. 'So Imperial Intelligence sent him here to "persuade" you back to Albion – or to murder you... With authority like that, he must be a player in his own right.'

'I suppose.'

'But he has no knowledge of the black ship that came from your Empire to Jade?'

'You heard what he said, Yoshi. It could have been a rogue mission, I suppose.'

'Yes, of course, but still sent by *someone* mighty!'

'I don't know who.'

'Faslane must have *some* idea who, back in your Albion, wants to kill you!'

Man shrugged, feeling an aggravating pain in his head again. Would he never be free of the Tears' taint?

'There are factions in the Empire. Now that the Queen is dead they will fight even more than before.'

'You believe that Elizabeth is dead?'

Man frowned. 'I don't know. But when we are in sanctuary, I will ask Mother Zandar. I understand she is a dream-walker.'

'In a dream she can travel 13,000 miles, find special knowledge and then return?'

Man smiled, though he rubbed his sore cheek, wanting to curse the Tears' name.

'It sounds like magic, doesn't it? It should. It is magic.'

Yoshi looked all round. 'You say you and the girls actually feel *him* here?'

Man said thoughtfully, 'It seems to me we are heading for trouble, Yoshi. An ambush using arms – or magic...'

'But we have scouts out, and the Sword Maidens rode on

ahead.'

'Yes.' Man was silent a moment, thinking about Sweet Snake, and the kisses of her twin sister. 'You think all the villagers who've seen us will keep quiet?'

'If Oatha's men come, one way or another they won't stay silent, will they?'

'His men are torturers.' Man admitted it: 'The country people will talk.'

'But what else could we do?'

'Nothing,' Man told his friend.

'Thanks,' Yoshi said. 'This responsibility feels huge.'

'You could have done nothing different,' Man said firmly. 'You couldn't order whole villages to be wiped out, just to keep our secrets! Win or lose, we are what we are; on the side of right!'

Yoshi clapped his shoulder, and they rode on together to the head of the column. They were proud to be leaders. Their samurai trotted at a mile-eating pace, three abreast. Several had spears. In their midst, Joah, the Voice and Keli rode ponies. Two Heads was striding just behind them. Man saw he had his great axe resting on one shoulder. Sanada also followed the women.

They all went loping along together. Man enjoyed the fast pace his horse set. Their riders were leading, their foot soldiers trotting to keep up. Man hadn't forgotten the peril they were in, though. He reached out with his mind, thinking of the Eye – and he thought he touched something magical.

Was that from the Eye, in this moment of peril? Or had Man accidentally touched *him*?

Man closed his eyes for a moment to concentrate; but there was nothing more. He remembered then what Joah had said about confidence being so important to magic. Was there some way of believing more in himself? If he did, there might be no limit to his power.

The road dipped down and they followed it. Man had a terrible feeling that Precious Stone had already crossed their path and gone up into the mountains. Maybe she'd be captured; maybe they'd never meet again. Man's doomed feeling increased. Then he saw, away to the south and east, a giant pillar of grayish smoke, not very different to the black stormclouds above The Waning.

'What's that? Is that from Mother Zandar's? Has it fallen?'

There was a silence. Yoshi also stared. Further away another pillar of smoke appeared.

The Voice came up. 'Lady Joah, what do you think?'

Faslane answered for her. 'It has to be something huge burning. But, whatever it is, it's too far away to be The Waning.'

The Voice sighed. 'That's one small mercy.'

'You think so?' Now Yoshi was pointing. 'That'll be our enemies, burning Waning ports and villages.'

Man was relieved it was not The Waning, but aggrieved by the violence. 'Yoshi, why that cruelty?'

'Oatha's people want to get our allies preoccupied, don't they? And not preoccupied with helping us.'

'So villages die to keep the Sword Maidens from getting to us!'

'Yes.' Yoshi turned to Far-Speaker Keli. He was emphatic. 'You must get through. Tell your Mother Zandar that we need armed friends here!'

The little novice looked right into Yoshi's eyes. 'You feel it too, Lord Yoshi?'

The Voice answered for her poet friend. 'We all feel *his* threat!'

Man felt something more specific, then: flashes of agony so powerful they made him flinch even through *his* barrier.

Now who might that be? Oh, it could be any one of us, or every one of us – if we get caught!

Yoshi leaned towards the Far-Speaker girl. 'Please!'

So Keli closed her eyes. Man could see the mental effort written plainly on her face. Then she opened her eyes again.

Man already knew what she was going to say and so he said it for her. 'Nothing.'

'No, Lord Emmanuel.' She sounded very sad. 'Nothing.'

They took the same path through the paddy fields and then up among the trees towards the mountains. Man kept turning his head, wondering where Nagaoka was, where his lovely Precious Stone was. But he saw neither.

It was not long afterwards that Kido trotted back to Ozawa, Yoshi and Man. 'I know this is a delay, sirs, but I think you'd better see this.'

When Man rode forward into the deserted village, he saw the scene with hypnotic intensity. The colors leaped out at him, the pale pink of flesh and the red of fresh blood. A naked woman had been nailed by her hands to an inn door. Beside Lady Joah

Words of Fury:

the young Far-Speaker began to sob.

'See what they've done to her!'

For Man a glimpse had been more than enough. He could not recognize the face. It seemed during the torture she had been disfigured. He really did not want it to be anyone he knew.

Then Man saw the chain around her neck, though the precious stone that used to be there had been forced from its setting.

That was how he knew who it was. He felt a howling rage build up in him, and a sorrow beyond estimation. His fists clenched.

It had to be Precious Stone.

'That's one of the Sword Maidens who went on ahead!' said Yoshi.

Man had never been angrier. He did not want to give those who had done this an honorable way out of life. He wanted to use his fists and feet to beat them to death, bone by breaking bone by breaking bone – and then start over again.

Ozawa was gruffly impersonal. 'She was probably found by the black sash cavalry and brutalized for information.'

'Then where are the cavalry now?' Faslane asked. He looked around. 'What if they're somewhere close?'

Man slid down from the saddle, raised his hands.

'Look at her!'

The scalped head hung limply, so there was no hair to provide an identity. She had been partly skinned, with her eyelids cut away. Man saw even stone-faced Ugaki was appalled. Scraps of red clothing and her broken swords had been left in front of the mortal remains.

Ozawa pursed his lips. 'Horsemen were here. Tracks – horseshoes – show dozens of them.'

'The same purity police cavalry we saw before?'

'That's my presumption. Nagaoka – you know him, don't you?'

'I do, and well. He is a torturer.'

'Our enemies are very bad people, Man.'

'They are.' Man's mind felt fogged by this horror. He needed to think straight. 'If you were our enemy and if you had men enough here, what would you do?'

Ozawa had been thinking through the options, because he answered without a moment's hesitation.

'If I could, I would get an armada to the shore here, and land men. I would then put my forces on all roads to The Waning, close each and every road, and lay siege.'

'You would close every last door against us, Ozawa-san?'
'Yes.'

Ozawa has seen how it will go, Man thought bitterly. So now we're trapped. There's no road ahead; there's only death – as it was for Precious Stone.

A man had kneeled to check the dead girl, and now he called over his shoulder.

'She's still alive!'

As they ran to her, the Maiden lifted her head. Scalped, she squinted her ruined eyes through a mask of congealing blood.

'Who's that?'

'I am Fujiwara-noh-Yoshi, Sword Maiden. You know me from before.'

'Ah, yes.' The broken voice was a dry croak. 'A party of black sash horsemen came galloping here. ...Nagaoka was the name given. At least he left me my tongue, so I can talk. You still have The One Who Will Change with you?'

'That is the name some give me,' Man said.

Precious Stone choked, the ruined eyes flickering about. 'They were in between you and sanctuary, so I ... had to find ... some way to make them leave.'

'I see,' Yoshi said.

'So I let them catch me.'

'You *let* them catch you!'

'So they would listen. But perhaps now,' the woman said, 'perhaps I wouldn't...' She coughed. 'The pain was... But when the black sashes tortured me, I said nothing. Not at first.' She was shaking her head from the pain and weeping from her pierced eyes so that tears mixed with the blood. 'Then they...'

Man laid a hand upon her bloody shoulder, and he saw Lady Joah making the Sign of the Cross. 'Save your strength!'

'I did save my strength, for this! I have to tell you ... what I told them...'

Man heard her coughing and choking; blood trickled out of her torn mouth.

'I told them I had come here in advance ... that you were still back on the mountain path behind me. Ah, my Emmanuel, they didn't believe me!'

'But...' Man's voice trailed off. So her misdirection had failed?

Words of Fury:

The Sword Maiden shuddered. 'That's when the man called Nagaoka took my eyes ... and *then* he believed me.'

'So they went back up into the mountains!' Man had to give her something for that, and it was sincerest thanks. 'You are wonderful. Tricking them might save us!'

She was restlessly turning her head and weeping even more blood. 'Others of the enemy may have set an ambush ahead, but you might possibly have a clear run to Miracle Island and then on to The Waning.'

'The mountains are impossible, and so is the east coast,' said Yoshi. 'So Miracle Island is our only chance.'

'Yes. Now leave me!'

'Rest,' said Man. 'You know we cannot desert you.'

'I will rest no more in this life.' The Sword Maiden coughed up new blood. Her head shuddered on her shoulders. 'Live for me,' she said, choking. 'And take revenge.' Then her head flopped down.

There was silence. Then Joah spoke with sad fury.

'Lord Oatha must be punished for this – and Nagaoka.'

'If we live,' Yoshi said quietly. 'Nagaoka's war party outnumber us, don't forget, and many more are coming.' He gave a harsh grin. 'Being cavalry, if they turn back soon, they'll catch us before we reach The Waning.'

'But you heard what this Maiden said; they may not turn back, and so we might escape!' said Ozawa.

'Yes.' Some of the strain had lifted from Joah's face. 'It's a chance. Let's go.'

Yoshi turned. 'Emmanuel?'

'My Precious Stone *died* to give us one last opportunity! She's sent Nagaoka into the mountains, to give us time. So I agree: the direct route to Zandar's – just as fast as we can!'

Lady Berenda still felt that she was walking to her own funeral. For *he*, after all, had his human forces coming here; and by magic he was himself besieging The Waning of the Moon. What place could there now be for her?

Probably no place at all. I have no future with *him*; I am utterly alone.

Unless she turned wholeheartedly to good, there was no future o any kind. But, realistically, how could someone so compromised as she really become good?

She told Hagiwara, 'I have felt Nagaoka, on the trail after

Man and the others. Others of our lord's followers are coming in from the eastern coast. Once Man is located, and soon he will be, all the forces of the Lord of the North will concentrate on him.'

'Then your Emmanuel is done – and so are we!'

'Though even for *him* it is a strain to oppose all the magic of The Waning.'

It was such a strain that even *he* could not do it all. Suddenly *his* pressure on her lifted.

Hagiwara felt that; he spun about. 'What is it?'

'*He* has had to concentrate elsewhere... So now I *feel* Man!'

'Go on.'

'He is telling the others how a dying Sword Maiden fooled Nagaoka and sent him off into the mountains! Oh, Nagaoka is a pure idiot! And fear has made him stupidly aggressive! While he is racing the wrong way through those mountain passes Emmanuel and the others will get to sanctuary!'

She turned to Hagiwara now, wondering how to slant her information. Sneer at the mistakes of a rival, treat this error as a tragedy, or make use of the mistake?

Hagiwara had turned pale. 'Lady, please tell *him!* Informing him and excusing ourselves might save us!'

She stopped, put her hands to her temples and tried to mind-speak to *him* with all the power at her command – though she did not dare use the ruby within her.

She tried again and again, but there was no communication with the Lord of the North. She turned to Hagiwara.

'It's no good. My former master will not hear me.'

Hagiwara turned his head this way and that, almost sick with desperation.

'Can you tell Nagaoka where Emmanuel is?'

'Even if I can, will he listen?'

'Frighten him! Make him turn back! If that foreigner makes it to The Waning, you and I will be iced over for all eternity!'

With the pressure of *his* mighty magic still reduced, she saw what she could do. A spell of Far-Seeing meant she found where Nagaoka was galloping on the road back into the mountains.

She concentrated, and made an image of herself there that was huge, much as Man had done back in Jade.

She paraded before Nagaoka.

'YOU HAVE BEEN FOOLED, LITTLE MAN! THEY ARE ON THE ROAD BEHIND YOU! GO BACK AND FIND THEM.'

She saw how he stared up at herself, the giantess. 'How do I

Words of Fury: 289

know this is *you*, lady? And, besides, isn't it too late?'

She answered that in the same great voice; but then she lost contact.

As soon as she came back to ordinary awareness, Hagiwara spoke to her. 'You made Nagaoka hear?'

'I did.'

Had she done enough for the Lord of the North to notice? Had she persuaded Nagaoka to turn back?

She feared that she had not.

'What now?'

'For our master, it's excellent, if Nagaoka obeyed. If he did, I cannot see Man getting to safety; Nagaoka will intercept him. But for us?' Berenda considered, pouting. 'I see nothing good.'

'But if you turned back Nagaoka – '

'So what? *If* Nagaoka has turned back, and I do say *if*, then the battle will likely be over before you and I can hope to arrive – with no thanks for us. And *if* our subordinate has not obeyed my avatar, then most likely Emmanuel and those others will arrive safely into the bosom of our enemies.'

'Freeze me! – Neither result will return us to *his* favor.'

'No.'

'Lady, I almost want to run.'

That was a temptation for Berenda, too. The sea gleamed between two steep hills. The sea was pathless, with no set roads, no checkpoints.

I might take a ship, and run as I once planned, and turn good. I have a power gem in me still, and surely *his* attention cannot be everywhere. I would be free!

But I would be alone, with a great enemy on my trail.

Or I can stay here and try to regain *his* trust.

She shrugged herself erect, and then walked on.

Or I can stay here and, secretly, oppose him!

Nagaoka had been leading, exhilarated by the charge up into the mountains. They would catch Lord Yoshi's party soon; he felt certain. He had the men and they were mounted. The enemy had fewer. Trees still clumped here, and he rounded a bend.

Lady Berenda was waiting for him. She was thirty feet tall and her legs straddled the roadway.

'THEY ARE ON THE ROAD BEHIND YOU! GO BACK AND FIND THEM.'

Wide-eyed, he backed away on his horse as he stared at the

giantess. 'How do I know this is *you*, lady? And, besides, isn't it too late?'

She sneered down.

'YOU HAVE HORSES, NAGAOKA, WHILE THEY ARE MOSTLY ON FOOT! FIND THEM! STRIKE! OUR MASTER WANTS ONLY THIS: EMMANUEL KINROSS, THE TWO WOMEN, AND THE EYE! KILL THE REST!'

That was plain enough.

'Back, back!' Nagaoka screamed at his men. 'The enemy is still on the fast road south! Back!'

It took Nagaoka a couple of minutes to turn their column around. In that time he lost it completely, raging and beating his own clenched fists on his war helmet. Then he sent his men galloping on in disorder, speed being everything now, so that before they gained sanctuary their enemies could be caught and destroyed.

'Hagiwara,' said Berenda, 'if young Nagaoka does intercept the Foreigner and his party, do you think the fight might possibly last long enough for us to arrive and help?'

Her companion had not noticed the ambiguity over who might be helped. She sighed, surrounded as always by the stupid and insensitive. There was that small secret part of her which was not *his*. In her mind, she celebrated what she might become.

'Lady Berenda, if we *can* get to the enemy before they reach safety and help beat them, that would please our master!'

'It would, more than anything – if we can do it!'

Now she looked up to heaven, to the south. She saw *his* mighty weaves, though to the untutored eye there was only dark cloud swirling above The Waning of the Moon.

She mopped at her brow with a sweat-cloth. Of course the Lord of the North was very powerful; he was also hateful.

Yes, hateful! – She wondered now if she could convince Hagiwara to change sides.

Then another strategy occurred to her.

'I wonder if we might just sit out this battle. Say Emmanuel then loses the fight and the Eye. Later I could sneak into this Waning of the Moon, and...'

'Ah!' He mistook her, of course. 'You could turn it *from within*, towards our master!'

'I *could* turn that place.'

If I have the courage, and the necessary luck, *I could even*

Words of Fury: 291

turn it towards me...

The afternoon grew hotter and hotter, or perhaps it was her nervous state.

Chapter Twenty-Eight: *The Disciple I Loved Most*

Heat, terrible sweltering heat, affected the Lady Berenda in her long black robes. Then there was a real surprise. She suddenly felt *his* cooling touch, his delightful stroking. She shivered in pleasure, mouth hanging open.

Then he spoke. 'YOU TURNED BACK NAGAOKA AND HIS CAVALRY.'

'Yes, yes!'

Fury exploded. 'EXPLAIN YOURSELF, BITCH!'

Terrified, she humbled herself completely, kneeling and kow-towing.

'They were sent in the wrong direction. I wanted them to come back, master! Then they could stop Man and get the Eye for you! I know I did you wrong, earlier; I confess it. I – I was *misled*, by the example of others. I beg you to forgive me!'

'ALL THINGS CHANGE, TILL I PUT AN END TO ALL CHANGE. NOW, DO MORE.'

'Master, how?'

'I PLAN TO LURE MY ENEMY ZANDAR OUT OF HER SANCTUARY. THE ONE CALLED "EMMANUEL", WHO MIGHT HAVE THE POWER TO DEFY ME, HIM I MUST ... REDUCE.'

'I gave him my special kiss!'

'I KNOW.' There was a silence. 'PERHAPS I WILL NOT NEED TO DESTROY ALL OF THE WANING. IF I WIN WITHOUT DOING THAT, I CAN PUT MY OWN PERSON IN COMMAND. WHO THAT PERSON MIGHT BE...'

He left the thought unfinished.

Of course they called the Lord of the North the Father of lies; but Berenda knew that was mere propaganda. Whenever it was convenient for him he kept his word. There would probably be *his* agents within The Waning of the Moon, but if not, if Emmanuel was defeated and Mother Zandar destroyed...

There will be a place of power for me!

'THIS "EMMANUEL"... TELL ME OF HIM!'

'I feel him coming down from the mountains,' said Lady Berenda, 'and he is not far from enemy headquarters.'

'BAD!'

'But our people are now coming up from the east coast, master. There are hundreds of black sashes – many already sworn to *you*. And Nagaoka – just as I hoped – is coming down from the mountains, with sixty men and more already following!'

'THEN WE MUST PREVAIL?'

She felt her joy diminish. 'The enemy are fighters and they have magic. If they access the Eye...'

'AH, THE EYE!' The bass voice throbbed with a mighty passion which she felt within her body. 'I CANNOT QUITE SEE, MY BERENDA. THE WANING HAS WARDS WHICH GENERATE INTERFERENCE WHEN THEY MEET MY OWN, AND I MUST HOLD BACK FROM TOUCHING THE EYE, OR ELSE...' There was silence for a moment. 'THE EYE IS DANGEROUS. PRESENTLY ITS USE IS BEYOND THE BOY EMMANUEL AND THE OTHERS, BUT IF THEY GET TO THE WANING...'

She raised two clenched fists. 'Oh, master, choose me to stop them! I will never again let you down!'

When there was only silence, she began more hopeless weeping.

'YOU...' At first he sounded angry. Then he said, 'YOU WERE THE DISCIPLE I LOVED MOST. BERENDA, I ACCEPT YOU AGAIN.'

When he said that, it had the force of magic.

So there could be forgiveness; there could be hope. She laughed her delight, dazed with happiness. She still had her secrets, still felt dirty, but in his presence she was overjoyed.

'Oh, Master, *I love you!* How may I serve?'

'JUST STOP THEM!'

Keli turned to look at Man.

'There was a moment just now when *he* let go his magic. I might then have touched some person in The Waning!'

'Mother Zandar could have heard you? And if she did, she'll send a force to help, or even come herself?'

'Perhaps,' said the young novice, 'though I can't say for certain. Still, we are not far.'

'Not far,' Man said, as he rode on towards the curved arc of waning moon, which rose up like a promise made of stone. He was totally committed; and he felt totally satisfied by his commitment. 'No, not far!'

The Voice came over to him. 'Man? Just for a moment things cleared, and I felt Nagaoka...'

'Well?'

'He did go back up towards the mountains, but somebody warned him.' Her face twisted. 'And now he's after us again.'

Mother Zandar remained in the Map Room with Sulina and Daisen, waiting for more battle reports. Already the invaders had taken several coastal villages – on the *east* coast now as well as the west – driving out the tiny Sword Maiden garrisons.

Then Zandar felt a sudden absence, which impressions then filled. She began to speak. 'Daisen, for a moment *he* stepped away from his station above us, and I think I heard...'

'Was it one of our scouts?' Daisen was eager. 'Was it Novice Keli? What did she say?'

Zandar's fingers moved above the living map, to the north of The Waning near where Miracle Island was.

'I couldn't quite hear,' she admitted, 'though it is good to know our people are close.'

'Even better if we knew they were close enough to get inside!'

Now Irizo came in. Her face was sad and serious.

'Nothing from Sweet Snake – or the three other parties we dispatched.'

'Are they dead?'

'In your place I might have asked "silenced?", but you are direct as always, Sulina.'

'Surely not all dead?' said Daisen, though there was little hope in her voice.

Sulina persisted. 'What about Novice Keli?'

'Nothing except that little flash of vision,' said Zandar. 'I will meditate, and look for her again.'

'The same silence from Four Rocks.' Irizo sighed at all the bad news. 'And I just spoke to Winter Morning.'

'The she-captain bravely led my bodyguard, when *he* came.' Zandar's compassion spoke. 'How is she?'

'Well enough, physically, though inwardly much changed.'

'How so, Healer?'

Irizo spread her hands. 'After seeing *him* break in here she will fight no more. She has shaved her head and taken vows as a Buddhist nun.'

'She has surrendered to fear? Sister, that surprises me!'

'Surrendered, Mother? That I don't know – though the Lord of the North is truly terrifying. Perhaps she has more faith in the power of prayer than the power of the sword.'

Words of Fury: 295

'Her replacement Hanake will fight – that I know – and so will I!' Sulina sounded utterly certain. 'And so I think will Man!'

Mother Zandar was tight-lipped. 'I have met young Emmanuel in dream, while you have not. And also...'

A faint booming sound came: it was from *his* besieging storm.

'Mother, you seem *un*-certain about The One Who Will Change.'

Zandar thought of lying; then she thought of merely concealing the truth; then she decided to stay silent about what she had done.

If my not-quite-lie is uncovered, it will be just as bad as a frank lie, and trust in me will be gone.

And yet if I did confess, I would make myself seem incompetent or worse – and that would do no good, would it?

I need to do something to prove I am still in charge. Whatever the danger from *him*, perhaps *this* is the time to go outside.

From horseback, Man explained to Yoshi how Nagaoka was coming for them again. 'Thank the Lord Precious Stone gained us time, but now we have to run!'

'If Nagaoka's still on his way down from the mountains, and the new black sashes are still close to the coast, maybe can run on south in between the two forces.'

Yoshi began waving his people on more quickly. He knew their time had almost run out.

After he checked his map, he turned to Man again. 'There's little tree-cover, just shrubs and paddy fields, and that river flowing to The Waning, which we must cross...'

Ozawa asked a plain question. 'Can we?'

'We must.'

Man threw in, 'Isn't the crossing at the river-island garrisoned by Sword Maidens?'

'My scout didn't get close enough to say if the Sword Maidens are still around, and Lilac hasn't reported back.'

'Fords and bridges are always good for ambushing!'

'Yes, Lord of Albion.' That was Novice Keli speaking to Man. 'But there is that island. We may cross – if only we can get there!'

'Miracle Island?' Yoshi had to smile. 'An auspicious name!'

A samurai spoke seriously. 'I know it. Lady Kannon

appeared there, to some wandering poet.'

Kannon was a female face of the Buddha, and often called the Goddess of Mercy.

'Appeared to some wandering drunk, more likely,' said Yoshi under his breath.

'I'd rather three or four loyal regiments appeared,' Ozawa said. 'Ah, I wish the Sword Maidens had all returned safely and told us that the roads to The Waning were open! If not, I wish I had carrier pigeons to send messages to Mother Zandar asking for help!'

'And I,' Man said calmly, 'wish I was the Emperor of Albion, with the Empire's treasury in my hip pocket, and a hundred dancing girls here to spend it on!'

Yoshi acknowledged the wry humor with a wryer smile. He looked up then, shading his eyes, and Man wondered if he was looking for more mech-birds.

Now he turned to Man and Ozawa. 'I know it's a risk, but I'm going to do this at speed. Every second now is gold. Man, can you hurry up the rear?'

'I will.'

Man stopped his horse, his fingers tapping the black stallion's neck as he let the column go by. Man looked them over as they passed. Forty-some samurai left, a couple of Sword Maidens and the fighting monk, and young Keli. The black sashes likely had hundreds close and more coming.

Poor odds, he had to admit.

'Faster!' Yoshi called, from the front.

Now Man felt another pulse of male power, and he turned to see slow-spinning blades of distortion over their destination. They would be there to chew up the Waning's defensive wards. Then there was a blow that shook the earth, and Man flinched. The Lord of the North was hammering at the door to The Waning, so strongly that Man felt it must eventually open.

When the last stragglers came up Man called out. 'Push on ahead! Push on!'

Man saw his fellows pick up the pace. Sweat was running down their faces. Then he went riding ahead. Joah was on her pony, with the Voice and Two Heads just behind her.

'Joah, is there any way *you* can get your friends in the monastery to send us help? Women with swords or with magic – ideally women of both sorts!'

She raised an eyebrow, every inch the aristocrat. 'From your tone, you find the notion of fighting women absurd.'

'I saw Sword Maidens often enough in Jade, though I suppose I do find it strange that some women fight with long swords.'

'You won't find it strange to be saved.'

'No, I won't, if it happens. Will it?'

Joah's hand tightened on her bridle. 'Mother Zandar knows we're coming.'

'But does she know *when*, or from where?'

'Emmanuel, don't you have any faith in your destiny?'

'No.'

She fanned her face without replying, hurt by his brusque answer. Therefore Man risked a gallantry in response.

'I do have faith in *you*, Joah: in your honesty and your beautiful soul!'

Man saluted her, and also the Voice from Afar.

Joah cooled her face with a fan as Man rode away. He was such a gentleman, sometimes; and then such a driven brute.

In that moment of thinking about Man, some other things in her mind finally snapped into place.

The logic was clear, though depressing. She turned and spoke to the Voice from Afar.

'You wanted to hear my conclusions? Well, here they are. We have seen many strange things, have we not, from *his* self-image a half-mile tall to the monsters on the black beach?'

'We saw all that and more!'

'Yet I did not see any great harm done to us.'

'Therefore?'

'Therefore the things we saw were mostly illusions, not so much to frighten us, for we are not children.'

'*I* was frightened, at the time.'

'I was, too! But I suspect the illusions were made for a purpose...'

'To...?' The Voice frowned.

'To take up our time and our attention.'

The Voice thought it over. 'If we are delayed, but not destroyed ... who might benefit?'

Joah let seconds go by before she spoke again. 'I cannot reach Mother Zandar. Nor can you, nor the holy Mother's trained Far-Speaker.'

'What is the link you are making?'

'Why, presently Mother Zandar is safe at The Waning, behind ancient wards that are – in some cases – over a thousand years old.'

'It's good she's safe.'

'Of course, but what if *he* has been playing with us – delaying us at the mountain bridge, for example, when his creature Yonai could have killed me easily, or killed Yoshi, or Emmanuel, or you.'

The Voice spoke honestly.

'Dear Lady Joah, I am out of my depth. What do I know about power politics or high magic? Please say what you think. You can trust me.'

Joah looked at her for several seconds.

'I know I can, but somehow it is hard to be direct. And yet I know that this mutual distrust is just what *he* wants.' Joah took a breath. 'I fear that *his* keeping us in danger but *not* destroying us has been deliberate. It will lead to one very, very bad thing.'

'You're scaring me, Lady Joah! What do you mean?'

'If *he* makes things seem bad but does not destroy us, then, to help Man and the rest of us all, Mother Zandar might feel obliged to leave the protection of The Waning.'

'And when she is away from her fortress – '

'Then *he* will strike her down.'

'Oh, that makes sense!'

'But, dear Voice, what can we do?'

'Lady, we are warned – you are who you are, and I am the Voice from Afar! We fight.'

The two looked at each other very directly, taking in each other fully.

'That's true. And now I will tell Man and Yoshi.'

Chapter Twenty-Nine: *Expect Nothing*

'So you think much of our journey has been delays, all organized by *him*?' Man asked in disbelief. 'Even his giant self-image of ice might have been little more than a trick?'

'Yes. We were not destroyed then, and I fear that was not our luck but *his* cunning. We are the living lure, to get Mother Zandar away from The Waning.'

The little novice understood at once. 'I will try to Far-Speak her, and give warning.'

Obviously *she* believed that Joah had guessed right. Keli's face changed, screwing up with concentration. Man watched and wondered.

Then the novice sagged; now there was despair on her face.

'You still can't get through?'

'Lord Emmanuel, *he* has besieged us!'

'Keep trying,' Man said. 'And let us know if you do make contact.'

Man might have said more; but just then there was shouting from the head of the column. He turned his horse and set off at a gallop.

He passed Yoshi, who was dismounted and examining a horse-hoof. Yoshi called out. 'Wait for me!'

Man didn't, because he had seen the single rider racing along the road towards them. As he galloped to meet the Sword Maiden, he saw heat-haze dance on the road.

He really, really wanted this to be Precious Stone.

Of course, it wasn't. The frantically waving rider was Lilac. When he saw her face he began to curse. Her news was going to be bad.

As Man reined in beside Lilac, the Sword Maiden almost fell from her pony. She had lost her helmet, and her bloodied red tongue was hanging out of a grey face. She saluted Man, though her eyes were already losing focus.

In spite of her hurts, she had enough left to gasp out her warning.

'Lord Emmanuel!' She spat blood, wiped at her slack mouth. 'Riders wearing the black are coming up from the coast road towards Miracle Island! Forty or fifty, with hundreds more coming!'

Man asked the key question. 'Is the island defended?'

'The garrison has gone.'

Worry came and deepened. 'Have the enemies seized the island?'

'No, but when they do they will have cut the road that goes to The Waning, and then you will be caught here in the open!'

'Is there no help on Miracle Island?'

'I don't know! Expect nothing.'

'We must seize that place before we can go on?'

'Yes!'

'What if we can't?'

'You *have* to... Take the island, defend yourselves ... hope that help comes!'

Man no more believed in hope, as against brute force, than his father did. In his memory he heard his father's voice: *How do you win? You get there first with the most men...*

Lilac choked, slumped, and then fell from her pony, face-down on the track. She was dead. It was only then that Man saw the three long arrows in her back.

He turned his gaze to the road leading to Miracle Island. On it, four covered wagons were following a string of pack-ponies onto the island, and people were everywhere. Man wondered if Keli's promised Sword Maidens might still there, or at least close. Above the little river-island was a watchtower, tall as a four-storey building, but no flags were flying there now.

Yoshi galloped up, two of his veterans riding with him and others like Ugaki running after. He looked angrily at Man.

'You should have waited for me!'

'I wanted to hear what she had to say, and lucky that I did – since she's dead now!'

'What did she tell you?'

'Black sashes on horseback are coming from the coast, maybe fifty with more following. They'll take the island and cut us off from Mother Zandar's!'

Yoshi beat his fists together. 'May Jehovah and Allah help us! We'll be caught in the open, and that'll be the end!'

'It will be, if the other side gets there first – and they're mounted!' The island was three-quarters of a mile away. When Man's experienced eye saw the dust-cloud approaching from the coast he understood the key point at once. 'Our foot soldiers won't make it in time!'

It was a cry of pain. 'No.'

He glanced at Yoshi, his eyes wild. 'But our horses might! I know we'll be outnumbered, but let's race the enemy!'

Words of Fury:

Yoshi's face lit up, though the odds were very bad indeed.

'You!' he yelled to Ugaki. The powerfully-built Ugaki was fast, but not as fast as a galloping horse. 'Enemies are coming to that island, but we want to beat them! Get the other foot soldiers there as soon as you can, and defend it!'

Ugaki waved to show that he had understood, and he started to sprint. Man saw the other men on foot follow him. They wanted to get to the island before the enemy riders could, though Man knew there was no chance of that. Only their few horsemen had the speed.

Man stood up in his stirrups, beckoning the rest of their riders.

'Those of you who are mounted, come with us now!'

Man and Yoshi raced forward, desperate to get to the island before the enemy, and hold them off long enough for their foot to arrive – but the enemy were well on their way.

'They have fifty horsemen, most in armor!'

'True, Emmanuel; but don't we have more heart?'

'You have the soul of a poet!'

'Not entirely! – Now, are the enemy banners on the far side of the river?'

Man leaned down beside his horse's neck. 'I think so!'

On the isle itself frightened civilians suddenly saw what was coming; they started to run away.

Man saw the islet clearly now. There were drinks stalls and some shops. A stone statue overlooked a walled garden shrine that was thick with tall flowers.

There were only two plank bridges, one on this northern side, and another on the far side where the first enemies would arrive.

Man saw their banners were held high. A leading squad, with a regiment to follow.

He wished he had picked up a shield.

Now he looked back quickly. He and Yoshi still rode in the lead, with five or six other horse-riders close behind. The Voice from Afar and the Lady Joah followed on their ponies, along with the mounted Sword Maiden.

Man and Yoshi galloped over the bridge on this side. A last few escaping civilians screamed.

It was chaos here, but Man reached the other bridge a minute or two before the first half-dozen black sashes, with Yoshi alongside him. They went on into the open on the other side of the river, two men to fight off fifty.

Man slowed his horse with his knees, got his bow from beside his saddle, loosed an arrow which swept a black-armored man right off his horse. Then he loosed another which – he regretted it – only wounded a horse. It was so maddened it threw its rider and then went galloping away. The black sash, foot caught in a stirrup, was dragged shrieking behind.

Yoshi's bow-work also brought down a man.

Then the first nine enemy horsemen were upon them. Man saw most had armor on, and of course he and Yoshi did not. Nevertheless he attacked with gusto. His sword cut away one spear-head and then he impaled its wielder. Leaning out from the saddle, one roaring black sash slashed at his head, but Man dodged back. He found he was behind another enemy and he cut hard with Words of Power. This man's helmeted head bounced away, torso sagging on the horse.

Man whirled his black stallion around. A new enemy almost reached him with a stabbing spear, but his parry meant the spearhead missed his throat by an inch. He hacked at the man's shoulder – not a perfect blow, but disabling. The man rode away cursing, blood pouring over him. Man drove his blade deep into another enemy, but then three swords were cutting at him.

'Here!' Yoshi yelled to the men attacking Man, wanting their attention, and as he rode on to get beside Man he bowled over a dismounted black sash. 'Here I am!'

From alongside Man Yoshi struck fast, but the two of them were heavily outnumbered by men in armor. The circle was closing. Man knew they'd be lucky to survive. He felt a sudden shock of fear. Now mounted enemies closed in on Yoshi and Man. Steel clashed on steel. Their swords cut at other, inferior swords. There was no shouting now, only the grunting of desperate men giving their fight everything. A spear-point slid past Man's ribs, and he stabbed the wielder in the face.

Then more of their own men were beside them. Abruptly the odds evened; two black sashes were killed. A mounted spearman came from behind Man to jab hard at the last black sash and then grab his horse's bridle.

'He's dead and I have his horse!'

It was young Sanada. He had always been a capable horseman.

'You won,' Man confirmed. His chest heaved. Sweat was stinging his eyes. 'Now, stay with me! We have to hold this bridge till the rest of our side arrives!'

'Archers, get here *now!*' Yoshi yelled.

Man and two others had their bows, and used them. More of their archers came and fired arrows.

Man saw young Sanada dismount. He stood alongside thick-set Ugaki. They formed up on the bridge with four other spearmen.

New enemies soon arrived. Man and the others were still outnumbered, but the short, sharp fight had scared off the purity police.

'We drew blood,' said Yoshi, satisfied.

Black sashes were not used to hard-fighting opposition. Beyond the south bridge they went galloping up and down the river bank without daring to attack – but they were between Man and the others and sanctuary.

When there were enough new arrivals to guard this side, Man and Yoshi went back to the other bridge.

Yoshi took tactical command. First he sent a sharp-eyed youth up the watchtower, then arranged the other defenders.

'You there! Throw water on the wagons and the wooden buildings! The black sashes will likely try fire-arrows, and I don't want to burn!'

Other squads were already tearing the planks off the two wide bridges, to make them as unusable as possible. The Emperor's samurai and Ozawa's men knew their work and did it quickly. Two Heads tossed Man a chainmail jerkin with steel shoulder-pads. He put it on and fastened it up.

There were four brightly-painted covered wagons left here. From the paintings on the canvas roofs, kabuki scenes of gods and goddesses and comic rustics, Man guessed the wagons belonged to some travelling theatrical troupe.

Man helped tip over wagons and put them broadside-on, two at each bridge, so they blocked both ways onto the island. The high-wheeled wagons were lightly made of wood but strong for all that, and the pulled-out baggage provided more shelter for the defenders.

The players themselves had been sensible and hidden themselves or fled.

They'll see drama enough today, Man thought sardonically. I wonder if Yoshi ever will write his epic. If he does, or someone does, how will I come out?

Now Yoshi came over, looking confident – though Man

wondered what the young Emperor's Man was really feeling.

'You put the wagons here to prevent enemies running straight onto this island? That's smart.'

'Have you ever heard of E'ropan wagon forts? Think of mobile castles.'

Yoshi nodded, and then lowered his voice. 'You're sure the holy Mother knows we're here?'

Man suddenly saw from Yoshi's carefully-concealed eagerness that he was desperate. All he could do to cheer his friend was to say, 'She will know we're close.'

'But not where we are?'

'I don't know! I *hope* she does, but what if *he* wants her out here with us?'

Yoshi was only murmuring now. 'Here, so, like Joah said, we can all be killed?'

Man looked at the whooping enemies on horseback, who were carefully staying out of arrow-shot – though occasional arrows came from them.

Their numbers are rising, but they're only doing theatrics now – it's amazing how taking casualties can damp down the fighting spirit. Ah, but once they get their reinforcements...

He spoke positively, though. 'Yoshi, you're doing the great job I'd expect!'

'Thank you. Maybe we have a chance after all.'

'We beat them to Miracle Island,' Man said. He felt a strange absence of fear now. 'We have secured this place and we can defend it! We already beat off the first charge. A handful of us and fifty of them! Remember that we beat twice our number of Takedas at Kagoshima, and the same when we invaded Kami Island!'

Yoshi had an impish look on his face when he smiled at Man. They were both bold survivors of first contact with the enemy, with their swords blooded.

'We did that, didn't we? Oh, let me live now, and I will make us immortal.'

'Eternal life? My old friend, that's strong magic.'

'I mean that someday all this will be a heroic poem.'

'With a happy ending?' Man asked, wondering how poetry could ever be truly heroic.

'Tragedy has more prestige!'

'Balls!'

Yoshi eyed him. 'Are you sure that your feeling about

Words of Fury: 305

Nagaoka is right? If they aren't coming back, we might have cut across higher up, and got to The Waning that way.'

Man gestured. 'Look!' Up on the mountain, the dust was rising. 'Those enemies are only minutes away. If not for Precious Stone's self-sacrifice, they would be here already, occupying the island and the road to The Waning.'

Sanada shook a fist. 'Yes, that's Nagaoka!'

Ugaki gave the young man a brief smile. 'Here is a chance for all of us to be brave.'

'I could do without it,' said Man, oddly deflated now. He was worried he would not live up to the standard Precious Stone had set.

Ugaki was quite certain. 'Courage is a human necessity. To display it is a soldier's duty.'

Man wasn't so sure.

'We're probably on our own. Look at all the sorcery above The Waning! Mother Zandar will have a lot on her mind.'

'Yes.' Yoshi waved at the black whirlwind over Zandar's base. 'Do you think you and our other riders could escape this fight and gallop to The Waning?'

Man scoffed. 'That would be desertion.'

'Take the Eye and go. You *should*. This might be your only chance!'

'Are you going to leave?'

Yoshi hesitated. 'No; but *you* ought to.'

Lady Joah came up on her pony. 'We have fought as one, for a good cause. I do not think any of us should run.'

'That's well said!' said Man, though he wondered if he might lose his life soon, and the Eye. Nevertheless he now felt exhilarated by the danger rather than scared. He saw another dozen or so riders coming up from the coast, with more following them. 'Enemy on the road east!'

He saw the Voice from Afar was praying.

'You really think we've done enough?' Man asked Yoshi.

A shout came from the ranks. 'Cavalry in sight, coming downhill!'

'Looks like we'll soon find out,' said Yoshi.

Man felt uncertain.

Should I have gone off by horse, taking the women? What if that would have saved a few of us, and the Eye? Was that the right thing to do?

I could still do it, maybe. I have a good horse under me, and the opposition riders have galloped here all the way from the coast, so you can bet their horses will be tired...

How can it be right to desert friends?

Man turned, shouted to everyone. 'Get ready to defend this place!'

This little island was an oval about sixty paces long east to west, narrower than that in its north to south width, with the river dividing here and then running on towards the south-east. Each river-branch had steep if low banks thick with green reeds. Man saw that the water, though low in this season, was still fast-flowing.

He checked the water's depth and flow by wading in till he was waist-deep. He was almost pushed off his feet by the current, and in mid-channel the water was even deeper and faster-flowing.

He came out, trying to pat water out of his kimono and leggings without much success.

'It gets so deep you'd have to swim.'

'A good barrier,' Yoshi said softly, 'especially for those of our enemies who cannot swim. We'll be in arrow-range everywhere, but there are walls and buildings to shield us, and the water barrier helps.'

They stood together in the middle of the island at the official checkpoint, a little sentry-house with a lowered barrier in between that and a public tea-stand.

An occasional enemy galloped up close and fired off single arrows, but with no effect – and two of the four men who tried it were hit by Yoshi's archers.

Now the two friends walked together to the east end of Miracle Island. Here a stone statue looked down on a glorious flower garden walled on three sides – chest high walls, but that was enough to make an excellent defense.

Faslane was standing in the garden with the Voice, both waist-deep in stunning colors from the flowers. Bees hummed pleasantly; the air was sweet-scented.

Faslane was gaping up at the statue.

When Man looked up too, he gasped.

Here was perhaps the loveliest lady he had ever seen. She was not Japanese but Hindian, with the large, tilted eyes typical of that people, and a smile as wonderful as her eyes.

Man pointed at the lady. 'It's as if I know her; but I don't know where from!'

Words of Fury:

'From your most tender dreams,' the Voice murmured.

'I can tell you don't know my dreams!' Man told her.

She pulled a mocking but friendly face. 'Thank goodness!'

'It's Kannon,' Yoshi said crisply. 'The Goddess of Mercy, Faslane! Know her?'

'Kwun Yum,' said the seafarer as he faced the statue, 'who protects mothers – and seamen. She is an avatar of forgiveness and mercy.' He turned to the others, gave a crooked smile. 'Today we will need both.'

'We'll need a miracle,' said Yoshi, suddenly sour. 'Let's see if this place lives up to its name.'

'It won't, not for everyone,' said Faslane, 'but there's one miracle already!' He pointed. 'The statue weeps!'

There was a murmur all around. Men and women pointed at the miracle tears, and soon there was much praying, to many gods.

Joah came close, to see. 'Even the old gods take notice – and my God, too.'

Ozawa bowed low to the statue.

'Kannon is a lovely face of all-compassionate Buddha. She was given eleven heads to hear mankind's cries of suffering, and a thousand arms to reach out to us and help us.'

'Amen,' said the Voice from Afar, and little Keli echoed her. The staff-wielding monk had also bowed his head.

'There will be much blood this day,' Yoshi said, shortly. He seemed less touched by sentiment, and kept looking at where the enemy approached. 'Men die, then women weep.'

Man looked up towards the mountains. The enemies coming from there were closer, now. The leaders were gradually appearing out of the dust.

Yoshi pointed. 'See the banner? The same black sashes, under Nagaoka's command.'

'What happens now, Yoshi?'

'Nagaoka's men will hit the north bridge. If they're an ill-trained enemy, as they may be, and we're lucky, as I hope we are, they and the others to the south and east may attack piecemeal.'

'Then we can stand them off?'

'Not for very long.' Yoshi sighed. 'I don't think there's much room for finesse, friend Emmanuel.'

Man looked round. They were surrounded; it was too late now to run. Infuriatingly, tauntingly, the Waning of the Moon's towers were in plain if distant sight.

'So we make our stand here, and hope Zandar and her women with swords put in an appearance?'

'Or we can surrender,' Yoshi said.

'No surrender!' Man said automatically, a strange echo of his father. He was still looking at the force galloping out of the mountains. He recognized one rider there, and rage distorted his face. 'That is Nagaoka! Oh, I know how to greet him!'

Yoshi flexed his hands. 'We both know how.' Now Yoshi stared. 'There are perhaps forty or fifty already with Nagaoka, and judging by the dust more are following.'

Man knew that Yoshi's force was smaller, though élite. He rubbed his fingers down his borrowed chainmail jerkin. With the others, he waited for Nagaoka between the overturned wagons blocking the torn-up north bridge.

'Three, four minutes, then they'll be here!' said the nervous youth up in the watchtower.

'Watch on both sides!' Yoshi called. 'Look-out, you must keep checking!'

Man knew others – the Tears, for one – were also coming. He felt a sudden pang, deep in his chest. He stared around at the others on the island, who were working desperately to protect this place, to protect Man himself, really; and now he felt utterly miserable.

'Dear Yoshi, Voice, you, Lady Joah, and you, Faslane – I see now I have brought you to this place, perhaps at the cost of your lives.' It was as if some darkness had been placed in his soul and was being made to grow. Shouldn't he just let the enemy take him? Then maybe his friends would be left alone, and survive. 'Really it is I who should be weeping. Yes. I should be weeping, and asking for forgiveness.'

Faslane's nostrils flared and he tapped his fighting-iron into his palm.

'Nay forgiveness needed, laddie. It is our battle, too.'

'Yes,' Yoshi said, very solemnly. 'There is no forgiveness necessary.'

'No, none,' said the Voice from Afar. She touched her crucifix, then set the same hand over Man's heart. 'But if you ask for it, my friend Emmanuel, I give you my forgiveness freely – whatever happens now.'

He knew he was cherished; he knew he counted. As courage flooded back into Man, he lowered his head. He felt absolved from guilt and removed from fear, and he wondered at how

Words of Fury: 309

those kindly words from his friends had so changed his feelings.

Lady Berenda glared at her hands, which had somehow betrayed her. The spell had seemed so powerful, and she had cast it with total belief. Then something in Man's soul had negated the poisonous self-doubt she had put into him.

'Good Hagiwara,' she said, trying to sound calm, 'Emmanuel has resisted my magic. His soul still shines with bright light.'

'Then what do we do?'

'If magic does not work we may have to confront him and the others directly.'

Hagiwara touched his sword-hilt. To kill The One Who Will Change would give the killer a name that would live forever.

'I look forward to doing exactly that. Please, in *his* name, lead us to the enemy!'

Now Nagaoka had eighty mounted men on this side of the river. He had already sent a messenger to those on the other side. There were about fifty or sixty there and their officer said there were more on their way. That was good: Nagaoka calculated the numbers were almost three to one in his favor. But how should he use them? The finest battle planning involved consideration before action; perhaps it would be best to wait for Lady Berenda, or for reinforcements.

Waiting wasn't how you got noticed by those above, though...

'We attack!' Nagaoka waved his sword. There might be a clever way to do this, though he couldn't see it; but still he wanted to encourage his men. 'We have numbers enough to sweep over the defenders!'

'You want to take our enemies before your superior comes, eh? You want to be a hero to Lord Oatha and the world!'

Nagaoka turned his head. Beside him on his great black horse was a black-armored samurai, a well-known warrior from the house of Takeda.

'No, Takeda-san. I just want to do my duty – and bring down this foreigner and his supporters.'

Takeda laughed in disbelief. 'Well, I do want to be a hero. I came from Kagoshima and allied myself to you black sashes for one reason: to kill the fighting foreigner Emmanuel.'

'When we win, rely on this: I will tell Lord Oatha even lending us your name was useful!'

Words of Fury:

Takeda arrogantly waved away this modest praise. 'My name was "useful"? Well, I will now do much more!'

Then he put on his helmet, and trotted forward.

Though he was unwilling to bravely lead, Nagaoka was also unwilling to be left behind. He waved for a general advance. His mounted men began to canter. Hagiwara, Oatha's right-hand man here, had talked about putting five thousand men around The Waning. No doubt he was coming here as quickly as he could, thought Nagaoka, with more men and the Lady Berenda. It might take days, but that would finish things for this gaijin 'One Who Will Change' and his so-called friends.

Of course, Takeda here was very famous, and Nagaoka had previously seen him go about his work with verve and lethal skill.

Either way Emmanuel was a dead man.

Words of Fury:

Chapter Thirty: *Perhaps More Than a Man*

Man saw one brave new samurai ride his black horse right up to the barricade on this side of the wrecked bridge.

'Show me the gaijin Kinross!' this man was shouting. 'Show me the gaijin Kinross!'

Even with the planks taken up, his wonderfully trained warhorse had kept its footing. He wore embellished black armor and his drawn swords were splendid.

Man trotted to intercept him, sword raised.

'Consider yourself shown!'

This was a chance to earn time, or death, or both.

This enemy slid off the panting horse and flourished his own blade without advancing. His black armor was inlaid with silver; his kimono was glowing cloth of gold; a huge leather pouch rode on one hip. Man saw he was grinning like a madman.

Man raised his hand so his own side would hold back. He had not given up hope about help coming, so he was happy to take up time by following bushido, the traditional way of the warrior caste here.

'Hold, hold! This is single combat and I've been called for!'

The enemy in black did not rush the assault, but did it all in the traditional manner.

'I am Takeda-noh-Yori, son of the famous Takeda-noh-Anato, once of Ashuri, now a Black Sash of the First Class! I am a poet and a warrior – a genius with the pen and with swords!' He glared through the eye-slit in his helmet. 'I see you, Emmanuel Kinross! What is *your* lineage, you foreign scum? I say you were born from a cockroach that banged its own mother!'

Man found the insult made him laugh. Nevertheless, he stepped into the calming ritual. At the end of it would be death.

'I was born the son of the Lord of Arms of all Albion; and you already know my name.'

'Look at you!' The voice was full of scorn. 'Though tall, you are hardly more than a boy! Your reputation must be lies!'

Man stared coldly at his opponent, till the man flinched.

'Your eyes are green jade! ...What are you?'

'What am I? A man, even if I am young. A foreigner, but now at home in this land. What else am I?' Man lifted his long sword Words of Power. 'I am the man who is going to kill you.'

In accordance with the way of the warrior, a space on the island was cleared.

Man weighed up his opponent. This Takeda was a famous fighter, from the famous family, and Man knew he had every reason to be full of hate. He was thick-set, powerful and well-stanced. And his wrist had a black dragon tattoo...

Takeda leapt forward, cutting down with his sword.

That speed surprised Man. There was a brief, fast exchange of blows; steel rang on steel. Man discovered his opponent was one of the best he had ever fought, and he also had armor to help keep him safe.

A cut from Takeda struck a steel shoulder-guard on Man, a blow which might have made him lose a limb.

At once Man retreated a couple of paces. Better to be cautious than dead.

They fought on and exchanged blows, then circled in front of dozens of spectators. The armor slowed Takeda. So, with some difficulty, Man held his own. There were shouts. He heard young Sanada blaring, 'Kill him, Emmanuel!'

Then he saw flickers of magic around his opponent's armor. That cunning magic amplified his enemy's strength.

Man took another step back, more fearful now. He felt his confidence evaporate.

With magic in his armor this one is just too strong for me...

Then he saw Precious Stone again, tortured, eyeless, murdered.

The rage that came helped him. He struck back again and again, blows too quick to follow and which Takeda could barely intercept. There was some fancy footwork from both fighters.

Man could not muster the subtle magic required to power up himself, but he could interfere with the magic the other man had – and he did.

Shortly Man realized he was a shade stronger than this Takeda, in spite of the poison in him from the Tears' kiss. He began to press his opponent back towards the bridge. With his long, powerful arms Man was chopping at head-height with his sword, and so forcing his armored enemy to do likewise.

Then there was an opening. Man stepped in instantly and forced up his opponent's sword. They were body to body, both of them panting. Man smelt sweat and leather. He risked a sweeping kick, and Takeda came down like a felled tree. He was flat on his back and panting hard.

Man showed him Words of Power's naked steel. 'You surrender?'

'Not to a foreigner!' The man raised his own sword again, eyes blood-mad, and then he jumped up – agile in spite of the armor.

Before Takeda could regain his balance Man stabbed him through the shoulder. The warrior staggered back, keening, though the armor had been some protection. His leather pouch came open, though, and something rolled away.

'See your hope die, foreigner!'

Man saw it was a Sword Maiden's head. The bonsai hair was crushed and dusty. The severed head rolled right to the river and fell in with a splash.

Man felt sickened.

Likely that was the end of the help they had hoped for. All the roaming Maidens were dead, Ozawa's scouts had no doubt been intercepted, and the Far-Speaker here had failed.

Despair touched Man's heart. What did it matter if he died?

Takeda saw his chance. Though he was wounded, he struck.

Man could not completely parry the stroke. He felt bright pain as one leg was cut. Takeda was foolish and paused to gloat, which gave Man his chance.

With a single two-handed slash he cut Takeda from shoulder to waist. Cut almost in two, the man toppled over.

Now he had finished this famous enemy there was chanting for Man from his own side. That cheered him and he hoped it encouraged the others. He knew his people would need cheering up before all this was over.

Then he turned to call forward the next opponent.

'Come on! Sword Maidens died for me! Now *you* can die for *them!*'

Nobody rushed forward. Indeed, they all turned their horses and rode away. Nagaoka went first.

Man tried to be positive.

We have a good view from the watch-tower. We have smashed both bridges; we have stone walls round the shrine to protect us; we have barricades here and we have supplies. There's a chance we can stand till we get relieved, Man told himself.

Surely Mother Zandar will have sent out her forces, or will risk coming herself...! Surely she will!

Though that might be just what *he* wants...

Man lowered his sword, profoundly disturbed.

'I think we've done well enough, so far,' Sanada murmured.

'What do you think, Lord Emmanuel?'

Man answered with brutal directness. 'We're alive, aren't we?'

Then Sanada was looking up. 'There's an odd thing, flying above! Is that a mech-bird?'

Man glanced up, saw, and frowned. 'There is something strange in how it flies.'

Ozawa pointed. 'It's heading away, south.'

'But that's where we're going!' said Joah. 'Now it's coming back! Look at it! I won't feel safe until we're inside The Waning ring-walls, if we ever get there!'

The novice Far-Speaker flinched. 'Oh, *he* just struck at The Waning again. Look!'

Man turned his head. A couple of miles off, that weird swirl of dark cloud over The Waning was turning quickly in on itself, a slow-motion unnatural whirlwind. Now weird blades of rainbow distortion – magic – began to rotate around The Waning like the spokes of a wheel. They stretched out over half a mile. Man gaped upwards as he felt the magic come and go, then closed his mouth.

The Lord of the North had power! Man grimaced at the cloud-pile. 'Whatever that spell is, it must be a mile high – and it's still growing.'

'It's the mother and father of all storms, and all *his* work,' said Joah. Man saw how shocked the women were by this display. Joah especially looked as if she had just had an unbelievably bad rumor confirmed. 'I think the Lord of the North has now besieged The Waning of the Moon.'

His courage had come back, but to Man this news was unmanning. 'You mean that sacred place is cut off? We're on our own?'

'Alas!'

The cloud slowly darkened and spread even further out. This affected their mood. Soon Man heard mutterings about the impossibility of approaching a place where *his* power was already so dominant.

The Lord of the North had come again to The Waning of the Moon. This time he was staying.

After a few more minutes one of the black sashes cautiously picked his way close enough for shouting.

'Listen, all of you! I am Nagaoka, senior samurai to the Lord

Oatha!'

'Nagaoka!' The name caught in Man's throat. 'He tortured Precious Stone!' Suddenly there was a blinding light in his head: fury. He lurched to his feet. 'I'm going to kill him!'

'No!' Sanada tried to pull him back into cover, but he was not strong enough. 'Please be careful! Don't empty her death of meaning by dying for no good reason!'

Those words struck Man hard. He squatted again, closed his eyes, tried to get back his self-control. 'Yes, you're right.'

Nagaoka continued to jeer: 'Why not talk? You must know there'll be no help for you now!'

Man wondered if this was true. Mother Zandar must know they were coming – he hoped. But then she might not know exactly where they were, and now *he* had besieged her home and probably cut it off from the world.

Nagaoka was shouting hoarsely. 'Don't expect anything from your women at The Waning of the Moon! That place is in the hands of my master, and he will never let it go! Look!'

Man did look. It was a wild show in the sky now: a vast whirlwind of black clouds was turning above The Waning. Now there were flashes of lightning there, and the thunder was frighteningly loud. Man found he was clenching his fists.

That is more power than I could have imagined. But then I saw his giant self-image, half a mile tall. I should have known how strong he is! The Waning of the Moon has been outmatched. So...

He hated to say it, even to himself; but he had to.

So already we are losing...

'It's only gaijin Kinross and the Lady Joah that we want! And they won't be harmed, I swear! Surrender them to me, Fujiwara-noh-Yoshi – with the Eye of Jade, of course – and then the rest of you can go on your way!'

Yoshi wriggled forward, swords trailing. Man noticed he too now wore some armor, hidden underneath his kimono.

Their eyes met.

'I could sell you to the enemy. Should I?'

Man laughed. 'They'd pay in false coin!'

'Even counterfeit money has some value – especially to the dishonest.'

'True. But, friend Fujiwara, think of your honor!'

'I'm thinking of my life. But if I think of my duty instead...' Yoshi sighed. 'Ozawa and I have told everyone to be especially alert, since this parley may be just an excuse to sneak up on us.'

Man had his bow held low now, and an arrow nocked. If Nagaoka showed his face...

'If we talk the talk, at least there'll be a delay before we have to fight the fight.'

'Yes. And delay is good. Isn't it?'

'It's better than defeat,' Man said dryly.

Yoshi considered. 'I hope it's enough of a delay for these people from the Waning of the Moon to fight their way to us, if they can, if they're coming.'

'Now you sound as if you hardly believe in them.'

'I have to believe in what Lady Joah says, my friend,' Yoshi said softly, wafting flies away from his face. 'And I suppose I have to believe in you. What else is there?'

Black sash Nagaoka bawled truculently, 'Fujiwara-noh-Yoshi, tell your foreigner to be a man!'

Yoshi rolled onto his back and addressed the blue sky in a loud, carrying voice.

'He is a man at the very least, and perhaps more than a man!'

The voice turned to honey, even more false than before. 'Brave Yoshi, son of a famous father, I am glad we can speak. Now, what do you say to my offer?'

'Let us discuss it! Is Lord Oatha with you? I want to deal only with the principal.'

'Surely he won't be here where we can get at him?' Man whispered. A thrill went through his blood. 'Or is he?'

'Lord Oatha would be pleased to speak to you, Lord Yoshi. He thinks of you often and praises you to your beloved father!'

Yoshi glanced at Man, raised an eyebrow. 'How flattering this Nagaoka is! – The slick, lying bastard.' Then he loudened his voice again. 'I thought your Lord Oatha was in Jade.'

A pause.

'He is not far. Lord Yoshi, if you came out to me, I could take you to him! Your safety is guaranteed.'

'Not good enough, friend Nagaoka. Can't you show him to me, at least!' Yoshi produced a hand-held crossbow, already cocked, which he loaded out of sight of the black sashes. He twisted, rose to his knees. 'I promise you I will deal with him!'

'Yes, yes, but for now you must deal with me! And I need an answer!'

'Very well.'

Words of Fury:

Yoshi tied his sash tightly. When Man saw Yoshi begin to stand he pulled at his friend, but it was too late.

Like a legendary hero of old, Yoshi stood up in plain sight of the enemy. His face was a map of dust marked by rivers of sweat, but his samurai topknot was neat. His hands, hanging loose and out of sight below his waist, held the crossbow.

'Let me see your face now, Nagaoka! I will deal honestly with you!'

A thick-set man also stood, smiling in assumed friendliness. He had been crouching behind the long row of horse feeding-troughs by the side of the road over the river.

'See my face, then, Lord Yoshi.'

The smile stayed on Nagaoka's face and his swords were not raised. Then he signalled.

But by the time the enemy arrows were in the air Yoshi had already fired his crossbow.

Nagaoka fell back, screaming. Yoshi's steel bolt had gone through both cheeks – just as Yoshi threw himself down.

Arrows bit into earth all around Man and his friend. After that volley finished Man jumped up and used his own bow. A man flung up his arms, swords flying away, and he died coughing blood. It was not Nagaoka, though others among the black sashes were also hit. Man saw that as he dropped flat again.

'Nagaoka, that torturer – that – '

Words failed him, just as violence had done.

Yoshi looked over. 'I've heard of being pinned down, but this –'

His green and gold kimono had flapped loose; and arrows to left and right of his chest had indeed pinned him to the earth.

Man eased the arrows out. They might be of use later, when his own were all shot.

Yoshi rubbed at the holes in the expensive silk. He was frowning very seriously.

'I just disliked those men before. Now I hate them!'

Man used his own bow again. A miss, but close. Then he slapped Yoshi's shoulder.

'You use that hate, friend Yoshi, the very worst way you can!'

Yoshi eyed him. 'You really are your father's son, aren't you? It's lucky for you I don't take after mine!'

Man said quietly, 'But I hear that he was like you: good at the bloody work.'

'You hear right, and in that at least I follow him.'

Now Man heard Nagaoka call the charge. His cavalry came on in a wild-riding wild-shouting column.

Man used his bow, hearing bowstrings twang all around him. Arrows flew out blindingly fast, found targets. Eight enemies went down immediately; another four were wounded but stayed in the saddle. Man saw that most of the others slowed.

The handful that reached the river's edge got riddled with more arrows, even before coming within sword-strike. He saw most fall. The remnant galloped away, desperately fast. Arrows from Man and cat-calls from others followed them.

Man was amazed.

So was Yoshi. 'We have defended our island against the odds, twice.'

Man said only, 'I won't say I've achieved anything, though, while Nagaoka is alive! I remember what he did to Precious Stone.'

'Then do what she said: live, to take vengeance!'

'I would like to. But soon we will find out if this island deserves its name. Our enemies have closed the circle round us, we are still miles from The Waning, and there is no help apparent.'

'You're right.' Yoshi gave a grim smile. Then he shouted, 'Banners, men!'

A banner-man rushed to do it. Man saw him unfurl four flags on long poles, planting each one firmly in the earth near the watch-tower. Man saw Yoshi's personal standard, a Fujiwara family banner, the Emperor's Man flag, and the red rising sun of the Empire of Japan.

Yoshi bowed to the flags. The rest of the party along with Man silently copied him. It was only now that Yoshi's banners were out, so ending his anonymity, that Man realized what Yoshi was expecting.

Extermination, and no one left on their side to tell the tale of heroic defeat.

Crouching under the shrine wall, Faslane watched the ceremonial raising of the four hard-flapping vertical flags, wondering what the different banners meant.

Then he turned to the Voice from Afar beside him. 'Your prince Yoshi is prepared for a serious encounter, isn't he?'

Words of Fury:

'Yes. The Prophecies tell us...' She sighed. 'There will be blood, Master Faslane. That is written, and I feel it coming. I think that's why Man never wanted to believe. He fights, but not from love of bloodshed.'

'And you? Do you believe in him?'

She was on her mettle. 'I do, absolutely.'

'Do you love him?'

She touched her cheek, looked away. 'I love him, of course I do. I've never met anyone braver, nor more caring. I would follow him to the end, and he knows it.'

'You know what my next question is.'

'Am I "in love" with him?' She gave a small, sweet pout. 'Is that really your business?'

'You know what I feel about you.'

'Actually, I don't. I've lived in a very different place to you, lived a very different life. How can I understand you?'

He looked gravely at her. 'I could explain myself, but this isn't the time or place.'

'No. – You realize I'm terrified, don't you?'

'I suppose most of us are.' He stroked her upper arm, tenderly, really wanting her to understand. He had had his duties; and any mariner's life was often lonely. Perhaps that was why he thought so highly of her now. 'If we live through this – and I know even at the best that many of us won't – what will you do then?'

'There is wonderful magic and wonderful art at The Waning of the Moon. I will ask them to teach me.'

'And then? I can't see you spending the rest of your life in such a place.'

'Why not?'

He smiled, touched her again. 'Because it sounds a little like a convent.'

'Well, more likely I'd live in Jade.'

'Don't you know how you'd be received in Albion? With your songs and your magic, I think that within a few months you'd be famous.'

'If I went – or was taken – to great Albion?'

'I'd love to take you there,' he said. He took her hand, and kissed it. 'I would.'

Yoshi stared at the four banners for one more moment. Then he waved Man close.

'The other side is using signal-flags. I know what's coming.'

'You know their codes?'

'I'm an Emperor's Man. I know many things. They're going to hit us from both sides. So check on Kido. Tell him what will happen. And tell him to watch the ronin and that Faslane!'

Man was disappointed that Yoshi still distrusted Man's fellow from Albion, but he didn't argue.

Man ran to where the walled garden shrine shrine to Kannon served as a strongpoint. Everywhere the veterans had worked hard to fortify the island, with sharpened bamboo stakes and tight-strung ropes. He looked into the garden on high alert, though pretty flowers grew in that sacred place and bees hummed pleasingly in the riotous colors. What if he had forgotten something? What if, when this place fell, it was his fault?

Man jumped up onto the wall, looked around. No new attackers were visible on the three or four trails that led down towards the sea. The remains of the cavalry that had attacked before were milling about far from the river.

Maybe Yoshi had misread the signals. Or maybe Nagaoka had lost his nerve.

Man jumped down. The samurai in charge here was scar-faced Kido.

'We beat off the first charges, and that was magnificent!' He was speaking to Kido, but making sure all the others could hear. 'Only now they're coming again.'

'There are always more enemies.'

Faslane nodded at that.

'Unfortunately they're enemies between us and The Waning.'

'You mean these fighting women cannot now come, Lord Emmanuel?' Kido shrugged. 'I never expected much from them. Anyway, given luck, we can fight here for a long while.'

That had sounded like an epitaph: but though Kido sounded downbeat, he also sounded strangely satisfied.

Man squatted down with him, avoiding looking at the terrible scar on his face. He waved a thumb at the three ronin Yoshi had found back in the village. 'What do you think?'

'I have my own men with me,' Kido said gruffly. 'All of us are keeping a watchful eye on Fudai and the other two. They will fight.'

'Are you certain?'

'Yes.' Kido suddenly slapped his shoulder and his voice became more excited. 'Look, there's open land in every direction. Even if one or more of them *did* want to desert, they'd never make it.' He shook his short bow in his right hand. 'I guarantee that.'

Too far to hear them, ronin Fudai eyed the horizon like an expert.

Man tried to plan how he and the others could hold off their enemies till relief came, but he could not.

What relief? There is no guarantee it will come. The Waning of the Moon has been stripped of its forces and already...

He looked over, to see the pillar of cloud above the fortress-monastery was taller and blacker than ever.

Then he turned to see Nagaoka's cavalry start back towards them from the high hills and the other enemy horse head up from the direction of the sea.

Man ran back to report to both Ozawa and Yoshi. 'I think the other side are getting ready!'

'And Kido?'

'He is behind stone walls and he seems confident enough – even about the ronin.'

'Good! Now if only more Sword Maidens could fight their way here...'

But Ozawa was staring above The Waning. Lightning struck at the fortress like stabbing blue-white spears. Man flinched. After a delay the sound of thunder rumbled to Miracle Island.

Mother Zandar can't leave now, Man realized, for that storm will tear her apart. So what happens to us? We make a good show of dying, I guess. But for what, exactly?

If I handed myself over...

No! I *have* to see this through with my friends!

Ozawa was still staring at the lightning, and the dark clouds corkscrewing above the fortress. 'See how mighty *he* is, where we wanted to find sanctuary!'

'It doesn't matter now,' said Yoshi. 'We must make this place ours, and fight as long as possible.'

Man acknowledged that bleak truth, and saw that Joah did too.

There was one last thing for Man to settle, though it was of supreme importance.

He had left the curiously-worked casket below a table.

Words of Fury: 322

Everyone knew it contained the famous Eye of Jade and its Talking Book, and Man had seen many people take a moment to touch the glimmering bronze. Afterwards, some whispered hopeful prayers. Others, mainly the hardest-looking men, simply nodded to themselves, flexing their sword-hand fingers which had touched the casket.

Having a miracle you can actually touch makes hope more real, thought Man. It was a comfort to him too.

Then he went to where the two women were opening medical packs to prepare for more wounds.

'I can't run about carrying the Eye, and I won't leave it in the open.'

Joah stood up. 'So?'

'So I want to leave it here, in your custody. Yes?'

'I suppose,' said Joah, 'but won't we be too busy to watch over it?'

'Then let me bury it.' He found a spade, and scooped out a hole in the earth. Then he put the casket in and covered it over. The Eye had once been so important; but what was it now, and what was he? 'I hope I can rely on you two to guard it.'

'Of course you can!' said Joah sharply. 'We all know how vital that gem is! With it we saved the city of Jade, and with it Lady Naosuke once saved the entire realm!'

'As you say,' Man said, with somber politeness. 'Now, can I put you to work?'

The Voice stared. 'When did I become your hand-maid?'

'Just now!'

Man put them both, and the walking wounded, to splashing more river water over everything that might burn.

'You expect fire arrows?' Joah asked, coolly, as she threw another bucket of water over the wooden shop walls. 'Or do you just want to see me sweat like a peasant?'

He wanted to curse her for her coolness; he wanted to use harsh words, but only to drive her back to a place of safety, and of course nowhere on this island was safe.

He made himself answer her politely.

'Fire will be an obvious tactic. They'll try anything to drive us out, and a fire here would do that. Remember this; defending ourselves here gives us a chance – while being forced out into the open is disaster.'

Irony was her response to his patronizing if well-meant explanation: 'What perception, sensei!'

Words of Fury: 323

'Have you ever,' Man asked, 'had a good thrashing?'

'For my education, several times.' Joah smiled and then wriggled provocatively. 'But surely we're too busy at this moment just for you to have fun?'

Men started laughing. Man, flushing, turned round to berate them.

But it was Sanada who was amusing all. He had dressed up in a farcical costume from a kabuki play.

'Dress like a demon!' Man told him. 'That will scare them away!'

'Even better, I'll dress up as *you!*'

There was more laughter. Man saw these men would not be easily scared, nor easily driven off this river isle.

Yoshi went to stand on the wall of the shrine, right alongside the lovely stone shape of Lady Kannon.

Man called, 'How does it look? Are they charging yet?'

'Come see.'

Man ignored a blinding pulse of headache and jumped up to stand with his friend. The lay of the land gave the defenders clear lines of sight all round; till night fell, there could be no surprise attacks. The first cavalry were still milling around and those on this bank were only just forming up again.

They had the numbers, though. Man estimated his side were now outnumbered maybe four to one.

'The channels of the river will be a good defense,' he said, determined to be hopeful.

'That's good,' said Yoshi, 'but there may not be a miracle today.'

'Why not? There will be help sent, surely.'

Yoshi cocked an eyebrow. 'Even if there is, will it arrive, my Man – and in time?'

'Have faith.'

'I do.' Yoshi looked around. 'But I won't say what my faith is in...'

For one long moment Man stared hard at his friend.

There was a shout from the sentry up in the watchtower.

'They're coming!'

Chapter Thirty-One: *The Boldness*

'I think I must confess to you, Daisen,' said Mother Zandar.

They were both in Zandar's study, preparing for a full meeting of the guidance council, which was the highest authority at The Waning. It could strike down full sisters and displace whoever was holy Mother here – and sometimes it had.

'Mother, I am in no way your superior, and there is no need for confession.'

'There is! And you *are* better than me, in every way.'

'No, you are stronger than me in every respect.' The two women let silence grow, though it was not comforting. 'Mother, you flinched! What is it?'

'I have tried to be alert to *him*, and to the souls of our scouts.' Annoyed that she had showed a weakness, Zandar rubbed at her scalp, then at her hidden eyes, as if it was possible to rub others' pain away. 'So often now I encounter death-agonies.'

'You have opened yourself up too much!'

'I have to. I *have* to help. If even one Sword Maiden, or one of Lord Yoshi's scouts, can reach us with a location…'

'How could they cross *his* vile cordon? If we with our power have to admit we are trapped, and without vision, what could an ordinary person do?'

'They could ask for help; they could *pray* – as I wish I could!'

The silence grew again.

'Mother, is there something else?'

Zandar had been brooding, and knew this private time was the opportunity.

'It is Man. You know I helped save him and the others from monsters upon the black beach?'

'That is to be celebrated.'

'Is it?' Zandar's hands pressed against her skull. 'My soul encountered his, at a very desperate moment for both of us. I was defeated. My Emmanuel was tortured with despair, and he could raise no power from himself. To help him, I…'

'Mother?'

'I did something dreadful.'

'What?'

'I saw he did believe in the power of the Lord of the North, and I made that belief flourish. In Man's mind our enemy told

Words of Fury:

Man that to save his friends he would have to admit the cold power into his heart...'

'What happened?'

'*And he did!*' There was a silence. Now Zandar regretted speaking. 'Young Man's soul had a touch of darkness already – and I made that worse.'

It was clear Daisen had not expected this. 'If Emmanuel crosses over to *him*...'

'All our battles here and elsewhere will have been wasted; and the Lord of the North will triumph.' Zandar blinked back tears from her blinded eyes. 'I am fearful.'

'Mother, Emmanuel will only turn if he is *already* prepared to do it. You have made nothing worse.'

'I fear I have. If Man turns to *him* – as he might, in desperation – the Lord of the North will harvest his soul.'

'Will Man despair?'

'Look at his situation, Daisen!'

There was no response to that. Then Daisen leaned forward, kissed her forehead.

'You are a good woman, Mother, in a terrible time. You did what you had to do to.'

Zandar folded her fists. 'In Jade they used to be interested in others, and celebrate the new and strange. Now foreigners there will be murdered, and foreign faiths and cultures exterminated. Even here, now that we are besieged, there is a nervousness sometimes edging into panic.'

Now Zandar swallowed. 'I wonder if words alone can stop that. Ah, if there was some way we could see outside, or if some brave scout came through to tell us where Emmanuel is, *then* I could do something! If not, then I must go out in challenge myself.'

'Mother, no! What if that's what *he* wants?'

Zandar turned her head in desperation.

'I don't care about that. Daisen, I must go!'

Daisen felt compassion as well as fear. It was so typical of the holy Mother to take responsibility for everything. But Daisen knew there could be no Far-Seeing out of this place now, and no returning scout could survive *his* siege. Mother Zandar was too valuable to risk outside.

There was only praying left.

Then Daisen saw Mother Zandar raise her blinded face.

They had both felt new throbs of power.

'What was that, Mother?' Daisen's voice became eager, now. 'I think I glimpsed something golden, something female. Could it be that the Lady Rishiri and the Princess Anamizu have arrived? Oh, we need their power!'

'That gold had a dark taste. I think it came from the woman who fought Emmanuel, the one called "the Tears", using some powerful gem.'

Daisen stared. 'She has the Eye? Oh, surely not!'

Zandar frowned. 'If I have been reading her correctly, she doesn't – though she's on its trail.'

'So much for your prayers for her soul!'

Zandar raised an eyebrow. 'It isn't wrong to hope.'

'No, but it's not always useful!'

'She isn't as much with *him* as she was, and such a change is a small miracle.'

'Mother! You helped change her heart?'

'For a time.'

Daisen's eyes narrowed. 'Though now she is *his* again?'

There was a long silence. 'I suppose.'

'Hah!'

Now Zandar stirred. 'If she is about to intercept Man and the others, surely we must get out and help them?'

'Mother, we – you – have this place to defend. We sent Sword Maiden parties, scouts and adepts. What more?'

'Oh, I am such a coward! I know I should go!'

'Our people knew the risks. And surely Oatha is not a big enough enemy to stop Lady Joah and The One Who Will Change – or Lady Rishiri and the princess?'

Zandar rubbed her fists together.

'Daisen, never forget who our real enemy is, and never underestimate that one – whatever mask he might wear. I may *have* to leave, may *have* to die.' She stared into blinded nothing, her lips twisting. 'Before I speak to the others, I must hide my fears. In a siege there is nothing more contagious than despair.'

'Of course I'm angry with stupid Zandar! We were summoned here where there's danger, where there will be a siege, and we were not even met, still less helped!' said Lady Rishiri. 'We have been let down! How can we help the poor creature Emmanuel if we do not even know where he is?'

'Though this Emmanuel is a "mere male", as you put it

before, I do not imagine he is a "poor creature", nor helpless!'

The two women were in a painted palanquin swinging from a frame held between four ponies. They were going south, on a little trail in between the mountains and the Shimabara seacoast. They had enemies, so their whole party was hidden under wards and their Sword Maiden escort was disguised in blue. Soon after they had landed a mech-bird had flown over their party, but after two passes it had flown away and so far there had been no follow-up.

Rishiri was elderly and rheumatic now, though splendidly dressed and made-up strikingly. She was very much the grand lady from Kyoto, where the Emperor had his palace. She had once commanded The Waning as a Sword Maiden and powerful adept, though her career as holy Mother had been controversial, especially at its end.

Princess Anamizu had been the senior Sword Maiden in Ezo, but when Mother Zandar summoned her and other women of power she had reluctantly passed on her command to Lady Egawa and took ship south.

'Princess, Zandar's "Emmanuel" might already be dead!'

'He *is* or *was* heading for The Waning of the Moon. If he lives, he might be in one of the magical dead spots *he* has made, where we cannot look.'

'I hate that word "if"!'

The princess ignored her companion's petulance, and slid back the forward window panel.

'The road ahead is empty, Lady. Have the people run, in fear of black sashes? Have they got ahead of us?'

'Surely not!'

'Why else would folk be hiding?'

Rishiri had closed her eyes.

'Oh, the lazy peasants are just hiding from their work!'

'I think not. I *feel* the threat around us.'

'What do you actually see?'

'To our left is blue; the sea.' A waving gesture gave Anamizu magically increased vision. 'I see only one sail, Lady Rishiri – but it is the red of our enemies!'

'I have the Blood Knot,' Rishiri said, flourishing her walking-cane with its ruby power gem at the head. 'And we are guarded by brave women. Let's not be nervous.'

The two women had rendezvoused at Obama, a small port on the north side of Honshu, and took ship there. When they finally neared Jade, they discovered it had already fallen to Lord Oatha. Then, while sailing to Shimabara, they had by-passed the half-mile-tall Lord of the North. Princess Anamizu had been shocked, while Lady Rishiri had mocked *him* to his icy face. But they had seen many pirate-red sails there and read the minds of evil men. The threat was even worse than they had anticipated.

To maintain secrecy they had rounded the Unzen peninsula far from the coast, landed at an obscure cove north of Shimabara Port and headed inland. Invaders were landing close behind. A half hour ago they had turned south, desperate to make The Waning of the Moon before *his* siege was complete.

Armed women on small horses were their outriders. Instead of the Sword Maiden blood red they were entitled to, they wore Rishiri's blue. It would be less noticeable.

'Lady, *he* and *his* will know we have been summoned, and they will be hunting us!'

'Ah, you worry too much! Think of me. Poor insulted *me!*' Rishiri complained. 'Summoned with such bad-mannered *urgency!*' Her wrinkled face was annoyed. 'That girl must think I am her serving-woman!'

'Mother Zandar is a high power and no girl; please be patient with her.'

It was a howl of pain. 'She took my place!'

'I know, aunt, but all things change. Your bloodline is as high as anyone's. You are sister to a former Shogun, and aunt to the present one and myself. You are so high Mother Zandar could not lower you, even if she wished to.'

'She does wish!'

Anamizu was vibrant and young. 'Aunt, would I have left my Maidens for a small reason? You know terrible fighting has been foreseen on Ezo.'

'Your brother will fight well.'

'Yes, but we have our own battle here. As Mother Zandar requests, we must help protect the Waning, and this Emmanuel.'

'A *foreigner*, who follows outlandish gods, will never be acceptable here!' Rishiri opened all the window panels, looked around, scowling. 'What does that girl know?'

'Zandar predicted that the Lord of the North would attack Ezo, and that happened.'

'Mere blood-raids!' Lady Rishiri flapped a fan at her face. 'Why, the North hasn't seriously challenged us for a decade, since that last attack on Jade!'

Words of Fury:

'Lady,' the younger woman said sternly, 'I was there for one enemy landing in Ezo.'

Anamizu was remembering how those demon warriors in silver and gold armor had come marching on, jetting fire. Though they had withdrawn from the village at nightfall, the fight had been truly frightening because it had been so one-sided – in the enemy's favor.

Rishiri's expression turned even fouler.

'If you're so bloody worried about Ezo, perhaps you should've ignored Zandar's hysterics and stayed to show the men what we can do!'

Princess Anamizu touched the hilts of her two swords.

'Do you think men will ever accept our power?'

Rishiri shifted on the padding again. 'Men, ah, men!' she said; a lifetime of wonder, loathing and addiction in her croaking voice. 'When it becomes as obvious as the nose on their faces or that wondrous organ between their legs, *then* they might take notice of our good sense and our power!'

The younger woman was still questioning.

'I have heard Mother Zandar has the greatest strength of any since the Lady Naosuke herself. Is that so?'

'She's a weak-minded fool!'

'She has commanded Sword Maidens in battle.'

'But *her* Sword Maidens are only po-faced girls swearing wan oaths. When *I* was a wild girl and carried the two swords, *I* swore oaths of a different kind!'

Lady Rishiri's hatred of her successor was dangerous: Anamizu knew that. She sighed. She had to keep everyone united enough to work together. Hatred and division would do *his* work.

'If we can assemble a sacred circle to do magic, we will need this Emmanuel and our strongest women, and that must include Mother Zandar.'

Lady Rishiri slammed shut the panels, then turned on one elbow and eyed the princess.

'Do not kow-tow to her! "Mother Zandar" indeed! I knew that young woman when...' She kneeled up, rubbed below her hips. 'Oh, my behind!'

The princess looked at Rishiri. In the gloomy interior it was hard to see, but she had the notion that the elderly adept was dripping sweat as she concentrated on hiding them from *him*.

The closed panels quickly made the palanquin stuffy, and it

rocked unpleasantly between the ponies.

What exactly Zandar planned the princess did not know. But it would be interesting to meet this Emperor's Man Yoshi and his *gaijin* friend, whether the young lord Emmanuel was truly the predicted one or not. Those two were becoming famous warriors both, and it was clear that 'the Foreigner' had man's power in magic to a stupendous extent. Both women had felt him shake the city of Jade to its foundations.

'That is power enough to stand off even the Lord of the North!' Princess Anamizu said aloud.

'Eh?'

Back in the present, Anamizu turned her head. 'Can we really beat *him* to The Waning?'

'We must, young Anamizu. For without us there will be no magic circle; and only such a circle can resist *him*.'

'I feel *his* presence, close over The Waning. He wants to get in! Won't he succeed?'

In Princess Anamizu's mind she saw the swirling column of thunderclouds – a tornado in slow motion – above that sacred ground.

Was it *possible* to hold off that much power?

Nagaoka's riders rushed in, to ride up and down the bank of the river. They howled madly, with those who had bows firing arrows.

A samurai next to Man was hit by a freak arrow. He rolled screaming in the dirt. An arrow had gone into his cheek and out of his mouth, impaling his tongue on the way. It was very painful though it wasn't mortal. A few others were also hurt. But the black sashes, having to approach without cover, took many more casualties even though most wore armor. The river worked well as a barrier and only a dozen managed to come over the ripped-up bridges.

Man went forward and killed the first enemy himself. A few others made it onto the island, and as Man fought them he heard shouting from the other bridge, which soon ceased. A win for the defense?

In case it wasn't, he went to help.

There was a worse struggle for this bridge, and it was well he had come. Many enemies fell in the bloody chaos here, so that this rush was finally beaten back, though it took minutes. The survivors ran away as the defenders jeered. Man saw that perhaps twenty of the enemy were left dead or grievously hurt.

He squatted with his back to a wagon, alongside Sanada. He was too tired to feel victorious, and, besides, the black sashes would be back. He was sweating badly and his face hurt now. He touched the Tears' kiss-wound. It was badly inflamed.

Not a good sign, he thought. Not good at all.

If I fail here...

He looked over at the two women.

Lady Joah kneeled by a hurt man, pressing a wet cloth to his forehead. Though the sun was still massively hot, her quilted travelling jacket was on. She did not wish to disturb the dying man by breaking off her care to remove it.

The Voice from Afar came over with another medical pack. She kneeled down beside Joah, her wide eyes on the wounded.

'Is there no magic you can raise to help us?'

'If I was attuned to the Eye, perhaps,' said Joah, vaguely. 'But not by myself. For *his* power has blanketed the area.'

'Are you sure Mother Zandar is aware of us?'

Joah made herself sound confident. 'I'm certain she knows of us; surely she will send help.'

'You say so, but look what's happened to The Waning! Even if she *can* somehow leave The Waning – will she? I'm scared that you are right, that *he* is doing this to lure her out, so that when she is away from all the protections...'

'We have powerful enemies. That is true.'

'You're not cheering me up.'

'Then pray.'

Yoshi heard that. He looked over and waved his bloodied long sword. 'Today I shall do my praying with this!'

The two women exchanged glances: the boldness of men.

Now Joah tied a bandage around scar-faced Kido's head. She remembered Father Sukomo saying that head wounds were tricky and always bled a lot. She got him to lie down and rest, and kept a hand on his forehead, trying to heal him.

It's so very strange, she thought, that as I give treatment to the wounded I forget to hate... Perhaps it's true that our love can be more powerful than our hates.

Kido opened his eyes. He still looked a bit dazed, but the bleeding had stopped. He thanked her briefly and then walked back to his post. The third wounded man had lost his left forearm to a sword-slash. He sat by himself, chalk-white face staring into nothing, right hand gripping his stump.

Joah met her friend's eyes. They were two very different people, but meeting now in intimate honesty.

'Dear Voice, if I could reach my sister, perhaps she could help...'

The Voice asked hopefully, 'You think the men here might ask for a ceasefire, while you try? Bloodshed postponed may never happen.'

'These men are warriors, and their blood is hot. Listen to a *female*, now they've begun to fight? I think not.'

'I know! Arrogant as always! Men! I don't know why we put up with them!' the Voice said, near to tears. The first wounded man, speared through the lungs, was beginning to choke on his own blood. His injuries were beyond their guesswork healing. 'Men are afraid of nothing, except showing a human weakness!'

'Indeed.' Joah wiped her forehead, squatted back on her heels. 'You have – known many men, I suppose?'

'Oh!' The Voice blushed. 'Can you think I'm that sort?'

'I am untouched, by – any of that, from any man,' Joah said, softly. 'So if I die now...'

'You will not die!'

'I want to live a long life. I want to find great truths and know true passion.'

'Yes!'

'Sometimes with Emmanuel I...' She looked at the Voice again; so tall and bright-haired, and usually so full of noisy confidence. 'What of you and men?'

The Voice looked away.

'I sing in bars, and I drink with many of the women who, well, the women who go with men for money – '

'Who "go with" men?' Joah sounded shocked. 'What do you mean?'

'Well, when I say "go with", what I mean is, well, all those sailors and merchants who are far from their wives, and haven't even seen a woman for long months...'

Joah said, calmly, 'Your lovely white skin shows up your blushes so nicely! I know perfectly well what you mean. I was only teasing.'

The high persons of The Waning listened, as Mother Zandar spoke with every appearance of confidence.

'There is much good news, though of course the great enemy

Words of Fury:

now has us under siege. You all want to know that we will be reinforced, and we will be. We have felt how Lady Rishiri and Princess Anamizu are nearing us. And, even more important, we helped The One Who Will Change, the Lord Emmanuel, land with the others on the "midnight beach" of Prophecy.'

'But *he* will be opposing all of our allies every step of the way!' said one elderly Sister, who was old enough to remember Lady Rishiri being in charge here. 'What if they don't ever arrive?'

Zandar took a breath. 'Of course it can be painful to be tested. Our friends, too, have had their strength sorely tried. After they landed upon the Beach of Monsters they fought their way through, all according to what Lady Naosuke saw three centuries ago. Though casualties were taken, that has to be good news. We *will* bring them here, along with my precious Eye of Jade.'

Zandar smiled, careful to project self-confidence before this admission: 'But now there is a difficulty. There has been a mass landing by our enemies to the east as well as the west, to south as well as north.'

There were smothered gasps in the map room. They had expected to be outnumbered, but not overwhelmed.

'As well as the magic surrounding us, our enemies will soon have the numbers to make a formal siege. And, I must tell you frankly, certain things have happened which are *not* in the Prophecies of Lady Naosuke in *any* version we have. We are in unknown territory.'

'Surely the first step is to find the Lord Emmanuel? Then he, with the Eye, can help us!'

Zandar turned her head. 'Indeed, Healer Irizo. Originally we sent two parties north to search for him, one to Four Rocks and another to a location close by. Each party had a full sister, but...'

'Well?'

'Neither party has been in touch.'

'Full sisters, *dead?*'

'That is our fear. More recently Far-Speaker Keli – '

'Mother, why do we need a physical search for our friends? We have magic!'

Zandar had always taken some comfort from this room, and the history it represented. Splendid paintings and maps hung upon the walls. The high ceiling was a blue night sky with a waning Moon pictured among the stars. From here, by tradition,

The Waning's wars were conducted. There were plan chests with drawers like closed mouths; some drawers, containing forbidden charts, were both locked and magically warded.

But what drew every eye was what they never spoke of, and which gave no comfort at all, only the reverse of comfort. This was the painted view of the waterfront where two giant towers had once stood. Now there was only smoking wreckage. Every heart, including Zandar's, wondered if that would be The Waning's fate.

She said smoothly, 'I regret to say that *his* weaves interfere with ours. Because of the Lord of the North, we can no longer see at a distance.'

'Then we are trapped here, blinded!'

There was a silence. One word especially had had the power to shock.

Blinded as she was, Zandar spoke without anger.

'You know I have sent out new search parties – Novice Keli and others. I am determined to get The One Who Will Change here, along with the Eye.'

'Exactly how, if we are now besieged!'

'We are far from helpless, Healer! As soon as I get a good idea of Man's location we will send a rescue mission.'

'Mother, I have already volunteered!'

Zandar smiled, ruefully. How young Sandella sounded, and how naïve her bravery!

'Daughter-Dear, you need not shout about your courage.' Mother Zandar folded her hands together. 'I am still waiting for that location. But if and when I get that information, whether from Lady Joah and the Voice from Afar, or from one of our Sworn Maiden scouts, or from an adept within these walls, you, Novice Sandella, will *not* be the first to leave the protections of this place.'

'Then who will it be?'

'It will be me.'

Incredibly, the novice continued to argue. 'But you can't go! Oh, holy Mother, it's too dangerous for you! And I want to go out and fight! So do others!'

That was open defiance. Most of those in the room were shocked.

'If I wait, then so must you – and these "others".'

'I know terrible things have happened to you, but you cannot use that as an excuse to do nothing!'

Words of Fury:

Sandella's statement was harsh, but to uninformed others it might seem fair. Zandar sensed her own support here was fading. Her side had taken many blows, and given few back.

'Novice Sandella, and all you "others", I promise you this much: before this is over, we will *all* have been put to the test. I will only let you and others go to fight if it is *not* some suicide mission.'

Something hammered at the Waning. The fortress quivered. Even in this assembly some of the women flinched or gasped aloud.

'Too late, Mother! *He* has come here now, so we are *none* of us safe, and we cannot leave!'

Sandella had spoken, and not even Zandar had contradicted her.

Zandar's magic senses swept up, and then encountered something that made her stomach lurch.

The High Healer was also shocked. 'Now *he* has broken through the outmost wards, and is squatting just above!'

There was a quiet kind of panic; a few shrieks and a general murmuring.

'*He* is overhead, yes, but still kept away,' said Zandar.

She would not admit it aloud, but of course Sandella had been right about everything.

Daisen whispered the truth. 'The Lord of the North has broken through *another* layer of our defenses!'

It was continuous hard pounding from above now. A little dust was shaken from the map room ceiling. People exchanged looks, especially the two sisters standing over the clock-face of the occult detector. This was about the size of a kettle-drum, with a black face divided into compass points. The silver pointer swung to show the source of the attacking magic, but instead of settling on a single direction it continued to swing in circles, never stilling.

They were completely surrounded.

Even Zandar could now see no way for her scouts to come back in without *him* attacking them – and she feared the Lord of the North would also attack if she or any other adept left.

'See, *he* is no gentleman; he has come early, to take us by surprise.'

'He has succeeded!' said Sulina.

'Perhaps it's good that *he* is concentrating on us. If not, he'd be attacking Lady Joah and our Emmanuel, and they're in the open,' said Zandar, trying to show something like confidence again. 'Trust in the wards, and in the power of prayer.'

'Now that *he* has come,' said High Healer Irizo, 'for you to leave us in such a crisis would be against all precedent – and it would also be suicidal!'

Zandar shrugged, irritable now. 'Times change.'

The thought of their home's holy Mother leaving put them all in a flutter. Some were afraid; but Zandar also saw that many resented being kept here away from the struggle. She realized no compromise to please everyone was possible.

Now the discussion became even sharper. Zandar interjected some hard truths, but stopped speaking when she realized she was making the tensions worse.

Then there was a sudden push to take a vote to confine Zandar to this supposedly safe place.

Zandar managed to avoid that vote being taken – just.

Then they felt the earth shake again.

'Is *he* going to attack?'

'Sooner or later he will again. But, for now, he wants us distracted – and trapped.' Zandar gave a grim smile. 'We must not be distracted, and I refuse to be trapped.'

'But the magical storm outside will only get worse – and to give help, we will need to get through it,' Daisen told the meeting. She turned to Zandar. 'And that can't be done safely!'

From love of me, she wishes to keep me safely confined; but my duty is different.

'I think there is a way,' said Zandar.

Sulina leaned forward. 'A safe way?'

'Safe enough.'

'How, exactly?'

Zandar did not answer. She realized the meeting was slipping away from her and she made the mistake of losing her temper.

'This talk does us no good! Where's your faith?' Shocked faces turned to Zandar, who had to struggle to recover her poise. 'I admit the thunder and lightning here is an unmanly fuss, even for ... whatever sort of man *he* may still be.'

Daisen said angrily, 'Mother, we can't do nothing!'

'Sister, you are implacable.'

There was silence.

Zandar gave an odd, child-like smile, and waved a hand at the map room walls. 'It's sad that we cannot summon help from the places pictured on our walls. That would be a mighty host.'

Daisen's words tolled like funeral bells. 'Not all the sorcery of all The Waning's adepts combined could do that.'

Zandar's voice sharpened. 'Sister, I said before you were implacable. Now I wonder if you are something worse.'

Daisen lowered her head. The accusation pained her dreadfully. For a while, no one spoke. Then Daisen rose.

'Mother, you plan to go outside, don't you?'

'I will go *anywhere*, to combat the Lord of the North!'

'You allow yourself heroic gestures. Are the rest of us not fit?'

Mother Zandar suddenly wondered if the betrayal that she would face in this place was already beginning – begun by Sister Daisen, her dearest friend.

Scorn came into her voice. 'Daisen, you wish to strike at the Lord of the North by yourself?'

'No, Mother. I know I would be ... inadequate. I would like your permission to use a power gem and also Sandella.'

'No! Fighting *him* cost me my sight. It might cost you more; and you are also risking our strongest novice.'

'Mother, I have already volunteered!'

In her white robes, Daisen stayed standing, very straight. To her and to all, Mother Zandar seemed small and tired. 'Mother, you want to leave our protections, but you mustn't!' Daisen shook two fists. 'Look what happened before. He *blinded* you! And then he *killed* you!'

'I assure you that I feel healthy.'

'Look, everyone!' Now Daisen took a white shroud from her pouch and shook it. It was imprinted with a dark outline: a human figure. Zandar's face could be recognized. 'I came here to proclaim a miracle! Life coming after death! Yes, resurrection!'

Some sisters and others knelt and crossed themselves. The word 'miracle' was repeated. Many looked at Zandar with awe. Others did not.

Ego and what feeds ego is so attractive, isn't it? thought Zandar. But I have to resist that sweet poison...

'Younger sister, I claim no such thing.'

'A miracle,' Daisen repeated. 'But your next death will be final!'

When she replied to that, Zandar's voice was unsteady.

'All of you know that I would sacrifice myself proudly for you and for this place. You cannot tie my hands. As I have said, *this is war!'*

Daisen kissed the image's face, then spoke with finality. 'Let us end this meeting. It can serve no purpose.'

'I forbid you to leave!'

'Mother, we cannot prevail without fighting, and we cannot fight from within this protection! And yet the *only* person you are prepared to risk is *you!*'

That said, Daisen began to walk away.

Zandar found she was shaking with fury. 'Come back! I did not dismiss you!'

It was as if Daisen hadn't heard her. She continued to walk away.

That terrible public argument had made Sister Daisen feel sick. When she walked out onto the battlements, she saw the sky above The Waning was all swirling black clouds now, and rain was descending in soaking sheets. But when she looked beyond the rain, the horizon a mile away all round was still summer-blue.

'I do believe you are right, Elder Sister!'

Sandella had followed her.

'I cannot thank you, Novice, for being right gives me no pleasure... I feel I am inciting mutiny. But I cannot be silent! For *he* is right here, and we have done nothing!'

This storm, and *his* thumping attacks, were all getting worse. Daisen and Novice Sandella shivered in the cold rain. They flinched from every lightning blast and then after-images seared their eyes; the crack-boom of the thunder shook the world.

'Why won't our holy Mother act?'

'What?'

'If we do nothing, we must lose! – Correct?'

Sandella had been unexpectedly fierce again. Daisen noted it would soon be time to promote the girl to full sisterhood.

'You quote me,' she replied, 'but, again, I do not thank you for it.'

'The One Who Will Change is outside these walls. While that brave man risks his life, we cower here like cowards! I am furious!'

Yes, Daisen thought, promote her – or discipline her severely.

In the back of her mind Daisen was still worrying about how

Words of Fury: 339

the Lord of the North had entered The Waning before – through Mother Zandar. Could he do it again through the holy Mother? Or perhaps through another?

All the more reason to let Sandella, and others prepared to fight, go against *him*...

Sandella suddenly winced, then rubbed her streaming eyes. 'This wetness hurts!'

Daisen's eyes also stung. Then she realized what this must be. The Lord of the North had opened a door from an alternate, and worse, world. She cupped her hands, shouted a message down the battlements.

'Everybody, take cover from the rain! Pass it on! This is *acid* rain! Take cover *now* – by order of Elder Sister Daisen!'

She sheltered with gangling Sandella in a glass summerhouse. Outside, the rain fell hard, poisoning the little fruit and vegetable and flower gardens of The Waning.

So much for self-sufficiency if there's a long siege now, Daisen thought. And with this evil rain *he* is even poisoning our water!

'If I do nothing... Elder Sister, I could not face myself!'

'You are only a novice.'

'So? As our holy Mother says, this is war, time to break precedent!' The girl peered at Daisen. She was upright and brave, though clearly frightened. 'Elder Sister, I cannot continue this way – and I feel you agree.'

'You cannot mutiny!'

'Yes, I can!'

A gigantic bolt of lightning ripped through the air just over their heads. The flash was tremendous. Electricity splashed violet and blue around the low wards; but for now the protection from *him* held.

Then a hooded figure walked out of the rainy gloom towards them.

On Miracle Island they fought on. Arrows flew from both sides. Then the enemy came again, in hordes. This time Man saw some thresh through the twin-branched river as others charged over the deliberately broken bridges. Men on both sides died, and then Man saw a Sword Maiden spitted on an enemy's spear. He took another leg wound himself in trying to help her. When he was recovering after it was healed he tried helping the two women with some second-rate healing of his own.

Meanwhile, numbers told. Even Ugaki came staggering back after defending Keli. There were a half-dozen sword wounds on his body – too many to help with, and all pouring blood – and an arrow in his chest. His left hand was on his right arm, and when it came away a huge slice of bleeding flesh hung down.

He squatted in front of Man, drooling blood, face dazed.

'I think I'm finished.' He clenched one massive fist; the other seemed paralyzed. 'If you see my sons... Ah, my sons!' He blinked at Man. 'But you won't see them before me, will you?'

In another few minutes Ugaki bled to death.

Mother Zandar pulled back her hood. Her blind, angry face turned from side to side.

'Daisen? Sandella? There were brave Sword Maidens who set out to get information about Emmanuel. I came to these walls to search for them. But what do I find?'

Daisen was full of anguish. 'I do have the right to question, Mother.'

'You cannot face *him* directly.' Now Zandar turned to Sandella. 'You want to believe that you can fight *him* by yourself, but you're wrong, girl – even with a power gem! We must wrong-foot him and use his own strength against him. That is my war strategy. Accept it!'

'Mother – '

'Obey!' Mother Zandar was firm, but here on the battlements in the shadow of *his* power she could not be both honest and optimistic, and she chose bleak honesty. 'You know we have tried to send Emmanuel help – but we do not know where he is!'

'If he lives, he must be somewhere.'

'Yes, yes, but we do not know where; and we cannot reach Lady Joah or Emmanuel to find out.' More thunder boomed around them, as if an evil god laughed. 'If even one scout returns – '

Daisen waved a hand. 'Nobody could get through this acid rain!'

'If someone can – '

'There's that word again – "if", holy Mother, if, if!'

Sandella said eagerly, 'Surely *his* magic might sometimes lift? In that interval we could Far-See, or go out, or others could come here!'

Zandar gave a mirthless smile. 'That sounds like Healer

Words of Fury: 341

Irizo, who was born for optimism.'

'Mother, what were you born for?'

'War.'

There was a silence. Zandar saw that her directness, as so often, made others uncomfortable.

She tried to explain. 'I know there is talk that we are not doing enough, but we must have patience. If you want to do something useful, help me scan the land around for a returning scout! If one returns with Emmanuel's location, I will risk going outside.'

'You ask for our patience,' said Daisen. 'For how long?'

Zandar said, 'Until things improve.'

Sandella replied. 'Mother, I can't wait to face him directly, and I am not the only one who thinks that way!'

'But you must wait, because I command it.' Then she put both hands on Sandella's face. 'Your fear might all too easily turn into dangerous fury. I know that temptation well. But the Lord of the North is not God and his power is not infinite! He is tiring, and his attention is in too many places.'

'You can't *know* that!'

'Listen to what I'm telling you! He *cannot* fight well in Rumoi, fight well in Jade, and also fight well here!'

Daisen said quietly, 'Perhaps he does not need to fight so well, to beat us.'

Chapter Thirty-Two: *We Thought We Were Heroes*

Even half an hour later, Sandella was still in a fury. The holy Mother, her idol, had dismissed her. From that last conversation it was clear that Zandar wouldn't do anything till it was too late, and Daisen would only wring her hands.

It's easy to shelter behind walls, thought Sandella, but it's wrong that my elders *won't* act.

That was why Sandella was in this corridor, which was the deepest and most secure place in all The Waning. By tradition, Sword Maidens and an adept Novice or even a Sister was always at the checkpoint set before the locked gate.

Sandella was strong and self-confident – some of the time – and this was her chance to prove herself. She met the guards with a pleasant look and a few humble lies.

' – on orders, yes.'

'You are young to be given such a task,' said the grey-haired Sister sitting here, knitting, with three Sword Maidens behind her.

Sandella's lies became even more humble, but then she made a boast which did happen to be true. 'I can be spared – but also I am very strong.'

So she was let through, and given many jangling keys. She walked slowly along the dark passageway. She felt reluctant now. The powers she wanted to unleash were just so mighty...

'Novice? What are you doing?'

That voice made her jump. Sandella whirled about to see who had followed her. Sister Daisen!

A confrontation with her would alert the Maiden guards, so Sandella kept her voice low.

'I have come to check our power, Elder Sister, and see how it might be used.'

'*You?*' Daisen seized her shoulder. 'You overreach yourself.'

'What is the alternative? To do nothing? Can you *honestly* tell me that you don't want to strike out now?'

There was a hesitation. 'I suppose it will do no harm to assess what powers we have, which might hurt even *him.*'

The two women walked on. This long dark passageway had a dozen iron-barred chambers. Each cell contained a padlocked and warded casket, some lined with lead. Sandella stopped to peer into one barred cell after another.

In spite of the closed lids, light flashed from the caskets. It

Words of Fury: 343

was a kind of pulsing music made from light. Sandella saw deep luminous green from an emerald, red coming from a ruby power gem, and pale but intense blue light from the famous diamond in the most remote cell.

Sandella breathed, 'The gems are all active!' She turned. 'Does that mean it's dangerous here?'

'Of course they are active – which of course means they are dangerous – for the Lord of the North passes over, and they know.'

'Sister Daisen! Are you telling me they are *alive*?'

'They are not true *kami*.' Daisen slowed her pace and then actually stopped. It was as if both women preferred to talk, now, rather than continue to the end. 'Some think they have volition and plans, but they are essentially gateways.'

'To what, exactly?'

Daisen gave a snort and pulled her robes tighter against the damp.

'If I knew the answer to your question, I would be the greatest adept ever – and I am not!'

'But you are strong, Elder Sister – though not so strong as I.'

'Our holy Mother is stronger.'

'Stronger than the two of us together?' Sandella was not given an answer to that. 'And surely *he* has the measure of her? She has fought the Lord of the North so many times and been defeated always.'

It came very reluctantly.

'You make the same case I have been making to myself.'

'You want to fight, don't you? – Just like me!'

'Yes – just like you.'

They walked on very slowly, in the shifting rainbow chaos.

'Which gem might you think of using, Sister Daisen? I am most familiar with the Red Star.'

'I want the Diamond Heart.'

Sandella stopped, and stared at her superior. That was no Eye of Jade, but it was the mightiest of The Waning's power gems – and therefore the most dangerous. 'No half measures!'

'We may only have one chance, so let our blow be mighty! Now, you have used the Diamond Heart, I think.'

'I melted part of the wall in the Hall of Challenge.'

Daisen chuckled. 'If only we might melt *him*, in the same way!'

'Is that possible?'

'How can I tell? The Heart is very, very powerful, but if we use it with you linked to me you should be safe enough.'

'I was not thinking of my own safety, Sister, but of the safety of this place; and of helping our army at Rumoi, where my blood sister Kinshi is!' Sandella took a breath. 'If we hurt *him* here, won't we protect our friends there?'

'I cannot argue with your logic.'

With that admission, Sandella walked on till her fingers touched the cold iron bars of the last cell gate, which had two immense padlocks. Already she had to shade her eyes from the electric-blue light within.

Now Daisen said, 'Even though we take this gem now, only afterwards will we decide about actually using it.'

The tall girl snapped back, 'I thought we had agreed to fight!'

'I did not quite say that.'

'But we know we have to, and we have the courage to act. Sadly, Sister, not all do.'

Daisen spoke sharply. 'What do you mean, Novice?'

'I know how brave she was. Is. Is, I mean. But I have to ask myself – and others – if she is the best leader we could have.'

There was a long silence. 'You want a more aggressive war leader? You have been planning?'

Sandella had the first key for the Diamond Heart cell in her hand. She turned away to unlock the first padlock.

'Thinking. Talking a little.'

'Talking with whom? A rash rebellious scheme might split the Waning!'

Sandella unlocked the second padlock on the gate and pulled it wide open. The casket was on a knee-high display table. Now diamond-white light with less blue was pouring out of the casket even though it was closed.

'If we do nothing, we are doomed anyway. A more aggressive plan is right. *I* believe it is right, and others agree.'

She glared back at Daisen, and then she stepped into the cell, holding the key for the casket. Eyes averted from the blinding intensity of the light, Sandella opened the casket's own padlock, which fell to the floor. Daisen had moved to stop her, but did not. Even though the lid remained closed, the increasing flood of light made them both flinch. The Diamond Heart was awake now and troubling the other power gems.

Then Sandella opened the casket and diamond light blasted

Words of Fury:

out.

When Daisen saw Sandella actually pick up the chain-held gem, she felt the beginnings of terror. The light inside the cell was a blue-white glare, but the light in the passageway behind Daisen was now a kaleidoscopic chaos far brighter than day. Rainbow colors duelled all along the passage. The gems had powered up. That might mean disaster, but there was nothing Daisen could do to restore tranquility.

'Sandella! Stand still!'

That was Mother Zandar, striding from behind them to the cell doorway.

Though she hadn't turned, Daisen saw the novice swing the Diamond Heart and shout out, 'I will not put down my weapons! Letting *him* go unopposed is deadly!'

'Sandella, tell me what you and those others have been planning!'

'To fight *him*, Mother, even if you will not – with *this*!'

Zandar confronted her closest friend. 'Sister Daisen! Isn't *this* mutiny?'

Sandella turned away from the casket. The angry novice seemed to wave the Diamond Heart on its chain, though Daisen was too dazzled by the glare to see clearly.

Zandar sounded furious. 'Is one of you – or both – *his* agent here?'

'Are *you*?' asked Sandella.

Daisen saw the novice straighten her back and spread her hands, ready to throw spells. The diamond glared light below her right hand. With it, Sandella could overcome even Zandar.

Daisen swallowed. Perhaps that had been the cold, cold plan, right from the beginning...

Zandar tapped fingers onto her chest, where a gem hung on a silver chain. This stone also shed light.

'Sandella, do not move!'

'Please, Novice!' Daisen said. 'You are endangering all of us, and this sacred place!'

'Mother, most of the novices agree with me! I cannot back down.'

Zandar spread her hands in her own threatening battle-magic gesture.

'Lay down the Heart! I won't ask you for names, but a house divided cannot stand.'

Words of Fury:

'I agree.' Tears had come to Sandella's eyes. She raised one hand, showing her stolen power gem again. Heat and light bubbled together in the small cell. 'That's why I'm doing this!'

The duel commenced in blasts of color so bright as to be stunning. Daisen stepped back, horrified. Violet light from Sandella met red light from Zandar, and was swallowed by it.

'Stop!' Daisen said. 'Sandella, you cannot threaten our holy Mother!'

The peace had been broken; this was to the death.

Static electricity crackled in the air, and then flashed along the walls and ceiling. It made all the women's hair stand on end.

The floor was shaking now. For a moment the stone walls turned transparent and seemed to buckle.

Then Daisen felt the electricity strike into her chest. She would have stepped in to end the fight, she would, but with a stopped heart could not. She gasped, slumping backwards.

A voice cried out, 'Sister!'

Daisen's back was against the wall and she slid down it as her breathing ceased. She was blacking out, dying.

'Look what you've done!' Zandar cried, to the girl. She stepped forward into the cell, one hand raised to throw magic ahead of her.

But then Zandar half turned and bent forward, to give life-saving assistance at the risk of her own.

From some place a million miles away Daisen felt Zandar's fingers scrabbling between her breasts, trying to re-start her heart with magic. Everything had stayed dark. Only after several terrifying seconds was this magic Daisen's salvation. Her pulse beat again.

When Daisen did manage to stand, she saw Sandella still posed to throw strong curses – and then the girl did. Ugly power clashed with itself in the cell. Magic fought magic in stupendous flashes of color.

Daisen was held by two weaves, one from Zandar, the other from the powerful young novice. Daisen could not even move. The others were willing to fight each other to the death, but still had compassion for the gemless bystander.

Daisen saw Zandar throw a hurricane of sleet to overwhelm Sandella, to bury her and hold her frozen when the sleet was turned to hard ice.

A gesture from the girl with the Diamond Heart turned the sleet into a blast of steam, a scalding explosion that rocked all

Words of Fury: 347

three women.

'You use *his* cold weapons, Mother!' Sandella taunted, 'Are you in *his* image?'

'You fool girl! I had planned to hold you still without wounding you!' Zandar's voice was huge and her expression was frightening. 'Stand down, or else!'

Daisen was kept to one side as the holy Mother and the novice fought with amazing weaves. The very air twisted and the walls shook. Sandella had great power, and Daisen saw it come in waves, amplified by use of the Diamond Heart.

Neither combatant had moved to the highest energy levels, yet, but Daisen knew that must come. When it did...

She saw Zandar flicking Sandella's weaves away without smashing them.

'Do you want to kill Daisen and me – and yourself? Are you mad, or in *his* hands?'

'I am in the Almighty's hands, Mother! If you are in the right, *fight me!*'

The building shook even more. Daisen saw cracks sprout up the stone walls, and then the floor went up and down like a ship's deck in a storm.

But that was not the most frightening thing. In this close combat the power was incredible and Daisen feared the effect unleashing so much energy would have on the other power gems. Most likely the woken gems would discharge, and that would blow up the heart of The Waning.

If they all vented at the same time, in a chain reaction, there would no longer be a Waning of the Moon.

There might not even be a Japan...

'Please stop this!' Daisen managed to force words out between her frozen lips. 'You injure our cause!'

Zandar glared at young Sandella. 'Unleash these gems and you will destroy everything!'

'But you were doing nothing! Let Daisen and I act! Then *he* will know he has been in a fight!'

Daisen saw that Zandar was looking wildly round her.

'I am trying to find Emmanuel and bring him here, but you play into our enemy's hands! Sandella, stop!'

'Not till you run or are destroyed!'

Something changed in Zandar's expression, which Daisen recognized. It was fear mixed with a desperate new hope. Then a decision was made.

There was a terrible gut-churning feeling as if the fabric of space-time itself was being wrenched apart, and a thunderclap. Then Daisen saw Mother Zandar step forward into darkness.

She was gone.

Sandella stared, then lowered her hands. The Diamond Heart powered down a little. The stone floor ceased its shaking.

'What happened? Have I *hurt* her? How could I do that?'

'She may be grievously injured, and I have no idea where she has gone! Sandella, release me!'

Sandella was still looking round. Multicolored light was everywhere, and all was thunder and chaos. 'Has Zandar taken that gem to give to *him?*'

That was the moment Daisen managed to release herself.

There was a pool on the stone floor where Zandar had stood. When Daisen knelt to touch it she found it burned her fingertips.

She shook the droplets off her hand. 'To avoid destroying you, or being destroyed herself, our Mother has gone outside – into the acid rain! Now she may *die!*'

Sandella lifted clenched fists, and the power she raised then was so intense that Daisen saw reality itself flicker around the girl.

'Oh, God, I have made myself responsible for *everything*!'

Daisen had been praying that the power gems might go silent now, but they did not. Terrified by the frantic color-changes and chiming coming from the gems, she took Sandella by the shoulder.

'No more! Please, no more!'

The jewels were ready to give up all their terrifying energies in one earth-wounding blast – and when that fury engulfed them both, Daisen pulled the girl to her and closed her eyes.

She was wondering if the coming destruction had been *his* plan all along.

The enemy withdrew from both banks, staying out of easy arrow-range but circling and whooping. The hot afternoon sun continued to beat down. Man realized his mouth was very dry. He took a long drink of water – but not from the bloody river. He shared the flask with the surviving Sword Maiden, and she thanked him with a look.

He could not help thinking of martyred Precious Stone. Why couldn't *she* have stayed, and lived?

Yoshi came back from another dangerous perimeter check.

Words of Fury:

Keli followed him.

Man turned to them. 'What about the road to The Waning? And, Keli, is help coming?'

'I went up the tower,' Yoshi said tiredly. 'The enemy has cut the road and it stays cut. Keli still can't get through. There'll be no reinforcements.'

'I'm so sorry,' the novice said. She was visibly upset. 'I've done what I can, but it's madness in The Waning, and *his* madness outside it.'

When Keli limped over to join the Voice from Afar and Lady Joah, Man felt his disappointment turn into blind fury.

'Joah said we would be helped!'

Yoshi looked over at the women. Now they were all flat out with exhaustion, and sheltering from the sun and enemy arrows under a tipped-over wagon.

'I suppose she still hopes Mother Zandar and her Sword Maidens will come.'

'You don't hope for that and I don't, either!'

'Why should we?' Yoshi shrugged. 'Even if it's dangerous for your Mother Zandar, she *should* have come!'

Man spread his hands helplessly, still feeling the terrible commotion in The Waning. Waves of chaotic power still came out, women's power amplified by gemstones. Perhaps *he* had friends within. Perhaps the fighting there was on his behalf. Even those within The Waning of the Moon might be turned.

'Man, with your magic, with the Eye, with the ladies ... surely there must be *some* hope?'

'I have been thinking of the Talking Book and the Eye,' Man said. He might as well tell Yoshi his thoughts, and the uncertain conclusions.

'And?'

'The Eye has living knowledge; did you know?'

Yoshi brightened. 'You mean it might help?'

Man flinched, as an invisible explosion of magic came from somewhere inside The Waning of the Moon; but then the disturbance ceased.

What kind of damage had been done, though? Who had been hurt?

Man didn't know, so, to arm himself, he tried yet again to reach out to the Eye with his mind. This time he seemed to detect a slight pulsing of warmth and light from behind the spectacle of this universe; but nothing came clear and there was no power there for him.

'I have tried to communicate, but there's nothing meaningful to me coming back, and certainly no power. I fear the Eye is alive, Yoshi, and has volition. Do you understand?'

'Explain!'

'The Eye has influenced humankind for hundreds of thousands years. I've come to fear that Book and Eye are in control – not us.'

Yoshi had a very sharp mind; he saw it, and grimaced.

'We thought we were heroes! And now you're saying we are just bit players, mouthing lines someone else – some*thing* else – has written?'

Man didn't answer, only pointed to the road.

This time the black sashes were forming up both north and south of Miracle Island. Man saw they would be hit from both directions, presumably at the same time. He realized that over a quarter of his own side now lay wounded or dead, while he could see the enemy had reinforcements arriving.

It would soon be over.

Words of Fury:

Chapter Thirty-Three: *We Have Made Our Stand*

Daisen hurried Sandella up to the battlements again. There she made a dome of protection to keep the acid rain from them, and then she looked out.

The horizon had vanished. Everything was ink-black.
'We must defend this place and find *her* – if we can!'
Sandella said miserably, 'Is the holy Mother lost out there?'
'I think she is. Or dead.'
'Can't we bring her back? I still have the Diamond Heart.'
'I don't know!' Daisen shuddered. She now felt she was linked to someone out there, someone in pain; and it might be their holy Mother. But whoever it was was being skinned alive. So was Zandar in *his* hands? 'I feel *his* power all around and it is increasing. I do not think *he* will let go now.'
'We must lose?'
'My hope and my faith are both failing.'
'Elder Sister, please! Surely we can still strike him!'
Daisen peered up through the black rain. 'We have all the power gems we could want, and they are awake. We can use them.'
'Won't that damage him?'
'He *is* the Lord of the North.'
'And *not* God!'

Man saw the Voice with her wonderful hair tied back, and sticky red blood splashed over her chest. She was working on a wounded man with Lady Joah. This man died, choking.
Joah stood up, face dazed. She held her golden cross, kissing it with her eyes closed. Then her lips were working.
Man stalked over there. He was still half mad with anger and fear. 'We need these allies of yours! We need Zandar and her Sword Maidens!'
'Do you think I'm blind – or stupid? I *know* we do!' Joah said.
'Is there no more you can do to bring them?'
'I tried my best! I did! Mother Zandar would surely come if she could – she *would* – but in the meantime *this* is how you treat me!'
And suddenly she burst into tears.
'I'm – ' Man scabbarded his sword, touched Joah's round shoulder. He felt guilty now. Why was he so hard on her, when

she had always been so loyal and kind, unlike her sister Lady Oki? 'I'm sorry, Joah. Really I am. I know you're trying.'

Joah shivered, still sniveling. 'I miss my father. I miss my sister. I miss Jade.' She blinked away more tears. 'I can't be brave all the time!'

Young Sanada was here, now. He kneeled beside her. 'Lady, do not weep! We are with you!'

'I know!' Joah swallowed. She touched the boy's forehead and then turned to Man. 'But I wonder… Did I do wrong, to bring you all here?'

Man blinked, at this surprise assumption of total responsibility.

'We *must* be here!' Sanada said loudly. 'Isn't that true? If we stand aside, evil will win!'

'True,' she said to him, and Man saw her give Sanada a small smile. 'Noble Sanada, you remind me of duty.'

'Friend Sanada, brave Sanada, you're right,' Man said. He saw Lady Joah kiss her crucifix again. For some reason Man felt reconciled to his fate, however bad it might be. 'Dear Joah, as for me, where else would I go? You and your father are all the family I have. And Yoshi and the others here are my only friends.'

She took his rough sword-hand, kissed his knuckles.

Man knew they would all fight on to the very last. Even though Sanada was bloody and bruised as any, the battle-light was in his eyes and he had taken on his share of enemies while protecting the women.

Still looking at the Lady Joah, Sanada now squatted with Man and Yoshi.

'It's strange. I feel released from fear.'

'Ashida's death has released you.' It was clear to Man that Sanada was the hero he had always wanted to be. He hoped the boy, now a man, knew it.

'He fulfilled Prophecy for me, didn't he? Now nothing says I must die. And even if I do…' Sanada turned his head to Man, and he was smiling. 'I saw how Ashida went into infinity. It's only a moment, however long, and then release forever.'

'Yes; it's only a moment, and then we are released.'

Sanada turned to look at the river. Man saw blood on the flowing water. Many corpses were entangled on the banks.

From the watchtower a high voice called out: 'Watch out! They're sneaking up!'

Man was pulling his sword out when he saw two men run

Words of Fury:

together towards Joah and the Voice. Though Yoshi used a throwing-knife, it bounced off the first man's breast-plate.

Sanada threw himself between the women and the assassins. His blade met the other swords, cut, thrust, parry – a blur. He couldn't fight two good men, but he just needed to gain time as Man ran to help.

Sanada shouldn't die, Man thought. Some other 'young man' already made the sacrifice the Prophecies call for.

He saw Sanada win his first fight though he was stabbed in the right thigh and badly cut on the chest. Immediately the second man stepped forward to take him on it was clear wounded Sanada had no chance.

Man and Yoshi called out together.

Their enemy whirled round to face them. His sword was raised high, so Man slid in low, legs twisting to bring the man down.

Yoshi struck once. A head rolled away and now the legs of the corpse were twitching. There was a whole lot of blood at the other end.

Man stood up. He was shaking badly.

Yoshi was shouting. 'Help us!'

Man ran to Yoshi and Sanada followed. Two Heads stood with them, bloody axe raised. Behind were Joah and the Voice and Novice Keli. Their magic swirled to confuse the attackers, but there was fighting everywhere on the island now. Man knew they were going to be overwhelmed.

'Fight!' he screamed out. 'No surrender!'

The women managed to throw some illusions in front of their enemies – enough for Man and the others to strike out at their distracted opponents and continue the fight.

Man killed well and easily.

When the surviving black sashes were driven back, Man looked over at Sanada and Yoshi.

'Another chance!'

Then an enemy bowman was here, sighting on Joah. He let fly.

Man saw somebody throw himself into the arrow's path. There was a scream. Sanada was still standing, though with the arrow gone through his right eye and out of his skull behind. He said only two things as he collapsed, truths Man would always remember.

'I did not die a coward! Prophecy is true!'

Man raised a hand, palm out in salute. Then he ran forward and killed the bowman with a single chopping gesture from the same hand. In a rage, he kicked the body.

Then he looked back at the corpse of their friend. Sanada probably wouldn't even get a burial; and nobody except the handful of friends here would ever know how Sanada had died.

'Sanada-san, you were a hero.'

Joah was in tears. She crawled over to Sanada, cradled his limp body, and kissed his bloodstained face.

Answering the call for help, Mother Zandar had made a whorl in space and then stepped through to this dangerous place. Black, burning rain flooded down from black heaven, though at this distance from The Waning there was a tiny glimpse of blue sky. Knee-deep in mud, Zandar used her lesser power gem to make a tiny shield overhead.

She pulled the acid-eaten girl to her.

'You called to me.'

'Mother…' The girl was dressed in dissolving scraps of red, and her two swords had discolored scabbards, though of course her skin was burned even worse. Zandar could both hear and feel as the girl gave great wrenching coughs, trying to wipe the acid from her face, trying to wheeze it up from her lungs. 'I am poisoned, and being skinned alive…'

'I can help you, but not here. This is *his* territory now.'

The girl was dazed. 'You can go back?'

'I think so, if I am helped; but perhaps I cannot take you.'

'If I must die, Mother, receive my news.'

'I have already.' Zandar gazed at the hurt girl in compassion. 'Your news must be communicated to others.' Zandar grimaced. 'Only, one of those others may kill me. – Now, give me your hand!'

A hurt hand reached out for Zandar.

Zandar's mind called, 'DAISEN! SANDELLA! BRING ME HOME!'

Would she be heard? If she was heard, would she be obeyed? Or would she be left here to die along with the Sword Maiden?

A moment passed. Nothing.

Zandar made a beckoning gesture as she murmured one final incantation – even though it was powerful enough to reveal herself to *him*. She had to take the girl with her, so she held the

Words of Fury:

Sword Maiden tightly and prayed. This meant she could not continue with the protection, and now the acid rain poured over them both. Zandar felt her own skin dissolving, the agony as if a saint had been plunged into fire.

Again: 'DAISEN! SANDELLA! HEAR ME AND BRING ME HOME!'

She was heard and she was obeyed.

In a flash of power, the mighty Diamond Heart opened the way through the dark. Zandar stumbled forward onto the Waning battlements, then fell to her knees with the unconscious Sword Maiden still clutched to her.

Sandella moved quickly to grab Zandar's power gem. A mad light was in her eyes, so mad that Zandar wondered if the girl now served *him*. As Zandar looked up, helpless and gemless but serene, she realized the girl had the Diamond Heart glaring light and was going to burn her down with it.

Zandar resigned herself.

Sandella's magic gesture stayed incomplete.

'Mother, you do not even defend yourself.'

There was a fury in Sandella that Zandar had often sensed, but in Zandar's cool presence it was fading.

The evil rain drummed on their protection. 'My daughter, need I defend myself – from you?'

'The Maiden ... you are doing good?'

'Yes. And now I ask you, too, to do some good!'

'Mother, when you arrived here you could have destroyed me.'

'Yes, but in the process I would let this Sword Maiden die. That I would not do, anymore than I would let Emmanuel and the others die – or you, my beloved daughter.'

'But you cannot prevent it,' said Sandella. It was something between a sneer and a sob. 'You don't know where they are, only that they are beyond our help, and dying!'

Zandar stood up, still holding the acid-burned Maiden, who had begun to blink and wheeze.

'We are all dying – but you are wrong about everything else. This Maiden knows enough! If you doubt my spoken words, look into my heart!'

Sandella's expression suddenly changed. All fury left her; love came back.

'Now,' said Mother Zandar, 'give me the weapon!'

Sandella handed over the Diamond Heart.

Blind Zandar held it in her right hand; she sighed heavily.

'Here.' She returned the mighty power gem to Sandella. 'I will trust you, little sister. Take up this burden for me.'

'Mother, I cannot! I am not worthy. You are in charge and I will follow you till the day I die!'

Zandar was stroking the Maiden's bonsai hair and smiling down, her expression like a Madonna's. Then she turned back to the young novice.

'You are powerful indeed, Sandella. You know that; I know that. But you must *earn* trust. Can you do that? Can you be a soldier for me?'

Sandella went down on her knees; that was her answer.

Mother Zandar rubbed Sandella's head for a moment, then stood back and held the slumped-over Maiden erect.

'Sandella, heal this brave woman!'

When the novice raised the diamond its pure white light first enfolded her, and then enfolded the whole group of them. The light transfigured everyone, and Zandar felt her own pains recede and fade. In the healing light she embraced the terribly scarred young Sword Maiden fully.

There was something desperate on Zandar's face; but there was also hope.

'Sword Maiden, you were poisoned, but now you will be healed!'

The young Maiden shuddered as the acid scars cleared up and her health returned. She touched the silver snake around her neck. Then, recovered, she looked out at the boiling black rain.

'Mother, you crossed *that*, in the face of *him*, to find me!'

'I did, for you have information. Tell us, please.'

The Sword Maiden went down on her knees, but her smile was ecstatic.

'Mother, *I know where Emmanuel is!*'

'Emmanuel!' Yoshi called urgently.

Again, weary to death, Man answered the call and came limping forward.

It looked even worse. Now black sashes came on behind wheeled farm carts, which they used as shields on both roads.

'The bastards are learning!' said Yoshi. 'The carts make them almost arrow-proof!'

Ozawa spread out his bowmen, to hit the enemies from the

Words of Fury: 357

flanks. Man saw the other side take some casualties even though they had that protection, but still the carts came on, with their enemies crowded behind them. He also saw bowmen had sneaked forward so that they somehow seemed to rise up out of the ground. Enemy arrows flew everywhere now within their own inner circle.

Ozawa's men and Yoshi's men were mostly unarmored; they had to take cover. Now the black sashes made screaming attacks from both sides at the same time. Man could tell some screams were pain, but others were triumphant.

It had finally happened: a war on two fronts.

The first enemies came out from behind the carts. A dozen armored men took the north bridge. Man could not will his exhausted body to go there and fight.

Then Keli came running up to the bridge, flinging illusions at the enemy – clawing monsters, hidden within blinding dust. That slowed them, though as that fight commenced even more enemies came in two spear-bristling columns, timed to arrive at the north bridge and the south simultaneously.

At last the enemy is being astute, thought Man, standing off from the killing. They attack us everywhere at the same time. We don't have the men to fight in every place.

The columns hit both bridges at almost the same time and turned into two hordes of screaming men. Man saw some enemies were holding up big makeshift shields, while others were flinging roped-up planks over the gaps. Others flung themselves into the two-branched river and threshed forward.

'We have to stop them this one last time!' said Yoshi.

Man looked down where Yoshi was crouching, but he was bleeding so much that Man thought he might be out of the fight or even dying.

So Man stepped forward in his place, a small shield in one hand and his long sword in the other.

As Man went to the bridge to help Keli, archers on both sides fired. Many of the black sashes were out in the open, and they suffered. Man's sword did more bloody work, but he was tiring now. He stabbed, cut, then even smashed one enemy face with the hilt of his sword.

It wasn't enough. In minutes Man's side lost control of both bridges.

'Keli! You've done enough! Get behind me!'

She stayed alongside, throwing more curses at the

advancing black sashes. Elsewhere, other enemies managed to scramble onto the island.

The whole of Miracle Island was a chaotic battle now, wild and noisy. The fighting monk who had been with the Sword Maidens smashed his long staff into the chest of one enemy, but then he took a blow from a fighting-iron on his shoulder and slumped down.

We *are* losing...

'Here!' shouted Keli. With magic, she pulled dirt out of the ground and flung it at the advancing enemy, temporarily blinding many of them. 'Eat it!'

A shadowy figure threw his spear; and Man saw Keli stagger back with that weapon in her stomach. She fell over and then he saw twitch about as she died.

Man had no time for grief. Ozawa got everyone to the battle-line at this bridge, even the wounded. The line held, just. A few of the other side started to step back, and then more did.

Man raced awkwardly towards the other bridge. Just then there was a scuffling within the defenders' ranks. Man saw one of the three ronin hired in the village – dog-face – stab the youngest, then quickly pick his way over the broken bridge towards the enemy.

'I'm on your side!' the traitor bellowed. 'Black sashes, I can help you win!'

The other ronin, Fudai, jumped up. He was tired-looking and grim, but he had a bow. Man saw him let go an arrow. It was suddenly sticking out from between the shoulders of the traitor. Dog-face took another step forward, wailing and waving both arms, and then he splashed into the river.

That seemed to dishearten the enemies there, and they too pulled back and then ran. Ozawa rounded up enough of his own side to also recover possession of this bridge.

For one more time Man saw his defenders had succeeded in defending.

Man went over to where Keli lay on her back. He felt tears come. She was a teenager, with many more years to come; and now she was dead.

Yoshi limped to where the senior ronin now kneeled beside the youngest, that mere grubby boy who was also dead.

Fudai stood up, face stricken.

'I apologize for the treachery of him out there, my lord Yoshi. To kill young –' Fudai was a tough warrior, wearied now but not a man to surrender. He waved a thumb over his shoulder. 'Let's find his body, then leave him to the crows and the dogs, please.'

Yoshi gazed into his eyes, then nodded. 'I will. And you are no longer ronin for hire; you are one of my men.'

'My lord!' Fudai bowed, then straightened up with shining eyes.

Yoshi came over to Man, squatted down beside him, stayed there panting.

Though still sickened by the many deaths, Man was impressed by what his friend had done. 'You've won loyalty from a wave man.'

'I believe I have.'

Yoshi smiled. Blood had splashed over him, but perhaps his wounds were minor. Man felt privileged that Yoshi was his true friend – who would certainly die for The One Who Will Change, and would probably die for his friend from Albion, too. And Yoshi was more than a lone hero, he was a leader.

Yoshi heaved himself up and pointed towards the distant coast.

'See?'

Man stared. There was dust from the road; lots of marching feet were approaching. Was this rescue? 'Is that Sword Maidens? Friends?'

A wounded man croaked, 'Are we saved?'

Man rubbed at his face. Was this truly relief? A few of the men began to smile.

The Voice from Afar looked away. 'I think that's more enemies.'

'Even more?' Man asked, appalled. 'In the name of Jesus! – Yoshi, can we stand them off?'

Yoshi's eyes gauged everything. 'Perhaps for one more time, Man.'

'And then?'

'We have made our stand on land belonging to the Goddess of Mercy. What better place?'

Man made some pulling and pushing motions with his arms, trying to loosen up weary muscles. He knew he had very little left to give.

'True.'

'Now make your peace with whatever God you hold in your heart; for without help we will die.'

Words of Fury:

A sentry bawled, 'They're coming again!'

Words of Fury:

Chapter Thirty-Four: *A Place Already Full of Magic*

'It will take time to assemble the necessary force,' Zandar admitted.

She glanced up to the dark, vaulted ceiling, and then to the water below. This dank place was stone-lined and full of river water – sacred water, which had a magic of its own.

What if Man surrenders to *him?* What if Man is turned before we can get to him?

Then she felt a death-pain. Who? It was Keli, the young novice, whose soul was leaving.

Zandar blessed her memory and her bravery. She had been devoted till the end.

Here Sword Maidens were arriving squad by squad. The senior she-captain Hanake formed them up. Zandar still hoped the Maidens, and her own magic, might be enough for a rescue – if it was done quickly enough.

But there was a balance to be struck, as so often in magic as in life. Zandar needed a strong force, but there was a limit to how much of a load she could take across, even to a place already full of magic like Miracle Island.

Anyway, my force of Maidens isn't enough, Zandar thought. Near the sacred island the purity police are hundreds strong and more are coming. And this 'the Tears' is close by, and there is also the strength of *his* magic...

My force isn't large enough, and I know *I'm* not enough... Oh, why can't I have more belief? Miracle Island, they call it. Miracle! Let us see what the truth is...

I already know the truth. We will arrive there only to find the dead!

Man picked up his bow and limped back to the wagon barricade. When he reached for another barbed arrow he found he had only seven left. He cursed under his breath as more and more mounted enemies assembled for another attack.

'Yoshi, they're going to win! What do we do?'

'Friend Emmanuel, this is Japan; capture is dishonor. Believe me, you do not want to be captured by the black sashes, or let the women be taken.'

Man glimpsed Joah and the Voice sheltering under the shrine-garden wall, working on a man who had an arrow right through his upper arm.

'I understand you.'

'You know how the ancient samurai escaped capture, and dishonor, and torture?'

'I know that, too, Yoshi.'

When Man looked left again he saw a burly man in red armor come splashing out of the river and run towards them. His sword was raised high. Man heard the Voice squeal, though she picked up a discarded short sword and stood up bravely. Man started towards them, then automatically ducked a thrown spear and lost his footing in the process.

Immediately he saw the Voice was going to die.

Two Heads ran up, huge axe raised – and he chopped the enemy. Two bloody pieces fell away.

'Thanks,' Man said.

'My pleasure,' said one head, grinning – though the other face had an expression of deep seriousness.

Then another man broke through, sword raised. 'Okada Joah, die! Kin'oss, die, die!'

Yoshi rose and grappled him, holding back his sword-arm, grunting with the effort. Man fought another man, and was cut in the leg again. It was a bright burning sensation, and when Man took a step forward his leg collapsed. He was on his knees when the enemy raised his two-handed sword.

Then he saw Joah jump on the black sash's back and clap both hands around his ears. The man screamed, hair smoldering from Joah's magic touch. Then he fell down, burnt-black blood coming from his ears, writhing for a moment on the ground before he expired.

Man saw her face; she was sickened by how she had killed. He managed to stand, though his hurt leg was terribly weak. Joah needed comfort; but what could he say?

'Look at you, stupid Emmanuel! Why are you so careless?' It was the Voice, having come forward with a bandage. 'Blood all down your leg again!'

Man looked there. It was true.

'I thought I'd wet myself...'

He winced, his leg gave way again, and he sat back down in the dirt.

'Funny man! The amount of beer and saké you drink, you can afford to lose urine much more than you can blood!'

Though Man wanted to give her some brave quip, he felt too exhausted. She clearly felt the same.

Words of Fury:

'I have no more healing magic, so must bandage up your thigh. Try not to do too much.'

He laughed.

Daisen came to Zandar now, with Sandella. 'Mother, this young woman finally burst through *his* power and spoke to Princess Anamizu and the Lady Rishiri.' Daisen rubbed a hand along her jaw. 'They are on their way.'

'They had better arrive! Otherwise there will be no circle.' Sandella spoke, still visibly upset.

'Mother, I am so sorry for what I did before!'

Zandar turned. 'You should be sorry, daughter. You almost destroyed me, and I almost destroyed you! Don't you understand I must protect The Waning whatever the cost.'

'Forgive me!'

'I did and I do. Nevertheless, I cannot grant your request.'

'Please, Mother! I want to join you. I want to *be* you!'

Zandar gave a grim smile.

'If you knew me better, you would not. I live in regret and pain. I do nothing but my duty and not what I want. It is ... not such an enjoyable life.'

This time Daisen spoke. 'Mother, your name will live forever!'

'My name! My name!' Zandar gave a sour chuckle, and shook her head. 'That is so unimportant! Don't you understand how late in the day it is?' Zandar spoke from the heart. 'I must soon go from this place. I believe I have a chance. But if I don't come back, don't think I died for nothing!'

'Don't leave us, Mother!' Sandella was in tears. 'Don't die!'

Die... Zandar thought of young Keli.

'You two know what to do. Hit where it hurts.'

Daisen was trying to sound assured. 'You will save Emmanuel, Mother!'

'I may not.' Zandar lowered her voice. 'You know there is that variant of Naosuke, which says we won't arrive in time.'

'That would be disaster!'

'It would, for poor Emmanuel. But if I take the Eye, even from his body – that will be more than something.' She sighed. 'Though I hope we can save that young man.'

'Mother? What if *he* gets this place, *and* the Eye – ?'

Zandar tried to hold back a shudder.

'Then above both gates to our home we must put new words.

"Abandon all hope, ye who enter here."'

She-captain Hanake came up then.

'Mother, we are assembled.' She lowered her voice, clearly furious. 'Please don't go risking yourself for one foreign boy!'

'The Savior I acknowledge was once just a boy, and foreign to us.'

'Yes, but – '

Zandar raised a hand. 'Daisen, if it all goes wrong, you know what you must do?'

Daisen could not speak, only nod.

Zandar was insistent. 'My beloved sister, my dearest friend... Please, reassure me!'

'Mother, if you fall and there is no Eye for us, I will still fight on. Then, when *he* is winning, the gems here will speak one last time. With them, I will end it all. If *he* inherits, he will inherit only blasted stones.'

'I thank you. If you can, save Irizo – and Sandella here. If not, let your end come together.'

Mother Zandar kissed both of them. Then Daisen and Sandella left.

The other side closed in again, and now more of them had spears to fight with and more were prepared to strip off and swim. Man found himself standing over kneeling Joah in the sacred garden beneath the statue of Lady Kannon. As Joah worked to heal a man, Man struck away enemy spears that reached from over the walls. He moved from side to side of the garden, screaming his defiance, lopping off spear-heads and twice human hands.

There were too many spears in too many hands.

A few eventually stabbed Man, making wounds in the forearms and biceps. Shallow wounds, but enough blood loss would be deadly. He realized he was a dead man walking and Joah was the same. Their eyes met. She rose, face determined. She had a sword in her hands and she moved alongside Man and began to use it.

Lady Joah was good, but it was not enough. The odds against them were too great. Man knew there would be no mercy when they were finally defeated.

Then another squad of cavalry came to the smashed-up bridge, shrieking war-cries as they slid off their horses.

Man dashed back there. There were two dozen screaming enemies. He fought them like a madman, hack, parry, hack again

Words of Fury:

– shoulder-charge one man while kicking another in the groin. He was forced back to the walled garden, lost in bloody chaos, screaming, slashing, stabbing – and once he even found himself driving a thumb into an enemy's eye.

He saw that man roll away. Man followed, stamped on his face and heard bones and teeth crunch; then he stabbed the man through the neck.

One down, but more enemies were coming, with more following them.

Man admitted the truth: *It will soon be over*.

Words of Fury:

Chapter Thirty-Five: *A Miracle*

By far-seeing magic, Berenda could glimpse the battle around Miracle Island. There was something deep in her that still made her want to help Emmanuel. It was perhaps some cruel impulse to keep him living longer, so that her master could see Berenda help destroy him; or maybe it was some protective impulse towards young Emmanuel and goodness itself.

Her heart was torn. What should she do?

She said out loud, 'Emmanuel and the others are about to be overwhelmed!'

Hagiwara responded at once. 'Then you must do something! If you don't, then our master wins, and we will have contributed *nothing* to his new world and will be surplus to requirements.'

'I dare not act if it means opposing *him*.'

'Look! *He* is squatting above The Waning! If this Emmanuel dies now, we will *never* be needed by the Lord of the North ever again!'

For various reasons she did not want Emmanuel to die. That meant she had to help him. It had to be done in a subtle way, too, so that *he* would not see – if that was possible.

Suddenly Berenda thought of the Voice from Afar, her young accompanist when she had performed as 'the Tears' in Jade. The Voice was there on Miracle Island, too, and she had always talked so much of the power of music.

Berenda saw what she might do, raised her hands, *did it*.

Man had been forced back into the walled garden where Joah was. He was never quite sure what happened next, but he suddenly seemed to hear music. It was a sitar, he thought. Then the stone statue came alive.

In the flesh, Lady Kannon was very lovely. Her honey-brown eyes met his, full of compassion.

'This is a miracle!' Man said.

She was so beautiful that he could hardly believe his eyes, and when she spoke her voice was beautiful too.

'And there will be another miracle, dear Emmanuel, for if you live we *will* meet again!'

She jumped from her plinth onto the wall with the gazelle-grace of a dancer. Louder Hindian music flooded the garden. It didn't seem to be sacred, more like an exciting dance-tune. Awed, Man now saw the Mother of Mercy undulate along the

Words of Fury:

walls. She crushed long bamboo spears under her feet, crushed the hands and forearms of enemies, though she did not ever kill.

So on this occasion Joah lived; so did Man.

The enemy died or fell back from the river island.

When they did, Kannon became stone again, lovely but lifeless.

Man was panting, shaking, and bloody. He found he was squatting behind a tipped-over theatre wagon again. Hadn't the women hidden there before? One hand was on his badly cut thigh, holding the lips of the wound together as blood ran. The bandage had slipped down to his ankle.

The fight would go on. Sooner or later he would take a wound that would be mortal.

The black sashes were retreating, though. His own side gave a ragged cheer; one bloodied Emperor's samurai even stood and raised a clenched fist. Man thought he had killed three with his swords this time and one with that bare-handed blow, and perhaps three with his bow.

But the enemy horsemen did not go far. They whirled around in a great shouting ring just out of easy arrow range.

Joah staggered over, and with the last of her power healed his leg with a finger-stroke. He knew he'd be scarred, but at least he had stopped bleeding.

I am weak, though; I am very weak now. If there was ever a time to call on *him* to save me, and my friends, that time is now...

Yoshi came. When he looked down at Man his face was drawn, and he held a wadded bandage to his stomach. Blood trickled there, and also from a slashed ear.

'I saw that beauty of a stone woman dancing on the garden wall. Did you see that, or am I imagining things?'

'You might say I actually danced with her – or alongside her.'

'It was a miracle. She saved us!'

'You know what Joah says. Sometimes prayers are answered...'

Yoshi squatted beside Man. His swordblade was bloody and his eyes were staring.

'We have hardly thirty of our side standing, and some are wounded. When the enemy next come...'

'They must not get the Eye, Yoshi.'

'Who's going to stop them? Man, we're done!'

That was the truth. Man looked around. There were tired, worn-down men squatting below the Goddess of Mercy. She was lifeless stone again, facing west towards Hindia and the homeland of the Lord Buddha. Men were sheltering behind the walls of her garden, where the flowers had been trampled flat. Man saw the other survivors were also at their posts. Two Heads came to stand above Joah and the Voice. His faces were both grim, his axe poised. Man realized that the Siberian would die before a hand touched the women. Joah and the Voice sat together still, but with knives in their hands.

Beside him, Yoshi stood up and gazed around, though he was standing in arrow-shot of the enemy. He was truly noble, brave, and loyal; and Man loved him.

'Yoshi? How many more have come, do you think?'

'Enough to...' Yoshi's words trailed off.

Man pushed himself to his feet. He saw more black sashes had arrived, and he still had the strong feeling from before that the Tears would add her magic to their sword-power. He saw the enemy all around, galloping, shrieking battle-cries.

'They'll attack soon!' Man's voice was still powerful, though he felt ready to collapse. 'When they do, you men, get on your feet!'

Some enemies headed for the broken south bridge. As if his body belonged to someone else, Man found he was drawing his bow, sighting on an enemy, and letting fly again and again. He thought he hit his targets, but they came on anyway.

Then suddenly they were all riding away. Man was alone again, with only dead men around him. He put down his bow, shook his bloodied sword and screamed out.

'I have Words of Power, black sashes! Come back and hear them!'

There was no enemy close enough to respond, but they would be back. Man lowered his sword. Many black-clad horsemen still rode up and down on both banks of the river. Man put his second-last arrow to his bow, stood up quickly, saw a horseman and let fly, then dropped down again.

'If it matters, you got him in the arm.'

Man turned his head. Dirk Faslane was crouching beside him, reddish hair plastered down with sweat. He stared at the man; at someone else from Albion. But who was he, really? Friend, or unfriend? Man felt doubt well up. Did this man truly want justice for his father the late Lord of Arms, and for Man

Words of Fury:

himself? Or was everything he said just trickery?

Faslane was still looking at him. A wrist-flip shook blood off his spiked fighting-iron.

'I don't know how we stood off the last attack.'

'A miracle,' Man offered.

'Will there be another?'

'I doubt it. Look at the numbers.'

Man began shivering, his consciousness suddenly sliding away. He jerked awake after a heartbeat. Was that blood-loss or plain exhaustion? Occasionally there were pauses in *his* interference, and then Man wanted to use his own magic: but he was so exhausted that magic, too, had deserted him. There was no sensible option now except surrender.

'We could maybe...' Faslane began.

Man narrowed his eyes, feeling a beserk rage within himself that was now ready to come out.

'You have something on your mind?'

Faslane rubbed at his sweat-streaked face. 'I have been honest with you.'

'Eventually.'

'I came here on a mission.'

'Only official historians would call it "justice". You came here prepared to do murder – to murder *me!*'

'I was sent here under Albion's orders, yes – but there'll be no murder now. Lord, I *believe* in you!'

Another mindless worshipper? Man rolled wearily onto his back. The sky above was blue. It would always be blue, though generation after generation died below.

He spoke the impossibilities with cutting irony.

'Thanks. So we just have to win our battle here, then go home to Albion and get me declared innocent and my father also, and then I, well, I...' Here his imagination faltered.

'You speak cynically, and not like the idealist I know you are. Where's *your* faith, Lord Emmanuel?'

The reproof had justice in it, but Man didn't bother replying in words; he just flung his hands up in the air and closed his eyes. He was aching and bleeding and he had come to the end of his strength.

'What do you expect from me? Albion killed their greatest hero – my father! Do you expect gratitude?'

'I expect you to clear your father's name.'

'What?' He rolled his head, eyed Dirk Faslane. 'That's

impossible. Especially since he's dead.'

'It has to be possible – if you want to clear your own name.'

'I don't do miracles!'

'Yes, you do.'

Man could not respond to that. He just lay there, staring at blue sky as Faslane continued.

'It's not even certain the Lord of All Arms is dead.'

'My father might be *alive?*' Man jerked up, his heart pounding.

'There was certainly no execution. I also know there was no body ever found.'

It was like a bright light shining out from Man; it was joy. He might not have been orphaned, he might not deserve to live in disgrace.

Then he tried to calm himself.

'Ah, that's nonsense, Faslane! We're just gabbling and speculating, while we wait for death!'

'I wanted you to know everything I know, Lord Emmanuel. Then you can make up your own mind about what to do. If you and I should live, please choose to return, and then I'll help you.'

This was at first hearing very cheering; but it was really only one more terrible responsibility.

'My father... Do you have any idea what his "treasons" were?'

'The case is sealed, even to the likes of me, but I was told that the accusation was "working for an occult power" – for *him*, that means.'

'But that's absurd!'

'I dare say – although there was evidence.'

'All lies! My father fought the Lord of the North!' Then Man saw the truth. 'You – or is it Imperial Intelligence – only *suspect* my lord father was innocent! Some of you think he *was* damned! And right now you can't prove a thing, either way!'

'Not from here, no. But think of what it would mean, to you and to the country, and to the world, if you could prove your father's accusers were wrong.'

'But if *you* can't prove him innocent, how can I?'

'If you came back to Albion, I think you could do almost anything!'

Man felt unexpected rage. 'If my father couldn't save himself when he was Lord of All Arms, what can I do?'

Faslane stared; there was perhaps compassion in that look,

and a seriousness that comes when death is faced.

'Perhaps that's something for the future, Lord Emmanuel – if we have one, eh? And I'm conscious now I'm in another country.'

'So?'

'So here I hear all this about "The One Who Will Change", and how important he is. Well, that makes you a savior, doesn't it? *Their* savior, in *their* land!'

A savior! Man toyed with his long sword, thinking once more about his father, who had obviously found out some dark secret to do with the Lord of the North – most likely a secret involving the great ones of Albion, perhaps even royalty...

He turned to Faslane. 'You think highly of me.'

'I *believe* in you. You've worked miracles. I've seen them – haven't I?' Faslane gripped his hand. 'You will win, or we will all die here with you!'

'But what,' Man said softly to his tempter, 'if you're really on the side of my father's killers?'

'No!'

'You already admitted you were given orders to kill me, if I'd been turned. What if you're here to lure me back to Albion, to death there?'

'Have you gone foreign in your mind? Your country needs your help, and maybe your father, too!'

'How can I help a dead man? My father can't be alive, or he'd have been speaking to me by magic.'

Dirk Faslane looked over at Man with bright, wounded eyes. Then he started to crawl away. Man was going to follow when there was more shouting off the island. The black sashes were working themselves up for yet another attack.

The man in the watchtower called down.

'The numbers are overwhelming!'

Man saw Yoshi stand up for a moment to risk a wide-ranging glance.

'He's right.'

Man grimaced, and he forced himself up. He was so dizzy that for a moment he could not even see – and then he did see the enemy, and the numbers were overwhelming.

There would be no return to Albion now, no miraculous cleansing of his lost father's reputation. Unless he turned and called on the Lord of the North right now, Man would die here. He wondered why he didn't feel more afraid.

Now Yoshi, in his bloodstained motley, croaked his last orders. 'Arrows, men! As many as you can! And fight for every inch of territory! And if they still break through, join me in the centre, and we'll fight to the death!' Then he spoke, absently, his own death poem.

> 'Fighting on the road
> We were only blood that spilled;
> Yet Heaven's eye has seen
> Immortal courage in our hearts.'

Fine words, Man thought, but no celebration of victory. In fact, it was a dirge – in ancient samurai style.

Man's healed leg was suddenly trembling again. Weakened, he sat down on a log. He saw Joah was sitting beside the Voice, who had her arm around Joah's shoulder. Man tried to smile; but the dead were scattered everywhere here, there was no hope, and he knew his expression would be ghastly.

So many are dead, now. Fukuzawa, I'm sure. Yonai, who had turned to evil. My lovely Precious Stone, and the other Maidens. Then Keli died too. Ashida, Ugaki, and my friend Sanada – and so many, many others...

As one, those black-armored horsemen turned. The enemy samurai on foot began to spread out in two big half-circles, all the way round Miracle Island. This time there was order in their movements. Every single enemy was involved, all the many hundreds of them. They started their approach again, slow and careful to start, but when they began to charge they would be overwhelming.

So it's finally over, Man thought, and we're done...

Yoshi shouted orders, getting everyone ready for a last stand. Then he squatted beside Man.

'What do you think?'

'They know we're exhausted – those of us who live – and too few to defend our perimeter. So this time it's going to be a mass attack all round. The armored riders will punch through any defense we can throw up, and the footsoldiers will envelope us.'

'I agree with you,' Yoshi said. He looked back at the women, raised a significant eyebrow.

Man found his hands were shaking. He looked down, willing the cowardice to stop. Nevertheless those hands would not cease their trembling.

'I hate to think of those bastards doing to the Voice and Joah what they did to those Sword Maidens.'

Words of Fury: 373

'Any decent man would hate it too.'

Man knew that Yoshi meant they should kill the two women before capture.

He found he was hefting his long sword, and staring directly at Joah, who now looked back.

What should I do, he asked her without words, when these men finally storm our circle? What if they take you alive, torture you like that poor scalped and blinded Sword Maiden, *turn* you?

Her eyes darkened; but then she nodded.

Rather than that, Emmanuel, give me the mercy of your sword.

If he could bring himself to do it, then he should do it. But Man blurted out to Yoshi, 'I don't think I can.'

His friend understood him perfectly.

'Then, at the last, will you cover me, Man – with your dying body if necessary? And I will do what has to be done for the ladies.'

'I will. Yes.'

'And then we can ... help each other into infinity.'

Man wondered, Will I wake up in heaven? Or in *his* cold place, where I probably belong?

'Yoshi, you would trust me so far?'

'I trust you to death, Emmanuel; and beyond.'

For a moment Man became English again; and he took Yoshi's hand in the two of his, and shook it.

'If only – ah, I might have showed you my father's castles, and Londres, and all our Albion greatness!'

'I would have enjoyed that,' Yoshi answered. Somehow he was still smiling. 'But, whatever happens now, it's been good – it's been a revelation – to have known you.'

Chapter Thirty-Six: *My Daughter*

Daisen and Sandella came to the doorway which led from the bastion to the ring-wall battlements. It was dark outside, under a stormy black sky which occasionally turned sickly yellow. Acid rain was still falling. Daisen scowled, and waved a hand over her head to make a dome of protection. Then she lifted up the metal casket and marched over to the table and chairs set out on the battlements below a summerhouse roof. Sandella followed, carrying the tea-things.

They were dry and comfortable. Daisen sipped the excellent tea and sighed in appreciation. Lightning struck at them again and again, furiously. It never quite reached them. Neither did the corrosive rain.

'He *has* noticed us!'

'Of course he has.' She looked over at Sandella, whose hands were shaking. 'You're ready, novice?'

'I – well, I suppose so.' Sandella was nervous, or worse. Keli had been a close friend. 'Though it must be too late for a rescue...'

Daisen gave her a stern glance, though there might have been compassion in the look. 'You wanted to fight, didn't you?'

'Elder Sister, I thought I did.' Sandella looked up at the terrible storm, then looked down again. 'But now we're actually confronting *him*...'

'You must have faith, my dear.'

Now Sandella rose to her full height and looked down upon the senior sister.

'I believe in you and our holy Mother. I believe in everlasting good, too.'

'Amen!'

Daisen raised one hand, and Sandella opened the casket.

From it, the blue-white light of the Diamond Heart lit them up from below.

Daisen rose, and stood with Sandella. Then she looked up at the all-black sky, eventually seeing where the heart of the Lord of the North's power was. It was so noisy with thunder now she had to shout to be understood.

'I make out *his* ugly shape overhead – you agree?'

'I, I think he is, yes.'

Daisen raised two clenched fists. 'Then strike!'

Lightning blasted up.

Settled on her pony, Zandar looked back over her shoulder. There she was, the slim Maiden with the bonsai hair, healed and pretty again.

'Thanks to you, we can find him.' Zandar touched the girl's face to read her emotions, which were all sincere. It was unlikely that Man and the others were still where this girl claimed, and even less likely they were alive. So unlikely, and yet the very name of the place... 'You saw them fight?'

'I did. Emmanuel – and the others... But they cannot last!'

'I know.' Now Zandar raised her voice so that its power filled this great space. 'Maidens! You are two hundred strong! Are you ready?'

From their shouting and their weapons-waving they were ready indeed. Zandar smiled in approval, touched by their brave loyalty.

Hanake beat a hollow reed on her hand as if keeping time in music.

'This magic you will attempt, Mother,' she asked, 'is it certain?'

'She-captain, nothing in life is certain. Magic may be beyond life – there is a big debate – but whether magic is beyond life and death, or the essence of life and death, it is very far from certain.'

Zandar took a deep breath, knowing she was soon to work the most important spell she ever had.

'Sword Maidens, we must not use magic when we arrive, but weapons!'

They cheered.

'Be bold!' When Daisen and Sandella struck, Zandar felt it, and then felt *his* power recoil. 'Maidens, follow!'

Zandar waved her hands to part the waters, but there was no visible effect on the long dark pool. Nevertheless she shook the reins of her pony, and headed down the ramp into the pool of river-water. When she submerged, there were not even bubbles left behind.

The throng of Sword Maidens followed her.

'This Emmanuel, is he now within The Waning?' Hagiwara peered ahead. The pillar of black stormcloud was now miles high, and The Waning was completely concealed by that darkness. He could glimpse the death-fight on Miracle Island, though. He turned to Berenda. 'Or is he not?'

She took another great breath. 'He is still trapped on the island.'

'Will Mother Zandar go out to help him?'

'She might.'

'Once outside, they will both be vulnerable.'

'Yes.'

'So that must be the time to hit them!'

She pouted her annoyance and hoped her worry did not show. 'They are so powerful... And the storm ahead of them, I do not think they can cross.'

'Lady Berenda, if they die from our master's storm, what have *we* gained? We should be in at the death! Then we have some chance to get back our place in *his* heart.'

'Yes.' Berenda flexed her fingers. In at the death. 'Follow me.'

She rode on quickly through a late afternoon that was still, warm and humid. Hagiwara came after her.

As Man looked at Yoshi, the Voice from Afar and Lady Joah, he felt his eyes prickle. Hard to think this was the end, when there had been so much faith and hope among his friends. His face ached, reminding him that the Tears' poison kiss was still working. Would it kill him? Not before the attackers did, Man realized as he looked again at his enemies' slow determined approach. They were in overwhelming numbers now. Was the Tears with them? She was certainly close.

A movement above attracted his eye. Several hundred feet up, a flying creature circled the island, its wings slowly beating. Might that be another drone?

'I don't know,' said Joah, wearily answering the question he had not asked aloud. 'Anyway, does it matter if Steel Angels come now? Surely death is death?'

Then Man flinched in surprise. There was light striking up from the Waning, the glow so fierce it was visible through all the cloud, so powerful that it might have knocked the Moon from its orbit.

It is women doing it, defending The Waning – or bringing on its destruction...

The lightning cut into the black clouds above the famed fortress, and where it touched *his* stormclouds they vanished.

Man felt *his* pain, and smiled. The Lord of the North had

Words of Fury: 377

placed himself here, and now he was suffering for it. Fury flickered in the sky.

'Man?' It was the Voice from Afar speaking. Man turned to look at her. 'What if the Waning is destroyed in this fight?'

'Even if we lose this battle, there'll still be good in this world.'

Their gazes locked; then she looked away.

Man felt a pulse of local energy, subtle and strange rather than strong. The Tears? A ripple of light had passed over the land. He looked towards its source, upriver. The Voice, too, stirred. There were thick green clumps of bush along the river there. Man saw a blue heron fly up; but that was not what had made him turn his head.

Only, when he tried to see the spell it wasn't exactly light. The green fields and the flowing water itself seemed different; but how, exactly, and what did it mean?

He saw Lady Joah jump up.

'Was that the Eye? Man, once you rocked the world! Try using it again!'

His mind felt for the hidden power gem, but nothing came back in response. He clenched his fists, caught between anger and despair. Magic in its nature was chaotic and irregular; it could not be relied upon.

But sometimes it worked, and sometimes it was mighty.

Yoshi was eager. 'Something?'

Man looked across the river to where dead men lay with dead horses, and arrows' tails stood up from the ground. It didn't seem to be magic from *him*, more of a man/woman thing... Man touched his swollen face.

Yes, it must be the Tears!

When light exploded up at *him* from below his own dark storm, Lady Berenda had hauled back at the reins. This fight-back was unexpected and she wondered if it might even be damaging the Lord of the North. And what about his helpers? Her mind's eye swept round, for miles.

'Master Hagiwara, I see more of us coming from both coasts, men who have read the black book and are sworn to *him*. These men are so many they must prevail.'

'So we are surplus?'

'No. I think all these men will be needed.'

He brightened. 'You mean that The One Who Will Change

Words of Fury:

won't be killed here?'

She turned on him in a fury. 'That won't make our master rejoice! If our lord's enemies escape and get to sanctuary, his fury will eat the world!'

Hagiwara had stopped dead on his horse. He paled.

'What if they do beat us to The Waning, and safety? Won't *he* then take revenge on his poor tools, such as ourselves?'

Berenda saw herself hurling white-hot thunderbolts at Man and his protectors, saw Man and those two girls destroyed. She herself was refreshed; they were exhausted, and so was this cowering 'Mother Zandar' who wouldn't dare come out to help them. Berenda *knew* she could stop Emmanuel and the others, or kill them, before they reached The Waning.

'I *can* intercept them, I can, and I *will* – '

She rode on, but her heart was divided. A secret part of her wanted to let Emmanuel go in peace. She had already helped Man by summoning Kannon through use of music.

Whose side should she be on now?

It took her minutes to decide, but when she did she smiled.

Man could still make his voice powerful. 'Everybody, get ready! I feel magic at work!'

He was aware of Joah staring upriver, just as he was.

'What are you two looking at?' Yoshi demanded.

Man said the truth reluctantly. 'A swirl of magic.'

'It's theirs?'

'Yes, I guess it's the other side doing some disguise, maybe while they bring up reinforcements.'

'So we should expect some nasty surprises?'

'You said it.'

Man tightened his grip on his long sword. He saw the blood-splashed Buddhist priest had also turned his head in the same direction, showing that he too was something of an adept.

Joah came closer to Man. 'Can we fight? Should we? Isn't the enemy just too strong?'

'No enemy is ever that mighty.'

Man tried to use the Eye again. He made the correct magical gestures, seeing himself slowly perform. He called out sacred words of power.

The great Eye did not respond.

Man had failed again. The afternoon here would end just as it had begun, in battle chaos and death.

Then more distorted light drew his attention back upstream.

Before it divided into the two bubbling parts around Miracle Island, the river ran through tall reed-beds. Man saw a line of tall reeds in mid-stream; a wrong thing. He was going to speak out, when there was a screaming from the island's perimeter. The enemy were shouting in unison. Man grabbed a small shield and kneeled in the partial cover of a wagon. The dead horse nearby had crapped itself and its urine pooled, but what did that matter? What did more reinforcements for the enemy matter? He knew now he was going to die, whether by magic or by steel.

The ring of enemies began to close in, swords beating on shields.

Man watched, sweating badly while his head throbbed. For almost a minute he had double vision. There could be no effective fighting from him now he was in this state. Man had lost. Joah was dead, so was the Voice, and all those he loved who were here with him.

He knew now he could give the gracious blows that would avoid humiliation and torture for his friends. He raised his bloodied sword. The Voice first, he thought. He looked over at her, planning how to take her by surprise. It would be instant oblivion for her. Joah was samurai, so...

It was then he heard Yoshi. 'Look there!'

'Not *more* enemies!'

Yoshi was pointing. 'Look!'

Man did, but his vision blurred again. He saw three dozen lithe persons stand up in the river and throw away the hollow reeds they had breathed through. Oddly, they didn't seem to be wet. Others appeared behind them, holding swords and long bamboo spears – most probably reinforcements for the black sashes?

Man raised his own sword and glared at them, half blind.

That Tears bitch used her magic to hide the final attack... Oh, how I hate her!

Man saw more of the quick, often shaven-headed warriors. Only magic could have hidden them. They came scrambling up from the greenery on both banks of the river, ululating.

Most wore partial armor, and they were too many to fight... A woman in white, on a pony, also appeared on the river-bank.

Then he noticed Yoshi seemed amused. A whole flock of arrows slashed in from the side, though only wearers of the black sash were hit. Man saw men with Oatha's mark on them die.

Words of Fury:

The new arrivals were all women wearing blood-red.

By a miracle, the statue of Kannon was dancing again, and smiling. When it turned back to unmoving stone that smile was still in place. Man saw Yoshi also dancing with joy.

He heard Joah say, 'Sword Maidens!'

He saw dozens of the warriors. A tall woman with beads woven into her hair seemed to be in charge and she was shouting orders. She and her fellows were killing Oatha's purity police quickly and skillfully, and soon the black sashes weren't just retreating, they were running.

Man realized it was all over when he saw Nagaoka gallop away on a black horse.

So he escapes justice – I should have known!

Man lowered his sword and shield, looking up in wonder at the blue sky. A single hawk-like thing winged towards the sun. It was possibly a drone, though Man didn't care now.

Yoshi hugged him, shouting triumph.

Then a beautiful, narrow-eyed Sword Maiden with bonsai hair was beside Man. She looked just like someone Man had known, and around her neck was the sweet snake symbol.

He was going to tell her the terrible news, but she put a hand on his mouth.

'I know what happened to my sister.'

Man found tears had come again. 'Then you know she died horribly, to save us.'

'Sweet Snake died for you! My twin gave up her life for *you!*'

There had been sorrow, but now joy overwhelmed it. 'Then you are – '

The living Precious Stone flung her arms round Man, kissed him hard. She was openly weeping and yet also smiling. 'Oh, my sister, may her name live forever!'

Man could not speak. He just touched the snake hanging from the narrow neck.

'She won! Don't you see that, Man! My Sweet Snake held them away long enough, and so saved you, and the future of the world! Now I want you to rejoice, in *her* name! Can you do that?'

Man exhaled hard, trying to take the truth of victory within himself.

'I can try.'

Then he looked round in wonder. Though he saw heaped bodies, this was a battle won. He took in a huge life-giving breath. It was superb to be victorious, to be samurai, to be

Words of Fury: 381

young.

    All those things *are* wonderful, he thought, but best of all is to be alive!

The Sword Maidens checked on the enemy lying here in heaps. The few survivors were killed. With Precious Stone at his side, Man watched it happen. The dead were everywhere on and around little Miracle Island.

    'There are so many of them, Yoshi!'

    'If they'd grouped together and struck us one hard blow...' Yoshi looked very serious now. 'We could not have survived.'

    'No,' Man agreed. He was looking at Sanada's corpse and wishing that he felt more than overwhelming relief at his own survival. 'This island deserves its name.'

    'It does,' said Joah, looking sidelong at Precious Stone. 'We thought you were dead. So the person with your "precious stone" –'

    'My sister. We sometimes swapped our charms, to share out the luck. She wanted my luck, and instead got my death!'

    'She had the power in her?'

    'A touch, especially the Foretelling,' said Precious Stone. She turned to gaze at Man. 'She knew what was coming.'

    'I will always honor her.'

    'Since she died to keep you alive, I will continue where she cannot!'

    'Amen,' said the Buddhist priest, holding his long staff one-handed.

    The Sword Maiden leader flung her arms around to give non-verbal orders, dispatching scouts – some in plain clothes. Man saw the enemy had retreated from the island; but more were coming up from the coast. His spirits sank.

    The Maiden strode over to Man and Yoshi.

    She bowed, then said throatily, 'I am Sword Maiden Hanake, my lords, first she-captain at The Waning of the Moon. You must be Fujiwara-noh-Yoshi, and you Emmanuel-noh-Kinross.'

    Hanake's bare arms were lean and muscular, and her strong features were vital and attractive. Man saw she was all woman as well as warrior. Unlike many, her head was not shaved – indeed her hair was in long black braids woven with gold and silver beads.

    'We are who you have named,' Yoshi said, bowing in return.

'And we thank you.'

Yoshi pointed out the others, naming them and making introductions where he could. The she-captain looked coldly at Man, before turning away to take charge again. Now she spread out a skirmish line away from the island.

Man looked at Yoshi. 'Was it something I said?'

Yoshi shrugged. 'Who knows?'

'Could Hanake blame me for all this slaughter?'

Precious Stone said, 'Man, to some people you are a trouble-maker – the biggest in history! – and you put our holy Mother and our home at risk.'

'I don't want your she-captain or anybody hating me,' Man fretted.

Yoshi shook Man's shoulders.

'We're alive, my Man. That's the main thing. And soon we'll be on our way!'

'You think it'll be easy? Do you? Look!'

Man pointed towards The Waning of the Moon, though nobody could now see it. The black whirlwind *he* had made had the place surrounded. Man glimpsed the Lord of the North's magic overhead. Occasionally the cloudy sky split, to reveal alien skies: once purple, then a deep ultramarine, and twice a poisonous-looking yellow.

'It looks impossible to get there, but we can hope!' said Lady Joah.

'Yes, we can,' said Man.

'I just spoke the second most important word in the language,' Joah said, smiling now.

'What is the most important?'

She answered without hesitation. 'Love.'

Man saw the Sword Maidens and Yoshi's survivors were exhilarated. This would be seen as a legendary fight; they would be famous.

The wounded were helped. Men and a few women had arrows in them or had been cut by swords. Even Yoshi had a little finger hanging bloody and loose off his right hand. Man, too, was still bleeding in several places.

They were healed one after the other by a thin-lipped Sword Maiden who wore a silver Eye of Buddah around her neck. A cold energy went through Man; he could feel the improvements this healer made, though her hurried work was far from perfect.

Precious Stone stayed close all the time, watching Man with

Words of Fury: 383

a tender expression but with her hands always on her swords. He felt protected and loved.

He also felt exhausted. He mostly wanted to go home; but of course he had no home. He looked at the bodies of the men who had died defending the circle. There was a big-jawed Emperor's samurai, and near him young Sanada. Man felt renewed hate for Oatha and Nagaoka. One day, he thought, one day...

The Voice from Afar came up. Her eyes were dancing and her red-gold hair had gone wild.

'Man! We did it! Thank you!'

Man forced a smile. 'Thank *you*.'

'Lady Joah here says...' She paused, and then was hugging her soul-sister Joah. 'We owe you, Man.'

'No.'

'Oh, yes.' Joah bowed low to The One Who Will Change, then eased herself away. Her black hair was pinned back neatly again, and blue flowers and jewels were glimmering there.

He had never seen her look more lovely.

The Voice turned back to Man, a rare seriousness on her face.

'I saw you use your sword.'

'Yes.'

The Voice regarded him. 'It seems so strange... Till a few days ago I'd never seen you draw your blade in anger.'

In anger? He felt his many healed cuts sting. He remembered those friends and allies who had died here. In anger? Yes. It had been done in anger, all his killing in response, and he did not regret any of it.

'May I look at your sword again?'

Man hesitated, then drew the razor-sharp steel part way out and handed the scabbard over. The Voice drew the blade out fully and held it in one hand. Now wiped clean, Words of Power glittered in the golden sunlight.

'You know it's centuries old, and famous. Supposedly it was blessed by Lalla Akiko Naosuke, who was a First Princess of Jade before she went to The Waning.'

'I know who she was. She deserves all her songs. You deserve a few, too.'

'Not me,' Man said quickly. 'I want to be anonymous.'

'That's no longer possible – if it ever was.'

Now the Voice held the long, curving steel very high, her fingers around the hilt. The blade was gleaming and immaculate.

'The Words of Power... "Freedom and change"!'

'Yes, that's what my sword says – and what I say, too. But don't touch the edge!'

She moved both hands along the hilt, made some two-handed cutting motions. Her eyes widened.

'Even in my untrained hands it feels natural.'

'Samurai swords take an age to make, but they're the finest in the world. The steel is hammered and folded again and again. Its edge will cut bone, plate armor – anything. Here.' He held out his hand for the weapon.

'And the grip?' She peered at it. 'What is this?'

'Sharkskin.'

Though his hand was still extended to take back his weapon, she still held onto Man's sword. 'I don't want to give this back to you.'

'You know that you must, and that I must take it.'

'I don't like what it does to you!'

'It allows me to do what is necessary.'

'And you're going to use it again, aren't you?' Now tears came to her eyes. 'Again and again!'

'If I have to.'

'There are things in you I could learn to hate...'

'Instead, forgive me for them!' He looked hard at her. 'Have you had a Foretelling? Have you seen me at war?'

She returned his sword hilt first, without answering.

Man felt the presence of very strong magic indeed and he turned to see its source. The Maidens here were suddenly looking joyful.

The small party approaching had in the middle a woman on a white pony, wearing a woman in a simple white gown. This was the person who had brought them here. This was Man's savior. Man had never met her in the flesh, but he knew her.

Tears now came from Joah. 'Oh, Mother, thank you!'

As the woman dismounted, Joah ran to her. Mother Zandar opened her arms wide, and took the sobbing girl into them.

'My daughter.'

Chapter Thirty-Seven: *I Have Loved, Too*

Though she hugged the Lady Joah, Zandar had already extended her magical awareness to Man. He was in pain. He had had many cuts to be healed and he was running a temperature, but he was trying to ignore the fever in his blood and mind.

Typical man! He does not want to acknowledge any weakness in himself.

When he realized who she was, she felt him stride towards her. A man in a hurry! She felt a sudden throb of power in him. She noted that Sword Maidens automatically gave way to him. Many were smiling, and some were awed. Only a few seemed to glare.

So he is loved and honored by my Maidens, though some see the damage he must do and the damage already done; but enough will gladly follow him!

Whenever Joah looked at Man her expression was ecstatic.

For a moment Zandar's heart melted. I have loved, too, loved one man beyond anything. Love is so very powerful.

Then she recovered her poise.

Ah, the young think only of today! They see one dynamic, attractive person and they think of undying love. They see one victory and their confidence is unbounded!

They don't see tomorrow's disaster...

Man stopped in front of the holy Mother, staring. She had a noble look, though her eyes were bandaged over. She was *strong*; so very strong in the power that he felt a little afraid.

'Safe, Mother!' Joah said, still huddled there in Zandar's arms. 'Safe!'

'You know I did not say that to you,' Mother Zandar told her, gently, as she stroked Joah's hair. 'And you cannot say "I am safe" and leave things to others. That is never right and it is not your destiny, dear Lady of Jade, and never will be.'

'I can't think of destiny now. I still live! Mother, you saved us!'

'No. You fought bravely to save yourselves and some of you died. And it isn't over. We must hurry! Never forget that *he* is watching!'

'Watching now?' Man asked her.

The blind face turned. 'Perhaps he doesn't quite *see*, though. This may be a small window of opportunity, Emmanuel from

Albion. Make the most of it.' Zandar raised her voice. 'Hanake, get everyone formed up!'

'I will, but I must prepare my force to receive another assault, for I see dust raised on the trails approaching us. Will we be here long? Should I occupy the island?'

Zandar said only, 'We must meet with Lady Rishiri and Princess Anamizu before we go, and I expect them to come from the north.'

The she-captain nodded, then went about her duties.

Zandar continued, speaking to Man and Joah both. 'There are still great battles to fight. We must meet our allies, stand off any more enemies, then find our way to The Waning –'

'Mother!' Joah begged her. 'You can't want me to fight! I've seen too much blood!'

He saw how tenderly Zandar held the girl, as Joah wept into her bosom where the crucifix was.

After she released Joah, Mother Zandar turned her face to the mountains; Man looked where she did, and saw horsemen up on the nearest high pass. They were neither running away nor approaching, only watching.

'I feel some strange power there...' murmured Zandar.

Man was very direct. 'That might be "the Tears" – and she's *his*.'

'Yes.' Zandar turned again to Man. 'Lord Emmanuel, you are The One Who Will Change; we have met in our dreams.'

'We have.' He found himself kneeling, for he saw the holiness in her. He took one of her hands in both of his and kissed it. 'Mother, I feel I know you.'

She touched his hair, which had come loose. He realized suddenly that she was exhausted from whatever magic she had done, and she was also trying to accumulate courage as well as energy.

'Emmanuel, you have been educated in your E'ropa. Tell us what came out of your East, and our North. Tell us what we face.'

'Why,' he said, standing and clapping a hand over the healed thigh wound, 'I only know stories, though they scared a light-minded boy. At the end of the Wars of Life,' Man began, and then remembered how his mother had told it to him. 'There had been billions of people on this Earth, too many, and science failed or turned evil. The rich took everything and let the poor go hungry. Then things broke down; people began to starve. They turned against one another everywhere, turned against strangers they had been taught to hate. There were massacres and genocide. The world was dying, Europe was a depopulated ruin. And then there *was* an invasion from the East. Many were men, of a sort; the rest were bloodthirsty creatures, ungodly and warped.'

He saw the Voice's eyes had gone wide. 'Monsters?'

'Monsters,' Zandar confirmed, 'sent by the cold lord of a cold land. Who is in Ezo, now. And in Jade.

'And, I have Foreseen, in your Albion.'

Man jerked away from the motherly Zandar. All the bloodshed and pain had made him savage.

'My homeland is in danger? Tell me how! Tell me who!'

He had a right to know, yes, he had a *right*; but when Zandar visibly hesitated to tell him he felt fury come.

The Lady Berenda looked down from the hills at Miracle Island. Tiny figures in red disposed of corpses wearing black sashes, throwing them into piles. It was less than a mile away, but it was another country now – and not *his* country.

'I remember when I was the Tears, back in Jade,' she murmured to Hagiwara. She did not even look at him. 'I had my power and my knowledge, and I had *his* love. It did not seem possible we could be defeated.'

'Well, the bitches in red won one battle – but we still have more men arriving! One counter-attack with everything we have, and we would roll over them.'

'You are *his* general. I will leave the martial arts to you. Myself, I have other ways to win.'

'Isn't this our best chance to regain favor? – No? Then what are you going to do?'

She turned to eye Hagiwara. With her veil raised, her expression was ghastly and vicious. 'I will show the world, and *him*.'

'You'll rebel against our master? Lady, please don't do anything crazy!'

She was cantering downhill towards the enemy.

Hagiwara felt he had no choice. He followed her and tried to feel good about it.

'Is the Lord of the North in my Albion now? Just tell me!'

Though Man was furious, Zandar did not falter. He still sensed supreme strength, hidden inside her self-disciplined mildness.

'There is evil in your birth-country, closer to you than you imagine.'

'No!' He wouldn't believe that. Not about his beloved home!

'It is true, my Emmanuel. Perhaps soon your Albion, which men do call "the dark Empire", will ally with the cold.'

'No!' Man said again. The mere thought of that alliance sickened him. He put his head in his hands and found he was swaying. 'I cannot believe that!'

But the black ship that earlier came to Jade from Albion had been *his* and on a mission from great Albion for *him*.

Zandar was very gentle now. 'But I see that you do believe it, my son.'

Now Dirk Faslane swore out loud. 'Never my Albion!'

Man turned to the Imperial Intelligence agent with relief.

'Dirk, it's like a sign from heaven that you are here. If the soul of my country is in danger, then I *will* go home with you – and I'll take the Eye!'

'Emmanuel!' Zandar was holding her anger in check. 'You can't possibly do that! Take the Eye, our salvation, away? We would have to kill you!'

Man spread his feet and his green eyes glared.

'You could try.'

She let her own fury free now.

'Do you threaten me? Don't you see that's what *he* wants? Always he divides our forces. If you leave us now, we lose; and if *he* wins here he will eventually win everywhere!'

Faslane was fierce. 'Lady, your heart is here. My heart is with my native land, and I bet my lord Emmanuel's is too!'

'There is only one world, and we are all its citizens. If you are both principled men, stay here with us and fight the good fight!'

Man was shivering. There was cold darkness coming; suddenly he believed his own country might turn.

That knowledge almost broke his heart.

She told him, 'Emmanuel, if you defend our country now, you also defend yours!'

'You are the Lord General's son, and true!' Faslane's face was a picture of tragedy. 'Help our Albion!'

'You must not desert the land that gave you sanctuary! You grew up here and you have been loved here!' Zandar was shouting now. 'You *must* help us!'

Words of Fury:

Man stood back from both Faslane and holy Mother Zandar. He had never felt so isolated, so unsure. Wasn't he important to this place, which had given him a home? Though he had been born elsewhere, Albion had rejected him; so surely his first loyalty ought to be to *this* place?

Probably Faslane read that in his face, because now the secret agent kneeled in the dust before Man and everyone.

'I am your man!' Faslane cried desperately. 'Before all, I pledge allegiance!'

Man was about to say something cutting. Then he heard his mother's warm voice, and his father's rough bold tones. They were Albion: but what did he owe them? What did he owe his home country, which had made him a traitor and likely murdered his father?

More to the point, what did he owe to this man Faslane he knew hardly at all and had often distrusted?

Faslane still kneeled, face humbled, looking up at Man. Everyone around – samurai, Sword Maidens, even the kabuki actors who had returned to the wagons – was looking on.

He could not deny this man; nor deny his own destiny. Man couldn't spoil the scene, which had a momentum of its own. He saw now what he was living for, saw what Lady Naosuke's Prophecies meant. He had to be part of a giant process of change, a moral change that would affect the world. It had to start here, and he had to get followers. So, in the old formal fashion, he did what he had often seen his father do. He placed his hand on Faslane's brow, and accepted his allegiance.

'You are my man! This is my man! And I will not see Albion go down to the Lord of the North, neither in battle nor because of high policy, without fighting! This I pledge by the honor of my name and the life of my soul, forever!'

Faslane was gazing up at him. 'I ask no more.' Man saw he looked both determined and very happy.

Zandar said fiercely, 'What about *my* land, which gave you a home?'

Man didn't enjoy being the centre of stares like this; nor the centre of so much belief and so many demands. Nevertheless he continued, putting a hand back on Faslane's brow so that his man was pledged too.

'I pledge also, by the honor of my name and the life of my soul, forever, that I will fight the Lord of the North in this country Japan, till death and beyond death!'

Words of Fury:

Faslane stood up, brushed dust off his knees.

Man hadn't realized how loudly he had been speaking. The promise he had given caused applause and cheering.

He had his followers now, even more than before. Followers, rather than friends!

Mother Zandar, though looking rueful, also looked proud. So did Lady Joah and the Voice from Afar.

Zandar mounted her pony. The Healed wounded who could not walk yet had been taken into a commandeered wagon; the fighting men and women had formed up in a column, with mounted and foot scouts out.

Man had already made sure the actors and actresses were helped, but now a bald-headed man came up.

'Lord Emmanuel, you interest me greatly; but so do the Lady Joah and the Fujiwara heir, and that golden exotic called "the Voice from Afar".'

'Why?' Man said to the man. He put the Eye's casket onto his back again, shifted its weight till it was less uncomfortable. 'You are the company's playwright, aren't you? Are you going to write about us?'

'Of course.' The bald head bowed. 'I am the force that shakes our company; I will create a legend for you.'

Yoshi raised an eyebrow at this unexpected rival. 'Comic or tragic?'

'Ah,' the man said wisely, 'surely that depends on how it all ends!'

Yoshi and Man laughed, though Man's headache was bad now.

'I suppose it does.'

The column had formed up, spear-points and sword-blades glinting. It was now the singing started.

"Who is the one who will break the realm?
The One Who Will Change, the One Who Will Change...
Who is the one who will save the realm?
The One Who Will Change, the One Who Will Change...
Who is the one we will follow to Hell?
The One Who Will Change, the One Who Will Change..."

'Yoshi,' Man said quietly, 'remember a lifetime ago, you and me on my houseboat, talking?'

'I remember.'

'All my ideas of conquest... A fine idea, if you're the conqueror. Not so good if you're on the losing side.'

'If Oatha and his fellows realize we lied to them, it will be death for us,' said Lord Okada, speaking very low and feeling much the same.

'Father-Sir, I know that. But we have helped my sister and her fellowship the only way we could. We distracted their enemies – the black sashes and the Steel Angels, both.'

'Yes; or we tried, at least.'

He stared over the port of Jade, out to sea where the sun was not far from setting. From upset, he was hardly aware of what he saw.

'Oatha's men have landed in Shimabara, and no doubt some arrived near The Waning. Even if those men believed us and rushed too far north, they might encounter Joah and the others anyway.'

'I tried to warn my sister by mind-speech.'

'Of course you did; but did Joah hear you?'

'I do not think so.' Oki gave a rare pout. 'But surely my sister, Yoshi and Emmanuel can look after themselves. Mother Zandar even more so!'

'You have powerful faith, Daughter-Dear. I hope you're right,' said Okada, struck by the absence of hope in his own voice. He looked back over the port city now, the quays, the great warehouses, the streets with their crowds, the perched-on-high Floating World. 'If only we can do something here!'

My loyal men! Irian Dall the Futurist! The persecuted foreigners! Surely some or all of them can help me!

His daughter's hand reached out for his.

Nagaoka's horse was foaming and maddened. When he pulled it up hard it reared and almost threw him. He scrambled off the frantic creature and fell down on his knees before Hagiwara and Lady Berenda and the new men who now followed them.

The wounds around his mouth made speech difficult. 'Lord, my Lady, they stood us off for a time – '

Hagiwara interrupted.

'Are you telling me you achieved nothing!'

'It was going well enough till those bitches in red came!' Nagaoka said, genuinely outraged. 'Hagiwara-san, they cheated!

They fought back!'

Berenda was also full of furious contempt.

'Yes, but there was no strong magic available to them and you *should* have caught them in the open. You had lots of *our* cavalry and *they* had only a few horses.'

Hagiwara said, 'Now how can this lady and I explain ourselves to Lord Oatha and – others, given the circumstances? You've put our lives at risk!' He sighed, then gestured for Nagaoka to stand up.

Nagaoka felt relief. He rose, still holding his horse's reins.

'Lady Berenda! These newcomers you have... If I had had them with me... Are these men legal?'

'Oh, many are legal recruits. This has all been planned for a long time – though the planners may not be familiar to you.'

Nagaoka stared, not understanding. Then Hagiwara gave him a rueful grin, which he returned.

'I worked over one Maiden, and took her beloved thing. Look!' Nagaoka showed off a precious stone, which glittered in his hand a little like an eye.

'You have done well,' Hagiwara murmured, 'so have a drink now, while the lady and I decide what to do.'

Nagaoka relaxed. He took the water-bottle he was given, bouncing the stone on his other hand. 'Please will you tell Lord Oatha how hard I fought?' Nagaoka took a long swig. 'And you'll both tell our lord who was to blame?'

'Indeed we will,' said the lady, sweetly.

Suddenly Nagaoka took a step back, clutching at his throat. His eyes widened and he looked outraged. He made horrible gurgling sounds, as if he had swallowed acid. His face flushed and his eyes bulged out. Then he collapsed on his back, twitching and choking.

Hagiwara spread his legs to avoid the fluids pooling as the poison finished its work.

'Yes, we'll tell Lord Oatha who was to blame.'

Mother Zandar made her voice calm and inviting. 'Man?'

'Yes?'

She used formal, ritual words. 'Will you help us, you who have given up so much? We need your help against the Lord of the Dark, who seeks again to conquer our world and the parallel worlds also.'

Man looked tired and confused and she wondered if he had

Words of Fury:

the strength to walk on. 'Mother, he came centuries ago!'

'He did, and now he has come again. Though he lost that fight, he placed the world on a knife-edge; and we are weaker now, while *he* is stronger. See?'

Zandar gestured at the black whirlwind over The Waning. The storm was a mile wide and lightning flared all around. The flashes were bright even this far away, and afterwards the thunder was deafening. Some lightning-bolts struck up at the sky, but they were few. Still, Daisen and Sandella were fighting back, fleeting sparks against a lightning storm, but perhaps enough to hold *his* attention.

She gave a grim smile. The Lord of the North always was easy to blind with fury...

There was a muttering among the survivors, though. Even Ozawa asked, 'We must go through *that*?'

'We will find a way,' Zandar said, and they believed her.

Now she heard the optimistic laughter around her. They were all together in the golden dusk, knowing a chance of safety was here.

She almost screamed in frustration.

Don't they realize that the Lord of the North is *here*? I am taking all of you towards him! And what if he turns his attention from The Waning and strikes us right now?

If he did, she had no idea how to confront him.

Alongside Zandar, Joah too was laughing again. Though she had been given the Five Touches, and that was mortal, it seemed she really thought the danger was over.

Is *she* the one? Is my nemesis walking with me, laughing but soon to challenge me?

Mother Zandar knew from Prophecy that a woman would come to The Waning of the Moon, a woman very strong in the power and also close to Zandar herself, who would come to hate her and betray her.

But, please, merciful God – not sweet Joah! I could not stand to be hated by *her*...

'You'll Heal me, Mother, and when I'm with you I will learn so much! I've never felt more hopeful!'

Zandar waved a hand in vague blessing. Joah knew no reason to hate her, yet; but she *would*, Zandar knew.

Oh, yes, darling Joah, when you know what I am and what I have done to you, you *will* hate me!

Zandar shivered now, a sour taste in her mouth.

'Mother, why aren't you happy? We have saved Emmanuel and the Jade Eye, haven't we?'

Zandar had gloomy secrets. She was leading her people not to safety but towards where Lady Rishiri and Princess Anamizu might be; only, she had no faith she could link up with them and bring everyone safely to The Waning. Not now *he* had her home besieged. And without the two women, there would be no magic circle, and without that she *knew* they must lose.

Faithless, I am, and without love – for I turned my back on the love I was given. And without faith, I can't perform my duty. May God forgive me!

Joah persisted. 'Mother, you look so sad!'

As well as being a dutiful pillar of faith it was Zandar's duty to be calm and positive. Lady Joah was famous; it was best to preserve her morale, even if Zandar had to twist the truth a little.

'There will be judgements passed on all of us, but your faith will be your salvation.'

'Oh, Mother, I know that!'

The young had so much confidence...

Emmanuel was moving wearily. 'Mother, how do we get inside The Waning – given that *he* is outside it?'

She gave him a wry smile. 'Earth, Air, Water, Fire... I have some power over all. Joah, you know how water can be mystic.' Zandar waved towards the running stream. 'And here is the sacred river flowing, changing always – making it almost impossible for him to make a spell against our passage.'

'Because what he would have to do magic against is ever-changing?'

'Exactly,' Zandar told her.

'So we avoid the black sashes and more fighting by using the "watery through-path", as in the Prophecies?'

'I am impressed by your understanding, young woman. Now, as soon as we link up with our allies, we go home.' Seeing that Joah was about to ask more questions, Zandar tried to change the subject. 'Lord Yoshi, I can say something to you.'

He eyed her, wryly. 'Some nice thing?'

That made her laugh. 'I cannot see where your road ends. But you must return to Jade, with the Emperor's secret mandate. Afterwards, there will be a great journey for you.'

Yoshi was bloodstained and exhausted, but he gave his cool smile.

'Back to Jade, Mother? There my sainted father is the

Words of Fury:

Emperor's Man in chief, not I. By now he has probably disowned me.'

'What he represents is yesterday. Only a new Japan can fight effectively; for swords and a little magic cannot be enough. We have to make Jade free, modern, and strong.'

'That task could be the size of a mountain!'

Man turned away from his Precious Stone. 'Or bigger!'

'Perhaps. And yet we should soon have powerful new allies with us: Lady Rishiri and Princess Anamizu.' She saw Hanake's signal that all was ready. She raised her voice again. 'Now, my friends, we go to meet our other friends!'

Their column moved off, heading for the island crossing.

'Well, we might need the princess and the lady right now,' Yoshi said. 'Look up!'

Flying in formation towards Miracle Island, their armor glinting brightly, was a mass of Steel Angels.

Chapter Thirty-Eight: *The Price*

Man saw the Angels come on remorselessly from the north, huge wings flapping. They were many.

Now he heard the holy Mother speak, voice hard with anger. 'Even a delay could finish us.' She raised her voice. 'Man, count them for me, and describe what they do!'

Man stared at the formation, as the sunlight glinted off their armor. Except for their beating wings, they reminded him of a more sophisticated version of his father's Iron Guard.

'Fifty Angels, with spears and swords, are slowing above us.' He stared through tired eyes, remembering how he had killed one mech-bird but seen others. 'They're forming an extended line above Miracle Island and the river. I think they want to drive us away from the water!'

Yoshi murmured, 'No escape by running. Not when our opponents have wings!' He sounded fascinated. He drew both his swords, laid them out on their scabbards, patted the hilts lovingly. 'If they land, I will fight them.'

'Fight?' Two Heads growled from deep in his chest. He banged big fists together, and this time the small head spoke, in a clear tenor voice that Man could imagine singing folk-songs. 'With friends that love me, like all of you, I will fight forever!'

Man said softly, 'Thank you.'

'Thank you, Lord Kinross,' both heads said together. A double smile came. 'It has been good to have a friend.'

'They won't land to fight,' Joah said. 'Why should they, if they can hit us from the air?'

Now the Angels came lower, maybe a hundred feet above ground. Man saw his friends on the island duck. One Angel settled on the watchtower.

So much blood, so close to escape, and now this!

'What do they want, Mother?'

The blind face somehow seemed to gaze at Man without visible eyes. 'The Eye, and to eliminate you.'

'The Eye's no bloody use!' he stormed, and the weight on his back seemed to increase. In a rage, he took off the heavy casket, then roped it to a pack-pony. 'Maybe we should just let it go.'

'You really don't know why the Eye won't work for you?' Zandar's voice became a whisper that only carried to those closest to her – Joah, Emmanuel and his Sword Maiden friend, and Yoshi. 'Emmanuel, if the Eye allowed you to pull too much

Words of Fury: 397

energy from it, you would die.'

That was a truth he felt within. For him to use the Eye, their great hope, would be death.

'Am I so weakened?'

'Aren't you?'

Man had to focus on himself. He realized he was trembling. Just as well he had stopped taking the weight of the Eye; it was too much.

'There, you see,' Zandar said, reading him. 'From one kiss every part of you is infected. If you use your power *you will die!*' In compassion, Zandar touched him. 'Your only chance is to be Healed at The Waning.'

Man turned away from the holy Mother, staring at the hovering Angels. All their wings beat to the same rhythm. They had spears and long swords, and darts in holsters.

Yoshi said only, 'What a piece of work is a *man*! How noble in reason, how infinite in faculty! In form and moving, how express and admirable! In action how like an Angel!'

'These Angels?'

'Ah, Man, each of us, in apprehension, is like a god! We are the beauty of the world! We are the paragon of animals!' Then his voice fell. 'And yet, to me, what is this quintessence of dust?'

Zandar said only, 'Yoshi, we are more than dust.'

'We are immortal souls!' said the Voice.

Man was trying to think up tactics that might help against enemies who could fly. Only, a pulse throbbed painfully in his right temple, and he couldn't think creatively at all.

Zandar felt her heart thump.

No doubt the Angels are only men of some sort encased in that shining steel, but they are in powered armor and they are not styled 'Steel Angels' for nothing. Sword Maidens are lithe and dangerous as leopards, but how can they match Steel Angels?

'We must stand them off!' she said, defiant to the end.

Man turned to her, and she was shocked by how pale and unsure he looked now. It was as if he was weakening by the minute.

'Can't we use your magic to disappear?'

'No, because Rishiri and Anamizu need my help to enter sanctuary – and I *must* have them with me. Also, if I use female magic now, *he* will know!'

'So we must fight *without* power?'

'Yes, Man.' Zandar made sure they all heard. 'Hear me! Be very careful! Angels are dangerous and *he* is lurking! Only when we get within The Waning will we be safe!'

Ozawa answered for them all.

'We understand, Mother.'

Ten Angels now landed on Miracle Island and folded their huge wings. There was a quick, brutal fight. After it was done the Angels herded the few survivors off the island.

We thought we'd won, she thought, and now I see we're going to lose...

Man put his hands to his head. 'More enemies to fight, and I am tired to the bone!'

Then a line of Angels was above them. She saw Man squint up and she entered his mind to see more.

As one, the flying Angels put their right hands into holsters hung from their belts, pulled out long darts, and in unison flung them down.

She saw that a couple of darts missed, but elsewhere samurai and Sword Maidens were terribly wounded or killed. A couple screamed.

Zandar's hands shook. She could not use her magic without revealing her position to *him*, and yet she could not leave her people here undefended. She looked over to The Waning in desperate hope, but there the evil mushroom-cloud was expanding. Even here they were falling into its shade.

Zandar tried to reach out with her mind.

'Daisen? Sulina?' If the women of The Waning Moon could hear her, and work with her, there was a chance she and the others might yet be saved. 'HEAR ME!' her mind said to them. 'I NEED YOUR HELP!'

More darts wounded and killed. Without her orders, though without panic, her forces were pulling back from the river-island.

Hear me, sisters! We need you! she thought.

But the area was still blanketed with *his* male power. She could not get through.

One brave Sword Maiden on a pony picked her way towards the nearest island bridge. She had both swords out. Zandar saw one of the line of Angels fly lower. A bolt of electricity struck out from him, splashing the Maiden with fire. Her burned corpse was blown into the river, and the wounded pony bolted.

Words of Fury:

She heard Yoshi shout. 'They hit us and we can't hit back!'

Then the Angel who had blasted the Maiden swooped low towards Yoshi and Man.

An electric shock now, thought Zandar, and The One Who Will Change will be changeless forever...

But Man was staring up, his bow held down by his left side. Then she sensed Man fire an arrow, followed by another.

Zandar was going to remonstrate with him over this foolishness. Then, incredibly, his steel-tipped arrow hit some weak spot, perhaps a joint in the armor. The flying Angel flinched, flinging up his arms. The other arrow also hit, this one in the groin. Suddenly, the wings were stiff, no longer beating. Head twisting in pain, the Angel came crashing backwards on the island near Kannon's garden.

Nobody was that good at archery. Nobody.

Zandar realized it anew. 'Emmanuel, you have cosmic luck! You *are* The One Who Will Change!'

In response the young man almost snarled. 'Am I?'

She felt the frightening amount of fury in him; and felt sorry for him – and also afraid.

Hanake spoke to a runner, then came up to Mother Zandar.

'Mother, we have enemies beginning to mass in the direction of the sea and also others coming down from the mountains!'

'What about Lady Rishiri and the Princess Anamizu? Remember, they may be disguised and warded!'

'Scouts have looked around on both sides of the river for over half a mile, and we cannot find them. And surely it's too dangerous to wait!'

Stray raindrops from *his* attack on her home spotted Zandar's forehead. She looked ahead; her river gateway to safety was only fifty paces away – but she did not have the princess and the lady with her.

Now other Angels landed by the river and drove away the last Sword Maidens and samurai. When those survivors had rejoined Zandar's main force, two more lines of Angels landed. They blocked the way back to the river.

Do they know I must re-enter The Waning by water? Surely their position can't be a coincidence!

The Angels came on in line abreast, stepping with a frightening machine-like regularity.

'Hanake! We must keep access to the river!' Zandar had to

order caution, though. 'Keep back from the Angels, though! They will be charged with deadly "electricity". They can't be touched or even speared in safety. Anything metal held close to them will become dangerous – and that *does* include your swords.'

Yoshi spoke to her while the Angels came on.

'Do you understand how hard that makes this fight?'

'Of course.'

'Mother? Man?' Yoshi asked now, cool as steel. 'Joah? This is where a little hocus-pocus could go a long way!'

'Women's magic will attract *his* attention.'

The Steel Angels came on, bizzarely in step. Their long swords and longer spears were raised. Their armor gleamed in the sunlight, though dark cloud was behind them.

Two Maidens and two Emperor's samurai ran to oppose them.

'No!' she heard Man roar. 'This is not about glory!'

Man's partisans fought Angels hand to hand, and it was not about glory. Zandar saw limbs go flying as the Maidens and the samurai were hacked to death.

Zandar shivered. Her force was retreating; soon it would break up into fleeing individuals who would be hunted down.

I don't know what to do!

A Sword Maiden was speared through the guts, and the Steel Angel lifted her high off her feet as she screamed and wriggled.

She felt Man come to her.

'Mother, we must fight them! Tell us how!'

'I know no more than you.'

'Our friends are dying!'

Perhaps if Rishiri and the princess had been here, there might have been a significant fight. As it was, when Zandar saw Joah fall weeping to her knees she finally gave up all hope.

For Man, the reverse happened. 'Mother!' He quoted her. 'Even without hope, we act!'

'How did you know I said that?'

He blinked, now looking somewhat dazed. 'I know because of what I am. So now...' He took the bridle of her pony in his left hand. 'We go forward together, for victory or for death!'

'Stop!' She was ashamed to hear the fear in her voice. 'We can't challenge them like this!'

Man's tired face looked up to her. 'Can't?'

She hated to say it, but there was no alternative. 'Unless you call upon *every* power available to you!'

'You mean the Eye?' He looked at her for some reprieve. 'I must have misunderstood you. Surely its use by me means death...'

She could not lie to him, and of course even if he died the Eye was a vast prize. 'There is no misunderstanding. Your destiny is what it is.'

It was clear to Man, now, though it was infinitely upsetting. He had to do what was right. In the process he would die.

He turned to look at the bronze casket, roped to the inoffensive pony. The Eye... He tried again to get through to it, and then again.

'There's no connection,' he whispered to Mother Zandar. In the overwhelming sound of *his* thunder, Man's voice was weak. 'The Eye is dead to me, and I am dead to it.'

'Try again!' Zandar said, and he heard her desperation.

Every second the Angels came closer, killing more of their people.

His mind and soul made one final attempt. *We are dying; you have to help!*

There was contact. He saw a shimmering green doorway right in front of him. He let go of Zandar's pony and he walked in.

It was the room all carved from green jade, in the heart of the Eye of Jade.

Here he immediately felt much stronger. 'Am I really so ill, from one bloody kiss?'

The Eye's Talking Book answered. 'Yes, young Man.'

'And if I let the power of the Eye go through me – ?'

'The infection will conquer you within the hour.'

He bit his lip, nodded. 'Suppose I do not use the Eye? Can Zandar defeat these Angels without me?'

'No.'

There was no escape, was there? 'Please... Look into me... Have I understood?'

There was a tiny pause; he nourished a tiny hope.

Then the hope was destroyed. 'You have finally comprehended self-sacrifice.'

Man nodded at the death-sentence. He stepped back through the magical doorway, to the golden afternoon.

They all stared at him with a variety of expressions. Some

looked stunned. Some, impressed by the magic, looked more determined than ever.

'You just stepped away from this world and vanished!' Yoshi said to him. 'That can't be.'

'It didn't quite happen that way,' Man told him. He turned to Mother Zandar. 'You know what I must do?'

'Yes.'

'Does Prophecy say that I die here?'

She hesitated before finally speaking. 'One variant says that, yes.'

Angels had spread out to block the road back to Miracle Island. They were killing Man's defenders. He thought about what to do for several heartbeats.

'Let's do what's right.'

Man stepped in front of Zandar, and reached out to her with both hands. She pulled away, and he sensed her hidden eyes going wide.

He persisted.

Was this an attack? Zandar flinched, for Man had so much power in him now she was afraid of him. Then energy flooded from him into her, more and more till she was shaking with it.

What had he done to her? What *was* he?

Their gazes met, living green eyes against murdered eyes. The connection was profound. She was then impelled to turn her head towards the fighting line.

If I use my female power, our enemy will know *exactly* where we are.

'Not if you act through me,' said Man, though she had not spoken aloud.

'When *he* realizes where we are, how long can we last?'

'He won't see anything significant. I am imitating *him*. Can't you feel what I'm doing? I am making male weaves with *his* stamp? The Lord of the North *won't* attack himself!'

She laughed once at Man's tactic.

Now Zandar stood up in her stirrups as Man led her even closer to the Steel Angels. She sensed he had some plan to give him hope, but when she tried to read him she could see no details, only somber colors shot through with blood-red. Men and women were just so different!

Then it was as if Man was only part of a much larger many-dimensioned Man made of light. She didn't understand it, though

Words of Fury: 403

now male magic throbbed here with earth-shaking force.

The line of Angels looked unstoppable. Then one came forward fast, pushing its way through a wooden hut. It sprinted towards her and Man, unnaturally quick, sword high.

Instantly, Man moved to intercept it, Words of Power in his hands.

He moved unsurely; he was going to be killed.

This Tears has infected him, and I can't have him *dying*! Come what may, it has to be magic!

Zandar linked herself with Man, and so to the Eye. She raised a finger, and then a word of dark masculine power was spoken out loud in Man's voice.

Magic flickered forward. The metal helmet was blown clear off the Angel's shoulders. A headless dead man staggered backwards and collapsed.

An Angel threw a spear at her. Man reacted instantly, knocking the spear away with a sword-blow. Now he looked and moved like a superman.

Zandar slid off her pony, and felt Man put a hand on her shoulder. Their enemies came on again. Wondering if she had made a terrible error, wondering if her magic had revealed her to the Lord of the North, Zandar raised her hands and struck again. Another Angel's head exploded, scattering red brains.

Surely the Lord of the North would notice her now?

But it wasn't really her power, though she was guiding it and helping it. It was what flowed through Man from the Eye, and it was straightforwardly masculine.

Together Man and she did more deadly magic.

Some Steel Angels burst into flame on the spot, dying with greasy black smoke coming from their steel-armored bodies. A few got by, but they were overwhelmed by crossbows which Man, shouting, arranged. The Sword Maidens had moved to overlap the enemy force. The few Angels who made it through them had armor pincushioned with crossbow bolts. They were mostly finished off by Two Heads' great axe – and still Man advanced.

I know how Man feels now, she thought. I feel it too. I could conquer the world!

Angry Angels flew low overhead, stabbing with their spears or trying to impale people with darts – but with identical gestures both Man and Zandar raised their arms. Electric energy blasted out, bringing down the flying Angels.

She saw a few had survived the landing, but then she exploded them by magic one by one. Metal and flesh flew hundreds of feet away.

Zandar disliked this murderous exercise; but she had been raised samurai and knew what was necessary – support Man, who was walking forwards and flinging power all around.

The last three Angels tried to fly away, but Man beckoned. Though their huge wings beat frantically, he hauled them down to earth.

There he killed them.

Mother Zandar saw how the armored dead lay sprawled around, many still trailing smoke. She sagged, thankful it was over.

'Emmanuel, I have never done so much before. Never, ever – even with the Diamond Heart. I am exhausted.' She stared hard at him. He was glowing with glory. 'But you blaze with power. You have all your magic again, and you saved us!'

Emmanuel shook his head, gaze sweeping the horizon for more enemies.

'Mother, that was the Eye.'

'The Eye is *you*, now!'

'No!' His voice was very harsh. 'I don't want to be that different.'

She almost laughed. Whatever men had, they were never ever satisfied!

But now Man changed his tone. 'What you did, blasting away men in armor... Useful, if *his* forces ever come to Albion.'

She read in his mind the outline of a bargain and responded at once. 'You wonder if my skill and power can help stand off an invasion.'

'Could you?'

'Of course I could help your Albion!'

'Will you tell me the price?'

In front of them all, she made her promise.

'If the day comes that *he* attacks Albion, I will stand with you, my Emmanuel. There would be nothing to pay. In our fight we are all one family even if we sometimes quarrel; for if we are not one family, we are doomed.'

She beckoned those behind

'Come on, everyone! Form up! We've alerted our enemies, so we have to go *now!*'

The only secure way to re-enter The Waning was close, but

Words of Fury:

Rishiri and Anamizu were not here, and without their presence there could be no magic circle.

Zandar had to find them, and soon.

Chapter Thirty-Nine: *That Isn't Logic, But It Is Magic!*

Man felt the power of destiny running through him. This was the great Mother Zandar he was with, and surely her friends the Lady Rishiri and Princess Anamizu could not be far. He felt that with their aid he would soon be able to touch the Eye freely. That would be needed, given the situation. He looked up at where *his* dark power had encircled The Waning.

But now there was hope.

Mother Zandar was giving orders. 'We will cross the river here at Miracle Island, and on the way to sanctuary we'll collect Rishiri and the princess!'

Sword Maidens ran. All were grinning though some were wounded. One with a purple orchid painted on each cheek even blew Man a bold kiss. He thought in pain of Sweet Snake and Lilac.

As his Precious Stone led over the little pony that carried the casketed Eye, she threw him a curious look.

'Yours, I believe.'

'We have a lot to talk about,' he said.

Without answering, she took his left hand.

'First, Precious Stone, why is the holy Mother taking this particular path to The Waning? Just to meet these two women?'

'She knows what do from the Prophecies. You must have faith.'

'I've been told that too many times!'

Precious Stone laughed, authentically merry. 'Relax! We're winning!'

He did relax, or he tried to.

Sword Maidens began to sing as they marched. Then the victorious men were chanting. Next, the Sword Maidens were ululating back. Soon both began to sing again about The One Who Will Change.

Everyone was positive. That suddenly included Man. Now he too felt happier than he had done for an age.

Why, he thought, this is victory, with The Waning and its powers close at hand, and strong allies waiting to join us.

Then the Eye-given power left him. He sagged, weak and without magic now, but there were others to take up the fight. He was offered his horse to ride again, and he took it. He felt too weak and dizzy to walk, and he worried that he was already dying.

Words of Fury:

Joah spoke in a low voice. 'Mother Zandar says *he* is furiously fighting The Waning. Like most men, *he* can only do one thing at a time. But of course that's only keeping him busy for now.'

Precious Stone asked her, 'Princess Joah, does the Lord of the North really hope to smash through all our protection?'

'Yes.'

The Sword Maiden shook her head. 'You have great knowledge of *him*.'

Zandar felt a tendril of power, light, casual, and just a probe – but it was from *him*! She touched her crucifix again.

'Mother, I felt that also!' It was Joah. 'Mother ... what if *he* comes here *in person?*'

'Pray that he does not, daughter.' She pointed ahead towards the rainy gloom over the Waning. 'Move faster, everyone!'

The pace picked up.

Zandar looked around again, twisting in her saddle. 'I feel women of power are close.'

'Friendly women?' Man asked.

'I hope it is Anamizu and Rishiri.' – Though it could be this 'Tears', she added, silently.

'But we're getting near to your magical door – aren't we, Mother?' said Joah.

Zandar shivered. The way was indeed near, but she was also so close to *him* now that her confidence was failing, and that made her indecisive. She couldn't wait for Rishiri and Anamizu indefinitely, because a long delay would mean that Emmanuel died; but surely she *had* to wait?

As Man rode on, wetness sprinkled him, blown from that twisting pillar of dark stormcloud ahead. It must be miles high now. Man knew with a certainty that could only depress him just how much power was in evidence now.

'Rain, from a summer sky,' said Faslane. He sounded puzzled rather than overawed, but of course he had little magical understanding.

Man had much more insight into the occult, and he sighed. Was his own death inevitable now? When *he* finally located them, here outside of the protections of The Waning, wouldn't he just destroy them? Even if he didn't, would Zandar actually find this Lady Rishiri and the princess? What if she didn't?

It was looking dark.

Then he heard the Voice from Afar laugh out loud.

'Raindrops!' She flung her arms around, alive and so very attractive. 'Ah! Is this the best he can do?'

Man blinked and laughed too, though others didn't. He saw Mother Zandar especially had a depressingly serious look, and then he heard her talking to herself. 'They must be here ... they *must* be!'

'Those mad skies from before...' said the Voice. 'I think they were from other worlds.'

Yoshi laughed, Man saw; but he thought the Voice was probably right. There were doors to other worlds that could be opened; but that wasn't necessarily good.

The great mushroom-cloud of black slowly expanded over their heads. Soon they were lost in a deepening twilight. Man wondered darkly if *his* black cloud would expand till it covered the entire Earth.

Light rain fell, stinging Man's face. He saw the more rain, the more Mother Zandar looked worried.

She was almost the only one, though. The others still went on gladly, some singing as they marched and others whistling. But Man saw that Faslane kept squinting up at the sky and then looking forward at where the clouds were a slow black whirlwind. Then more rain drummed down, soaking everyone.

Mother Zandar looked too grim to talk to, so he turned to Joah.

'This is going to turn all local roads to mud!'

'That will not be relevant now. There's a better way,' Joah told him, stepping daintily. 'Mother Zandar is powerful in water magic – that's how she got here. When we pick up Lady Rishiri and Princess Anamizu we will go into the sacred river and emerge a lot closer to The Waning of the Moon. We don't cross the intervening space at all.'

'Now that isn't logic, but it *is* magic.'

'Only, because of the ancient wards, we must every one of us be pure.'

Man laughed as he looked at Joah's weary, noble face. That was one beautiful woman, pure in heart, strong and lovable!

Then what she had said struck home.

We must *all of us* be pure... But what of me? I named *him* as Satan, and later I actually called upon *him!*

What does that make *me*?

Nothing good...

Man squinted through the falling water. The rain irritated his eyes, and he blinked again and again.

Mother Zandar bent her head down to him. 'The rain is not dangerously acid yet, but I fear what is coming.'

Man turned to her, jaw sagging.

Acid rain?

They were all walking towards that storm. The rain fell in torrents now. He saw how the river beside them began to flow faster, and then he heard it roar.

He had to shout to Mother Zandar.

'Are your friends Rishiri and the princess on the other side of the river? How will they cross?'

'Downstream there is another bridge,' Zandar told him.

Faslane squinted up at the rain. He was drenched. 'What if the bridge doesn't hold?'

'It must.'

Of course that didn't quiet the sea-pilot. 'But what if it doesn't?'

'Let's cross that bridge when... Oh, you know what I mean!'

A cold wind came, and then turned even colder. Man found himself shivering, as sleet blew. Thunder tolled again.

He heard Yoshi bawling at him over the rumbling.

'All this ungodly noise! It's worse than you singing!'

Man smiled, though his teeth were chattering because of the fevers in him and the cold outside. 'Surely nothing could be that bad!'

'I disagree, and cite your snoring!'

Joah was looking around, frowning in disquiet. 'This rain...'

Man was already soaked and chilled to the bone; what more power could some rainstorm have?

He found out when there was a terrific flash just overhead, along with a bang loud enough to shake the earth.

He saw Zandar had flung her arms into an arch above her head. Only her instant gesture had deflected the lightning.

Man was certain. 'That's *him* – using weather as a weapon!'

His stallion had almost thrown him, and there were screams from burned samurai and Sword Maidens. He saw Zandar was shaking as she gestured more defenses into being.

Man stopped, and turned from where the river seemed about to burst its banks to stare at Joah. The rain was thick enough to be blinding. 'Will this rain help Zandar's magic or dilute it?'

'You don't understand!' Storm-noise almost drowned out Joah's voice. 'The new shape and depth of the river may be too different for her spell to work!'

'You mean we're trapped here?'

Her face gave the answer.

Man saw just how *he* would want it... Get us all outside, get us important targets together ... then *strike*.

Zandar raised her crucifix in one hand. 'Lady Rishiri! Princess Anamizu! You must find me – *before it is too late!*'

She cocked her head, as if she could hear an answer, but if there was a reply it did not please her.

Joah shouted over the thunder, 'We need something to shield us while we wait for them! Mother, try for a Dome of Protection!'

Man felt Zandar's power throb up and out, but it seemed uncertain and she confirmed that.

'I cannot do this for long!'

Yoshi bawled, 'If we stay here it's the end! Can't we rush on, even if we take casualties?'

Then twin bolts of lightning struck behind and there was a wash of fire from that direction. Screaming came from back in the column, and the milling people there were driven forward.

Next, lightning struck in front. To his shame, Man ducked. He slid down from his kicking horse. All the horses and ponies were panicking. More lightning strikes hemmed them in, and each time *he* struck a few persons on the edges of the party were wounded or even killed. Soon the column was crushed into a circle of wet and frightened people.

Man rubbed at the icy water streaming over his face. Its acid burned his eyes.

'We have to get inside your walls!' he said to Mother Zandar. 'We must go forward or die!'

Zandar gestured magic again, but he saw how little strength was left in her.

'All my power goes on keeping us protected! I can do no more!'

Purple-white lightning exploded not far ahead of Lady Berenda. 'There!' she said. 'Now *he* takes a hand!'

Hagiwara glanced at the black sashes marching behind.

Most were newly recruited, but there were many. By tomorrow night there should be thousands.

He turned his head to look forward again. Rain was no deadly weapon, though lightning could kill. 'I still don't understand why our Lord – as you told me – ordered our human forces not to attack.'

'Have the gates of death opened for you to peek beyond, little man?' Berenda's voice sounded ecstatic now. 'No, no, no! Never mind their vaunted walls! I can foresee what is coming!'

She laughed, stroked a fingertip through the air, and made a scene in three dimensions for him. It was The Waning, with the earth erupting under it. Hagiwara saw how its towers and ring-walls collapsed and its Moon came crashing down.

He blanched. 'Aren't we too close?'

'His storm is focused on The Waning – but there's enough to submerge the land. Every step will bring them closer to drowning.' The rain turned chill. 'Hagiwara – !'

'What?' The gale turned icy cold and he had to grab her and shout over it. 'Lady, it's so bloody noisy I can't hear you!'

She unloosened his grip. 'I think our master is making a blizzard.'

'But we're here too!'

'Other servants will take our places.' When she did speak again, it was not to Hagiwara, but to an almost infinite greatness. 'Though I walk through the valley of the shadow of death, I will fear no evil; for *you* are with me.'

Hagiwara felt his hair stand on end.

Lady Rishiri's Blood Knot gem was pulsing, and her own amplified hatred had made it a vicious weapon. But now she felt vital male energies focus on their rocking palanquin.

Yes, that's *him*. Rishiri felt a bit afraid. What is the brute up to?

Princess Anamizu's eyes opened wide. 'Beware!'

Rishiri gestured protective power only just in time. In all directions eye-blinding lightning bolts exploded.

'He's found us now,' the old lady said. She glared out from her window, but there was nothing except dark rain to see. It was only her magic that revealed to her the threatened humans ahead. 'All the people with Zandar have been stopped!'

Anamizu made a magical glow in the interior, which showed Rishiri the princess's haunted look. '*Zandar* needs help? Then we are truly desperate!'

'No! *We* are fine. But a rescue of this upstart "Mother" and her boy... I refuse. It is *not* my duty to help imposters!'

'It *is* your duty to help!'

Rishiri glared even more, but did not renounce duty. After a moment she spoke again. 'Anyway, before giving assistance we must somehow cross this river...'

'In this flood, is that even possible?'

Rishiri said nothing.

They had been stopped, but now Man felt women's power in the chilled wet dark. 'Mother! That must be your Rishiri and Anamizu. Oh, they're strong! I see why you want their help.'

Man looked up at the dangerous black sky. Under Zandar's dome of protection water and lightning could not penetrate – for now.

More bolts hit home, close by. Man and the others were shocked as well as deafened. He worried that they would all be held here, as *he* struck again and again. Eventually Zandar's dome would shatter, and then they would die.

The Voice tried to sing up some sorcery, but he heard her voice crack and die away.

Then the thunder spoke in *his* voice: 'SURRENDER!' The emphasis was on the third syllable. 'SURRENDER!'

Man grimaced. Was there any chance of help, from anywhere at all? He had lost touch with the two new women, but perhaps something useful was happening inside The Waning? Man sensed they were again throwing power into the sky, and that was distracting *him*, even hurting him.

Zandar spoke so that only Man could hear her. 'There is some flaw here.' She looked at Man, and then at the Voice from Afar and the Lady Joah. 'My dome is – not what it should be. It might break.'

Joah reached out for the Voice's right hand and for Man's left hand.

'Form a magic circle! Women and men together!'

Man pulled back. Probably it was the Tears' bloody kiss and the illness it had caused, but he had lost all faith in himself.

'I have nothing to contribute! Do it with women's magic.'

'But the greatest power comes from togetherness!'

A lightning-bolt exploded just over Man's head, and his clothes and hair stirred from the electricity. Some childhood part

of his mind recalled that wet allowed electric power to spread...
He saw that this, too, was most likely part of the enemy's plan.
When their protection failed, which was inevitable, they would
all be killed.

With his mind, Man reached out for the Eye just as hard as
he could.

'What are you doing?' The Voice's wet fingers were on his
neck, caressing, perhaps dangerous in their desperation. 'I felt
you try to do something!'

'I can't do a thing. You help our Mother!'

The cold rain had turned to cold sleet. Then he sensed a
sudden blaze of energy behind his back. Was it the Eye, or
something new? This force was so powerful he didn't dare turn.

'If that's the Tears...'

'What?' Zandar asked.

Man held his head, suddenly nauseous. Unless he was
helped soon he could not live. 'Whoever it is, they're on the
wrong side of this flood! Do you expect people to walk on water?'

'You should have more faith, my Emmanuel; there is a
bridge.'

Afraid that a fresh, viciously determined Tears was coming,
Man shouted at the holy Mother. 'In this weather and in this
flood you can't even *find* a bridge!'

Then he felt the personalities within the power that was
approaching. Now he turned his head, less afraid he would see
her. Instead, in the dark on the other bank of the river he
glimpsed a dome of light.

Now Man saw enemy lightning begin to cascade around this
second dome. The newcomers were allies, then!

Man's optimism rose.

When Rishiri and Anamizu reached the river, lightning struck
ahead where sleet had turned to falling snow. Lady Rishiri
squeezed her eyes shut. She did not want to see their situation.
Then courage gathered – though she desperately needed a drink
– and she opened her eyes and spoke with harsh apology. 'Lord
Buddha, forgive me for my sins. Princess, forgive me for my
fears!'

'Your bravery was famous, lady, and still is.'

Rishiri had to smile; she loved flattery. 'You know what we
must do!'

In the dark palanquin Princess Anamizu's voice was full of

doubt. 'Can we really get to Zandar and the others, before *he* destroys us all?'

Rishiri spoke with ultimate grimness. 'We must.'

'Even if we do meet, where can we go then?'

'Oh, give me a little to hope for! The young fool "Zandar" does have some skill.'

Now a huge lightning-blast struck close by, powerful enough to shake the palanquin and spook the horses badly. There was the stink of ozone.

The Lord of the North began flogging them fiercely. He was truly powerful, though Rishiri knew that *he* was also a fool. A single strike with everything he had would have been much more effective than all this furious flailing.

Unless he was holding off till they were all together...

Anamizu said only, 'When I see your lips move I wonder if there are prayers being mouthed, and, if so, to what god, or what devil?'

'You know the nature of my soul, princess. You also know you have no choice except to trust me!'

'You are correct.'

The old lady cackled, as if that was a wonderful joke. 'Now, light up the path ahead!'

The princess managed that. Rishiri peered ahead into the erratic glow. The path had already been submerged by knee-deep muddy water. The bridge itself might have been destroyed. Even if it hadn't, now the river was in full spate it was hidden underwater.

'Perhaps if we both stepped in...'

'No!' Anamizu said. 'We'll be swept away!'

'We cannot wait.'

The old lady slid out of the palanquin. The cold flood took her around the knees. Meanwhile wind shrieked around her and snow struck her face.

Expecting to be swept off her feet but deciding to chance it, Rishiri stepped into the full, racing river. She tried to establish what was underfoot. Was this the planks of a bridge? It might be. Then lightning flared again, and the simultaneous thunder stunned her. She lost her bearings and stumbled. Now she was on her knees, icy water rose up to her chest. She moaned, fearing she would drown.

Where was this young Emmanuel? Even in dying, perhaps she could help him!

Words of Fury:

Rishiri reached out, and her mind sensed great soul-force all around. It was not just the Lord of the North who was focusing here.

Emmanuel...

She made contact with him.

For a moment she was overjoyed, but then she realized he was too feeble to be The One Who Will Change. Those who said he was were fools. The magic this young man had was weak, and she felt the fever in him as he touched his swollen cheek. Now she read him, thoughts and emotions both.

Man knew he was losing and he hated himself for it.

Rishiri understood that. The icy water was killing her; it would be all too easy to give up. But Rishiri wanted to live, to take revenge on all her many enemies. Using her cane, she forced herself up in the flood. The horrible arctic wind *he* made was blowing counter-clockwise around The Waning; that gave her a direction, and she pressed on over the flooded bridge.

When lightning flashed again above the river, it was actually useful to her.

There!

It had revealed Zandar's party. A few riders, but mainly Sword Maidens on foot – perhaps two hundred. There was power among them, though Man's was almost insignificant.

Rishiri saw another electric bolt strike towards them from *him*, but Man had already flung up an arm to ward off the electric attack.

The Lord of the North recoiled.

It was only then that Lady Rishiri truly knew. In angry surprise, recognition was torn out of her.

'Princess, Zandar may have been right!' Then more and more energy flickered up in Man. Soon he was blazing with silvery-white power, so that Rishiri became frightened. Nevertheless, she shouted back to the palanquin, 'Follow me towards that power blaze! Foreigner or not, that boy *is* The One Who Will Change! We have to get to him!'

Rishiri was sobbing for breath. The waist-deep icy water had almost paralyzed her legs. Her teeth were chattering, those that remained, and melting snow humped on her shoulders.

She beckoned behind. Anamizu and the others *had* to follow!

If they did not, Lady Rishiri might as well drown herself in this wild river, and take the princess with her.

Words of Fury:

Chapter Forty: *We Have Darkness In Our Light*

Through the sleet, Man saw a lit-up dome approaching. Shadowy figures were within – horses and riders, a palanquin. The procession was led through the flooded river by a small swaying figure with one hand raised.

As he knew something of the Shogun, Man had heard of Princess Anamizu, but Lady Rishiri was unknown to him. He noticed Zandar didn't look happy. Was that a sign the newcomers might be unhelpful? Or did it mean that the new women couldn't do enough with the power, and so all was lost?

The sky was full of exotic lightning. Man saw insanely heightened colors exploding everywhere. The blasts were strong enough to feel like blows, and the other dome of protection was being hit by lightning almost all the time.

'Look at that!' The Voice was pointing. Then she turned her head. 'I wonder how long they can survive!'

The wild river tried very hard to sweep Rishiri away. It took everything she had, to force a way over against *his* resistance and *his* weather. She shivered; she thought she might faint away and drown. Nevertheless, taking one step at a time, she managed to cross.

The others followed her.

Rishiri waited for them. Once they were all on her side of the river, soaking-wet Rishiri was helped back into the palanquin.

'Lady, you were magnificent!'

'Wasn't I just?' Rishiri cackled, pleased that she had not fainted. She rubbed at her legs to restore the circulation. 'And more magnificence to come, eh?'

Though their own dome flexed every time it was hit and it sometimes changed color, for the moment she saw it was surviving all that the Lord of the North threw at it. Rishiri squinted through the hail as lightning splashed the other shield again. Was there something not quite right there?

Now the edges of the two domes touched. Both domes stopped moving because neither dome, neither magic, could prevail.

'The two shields must become one, Princess!'

Anamizu, very shocked, said, 'It would be mad to let slip our protection!'

Words of Fury:

'Of course.' Rishiri felt her brave old heart thump at the inside of her chest. 'But what alternative is there? – None... So, Princess, raise up our shield!'

'No. I dare not! It would let *him* in!'

'It must be done, or we stay here until we die!'

Anamizu's lightning-lit face showed fear. Nevertheless she raised both hands, with palms up.

Rishiri saw there was now a space below their shield as it tilted back. Icy wind blasted in, driving the hailstones almost horizontally – and Rishiri felt *his* anger drive the storm.

She shrieked vocally and in mind-talk, 'Zandar! Wherever you are, let us in *now*, or we all die!'

Rishiri saw Zandar was in the middle of the big, sodden group, mounted on a pony. Her expression was dead.

Then an oddly familiar-looking girl bent towards Zandar and said something. Might that be the renegade Okada daughter?

The advice was taken. Now she saw how Zandar's own shield rose, flexing as it weakened.

'Their dome won't hold, nor will ours!' Princess Anamizu yelled.

Rishiri knew the risk had to be taken. 'Lift!'

Their own dome rose further, but then their power lost focus. Instantly Rishiri's shield was torn into rags. She made a grabbing motion to hold on to these last shreds, but the hailstones and the wind buffeted them. Rishiri was shivering terribly now, and wondering about freezing to death. Then she felt *him* above – and then *saw* him – saw his huge drawn-back fist, about to smash them into the earth...

What human magic would serve, against *him*?

Somehow Rishiri knew what to do. After all, she had fought this Lord – and his predecessors – before...

'Join together!' Rishiri tried to shout to Zandar. 'Make the two shields into one!'

That did not happen, and her own neglected shield was little more than flapping rags now.

Lady Rishiri cursed spectacularly. Though she was blinded by the stinging hail that also thundered on the palanquin roof, Rishiri made some subtle gestures *he* would not expect, and then spoke strong words.

Now her power touched Zandar's. Even as the weaves meshed together, Lady Rishiri wove more. It felt natural and good to work together this way, and Rishiri laid aside selfish fury. Her work was quick and sure, and so were the weaves of the fool girl some other fools called 'Mother'. They were making magic together as if they'd practiced for years.

'At the same moment!' Rishiri said to her inheritor at The Waning of the Moon, the woman she hated, the woman she must now save. If their timing was off, *he* would smash them into a pulp. 'Three – two – one – *now!*'

Rishiri and Zandar made the two domed shields one.

'Yes!' said Zandar.

A second later *his* fist struck down. It hammered their shield a couple of feet deep into the earth. The air was so compressed it stabbed their ears.

Nevertheless there were no casualties. Inside her palanquin Rishiri sagged back, panting, realizing her face was running with sweat as well as melted hail.

That had been close...

Riding her pony, Zandar came over to the palanquin.

Rishiri saw the bandage, and was shocked. 'You're blind!'

'No. It's simply that I've lost the use of my eyes!'

Some might call that bravery, but Rishiri bridled at the familiar arrogance. Zandar was a mere girl self-promoted far beyond her worth. Rishiri felt fury rise in her again, as acid-sour as alcoholic vomit. She flicked her right hand, and her own lightning struck back at the sky – though still *he* called out, 'SURRENDER!'

Zandar told her, '*He* is back in Ezo, Lady! There's nothing here to hit.'

'It relieves my feelings somewhat, so-called "Mother", and I assure you it does hurt him. I should be angry with how you have failed everyone, though I never had much hope in you. But when I see you now, lost to the light of the world, and see the sickly state of Joah, and poor foreign Emmanuel *dying* when you were tasked to protect him...'

'Enough – please!' said Zandar. 'Follow me, before it's too late.'

'Follow *you?*'

'There is no one else.'

'There is myself, who is...'

Zandar leaned forward. 'Forget you and me! Forget your selfish pain! Think of the world!'

'Ever the optimist!' Rishiri jeered. Hatred for this young

woman tore through her insides, with a birth-pang pain.

'On this I agree with her, Lady Rishiri,' Princess Anamizu said severely. 'We must try to advance!'

'You think you can get to The Waning of the Moon without me?' The old lady cackled, showing toothless gums. 'Oh, what do you green girls know? If only I'd been left in charge as I deserved – !'

Zandar made a subtle hand-signal to the Voice, and the foreign girl understood. Zandar's voice called right across the protected area, its volume getting everyone's attention.

'We have to move! Form up! Then we will do it at a run!'

Everybody – women, men, Sword Maidens and samurai – obeyed without question or hesitation.

Rishiri knew then, as she had really known for a long time, that it was too late for her. Once she had been First at The Waning, but that time would never come again. She understood that clearly now. For the survivors, bedraggled and burned though they might be, all cheered Mother Zandar as they obeyed.

In the blinding hailstorm Man and the others followed the irregular riverside track. He wondered why they did not strike out directly for The Waning, or use water magic here, but he had to assume that Zandar knew best.

They could not keep up a good pace, though. In many places the track was deep in muddy water. Lightning struck down again and again, burning over Man and the others. He felt somewhat protected, for Mother Zandar and the two great ladies were working together to shield them. Most of the lightning was diverted harmlessly. The column progressed, if slowly.

'Thank all the gods for those new ladies!' said one Sword Maiden, fervently. 'They know how to shield us from *him*, and I am grateful!'

Man saw the golden weaves rising. Most were centered on Mother Zandar, though many were woven by Lady Rishiri and the princess. Nevertheless they all knitted together perfectly. The elastic webs took *his* great blows but did not break. And yet Man saw some weakening touch of darkness in the protection, and enemy power did sometimes leak in.

Can it be that Zandar is secretly compromised?

Man could not believe that, not about her.

But it was *someone*...

Then perhaps it was one of the new people? He turned his

head, looking at their palanquin and the guards around it.

He knew there was wrongness; he did not know exactly where it was.

It was very, very cold now, with the hail still lashing, and the light almost gone. He turned, saw Zandar was tired, saw the uncertainty in her. Would her magic protection last much longer?

The river had broadened considerably since they left Miracle Island. His heart missed that place, and the miraculous power for good there.

Here, lightning struck close by again, with some leaking through. It was hot enough to burn flesh and there was some screaming from the newly wounded.

Yoshi ducked his head again. 'You know more of magic, Man. Are we going to make it?'

Zandar had already hinted her water magic would probably not work on this floodwater, so he didn't give Yoshi a direct answer. 'We have powerful adepts with us.'

'And a more powerful enemy above!'

'Yes,' Man admitted.

Now he looked at the embittered face peering out from the palanquin. Rishiri looked sour and wicked: could she really be on his side? She scowled up at dark heaven, whispering magic curses that turned the shivery air ice-blue.

'Precious Stone, who is this "Lady Rishiri"? She looks like a murderous elf who drank an aging potion and then went mad!'

His Sword Maiden shouted over the storm.

'She is a noble-born with great power – though she is, I understand, arrogant and misguided. Before my time Lady Rishiri was in charge of The Waning, but was erratic and drunken and often malicious, and took too many risks to fight *him*. She was therefore deposed.'

'So she's a Sword Maiden and adept?'

'Yes, and very strong; and when she was sent away Zandar was invited here to take her place. There is much bad blood between her and the present Mother.'

'Are they going to fight?'

Joah answered that, face ghastly with strain as she kept up her share of the mighty protective magic. 'I feel their mutual fury. When it comes out, we are done!'

Mother Zandar cantered her pony towards them.

Joah said, 'Mother, better to end it all here!'

'What?'

'We would keep our souls, even if *he* gets the Eye and the Diamond Heart and all!'

'If he does win here,' Zandar said calmly, 'then the world falls. Compared to that, *all* our lives and souls together are of little importance.'

Joah suddenly sat down in a shallow spot, holding her head in her hands. She looked wretched. The Voice and Yoshi combined to help the mudstained girl back to her feet.

Man had ridden forward too late to assist. He was ill and he had slowed up.

The widening river was only a few paces away now, and flowing dangerously fast. Wanting the truth, Man turned to Mother Zandar.

'You say there is magic in this river.'

'There is.'

She was so mild he felt his own fear and fury mount. 'Well, his flood of rain has made the river run too quickly to be safe. If we step in, we'll be swept away.'

'I know that, Emmanuel.'

Man said, 'Well?'

'There is a way back, *if* we believe, by means of magic.'

'Then we might still be saved!'

'I hope so.'

Man shivered. 'But how?'

'There is a way to journey on, which *he* may not know!'

Joah shouted, 'He *will* know it! Believe me! *He* knows *everything!* And whatever spell has been made, the river's changes will invalidate your work!'

'To despair is wrong and surrender is worse.'

Man stared at Joah; and when she did not respond, Mother Zandar gave her a frown but said nothing more to her. Instead, Zandar led everyone on to some long fish-pools parallel to the river. The pool closest had a wooden roof and walls. Zandar dismounted, and led the way in. Man got off his black stallion and followed her. Their dome was still overhead, shuddering as it took punishment.

It was too dark within to see much, except when the lightning-bolts hit. In those flashes Man saw the shed was only a big empty space, with steps leading down into the long glistening pool. Shivering, he felt no pure magic here at all. The others too looked subdued. He could not see how being here helped them –

Words of Fury:

unless there was a half-mile-long secret way to The Waning!

He shouted to Zandar, 'Are we looking for a tunnel?'

Then he became conscious of the hail drumming on the roof; *his* hailstorm, frighteningly loud, so loud it had drowned out his words and his hope.

By now, any such tunnel would be flooded...

Zandar called over her shoulder. 'All of you, come inside!'

It was an incredible crush, but they managed to get everyone in. Two hundred Sword Maidens and samurai had crowded in after the holy Mother and Man.

'*He* knows we're here,' said Lady Joah. Another lightning-flash showed her looking like a drowned rat, her breath steaming in *his* cold. 'I think he plans a blizzard. We're finished.'

But Man was now watching Mother Zandar. She was standing at the head of the steps that went down into the pool. Her expression was calculating and grave.

The Voice saw it first. 'The water here is a run-off from the river.' She turned her head. 'Man, *this* is also the sacred river! And the pools here must be just as they were before the storm!'

So the old spell might still work! He saw how being *exactly* here might help them. That was just as well, as The Waning was over a half mile away and they could not possibly get there through this storm. He shivered, hugging himself.

'Mother?' he asked. 'Isn't it time?'

Suddenly Zandar was gesturing magic and speaking magic, and there was light around her, warming and gold.

When she completed the spell she turned and bawled out, 'This is magic of earth and water, using a river sacred for two thousand years! Magic has made a water door for the pure in heart! People, we are almost home!'

Man heard the cheering and saw the relief. Zandar looked as if joy and raw pride were fighting with her self-restraint.

But Lady Rishiri stood off to one side with the tall princess. She kept looking from Mother Zandar to Joah, and Man saw she was both disdainful and furious.

That made him worry about the future – if they even succeeded in escaping from this place.

Zandar called proudly, 'I will be last to leave, to hold the doorway ajar! Now I need someone to open the way!'

At once Man took a step forward, though he felt dizzy and stumbled. Ozawa caught him.

Precious Stone had been quicker to volunteer. 'Mother, I

Words of Fury:

will do it for you. I am like my sister – not afraid!'

Zandar touched the Sword Maiden's head in a blessing.

'Then lead us! All you pure others, follow brave Precious Stone!'

Man saw his Sword Maiden move to the steps leading into the water. She was breathing hard, and not so bold now. Perhaps she had a particular fear of drowning. Man saw her turn; their eyes met and she blew him a kiss.

Next to Man the Voice from Afar was praying aloud.

She-captain Hanake spoke quietly, to Man and the other newcomers. 'There are wards here to keep out any servants of *his*. Only the good-hearted can travel.'

'Amen!' said the Voice from Afar.

Man watched Precious Stone feel her way cautiously down the slippery steps. Soon the water was around her knees, and then waist-deep. Drawing her two swords, she turned and bowed very low to Mother Zandar and then to Man.

Man was exhilarated now. He was going to see a miracle: see his very own brave Maiden breathing underwater and taking a short half-mile step to The Waning of the Moon.

Precious Stone stepped down and water closed around her head. The Voice from Afar raised two clenched fists in a sign of triumph and there was a babble of hopeful words. Only Faslane, right beside her, looked dubious.

Instead of a miracle, Man saw Precious Stone pull her head out of the water. She had been beginning to choke. He saw her back out of the water, dripping wet and coughing.

'Mother! I could not breathe!'

'But it must be possible! It must! The magic allows no one tainted by *him* to pass, but we are all pure!'

They were crowding under the roof, where *his* big hailstones pounded even more fiercely than before. It made Man think of a maddened animal clawing to get in.

Lady Rishiri's croaking voice challenged them all.

'If the sacred way is closed, it must be because somebody here has let *him* into their heart!' Lightning showed Man how she stared first at Yoshi, then at the Voice, and then back at Yoshi. 'Is it you, you sprig of the Fujiwaras? Or you, outland girl? Tell me! That person must confess and be sacrificed, or it all ends here!'

Be *sacrificed*? The Voice? Man tried to dismiss that accusation; he knew her character. But Yoshi had opened his mouth, then closed it again. Rishiri's words had shaken him.

Was Yoshi *his?* Man knew his friend could be violent, even cruel. He suddenly remembered Yoshi in a screaming rage, with a bloody sack of skin in one hand and a skinned-alive enemy in the other...

But he can't be a traitor; he's done too much for me!

The old lady sniffed, turning to Zandar.

'We have darkness in our light; such weakness is deadly. Is it you?'

Zandar turned on her in a fury. 'You imagine there's something wrong with *me?* Well, I could destroy you with a single word of power – and perhaps I should!'

Another hammer-blow dented their protective dome. Man felt the corrupted shield could not last much longer.

Lady Rishiri was bellowing. 'Admit it, "Zandar", you young fool! Someone here has the taint of *him!*'

'Rishiri, this is more of your poison!'

Zandar had sounded appalled, but now Lady Rishiri turned to her, raised a finger and made a sign. Man saw the magical gesture was something to do with thought or logic.

Zandar staggered away from some terrible realization, and what she said then took away all hope.

'Lady Rishiri, you have seen the truth!'

Rishiri wasn't looking at Yoshi any longer. She was staring directly at Man. He felt her power now, rolling from her in waves. He knew he was very, very close to death.

'It isn't me!'

'What if you lie?'

'I'm not!'

'But one among us does have *him* within!' she said.

Is that one *me?* Man wondered.

He felt guilt twist inside him. In a desperate moment when his friends had been close to dying, Man had allowed the Lord of the North to touch his soul. Because of that well-meant treachery, all his friends here would die – though Man somehow knew he might still save himself.

If I turn to *him*, and I can, he *will* save me – ! I don't have to die!

Man had hardly any Foretelling power, but he suddenly saw himself as a powerful tool for the Lord of the North. He saw himself cutting throats, destroying towns and cities, and all the while laughing along with his master.

Words of Fury:

If I turn to him, my soul will certainly die, but I will live...

'Man!' It was the Voice from Afar. 'Please, please help us!'

She believed in him; but Man knew she was wrong and he had to confess. He *had* to. He would not turn, though. He decided that. No, he would instead die, they *all* would, but still he might save his soul and theirs.

'The Lord of the North has touched a heart,' he began.

Joah spoke. 'Indeed he has.'

Man felt fury at himself and at the world; a fury much like *his*. He realized he had things in common with the Lord of the North, though he hated his master.

Could even Joah forgive me now? No, of course not...

But the Lady Joah was continuing to speak. 'And who is the one stopping our progress, the one with *his* taint?'

'That one will ruin this journey, and fail the world!' said Zandar.

'That is so.' Joah had a sad but brave smile. 'And it is me.'

No! Man felt devastated. Not Joah; it couldn't be *her*!

But he saw from her expression that it was.

Words of Fury:

PART THREE

There is a war between darkness and light in every world. In the world of this story there is one possible sanctuary in all of samurai Japan: The Waning of the Moon. But that monstrous cold enemy, the Lord of the North, is determined that it will fall...

Prologue to Part Three: *A Mile of Freezing Storm*

As melted snow from the blizzard outside dripped through the roof, Man listened to Lady Joah confess. Her voice was surprisingly calm and unapologetic.

He still didn't believe her. 'You can't have deceived us all this time! Joah, you fought *him* so hard! Somebody else *must* be the traitor.'

'I thought someone would realize. In Jade my own sister caught me doing blood magic. And you, Man, when I was so useless opposing *him* that night on the balloon and afterwards I was *sure* you'd guess...'

Joah lowered her eyes, shrugging.

Perhaps it's true, perhaps she has been ruined by the Lord of the North.

No; that's not possible. – *Is it?*

Man swept wetness off his hair. It was dark here, but he looked hard at Lady Joah and then ground out angry words. 'You've really been living a lie for... How long?'

She shrugged again. Rain, endless freezing rain, still came dripping down.

'Lady Joah, you are an Okada, from a line of samurai heroes!' This was Princess Anamizu. 'Why did you fail us?'

This time Joah pouted. 'I had to test *him* for weaknesses, and I did.'

The Lord of the North was the all-powerful epitome of death and cold – and Joah knew that; she *couldn't* have been turned to evil.

'Oh, you pretty fool!' Zandar raged, and a lightning-flash showed Man her tears. Mother Zandar the strong and faithful, with a human weakness! 'Joah, our weaves are tainted, because of you! We cannot take that one step to sanctuary, because of you! We will die here, because of *you!*'

When lightning came again, Man saw the famous family

pride in Joah's face – and from her mutinous expression it was clear her confession was true. They were all trapped. Man's friends; Mother Zandar; the brave Sword Maidens; all were condemned. Man felt sick and full of anger.

He had to know if any act of self-sacrifice might save them. 'Joah, is there anything *I* can do?'

'I cannot help you, Emmanuel, and I cannot be helped. Make your peace with *him*.'

'Never!'

Everywhere the water rose and he saw the fishpond here overflow. There was no ark. Everyone's fear now was drowning, while before it had been freezing. Joah's corruption meant they would stay trapped in this ramshackle shed; and that meant death.

Joah was staring around now, as if woken into day from some bad dream. 'If I said I was sorry – '

Lady Rishiri glared. She was a very fierce old lady. 'Girl, it is too late to repent!'

Man felt the nervy crowd shift. There were two hundred people crowded in. Mother Zandar and Man were at the front, with Sword Maidens pressing behind. There was no more to be said. The wind battered the roof and Man saw it flex. It couldn't last much longer.

Was there any way to escape? Man knew there was cold outside, acid rain, evil and fury...

Suddenly the Voice from Afar was looking up. 'This quarrelling means the Lord of the North has found us!'

Man's best friend Yoshi also squinted up at the wooden roof, which was shaking. 'What makes you say so?'

A blast of wind ripped the roof clean off.

'That!' said the Voice.

Man and others were sent sprawling. Riders had been blown out of the saddle. With no roof above, Man and all the others were drenched again. Everyone now felt the incredible pressure of the Lord of the North bearing down from the black sky.

Yoshi nudged him. 'Man? We can't make it to The Waning by magic?'

Zandar shouted over the storm-wind. 'Not with the water so changed and *him* so close!'

Yoshi just looked sad. 'Then we will be sacrificed here.'

Joah was still proud. 'Realize this, I *had* to see *him*. All was done from a good intention!'

'From arrogance!' Zandar snapped.

Man saw with horror that Joah's arrogant sneer was *him*. The Lord of the North had eaten into her soul.

But now Zandar showed her steel.

'My friends, we must try to get to sanctuary on foot. We may not succeed, but we can at least let *him* know he has been in a fight.'

There was almost a mile of freezing storm to get through, and Man knew that was impossible. Their story would end here; Joah had seen to that.

Zandar hadn't finished. 'So, Lady Joah, you *must* be untainted!'

Joah's response was somewhere between a pout and another sneer, sly and wicked both. 'All of you put together have not the power!'

'Joah! Kneel down and ask forgiveness!'

Lady Joah made a disdainful gesture. 'You cannot think you can command *me*?'

'For all of us you must put aside your pride! Kneel!'

'Never!'

Man knew that his friend Lady Joah was now the Lord of the North's agent and could not be saved. The old enemy had won and it was over for the human race.

Zandar placed her hands on Joah's shoulders and Man saw her try to force the girl down.

Words of Fury: 429

Chapter Forty-One: *Every Diabolical Legion*

Man saw most people were now looking hopelessly up at the black, roiling sky. Without orders, a few of their party – some of the samurai who had come with Man, Sword Maidens owing allegiance to Mother Zandar – were beginning to slip away into the unnatural night.

This was the end, was it?

Man exploded. 'We have to resist! It can't end this way!'

Joah tried to pull away from Mother Zandar, but to Man's surprise Zandar – though slight and not tall – had the power to force Lady Joah down into the mud.

Now Joah was kneeling, the holy Mother put a hand to her forehead. Zandar held her hand there and her lips moved; an incantation.

Joah began to twist and moan.

Man felt the earth tremble. From Joah's expression, *he* was deep inside her, and he would *not* go quietly. Would they all be destroyed in an earthquake, or drowned? Man realized Zandar's spell was either/or: either it would free his lovely friend Joah, or destroy them all.

Now Lady Joah was mumbling obscenities that made Man flinch. Once she actually spat at Mother Zandar.

'Be silent,' said Zandar, speaking to the horror inhabiting Joah. 'Be silent and come out of her!'

Joah's face suddenly blanked.

Now holy Mother Zandar began to chant. Man recognized Latin, very ancient. The words throbbed with power.

> *Exorcizamus te, omnis immundus spiritus*
> *omnis satanica potestas, omnis incursio*
> *infernalis adversarii, omnis legio,*
> *omnis congregatio et secta diabolica!*
> *Ergo draco maledicte*
> *et omnis legio diabolica*
> *adjuramus te!*
> *Cessa decipere humanas creaturas,*
> *eisque aeternae Perditionis venenum propinare.*
>
> *Vade, Satana, inventor et magister*
> *omnis fallaciae, hostis humanae salutis.*

Words of Fury:

> *Humiliare sub potenti manu dei,*
> *contremisce et effuge, invocato a*
> *nobis sancto et terribili nomine,*
> *quem inferi tremunt.*

The world-shaking grew worse; *he* was *not* leaving his victim.

At once Zandar turned. 'Emmanuel, speak the words with me!'

So now Man began to chant the exorcism himself, and so did others. In speaking he felt whole and powerful again, and he knew these were truly words of power.

> 'We exorcise ye, every impure spirit
> every Satanic power, every incursion
> of the infernal adversary, every legion,
> every congregation and diabolical sect!
> Thus, cursed demon...'

Joah shrieked curses now, so it seemed the entire earth shook. Man spoke on, afraid but dutiful.

> 'and every diabolical legion
> we adjure ye!
> Cease to deceive human creatures
> and to give to them the poison of eternal perdition!'

He saw Joah threshing about. She cried out again, frothing at the mouth. Could she really take this, and live? *He* fought hard to hold onto Joah, so that the very air distorted around the kneeling young woman and Mother Zandar. Man knew his side was losing, and to fight the Lord of the North was like trying to manhandle a mountain. The whole world shook, but the holy Mother was not daunted. With the help of the Voice from Afar, Zandar's voice chorused.

> 'Go away, Satan, inventor and master
> of all deceit, enemy of humanity's salvation!
> Be *humble* under the powerful hand of God
> tremble and flee! – I invoke
> the sacred and terrible name
> at which those down below tremble!'

Words of Fury:

Joah's eyes rolled up and she fell face-down into the mud.

Immediately Man pulled her up, and held her slack body close. Was this a complete collapse, or death? Was she even breathing?

'For God's sake, don't give up!'

Leaning over his arms, she coughed up dirty water, but then lifted one hand. To his surprise, the bedraggled girl was smiling.

'Man, *he* has been driven from me! Mother Zandar, you have expelled the Lord of the North. I am pure and whole again. *I have been saved!'*

Shivering in the sleet, Man held that small, proud figure against his chest. For now Joah was redeemed and so they all had a chance. In some ways The Waning of the Moon, their sanctuary, was not so far – though in another sense it was infinitely distant.

Nevertheless, there was hope.

Along with everyone else, Man rejoiced.

Chapter Forty-Two: *We Must Move On!*

Now he had seen Joah's salvation, Man made a decision. He was weak and drenched, but he knew what their only chance was. He managed to re-mount his horse and shout. 'We must move on!'

He felt ghastly and probably looked worse – but he was determined that he *would* go on, and take his people with him.

Though icy sleet drummed on them all, Man had found renewed strength. That invigorated Yoshi and Ozawa, his samurai friends. With the Sword Maiden she-captain Hanake, they got everyone formed up in the roofless shed. Meanwhile the women repowered their dome of protection, the shield from *his* magic and *his* storm.

Man led the party out.

'I don't know if we can find the road!' Mother Zandar said, holding her pony's reins and shivering. Snow caked her hair. 'Yet we must. It goes to The Waning.'

Yoshi tried to push the sleet from his face. 'There are no roads left – it's hopeless!'

'*I* know where your Waning is.' Faslane had shouldered his way forward. He was the seaman sent here from Man's homeland, great Albion. 'This storm swirls counter-clockwise. If we keep the wind on our left and press on, we will come to storm-centre eventually – your Waning of the Moon.'

Man was grateful; he didn't know if they would or could arrive, but they couldn't get lost.

'You have your uses, sea-pilot!' Yoshi called to Faslane.

The seaman gave a well-meant mock bow at the compliment, and Yoshi laughed.

As joint leaders, Man and Mother Zandar pushed on.

Man guessed this had been a decent road once, but in places it was already deep in water, flowing water which threatened to sweep everyone downhill. Man had to struggle to keep his horse steady. The mud was sometimes knee-deep. He was dismally aware that if he slipped off his horse he would most likely drown.

Lightning flailed just ahead and the lightning-bolt somehow bent under the edge of their shield and then up again, hitting someone. Man flinched, as his horse reared and almost threw him; he had to take a moment to soothe it. He had been so drained by the long fight that now he was rolling about in the saddle.

The lightning had incinerated a mounted Sword Maiden and

her blackened bones had flown around dangerously. A smoking pelvis and thigh-bone embedded itself in the mud between Yoshi and Man. For a moment they both stared at the human remains.

The Voice from Afar shouted out anger and despair. 'I told you! The Lord of the North *does* know where we are!'

Man raised two clenched fists. 'We still have to keep moving!'

'We can do it!' Ozawa was pointing determinedly – though through this sleet nobody could see The Waning. 'It's only a mile or so!'

It might as well be hundreds of miles, Man thought. He had to fight to get beside Zandar on her pony, and twice his horse stumbled and almost went over.

They went on a hundred paces, then another hundred. In some places their footsoldiers had to wade, but nobody faltered or gave up, even though the dark had swallowed them completely.

It was slow progress, inch by inch. All the time they were beaten down by the storm. Some hailstones came, egg-size; they hurt.

'Mother, how are we doing?'

'Our shield is frayed, Emmanuel. I fear I have played into *his* hands, as the girls suspected. I have assembled our mightiest powers, our gems and you – and now *he* has the one target.'

'You think he did plan it?'

'If he wins here, *he* wins everything!'

'But if there is help – '

She raised a hand in tired dismissal. 'At The Waning Daisen and the others have been fighting *him* for hours. They are exhausted.'

'You can't mean we must give up?'

He couldn't believe it would end this way, after so much effort, so much sacrifice.

Now Man's horse slipped again on the mud and this time went down. He rolled off it, landing on his knees with cold water flowing up to his waist. For a moment he thought he would never get up again. His legs didn't work properly and his teeth were chattering. But then brave, witty Yoshi got him to his feet, with the help of Sword Maiden Precious Stone.

He knew he had friends. He knew he had their loyalty, and was loved.

'No, Man,' Mother Zandar told him. 'I did not say "give up", and I never will.'

Ozawa was dragging one leg, but did not flag.

'Almost there!' he told them. He was panting and exhausted but Man knew Ozawa would never give up. 'Almost! What's a half-mile more?'

For that, Man loved him.

'Yes, we're close!' said Precious Stone.

Blinking through the cold sleet, Man saw a tall waterwheel, one-third submerged and spinning madly. Four roads crossed here. He saw a great milestone, with city names and distances carved under the Eye of Buddha and the Cross.

There was London, there Moscova, there Johannesburg, and there Mumbai...

In the gloom ahead Man saw their broad path was now lined with shops and tea-houses and taverns. When he got closer, he saw they were all shuttered and dark – long since evacuated, he guessed.

He walked on, awkward but determined, leading his black stallion. Soon the water and mud was less deep, and the air less chill. Man took all that as a good sign.

'It is,' said Zandar, leaning down from her pony just as if he'd spoken aloud. 'This is where our protections begin.'

That was cheering to hear; and they all felt cheered. Man got on his horse again.

Beyond where the road finished was some tall structure, its pale shape hard to make out in the sleet-swept darkness.

Then he saw it was a gatehouse, guarding the way, with a flooded moat behind it and then faintly visible high ring-walls.

'The Waning is *here!* We have arrived!'

They were in a trap, true; but now he felt they might escape.

The Voice was working on something, Man saw from her movements. As she worked, some more of the darkness cleared. Perhaps she could not directly oppose *him*; but she had brought a little light.

Yoshi was gazing into the air. 'Look up, Man! The *size* of that! Surely it's enough to scare even *him!*'

Man stared wide-eyed at what was held high above the fortress on two giant pillars.

It was that huge crescent slice of yellow Moon which gave the psychic fortress its name. So close, its immensity was terrifying, and the sheer scale of it produced a powerful sense of wonder in Man. Within the ring-walls Man now glimpsed

Words of Fury: 435

strange towers, but high above all was that stone arc meant to represent the waning Moon – which *would* wax again.

Man knew he was seeing one of the miracles of this world. Of all the things he had seen in this land, only the two Welcomer statues at Jade were made with similar dimensions.

'I feel a trembling go up in the air!' The Voice from Afar turned to Mother Zandar. 'This must be where your wards of protection are anchored.'

'You are correct,' said Zandar, smiling.

The gatehouse had a lowered portcullis. Beyond, on the far side of the flooded moat, Man saw a grey square shape looming up.

Precious Stone pointed at it. 'Our inland-facing entrance: the famous Mountain Gate!'

Man remembered Yoshi's living map.

Faslane leaned on Man's thigh. 'It looks strong enough to withstand God Almighty! If we can only get within...'

They all marched on, at a quick easy pace now. Man's mood lifted even more.

Almost home!

As they came closer, Man could see the high ring-walls were painted. He saw the green crescents of Islam, the golden all-seeing Eye of Buddha, and the white crosses of Jesus Christ.

'The sleet is cold but harmless.' Zandar was trying to strike an optimistic note. 'Fortunate, as the rain before was acid.'

That was another piece of good news.

'Prophecy now becomes plain truth,' said Mother Zandar now. 'We have arrived with The One Who Will Change. We will be welcomed!'

But when they neared the gatehouse they had to stop, for lightning flared down. Man saw their dome had diverted it, but still they milled about helplessly as lightning struck again and again.

Over the ring-walls Man glimpsed a steeple and what looked like a mosque minaret. He also saw gold and silver flashes – spells, warding off *his* attacking power. But then snow swept in, and he lost the reins again and almost tumbled.

Fortunately Yoshi saw what was happening. 'Here, Man, I'll help you!'

Man was grateful, and leaned a little on Yoshi as his friend recovered the reins for him and handed them back.

Man touched his cheek, which now hurt badly. That was the

poison kiss from the Tears, one of the Lord of the North's strongest sworn servants.

Precious Stone pulled Man's head close so she could speak into his ear.

'Can you still ride? You look ill!'

'It doesn't matter if I can ride or not. There's no more road! – Why don't your friends raise the portcullis?'

'In a crisis like this the gatehouse should have a double Maiden guard, but I don't know where they are.'

Faslane glared at Zandar.

'Won't your people open up for us? Or are they *turned*? What is happening?'

Man saw no sign of life in the gatehouse. What if *he* had murdered everyone within? What then?

So near, Man thought, and yet so very far...

Here in the open it was still golden, a summery afternoon, but Lady Berenda stared ahead at the dark whirling storm which hid the immense fortress that was her destination. She was restored to the favor of the Lord of the North, and her pride puffed her up. She was again *his* beloved.

Only fools call pride a sin, she thought.

There were badly-formed ranks of black sashes, mercenaries, and *his* sworn followers behind her, but she ignored them. They would be for another battle, probably on another day.

'We are strong, aren't we?' asked Hagiwara, the black sash, hoping for her reassurance.

She gave him nothing.

Instead, she looked at the lightning playing about The Waning of the Moon, and the mushroom-cloud of black above it. Somewhere in there, and she could make a good guess where, she would find Man and Mother Zandar and the others.

'I feel Emmanuel; I can pursue him, and hurt him – like *this*.'

Man clapped a hand to his face, where he had felt another clawing pain. The Tears, no doubt. If she actually caught up with him, now that he was so weakened...

It really won't be good – and that's an understatement. We need help to enter this place we *have* to enter, but where is our help?

He looked hard at the lowered portcullis. It had metal bars thick as human thighs and it was clearly impassably strong. The gatehouse and its portcullis protected the drawbridge – of course it was raised – that led over the moat to the massive Mountain Gate itself.

You'd think they'd be glad to see us, Man told himself. That is, if any of them are alive... His mind produced a hideous picture: *him*, huge in his black armor, the only one left alive in the fortress, waiting for them.

That isn't impossible; in fact, that's how this might end...

'Where the hell is everybody?' said Yoshi, sounding furious. 'Where is our welcome?'

The gale picked up so that now it howled. Man shivered again and again as the sleet flailed him.

Then Zandar pointed. 'Look! I think we still hold The Waning!'

She actually sounded relieved. Man saw shadows at the tall arrow-slit gatehouse windows and also on the ring-wall battlements.

Sword Maidens – or enemies?

He and Precious Stone waved.

'They are Maidens!' she said at last.

On the ring-wall battlements and the gatehouse windows were Waning Sword Maidens, waving encouragement back through the hail.

'*Now* we have people in the gatehouse!' Zandar said.

She-captain Hanake spoke. 'I had feared the former crews were murdered.'

'Why should they be dead?' Ozawa asked. 'I presumed the gatehouse was safe behind the fortress wards.'

Zandar said, slowly, 'Magic is neither exact nor predictable.'

'But it *is* mighty,' said the Voice.

'It can be,' Zandar acknowledged.

The giant metal portcullis was still lowered, though, and beyond that the drawbridge over the moat was still raised. Everything was closed against them.

Yoshi said, 'Surely they'll open up now?'

Joah shook her head. 'Not if it's unsafe for The Waning.'

Yoshi flared up at her. 'But if we die outside, what sense does your Waning staying shut make?'

Maidens were at the gatehouse slit windows, while others worked capstans to raise the portcullis.

Man saw the portcullis at last begin to wind up, though very slowly.

'Well, the Maidens there want us inside.' Ozawa smiled, but it was a grim look he had. 'If this is our chance, let's take it.'

'Yes indeed!'

Man spread his shaking hands. In this fight he had already drawn more power than he could handle, and he suspected that excess was killing him. Time was his enemy now.

When lightning struck close by, his horse tossed its head. He quieted it as best he could and then dismounted awkwardly. A Sword Maiden took the reins for him.

The portcullis was still coming up.

Suddenly there was a flicker of masculine magic ahead. Now Man saw ice speckle the world. His breath turned to steam in the freezing air, and he shifted his feet in the calf-deep mud.

Old Rishiri growled, 'If this mud is turned to ice, we could all be held here in a man-trap till we are frozen to death.'

When Man sucked in a breath of air it was so cold it burned his lungs. Rishiri had a point.

Freeze you, Lord of the North, he said silently. We are *not* going to lose, even if many of us must die...

Zandar shouted encouragement. 'My Sword Maidens are opening the way! They, Man, will be first to greet you!'

It was as if *he* heard her; perhaps he did. Suddenly *his* lightning flared everywhere in the gatehouse. Man saw sparks in every room in the building. Windows blew out and he heard screaming within. Fire showed briefly.

Man could smell the aftermath, smell burnt wood and paper – and roasted flesh. There was a metallic clattering, and he saw the portcullis come down again to block the roadway.

Ozawa looked sick. 'Lord Emmanuel, what's happened?'

'What do you think?' Man didn't need second sight to know. '*He* fried them alive, and we are still trapped!'

They all milled about within their protection, helpless and harried.

'Is *he* winning?' Hagiwara asked Berenda, looking in the same place as her and gripping her shoulder tightly. He, too, had sensed the Lord of the North attacking.

'As Zandar and Emmanuel try to enter, our lord kills their followers, and soon he will kill them.'

'I would not want to be in that fight,' Hagiwara said

honestly. With his free hand he touched his steel breast-plate, heart high. 'One way or another there will be many dead.'

She scowled at his unmannerly fingers as they worm-writhed.

'You are correct. But we ourselves must now advance to The Waning of the Moon. Our enemies may die at our Lord's hand before the walls, but perhaps we can assist him. Then The Waning will be leaderless, with all hope gone.'

'We can go in on his behalf!'

Or *I* can go in, at least, thought Berenda. And if I do, I will enter for my own reasons.

Cold snow fell now, humping white over everything. Man's teeth chattered again and he felt *his* cold nip at his flesh.

The Lady Rishiri was grinning madly. There was snow on her shoulders. 'His trap is sprung!'

Yoshi sneered at her. 'Tell me something I don't know!'

She was cackling laughter. 'There are inches of snow coming! Fatal – or so *he* thinks!'

Suddenly Man was scared of her arrogant wild laughing and her mad eyes.

She's a bloodthirsty one, made for war... If she was a man, she'd be unstoppable, Man thought.

He was bluntly practical. 'We must get within, or we die!'

Ice gleamed everywhere now.

The Princess Anamizu had come up. She had snow on her but was trying to ignore it.

'I hope my friends back in Ezo are having more luck fighting *him*. At least there the Lord of the North is flesh and not untouchable magic.'

'It's lucky for us he *is* up there,' Rishiri said. 'He's spreading himself thin, the fool!'

A fist of power smashed down on their dome, driving it into the earth and stabbing pain into their ears.

'You call *this* "spreading himself thin", do you?' Zandar snapped, although Rishiri only sniffed.

'We can't move!' Faslane marveled. 'We're going to be held here, till...'

'Till we freeze or we're smashed flat,' Man finished for him. He turned to the women. 'Look, we have the Eye – '

Joah was small in stature but great in intensity.

'It's too late. You must see that! And afterwards *he* will

collect our power gems and use them all for *his* conquering!'

Man let words form on his tongue, though he did not speak aloud. *Afterwards means when we are all dead...* He saw the enemy's tactics clearly enough. The gatehouse portcullis would stay down. Then either their own protection would fail, or when the dome was eventually driven down upon them they would be crushed. The Eye and whatever Zandar was using would then be recovered from the pulped corpses – just as Joah had said.

So Man knew what he had to attempt. He knew, though he had not the faith. He turned to gaze at the pack-pony where the Eye was. The beast looked back with wary but trusting eyes.

The Eye... Man reached out for that ancient power.

Did *he* know what Man was trying? Maybe he did, because now another mighty fist of power crashed down on their protective bubble. Man saw the edge of their dome driven into the made-soft earth.

Their dome had held – this time. Next time or the time after that he knew it would disintegrate. Man swallowed.

'At least it's stopped snowing,' Faslane said. 'Maybe he really can't do too many things at once, eh?'

'No.' Joah spoke, miserably. 'I was right in what I suspected before. We were led here to be slaughtered!'

If there was a time to wake the Eye, this was it. Man knew a second use would kill him quickly; but what alternative was there? Burned people still screamed around him, and from the expressions of the others huddling here there was nothing good to hope for.

Man tried again.

'You in the Eye,' he began, sounding ridiculous even to himself.

'Nothing will happen from what *you* do, you young fool!' Ancient Rishiri addressed her contempt to him, before she turned to her rival. 'Zandar, the boy is ruined and useless! You've lost!'

In Man, the words echoed powerfully.

I *have* lost, yes, to the dark and the cold, lost to the deep mud here and the lightning overhead.

Yes, he said to himself, but this isn't all about me...

Man turned to Zandar and the women. 'Mother, and you, Joah, and you, Voice from Afar – yes, and *you*, Lady Rishiri and the Princess Anamizu – can't all of you combine and *force* your way into The Waning?'

Words of Fury:

Rishiri and the princess exchanged glances. They did not look positive, but they had not dismissed the idea.

Zandar responded directly. 'Man, you know how strong *he* is!'

He eyed the holy Mother coldly. Her failure here was big as his own.

Now purple-white lightning struck just to this side of the gatehouse. That magic-made lightning did not fade. Instead, Man saw it spread out left and right. Now a wall of electricity made a deadly, sizzling barrier in front of them.

Man bit his lip. 'The lightning, made by *him, will* keep us out!'

His heart was hammering. Unless those inside could mount a rescue, he and the others could only linger till they expired.

Then Man felt danger coming. 'Watch out!'

Another lightning-bolt struck beside them, then another and another, on and on.

A hundred lightning-bolts struck down simultaneously. Man felt the power like blows to his chest. People fell down from the sheer shock. A couple did not get up again.

A few of the most frightened had moaned out loud and Man wondered if he had. Fear made them all crush together so tightly now that one serious blow from above could kill them all. Their dome of protection was flickering and was almost useless, or so it seemed to Man. He wanted to step in with his own powerful magic; but what the Eye had given to him, the Eye had afterwards drained away. It had left him even weaker than before.

I couldn't fight a kitten and win...

Then Man saw what the new lightning had done.

'I don't believe it!' He wiped stinging sleet from his face, the last residue of the acid rain. 'That's impossible!'

'It's only impossible by logic,' Princess Anamizu said. She too was on foot now and thick with mud up to her waist, with snow on her hair and shoulders. She shivered violently. 'It's not impossible by magic.'

The lightning had made two giant apes out of roaring light. They now stood before the lowered portcullis, almost as big as the gatehouse. They snarled, showing clawed paws big as a man, impossible to pass.

Lady Rishiri stood with the princess in the filthy mud. Her face was a child's picture of fury. Then she turned to Zandar.

Words of Fury:

'The way must be cleared, you stupid bitch!'

Zandar flinched, but it was obvious to Man why she didn't move. For *his* wall of lightning burned, and that and the apes made an impassable barrier between them and the gatehouse.

Nevertheless, Rishiri sent two samurai spearmen forward.

'That won't work,' Man said. He was angry at this waste of lives, but not brave enough to act.

Each ape approached a spearman, and channeled electricity into their bodies.

The two men stood there screaming as they were electrocuted, their flesh first steaming and then burning till it charred. Finally two blackened skeletons fell to the mud.

It was much like what had happened when the Empire of Albion's steamship had been driven from Jade; but this time Man had no access to power gems for a fight-back. He clasped his hands together. He *had* wanted to fight, but he knew now he would be defeated – and after he died they would still be locked out of The Waning of the Moon.

Zandar eyed Man. Her expression was tragic.

'My Emmanuel! You were supposed to change everything!'

'Instead,' sneered Rishiri, 'you've changed nothing at all, you useless clod of masculinity!'

Though he was shivering, Man smiled politely. 'I love you, too.'

Words of Fury:

Chapter Forty-Three: *Stars and Galaxies*

The Cube Castle in Jade had come alive again, and its Steel Angels regularly flew in and out. Irian Dall considered that new traffic as he walked the city's waterfront in the dusk. Before, there might have been five or six exits and entrances in a week. Now there was ten times that every day. And the mechanical drones flew continuously. Two always circled high in the air to watch the city, which he found ominous.

The Man in the Castle – the ancient *thing* in the Castle – is finally taking a hand. The castle and its Angels want to destroy all progress and stop change, thought Dall. That means Emmanuel is in danger, and every Futurist including me.

Dall walked on, alert, hearing water lap the quayside stones. He was still thinking over his meeting with Lord Okada, the deposed ruler of the city.

How can I help Okada? I need him as a living, free ally, Dall thought now, for if Oatha does win control here, my side goes down. Can I get Okada out of his prison? Can I possibly get enough armed men to do that?

Irian Dall really wanted to help. If Lord Okada was rescued, he could bring over his loyal regiments, and then there would be a chance for a freedom-saving uprising.

Dall stopped to listen to two street musicians. A young man from Eire played a kora, the strings making sparkling sounds. The bright-eyed young African squatting opposite him played wailing Eirish pipes in counterpoint.

It was a brave, wild tune. Dall didn't want it to end; nor did the small audience. They were all cheering what might soon end, dropping coins into the cap left for their offerings.

When it did end, Dall went over to the musicians, tossed them silver.

'You know Oatha's order?'

'Aye,' said the Eirish boy.

'From midnight, you must stop playing "foreigners' music".'

'He calls our tunes pollution!' the African said.

'So he does, so he does, and we know that man's penalty,' the kora-player announced.

'Amputation,' said his friend, shuddering.

Then the two rose, smashed their instruments right here, and tossed the wreckage into the water. They walked away arm in arm, singing defiantly.

Amputation, just for playing foreign music!
Irian Dall was a strong man, but he almost wept.

There was another blow from *him*. The impact was so loud Man covered his ears, and so did others. The blow had brought the roof feet lower.

Joah was quite right. It is too late. ...Unless we can make a deal with *him*, Man thought. What if I offer the Lord of the North myself, or the Eye of Jade?

But, as Joah said, when we are dead *he* will get the Eye anyway, and also the power gems Zandar and the new women have brought. So why should he deal?

Lady Rishiri looked up, sneering even though the hammering on their protective dome had terrified everyone else.

'Well, *he* has us, good and proper!'

'We should have known!' said one of the Sword Maidens. 'He is just too strong! He made an idol of himself, to be worshipped!'

Rishiri turned, glared. 'So?'

'Lady, he made a self-image out of ice *half a mile high!*'

Rishiri fluttered a disdainful hand. 'Men always boast about their size.'

Man put both hands to his head. Where was the power of the Eye? He tried to reach through the darkness for it; but there was no contact.

Somehow Rishiri sensed what he was doing.

'That will do you no good, boy,' she rasped. 'You have that woman's death-kiss at work in you. Both Book and Eye are beyond you now.'

Man stared hopelessly at the burned-out gatehouse and the lowered portcullis.

This secret cellar was a House of Progress, kept in gloom to prevent the worshippers easily recognizing one another, and with a device to distort with echoes whatever was spoken. Dall had checked everything before beginning tonight's service. Futurists were of necessity bold; but those who lived were also cautious.

Though caution was not the note sounded now, among the Futurists Dall had selected.

'Oatha wipes out our culture, first our music!'

'And our businesses! "Registration" of aliens and their

commerce, fines and arrests!'

Another voice snapped, 'We know what he plans!'

'He and the patriotic societies boast about our extermination.'

'Then we must resist; we must.'

Dall liked the attitude, though perhaps not the lack of caution.

'We all want progress here, but can we really fight Oatha's black sashes, and the Angels?' Dall asked them, soft-spoken in the gloom. 'We have the right ideas, but ideas do not usually win battles.'

'Better to die on your feet than on your knees!'

'We would not be alone,' another voice insisted. 'Okada's men are no lovers of the black sashes, this is known!'

'This is known!' said another, perhaps a young girl.

An older man with a thick E'ropan accent spoke next: 'We have to have revolution to protect ourselves.'

'Better to die on your feet,' said the insistent voice from before, 'than on your knees.'

Revolution, Dall thought. He savored the word. He had been contemplating the rescue of Okada. If he could do that, no doubt Lord Okada could bring over thousands of samurai; then Oatha would really be in a fight.

Yes, with Okada a free man, the purity police would lose – if it wasn't for those Steel Angels!

Irian Dall began the ceremony, which he would lead. There was praise for the future; there was hope for the future. Led by Dall they all chanted out loud. 'Embrace the new and strange! Embrace the stranger here!'

Each person present hugged whoever stood by them. It was a symbolic embrace of real, warm life in this dark place and time.

Dall gave faith to his people by showing them wonders, in a wall which had turned into a 3D screen. He showed people alternate futures and let them glimpse the worlds round the corner from this one.

In one sequence there had been hunch-backed vehicles with glaring headlights, flitting at mad speeds along strangely constructed roads at night.

There had been great fleets of flying machines.

There had been a lit-up ship large as a city, sailing an ocean that was Earth's blue.

Words of Fury:

Lastly, a spherical ship blasted off from an ocean, heading for the stars.

'This is our past and our future, if we earn it! This is science, this is progress! In our future there will be no more hunger,' he said, beginning the creed.

'Amen!'

'In our future there will be education, travel, and peace for all!'

'Amen!'

'There will be hope eternal!'

'Amen!'

That said, Dall let silence descend. Finally he spoke. 'Now, let me explain to you the truth about our battle. There is a war between light and dark, heat and cold, life and the opposite of life. This is true above, and also here below.

'In this universe is dark matter, which holds our cosmos together. This means that structure is possible, life is possible, and because the universe will hold together forever there will always be a future and time will never end; ultimately, therefore, there will be no death.'

'There is no death!' someone echoed.

'Life and universal progress are the positives we worship.

'Now, humanity's great enemy the Lord of the North is the local face of another principle of this universe, the dark energy that drives everything apart, causes structure to turn into cold chaos, and entropy to triumph as things fail and fall apart.

'Now, *he* says that his victory is inevitable; he says that the final truth is cold and the dark, dark absence of light and life – he says that always – but *I* say that he lies...

'Look now!' Dall said triumphantly, for he had lived what he spoke of. 'Look at the light, and have faith! Look!'

At Dall's gesture, the blank wall became a screen again. In it, the gates of the universe opened.

There were giant red stars, emerald-green stars, blue stars. There was the Milky Way, a spiral of light made from billions of stars. Then there was a sombrero galaxy twenty-eight million light-years from Earth, with its glaring white heart circled by incredible dust-rings. There were other pictures now, overwhelming in scale: colliding galaxies, glowing orange, violet and purple, galaxies like flowers, and galaxies erupting energies on a scale inconceivable to humans.

'If we survive, that will be our future, and it *is* worth fighting

Words of Fury: 447

for! Look at those stars and galaxies, and worship! For one day the stars will be ours!'

Words of Fury:

Chapter Forty-Four: *The Connection is Live*

When the Lord of the North's next blow came, the dome shuddered even lower. Crouching, Man took Joah into his arms. 'Lady!'

She stroked his cheek, crying abundant tears. 'Oh, how we tried, Emmanuel.' She rubbed a hand under her running nose. 'What a way to die... I must look terrible.'

'No. You look wonderful – and whatever has happened before, wonderful is what you *are*.'

He continued to hold her, though she was soaked through and muddy and so was he. At least the snow had stopped and the air had turned a trifle warmer. Finally her arms came around him.

Yoshi was huddled up and shivering. He looked over at Man for something positive. 'Are you praying, my Man?'

'In my own fashion!'

'What do we do now? – We must do *something* before we freeze to death!'

'My father broke into many fortresses! The question is, what would *he* do?'

'Tell me!'

Man wanted to come out with something bold; but no ideas occurred. He touched his forehead, blinking and shivering. Ice had covered over the moat and the ring-walls, and more snow fell.

Is this the way we all die – murdered by *his* power to freeze?

Man had no plan at all. Above, he saw a giant, ghostly arm – with *his* big steel-gauntleted fist on the end of it. The arm started to go up again. When it came down Man knew their dome of protective magic would be smashed.

'Another blow and we will be paste.'

'That portcullis has to be raised!' said Yoshi angrily, and then looked round. 'Can't we get somebody into the gatehouse?'

Heads turned and questions were shouted, but nobody volunteered except for one.

'I will go!'

Then Lady Rishiri twisted one wrist, and the protective dome tilted way over. That made a gap, which allowed an athletic Sword Maiden to run out.

It was Precious Stone. Man would have shouted at her, told her to return; but he knew she was as brave as himself, or braver.

She was too clever to take on the apes. Instead she used her wonderful agility to dodge between them, and when she reached the fence of electricity she crawled under it through a flooded ditch. She sprang up, looking back for a moment. Then she put a hand on the portcullis bars but immediately pulled it back.

'The metal is still hot!' She turned her head to see Man one last time. 'That must be from all the energy that ran through it!'

But then she bravely swarmed up the portcullis right to the top. She stayed there looking in, and then vanished inside.

'What can one person do, however brave?'

Man turned to Ozawa and answered in one word: 'Try.'

But then he saw Ozawa draw his own long sword and look at the gatehouse.

'Don't!' Man said to him at once.

He stepped forward to Ozawa, waving his arms to stop him.

'We must try something!' Ozawa cried.

'Well don't try dying, especially for no good reason!'

When his Maiden came to a smashed window, Man saw how very wide Precious Stone's dark eyes were. She cupped her hands around her mouth. 'They're all dead, inside. All of them are dead!'

'And soon we join them,' Rishiri snapped, 'because of you, Zandar!'

Man looked over, to see Lady Rishiri and Zandar duel with glares. There would be no help from them.

Precious Stone told them, 'The portcullis chains are all melted together, and the capstans ruined!'

That meant the portcullis would stay down.

Man shifted his feet. What could he do? Not enough. Not nearly enough.

'Man!' The Voice from Afar looked into his eyes. 'I feel *him* above us, and he's going to strike again!'

And when he does...

Man knew there was only one thing to try, though it had failed before, and even if it succeeded now would make him die. But others had already sacrificed themselves, so Man needed to find equivalent courage.

When Man's mind reached for the Eye there was no obstacle this time. He immediately touched it. He let the warm trickle of power from the Eye grow into a torrent, which soon filled him to the brim. His vision sharpened, and now he could hear every small sound within the dome of power and outside. But there was tension in his flexing body, and his chest was heaving for air.

Man knew the women here could sense the power rippling out from him, for they stepped back. Now he was strong again, they were all afraid.

When he looked up he saw the giant fist was almost ready to smash down.

I can't stop *him!* If I let serious power flow through me, I will *die*... And yet if I don't, it will be the end for all of us.

He felt so lonely, but he would not be a deserter from this war. Though the cost might be his life, he had power and renewed faith: faith enough to move mountains!

'Let me try something.'

He took his horse's bridle and led it through their magical protection as if it was made from spider webs. Now *his* glowing electric barrier was ahead, along with the two luminous apes.

'No!' Zandar was shrieking behind him. 'Come back! You'll die!'

Yes, I will, Man thought. It was not a thought that shocked him or even made him sad. I *will* die, unless...

Unless I am helped.

The apes, thirty feet high, loped towards him.

He did not run. He felt more warm power pour into him from the Eye and he knew he was literally glowing. He raised both his left arm and his right arm. Immediately the two giant apes stopped as if they had collided with a wall. They roared and gibbered, held at bay.

Lady Joah shouted, 'Make them touch – positive to negative!'

It sounded like good advice. Man gestured with his fingertips. Though they howled in protest, the apes each reached out one long arm towards one another.

When he forced their lightning-made paws to touch, the short circuit made an explosion of blue light.

When Man could see again, the wall of lightning was still there but the giant killer apes had gone. Touching the barrier would be death; but perhaps there might be a miracle.

He made a two-handed pushing-forward gesture.

In the middle of the portcullis metal bars were blasted clean away, while other bars were bent back. There was space to ride through three abreast.

Was that his own power working now, or was it the Eye's?

Words of Fury:

And did it matter?

Maybe not. It was as his father often said: winning is *everything*.

Now Man looked up into the sky and glared at the Lord of the North's ghostly fist. There was power even in Man's look. The fist seemed to fade away...

Mother Zandar, face full of expectation, turned to Man. 'There's still the lightning ahead of you, and the moat to cross!'

That was true, so now Man growled deep in his throat and sent his raw magical force to clear a path through their enemy's high voltage. His power lifted the lightning to just above head-high and held it there. Man kept the connection to the Eye, though suddenly he felt loose-limbed, dizzy and strange. He could barely scramble back onto his horse, but he did, and then he slowly rode forward.

Now I live, or I die!

As Man and his horse approached the shimmering barrier ahead he raised both hands, palms up. Though he had to push on against increasing resistance, he felt the lightning respond, sizzling furiously. He made the barrier shift upwards, till it was just clear of his head.

At once Mother Zandar shouted, 'Move, everyone! Move on!'

She came up to Man to ride alongside him, and then he and Zandar went forward together. He kept his head lowered to duck the lightning, and then he and the holy Mother were in the wreckage under the gatehouse. Precious Stone dropped down from a murder-hole and ran beside Man. He wanted to smile at her, but there was only determination in him now.

Ahead was the wide moat's ten yards of water, and the steep glacis slope that led up to the ring-walls and the Mountain Gate.

Zandar put a hand on his biceps and then pointed ahead. 'The drawbridge is still raised!'

He saw easily through the stone and metal of the gate, saw the mechanisms within. At once Man realized what to do. He waved two flat hands and sent his power into the great gate. From inside there came a rapid clanking, and then the drawbridge came down.

Behind them there was cheering.

In the great gate was another metal portcullis, this one four times the height of a man. Behind the portcullis were giant metal-braced wooden doors. They had protective hex signs painted on them, in clashing shades of white, blue and purple that hurt his eyes. Only if the portcullis could be raised and the gates opened would they finally reach sanctuary.

He heard Zandar speak, and he turned to her. 'You're telling them to raise the portcullis?'

She smiled briefly, suddenly looking much younger.

'I wasn't so direct. I was praying to Our Lady. "Make Him take up the weary, O blessed lady, and establish them safe in His stronghold. Amen!"'

'Amen to that,' he responded. He was indeed weary. So were they all. And yet they all deserved to be safe in the stronghold ahead.

She threw her head back. 'Raise the portcullis!'

Sword Maidens began to work twin capstans; the metal barrier was slowly hauled up.

'Let me!'

Man sent his power into the mechanisms, and worked also on the huge doors. Soon the portcullis was raised and safely pegged, and the giant hexed doors had also parted.

The Mountain Gate was open at last.

'Sanctuary!' He felt exhilarated. 'We're in!'

Zandar turned to Man, overjoyed. 'You have opened the way!'

Yes; I finally have.

He smiled at Mother Zandar, bowing in the saddle. She bowed back, and gestured for Man to go first.

Of course, he would not go before her. They rode towards the Mountain Gate together. Man felt the ancient wards of The Waning, made by men and women working together all those centuries ago, open up for him. Riding over the drawbridge, he heard their horse-hooves hammer the planks.

The others followed.

Just within the fortress was a giant tori gate with rope on it. Zandar took him through that, too. He still felt ill underneath the exhilaration, but he was determined. There was another huge blow from the Lord of the North then. The whole fortress-monastery quivered, but Man felt sure it was unharmed.

'You can do nothing, now, enemy!' That taunt was from the Voice. 'You have missed your chance!'

He has, Man thought. He really has!

Man felt he was at last in safe hands. They were home.

There was a road ahead which tall, plain buildings lined. Everywhere Man saw people, many holding torches. All were

Words of Fury:

silently staring.

Mother Zandar took his arm.

'We have fulfilled Prophecy, saved ourselves and the world. Savor this, my Emmanuel.'

Man suddenly felt uncomfortable. It was as if Zandar's helpful grip was meant to make him a prisoner.

And why are they all looking at *me*? Do they expect some magical stunt? Do they want me to change the world in front of them? How can I?

He wondered if this was modesty – or cowardice. He pulled his arm from Zandar and moved away from her, but for some reason he couldn't make himself go ahead of her.

'Be welcome here, prophesied one!' someone in the crowd called.

He heard others start to laugh and celebrate, and though he was dying he wanted to join in. He became aware of Yoshi riding close, with one deliberate hand on the bridle of Man's horse.

'I don't need your help!'

'I think you do, my friend,' Yoshi told him. He smiled hugely at the people who lined the roadway, but the face he turned to Man showed concern. 'You're swaying in the saddle, though usually you're a masterful rider, and one side of your face is really swollen now – where that sexy bitch kissed you!'

Man said nothing, only shivered because he was cold. Then he was pouring with sweat because he had a fever.

This isn't good at all; I'm very ill. Still, the healing here is the best in the realm.

He waved, and the watchers waved back.

Somehow that connection with her *is still here...*

'I gave him my kiss, and the connection is live,' Lady Berenda said under her breath. She knew if she was closer she could physically follow him in. 'The connection *is live!*'

With her mind, she followed Man into sanctuary. Her mind roamed around him, and then around that ancient place. The fortress was truly mighty. She sensed it housed thousands of souls and much magic.

Though Emmanuel had for now escaped the Lord of the North's justice, Berenda still felt for him and she secretly rejoiced in his escape. She had helped him, she had learned a little more about being good, and she regretted nothing.

Even though Man must now die...

Man rode on into an open space, and stopped. It was warm and summery. In The Waning it had probably never been cold. His face throbbed, though; and it was difficult to breathe.

He was distantly aware of people coming up to him. They were almost all women. A few of them he thought he knew, though he could not quite place them. He saw some were in sandals and white robes like Mother Zandar, with the crescent Moon in silver and the scarlet cross on their backs. Others were proud Sword Maidens wearing blood-red kimonos and two swords.

'The One Who Will Change! The One Who Will Change!'

He was pointed at and touched, and sometimes had his hands kissed.

A tall woman in white came up. Her expression was an incredible mix of relief, anxiety, and joy.

'Sister Daisen!' said Zandar. 'I have returned, and now I present our friends!' She turned her blindfolded face around. 'Without dear Daisen this would never have worked!'

Smiling, and now also crying, this woman bowed very low to Mother Zandar.

'Welcome back, Mother. And welcome to you, Lady Joah, and Lady Rishiri, and Princess Anamizu.'

The princess spoke, with a ritual sound to her words. 'This is the waning of the moon, but it will wax again! I am a woman of power, and I crave sanctuary!'

'This is a place of safety for all,' Daisen said, following the rite, 'and you have asked for sanctuary, and it will be granted. Whatever has happened before, from now on everything can be different!'

There was a great cheer at that, which continued for half a minute.

Lady Rishiri's thin lips twitched. 'This is a sour and impersonal welcome!'

Mother Zandar eyed her, then looked away to Man. 'Emmanuel, ride on with me.'

She began to canter forward. He came with her.

Now Sword Maidens stood on both sides of the road, hundreds of them, some holding flaring torches. Many raised clenched fists as they saw him. Their faces were ecstatic.

Mother Zandar called out: 'Behold! This is the man!'

The crowd shouted in triumph.

Words of Fury: 455

Man also gave a clenched-fist salute and called back in gratitude, 'The Waning of the Moon! Life for us all! And darkness eternal for *him*!'

Then a thunder of drumming began; taiko drums in massed ranks. Man recognized a martial rhythm and began to move with the beat. It was deafening, and the cheering grew till it was almost as loud as the drum-rolls.

We have won, and now perhaps I can let go of life, and move on...

He wanted to let go.

As he rode forward, Mother Zandar fell back. There was a clear space around Man now. A pure white light seemed to shine above his head, brighter and brighter. The light circled him, and showed new people appearing one by one.

Not exactly new, though. First came some samurai of Ozawa's he hardly knew, and then One Arm from back in Jade with his arm around a scared-looking boy.

Man saw now they were the dead; the people who had died to get him here.

The dead were mostly smiling, and why not? Man supposed they were all pleased to know for certain there was an afterlife. That bear of a man Ugaki looked overjoyed as he marched along, swinging his thick arms and sometimes waving at the cheering crowd. Keli came walking behind him, her face dazed with happiness. Sanada walked there, too, waving once at Man. He was healed of all wounds, and his face was full of pride.

Man heard a soft voice. Recognizing it, he immediately turned.

Brave Sweet Snake was there, arm in arm with the other Sword Maiden, Lilac, who had also been martyred.

'Emmanuel!' Now Sweet Snake had his attention, she blew him a kiss. Both the dead women were smiling. 'Now you are here it was worth it, all! – And perhaps we will meet in the life after this, and there embrace!'

Man raised his hand in salute. He realized he was crying. 'I hope we do!'

A crowd of Sword Maidens came next. Man presumed they had been killed at Miracle Island or in the gatehouse. They waved excitedly.

The last person to appear was Yonai. He did not look pleased; only shocked. When he turned to look at Man his expression was frightened, but it was also a begging for forgiveness.

Man held Yonai's gaze. It was impossible to forgive, even if he wanted to. Yonai had cut Joah; he had almost handed them all over to the Lord of the North.

Both things were unforgivable.

Yonai continued to stare a desperate plea as he walked with Man towards the one destination that all humans share.

Finally, Man raised his hand in a brief salute – not forgiveness exactly, but acceptance, and a moving on. At this sign Yonai too began weeping, and then he bowed very low. Man saw him vanish first. Then, one by one, all the dead went away.

Sweet Snake was last to go, looking from Man to her twin sister and then back again. There was love in her eyes.

'Stay with my sister, my Precious Stone! Love her, as she loves you! Do you promise, Man?'

'I will never stop loving her and you, I will never forget you all, and I will *never* surrender!'

With a little wave, Sweet Snake too went into the shadows.

Had that really been people from the afterlife, or some waking dream? Man didn't know, but he was incredibly moved.

His procession went forward again. Everyone was cheering and flowers were thrown. Man saw many buildings, some close by and others looming up in the distance. One building was a many-sided giant pyramid of colored glass, lit-up from the inside. There also seemed to be a church steeple and a mosque tower, close together.

'Look!' Faslane said in awe. 'It's as if different ages have come together.'

Yoshi was also looking around. 'Maybe they have.'

'I've seen nothing like this in Albion,' said the pilot.

Man heard Yoshi say lightly, 'We're not in Albion now, my friend.'

With the last of his strength, still wondering where the dead had gone to, Man went riding on with his friends.

Words of Fury:

Chapter Forty-Five: *You Have No Dominion*

Through Man's eyes, Berenda was seeing wonders. Though The Waning of the Moon was a working power centre, some of it was beautiful, and much was toweringly impressive. She saw actual towers. One was a lit-up glass construction, one was a steeple, another was a mosque tower, and she saw other things harder to describe. Incredible buildings had been brought from all over the world – including a parish church that had a connection to some place called 'Stratford-upon-Avon'.

There was nothing ugly here; and almost everything in this place was noble.

Yes, I am *truly* impressed. It is uplifting merely to be here. This place could transform anyone for the better.

As Man rode forward, she could see hundreds applaud him. Many of them threw flowers. She sensed power almost everywhere here, mainly female but not entirely. There were hidden 'gates' that might be used to travel to other worlds, or possibly even other times.

Hagiwara tugged at Berenda's shoulder and that broke her concentration. She looked over at her co-leader. Now she was no longer able to see through Man's eyes she was furious with Hagiwara and was about to tell him so, but then thought better of it.

Behind them both, the new arrivals had formed up in the moonlight. Their party was mainly black sashes with out-and-out mercenaries, and many hundreds strong.

'When our master speaks again, Lady Berenda, I will propose an early attack. We will have thousands of allies in place before dawn, and they have only a few hundred Sword Maidens and samurai survivors to oppose us.'

Hagiwara had a sneer as he tossed some looted sparkling stone in one hand. He was full of that piggish male self-satisfaction. She disliked almost everything about her escort, but she gave him a cold smile that was meant to be disarming.

'You presume much.'

Hagiwara shrugged. He had resumed his arrogant bearing; he really imagined he was again Lord General-to-be.

'I mean no disrespect to you, lady. I know you have regained your place close to *him*. But I have fought in battles before, some involving magic, and because of that I hope to be appointed to mastery here.'

Excluded, she stared at the lit-up Waning from the outside. There were those fantastic towers above the painted ring-walls. In spite of all the danger there were happy people within.

She felt a strange mash-up of emotions – distaste, anger, and also longing.

'If only I was within, *he* would not need your man's tricks and your simple-minded brutality.'

Hagiwara's lip curled. 'Lady, you are *not* within, and those ring-walls now hold Zandar, Rishiri, the princess Anamizu – and The One Who Will Change. They will not go down easily. And even you admit the wards around those walls are powerful.'

'I know they are, better than you. You have a pebble's weight of power, while mine outweighs a mountain.'

Hagiwara just shrugged again, and that annoyed her even more than before.

'Lady, we both serve *him* in our different ways. When *he* comes here tonight I am sure it won't be a discussion, it will be orders.'

Then fire flowed up and down Berenda's spine. She flung back her head, opened her mouth, and began moaning.

When the Lord of the North spoke in her head he went straight to the point. 'MY BERENDA, IT SEEMS THERE HAS BEEN WEAKNESS AND TREACHERY, SO MY ENEMIES MADE IT TO SANCTUARY.'

'I will help bring them down, lord!'

'I HAVE THE POWER, BUT THE ENEMY HAS POWER TOO, AND TONIGHT THERE WILL BE A BATTLE.'

'Master, please!' She felt an insane eagerness to submit, and wondered if that emotion would last. 'There must be ways I can help you!'

'THERE WILL BE, BUT FOR NOW STAND BACK.'

Then *he* went, hurriedly, with no further explanation.

Puzzled, Berenda looked over at Hagiwara, who had always been jealous of this intimate, direct communication between her and their master.

'What did you pick up from me and *him?*'

He gave that slick smile. 'I think we have been ordered to be patient?'

'We have. For now, our master does not want us in the fight.'

'Then we wait.'

Hagiwara tossed up the precious stone again, and she was so

Words of Fury:

annoyed by his lack of deference that she used a flick of her power to snatch the stone. She brought it to the palm of her hand, and when it was there she examined the gem carefully.

'It is a power gem of sorts, though almost insignificant.'

'I took that from Nagaoka, who took it from one of the Maidens he interrogated.' Hagiwara was annoyed. 'By right of conquest, it is *my* souvenir!'

She touched her stomach; the ruby that *he* had made her swallow was still there. She still felt angry over that disgrace.

'You won't mind if I keep it, lady? It will bring back happy memories.'

She sneered at this presumptuous man, and slipped the stone into the small pocket sewn below her breasts.

'It's best if it stays with me. It may have a power which I can use.'

Hagiwara lounged back, spread his hands.

'All things come to those who wait, they say. I won't argue, this time.'

That was close to open defiance; though not close enough for Berenda to become furious.

Instead, she gave what was meant to be a sweet and encouraging smile. 'When we take The Waning, there will be fortunes to loot, and many women for you to exercise yourself upon.'

Hagiwara swayed even further away from the campfire's flickering light. 'Unless there is no Waning left to occupy. Don't you feel how the powers contend?' He turned his head, for light had exploded within the Waning. 'If more power comes down our master will level the place!'

She saw fire pour down upon that nest of enemies and heard the roaring, as of a great furnace.

Perhaps this was when The Waning of the Moon would be destroyed.

Man didn't feel like a winner now, still less like anybody's savior. He felt hot and feverish, and he was so dizzy he saw the ground dip up and down.

Nobody showed they were aware of what he was going through. They thought he was a hero; but Man knew he was only a man who had suffered, and would suffer more.

Now he saw Mother Zandar give a sunny smile, and extend her hand. 'Emmanuel?'

Her hand was surprisingly soft and small when she took his. Then she raised his right hand.

Immediately there was shouting from the folk here. 'Freedom and change! Freedom and change!'

Those words had been important once; but Man had forgotten their meaning.

When Man got off his horse all his movements were awkward and he felt sick. His manners stayed Japanese, though. He bowed low to the holy Mother, and then thanked the Sword Maidens who led away his horse.

But Lady Rishiri made a great complaining fuss.

'Don't try to stampede me, "Mother", or give me orders! We have to talk.'

'Do we?' Zandar's expression turned grim as she stared at the great lady from Kyoto. There's trouble between those two, Man thought. 'I suppose we do. But not here and not now!'

Rishiri bared what remained of her teeth.

Man swayed on his feet. He was ashamed of his weakness.

Precious Stone supported him. 'You're ill! Was that from *her?*'

He spoke through gritted teeth. 'Yes, "the Tears".'

Faslane, Joah and the Voice had also come protectively close. Man looked round, blinked. Was his illness so obvious?

He wondered what to do. There was probably something in the Prophecies about how to act; but now he had no desires left, no intentions, no plans. He felt like a docile lamb being led to slaughter.

Zandar said, 'Emmanuel? Your men must give up their weapons, and go to our male barracks. That is our rule.'

That was so briskly spoken it was annoying. But before Man could respond, Yoshi asked her, 'Our men will be fed there, and have their wounds treated?'

'Yes; they, and you, will have the full hospitality of The Waning. We appreciate you have been loyal to The One Who Will Change. You officers can stay with us, for now.'

A senior Sword Maiden and a dozen of her women came to escort the surviving samurai away. Man saw how exhausted they all looked, and even after magical healing many showed wounds. And there were so few of them…

In Albion style, Man shook their hands and thanked everyone – those who had survived, that is. Then, as well as Joah and the Voice from Afar, he was left with Yoshi, Ozawa, and

Words of Fury: **461**

Faslane.
 Now two other Sword Maidens opened double doors in the wall ahead. This revealed a shadowy, more private courtyard, with niched wall-lanterns.
 When Man saw the bare cobblestones ahead, he suddenly felt sick to his stomach.
  It could be the floor of a slaughterhouse. Is it here that I die?
  Zandar waved Man and his friends forward.
 'Please go on, while I make arrangements for the Lady Rishiri here and Princess Anamizu, and also you two girls from Jade.'
 'I cannot leave Emmanuel,' said Joah.
 'Nor I!' said the Voice, hotly. 'You're powerful, Mother, and we love you – but I loved him first!'
 'Do what this Lady says,' Man told them dazedly, though he was touched by their loyalty. 'I see sincerity and goodness in her – as well as other things.'
 Mother Zandar frowned, but now there was another question he wanted answered.
 'What will happen to us?'
 'Emmanuel, we will try to make you comfortable, and also Lord Yoshi, and Ozawa-san, and this gentleman Master Faslane. I will send serving-women and healers to attend you.' She pointed at Yoshi. 'You had healing, but you still bleed. We can do more.'
 Lady Joah answered for them all. 'Thank you for everything, holy Mother!'
 The men all bowed to Mother Zandar, then followed Man. From the courtyard walls lanterns flickered light. There was the sound of tinkling water. The fountain gave the air a fresh watery smell. Flowering plants climbed the walls, their scents thick and sensual in the night. Man was almost certain *his* hand had never polluted anything here.
 Zandar replied to the comment Man had not made aloud.
 'You are right. *He* cannot enter; we are warded.'
 Man's voice was eager. 'You mean we are safe?'
 'No, only that we have protection.'
 Then a great light came on in the sky. Man gasped. All the stone arc of the waning Moon above was lit-up yellow now.
 'Our symbol,' Zandar said. 'Now *his* storm is gone, our lunar light will show *him* and all his followers we are here and not afraid!'

Man saw there was another part of this Moon, a dark part only faintly visible and not quite solid. The whole made up a sphere – a ghostly Moon that was a round planet, with dark seas, craters and rills, and uplands in lighter colors.

'Another world, as you told me!' he said to Joah, remembering talk of cities on the Moon.

Were those cities real in this age? Or had Joah the Futurist been talking of a future time, which the Moon here modeled? Or had she meant the past? Man tried to puzzle it all out, but his thinking was fuzzy.

As he walked on, Man stumbled. Pain clenched again in his stomach and stabbed his cheek. It would be very embarrassing to throw up now. He knew he desperately needed healing, but he feared his sickness was beyond that.

Perhaps Joah sensed his trouble. One of the Maidens had given her a pink-flaring torch, which spluttered in her hand. She came closer to him.

'Man? What's happening to you?'

He saw her face was pale and drawn, but very noble now. He thought of the Five Touches given to her by Oatha, and imagined how those cunning poisons would be working within her. He wanted to speak words of comfort, but he was so tired those words would not come. Instead, he spoke the truth.

'You mean what's happening to *us?* Lady, lady, we've made ourselves vulnerable, now when we *should* have been so strong!'

'Aren't we safe here?' Joah shivered, her eyes widening. 'Surely we are!'

'If *he* comes and strikes now,' Man said, remembering a phrase of his father's, 'I would be as much use as a chocolate sword...'

He felt wild, chaotic thoughts well up, he saw images from a hundred different futures, images which whirled around and fought one another without ever becoming clear. There were good times possible, and very bad times. Prophecy said he could help the good and fight the bad.

But that was wrong. Now he was dying; he had no future, and knew it.

'Heal me!' he mumbled to no one. 'I am desperate!'

He realized he was shamefully stained with sweat and blood. For a moment he put his aching head in his hands.

Two peacocks appeared, spreading their splendid tails in a miracle of color.

Words of Fury: 463

Joah raised her torch high to see the wonderful creatures more closely, and then turned to Man. When their eyes met she took another half-step towards him. Her face showed nothing but love.

'The peacocks show off for the hens!' said Man, laughing in madness.

Joah said nothing, then turned away and tossed the torch into a pool. It quenched with a hiss. Precious Stone simply stood by the pack-pony with the Eye. Her hands were on her hips, eyeing the lady from Jade. Joah scowled back at her.

A few of the other Sword Maidens here seemed to be hiding smiles, though Man had no idea why.

I can't read this world at all. I'm ill, ill...

When he tried to walk on he began staggering. His headache now felt like an ax-blow. He went over to where the Eye was, unfastened the ropes, lifted the casket – and almost dropped it. It had an immense weight and it seemed to shake in his arms as if it was alive. He was trembling as he lowered it to the flagstones.

Ozawa and Yoshi came closer. Their faces asked Man how he was.

'I don't know what's happening to me!'

He hardly knew who he was any longer; but he had been made weak. He would welcome the grave, and he knew the grave would welcome him.

Daisen put a hand on his forehead, pulled it off instantly.

'You're boiling hot!' She blinked, turned to Mother Zandar. 'He must be dying!'

Am I dying? Man wondered. Who am I? I know I am not what I thought I was...

He was a stranger to himself. Then he blinked at the people who seemed to be whirling around him in some fever madness. Who were they?

He shivered; and then he sensed something overhead turning very wrong. What was it? Man felt a strange, dark power begin to curl around him, licking away at him. It was like the Eye, in reverse. He was suddenly very afraid.

'Emmanuel, you need help!' said Joah.

'I look ill? Is that what you're saying?' He felt fury. 'I am ill, made ill, because *he*...' He shuddered. 'No, actually it was *her*, and I...'

Man could not begin to explain. He felt stupid and knew he

had sounded the same. He felt terrible pain from the Tears' bloody kiss, and he worried he was somehow helping her and her master just by being here.

There was a thought there, a very important thought, but it did not become clear.

'Man!' Joah took his hands in both of hers. 'I'm looking into you. You see something dreadful coming!'

Now he heard Daisen saying, 'In the Prophecies, I think in secret variant 7, it says that if The One has a fever when he arrives, the Lord of the North will enter through him and...'

She gasped, and stepped away from Man.

Man pulled back from Joah and screamed out his realization. 'All my journey here was *him*, tricks by *him*, to get me weakened and into The Waning. *I'm just a stepping-stone!*' Pain pounded in his head. 'My coming here with the Eye has made a hole in what shields us *and now he is coming!*'

'You're right!' Zandar said. She sounded truly appalled as she looked up at the night sky. It had cleared. Man saw it was full of shaking stars. She raised her hands. 'We must repair the weak point.'

'How? Some was done as men's work, from the long ago! How can unassisted females repair men's work?'

'Daisen, we must try! Help me, all of you! And you, Man!'

'There's no time left,' Man told them hoarsely.

Now he could see Rumoi, and how *he* was laughing, and making *his* connection to this place.

He saw a fever-Joah take a step towards him. 'We must – '

'No!' Suddenly Man was raving. 'All of you, back off!' He clenched his fists, wanting to shout out with the pain. He was right where the strongest enemy in the world was aiming; and he had never felt weaker. 'I'm the target, so when *he* comes I'll be the one hurt! I'm going to die, but I won't take you with me!' Man pushed the Voice away, and Joah, and then Precious Stone. He barely recognized them, but knew he was putting his friends into danger. 'For God's sake get away!'

Yoshi caught Joah, held her back. Man heard his voice come from a million miles away. 'Emmanuel knows something!'

'Yes!' Zandar said. 'Do as he says! Back to the walls!'

Man saw his friends backing away. Suddenly he was in the middle of the courtyard by himself. Everyone else was in the flickering lamplight by the walls. He saw now the walls had writing, which burst into color – written spells and hex signs.

Words of Fury:

Those spells were not protection for him; they were protection *from* him.

This had all been foreseen.

Man flung down his swords; they wouldn't help. Then he turned around in a complete circle. The power that was coming to destroy him was overwhelming, but he wasn't running.

He glared up into the quivering, star-speckled sky, then shook one fist.

'It's better to die on your feet than die on your knees, and I will!'

Yoshi stayed close to this Mother Zandar. He had hoped she had a better understanding of what was happening than he did, but what he was seeing now made his skin crawl.

'Man looks as if he has gone mad!'

Zandar spoke softly. 'That would be easier than what is to come.'

'You think he's going to die, don't you?'

'There is a passage in the Prophecies – '

'I *hate* that *bloody* book!'

Now Man rose up on his toes and stared about him. 'What place is this?' They saw he was whirling his arms in desperation. 'I feel power all around, and none for me!'

Yoshi demanded, 'Can't we help him?'

Zandar said one word: 'No.'

In tears, Man cried out, 'I am all alone!'

Mother Zandar made the sign of the cross.

Then Yoshi saw it begin.

Lightning struck down from the sky – searing and hot. It blasted Man for seconds.

Yoshi flinched in horror as Man's hair and clothes were burned away by the electric-blue lightning which wrapped itself around him. He heard Man scream continuously, even though the furnace-roar was deafening. The Voice fell onto her knees, hands over her ears. Yoshi saw that she was crying.

'Oh, be brave!' Precious Stone was wringing her hands. 'Be brave, my Emmanuel!'

Joah merely stared, her face stricken. 'Man is our sacrifice.'

And Yoshi saw he was.

At last, *his* lightning ceased.

Somehow Man, or what remained of him, was still standing – but Yoshi knew that nobody human could have survived.

Words of Fury:

Smoke was rising from the charred fragments of Man's clothes, and most of his hair was burned away. He was shaking. A few electric-blue flames still flickered over his body, and Yoshi saw how he blinked blinded eyes.

Intending to help, Yoshi took a desperate step forward, though he was no healer and this disaster was far beyond his power to correct. Maybe he could pull Man somewhere safer...

Man crashed down like a felled tree and did not move.

'Well, that's that,' Lady Rishiri said briskly. 'You've lost him, "Mother". The One Who Will Change is dead.'

Yoshi saw her glare at dead Man, then glare up at the sky, and lastly turn the same hard expression onto Zandar. As it all struck home, Yoshi felt his eyes widen. 'He must not be dead!' He turned to Zandar. 'We were told this place would be safe!'

Nobody replied to him, except the old woman from Kyoto.

'There is no safety. This is war!'

Smoke and steam still rose up from the corpse, and no one dared approach it.

So *he* has won, Yoshi thought dismally. We fought so hard to get here with Emmanuel and the Eye, and all for nothing!

'You are a failure, "Mother" Zandar!' said Lady Rishiri, spittle flying from her mouth. 'Give your command over to me, and I might salvage something!'

'It wasn't supposed to end like this!' Zandar cried.

That gave Yoshi no comfort. What now? With no assistance to expect, no doubt a siege of this place. Then death for all? He looked around. There *had* to be a way of escaping, of getting to some place where he might fight back.

Then Daisen pointed up. 'The wards above are broken open! Look!'

'A hole in the protection big enough to admit...' Zandar's color turned to ash. 'The repair failed. *This* is what was Prophesized!'

Yoshi realized what she meant, for in the cobbled courtyard a huge shape was slowly solidifying. For now, the moon shone through the dim colorless outline, but to Yoshi it looked much like a giant in black armor.

'Fetch every sister with significant power!' said Zandar. 'And Sandella, yes, bring her here to the fight!'

Zandar's voice was still strong, but the only reply was hopeless.

'There is no time for that.'

Words of Fury:

'I know, Daisen,' said Zandar, without even a ritual mention of hope. 'I know.'

There was a series of clicking sounds, much as if bones snapped into place. Then the black knight was three-dimensioned, and very, very real. He was thirty feet tall.

A long armored leg took a step; the helmeted head began to look round and down. Though his eyes were hidden by a face-guard, Yoshi saw a triumphant smile.

Yoshi suddenly realized what he was seeing.

'*He* is arrived! It's the Lord of the North...'

'Meet your new lord, come to complete his conquest!' Rishiri rasped to everyone. The worst had happened, and she almost sounded satisfied. 'The Waning of the Moon has fallen, and now we will *all* be slaves.'

Yoshi felt sick to his stomach. He didn't know whether to run or try to fight; probably either would be useless.

The giant settled himself comfortably on his feet, nodding to himself. There was great power there. Even Yoshi found himself wanting to kneel, and a couple of the others actually did.

Man's corpse was lying at the steel-shod feet of the Lord of the North – the first of many sacrifices.

The doomed whisper came from Mother Zandar. 'If Sandella could attune to the Diamond Heart and then...'

'It would do no good,' said Lady Rishiri. She sighed. 'Believe me, it would do no good at all.'

Then Yoshi saw Man's corpse twitch, and his eyes blink.

'Look!' Yoshi pointed. 'He moves!'

'This might be the pre-ordained black miracle!' Zandar was trembling. 'If the Lord of the North has made Man his own – '

Was this *his* dark magic, making use of a corpse? Yoshi remembered what had happened at Queller's, back in the city of Jade.

He saw the charred body struggle now, as if within invisible ropes.

The Lord of the North was solid. If he saw Man, he did not yet deign to act.

Man's corpse sat up, and Yoshi saw eyes open in the blackened face. The eyes were still that surprising green, but they looked as if they were staring out from hell. Then the Man-thing was on its feet. It staggered forward blindly with its burned-black arms thrashing about.

The Voice gnawed her knuckle till blood came. 'It's like that

Words of Fury:

animated corpse in Queller's!'

'Yes,' said Yoshi hopelessly. 'Now *he* is making a puppet of another dead man – my Emmanuel!'

No one came to help. Not even Yoshi, though he would have died for his friend.

'Is this Prophecy being fulfilled?' Rishiri snarled to Zandar. 'Is this salvation? The twitchings of a dead man?'

'I know I am not stronger than Prophecy,' Zandar whispered. 'I can only hope that Emmanuel may be.'

The Lord of the North was solid and real now.

Man was tiny and feeble. He staggered to the ancient bronze casket. He opened it with fumbling fingers, obviously unable to see, and then took out the Eye with his left hand. Yoshi flinched, for the dangling power gem glowed searing green. Its light changed hue continually, but it was always intensifying.

'How can he stand the light?' That was Precious Stone. 'How can he stand it?'

The glow soon completely surrounded Man.

The giant looked down, still smiling, perhaps pleased with his toy.

Is Man enslaved: *owned?* Yoshi wondered. Or will he now be a fully willing tool?

Man began screaming again, though now it had the tone of rage.

He rocked backwards, as if surprised. Then Yoshi saw the Lord of the North take a step forward, raising a steel-shod foot to stamp down on Man.

So our enemy is just toying with my friend, before grinding him into paste!

Man stumbled away from the descending foot. He was panting frantically. Then something ghostly surrounded him, man-shaped and as tall as the Lord of the North.

'It is his soul, made larger,' said Lady Joah.

Yoshi asked eagerly, 'Then it might turn into a fight?'

'It is still hopeless. Drawing so much power means that Man will be soon erased.' She turned away from the murder-scene. 'Our friend is dying right in front of us!'

Yet Yoshi could not and would not look away.

The soul-shape suddenly tried to grapple the Lord of the North. Immediately *he* pushed back, laughing his profound bass laugh.

The soul of Man would not be pushed away permanently. Its

Words of Fury:

feet scrabbled, smashing through cobblestones to get a better grip. Then it flung both its arms right round the Lord of the North's huge chest.

The soul began hugging very hard.

'I don't believe it,' said Mother Zandar. She sounded stunned. 'This is impossible.'

Nevertheless, thought Yoshi, it is happening.

Now *his* metal armor started to creak; several rivets popped out. Still Man's soul did not let up. There were snapping sounds as the plate armor folded. Unable to move in the bear-hug, the Lord of the North began to scream.

There was more screaming as *he* was flattened – his arms whirling uselessly – and then *he* was suddenly gone.

Daisen said it for everyone. 'I can't believe it – but I must! Our Emmanuel has beaten him!'

Man's soul faded now; but his fight was won.

Cheering began. Precious Stone grabbed Faslane and the Voice from Afar, and kissed both of them.

'Oh, what a victory!'

'Only,' said Daisen, 'the hole above means *he* can return.'

Yoshi looked away from Daisen, depressed; *he* had only retreated!

A girl in white came racing up. Yoshi heard her addressed as Sandella, heard frantic talk about repairing the wards. Yoshi heard the opposite of calm confidence. His side were still the losers, it seemed.

But before more plans could be made, Man acted.

His right hand made a fist. He punched up at the sky.

Lightning roared up from him in a continuous furnace-blast. It lit up the night, a true pillar of light that was soon many miles high.

Then the flaring energy began bending over towards the north.

Yoshi realized what Man was doing before anyone else. 'He's hitting our enemy!'

'I don't believe this!' Lady Rishiri had paled. She leaned forward on her cane. 'Emmanuel has actually hit where *he* is!'

Terrifying power flowed out from The Waning. Yoshi knew it must be causing damage wherever it was earthing itself.

The blast of electric fire continued for several seconds.

'Is the Lord of the North dead? *Is he?*'

It was the young novice shouting.

When his fire-throwing stopped, Man slowly crumpled. Yoshi and Precious Stone moved fast enough to catch him. Together, they lowered him gently to the cobblestones.

The Maiden pressed an ear to Man's chest.

'Mother! There is no heart-beat! *Mother!*'

Zandar shouted, 'Alert the High Healer! Get Irizo here!'

Rishiri sneered. 'As always, you are too late.'

Yoshi stared around. *Was* the Lord of the North injured, or even dead? And what about Man? Was it too late for him?

Not according to Zandar. 'I will not surrender Emmanuel!'

'Zandar, you fool, don't look at me with such hatred! Can't you feel it?'

Yoshi saw Zandar blindly gather her robes around her. 'Feel what, Lady Rishiri?'

'Emmanuel is *gone!*'

'He cannot die now, not this way, not after what he has done!'

'All of us die. That is the truth to live by.'

Daisen and this Sandella were forming some of the women of power into a unit for defense. Perhaps, thought Yoshi, *he* will not re-enter so easily...

Lady Rishiri was still leaning on her cane and making a first bid for the power she longed for.

'With Emmanuel dead, the only question now is what sort of funeral might be appropriate. I should be in charge of it, of course. I want to help his legend, so... – Even though he was Albion Christian, I'd prefer Buddhist rites, with Shinto elements as appropriate. At the last, dear so-called "Mother", we should adopt him as our own. For this Man, that you proclaimed as "The One" and brought here as "The One" – well, life is emptying out from him!'

'He must not die!'

Lady Rishiri sounded unexpectedly gentle now. 'Death! Ah, Mother, you have no dominion there!'

Chapter Forty-Six: *Now We're Prisoners*

Mother Zandar would not allow Man to die; she just *would not*. But for now she stayed looking up at the night sky, still watching for dangers.

'Everyone with serious power, watch the skies!' She knew the wards were ineffective in part and would have to be rebuilt, if that was possible. After a minute Zandar continued in a more normal voice. 'Sandella, stand here with me!' She sensed the girl moving closer.

Man was stretched out on the cobblestones, almost naked in the flickering torchlight. His blackened skin was still steaming. His mouth hung open and he did not appear to be breathing.

Zandar yearned to help him, but she knew her protective powers had to serve all The Waning. She kept looking up. There was the real Moon, set among glimmering constellations; but there was a hole in their protections and she could not help the earthbound now. Zandar could only hope that the incredible energies Man had thrown north would have weakened their enemy, or more.

A quick glance showed her that the two girls from Jade and a young Sister who was a healer were kneeling beside Man now, along with Precious Stone.

'Help Man to our infirmary! *Now!* – And bring the High Healer to him!'

Some people ran.

Daisen spoke very softly. 'Mother, I am ready, and the Diamond Heart is here to help ward off him.'

'I commend you,' said Zandar. She raised her voice. 'I am sure the Lady Rishiri will use her power to assist us.'

The old lady snorted, but did not refuse outright.

Now Zandar turned her head, to see Man being put on a makeshift stretcher.

'You should follow Man into shelter, Mother.'

'Sister Daisen, I won't desert my post.'

Daisen threw her superior a wry look.

Zandar kept her face expressionless and her voice conversational. 'I did not think even The One Who Will Change could be so strong, but *he's hurt the Lord of the North!*'

'Might've killed him,' Sandella murmured.

'That can't be!' said Albion's Faslane.

Daisen said, 'I have looked North, and at the very least *he* has been hurt!'

'Till there is proof, we must stay alert!'

A peacock-cry split the night. More water ran. It was strange to feel all this tension, when the night was so calm and lovely.

Mother Zandar was trying to remember certain verses from the Prophecies – verses dealing with alternate futures. For now they had escaped destruction, but the future that had just arrived looked and felt particularly bad.

Without Emmanuel, how can we have *any* hope?

The constellations all looked stable now; they did not shake. Zandar let several more heart-beats come and go.

'I feel *he*...' Sandella paused. 'I certainly feel he is not close just now. If he lives, gone back to Ezo, do you think?'

'Perhaps, and let's hope he's dead – or at least never comes back!'

For without Emmanuel and the Eye...

Zandar sighed, and opened her arms to the moonlight, reaching out to bright mother Moon. She wanted to take this last chance to embrace pure light.

For Joah was poisoned. Emmanuel was infected and lightning-burned. Weren't they both sure to die? And what if they were given successful Healing, only to become enemies?

Zandar knew that might happen. Rishiri was already a vicious opponent. And if Lady Joah ever discovered Zandar's discreditable secret, she too would learn hate.

If I have too many enemies here, then this sacred house will fall, and that will be the end of everything.

Zandar had wanted so much to save everyone, to say 'by grace you have been saved through faith' as it said in Ephesians; but she had failed.

Where is my faith, now? Zandar asked herself. *I have so much need of it!*

Then the stars rippled again. Zandar flinched. Was that *him*? She felt underpowered and tired now. The others might have more power left, of course, and Sandella had the Diamond Heart. Still they were all in deadly danger.

'Yes, that is the Lord of the North – but I'm watching him!' Daisen eyed the sky. 'He is looking for any weakness here.'

'It is even more intimate than looking; he is actually testing the wards.' Zandar knew she herself couldn't fight *him* off for longer than mere seconds; she could only hope he wouldn't strike. 'If he finds a serious weakness...' She shivered.

Daisen said only, 'I wish Man – or that I or you – could use the Eye!'

Lady Rishiri stood waving one hand, ready to strike in defense of The Waning. But when she glared at Zandar, Zandar flinched from the visible hatred. Now she actually regretted summoning the older woman here, though the power she had was much-needed.

Then the stars overhead trembled again, and for a moment Zandar seemed to see *his* translucent shape. Hurt or not, *he* had returned.

'Watch the skies!' Zandar said again. 'Watch the skies!'

They did, all on guard together, spaced out in the courtyard.

Although it might cost them their lives, they were doing the right thing.

After that incredible fire-fight ended, and without introduction or explanation, Yoshi, Ozawa and Faslane were herded away by six Sword Maidens.

As he and the others were politely relieved of their swords, Yoshi tried not to sound plaintive when he asked their escort, 'What of my friend Emmanuel?'

'The One Who Will Change,' Ozawa explained.

'It is all women's business,' said the Maiden leader.

'No, it isn't!' Faslane snarled at the Maiden. 'That was bloody well *him*, the *male* who is Lord of the North, giving this place a kicking! And then we all saw Emmanuel – a *man* – kicking back! He risked his life to protect all of you!'

'Don't presume to give commands here, you man! I am Sword Maiden Ice, trained by she-captain Nagisa to follow orders, but not orders from *your* sort!'

This disagreement could get serious, Yoshi thought. Their boss Nagisa sounds like a narrow-minded bitch. Will we have to fight her Sword Maidens?

He eyed the six guards. They were fit-looking women. All bore the two swords, and looked confident in their skills. They stared back at the three men with hauteur.

A matronly woman arrived, keys hanging from her sash.

'Lord Yoshi? Come, please.'

'To where? And why?' Yoshi said. He would not allow himself to be ordered around as if he were nothing. 'I am an Emperor's Man and a famous warrior, and also the closest friend of Emmanuel from Albion!'

'I hear what you say, sir.'

'Then take me to my friend.'

'I have different instructions, Lord Yoshi, which I must obey.'

'You must, but why should I?'

As one, the Sword Maidens took a half-step forward. For a moment it seemed that violence might break out; but Yoshi knew he and his company were outnumbered and without swords, and in a place where there was mighty magic.

The housekeeper said, 'If you can please follow me to the male visitors' quarters...'

Yoshi parted his empty hands.

'We were told we were among friends here – allies and friends!'

'And so you are,' said one of the Sword Maidens, older and muscular and with a scar on her jaw.

'We have fought *him* too!' said Faslane, bitterly.

'I'm sure,' said the housekeeping woman. 'But, please, follow...'

Yoshi did, leading the other men. He kept his eyes on the sky, but there was no more fire.

They were led to a low stone building, windowless on the ground floor and with a massive iron-nubbed door that could be barred from the outside.

Faslane stared at their prison. Then he turned to Yoshi, as if he expected some strong reaction.

Yoshi only parted his hands again. He was bleeding, and he did not feel up to a battle.

They were led in. A lightstone in a fancy holder on the wall gave the corridor plenty of illumination.

'Take any room, my lords. There's a bath-house at the other end of the corridor.'

Each windowless cell Yoshi looked into was bare, though Yoshi presumed there'd be rolled-up futons and small sacks of rice in the cupboards, to go as beds and pillows on the tatami mats.

He still felt annoyed to be ordered about so much.

'Man.' The housekeeper glanced over at Ice, then at another of the Sword Maidens. Yoshi persisted. 'Have you let him die?'

Ice sneered. 'I have no news to give you.'

Yoshi felt fury build. He wanted to strike this insolent girl in blood-red.

Words of Fury:

'Your reticence is an insult. Tell me what you do know! And if you know nothing, find out!'

The young Sword Maiden glared back, but the woman with the scarred jaw spoke instead. 'Lord Yoshi, sir, you best speak to Sister Daisen about this, soon as she's free.'

'When might that be?'

'When she says!' Ice told them.

The older Maiden said quickly, 'After what happened tonight, please understand that she is a mite busy.'

Ozawa stepped forward. 'We are Man's true friends and among his first followers.'

Yoshi backed Ozawa up. 'And we deserve the truth about him!'

'We are the same as you three. We have planned for many years to help The One Who Will Change. We are all followers!'

Yoshi took Ice's wrist – not the one above her sword-hand, of course. Ice instantly disengaged her hand. The light of violence was dancing in her eyes.

Suddenly Yoshi was saying to himself, Not here, not now, not yet – we must not fight these people!

The older Sword Maiden spoke again. 'Later there will be a proper welcome for you all; green tea, ceremony, and perhaps even a word from our holy Mother. Now a healer will visit you – for you are cut, Lord Yoshi.

'I hope you will excuse us, but we have our duty. We must respectfully ask you not to go beyond the outer door, which will be guarded by me and my sword-sisters.'

When the Maidens had all given formal bows and gone, and the door was closed and barred, Faslane turned to the others.

He was furious.

'Where's Man? I hate these Sword Maidens for not telling us!'

'They may not know themselves. Don't forget, we left the great ones of this place watching the sky,' said Ozawa. His voice was pitched to take away some of the tension. 'Having taken our dying friend Emmanuel, of course.'

So someone else realized Man had died! Yoshi scowled. 'You are very polite.'

'Polite?' Ozawa smiled inscrutably. 'Ironic, friend Yoshi. I am ironic. And, of course, concerned we are being excluded.'

'Yes, the high-up women here will no doubt make plans for us.' Yoshi's scowl deepened; he was in pain from the long fight and bleeding again. 'Plans I'll delight in upsetting.' He banged fists together. 'Did you see how Man shook heaven! What have they done with him!'

Faslane grimaced, tapping at his belt where the spiked fighting-iron had hung. 'A pound to a penny says they won't tell us!'

Ozawa sounded grim. 'We risked everything to bring our friend and the Eye here, so that Man could learn its ways with the help of the women here – and then stand up to *him*.'

'Aye! We bled to come here, but now we're prisoners,' Faslane said. 'We ought to fight our way out!'

Probably Faslane was right; but what could they do right now? Yoshi was wounded, bloody, and weary. He considered what Man would have done in his place.

'Let's have a little patience. Man would want that. I feel safer here than I did on the road, and I bet you two do too. And if our friend is dead, we will give him a splendid funeral, and move on to continue the fight!'

Once in his own cell Yoshi laid down in the dark and tried to rest. There was nothing good to think about. He was face-down on the bed, naked and panting. He had a cloth held to his stomach, where he was dripping blood. Had he been left here behind a locked door to die? Where was Man? Was there *any* chance he had survived, or was it time for elegies?

Yoshi had had faith in Man's role; now that faith had failed. There would be no freedom, no change.

He wondered what was happening back in Jade, especially with his father.

I sent him that messenger. Will he search out *his* high Son in the city? Or will he think me a fool, or, worse, a traitor?

Of course he will do as always, and think the worst of me! – And yet I know we *must* change the world – or die! That's why I became a Futurist. Man was right and Joah *is* right. This world must be opened up and changed.

Yoshi closed his eyes and divided his mind into two. One part began roughing out that elegy for his friend Emmanuel. The other part made plans for war.

Then someone came in, holding a lamp. Blushing, Yoshi reached behind and pulled a sheet over his body.

Stern but well-meaning eyes glinted. 'No need for shyness, boy. You have nothing I haven't seen before.'

He raised his head and managed a little tired defiance. 'That

Words of Fury:

doesn't mean I want to show off what I do have.'

She touched his bare shoulder. 'I am the High Healer, Sister Irizo.'

'And my name is Fujiwara-noh-Yoshi, and I've bled all over your bedding.'

'No matter, young man. A laundry bill is a small thing. Now,' she said, 'I am the finest Healer in The Waning of the Moon, which means in all Japan. Let me look at your wounds.'

Yoshi was about to sneer, and then was humbled by the confidence of her expression.

'I'm yours,' he said. 'On one condition.'

She smiled wryly. 'You are a spirited young warrior, aren't you? I like that.'

'And a poet.'

'I like that even more. But you are in no condition, and no position, to make conditions.'

'How is Man? Is he – dead?'

She put a hand on his forehead, in motherly fashion – a cool and welcome hand.

'You know this already: all of us must die. All we can do is to follow duty, and die in the right way.'

Their eyes met, in mutual respect.

'I understand you, Sister Irizo. Do what you need to do.'

She pulled the sheet away, studied his bare body, then laid her hands on him.

'You are the worst hurt; a slash across the stomach, your right ear has been cut almost in two and the loose little finger has only been inadequately healed. And you have lost much blood!'

Yoshi just felt so very tired... He had vaguely realized he was still bleeding, but the sticky red pool on his futon was wide. It came to him that he might be dying.

'I had some Healing.'

'Lucky for you, else you would already be dead. Now, I must do my work.'

The healer washed him all over in some astringent fluid, tutting over Yoshi's wounds as she cleaned them. Then she went over every hurt, one by one. It was as if warmth and then cold came out of her probing fingers. Sometimes Yoshi gasped, though more from the strangeness of it than from pain.

'There,' she said. 'Lost blood, of course. But you're young and fit, with a great power to heal... I will prescribe appropriate drinks, with much fresh beetroot. How do you feel?'

'How do I feel, Sister?' Yoshi touched what should have been wounds and were not even healing scars. He breathed in and out, feeling relaxed and free of pain, though he was still exhausted. 'I feel healed! You are a genius!' He took her hand, kissed her ring. 'Thank you.'

Irizo stepped away, holding her white robe clear of the bloody garments Yoshi had left on the floor.

Even without Man, Yoshi thought, they have *powers* here. Perhaps there is hope left.

For long minutes Zandar had looked at the night sky where the moon and the stars were. The night below the giant waning Moon was warm and humid. All *his* sleet and ice was vanished from the land around, as if it had never existed.

Then Rishiri addressed her, very calmly, and without looking away from starry heaven. 'You know we are both strong in the power.'

'Yes,' said Mother Zandar.

'Then relax a little; have faith.'

'I do have faith, Lady Rishiri. It just may not be enough faith...'

But the other women's strength gave Zandar comfort, and anyway it was too late for second thoughts about summoning Rishiri and the princess. The regulations about sanctuary were clear, and it didn't matter that Lady Rishiri was a personal enemy. Princess Anamizu was almost equally distinguished, brave, and powerful in the art – and as far as Zandar knew had no particular reason to dislike her.

Of course, there is Anamizu's friendship with Lady Rishiri... Days of hearing me insulted and despised must have had some effect.

At last, Daisen spoke.

'I see no sign of *his* evil.'

'No.' Zandar lowered her hands and felt some of the tension ease out of her body. 'Not at the moment, at least. But no doubt *he* has his plans for us.' She glanced around. 'Any of you have an idea what his plans might be?' Nobody responded. 'Joah?'

Joah shook her head.

Daisen gave Zandar a brief wry glance, but did not speak.

A messenger ran up and said, 'Mother! The Healers are assembled – with Sister Irizo!'

Words of Fury: 479

'Then I will come – praying all the way.' Zandar looked into the dark sky, then away from it. 'Daughter Sandella?'

'Yes, Mother?'

'You wanted a war, or said you did. Is it to your liking?'

'No, Mother!'

'Stay here anyway – and if *he* returns, give him some licks! Daisen, please supervise our defense as guardian-in-chief!' She turned her head a little more. 'That is my request to you, too, Lady Rishiri: please guard our home!'

'I am like you in one thing only,' the voice rasped. 'I do not wish to see this wonderful place fall to *him*.'

'If we all do our duty, perhaps it won't!'

Zandar's guards had closed in and she was about to follow the messenger when Rishiri called out to her.

'So-called "Mother", admit you have failed!'

Zandar whipped round, annoyed. 'How can we have "failed" when we are still fighting?'

'You're trying to give disaster a good name, but nobody is fooled! I say, give up your power to one who deserves it!'

'I already have, for only God deserves that kind of power, and He already has it.'

Then blind Zandar swept away, accompanied by her bodyguards.

The underground infirmary was a cool place, with clean whitewashed tunnels. Waiting for Zandar were four women, who were among the five finest healers in The Waning.

There was one absentee.

Zandar felt shocked. 'No Sister Irizo? Where is she?'

'When she came here she scolded us and then went to see the men Lady Joah brought.'

Zandar was both puzzled and hurt.

'She would not help Emmanuel? But he was grievously hurt!'

There was no reply; even these women could feel awkward. Of course, Zandar knew the one obvious reason for Irizo's absence. Death could not be healed.

Sickness crawled into her belly.

'Why are you all so afraid? I won't believe Emmanuel has finally died, I just won't!' She shuddered, and then Mother Zandar's strength gave way. Weak and dizzy, she almost fell. She leaned on the wall, her head bowed. Her voice was small. 'We always knew we might lose.'

'That was the bargain, holy Mother.'

'Yes. A chance – with no guarantees.' The others saw her lips move in prayer. Then she straightened up, nostrils flaring, and her voice rang out proud and clear. 'But we also always knew that we would fight to the very end!'

'Amen!'

'I am the most potent of all of us,' said Zandar. She felt strong again. 'I have fought *him* face to face when I expected to die, and taken wounds doing it. I *will* find Man!' Zandar understood that Man was a corpse, but it was important that her sisters and everyone else in The Waning did not take that tragedy as the end. 'Now he is dead, I will bless his flesh before the funeral, and make new plans for our war!'

Again, nobody responded.

Zandar groped her way forward to the futon. When she felt what was in it, she flinched. 'Why have you brought me to this bed?'

'We had wanted your help, holy Mother.'

'But – the bed is empty!'

'Yes, *now* it is.'

'The Lord Emmanuel has gone?'

Zandar felt a tightness round her heart. Had Man recovered so much that he had simply walked away? She was going to ask the others, and then realized they would have given her that good news immediately.

There was one last question to ask. 'Ah, my sisters, my daughters – *where has he gone?*'

'As he died, he vanished – along with the Eye.'

'No!' Zandar felt frantic now. This news was bad beyond anything. 'We can't have lost *both!*'

'Mother, I think we have.'

Words of Fury:

Chapter Forty-Seven: *Unconditional Love*

Joah had been taken to the Novice House along with the Voice from Afar.

There, Joah looked round the empty entrance hall. Except for a couple of plump housekeepers, it was deserted. 'Where is everyone?'

The head housekeeper bowed very low. Joah realized she was already known here. The Prophecies, no doubt; or some kindly advance words from the holy Mother.

'Lady Joah, everyone with the power, however young and untried, has been ordered outside to take part in the defense.'

There were two lightstones here, on tall stands with mirrors behind them. The Voice had touched one glowing stone and then turned round. Her face was almost ecstatically proud.

'Joah, dear Joah! To think we fought off *him!*'

My singing friend is always optimistic, thought Joah, while I have worked blood magic, been given poison touches, and associated with *him*. I see the dark and I know the dark.

'That's true, dear Voice, and Man *crushed* him – but at such a cost!'

The Voice stared at her, now. 'Man was taken to the infirmary, and they have wonderful healing here. I know he was terribly hurt, Joah, but...'

I am secretive when I need to be, and a planner always. But I also know all our plans can fail.

Joah looked up at the ceiling and imagined the sky. 'The wards still have a hole, though a patch is over it. Let's hope *he* doesn't come back.'

'Do you really think Man is dead?' Tears flashed in the Voice's blue eyes. 'Have they concealed that? Surely holy Mother Zandar would tell us!'

'I'm sure she would,' Joah lied. 'But this *is* war, there have been casualties, and there will be more.'

'You are samurai-raised. You could be a Sword Maiden if you wanted, and you know the Prophecies. I bet you've been planning for this!'

Joah said wryly, 'As you know, I do know the enemy – *did* know the enemy – quite intimately.'

'I want to hit *him* again,' said the Voice, and Joah understand that desire. 'Man *hurt* him, which is what *he* deserves, and we can hurt him, too – or kill him!'

'Perhaps, if luck is with us.'

I know we *can* hurt him, and we have; but that chance may not come again, at least not for me.

Joah admitted it, though only to herself.

I *must* be helped. Otherwise, this is where I will die.

Zandar went back outside. Her head was aching, but in her soul it was worse.

Without Emmanuel, with my dear Lady Joah dying, what can we do?

At best we can only stay here behind our defenses, and watch the skies while his forces sweep over this land and the world; and what is the good of that?

I am so lonely and full of fear...

As she walked, Zandar was trying not to weep.

What's happening to me? I cannot stay like this! Better if I fling myself down from the highest tower we have. If my only faith is in the darkness to come, I might as well join *him!*

She made herself stop her hurried walking, made herself breathe the night air with a semblance of calm. A couple of Maiden bodyguards were ahead of her, and now Daisen came over.

'I have left the princess in charge, and let go our two girls from Jade. It seemed safe, for now I think heaven is empty of malice.'

'Empty of malice; that is good! I only wish our home was similarly empty.' Zandar sighed. 'Who led, in repairing the wards?'

'I'm sure you can guess. Actually, she has some very clever techniques indeed in her palette of skills.'

'She always did. That was never the problem.' Zandar and her friend both gazed up at the dark sky for some while. 'Yes, it is quiet there, and perhaps the wards were effectively patched. Oh, Daisen, our heaven is full of stars, though with my ... wound ... I cannot always see them.'

'But they are always there, Mother.'

Somewhat comforted, Zandar went striding on.

The cool night kissed her cheeks sensuously, reminding her of her long-lost husband; and suddenly she was quite certain that her life had taken a very wrong turning. She wondered if someone exterior, or a *thing* like *him*, was working on her soul. That did not seem likely. For he was male; surely she would see

Words of Fury:

what *he* did to her.

Nevertheless her spiritual crisis grew worse.

Perhaps I should not have come here, though I was told I had to; perhaps I should not have deposed Rishiri, though everyone except her said it was necessary.

By ugly coincidence, when Zandar rounded a corner Lady Rishiri was here, watching the skies alongside the Sword Maiden princess. The old lady's defensive weaves had domed the entire Waning, and they were cunning as well as powerful.

Zandar was going to pay a compliment, but then Rishiri saw her and came strutting up. Her cane's ruby glowed a malicious red, and showed up harsh lines in her face.

Lady Rishiri adopted her usual tactics: she attacked at once. 'Zandar, you let Man die! You are responsible!'

Zandar straightened. 'You are correct. I *am* responsible.'

Those words somehow made Rishiri go silent, though Princess Anamizu frowned.

Zandar suddenly feared that she was making an enemy of Anamizu also, so she returned to stiff courtesy.

'I beg you both, in this emergency let me be about my duties. I thank you, lady, and you also, princess, for what you are doing. But please remember that for now at least you two have no official standing here.'

By magic, sightless Zandar watched the other two women bow. Lady Rishiri's face still showed fury, and even the princess frowned.

Then Zandar left with her escort, and went down to the Map Room.

No doubt Daisen sensed her mood. 'Mother, even by existing here against *his* will we will be a beacon of hope.'

Zandar wove a charm so that they could not be overhead. 'Yes; to defy *him* and exist is a hope for all. And if I can form that magical circle – why, even without the Eye, we may have the power to humble the Lord of the North!' Then she lowered her voice more, though supposedly only Daisen could hear. 'But that plan cannot be discussed yet. Now, let us hope we get news of Emmanuel.'

Zandar had given orders for her most powerful adepts to search for Man and the Eye.

'Is good news possible, Mother?'

'In heaven or in hell, he must be found! So must the Eye!'

As she entered the long room, Zandar tried to look gracious.

Female faces turned to her; not all were welcoming. Here, among pictures of mysteries, Zandar automatically went to the head of the long, lacquered table. She kneeled there, composed.

Attendance was thin, as most of her Sisters were outside on defensive duties. Zandar realized that might work to her advantage.

Daisen came, to her right. Opposite Daisen kneeled Sulina, with the chief Healer close by. Other important women were further down the table, while others of lesser status waited in the shadows.

Zandar knew *he* was supreme at creating defeat and dissension even out of victory, and some here might only see her failure: for the loss of The One Who Will Change was a disaster. She was wondering if she would retain her place. Lady Rishiri had been deposed. It could happen.

It better not happen to me. I have all the plans – and most of the determination.

Zandar spoke positively.

'Let us be optimistic. We have warded our Waning, and peopled our walls with Sword Maidens and strong Sisters. We cannot be seized by surprise, and we can stand off any siege for a long time.'

There was some applause. She politely raised a hand, her smile more relief than anything.

'There have been difficulties, but the One Who Will Change and his mighty power gem the Eye have been taken within our walls, and so has Lady Joah. We also have Lady Rishiri and Princess Anamizu with us. That is a force indeed.'

Sulina pursed her lips. 'True, holy Mother, but can we bring that power to bear? Man is ... well, it's best left unsaid.'

Zandar sensed how Irizo's head turned, and she wondered if the High Healer had some relevant secret. 'So there is no news of him?'

'None,' said Sulina, 'and I have been monitoring our search with my Far-Seeing. But we will continue to look.' When Zandar said nothing, Sulina went on. 'Lady Joah is ill and her cure may be beyond us, and most of our Sword Maiden force went North.'

Zandar nodded, gravely. 'We still have a strong heart here.'

'What can you mean by that?'

'Sulina, be more respectful of our holy Mother! By undermining her authority you undermine all of us!'

Sulina's face shuttered. She looked away from Daisen and

Words of Fury:

bowed slightly to Mother Zandar. 'I meant, of course, no disrespect. I simply want to face facts.'

The audience stirred, and Zandar felt their concern.

Then she-captain Hanake arrived. She bowed low.

'How is our human defense?'

'Ready. Of course, when you and I and the others came in by the Mountain Gate, it was damaged. In view of that, I have concentrated our Maidens there, while artisans are working to repair the hurts.'

'That's sensible,' Zandar said, impressed by Hanake's efficiency – though the young veteran was clearly stressed from the rescue of Man and his party and what she had seen afterwards. 'I have placed most of our strongest adepts outside, watching out for *him* in case he tries to come from above. Who is at the Sea Gate?'

'That's Nagisa. If there's an attack, she'll be aggressive.' Hanake gave a small, grim smile. 'She has her reputation to consider.'

'I think there'll be no attack tonight.'

'I hear you, Mother. But tomorrow, or the day after, the human storm hits us... For now, though, Sisters and extra Maiden guards are posted on all the walls.'

'An excellent precaution – though now the night seems quiet,' Zandar told the others, wanting to give an impression of confidence.

'Mother, on our journey back we encountered purity police in great force, and you tell me more are coming. I cannot relax.'

Was that a subtle rebuke? Zandar frowned.

Now the senior she-captain bowed again, and took her place at the other end of the table.

Ah, we came so close, Zandar thought, deep in the guilty misery she had to conceal. We hurt *him*. But we lost our Emmanuel, and because of that we are further from victory than ever!

'She-captain Hanake,' said Sulina, 'what say you about our strategic situation?'

'We had to give up so many of our brave girls, and send them so very far, to Ezo in the North. That is known.'

A cold-faced, elderly Sister leaned forward. 'So you conclude – ?'

'We are weakened, and as well as the magic from *him* there are human enemies around us – with more arriving.'

Sulina asked, 'Do we know how many?'

Daisen answered this. 'Hundreds are here in Shimabara already, and still more are heading here.'

'Hundreds more? Or thousands?'

Zandar thought it best to be honest. 'Thousands more will come. We will have a better idea by tomorrow night.'

'So many enemies,' said a shocked Sister. 'So many, many enemies!'

'They are outside. We are within these walls.'

'But, Mother!' Hanake sounded very serious. 'It's clear that we will be cut off. We will be on our own.'

Zandar fanned herself. 'Yes, we must withstand a siege.'

'Until when, Mother?' Sulina asked.

'Until relief comes, daughter, or till we empower ourselves with the Eye or in some other way.'

Sulina pressed the point. 'What "relief"? Lord Okada of the Jade has sometimes been helpful, but now he has fallen from power. I thought that our "relief" would be The One Who Will Change – and the Eye.'

'Yes.'

That answer did not satisfy. Zandar felt the disquiet turn towards anger.

'Then, short of a miracle, there will be no more reinforcements!'

Another aggrieved voice asked Zandar, 'What exactly is happening with Emmanuel and Lady Joah?'

'We all saw Man's power – saw the truth of Prophecy! Irizo and I will see Lady Joah together. There is hope.'

Sulina was angry. 'Mother, please! Long ago Joah went over to *him!* And as for Emmanuel, he was destroyed!'

Zandar touched her rosary. This was not the atmosphere she had hoped for, but the atmosphere that she had long feared. The Waning of the Moon contained sensitive, quarrelsome women. They were not exactly a brutally-disciplined army.

And I am not universally loved. I have disagreed with many and some are angry. To some I am crude and abrasive; they despise me. Already Rishiri hates me; but if Joah comes to feel the same – and she has cause – I could not bear it.

'Hope may have setbacks; but hope is never destroyed!'

'No, but *life* may be destroyed!'

The argument continued. No firm plans were made.

Zandar saw the situation clearly, and she suspected others

did, too. Though the Waning was ready for a siege, the initiative had passed to the enemy.

The woman of power once known as The Tears was now Lady Berenda. She had stayed in the saddle to watch by magic the dying man being carried to the Waning's infirmary. Berenda had Far-Seeing, and saw how women had quarreled around the stretcher. She smiled, now. Some in that place would betray one another, would despise and be despised, and then the end would come.

Mother Zandar had more and more enemies, and a lack of confidence in herself. Lady Rishiri, as always, verged on evil.

All this dissension among the enemy made Berenda feel wonderful. She had worked on Zandar's soul, imitating there the darkness that had been put into Joah.

That so-called 'Mother' dared pray for me! Now she has received her prayer-power back, and I have put cold corruption into her soul. She is vulnerable, and The Waning is vulnerable. It could be turned and so could she!

She decided to tell her master, and tried hard to do that. But when her mind-voice spoke, there was no answer.

They were an immense distance apart, the Lord of the North and she. She rode on slowly, alone. She was actually fearful that *he* had been hurt in the fire-fight.

Finally, she reached the road that went down from The Waning of the Moon up there to the sea and the port behind her. There was no one here. The road was empty, and she was quite alone.

Have I been deserted again? Surely not! Surely I am *loved*. This silence from the great Lord is no more than a test...

But for now her prayers were either not heard or were left unanswered.

After a chance to bathe, change, and rest, Joah was escorted into a six-sided mirrored chamber. She saw Mother Zandar and four other women were kneeling around a black table. Two were sisters all in white, like Zandar. Another woman wore something colorful, and the frowning she-captain Hanake was in Sword Maiden blood red. Joah saw the three in white all had the crescent Moon in silver and the scarlet cross on their backs.

Zandar's fan flapped. 'Well, daughter?'

Christian icons hung on the mirror walls, which showed

them all an infinite number of self-images. There were no servants here, and clever weaves prevented eavesdropping.

This was a safe place. This was a chance to get answers. Joah bowed low. In this context she felt very young and inexperienced.

'You have welcomed me, and I – feel I know you, Mother, from all we shared. And also I feel that I do not know you.'

Zandar said to the others: 'We have met in our dreams, this young lady and I, and dream-talked many times. She is very powerful, and she has helped Man – as predicted in Prophecy.'

'But she *did* ally herself with *him*,' said the sultry woman dressed in russet and gold silks.

She showed much bosom, wore jewels, and was doused in a spicy perfume. But Joah felt her power, and her personality. Suddenly Joah saw how she herself was seen: a wonderful child, with great potential – but wayward and tainted by her connection to *him*.

Zandar introduced the adept. 'This is Sulina, learned and powerful.'

Sulina continued to look at Mother Zandar. 'Though Lady Joah may now be healed of that moral wound, I cannot forget it, nor how she came by it.'

Zandar's voice turned sharp. 'Sulina, Lady Joah has turned her back on *him!* She is as close to me as my own true daughter could be, and we will trust her in the same way. Now, Lady Okada-noh-Joah, this is Sister Daisen, my secretary and chief aide.'

Joah bowed, very formally.

'And you will recall Hanake, our chief she-captain.'

Joah remembered being besieged on Miracle Island, knowing that *his* forces must win there. It was true Mother Zandar had created a path from The Waning, but most of the actual fighting had been done by Hanake's Sword Maidens. Joah felt gratitude.

'Thank you for what you and your Maidens did.'

Zandar extended a hand towards an older, motherly woman in white who seemed at a slight remove from the others. 'And Sister Irizo here, who you met before, is our most famous Healer.'

Joah asked at once, 'How is Lord Emmanuel?'

The women exchanged glances. They were good at keeping blank faces, but Joah sensed distress. Finally, Zandar nodded.

Words of Fury:

The Sister called Daisen tried to explain.

'He is...' Daisen sought words. 'Gone away from us.'

'Ah!' Joah's expression hardly changed, but she began to weep. I loved him, and he never ever believed it! 'Is there no hope?'

'Hope for a miracle, daughter; and believe.'

'I will, and I do!'

'Nevertheless, we must plan now, eh? Kneel with me.' When Joah did, Zandar rubbed her shoulder. Joah admired the compassion in Zandar's face, though her blinded eyes were hidden by a white bandage. 'His sacrifice was not in vain. Man fought off *him* – and hurt him.'

'Yes, he did!'

'Indeed. Otherwise, the Lord of the North would have come here, and all would be over.'

Joah showed some of her steel. 'So Man saved us, and now we can continue to fight!'

Zandar did not follow up that comment. She regarded Joah with unseen eyes, in the spirit of a mother looking on a beloved if errant daughter.

Joah did not lower her gaze. She realized she and the woman Zandar were much of a height, and her own power might someday be on a similar scale.

'Joah, you thought very highly of Man, didn't you?'

Suddenly Joah found herself blushing. She wiped away tears on her sleeve. 'I ... know how important he was. From reading the Prophecies, you understand.'

'Yes,' said Zandar, 'and also because of his birth in Albion.'

'And who he was born to there.'

'Indeed. – And there are Prophecies in great Albion also, aren't there? But you are important, too.'

Daisen added, 'The power that is still largely latent in you is very great. One day, with training, you will be like our Mother Zandar.'

'Mother, right now I don't feel powerful at all.'

'But one day you will,' Zandar said. 'When I was your age, I also ... lacked faith. But you saved Man before, and there is more to come for you – perhaps something incredible.'

'You have had a Foreseeing?'

'If I have, you know I cannot tell you directly. But I see a wonderful journey for you.'

'*If* I live.'

Words of Fury: 490

'Yes. If you live ... if ... and you have been given the Five Touches.' Zandar looked at the other women, then turned back. 'Lady Joah? May High Healer Irizo examine you? Undressed, if you please?'

'Of course.' Joah stood. She stripped quickly, and soon stood there naked, bare breasts and loins on display. Now the healer could check her, and give good news or bad. 'You have seen to our wounded?'

'They have all been helped. I saw to the Lord Yoshi myself.'

'I thank God, and also you!'

First the Healer would check her against the Four Natures, and then the Five Flavors. As the others watched, Irizo's long fingers probed at Joah's head and body. There were some wounds, of course, especially around her neck. They were hardly visible now.

'Healing. Your foreign friend?'

'The Voice from Afar has power in her songs and in her fingertips.'

Irizo smiled, and then examined Joah's tongue. All the while now she was asking Joah questions about her health, sometimes going close to Joah and sniffing. Everyone knew that many diseases had their own particular and peculiar odors.

'You are very skilled, Sister Irizo,' said Joah.

'I practiced for many years to be the best, and I am.'

Joah made herself smile, though wanly.

Mother Zandar tapped Joah gently on the shoulder. 'You really are in good hands.'

'Then let me do my work, please,' said Irizo.

Now Irizo produced jewels, the first blue and the second glowing a deep, rich red. Joah felt them resonate with subtle power. She felt a sudden rush of optimism. These people had power; they could help. The High Healer held the gems close to Joah and looked into them as she ran them over Joah's body.

Joah wanted to ask many questions, but did not dare. She still felt very young to be here among these women of such power and wisdom. It took a considerable effort to hide that feeling of inferiority.

Irizo sighed, and put the jewels back into a black case.

'Your *qi* has been badly tainted, dear. Your pulse is very slow, too. There is a terrible imbalance in all your body's functions, and the imbalance is getting worse.'

'You know why?'

The healer nodded. 'I find cunning poisons in you.'
'Yes,' Joah acknowledged. 'From the Five Touches.'
'Given in the presence of the Jade Eye?'
'As Oatha held the Eye,' Joah admitted.

She saw Mother Zandar bite her lip. Obviously this was not the news she had hoped for.

'We will do everything we can, my daughter. We are forming a circle, and then perhaps...'

Daisen interrupted. 'It's just that we expected you to have the Eye, and an Eye under control! Instead, you have Oatha's poisons in you, but Man is gone, and the Eye with him!'

'I know what the plan was. And I would have followed it,' Joah said, tartly. 'Too bad Lord Oatha did not, and nor did *he*.' In spite of her defiant attitude, Joah did want to serve. 'Mother, you must have many questions about what I know, and who I know. Please ask.'

Zandar glanced over at Daisen, then back to Joah.

'Joah, you know Emmanuel, our "Mr Foreigner", better than anyone, and you are familiar with the Prophecies of Light...'

Sister Daisen asked, 'Back in Jade, what did he say about himself? Did he openly claim to be The One?'

'He claimed nothing. He didn't want to believe and to the very end I don't think he *did* quite believe.' Joah threw up her hands. 'To him Lady Naosuke's prophecies are little more than speculation, and, worse, he was a natural rebel. To him, if he *did* wholeheartedly believe, he would be made a slave by her words.'

'Ah! You understand him to the core, don't you?' Mother Zandar looked sadly over to Daisen and Irizo. Without speaking, Irizo calmly moved her glowing gems over Joah's naked body. 'So he lacked the necessary faith?'

'Faith can move mountains!' Daisen said.

'And lack of faith moves ... nothing at all,' Zandar responded. To Joah, she sounded sweet and bitter at the same time. Now she saw the holy Mother touch her hidden, blinded eyes. 'So perhaps Emmanuel was not really the one, and it's a mere string of coincidences that made us think he was... But you, Joah? What opinion do *you* hold?'

'It's not opinion, Mother,' Joah said firmly, lip curling.

'You seem very confident, my girl!'

'Because I have seen the truth. I saw what he did today – as *you* did. Earlier, he came "from the sea" and he is "different blood". He has the power though he is scared of it, and therefore scared of himself; but in Jade he rode the winds and I saw him kill Albion's flying snake. There can be no doubt. He *is* The One Who Will Change.'

The words tolled like a funeral bell. 'He was. And now,' said Zandar grimly, 'he is gone.'

Joah stared accusingly. 'What do you mean, exactly? Tell me!'

Mother Zandar slapped her bare buttocks.

'You will make no demands here, girl! You are not even a novice!'

Joah rubbed the inflamed flesh with both hands and glared in response to her disciplining.

'You know who I am. I count!'

The women looked aghast. But finally Mother Zandar nodded.

'Yes, I know who you are, and I love and cherish you – and you *do* count. But I must demand your obedience. You know The One Who Will Change; but I know much more!'

No one spoke. Joah continued to glare.

Then, without Joah having to formally submit, they gave her white novice robes of The Waning, and Joah dressed herself in them, and for a few moments felt she belonged.

Then a Sword Maiden was admitted with a message. 'Mother, she-captain Hanake, the electric barrier round The Waning has all gone!'

Daisen looked satisfied. 'Even *his* power has limits.'

Joah scowled; they didn't really believe that Man had hurt *him*, and they didn't want to see it – or acknowledge that because of Man everything had changed!

'I think *he* sees there is no point to the barrier, now,' Zandar explained. 'Those he wanted to keep outside are safely inside. And now our wards are replaced, *he* cannot enter.'

'Holy Mother, that is a relief,' said the Sword Maiden, bowing low.

'So, Maiden, return, and tell our she-captains to keep up a good watch. Maybe by tomorrow, and certainly sometime soon, there will be more magic coming against us, and vicious ungodly humans.'

When the Maiden went, Zandar turned to face Joah again. The other women also gave Joah measuring looks that made her uncomfortable. She looked back without flinching, though.

They were all so self-confident. Surely they would be able to

Words of Fury:

help?'

Joah tried very hard to keep her voice level.

'And what about me, elder Sisters, Mother?'

'You were to work with young Emmanuel, and guide him to oneness with the Eye.' Zandar took a breath. 'He would have learned, I'm sure.'

'And then?'

Mother Zandar shifted minutely. 'We would have worked together to clean out your system.'

'So you need Man, fit and healthy. And you need the Eye – under his control.'

'Ideally.'

Now Joah's voice became eager. 'But still I can be Healed?'

'As you know, your condition is grave,' Irizo said.

Joah fanned her face. 'I do know; for now I see into you.'

'Oh? I did not know you had the skill.' Irizo gave a sad smile. 'And what do you see in me?'

'That I am dying.'

Joah continued to smile and fan her face, but she wanted to shriek. There was no hope at all now. This was a death-sentence.

'The Eye may be recovered,' said Daisen swiftly, 'and your young Man might return from anywhere except the grave.'

'And if not,' said Joah bravely, 'I must die.' She found she was wringing her hands together. 'What precisely will happen to me?'

'There are herbs and potions to treat your symptoms.'

'Herbs! Mother, I know blood magic,' Joah said harshly. 'I know the dark arts – to an extent. So please tell me the truth.'

'You already know how it will end. Lady Joah, do you really need us to say it aloud?'

'Then I will! First, I will be in great pain, and I will go blind. I will be incontinent. I will suffer terribly, and only death will release me.'

The sentence had been spoken. There was a long silence.

'You are brave to envision it, braver still to speak it.' Zandar moved her head, though of course Joah knew she could not see. 'Sisters, I would be alone with my brave daughter.'

The others left, giving admiring murmurs about Joah's courage.

Zandar spoke again. 'We have powerful Healers in this place, and soon there might be a Circle here.'

'What if there *isn't* a circle? I know the Prophecies, Mother!

Words of Fury:

There may not be a happy ending. *I* am *dying* and your Healing may not work!'

'There is no healing death; and that awaits us all. I and my Sisters will pray for you, and one way or another you *will* be released from your pain.'

'Mother!' Joah was terribly ashamed of her own sudden tears. She gave a heart-rending sob and stumbled forward. 'I don't want to die! I don't want to die!'

Zandar embraced the dying girl with complete and unconditional love.

Words of Fury: 495

Chapter Forty-Eight: *Sanctuary*

Berenda reined in her horse again. In full night, The Waning seemed quiet and certainly there was no sign of a siege. But they were prepared. The great Sea Gate a half-mile in front of her was thick with defenders, and she sensed women of power on the ring-walls, weaving magic to stand off any enemies.

Can they hold out? I mean, with Joah poisoned and Emmanuel dead, how can they fight on?

Most probably they *can* hold on. My lord has made several different attacks, and still this Zandar is in power and her mighty soul-fortress has not fallen.

Her faith in *him* was slowly failing. She had seen little groups of Sword Maidens taken in without any trouble at all. They were survivors of the scattered garrisons which had fought the invasion, and they would reinforce the Maidens here.

Now Berenda looked out to sea. There were boat-lights there, and not all would be *his*. Impossible dreams came to her, dreams of leaving, of escape by sea...

In her fear of losing all her faith again, she prayed to *him* with especial force.

'Master, I have acted! Master! – Lord of the North, I call upon you! Please speak to your servant! Please, please!'

There was silence from the Lord of the North; only the usual night-noises could be heard. Berenda wondered if she should fall back, now, in case of enemy patrols. It would not do to be captured. Again, she felt an urge to run, to some place where she might be free.

I will try one last time. 'Master, eternal lord, I beg you! Please respond! I need you!'

Of course, even the darkest of true faiths has power.

'I HEAR YOU, LADY.' There was a silence. 'KNOW THAT I HAVE PLANNED MY ASSAULT UPON THE WANING, UPON THOSE WORMS MY ENEMIES.'

'Master, wouldn't it be best to take them undamaged, to be your slaves? After all, they *are* women of power!'

'TO TAKE THAT PLACE INTACT, I NEED FRIENDS WITHIN.' There seemed to be cold laughter now, and she glimpsed a little more of his subtlety. 'LADY, YOUR PLAN WORKED! THE ENEMY WOMEN ARE LOCKED IN THEIR FORTRESS ALONG WITH ALL THEIR POWER GEMS. NONE SHALL LEAVE IT, AND THERE WILL BE NO RESCUE FROM

Words of Fury: 496

OUTSIDE.'

Another long silence. 'Lord?'

'IF THAT BOY HAD LIVED, WE MIGHT NOT HAVE BEEN ABLE TO BRING HIM OVER. HE MIGHT HAVE DARED TO FIGHT ON. BUT IF HE IS TRULY DEAD...'

'He is gone,' she said. 'Oh Lord of the Dark, I felt him go! – With me in his blood, diseasing him, as well as those hurts from your power, how could he possibly live?'

'THEN ONE WAY OR ANOTHER WE MUST WIN.'

'For *you* – starting here – I can win the world entire!'

'THEN DO SO!'

With that approval given, Berenda cantered her horse forward. She knew what to say, and what to do when she was inside those high walls. The sea was at her back and the Waning of the Moon was ahead. Full of joy, she spurred on her horse, and began to gallop along the empty moonlit road.

Here at the Sea Gate the young she-captain Nagisa was in a fury. How could she prove her quality with no-one to fight?

'Our so-called betters are too busy "watching the skies" to actually strike at *him!*'

'True,' agreed the newly-raised Sister Opal Green.

Nagisa had more to say. 'At the Mountain Gate, when they brought home The One Who Will Change, there was a fire-fight!'

'That was bravery, and they will sing of it for a thousand years!' said another of the Sword Maidens.

Here there was no gatehouse on the other side of the flooded moat, and the battlements Nagisa commanded overlooked a broad dark road, which led down to the sea and the port there. In this time of crisis the road was watched all the time – or at least it was supposed to be.

'Yes, they *will* sing,' Nagisa raged, '*but we weren't there!*'

'Because our duty placed us here,' said a grizzled Sword Maiden, Rock of the Garden, as if to an impatient child.

'But here there can be no heroic defense because there is no attack!'

Opal Green stood right beside Sword Maiden Nagisa. She was even younger than the she-captain, but she had been well trained in aggressive magic.

'I agree.' Opal Green's voice was sweet and high, though she was always trying to make it rough and war-like. 'I *know* there is no enemy magic in front of us; none. I hardly know why I am here, when I could have been fighting at the Mountain Gate!'

'Yes, we have been excluded from glory.'

'Quiet is safe, she-captain, and being patient is wise,' said the veteran Rock. 'Fury is not wise. In the weak-minded it can even overwhelm duty.'

Nagisa rattled her fingers on her armor. 'What glory is there in being sensible? – Or do you think being sensible is better than having a wonderful reputation! Ah, always that old woman Winter Morning was given pride of place!' Now Nagisa turned to address her Sword Maiden troops. 'But even though Winter Morning is gone, Hanake is made senior she-captain, and not me!'

'Please!' Rock touched the hilt of her long katana. 'That promotion has been decided.'

'Am I not as brave as her?'

'Yes, but Hanake is famous – '

'Where is *my* chance for fame?' Nagisa still seethed over the opportunities she had been robbed of. Occasionally Sword Maidens were sent out as mercenaries, or to help the authorities; otherwise they made up garrisons that were rarely attacked. 'Where is *our* chance? Even Sweet Snake and her sister were allowed to leave and join the fight!'

Even before that, most of the other Sword Maidens had been sent to Ezo, to actively defend the realm there. Those left behind resented it, especially Nagisa and her admirers. For weeks now adepts had passed on stories of bravery up in the North. Every tale of heroism had infuriated Nagisa more.

'When we are besieged there will be chances enough to be brave, if by then it matters.'

That grave truth from Rock of the Garden silenced them. Looking out again, Nagisa saw moonlight bright on the distant sea. A few ship-lights visibly moved. She sighed, thinking again of the big fight around Rumoi port up in Ezo where the other Sword Maidens were.

One of the younger girls pointed out that there seemed to be several fires in the night now.

As before, the veteran Rock explained it. 'Our enemies will be burning villages they seized, to secure the land around.'

'Let them come here and try it!'

'She-captain, they'll be with us soon enough. Likely they will bring siege-engines, and certainly *his* magic.'

'Rock of the Garden, you sound nervous! It's impossible for

this place to fall. Some of you might be afraid of the Lord of the North, but I am not!'

Nagisa's boast was followed by silence. She realized she had sounded like a weak person trying to be strong. She writhed in embarrassment.

Rock threw in, 'Tomorrow or the next day our enemies will come: *his* friends, and black sashes, and all those who hate free, powerful women.'

'Or perhaps they won't. Perhaps even *he* is not as strong as they say and our commanders here fear him over-much!'

In arguing, they had again turned their attention from the road.

Then some sentry Maiden saw the single rider and called out.

Nagisa turned her head. One moment the dark road had seemed empty; then there was this horseman lashing a maddened horse.

Shouldn't we see that as magic, and send to the senior Sisters? Opal Green is spirited, but young and inexperienced.

For a moment, for no reason at all, Nagisa suddenly felt a great wave of fear wash over her.

A youngster spoke quickly. 'Shouldn't we open the gates? That man is being pursued!'

When I open the gates I will end this shameful fear...

That attitude was wrong; now Nagisa tried to think like a Sword Maiden. Ordering the gates opened was premature, surely – even dangerous? 'I see no pursuing enemies.'

'Would we see magic, she-captain?'

'True.'

'I see no magic, and *I* am the expert!' said Opal Green.

Nagisa thought aloud, 'Anyway, what harm can one person do?'

Now the veteran Rock spoke again. 'What if it's some trick? We should be cautious.'

Nagisa turned to the young, battle-eager Sister with her. 'Sister Opal Green, what do you say?'

Opal Green was full of fighting spirit.

'I say wars aren't won by being cautious!'

The rider reached the moat and drew rein savagely; the horse reared. Of course, the drawbridge was raised, and with the flooding the moat was especially wide.

Beside Nagisa, the Sister had also looked down. 'There is a

Words of Fury: 499

power about that person.'

'*His* power?'

The young Sister had never encountered one of the Lord of the North's adepts in the real world; but she didn't like to admit her ignorance.

'I think not. No. Very probably the newcomer is a friend to this place.'

Nagisa looked at the horizon where the dark and sparkling sea was, looked at the unmanned checkpoints on the dark road that went down to the port. There was nothing unusual.

Then why do I feel so uneasy?

She shifted the responsibility. 'Then what say you, Sister Opal Green? Admit?'

The Sister licked her lips. 'Yes. – No! Not yet. I mean, it *could* be a dangerous man.'

The rider below had a cap, which was now taken off. Sighing, the rider shook out long black hair. Now this tall person, oddly glamorous in the moonlight, looked up at the battlements.

'Aren't you expecting me?'

'More adepts *are* expected, Nagisa,' the Sister said. 'This very night Lady Rishiri and Princess Anamizu arrived. The holy Mother has summoned assistance from far and wide.'

The veteran Rock growled, 'Yes, but the last complete stranger who demanded a place among our adepts didn't have the power to light a candle! Lady Sulina told me so herself.'

'This one will be different,' the Sister told them. Her voice was shaking. 'I feel power.'

Nagisa leaned forward and called out, 'You at our gates! Identify yourself!'

When the stranger plucked it off, the long black hair was revealed to be a fine wig. The striking, finely-proportioned head was mostly shaved; but from the centre sprang a few woven black locks braided with silver thread, almost in Sword Maiden style.

'Look!' said a Maiden whose own hair was in similar braids and dyed green. 'It's a woman!'

'I am a true daughter of the power, and you all know it! Let me in!'

The rider's voice was a thrilling dark contralto, and in the moonlight her smile was heroic and perfect. As one, the Maidens all leaned forward to see her, each one of them strangely touched.

Nagisa made herself stand taller, and kept her hands on her two swords. 'Archers, nock your arrows!'

The woman below threw her head back and laughed magnificently. 'You don't trust me? You must. And you will. Now, let down the drawbridge, raise the portcullis, *and admit me!*'

Nagisa called down in response, 'Not after curfew! Now give the password, or leave and try again tomorrow!'

The superb voice spoke out thrillingly: '"This is the waning of the moon, but it will wax again. I am a woman of power, and I crave sanctuary!"'

'Ah!' said the young Sister, face lighting up with emotion. 'She knows the words!'

Nagisa did not move, nor speak. Something unknown held back her decision. She wanted to admit this woman, and also did not want to admit her.

Now the voice from below spoke harshly. 'Listen to me! I am a *true* Lady of Power, and I am here to help. *Invite me in!*'

The rider had not specified who was to be helped, but none of the defenders noticed that.

Quite suddenly Sister Opal Green shouted down to her. 'You have asked for sanctuary. It will be granted. Lady, please enter!'

Though another had made the decision, the young she-captain gave orders. The broad drawbridge was lowered and the portcullis behind it was wound up. The way was open now.

Elsewhere, there were tears and mourning, for the loss of Man and all the hope he had represented.

Here at the Sea Gate Berenda, who had once performed as the Tears, entered sanctuary and was made welcome.

Words of Fury: 501

THE WORLD OF 'WORDS OF POWER' – PLACES & PEOPLE

THE BOOKS, IN ORDER
Words of Power**, **Words of Fury**, **Words of Darkness**, **Words of Light

HISTORY
Imagine early 17th century samurai Japan, a closed society, with Europe and new faiths arriving. This is where the first four books of **Words of Power** are set.

The most powerful European state coming to Japan is Albion. The Empire of Albion is like our world around 1820. Its capital London (Londres) is a city of over 500,000 souls. Already Albion has conquered much of Europe, using world-beating steam-engine technology. At great cost, the so-called 'Empire of Blood' has also fought the icy occult power known as 'the Lord of the North'. This enemy is more than human, but Albion's famed general, Lord Kinross the Lord of All Arms of Albion, won famous victories against him.

However, this Kinross was then arrested as a traitor and 'vanished'. The Lord of All Arms' young son, the orphan Emmanuel-John Kinross, 'Man' to his friends and enemies alike, has been spirited away to presumed safety in Japan. He lives in Jade, Japan's only open city. This is a cosmopolitan port which trade and freedom have made rich.

Jade is hated as a mongrel place by many, and its ruler Lord Okada is deposed by Lord Oatha, the infamous black sash leader. The Okada family (Okada himself, and the two princesses Oki and Joah) are either imprisoned or forced to run. Young Emmanuel (Man) also escapes. The only sanctuary possible for Lady Joah and Man is the psychic fortress The Waning of the Moon. On the way, Man must fulfill the 'Naosuke Prophecies'. If he and Lady Joah fail, or turn to the Lord of the North, or die on the journey, their world will end – and our world too.

MAGIC
In this universe, magic can be done by physical spell-making, or by gesture and spoken words of power. Only the greatest adepts

Words of Fury:

can do magic by mental exercise, with nothing external. Prayers can be answered – but, as everywhere, some pray to dark gods. Magic is very powerful here, a mystic thing which does not follow rules of logic: but if you believe in a higher power, or *truly* believe in yourself, you can sometimes do wonders.

PEOPLE

IN THE CITY OF JADE
Lord Okada – deposed overlord
Oki – his daughter, a strong adept
Lord Oatha – leader of the purity police (the black sashes), victor over Lord Okada
Oatha's chief aides: his deputy, **Aoki**, a young high-born samurai, and **Yamagata**, an angry old bigot
Lord Fujiwara – chief Emperor's Man in the province, who is above all ordinary law
Queller – former agent of the Lord of the North, now deceased

ON THE JOURNEY TO THE WANING OF THE MOON
Man (Emmanuel) – exiled son of Albion's Lord of All Arms, and the presumed 'One Who Will Change' of the Naosuke Prophecies, who aims to save the realm of the Rising Sun from the Lord of the North
Yoshi (Fujiwara-noh-Yoshi) – poet and fighting samurai, son of Lord Fujiwara the Emperor's Man, and best friend to Man Kinross
Joah (Lady Joah, Okada-noh-Joah) – princess of the city of Jade, daughter of its overthrown lord, powerful magician and secret Futurist, and Christian
The Voice from Afar – young singer of Albion descent, famous in the port and elsewhere, and a magical power in her own right
Dirk Faslane – newly-come sea-pilot much more than he seems, sent from Albion on a secret mission

Ozawa – a captain of samurai, friend to Man, old ally to Yoshi
Ugaki, **Kido**, **Yonai**, **Ashida** – samurai companions on the journey to The Waning

Sweet Snake and **Precious Stone** are twin sisters, Sword Maidens sent by Mother Zandar to help Man

FOLLOWERS OF THE LORD OF THE NORTH
Queller – deceased in Jade
The Lady Berenda – performer once known as 'the Tears', who is a high-strung mystic, a sensitive soul and brute murderer, and in her mind *his* favoured adept
Hagiwara – black sash military commander, high Son of the Cold, and a man of unmatched ambition
Nagaoka – a leader of black sash cavalry
Other black sashes and mercenaries also follow the Lord of the North (not all knowingly)

IN THE WANING OF THE MOON
The Waning of the Moon is a psychic powerhouse set up for women, especially for women of power. It was the base of the seer Lady Naosuke. (Centuries ago, Naosuke's magic made a divine storm that saved Japan.) The Waning has Sword Maidens, young women trained as samurai; great scholars and artists; and, most famously, female adepts of the magical Arts (Healing, Far-Seeing, etc.). These persons include:-

Mother Zandar – the leader of The Waning, from an exalted samurai family, and an adept of almost matchless power, though in a fight against the Lord of the North she was blinded
Daisen – Zandar's chief aide and admirer
Irizo – the famous, compassionate High Healer
Sulina – a clever, passionate adept, not in holy orders
Sandella – an outwardly humble but secretly headstrong young novice, whose dangerous power already almost equals Zandar's own
Winter Morning – first she-captain of Sword Maidens, who is prepared to confront anyone – or anything
Hanake – the young she-captain promoted to Winter Morning's place
Nagisa – an angry young Maiden who is Hanake's rival

ELSEWHERE
Coming urgently at Zandar's request to help The Waning are:-
Lady Rishiri – former Sword Maiden, now retired to the Emperor's court in Kyoto. Rishiri was deposed from ruling The Waning, and is famously foul-mouthed, aggressive, and heroic, and also said to be rashly dangerous to everyone, including

Words of Fury:

herself
Princess Anamizu – Sword Maiden commander recalled from the fight against the Lord of the North in the northern island Ezo

COPYRIGHT INFORMATION AND AUTHOR'S WEBSITE

Copyright © by Ritchie Smith, 2017

Ritchie Smith hereby asserts his right to be identified as the author of this Work, in accordance with the Copyright, Designs and Patents Act 1988 (UK)

This novel is a work of fiction. Names and characters are products of the author's imagination, and any resemblance to actual persons, living or dead, is entirely coincidental.

All rights reserved. No part of this publication may be reproduced, stored in any retrieval system, or transmitted in any form, or by any means, including electronic, mechanical, photocopying, recording, or otherwise, without the prior written permission of the copyright owner.

Thank you for reading. You are very welcome.

For more information about the author and future projects in the *Words of Power* series, please go to the Website:-

www.ritchievalentinesmith.com

Made in the USA
Columbia, SC
13 April 2017